"Penny is the doyenne of the modern blockbuster.   *ur*

"The bestselling British novelist Penny Vincenzi is poised to fill a gap in the American realm of Cinderella fiction. With so few current writers able to summon the quaint allure of such women's fiction without stooping to sensationalism, Ms. Vincenzi really is an anomaly."

—*New York Times*

"British bestseller Vincenzi pulls out all the stops in this orchestral saga . . . the women are, without exception, multifaceted, smart, and brave, and their happiness is hard won. The book offers major escape and abandon for summer."   —*Publishers Weekly* (starred review)

"She's the plot-twist queen."

—Adriana Trigiani, author of *Big Stone Gap*

"An absorbing tale rich in seductive intrigue and emotional impact. Vincenzi, wildly popular in Britain, will please her growing American audience with this compelling tale of loves lost and found."   —*Booklist*

"Penny Vincenzi's *Sheer Abandon* is the work of a master, offering a large cast of amazingly three-dimensional characters involved in an expertly manipulated plot . . . Full of snappy dialogue and provocative moral implications, Vincenzi's novel makes it very hard not to care."

—*Newsday*

"Well drawn characters and engaging style. Vincenzi keeps things humming."   —*People*

"Never less than deliciously readable, and the pace never flags."

—*Daily Mail*

SHEER ABANDON

· · · ·

ALSO BY PENNY VINCENZI

•◆•

No Angel
Something Dangerous
Into Temptation

A NOVEL

SHEER
ABANDON

Penny Vincenzi

BROADWAY BOOKS

NEW YORK

PUBLISHED BY BROADWAY BOOKS

Published in the United States by Broadway Books, an imprint of
The Doubleday Broadway Publishing Group, a division of Random
House, Inc., New York.
www.broadwaybooks.com

Originally published in the United Kingdom as *Sheer Abandon* by
Headline Book Publishing, Ltd, London, in 2005. A hardcover
edition of this book was published in 2007 by Doubleday, by
arrangement with Headline Book Publishing.

Book design by Ellen Cipriano

Library of Congress Cataloging-in-Publication Data
Vincenzi, Penny.
Sheer abandon : a novel / by Penny Vincenzi.
p. cm.
1. Abandoned children—Fiction. 2. Female friendship—Fiction.
I. Title.
PR6072.I525S54 2007
823'.914—dc22
2006035917

ISBN 978-0-7679-2625-6

PRINTED IN THE UNITED STATES OF AMERICA

3 5 7 9 10 8 6 4 2

*For my four daughters,
Polly, Sophie, Emily, and Claudia, for
every possible kind of help and support in
a very long year.*

Acknowledgements

·   ·   ·   ·

I have been bothering even more people than usual in my quest for back-ground information for *Sheer Abandon*; the book covers a rather large landscape. First of all, I would like to thank the many people who had been abandoned or adopted or given their own babies up and who shared their experiences with me so generously; and then the politicos, as I think of them, both MPs and political journalists, all of whom made the work-ings of the House of Commons feel both wonderfully intriguing and al-most comprehensible; the lawyers and medics who answered all my questions so patiently; and of course everyone who shared their memories and experiences of traveling and backpacking with me.

I am very, very grateful to all those wonderful people at Hodder Headline who published the book so brilliantly in the UK; and to Tim Hely Hutchinson for welcoming me so warmly into the Headline fold.

And so much gratitude to Steve Rubin, publishing supremo, who has welcomed me equally warmly into Doubleday and the US fold; and everyone Over There who is publishing me with such inspired passion. Most notably, Deborah Futter, my editor, whose enthusiasm is a total joy;

Dianne Choie, who keeps the nuts and bolts neatly lined up; and Alison Rich, who is making sure everyone the length and breadth of the United States knows about the book.

Huge thanks to Clare Alexander, my wonderfully supportive agent, and in memoriam Desmond Elliott, so well known on both sides of the Atlantic and who looked after me and my books for so long and is, I am sure, now brokering astounding deals at the great publishing lunch in the sky.

And, finally, my husband, Paul, so unfailingly there for me, so swift to respond to my frequent wails of despair, and so unselfishly ready to share in my (rather rarer) whoops of delight.

As always, in retrospect, it looks like a lot of fun. And I think it really was.

The Main Characters

· · · ·

JOCASTA FORBES, a dazzling tabloid reporter
NICK MARSHALL, Jocasta's political-journalist boyfriend
CHRIS POLLOCK, their editor
CARLA GIANNINI, a fashion editor

JOSH FORBES, Jocasta's slightly hapless brother
BEATRICE FORBES, Josh's barrister wife
HARRY AND CHARLIE, their small daughters

GIDEON KEEBLE, a retailing billionaire and political benefactor
AISLING CARLINGFORD, one of Gideon's ex-wives
FIONNUALA, their teenage daughter

CLIO GRAVES, née Scott, a charming and clever doctor
JEREMY GRAVES, her overbearing surgeon husband
ARTEMIS AND ARIADNE, her sisters

MARTHA HARTLEY, a brilliant corporate lawyer
PAUL QUENELL, her boss
ED FORREST, Martha's lover
PETER HARTLEY, Martha's father, a vicar
GRACE HARTLEY, his wife

KATE TARRANT, a beautiful teenager, abandoned at birth
HELEN AND JIM TARRANT, her adoptive parents
JULIET, Kate's sister
JILLY BRADFORD, Kate and Juliet's glamourous grandmother
SARAH, Kate's best friend
NAT TUCKER, Kate's boyfriend

JACK KIRKLAND, a politician and leader of the Centre Forward Party
MARCUS DENNING, CHAD LAWRENCE, and ELIOT GRIERS, all
  prominent members of Parliament
JANET FREAN, a dynamic having-it-all politician
BOB FREAN, her husband

FERGUS TREHEARN, a public relations consultant

SHEER ABANDON

. . . .

Prologue

. . . .

People didn't have babies on aeroplanes. They just didn't.

Well—well, actually they did. And then it was all over the newspapers.

"Gallant aircrew deliver bouncing boy," it said, or words to that effect, and then went on to describe the mother of the bouncing boy in some detail. Her name, where she lived, how she had come to be in the situation in the first place. Usually with a photograph of her with the bouncing boy and the gallant crew.

So *that* wasn't an option.

She couldn't have a baby on an aeroplane.

Ignore the pain. Not nearly bad enough, anyway. Probably indigestion. Of course: indigestion. Cramped up here, with her vast stomach compressed into what must be the smallest space in the history of aviation for what?—seven hours now. Yes, definitely indigestion . . .

Didn't completely solve the situation though. She was still having a baby. Any day—any hour, even. And would be having it in England now instead of safely—safely?—in Bangkok.

That had been the plan.

But the days had gone by and become a week, and then two, and the date, the wonderfully safe date of her flight, three weeks after the birth, had got nearer and nearer. She'd tried to change it; but she had an Apex seat; she'd lose the whole fare, they explained very nicely. Have to buy a new ticket.

She couldn't. She absolutely couldn't. She had no money left, and she'd carefully shed the few friends she'd made over the past few months, so there was no danger of them noticing.

Noticing that she wasn't just overweight but that she had, under the Thai fishermen's trousers and huge shirts she wore, a stomach the size of a very large pumpkin.

(The people at the check-in hadn't noticed either, thank God; had looked at her, standing there, hot and tired and sweaty, and seen simply a very overweight girl in loose and grubby clothing.)

So there was no one to borrow from; no one to help. The few hundred she had left were needed for rent. As it turned out, an extra three weeks' rent. She'd tried all the things she'd heard were supposed to help. Had swallowed a bottleful of castor oil, eaten some strong curry, gone for long walks up and down the hot crowded streets, feeling sometimes a twinge, a throb, and hurried back, desperate to have it over, only to relapse into her static, whalelike stupor.

And now she had—indigestion. God! No. Not indigestion. This was no indigestion. This searing, tugging, violent pain. Invading her, pushing at the very walls of the pumpkin. She bit her lip, clenched her fists, her nails digging into her palms. If this was the beginning, what would the end be like?

The boy sitting next to her, as grubby and tired as she, whose friendliness she'd rejected coldly as they settled into their seats, frowned as she moved about, trying to escape the pain, her bulk invading his space.

"Sorry," she said. And then it faded again, the pain, disappeared back where it had come from, somewhere in the centre of the pumpkin. She lay back, wiped a tissue across her damp forehead.

Not indigestion. And three hours to go.

"You OK?" The boy was looking at her, concern mixed with distaste.

"Yes. Fine. Thanks."

He turned away.

·   ·   ·

They had landed; everyone was standing up, pulling their luggage down from the lockers. The moment had coincided with a very violent pain. She sat in her seat, bent double, breathing heavily. She was getting the measure of them now; they started, gathered momentum, tore at you, and then departed again. Leaving you at once feebly grateful and dreadfully fearful of their return.

Well, she hadn't had it on the plane.

For the rest of her life, when she read of people describing bad experiences of childbirth, of inadequate pain relief, of briskly bracing midwives, of the sense of isolation and fear, she thought they should have tried it her way. Alone, in a space little bigger than a cupboard, the only pain relief distraction therapy (she counted the tiles on the walls, more and more as the time went by), her only companion a fly buzzing relentlessly (she worried about the fly, the dirt and disease it might be carrying, looked at it thankfully as it suddenly dropped, exhausted, on its back and expired). And then there were some brushes and mops and some clean towels—thank God for those towels, how could she ever have thought one pack of cotton wool would be enough? Her isolation was absolute, her only midwife herself and her precious book, propped against the wall as she lay on the floor, studying its explicitly sanitised diagrams desperately, heaving her child into the world. How could she be doing this, so afraid of pain she couldn't have a filling without a local anaesthetic, so clumsy she could never fasten her own Brownie tie?

But she did.

She managed because she had to. There was nothing else for it.

And when it was all over, and she had cleaned herself up as best she could, and the room too, and wrapped the baby, the tiny, wailing baby, into the clean sheet and blanket she had packed in her rucksack (along with the sharp, sharp scissors and ball of string and large bottle of water which was the nearest she could get to sterilising anything), she sat on the floor, slumped against the wall, feeling nothing, not even relief, looking at the baby, quiet now, but breathing with astonishing efficiency, its small face peaceful, its eyes closed.

It was over. She had become a mother; and in a very short while she would be one no longer, she could walk away, herself again, free, unencumbered, undisgraced.

She could just forget the whole thing. Completely.

It was over.

Wonderfully, neatly, absolutely over . . .

The Year Before

·   ·   ·   ·

They sat there in the departure lounge, on two separate benches, consulting the same departure board: three girls, strangers to one another, the faded jeans, the long hair, the beaded friendship bracelets, the sneakers, the small rucksacks (vastly bigger ones already checked in) all marking them out as backpackers, and about-to-be undergraduates. With school and parents shaken off, a few hundred pounds in their new bank accounts, round-the-world tickets in their wallets, they were moving off to travel a route that would take in one or all of a clearly defined set of destinations: Australia, New Zealand, Thailand, Nepal and the Himalayas, and even the States.

They were very excited, slightly nervous, above all impatient for the journey to begin; constantly exchanging looks, half smiles with one another, moving slowly physically closer as more and more people filled the lounge and the space surrounding them.

It was the announcement that brought them finally together: the announcement that their flight to Bangkok had been delayed for three hours. Their eyes met, eyebrows raised, and they all stood, picking up their bags, moving towards one another, smiling, annoyed at so early an interruption to their journey, and yet welcoming it as an excuse to meet. They settled at a table, and, over some fairly unpleasant coffee, began to talk. Jocasta Forbes, tall and skinny with wild blond hair, opened the discussion; she was travelling, she said, with her brother Josh, "If he ever turns up. He's the baby of the family, totally hopeless."

"Like me. I'm the baby too," said the second, "pretty hopeless as well I'd say . . . Clio," she added, "spelt with an 'i.' Clio Scott." She was neither tall nor skinny, distinctly plump indeed, but extremely pretty with dark curly hair and big sparkly brown eyes.

"And I'm the eldest," said the third. "Martha Hartley . . . Not sure if I'm hopeless or not." She smiled at the other two; studying her they felt sure she was not. Martha was not pretty in the conventional sense; she was small and pale with long straight brown hair, but she carried an air of quiet assurance with her that Jocasta with all her wild beauty lacked.

They chatted easily after that, discovering one another, liking one another increasingly; interrupted by Jocasta waving furiously across the room. "At last. You made it. Wow. Well there he is, everybody, my brother Josh."

Martha and Clio watched him coming towards them; he looked so like Jocasta it was almost shocking. The same wild blond hair, the same dark blue eyes, the same just slightly crooked smile.

Edgy suddenly, Jocasta introduced him. "You're incredibly alike," said Clio, "you could be—"

"We know, we know. Twins. Everyone says so. But we're not. Josh, why are you so late?"

"I lost my passport."

"Josh, you're so hopeless. And fancy only looking for it this morning."

"I know, I know. Sorry."

"Was Mum OK, saying goodbye to you? He's her baby," she added to the others, "can't bear to let him out of her sight."

"She was fine. How was your dinner with Dad?"

"It never took place. He didn't get back till twelve. And this morning he had to rush to a meeting in Paris, so he couldn't see me off either. What a surprise."

"So how did you get here?"

"Oh, he put me in a cab." Her expression was hard; her tone didn't quite match it.

"Our parents are divorced," Josh explained. "Usually we live with our mother but my dad wanted—"

"*Said* he wanted," said Jocasta, "to spend yesterday evening with me. Anyway, very boring, let's change the subject. I'm going to the loo."

She walked away rather quickly.

There was a silence. Josh offered a pack of cigarettes, and Martha and Clio each took one. Josh's arrival had brought a tension into the group that was a little uncomfortable. Time to withdraw, at least until the flight . . .

Their seats were far apart, but they managed to spend some of the flight together, standing in the aisles, chatting, swapping magazines, comparing routes and plans. They would all be going in different directions after a short time in Bangkok; even Josh and Jocasta were splitting, starting out together only to make their parents happy. They spent three days together in Bangkok, three extraordinary days in which they bonded absolutely, adjusting to the souplike heat, the polluted air, the uniquely invasive smell—"I'd call it a mix of rotting vegetables, traffic fumes, and poo," said Clio cheerfully—staying in the same bleak guesthouse on the Khao San Road. It was an incredible and wonderful culture shock—hot, noisy, heaving with people, alight with Technicolor flashing signs, lined with massage and tattoo parlours and stalls selling everything from T-shirts to fake Rolexes and illicit CDs. Every other building was a guesthouse, and all along the street neon-lit cafés showed endless videos.

The girls all kept diaries, writing in them earnestly each night, and evolved a plan to meet in a year's time to read of one another's adventures.

Jocasta inevitably took hers particularly seriously. Reading it many years later, even while wincing at a rather mannered style, she was transported back to those early days, as they moved around the filthy, teeming, fascinating city. She felt the heat again, the nervousness, and along with it, the sense of total intrigue.

She tasted again the food, sold from stalls on the street, tiny chickens, "the size of a tenpence piece," stuck four in a row on sticks, to be eaten bones and all, kebabs, even cockroaches and locusts, deep-fried in woks; she stared out again at the waterfalls of warm rain hitting the streets vertically, which, in five minutes, would have them ankle-deep in water—"Bangkok has the opposite of drainage"—shuddered again at the shantytown ghettos by the river, and smiled at the incredible near-standstill of traffic which filled the vast streets all day long, the overflowing buses, the tuk tuks—motorised three-wheel taxis—hurtling through the traffic, and the motor scooters transporting families of five, or occasionally glamorous young couples, snogging happily as they sat in the midst of the fumes.

They went to Pat Pong, the red-light district, and watched the lady-boys plying their trade—"You can tell they're men, they're much better turned out than the women"—to the post office to write to their parents and tell them where they were, checked the poste restante desk where a horde of backpackers queued to pick up letters from home, messages from friends arranging meetings; they water-taxied through the stinking canals, shocked at the poverty of the hovels where the river people lived, wondered at the gilded and bejewelled palace and temples, and visited the shopping centre, packed with Gucci and Chanel—"This is mostly for rich men's mistresses apparently, and you can get real tea, not the endless Lipton's, wonderful!"

What none of them wrote about—with that year-off meeting in mind—was the other girls, or even Josh, but they learned a great deal about one another very quickly in those three days. That Jocasta had fought a lifelong battle with Josh to gain her father's affection and attention; that Clio had grown up miserably envious of her older sisters' beauty and brilliance; that Martha's jokey complaints about her straitlaced family masked a fierce defensiveness of them; and that Josh, easily charming, brilliant Josh, was both arrogant and lazy. They learnt that Jocasta for all her wild beauty lacked self-confidence; that Clio felt herself acutely dull; that Martha longed above all things for money.

"I do plan to be really rich," she said one night as they sat in one of the endless bars, drinking one cocktail after another, daring one another to eat the deep-fried bugs. "And I mean *really* rich."

And when they parted, Clio and Jocasta on their way down to Koh Samui, Josh for his trip north, and Martha for a couple more days in

Bangkok while deciding exactly what to do, they felt they had been friends for years.

"We'll ring each other when we get back," said Jocasta, giving Martha a last hug, "but if one of us doesn't, we'll track her down somehow. There'll be no escape."

But they knew there would be no need for tracking down; it would be a race to the phone. They would want to see one another again more than anything in the world.

PART ONE

Chapter 1

. . . .

She always felt exactly the same. It surprised her. Relieved. Excited. And a bit ashamed. Walking away, knowing she'd done it, resisting the temptation to look back, carefully subdued—she could still remember old Bob at the news agency telling her one of the prime qualities for a good reporter was acting ability. Of course, the shame was pretty rare, but if it was a real tragedy, then it did lurk about, the feeling that she was a parasite, making capital out of someone else's unhappiness.

This had been a horror to do; a baby in its pushchair, hit by a stolen car; the driver hadn't stopped, had been caught by the police fifty miles away. The baby was in intensive care and it was touch and go whether he would live; the parents had been angry as well as grief-stricken, sitting, clutching each other's hands on the bench just outside the hospital door.

"He'll get what—three years?" the young father had said, lighting his ninth cigarette of the interview—Jocasta always counted things like that, it helped add colour. "And then get on with his life. Our little chap's only had eight months and he could be gone forever. It makes me sick. I tell you, they should lock them up forever for this sort of thing, lock them up and throw away the key—"

She could see her headline then, and hated herself for seeing it.

While she was in the middle of writing her story, she got an e-mail from the office: could she do a quick piece on Pauline Prescott's hair (a hot topic ever since her husband had made it his excuse for taking the car out to drive a hundred yards); they would send a picture down the line to her. Jocasta, wrenching her mind off the desperately injured baby, wondered if any other job in the world imposed such extraordinarily diverse stress at such short notice. She filed that copy via her mobile and had just returned to the baby when her phone rang.

"Is that you, Miss—"

"Jocasta, yes," she said, recognising the voice of the baby's father. "Yes, Dave, it's me. Any news?"

"Yes," he said. "Yes, he's going to be all right, he's going to pull through, we just saw him, he actually managed a smile!"

"Dave, I'm so glad, so very glad," said Jocasta, hugely relieved, not only that the baby was going to live but that she was so touched by it, looking at her screen through a blur of tears.

Not a granite-hearted reporter yet, then.

She filed the story, and checked her e-mails; there was an assortment of junk, one from her brother telling her their mother was missing her and to phone her, a couple from friends—and one that made her smile. "Hello, Heavenly Creature. Meet me at the House when you're back. Nick."

She mailed Nick back, telling him she'd be there by nine, then, rather reluctantly, dialled her mother's number. And flicking through her diary, knowing her mother would want to make some arrangement for the week, realised it was exactly fifteen years to the day since she had set off for Thailand, in search of adventure. She always remembered it. Well, of course she would. Always. She wondered if the other two did. And what they might be doing. They'd never had their promised reunion. She thought that every year as well, how they had promised one another— and never kept the promise. Probably just as well, though. Given everything that had happened . . .

Nick Marshall was the political editor on the *Sketch*, Jocasta's paper; he worked not in the glossy building on Canary Wharf but in one of the shabby offices above the press galleries at the House of Commons. "More like what newsrooms used to be," one of the old-timers had told Jocasta. And indeed many journalists, who remembered Fleet Street when it had been a genuine, rather than a notional, location for newspapers, envied the political writers for working at the heart of things, rather than in shining towers a long cab ride away.

It always seemed to Jocasta that political and newspaper life were extraordinarily similar; both being male orientated, run on gossip and booze (there was no time in the day or night when it was not possible to get a drink at the House of Commons), and with a culture of great and genuine camaraderie between rivals as well as colleagues. She loved them both.

Nick met her in Central Lobby and took her down to Annie's Bar in the bowels of the House, the preserve of MPs, lobby correspondents, and sketch writers. He ushered her towards a small group in the middle; Jocasta grinned round at them.

"Hi, guys. So what's new here? Any hot stories?"

"Pretty lukewarm," said Euan Gregory, sketch writer on the *Sunday News*. "Labour lead shrinking, Blair losing touch, shades of Maggie, too much spin—you name it, we've heard it before. Isn't that right, Nick?"

" 'Fraid so." He handed her a glass of wine. "Pleased to see me?"

"Of course." And she was, she was.

"Good thing somebody loves him," said Gregory. "He's in trouble here."

"Really, Nick? Why?"

"Over-frank on lunchtime radio. Spin doctors very cross!"

"I wish I'd heard you."

"I've got it on tape," said Nick with a grin. "Good. I'm going to take you out to dinner."

"My God. What have I done to deserve this?"

"Nothing. I'm hungry and I can see nothing interesting's going to happen here."

"You're such a gentleman, you know that?" said Jocasta, draining her glass.

In fact Nick *was* a gentleman; nobody was quite sure what he was doing in the world of the tabloid press. His father was a very rich farmer and Nick had got a double first in classics at Oxford. He had rather old-fashioned manners—at any rate, with the older generation—and was much mocked for standing when a grown-up, as he put it, came into the room. But he had developed an early passion for politics and after an initial foray into the real thing had decided he could move into the corridors of power faster via the political pages of a newspaper. He was a brilliant investigative journalist, and came up with scoop after scoop, the most famous, if least important, of which was the revelation that a prominent Tory minister bought all his socks and underpants at charity shops.

It had been love at first sight, Jocasta always said, for her. Nick had walked into the newsroom of the *Sketch* on her first day there, fresh from a news agency in the west country, and she had gone literally weak at the knees. Told he was the political editor, she had assumed, joyfully, that she would see him every day; the discovery that he only came in for the occasional editors' conference, or one-to-one meetings with Chris Pollock, the editor, was a serious blow. As was the news that he had a girlfriend on every paper. She wasn't surprised; he was (as well as extremely tall: about six foot four) very good-looking in an untidy sort of way, with shaggy brown hair, large mournful brown eyes set deep beneath equally shaggy brows, a long and straight nose, and what she could only describe rather helplessly as a completely sexy mouth. He was very thin and slightly ungainly with large hands and feet, altogether a bit like an overgrown schoolboy; he was hopeless at all games, but he was a fine runner and had already done the New York as well as the London marathon, and could be seen early every morning, no matter how drunk he had been the night before, loping round Hampstead Heath where he lived.

It was not entirely true that he had a girlfriend on every paper, but women adored him. His secret was that he adored them back; he found them intriguing, entertaining, and treated them, certainly initially, with a rather old-world courtesy. When Jocasta Forbes arrived on the *Sketch* he rather miraculously had no one permanent in his life.

She had pursued him fervently and shamelessly for several months; she would feel she was really making progress, having flirted manically through evening after evening and been told how absolutely gorgeous he thought she was, only to hear nothing from him for weeks until some newspaper happening brought them together again. She had been in despair until one night, about a year previously, when they had both got extremely drunk at a *Spectator* party, and she had decided a proactive approach was the only one that was going to get her anywhere and started to kiss him with great determination. Unwilling, this time, to leave anything to chance, she then suggested they go back to her place. Nick declared himself hooked.

"I've admired you for so long, you have absolutely no idea."

"No," she said crossly, "I haven't. I've made it very clear I admired you, though."

"I know, but I thought you were just being kind. I thought a girl who looked like you was bound to have a dozen boyfriends."

"Oh for God's sake," said Jocasta, and got into bed beside him and their relationship had been finally—and happily—sealed.

Although certainly not signed. And it troubled Jocasta. She stayed at his flat sometimes, and he at hers (in which case it was Clapham Common he loped across), but they were very much an item, recognising that the next step would be moving in together. Nick said repeatedly that there was absolutely no hurry for this: "We both work horrendous hours, and we're perfectly happy, why change things?"

Jocasta could see several reasons for changing things, the strongest being that they had been together for well over a year and if they were so happy, then that was a very good reason indeed to change things. There was also the fact that she was thirty-three, which meant that next birthday she would be thirty-four and everyone knew that thirty-five was the age when being single stopped being a statement of independence and started being a worry. She loved Nick, and she was fairly sure he loved her, although he seldom said so, and usually then with that preface so hated by women: "Of course." And she felt, with increasing intensity, that the time had come for some proper commitment. At the moment, it seemed no nearer; and it was beginning to worry her. Quite a lot.

"Where are you taking me then?" she said, as they walked into the long corridor.

"Covent Garden," he said. "Mon Plaisir. I don't want to see anyone in the business tonight."

This was unusual; one of the downsides of having a romantic evening with Nick was that he was so in love with his job and so deeply fond of everyone he worked with that she often thought if he ever did get around to proposing to her, and was down on his knees and he saw Trevor Kavanagh from the *Sun* or Eben Black of the *Sunday Times* across the room, he would call them over to join them.

"So," he said as they were finally settled at Mon Plaisir, "tell me about your day. You do look tired, Mrs. Cook."

"I *am* tired, Mr. Butler."

They had once gone to a fancy dress party as the cook and the butler and used the names occasionally in their e-mails (the more indiscreet ones), whenever a code was necessary.

"But it was OK. One tragedy, one trivia—Mrs. Prescott's hair. I do get so tired of doing those stories."

"But you're so good at it."

"I know that, Nick," she said, and indeed she was good at it; she could get into anyone's house, however many other journalists were on the doorstep, make her way into anyone's life, it was all part of her golden charm and, to a degree, she knew, the way she looked. If it was a choice between talking to a male reporter in a sharp suit or an absurdly young-looking girl with long blond hair and wide blue eyes, whose face melted with sympathy for you and whose voice was touched with feeling as she told you this was the worst part of her job and she absolutely hated having to ask you to talk to her, but if you could bear it, she would make it as easy as possible—then it was not a very difficult decision. Jocasta got more bylines on human-interest stories, and what were known in the trade as tragedies—and also those about celebrities caught with their trousers literally down—than almost anyone in Fleet Street. But she was weary of it; she longed to be a feature writer, or a foreign correspondent, or even a political editor.

No editor, however, would give her that sort of chance; she was too valuable at what she did. In the predominantly male culture that was newspapers, a dizzy-looking blonde with amazing legs had her place and that was getting the sort of stories other reporters couldn't. Of course she was extremely well rewarded for what she did, she had a very generous expense account, and most of the time she was happy. But as in her relationship with Nick, she was aware that she wanted more.

"Anything happen to you today? Apart from your scoop?"

"I had lunch with Janet Frean."

"Should I be jealous?"

"Absolutely not. Very nice, I'm sure, but a Wonder Woman type, politician, five children, famously pro-European, sacked from the shadow cabinet is not for me. Actually, I don't exactly like her, but she's an incredible force to reckon with."

"So?"

"So, she's pretty sick of what's going on in the party. They're all feeling depressed. Saying that the party has got everything wrong. That they'll never get in again, that Blair can walk on water, however often it looks like he'll drown. There's talk of some of them doing something about it."

"Like what?"

"Well, like making a break for it. Forming a new party with a few right-minded people within the party."

"And do these people exist?"

"Apparently. Chad Lawrence, for a start."

"Really? Well, I'd vote for him. Most gorgeous man in Westminster. According to *Cosmo* anyway."

"Which won't do him any harm—women voters by the dozen. And then they have a couple more quite senior and high-profile people in the party onside. Most notably Jack Kirkland."

Jack Kirkland had risen from extraordinarily unpromising beginnings—and indeed unlikely for a Tory—from a South London working-class family, to a position as minister for education in the Tory party; his journey from grammar school to an Oxford first was extremely well charted in the media.

"So where is this leading, Nick?"

"A new party. A party just left of centre, but still recognisably Tory, headed up by a pretty charismatic lot, which will appeal to both disillusioned Blair and Tory voters."

"That's what every politician since time began has said."

"I know. But there's a growing disaffection with Blair, and there are a lot of instinctive Tory voters out there, longing for change. If they could look at someone new and strong and say, 'Yes, that's more like it, I could go for that,' Kirkland and his merry men could do rather well."

"And what does this Frean superwoman want you to do?"

"Get the editor onside. Get the paper to support them. When the time comes. I think maybe he would. He's a Tory at heart and the whole thing will appeal to his romantic nature."

"Romantic! Chris Pollock!"

"Jocasta, he's terribly romantic. Not in your women's fiction sense, but David and Goliath, triumph of the underdog, that sort of thing. And our readers are precisely the sorts of people Frean is talking about. They've got to get some funds together and more people onside. There'll be a lot of plotting—which'll be fun. I would say by conference time it'll all be boiling up nicely."

His large brown eyes were brilliant as he looked at her; she smiled. "Is this another exclusive?"

"At the moment. Obviously they chose the finest political editor of the lot."

"Yes, I suppose so." She looked at him. "Maybe," she said thoughtfully, "maybe this could give me my big break. Be my first proper story. You never know."

"Jocasta, I adore you, but this is not a human-interest story."

"It might be. I bet Chad Lawrence has an intriguing private life for a start." She looked at him and took a deep breath. "Nick, there's something I really want to discuss with you. Speaking of human interest . . ."

But he dodged the issue, as he always did, told her he was tired and he just wanted to take her home and curl up with her and think how lucky he was. Feebly, she gave in.

◆

Martha looked out of her office window and saw the first streaks of dawn in the sky. She had worked all night. Of course it was July, and dawn came pretty early: it was only—she glanced at the three-faced clock on her desk, showing London, New York, and Singapore time—only just after four. It seemed much harder in the winter, when the nights were long and the streetlights were still on at seven thirty in the morning. People always said how exhausting it must be, which irritated her. She enjoyed the all-night sessions, found them exciting; and perversely she never felt remotely tired. Adrenaline boosted her all through the following day, she seemed to become high on her own nervous energy, only collapsing as she closed her front door on the day and the deal, poured herself a drink, and sank into the hottest bath she could bear—often to fall asleep and wake an hour later to find it cooling rapidly. People warned her it was dangerous, that she could drown in it or have a heart attack, but Martha pooh-poohed this. It was what she did, she said, how she ran her life, it suited her, and as in so many other tenets of hers—like only eating once a day, or never taking more than one week's holiday at a time—it had always worked very well. Martha was extremely sure that what she did was right.

Although recently she'd been having just a few doubts . . .

Anyway, she had finished now; she had only to get the document typed, complete with its final changes, ready for sign-off. She rang the night secretary, got no asnwer, and rang again. She'd obviously gone walkabout. They were always doing that, gossiping in one another's offices. Very annoying. Well, it would have to go to the word processing centre. She took it down, told them to call her when it was done, and decided to get her head down for an hour and a half in the overnight room and then go to the gym and come back to the office. With the clients coming in and the deal closing at noon, it was terribly important nothing went wrong now. It was one of the biggest acquisitions she had worked on— one financial services company taking over another, made more complex by the worldwide offices of both and a very quixotic CEO in the client company. And the whole thing had begun as a management buyout that had gone wrong in the other company, and the acquisition was salt in the wound of the main protagonist; he had been dragging his feet, looking for a white knight until the eleventh hour, and raising objections to almost every clause in the contract.

But they had done it. Sayers Wesley, one of the biggest, sleekest operations in London, had fought a mighty battle on behalf of their client, and won. And Martha Hartley, at thirty-three one of the youngest partners, had been in control of that battle.

She was happy: very happy indeed. She always felt the same at this point, her muscles aching as if the battle had been a physical one and light-headed with relief. She had sent her assistant home to get a few hours' sleep and the poor exhausted trainee as well; she worked best on her own in these last-lap hours, undistracted, her head absolutely clear.

What was more, she had earned a great deal of money for Sayers Wesley, which would be reflected in her salary in due course. Her £300,000 salary. Her dream of becoming rich had certainly come true.

Her father had asked her, quite mildly, the last time she had gone home, what she did with her earnings; she had appeared, to her irritation, in a list of the up-and-coming women in the city, the new nearly millionaires it had said, and her family had been shocked by the amount she earned. She didn't tell them it had been underestimated by about twenty thousand.

"Spend it," she had said.

"All of it?"

"Well, I've invested some of course. In shares and so on." Why was she feeling so defensive, what was she supposed to have done wrong? "And bought that time-share in Verbier. Which you could also call an investment—I let it if I don't go there." Which she hadn't for the past two years, she had been too busy. "My flat was quite expensive"—she hoped he wouldn't ask how expensive—"and that must be worth at least twice what I paid for it. And I give a lot to charity," she said, suddenly nettled. "Really a lot. And I'm ready and waiting to help you and Mum buy your retirement bungalow."

This was a sore point with her parents. One of the things about being clergy was that you never owned a house, you lived in church accommodation, never had that huge investment most people did nowadays, to cash in on at the end of their lives. Pride had so far kept Peter and Grace Hartley from accepting money from their children, but it was beginning to appear inevitable—and painful. Martha knew that and was as discreet as she could be about it; but there was no very satisfactory way of saying, "Look, Mum and Dad, take thirty thousand, you need it more than I do."

She had the money in a high-interest-bearing account; had saved it without too much difficulty over the past five years. It almost frightened her to think she could do that.

But most of her life was appallingly self-indulgent, and she knew it. Her apartment was dazzling, in one of the most sought-after high-rise buildings in Docklands, with huge sheet-glass windows and coolly pale wood floors, furnished from Conran and Purves & Purves; she owned a soft-top Mercedes SLK, which she used only at weekends; she had a walk-in wardrobe that was an exercise in fashion name-dropping, Armani, Gucci, Ralph Lauren, Donna Karan, and a stack of shoes from Tod's and Jimmy Choo and Manolo Blahnik filed in their boxes in the fashionably approved manner, with Polaroids stuck on the outside for instant recognition. And she worked on average fourteen hours every day, often over the weekend, had a very limited social life, hardly ever went to the theatre or concerts because she so often had to cancel.

"And what about a boyfriend?" asked her sister, married now for seven years with three children. "I suppose you just go out with people in your own line of work."

"Yes, that's right," Martha had said briefly, and it was true; she had had two rather tidy relationships with solicitors on a similar level to her, and one heartbreaker of an affair with a third, an American who had just happened to be married and failed to acquaint her with the fact until it was too late and she was helplessly in love with him. Martha had ended the relationship immediately, but it hurt her horribly, and a year later she was only just able to consider going out with anybody at all.

She wasn't lonely exactly, she worked too hard for that, and she had a few good friends, working women like herself with whom she had dinner occasionally, and a couple of gay men she was immensely fond of, who were invaluable escorts for formal functions. And if an empty Sunday stretched before her, she simply went to the office and worked. But somewhere within her was a deep dark place which she tried to deny, which drew her down into it during her often sleepless nights, usually at the news that yet another friend was settling into a permanent relationship; a place filled with fears: of a life that was not merely independent and successful but solitary and comfortless, where no one would share her triumphs or ease her failures, where fulfilment could only be measured in material things and she would look back with remorse on a life of absolute selfishness.

But (she would tell herself in the morning, having escaped from the dark place) being single was perfectly suited to her, not only to her ferocious ambition; nobody messed up her schedule or interfered with her routine, no untidied clothes or unwashed cups or unfolded newspapers destroyed the perfection of her apartment. Apart from anything else, it meant her life was completely under her control.

She walked back into her office at six, having studied herself in the mirror as she left the overnight room; she certainly didn't look tired. She actually looked as if she had had a good night's sleep.

Martha was not a beautiful girl, and certainly not pretty; she was what the French call *jolie laide*. Her face was small and oval-shaped, her skin creamy, her eyes dark and brilliant, but her nose was just a little too large for her face, a patrician nose, and she hated it and from time to time she considered having surgery, only to reject it again on the grounds that the time could not be spared. Her mouth also displeased her, too big again, she felt, for her face, although her teeth were perfect and very pretty. And as for her hair . . . a lovely gleaming brown certainly, but very straight and fine and requiring endless (and extremely expensive) care simply to produce the easy swinging bob that looked as if it could be washed and left to dry on its own.

And yet people always thought her gorgeous: glossy, perfectly dressed, and wand-slim. Her appearance was the result, like everything else in her life, of a great deal of hard work.

There was a weary-looking Asian woman plugging in a vacuum cleaner in her office.

"Lina, good morning. How are you?" Martha knew her quite well; she was always there at six, her weariness hardly surprising, since this was the first of three jobs that she did each day.

"I'm sorry, Miss Hartley. Shall I come back later?"

"No, no, you carry on. How are you?"

"Oh, I'm pretty well. A little tired."

"I'm sure you are, Lina. How are the family?"

"Not too bad. But Jasmin is giving me trouble."

"Jasmin?" Martha had seen pictures of Jasmin, a beautiful thirteen-year-old, adored by both her parents.

"Yes. Well, it's the school, really. It's a bad school. Like most schools these days, seems to me. She was doing so well, in her last school, working so hard, getting such good marks."

"And now?"

"Now she's bored. Not learning anything. She says the teachers are rubbish, can't keep any discipline. And if she tries to work, she gets teased, told she's a . . . boff. You know what a boff is, Miss Hartley?" Martha shook her head. "A boffin, someone who studies all the time. So already she's slipping. And you know they said at her last school she was university material. It's breaking my heart, Miss Hartley, it really is."

"Lina, that's terrible." Martha meant it; it was the sort of waste she hated. "Can't you get her into another school?"

"All the neighbourhood schools are bad. I'm thinking of taking another job, in the evening at the supermarket. So I can pay for her to go to a private school."

"Lina, you can't. You'll be exhausted."

Lina's eyes met hers, and she smiled. "You're a fine one to talk about exhaustion, Miss Hartley. Working all the nights."

"I know, but I don't go home and care for a family."

"Well, the way I see it, no point caring for them if they're all going to end up on the social. Half the teenagers on the estate are unemployed. No qualifications, nothing. Only way out of it is education. And Jasmin isn't going to get it if she stays where she is. I've got to get her out of it. And if it means me working harder, I'll work harder."

"Oh, Lina!" God, this sort of thing made Martha angry. How dare this ghastly system write off children as they did, denying them their most basic right, while swearing via their absurd league tables that standards were rising. She'd read only the other day that a large number of children were arriving in secondary schools still unable to read. Why should people like Lina have to work themselves literally to death to provide what their children should have by right? But there were only a very few grammar schools left and she had heard only the other day some education minister pledging to see them all closed by the next Parliament; going as they did, he said, against the comprehensive ideal. Some ideal . . .

"I'm sure she'll cope," she said rather helplessly to Lina. "Bright children always do. She'll make her way somehow."

"Miss Hartley, you're wrong. You don't know what it's like there. And no child wants to be the odd one out. If all Jasmin's friends turn against her because she's trying to do her schoolwork, what's she going to do?"

"I—don't know." She wondered suddenly, wildly, if she should offer to help pay Jasmin's school fees—but what about all the other Jasmins, the other bright, wasted children? She couldn't help them all. And it wasn't just education; her father was always telling her of elderly parishioners waiting two years for hip replacements and lying frightened and neglected in dirty wards run by hopelessly overworked nursing staff. But what could she do? What could anyone do?

She checked her diary, to make quite sure that there were no outstanding personal matters to attend to, no birthday cards to be posted that day—she always kept a stack ready in her desk—and no pressing phone calls to make. But it was all under control. She had sent her sister some flowers: she always did remember her birthday. It was the day they had all met at Heathrow, and set off on their travels. And she had said how determined she was to be successful and rich. She wondered if the other two had done as well as she had. And if she would ever see any of them again. It seemed extremely unlikely. And it would certainly be much better not to.

Clio wondered if she was brave enough to do it. To tell him what she had done, tell him why. He wouldn't be pleased. Not in the least. So—oh, Clio, come on, pull yourself together. You may be about to get married, but you're still an individual. Go on, pick up the phone and tell him, or at least tell him you want to talk to him. This is your fiancé you're confronting, not some medical board . . .

"Hello? Rosemary? It's Clio Scott. Yes, hello. Could I speak to Mr. Graves, please? What? Oh, is he? Oh, all right. Must have been a very long list. Well—could he ring me, please? When he's through. No, I'm at home. Thanks, Rosemary. Bye."

Damn. No getting it over quickly then. Still time to change her mind. But—

Her phone rang sharply, made her jump. Surely Jeremy hadn't finished already.

"Clio Scott? Hi. Mark Salter here. Just wanted to say how very pleased we are that you're joining us. I'm sure you'll enjoy it and we can certainly use you. When are you actually joining us? Good, good. Sooner the better. I believe you've had the nerve to ask for time off for your honeymoon. Bloody cheek. Well, look forward to seeing you then. Bye, Clio."

She'd liked Mark Salter. He was a senior partner in the practice and one of the reasons she'd wanted the job so much. That, and the proximity to home. Or rather what would be home. That was something she could tell Jeremy. That one of the things she had based her decision on had been that the job was so near Guildford. He should like that. Surely . . .

"I don't understand." They were sitting at an outside table in Covent Garden in the early-evening sunshine; his face—his slightly severe face—was as much puzzled as angry. If you'd asked for an actor to play a surgeon, Clio often thought, he would have looked like Jeremy, tall, very straight-backed, with brown wavy hair and grey eyes in a perfectly sculpted face. "I really don't. We agreed—or so I thought—that you'd only work part-time. So that you could support me as much as possible. And get the house done, of course."

"Yes, I do know, Jeremy." She waved the hovering waiter away. "And I know I should have consulted you before I accepted. But—initially—it was a part-time job. But there were two, one full-time. And they just rang up and offered me that, and said they had to know right away, as there were others—"

"I'm sure they'd have waited until you'd discussed it with me."

"Yes, of course. But—" Inspiration hit her. Slightly dishonest inspiration. "I did ring you, Anna must have told you. But you were in theatre. And I had to—to make the decision. I can't understand why you mind so much. You know I've done the GP course, we agreed it would be ideal—"

"That has nothing to do with whether you're working part- or full-time. And if you really can't understand it, then I would say we're in trouble."

"That's ridiculous." She took a gulp of wine. "I'm not going on the streets. I'm going to be a GP. Pretty near the house we'll be living in. We need the money, you know we do—"

"Clio, being a GP is a pretty full-time job. And then you'll be on call, often at night, at weekends—"

"You work very full-time," she said, meeting his eyes stormily. "What am I supposed to do while you're operating six days a week? Polish the nonexistent furniture? I'm a trained doctor, Jeremy. I love what I do. It's a wonderful opportunity for me."

"The fact that I work so hard is all the more reason for you to be there when I am at home," he said. "It's not easy, my work. It's physically and mentally very hard. I'm trying to make my way in the world. I need support, and the absolute certainty that I'm going to get it."

"Look," she said, playing for time, knowing that actually she was—to a degree—in the wrong. "I'm sorry if—if I should have consulted you more. But I do find it hard to imagine I won't be at home when you are. Ever. And I got an estimate for the work on the roof today. You know, having it all reslated. Ten grand, Jeremy. Just for the roof. I don't think even doing your private list on Saturday mornings is going to make that sort of money, do you? Not at the moment. When you're a senior consultant, of course."

"And until then I have to do without your support? I see."

"Oh, Jeremy, stop being so ridiculous." Clio was losing her temper fast; that was good, it was the only way she ever found the courage to face him down. "You're twisting everything. Of course I support you. My hours will be very proscribed and I won't be travelling for hours to get to work. And the money I earn can go on the house, make it all happen sooner."

"I'm beginning to think we should never have bought that house," he said, staring moodily into his drink. "If it's going to be that much of a burden to us."

"Jeremy, we knew how much of a burden it was going to be. But we agreed it was worth it."

As they had; after falling in love with it, a beautiful early Victorian farmhouse, in a pretty village just outside Godalming. It had been going for a song, as Jeremy had said, and as he always added, it was going to cost them a grand opera to make it habitable. Neglected for several decades, with every sort of rot and damp, it was nevertheless their dream house.

"We can live here all our lives," Clio had said, looking up at the rotten, damp-stained ceiling, on which sunlight nevertheless still danced.

"And that room next to the kitchen will be absolutely superb for parties," said Jeremy.

"And as for the garden," said Clio, running out through the rotten back door and into the overgrown jungly mess that seemed to go back for miles, and was overlooked only by a herd of cows in the meadow beyond, "it's just wonderful. All those trees. I do so love trees."

So they had offered the absurdly low asking price—and then hit reality as the work estimates began coming in. Which was one of the reasons she had been so extremely tempted by the full-time job. One of them . . .

Jeremy and Clio had met when she was a houseman at University College Hospital and he a senior registrar; she could never quite believe that she had managed to attract someone as handsome and as charismatic as he was. (She was later to discover that he recognised in her—probably subconsciously—a certain willingness to be told what to do, and a rather disproportionate respect for intellect and success.)

She had fallen helplessly in love with him, and the hurt when he made it very clear to her that it would be many years before he could consider any sort of proper commitment had been profound. Desperately humiliated, she had fallen into a relationship with one of her fellow housemen; he was funny and fun, and was very fond of her, as she was of him, but after two years of almost living together, as Clio put it, she arrived unexpectedly at his flat late one night to find him in bed with someone else.

Horribly hurt and disillusioned, she set herself against men altogether for a while, and did a series of hugely demanding hospital jobs, finally settling on geriatrics and a consultancy at the Royal Bayswater Hospital.

"It may sound depressing, but actually it's not. Old people are so much more courteous than most patients and so grateful when you can do something to help," she said whenever people expressed surprise at this most unglamorous of choices.

It was at a medical conference on geriatrics that she met Jeremy again; he was a consultant at the Duke of Kent Hospital in Guildford and lecturing on orthopaedic surgery in the elderly, and they were placed next to each other at dinner.

"So, are you married?" he asked, after half an hour of careful chitchat; and, "No," she said, "absolutely not, what about you?"

"Absolutely not, either. I never found anyone who came anywhere close to you."

Recognising this as the smooth chat-up line that it was, Clio still found it impossible not to be charmed by it; she was in bed with him twenty-four hours later.

A year later they were engaged; now they were a few weeks from being married. And she was generally very happy, but at times filled with a lurking unease. As she was now.

"Look," she said, resting her hand gently on his, "I'm really, really sorry. I never thought it would matter to you so much." (Liar, Clio, liar; it was an unexpected talent of hers, lying.) "Let me do the job for six months. If it's still bothering you after that I'll leave. I promise. How's that?"

He was silent for a moment, clearly still genuinely hurt.

"I just don't understand why you want to do it," he said finally. "You could have such an easy life, do a couple of geriatric clinics at the local hospital, or even a family planning clinic—"

"I hate gynae," said Clio quickly, "as you very well know. And I don't want an easy life. Let me give it a go, Jeremy. I promise it won't interfere with your job. Promise!"

"All right," he said finally, "but I really don't expect to like it. Now can we please order? I'm desperately hungry. I've done three hips and four knees this afternoon. One of them really complicated—"

"Tell me about them," she said, summoning the waiter. There was no swifter way to ease Jeremy into a good mood than listening to him intently while he talked about his work.

"Well," he said, sitting back in his chair, having ordered a large fillet steak and a bottle of claret, and clucked as always over her grilled sole, telling her she starved herself, "the first one, the first hip that is, was very moth-eaten, so I had to—"

Clio tried to concentrate on what he was saying; a couple had settled down at the next table, both obviously backpackers, sun-bleached and skinny . . . just as they had all been. She hadn't been skinny, of course: not at first anyway. But later . . . She often found herself thinking of the three of them at this point in the year, when London was filled with backpackers, about what the other two might be doing and how well they might get along together now. Probably not well at all; and even more probably they would never find out.

Chapter 2

· · · ·

"She would have let me go! I know she would. My real mother. She'd want me to have a good time, not keep me locked up at home like some kind of nun. I just wish she knew how you try and spoil everything for me. And I'm going anyway, you can't stop me."

Helen looked at the flushed, furious face, at the hatred in the dark eyes, and felt sick. This was the only thing she found almost unbearable, when Kate used the fact that she wasn't really her mother against her. She knew it was only her age; she had been warned about it by social workers, by Adoption Support, and by the adoption agency all those years ago, that there was bound to be trouble sometime and it would probably come when Kate hit adolescence. "They have to have something to kick against," Jan had said, "and she'll have that ready to hand. She'll idealise her birth mother, turn her into everything you're not. Just try not to let it get to you. She won't mean it."

Not let it get to her? How could you not, when this was someone you loved so much, lashing out at you, wanting to hurt you, turning from you? Someone you'd cared for all her life—unlike her birth mother!—someone you'd sat up feeding what seemed like all night, nursed through endless childhood ailments, someone you'd comforted, petted, soothed, someone you'd wept over, rejoiced with, been proud of. Someone you'd loved so much . . .

Helen felt the searing sense of injustice in her throat. The urge to say something childish, like "I hate you too," or even "Your real mother hasn't shown much interest in you so far," was violent. "Don't be silly, Kate," she said smoothly. "I don't keep you locked up and I don't want to spoil everything for you. You know that. I just think you're too young to go to the Clothes Show on your own, that's all."

"I'm not going on my own," said Kate. "I'm going with Sarah. And I *am* going. I know why you don't want me to go, you don't like Sarah. You never have. You'd like me to be going round with someone like Rachel, some stupid boff who likes classical music and speaks what you call properly and wears what looks like her mother's clothes. Don't deny it, you know it's true. And don't bother calling me for supper because I'm going up to my room and I don't want any. All right?"

"Fine," said Helen, "absolutely fine."

Adoption Support would have been proud of her, she thought. It wasn't a lot of comfort.

Later, after supper, when Kate had appeared to make a piece of toast with the maximum amount of noise and mess and gone back to her room, all without a word, Helen had asked Jim if perhaps they were being rather too restrictive.

"She is fourteen and a lot of her friends are going."

"Well, she's not," said Jim, picking up the paper, leaving Helen to clear away. "She's too young and that's that. Maybe next year, tell her. That'll calm her down. Thanks for a nice supper."

Helen started to unload the dishwasher, and think—as she always did on such occasions—about Kate's mother. She supposed she would have let Kate go to the Clothes Show. She would have been that sort of person. Liberal. Fun. And, of course, totally irresponsible . . .

She probably wouldn't have got landed with the washing up, either.

Much, much later, after she had gone to bed, she heard Kate crying. She waited for a while, hoping it would stop. It didn't.

She eased herself out of bed, very carefully so that Jim wouldn't wake, and went quietly along the corridor. She knocked on the door.

"Can I come in?"

There was a pause; that was a good sign. If Kate shouted "No" at her, a conversation was out of the question. Helen waited. Finally: "Come in."

She was lying facedown, her tangle of blond hair spread on the pillow. She didn't move. "Sweetheart, please don't cry. Want a drink? Some cocoa or something?"

"No thanks." The "thanks" was a good sign too.

"Well, want a chat then?"

Another silence; then: "Don't care, really." That meant she did.

Helen sat down on the bed, very carefully. "I'm sorry, sweetheart. About the Clothes Show. Dad and I did talk about it again."

"And?" Kate's voice was hopeful.

"I'm sorry. Next year, maybe."

"The others won't even want to go next year. They'll be doing something else. Mum, I'm fourteen. Not four. There'll be loads of people there my age. God, Dad is such a dinosaur!"

"Not really," said Helen, struggling to be loyal. "We both feel the same. I'm sorry. Look, how would you like it if we went shopping tomorrow? Spent Granny's birthday money?"

"What, and bought some nice white socks or something? No thanks." There was a silence. Then Kate said, "Mum . . ."

"Yes?"

"I don't really hate you."

"I know you don't, sweetheart. I didn't think you did."

"Good. I just feel so—so angry sometimes."

"Most people of your age do," said Helen. "It's part of growing up."

"No. I don't mean that. Of course I get angry with you. You're so"— her lips twitched—"so *annoying*."

"Thanks."

"That's OK. But I mean—angry with her. With my . . . my mother. If I knew why she did it, it might help. How could she have done that? How could she? I might have died, I might—"

"Lovely, I'm sure she made sure someone had found you. Before she—she went away."

There was a long silence, then Kate said, "I want to know about her so much. So, so much."

"Of course you do."

"She must have had her reasons, mustn't she?"

"Of course she must. Very good ones."

"I mean her life must have been very difficult."

"Very difficult. Impossible."

"It must hurt to have a baby. So—to do that all by yourself, not tell anyone—she must have been very brave." Helen nodded. "I wonder sometimes how I'm like her. In what ways. But I don't think I'm that brave. I mean, I wouldn't have a filling without an injection for instance. Having a baby must hurt much more than that."

"Yes, I think I would say it does. But Kate, you don't know what you can do till you have to."

"I s'pose so. And then I think, what else do I know about her? Hardly anything. Except that she was terribly irresponsible. Is that what worries you about me? Does it make you extra fussy, do you think I'm going to go off and sleep around and get pregnant? I suppose it does."

"Kate, of course it doesn't. Don't be ridiculous. We would never think that."

"Well, why are you so old-fashioned and strict then?"

"We just want to take care of you, that's all. It's—"

"I know, I know, it's a wicked world out there, crazed drug dealers and white slave traffickers on every corner. Especially at the Clothes Show."

"Kate—" Helen looked at her and saw she was half smiling.

"It's all right, Mum. You can't help being senile."

"No, I can't. Sorry. You all right now?"

"Sort of. Yes. Thanks for coming in."

Helen had reached the door when Kate said, "Mum. What would you think about me trying to find her?"

"Your birth mother? Absolutely fine, sweetheart. Of course, if that's what you want."

"It is. Yeah."

"Right then, of course you must." She hesitated, then: "If there's any way I can help—"

"No, it's OK." The small face had closed up again. "I'd rather do it on my own, thanks."

Thank God for the darkness, Helen thought, closing the door quickly; otherwise Kate would have seen her crying.

Sometimes, she thought, as she drank the sweet black coffee she always turned to in times of crisis, sometimes she wished she'd ignored all the conventional wisdom and not told Kate the truth. Not, of course, said that she was her natural mother, but that her own mother had died and she had adopted her because of that. It would have been so much easier for a child to cope with. How could a small person of seven—which was the age Kate had been when she had actually framed the question, "What happened to my other mummy?"—possibly digest the news that her other mummy, her real mummy, had abandoned her in a cleaning cupboard at Heathrow airport, leaving her without even a nappy, wrapped in a blanket, and not so much as a note? Helen had dressed it up, of course, had said she was all tucked up in a blanket, nice and warm and snug, and that her birth mother had made quite, quite sure she had been safely discovered before going away. At the time Kate had appeared to accept it, had listened very intently and then skipped off to play in the garden with her sister. Later she had come in and said, "I've decided I probably am a princess."

"You are *my* princess," Jim had said, having been warned that the dreaded conversation had finally taken place, and Kate had smiled at him radiantly and said, "Well, you can be my prince. I'd like to marry you anyway."

Life had been so simple then.

But of course you couldn't lie to·them because as they grew older more and more questions would be asked. If the birth mother had·died, where was her family, where were Kate's grandparents, surely they'd want to know her, and her father for that matter? And did she have any brothers and sisters, and— No, it would have been impossible to sustain as an explanation. The truth had to be told.

They had several friends with adopted children, made through all the counselling and support groups. Adoption was a fact of Kate's life; indeed when she was very small she had asked everybody if they were adopted. Told that she was special, that she had been chosen by her parents rather than just been born to them, like her sister, Juliet (arriving to her parents' enormous surprise and pleasure just two years after they had adopted Kate), she had for a while been entirely happy about it, had never seemed to give it a great deal of thought; until one terrible day when she had come home from school, aged nine, crying and saying that one of the girls had been teasing her about being adopted.

"She said if my other mum had loved me she wouldn't have left me."

"Now, Kate, that isn't true," said Helen, panic rising in her as she recognised the beginning of the real problems that faced them all. "I've told you, she wanted a happier home for you than she could give you, she wanted you to go to people who could care for you properly. She couldn't—I've explained that to you lots of times."

Kate had appeared to accept that at the time, but as she grew older and sharper and the truth became balder and uglier, it troubled her more and more. She stopped talking about her other mother, as she called her, pretended to any new friends that Helen and Jim were her real parents, and then a little later, constructed elaborate lies about a mother who had died in childbirth and entrusted her to Helen, her oldest and dearest friend.

Which was fine until other friends, who knew what had really happened, had revealed it. And so in the end, there was no more pretending. And she had to learn to live with the ugly truth.

Helen's mother had been very supportive as Kate grew increasingly difficult; having said that she had feared it would happen all along, ever since Helen had told her they were adopting a foundling (as they were still called), she then also told Helen that she wouldn't say it again. Which she didn't and moreover proceeded to do all she could to help. This mostly consisted of slipping Kate ten-pound notes, taking her on shopping expeditions—"Of course I know what she'll like, Helen, I'm in the fashion business, aren't I?"—and treating her to expensive lunches at smart restaurants. Jim disapproved of the whole relationship, but as Helen pointed out, her mother was a safety valve, someone Kate could talk to if she felt she needed it.

"Why can't she talk to us, for God's sake?"

"Jim, I sometimes despair of you. The whole point is there are things she can't talk to us about. Things she thinks will upset us, things she won't want to tell us. Better my mother, who she sees as someone rather raffish and naughty, than that dreadful Sarah."

Jim didn't argue. Helen knew there was another reason he didn't like her mother: she favoured Kate over Juliet. Which was on the face of it illogical, since Juliet was Helen's own child; but she was also Jim's, and had many of Jim's characteristics. She was a very sweet child, and extremely clever and musically gifted, but she was quiet and shy, with none of Kate's quicksilver charm, and she found Jilly Bradford rather daunting.

It had been one of the most glorious days in Helen's life—her wedding day and that of Juliet's birth being the others—when Mrs. Forster from the adoption agency had telephoned to say that there was a baby who they might like to consider adopting. "She's a foundling," Mrs. Forster had said, "so there could be no question of her ever going back to her birth family." Helen had actually been reading about the baby in the papers—she had made front-page news, as such babies always did—and there had been photographs of her being held by a phalanx of nurses at the South Middlesex Hospital, her small face almost invisible within the folds of a blanket.

BABY BIANCA the caption had said. "So called by the nurses because she was found in a cleaning cupboard at Heathrow airport (Bianca is Italian for 'white'), now five days old." It went on to say that the social services were hoping to contact her mother who might be in need of medical attention, and appealed for anyone who had noticed anything untoward at terminal three at Heathrow airport, on the night of August 16, to contact their nearest police station.

"How could anyone do that?" Helen had said to Jim, and when Baby Bianca was finally handed to her by the foster mother, Helen felt that, to a degree, she already knew her.

Helen had been very nervous, driving to meet Bianca for the first time; what if she didn't feel anything for her? What if the baby started screaming the minute she saw her, sensing her complete inexperience and incompetence? What if she just proved to be totally unmaternal? But it was love at first sight; Bianca (shortly to become Kate) opened large blue eyes (shortly to become deep, dark brown) and stared up at her, waving one tiny, frondlike fist, making little pouting shapes with her small mouth, and Helen knew, quite simply, that she wanted to spend the rest of her life with her.

Today had not been one of the happiest days of her life, though. She poured herself a second cup of coffee and tried to face the reality of that small, dependent creature, who had become in some strange way as surely her own flesh and blood as her natural daughter, seeking out the woman who had actually given birth to her and perceiving her as her mother.

Whoever that woman was, Helen thought, and whatever she was like, she would undoubtedly want to kill her.

Chapter 3

· · · ·

"Jocasta! Attempted suicide. Village near Hay Tor, Dartmoor. Go!"

God, this was terrible, this foot-and-mouth epidemic, she thought, turning her car onto the A303. Every day there were more cases, hundreds of them; the shocked face of Nick Brown, the agriculture minister, appeared every day on the television, usually followed by shots of Tony Blair looking carefully ill at ease; they both spoke (also every day) the same platitudes, the fact that it was being contained, the outbreaks were being carefully monitored, if everyone obeyed the strict regulations laid down by the government it would shortly be under control. It hardly seemed like that. Farmers were in despair, their farms under siege, the dreadful pall of smoke drifting from the funeral pyres of cattle, large tracts of the countryside silent, the fields empty of livestock. The royal parks, Richmond and Hampton Court, were shut, and even the Peak District and the Yorkshire Dales were closed to walkers; the land itself seemed dark and despairing.

Jocasta had done a few stories already, but none as desperate as this—although Nick had said half the farmers in the country would be found hanged in their barns if the government didn't do something soon. There were terrible stories of bungled shootings of animals by the police, of huge heaps of unburied cattle in once-lovely meadows, of a dreadful stench drifting across a five-mile radius of each one.

"They should get the army in at least," Nick said. "Do the job properly. What do these idiots think they're doing, messing about with volunteers?"

Jocasta felt half afraid of what she might find at Watersmeet Farm on the southern edge of Dartmoor.

It was after two when she reached the farm. The gates were barred, disinfectant buckets and beds of straw on either side of them. There were at least half a dozen reporters standing around, and as many photographers, and several police cars as well. She jumped out and asked one of the reporters she recognised what was happening.

"The chap's all right, apparently. But the wife's desperate. Whole herd slaughtered yesterday, over there, behind the farmhouse. It's horrible. Poor people. Children in there, too. Anyway, you won't get in, Jocasta. Not even you. *Daily News* has just got very short shrift. Offered money as usual."

"Well, I'm going to try my luck," said Jocasta.

"If you crack this one, Jocasta, I'll eat my notebook."

Two hours later she called and told him to start munching. She had gone to the village shop, where she had spent an enormous amount of money on things she didn't want and listened sympathetically to the woman talking about the misery the entire area was enduring, how her own trade had dropped by half, how the whole of the countryside seemed to be dying along with the cattle. "I'd so love to talk to the poor farmer's wife," Jocasta said.

"Well, I don't know as she'd talk to you, but I could ask her sister what she thinks. She lives next door to me. Angela Goss her name is."

"Do you think she'd mind? I'd only want a very short time with her."

Angela Goss said she'd see her, but only for a minute. "And don't think I can get you into the farm, because I can't."

"Of course not," said Jocasta. What Angela Goss did arrange was for Jocasta to speak to her sister on the phone.

It had been the noise at first, she said, the endless firing of the rifles and the cattle bellowing. They had tried not to listen, had put loud music on, but they couldn't help it. And then the silence, it had been awful, that dead, heavy silence, and watching the ewes leading their lambs, some only a couple of days old, into the meadow to be slaughtered.

"They say there's no sentiment in farming, but Geoff was crying, same as me. Course they promised they'd dig trenches, but they didn't have the equipment, so they're piled up there, these beautiful animals in a great horrible heap, starting to smell. It's criminal, it really is."

Her husband had been very quiet the day of the slaughter, she said, hardly speaking; it was the following morning quite early that she'd re-alised he was missing. "I found him in the cowshed; he'd driven his car in, and put the hosepipe through the window. I got him out, just in time. But what for, I'm wondering? What's he got now? Just this ghost of a place. And what's it done to the children, all of it, I'd like to know? What a memory to carry through their lives. I—I must go now," she said, her voice breaking. "You'll have to excuse me. But you'll tell them, won't you, your paper, what it's really like, the loss of a future. It's like some terrible bad dream. Only we're not going to wake up."

Jocasta filed her story and then drove back to London, wondering how many of the farms she passed were living in the same nightmare.

"I can't tell you how awful it was," she said to Nick on the phone. "It's a kind of living death they're all in. Poor, poor people. They feel so let down and so ignored."

"You sound tired, sweetie."

"I *am* tired," said Jocasta irritably. "I've just driven three hundred miles. I feel about a hundred years old."

"Poor old thing. Would you like me to tuck you up in bed with some hot milk?"

"Well, you can tuck me up in bed with yourself. That'd be nice. But I'm going into the office. Chris wants to see me. Not sure why."

"Good luck. I'll see you later. I'll be at the House. If I'm not in Annie's, I'll be up in the press dining room."

Chris Pollock was young for an editor—only forty-one—and was famously easygoing until he wasn't, as one of the reporters had told Jocasta on her first day. He would remain calm and patient in the face of quite considerable crises, leaving his staff to work without too much interference from him—until they either made a mistake or missed a strong story that another newspaper, most notably the *Mail*, had got. Upon which he became incandescent with rage and the unfortunate reporter—or section editor—was first bawled out and then left to stew for several days before being summoned again, either to be fired or told they were to be given another chance. This was an inescapable process and there was absolutely no knowing which way it would go.

He had his philosophy of the paper—"soft news with a hard centre"—and expected all the journalists to know what he meant. What it did mean was the human stuff on the front page, "and I don't mean bloody soaps, I mean people-slanted stories"; an adherence to the paper's politics, "right with a dash of left, just like New Labour"; and fairly hefty, well-written slugs of news on pages three, four, five, and six. The *Sketch* was also very strong on its female coverage and ran ongoing campaigns about things like health, child care, and education.

As Jocasta went in, Chris was sitting with his back to the window, the lights of London spread out beneath him; he smiled at her. He was an attractive man—short and heavily built, with brilliant blue eyes and close-cropped dark hair—and he had an energy that was like a physical blow. He had a great deal of success with women.

"This is a great story." He thumped a page on his desk. "Brilliant. You did very, very well. See what we've done with it."

Jocasta looked: it was a whole page, and there was the photograph

Angela Goss had given her of Geoff Hocking and over it a headline that read THEY KILLED HIS CATTLE. HE TRIED TO KILL HIMSELF, and underneath as a caption, "The idle farmer on the silent farm."

"That's great," she said. "I'm so pleased you kept that in. About the silent farm."

"It's a good quote. Anyone else get in?"

"Don't think so."

"Good girl. Anyway, nice big display for you."

"Yes. Thanks, Chris."

He sat in silence for a moment, looking at her, then he said, "This is the front page, you know. Did you realise that?"

Jocasta, already overwrought and upset, burst into tears.

"The front page!" she said to Nick. She had found him in the press dining room and had dragged him out onto the corridor. "I got the front page." And she was actually jumping up and down. "Isn't that great? Isn't that fantastic?"

"Bloody fantastic," he said and gave her a hug. "You're a genius. How on earth did you do it? I've been watching the news, it looked impenetrable."

"Let's just say I boldly went where none had gone before."

"Very boldly. Clever girl."

"Actually," she said, "I have to tell you it wasn't all that difficult. Come on, you can buy me some champagne. I can't believe it! My very own, very first front page."

Her phone rang endlessly next day. Everyone had seen the story, wanted to congratulate her. Her mother called, Josh called, and even Beatrice, her rather daunting barrister sister-in-law.

"I think it's thrilling," she said, her clear-cut voice warmer than usual. "And it's such a very good piece of reporting. I'm extremely impressed. Those poor, wretched people. Well done, Jocasta. Very well done."

"Thank you," said Jocasta. "And thank you for calling."

"My dear girl, anyone would call. It's a great achievement."

But not anyone would call. The one call she had been waiting for, longing for, did not come. Her father as always had chosen to ignore her. And it hurt: dreadfully.

The doorbell ringing endlessly broke into her heavy first sleep; she'd had a very long and tedious evening and hadn't filed the story she'd been on until midnight. Nick was working late and going home to Hampstead and she had been looking forward to a long, uninterrupted sleep. She stumbled down the stairs, shouting curses at Nick—he forgot his keys at least once a week—and opened the door to a dishevelled and wretched-looking Josh.

"Can I come in?" he said. "Beatrice has turned me out."

It was a wonder she hadn't done it before, Jocasta thought, sitting him down on her sofa, going into the kitchen to make him some coffee. He'd had his first affair a year into their marriage, and six months after the birth of their second child, he had done it again. A year after that he had what he swore was a one-night stand with his secretary; Beatrice had said then that the next time would be the last. Now she had discovered an affair that had been going on for five months with an English girl working for the Forbes Parisian office and, true to her word, had literally locked him out of the house.

"I'm such a fool," Josh kept saying, "such a bloody fucking idiot."

"Yes you are," Jocasta said, looking at him as he sat there, tousled head in his hands, tears dripping rather unromantically onto his trousers. At thirty-three he still had some vestiges of the beautiful boy he had been, with his blond hair, his high forehead, his rather full, curvy mouth. He was distinctly overweight now and his colour was too high, but he was attractive, and he had a slightly helpless, self-deprecating charm which made women want to take care of him. He was always late, very untidy, and endlessly good-natured; everyone loved Josh. He wasn't exactly witty, but he was a very funny raconteur, he lit up a room or a dinner table, and had that most priceless social gift of making others feel amusing too.

Jocasta had always thought that Beatrice, less naturally charming and attractive than he, must find it trying, but her attitude towards Josh was one of slightly amused indulgence, and she tolerated much of his bad behaviour with immense good nature.

Beatrice was not beautiful, but there were things about her that were: her eyes, large, dark, and warm (distracting from a heavy nose and jaw); her hair, long, thick, and glossy; and her legs, longer even than Jocasta's and as slender. She was, at the time she and Josh met, already making an awesome reputation for herself as a criminal barrister. Josh was drifting through life, ostensibly being groomed to take over the family company. He had given up law even before leaving university, and had read philosophy instead. He had then spent a year auditioning for various drama schools, all of which rejected him, and, finding himself unemployed and unable to finance his fairly expensive lifestyle, had finally gone to his father expressing a rather unlikely and sudden interest in the Forbes business.

Ronald Forbes had not greeted this news with the enthusiasm Josh had hoped for, but he said he'd give him a taste of it and see how he liked it. The taste was not too sweet; on the first day Josh was not given the plush room he expected in the London office, but a lesson in driving a forklift in the factory at Slough. After a month, he progressed to the assembly line and thence to the sales office, where he learnt to use the company computer. He had perversely quite enjoyed the factory period, but this was mind-numbing; he stopped trying, kept calling in sick and taking longer and longer lunch hours around the pubs of Slough. His father sent for him and told him if he didn't pull himself together he'd be fired; Josh told him that would be a happy release.

That had been the day of the dinner party at which he'd met Beatrice.

Less than a year later they were married. People who didn't know them very well could never quite understand their relationship, why it worked; the simple fact was that they needed each other. Josh needed order and direction; and Beatrice, who had been born ordered and self-motivated, needed the emotional and social support of a husband who also had plenty of money, criminal litigation being the least financially rewarding branch of the law.

She was hugely attracted to Josh, she found him surprisingly interesting, and he was potentially very rich. Josh had discovered that Beatrice was a great deal less confident than she seemed, that she had a sexual appetite which was quite surprising given her rather stern personality, and also that she was the first person he had met for a long time who seemed to think he had any real potential for anything.

"I think you could do wonderful things with that firm," she said (by the Monday evening she had looked it up on the Internet and assessed its potential), and sent him to his father to apologise and to ask for his job back; a month after that, when he was working genuinely hard, she invited

Ronald Forbes to dinner with her and Josh. They impressed each other equally.

"I can see he's difficult and incredibly authoritarian," she said to Josh afterwards, "but he's got so much drive and energy. And I love the way he talks about the company, as if it was someone he's in love with."

"It is," said Josh gloomily.

Ronald Forbes in his turn found Beatrice's intellect, clear ambition, and intense manner engaging; he told her she was exactly what Josh needed and said he hoped he would be seeing a great deal more of her in the future. Beatrice told him she hoped so too.

Six months later Josh was appointed deputy sales manager for the south of England and given the longed-for London office, and Beatrice told him she thought they should get married. Josh panicked, and said maybe one day, but what was the rush, things seemed fine to him as they were, and Beatrice said not really, as she was pregnant.

"As if," Jocasta had said to her mother, who deeply disliked Beatrice, "a girl like her would get pregnant by accident. I bet she decides exactly when she ovulates as well as everything else. God, he's an idiot."

But Josh surprised everyone—including Beatrice—by acknowledging his responsibilities and agreeing that they should marry. They had a small but beautifully organised wedding at Beatrice's home in Wiltshire, and a honeymoon in Tuscany. Ronald Forbes was as delighted as his ex-wife was not.

Beatrice had worked until she was eight months pregnant and returned to her chambers two weeks after the birth of Harriet—known as Harry. Two years to the day after Harry's birth, Charlotte—inevitably called Charlie—was born.

That had been two years ago. Josh was now deputy managing director of Forbes Furniture, and working just hard enough to keep both Beatrice and his father satisfied. Beatrice had switched from criminal to family law, as being more compatible with family life and running their large Clapham house and hectic social life with apparent ease. The fact remained that domestic abuse cases were funded by legal aid and therefore still not especially lucrative; Josh paid most of the bills.

Jocasta wanted to dislike Beatrice, but she never managed it; she was, for all her bossy manner and workaholism, surprisingly kind and genuinely interested in Jocasta's life and career. Nick adored her, he said she was the sexiest sort—"I bet she puts on a gym slip and sets about old Josh with the cane"—and was charmed by the way she always read his column, and discussed whatever story she had most recently read with great seriousness, as indeed she did Jocasta's. There was absolutely no doubt in anyone's mind, both within and outside the family, that Beatrice was the perfect wife for Josh.

"Why did I do it, Jocasta?" he moaned now, between sips of coffee. "Why am I such an idiot?"

"No idea," said Jocasta. "But I have to say, it's Beatrice I feel sorry for. I'd have slung you out the last time. And you realise Dad will be on her side, don't you? He won't let her starve."

"Don't think I haven't thought of that, either," said Josh. "I don't hold a single card, do I? What can I do?"

"You can't actually do anything. Except wait for a while. And keep telling her how sorry you are. You've got one wonderful thing in your favour. And it just might be enough."

"Jesus, I hope so. I'd do anything, anything at all, if I thought there was a chance she'd forgive me."

"I suspect she's heard that before."

"Yes, all right. Don't kick a man when he's down. So—what is this one wonderful thing?"

"I think," said Jocasta, and her voice was slightly sad, "that she loves you."

•◆•

Martha raised her lips to the silver chalice and took a sip of wine, struggling to concentrate on the moment, on the fact that she was taking the Blessed Sacrament. She never could, of course. Not completely. She had moved so far from her father's church, her parents' faith, that she only went to church when she was staying for the weekend in Binsmow. It pleased them, and it charmed the parishioners; the fact that she felt an absolute hypocrite was immaterial. And in a way she enjoyed it, savouring the peace, the reassurance that nothing had changed.

She stood up now, walked slowly back to her seat, her head carefully bowed, taking in nonetheless the fact that the church was three-quarters empty and, apart from a few—a very few—teenagers, she was the only person there who could be called young. How could her father do this week after week, year after year? How could his own faith withstand what seemed to Martha the humiliation of knowing that his life's work was for the large part rejected by the community? She had asked him once, and he had said she didn't understand: St. Andrews was still the centre of the parish, it didn't matter that the congregation was so small, they turned to him when they needed him, when illness or death or marriage or the christening of a new baby required his services, and that was enough for him.

"But, Dad, don't you want to tell them they should have done a bit more for the church before expecting it to do things for them?"

"Oh, no," he said and his eyes were amused. "What good would that do? Alienate them, and fail them in their hours of need? Martha, I believe in what I'm doing and I've never regretted it. And it enables me to do some good. Quite a lot of good, even. I like that. Not many professions allow it."

"I suppose you mean mine doesn't," she said irritably.

"I didn't. I wouldn't dream of drawing such a comparison." But she knew he would.

She had come down this weekend very much from a sense of duty; her sister had called her to say that her parents were a bit low.

"Mum's arthritis is bad, and Dad gets so upset because he can't help. I try to cheer them up but they see me all the time, I'm not a treat like you are. You haven't been for months, Martha."

"Well, I'm sorry," she said. "I've been—"

"Yes, I know how busy you've been." Her sister's voice was sharp. "I've been quite busy too, actually, trying to cope with work and the children. Even Michael gets down more than you do."

"Yes, all right," Martha said. She was tempted to say it was easy for Michael, their brother, who was in his first year of teaching, and had a great deal of spare time, but she didn't. In any case, Anne was right: she didn't come down much.

"I promise I'll come very soon," she said finally. "I really do promise."

"Good," said Anne and rang off.

Martha wished she could like Anne more. But she was so—so sanctimonious, so much too good to be true. She was married to a very hardworking, poorly paid social worker, and they had three children, no help in the house, only one car, and Anne had a job as a special needs assistant at one of the local schools to make ends come a little nearer to meeting. On top of that she did a lot of volunteer work and even helped her father in the parish, now that their mother was finding it difficult to cope. To Martha it looked like the life from hell; especially being married to Bob the Social Worker, as she thought of him, rather like Bob the Builder. Martha actually felt Anne would be better off with Bob the Builder; at least he would be some practical use around the house. Bob Gunning added acute unhandiness to his other shortcomings, and all the DIY jobs were done by poor Anne. There really did seem to be very little joy in her life.

Martha could see how excessively irritating her own gilded existence must seem to her sister, not just the apparently limitless money, with only herself to spend it on, but the way she did find so little time to visit, to help their parents—other than financially, which in any case they would accept only under extreme pressure. And although she had come down this weekend, it would be the only one for some time, she knew; the general election was looming and that always resulted in a lot of work, as the money markets became jittery and the big corporations swung into action to accommodate any changes.

Not that they would be very remarkable; Blair continued to sit high in the polls, smiling purposefully, making empty promises. He would get in again; there was no doubt about it.

"Things are pretty bad around here," her father said.

"In what way?" She took his arm as they walked back.

"The countryside has been dreadfully hit by the foot-and-mouth business. There's an air of depression over everything."

"Really?" said Martha. She had read about the foot-and-mouth tragedy of course, but sheltered as she was in her glass tower in Docklands, it had somehow lacked reality.

"Yes. Poor old Fred Barrett, whose family's had a farm just outside Binsmow for five generations, has struggled on until now, but this has finished him. He's selling up. Not that anyone will buy the farm. And then I've got God knows how many parishioners waiting to go into hospital. Poor old Mrs. Dudley, waiting eighteen months now for a hip replacement, in real pain, and still they tell her another six months. It's criminal, it really is."

"Everything's a mess," said Martha, thinking of Lina and her daughter Jasmin. "Absolutely everything."

She walked into her mother's bedroom; Grace was lying in bed, looking pale.

"Hello, dear. I'm sorry I'm not seeing to breakfast. I slept so badly; the pain wakes me, you see, and then I get back to sleep around six and don't hear the alarm."

"Oh Mum, I'm so sorry. Can I get you anything, tea, coffee . . . ?"

"I'd love a cup of tea. I'll be down in a minute."

"No, I'll bring it up," said Martha. "Spoil you a bit. Is the pain very bad?"

"Sometimes," said Grace. "Not always. You know. Grumbles away."

"What does the doctor say?"

"He's referred me to a consultant, but there's a year's waiting list at least. In the old days, when we still had the local hospital, it would have been much quicker. But it's gone, of course. Dr. Ferguson gives me painkillers, which help, but they make me feel sick."

"Mum, won't you let me pay for the orthopaedic consultant at least? You could see him so much more quickly. This week probably."

"No, Martha. We don't believe in private medicine. Or jumping the queue—it's immoral."

"You might not believe in it," said Martha briskly, "but it would stop you being in pain. Wouldn't that be worth it?"

"Martha, we can't be beholden to you. It's not right."

"Why not? I was beholden to you for all those years. And suppose it had been me? When I was a little girl. In pain, not able to see a doctor for more than a year. Wouldn't you have thought anything was worth it to help me? Wouldn't you have set your principles aside?"

"Possibly," said Grace with a feeble smile. "I suppose . . ."

"Good," said Martha, seeing victory. "It's no more than you deserve. I'd much rather spend some of that disgraceful salary on you than on some new Manolos."

"What are they, dear?"

"Shoes."

"Oh, I see. Some new style, is it?"

"Something like that," said Martha.

After lunch her sister called. "My next-door neighbour, she's a widow"—she would be, Martha thought—"needs help. Her son's car's broken down and he needs a lift back to London. I said I was sure you wouldn't mind taking him."

Martha felt disproportionately outraged. She did mind, very much. She had been longing for the peaceful drive back to London, with her stereo playing, catching up on phone calls, having the time to think . . . and of course *not* to think. She didn't want some spotty lad sitting beside her for three or four hours, requiring her to make conversation.

"Couldn't he get the train?"

"He could, but he can't afford it. Martha, it's not much to ask, surely. He's quite sweet, I've met him."

"Yes, but—" Martha stopped.

"Oh forget it," said Anne and her voice was really angry. "I'll tell him he'll have to hitch a lift. You just get on back to your smart life in London."

Martha promptly felt terrible. What kind of a cow was she turning into? Anne was right, it wasn't a lot to ask. She just didn't want to do it . . .

"No," she said quickly, "all right. But he'll have to fit in with me time-wise and I'll drop him at an Underground station, all right? I can't spend half the night driving round London."

"You're so extremely kind," said Anne. "I'll tell him then. What time exactly would suit you, Martha? Fit in best with your very heavy time-table?"

"I'm leaving at about four," said Martha, refusing to rise to this.

"Could you make the huge detour to pick him up? It would take at least fifteen minutes."

"I'll pick him up," said Martha.

Anne came out of her house as Martha drew up; her sniff as she looked at the Mercedes was almost audible.

"So good of you to do this," she said. "He's all ready. We've been chatting, haven't we, Ed?"

"Yes. Hey, cool car. It's very kind of you, Miss—"

"Hartley," said Martha. She had been fiddling with the dashboard, not looking at him; she took in only the voice, the classless young London voice, and sighed. It was going to be a terribly long drive.

Then she got out, took off the sunglasses she had been wearing—and found herself staring at one of the most beautiful young men she had ever seen.

He was quite tall, over six foot, with messy short blond hair and astonishingly deep blue eyes; he was tanned, with a few carefully scattered freckles on a perfectly straight nose, and his grin, which was wide, revealed absolutely perfect white teeth. He was wearing long baggy shorts, a style she hated, trainers without socks, and a rather crumpled white shirt; he looked like an advertisement for Ralph Lauren. Martha felt less resentful suddenly.

"Mum's at church, but she said I was to thank you from her," he said. "Shall I put my bags on the backseat?"

"Yes, do," said Martha. "Well, Anne, sorry not to have seen more of you. Next time, perhaps."

"Perhaps," said Anne. Her tone was still chilly.

"This really is very kind of you," said Ed again as they pulled down the road. "I do appreciate it."

"That's all right," said Martha. "What happened to your car?"

"It just died," he said. "It was just an old banger. Present from Mum for my twenty-first. She said I shouldn't take it on long journeys. Looks like she was right."

"So what will you do?"

"Goodness knows." He looked round the car. "This is really cool. Convertible, yeah? I don't suppose you use this much in London."

"Not during the week, no," said Martha. "Not much use for a car where I live."

"Which is?"

"Docklands."

"Cool."

"Quite cool, I suppose," she said, hoping she didn't sound like some pathetic older woman acting young.

"And you're a lawyer?" he said. "Is that right? Do you get all dressed up in a white wig?"

"No," she said, smiling against her will. "I'm not a barrister. I'm a solicitor."

"Oh, right. So you do people's divorces, help them buy their houses . . ."

"No, I work for a big city firm. Sayers Wesley."

"So—you work all night, see big deals through, that sort of thing."

"That sort of thing." She glanced at him; he had put a baseball cap on back to front, another thing she hated; impossibly, it suited him.

"And earn a fortune? Yeah?"

"I don't know how you would define a fortune," she said coolly.

"Sorry. I didn't mean to sound rude. I just get interested in people." He turned to smile at her, an astonishing, beautiful smile.

"So I see. What do you do?"

"I'm just temping at the moment," he said, "doing IT stuff. It's pretty boring. But I'm going away in a couple of months. It's paying for that."

"Where are you going?"

"Oh—Thailand, Oz, all that stuff. Did you do that sort of thing?"

"Yes I did. It was great fun."

"Yeah, hope so. I should have done it before uni, really."

"How old are you, Ed?"

"Twenty-two."

"And what did you read?" she asked. "At university?"

"Oh, English. My dad wanted me to read classics because he did. But I couldn't face it."

"I'm not surprised," she said and was reminded suddenly and sharply of Clio, pretty plump little Clio, saying almost exactly the same thing, all those years ago. Clio who had wanted to be a doctor, who— Enough of that, Martha. Don't go back there.

"I kind of wish I had," he said, "it would have made him so happy. Now that he's died, it seems something I should have done for him."

"Yes," she said, "I can see that. But you're wrong, you know. You have to do what's right for you."

"Yeah," he said, "that's what I think, really. But just sometimes . . ."

"Of course. I'm sorry about your dad. What—what was it?"

"Cancer. He was only fifty-four. It was awful. He kept putting off going to the doctor and then there was a long waiting list to see someone, and—well, the whole thing was a mess really."

"It must have been very hard for you. How long ago was this?"

"Three years," he said. "I was at uni and it was really hard for my mum. Your dad was so good to her. She said he helped her get through. He's all right, your dad. Your sister's pretty nice too."

"I'm glad you think so," said Martha.

He turned to look at her consideringly.

"She's not too much like you, though," he added, and then blushed. "Sorry. You'll be putting me out on the road next."

"If you'd told me I was like her, I might," said Martha, smiling.

"Yeah, well you're not. Of course, she must be much older than you."

"Actually," said Martha, "she's two years younger."

"You're kidding!"

"I'm not."

A silence, then: "That is just so not possible," he said.

"Ed," said Martha, "you just made my weekend. Tell me, where did you go to uni?"

"Bristol."

"Oh really? That's where I went."

"Yeah?" He turned to smile at her again, then said, "I bet you were in Wills Hall."

"I was," she said. "How did you know?"

"All the posh people lived there. It was a public-school ghetto. When I was at Bristol anyway."

"I'm not posh," she said indignantly, "and I certainly didn't go to public school. I went to Binsmow Grammar School. When it *was* a grammar school."

"I went there," he said, "but it was a complete dump by then."

He must be very bright, she thought, to have got into Bristol from a bad comprehensive. And it was bad; her father was on the board of governors and often talked despairingly of it.

They reached Whitechapel about eight thirty. "This'll do fine for me," he said. "I can get the tube."

"OK. I'll just pull over there."

"It's been really nice," he said. "Thanks. I've enjoyed it. Talking to you and so on."

"Weren't you expecting to?"

"Well, not really, to tell you the truth. I thought you'd be—it would be—"

"What?" she said, laughing.

"A bit of an ordeal. Actually."

"Well, I'm glad it wasn't."

"No, it absolutely wasn't." He got out, shut the door, then opened it again. He looked at her rather awkwardly. "I don't suppose," he said, "you'd like to come for a drink one night?"

"Well," said Martha, feeling suddenly very uncool indeed, almost flustered, angry with herself for it, "yes, that would be nice. I'm afraid I—well, I'm afraid I work very late quite often."

"Oh, OK," he said. "It was just an idea."

He looked mildly dejected and very awkward.

"No, I didn't mean I couldn't," she said quickly. "I'd—well I'd like that. But I'm a bit hard to get hold of. That's all."

"I'll try and manage it," he said and smiled at her. "Cheers. Thanks again."

"Cheers, Ed. It was my pleasure."

"And mine."

He shut the door and loped off, pulling a Walkman out of his rucksack; she felt quite sure she would never see him again. Especially if he was going travelling.

And she started thinking, as she had not allowed herself to do in church, of those first heady days, the ones when it was still all right . . .

She had decided to go down to the islands after all. After two more days, Bangkok had become claustrophobic, and everyone she met talked about the islands, the beauty of them. What was she doing, missing so important a part of the grand tour?

She travelled down to Koh Samui alone by train overnight. The train had cabins, sleeping six, with small lights; it felt rather colonial, a bit like an economy version of the Orient Express. A uniformed attendant made up the beds and urged them into bed almost as soon as the train left the station. Martha had already eaten—a smiling Thai had taken her order as the train stood at the station and cooked her a delicious meal on the platform—and she lay down obediently and fell asleep almost at once, waking at some time in the middle of the night at Surat Thani where she was transferred by bus to the ferry and a four-hour journey by sea to Koh Samui.

She had made friends on the boat with a girl called Fran who'd been told the best beach was Big Buddha and, for want of any further information, they took the taxi bus there—and felt the world had entirely changed.

Martha never forgot not just her first sight of the long tree-lined sweep of beach but her first feel of it, the soft white sand, the warm air, incredibly sweet after the gritty stench of Bangkok, the tenderly warm, blue-green water. She and Fran found a hut, rather grandly referred to as a bungalow, for two hundred baht a night and thought they would never want to leave it. It had a shower, a veranda, and three beds. Time slowed; they drifted through it.

After a few days, with no sense of surprise at all, she found Clio staying a few huts along; it was easy to find people, you just asked around the beach and the bars and if they were there, you found them. Jocasta had already moved on, had gone north. "But she said she'd be back," said Clio vaguely. The life encouraged vagueness; it was timeless, aimless, and wonderfully irresponsible.

Where you lived was defined by the name of your beach: people didn't say, "Where are you staying?" but "What beach are you on?" It was immensely beautiful; after the filth and squalor of Bangkok it did seem literally like paradise, the absolutely clear water, the palms waving above it, the endless white sand. Big Buddha sat at the end of the beach, at the top of a huge flight of ornate steps, painted a slightly tatty gold; his stern eyes followed you everywhere.

It was the rainy season, but still extremely warm; it was actually more comfortable in the softly warm sea when the rain fell. They spent a lot of time in it. And because it was the rainy season, there were the most wonderful sunsets, orange and red and black, hugely dramatic; everyone just sat and watched them as if they were an entertainment, rather like going to the cinema. Only the sunsets were nicer, Martha said . . .

They spent a lot of time sitting on their veranda, hour after hour, talking and talking as the day turned to dusk and then to dark, not just to each other but to anyone else who happened along. The ease with which relationships were formed fascinated Martha, growing up as she had in the strict society of Binsmow. One of the things she most liked was the way everyone was accepted just as they were, part of this one great, easy tribe. Nothing else mattered, there was no snobbery of any kind; you didn't have to have lots of money or the right clothes. You were just a backpacker, nothing more or less than that.

On the third day she and Clio hired a motor scooter and drove inland down the bumpy rough tracks. They found some deep pools, with great waterfalls dropping into them, and swam lazily for hours, discussing how they felt already changed into different people; easier, more confident, happier people. Martha grew fonder and fonder of Clio; she was so sweet, so eager to please, so good-natured. And so lacking in self-confidence: it was strange, Martha thought, she was so pretty. OK, a bit overweight, but from the way she went on, you'd have thought she was a size 20. Those sisters of hers obviously had a lot to answer for.

There were downsides; Martha's stomach, always delicate, was almost permanently painful and she suffered from diarrhoea endlessly.

"My periods seem to have gone up the spout," she said to Clio one morning. "One started in Bangkok, then stopped after two days, and then I got one again yesterday, and now that seems to be over." Clio, in her capacity as medical adviser, had been reassuring, said it would be the complete change of food, climate, routine. Martha had tried not to worry about it, and after a few more weeks succeeded. It was all part of this unfamiliar new person she had become, relaxed, easy, untroubled by anything very much. And very, very happy. She found herself waking up every morning thinking, What can I do today? and knew she could do it, whatever it was.

She felt she had conquered the world.

Lucky, lucky Ed, with all that ahead of him.

Chapter 4

· · · ·

Dreadful sobs came from the room: dreadful sobs telling of dreadful grief. It was the third time Helen had heard them over the past few months; she waited a while hoping they would ease.

The first two had been the result of Kate's so-far fruitless search for her birth mother. She had told Helen what she intended to do the first time, and Helen had listened, her heart sinking at the inadequacy of the plans, not daring to criticise or even make suggestions. She had merely smiled at her brightly, hugged her goodbye as she set off; and waited, sick with anxiety, for her return.

It had come a very few hours later; the front door had opened, slammed shut, there were running footsteps up the stairs, her door shut— and the sobs began.

She had waited fifteen minutes, then followed her up the stairs and knocked on her door. Kate was lying on her bed, swollen-eyed, resentful, angry with Helen.

"Why didn't you tell me?"

"Tell you what?"

"That no one would still be at the hospital? People who were there when I was found. Why didn't you tell me?"

"I didn't know. How could I?" Helen tried to be patient. She sat down on Kate's bed and tried to smooth her hair, but Kate shied away from her.

"Look," said Helen, "why don't you tell me what happened?"

Kate had gone to the hospital, the South Middlesex, to outpatients (not having any idea where else you could go for help); they had looked at her, she said, as if she were mad.

"I mean, is it such a lot to ask? I only wanted to know who'd been on the baby unit in 1986. They just said had I got a letter from anyone? As if I was going in to have an operation or something. I said no, and they said they really couldn't help, I'd have to write in, so that my request could be guided through the proper channels. I mean, please! Anyway, then I followed the signs that said Maternity Unit. It was on the third floor and when I got there, there was this sort of waiting room full of these hideous pregnant women and more of these stupid women on the reception desk. They said there wouldn't be anyone still working there and I said how did they know? And they said because no one had been there more than seven years. So then I said what about the cleaners or something? And they said the cleaning was all done by outside agencies now, and then it had been done by staff. So I said what was the name of the agency and they said they had no idea. I saw one of them look at the other and raise her eyebrows and I just walked out. And then as I was walking down one of those endless corridors I saw a sign that said Administration Offices so I went in there."

"And?"

"And there was only one nerdy man in there and he said nobody was available on Saturdays, and I said oh, really, what about him, and he said he'd just come in for half an hour. I said that didn't make any difference,

I wanted the names of some people who'd been working there fifteen years ago, and he said that was classified information and couldn't be handed out to anyone. He said if I wrote in, they might consider my request. And that was that."

"Well," said Helen carefully, "why don't you write in?"

"Mum, they're complete morons. They don't know anything. And they don't want to help."

"Did you tell any of them why you wanted to know?"

"Of course not. I'm not going round like some sad thing looking for her mother. Having everyone sorry for me."

"Kate, my love," said Helen, "I think you're going to have to. Otherwise your reasons could be very dubious indeed. Just think for a minute."

Kate stared at her; then she said, "No, Mum, I can't. I'm not going to do that. I'll do this in my own way. I know what I'm doing."

"Good," said Helen.

She did nothing for several months; then she had gone to Heathrow and made for the information desk; how could she make contact with one of the cleaners?

"Do you have a name?" said the overdone blonde, pausing briefly from her interminable computer tapping.

"No."

She sighed. "Well then, dear, how can we help you?"

"You must have a list of people."

"Even if we did, if you don't have a name, what good would a list do? Is this a complaint or something?"

"No," said Kate, "no, it's not."

"So what is it?"

"I—I can't tell you."

"In that case," she said, returning to her tapping, "I don't think I can help. You could write in to HR if you like."

"What's HR?"

"Human Resources. Now if you'll excuse me, there are people waiting. Yes, sir—"

And she indicated to Kate to move so that she could talk to the man behind her.

Kate felt the same despairing panic as last time. She went over to one of the cafés and bought a Coke and sat looking around her at all the cleaners and porters. Some of them were quite old. They must have been there for at least fifteen years. And they must all know one another. Bound to. She finished her Coke, and went up to a middle-aged Asian woman wiping the tables; she asked her how long she had worked there.

"Too long, my dear, much too long." She smiled, a sweet tired smile.

"Fifteen years?"

"Oh, no."

"Do you know anyone who has?"

"I could ask around for you, I suppose. Why do you want to know, my dear?"

"I can't tell you that. Sorry. But it's nothing unpleasant."

"I'll see what I can do."

Kate sat for a long time, watching her ask several of her fellow workers. She saw some of them smiling, some of them raising their eyebrows like the nurses, all of them shaking their heads. Finally an officious-looking man came up to the Asian woman and asked her something; she stopped smiling and pointed in Kate's direction. He walked over to her.

"Excuse me, miss. Is there a problem?"

"No problem," said Kate. "I'm just looking for someone."

"And who would that be?"

"Someone who was working here fifteen years ago."

"And why would you want such a person?"

"I'm afraid I can't tell you."

"In that case, I must ask you to stop wasting my staff's time. If you have a request, you must make it through the proper channels. Write in to the HR department. But they won't help you if you don't have a very satisfactory reason."

She caught the tube back to Ealing and spent the afternoon in her room.

That day she wouldn't even allow Helen in.

And now, today, more sobs. Helen braced herself, knocked at the door. She couldn't leave it; and besides, she thought she knew what the sobs were about. Tomorrow was Kate's birthday; how it had upset her for the past few years.

"Kate? Darling, can I help?"

"No. Thanks," she added, after a pause.

"Not even to listen?"

"I said no."

"Fine. Well—"

The phone rang; gratefully, Helen went to answer it.

"That was Granny," she said, walking into Kate's room. "She wants to take us all out tomorrow night. To celebrate your birthday. Isn't that nice?"

"Where to? McDonald's?"

"Kate, don't be rude, dear."

"Sor-ry." The word was dragged out, in an exaggerated pretence at politeness.

"To Joe Allen. In Covent Garden. She says it's great fun."

"Joe Allen?" She struggled to stay disinterested, gave up. "Well done, Gran. She's so cool."

"I'm glad you think so. You sure there's nothing you want to talk about?"

"Mum! I said no!" But she smiled at Helen, gave her a quick hug. "I'm OK. Honestly."

Relieved, Helen went downstairs to tell Jim about Jilly's offer; he wasn't at all pleased as she had expected, said he didn't think they should go.

"We always celebrate birthdays at home. It's a family tradition. And you've already made her cake. What are you supposed to do with that?"

"Have it before we go. Or when we get back. Jim, I think it's important that we go. And it's very generous of my mother. Can I please ring her back and say yes?"

Silence. Then: "I suppose so," he said grudgingly.

"Good. Thank you."

She went to phone Jilly, to say they'd all love to come. Heavens, life was difficult. And of course, the evening itself wouldn't be exactly easy, either; the tension between her mother and Jim was always there. However hard they both struggled to hide it. But—for Kate it would be worth it. Like so many things . . .

Jilly had pretended right from the beginning and to absolutely everyone that she liked Jim enormously. In fact she found him boring, self-righteous, and—yes, she admitted to herself—just a bit common. He even looked rather common, with his brown, neat hair and his slightly round face, and early middle-aged spread. The sort of person Helen would never have married, if things had been different. Different from Jilly being so cruelly widowed, when Helen was only three, and being left not only lonely but very hard up. With admirable courage and determination, she had exchanged her smart Kensington Mews house (of disappointing value, due to its short lease) for a modest Edwardian villa in Guildford, taken a shorthand typing course, and spent the next ten years working as a part-time secretary.

She could have married again; had had several offers. But Mike Bradford had genuinely been the love of her life, and she hated the idea of anyone becoming Helen's stepfather. Helen was her life's work; she was not having it thrown away on some mediocre man. Only—Helen had thrown herself away on precisely that. Very mediocre. It was dreadfully depressing. Of course Jim was extremely clever, you didn't get to be deputy head of a comprehensive school at the age of thirty-eight if you weren't. But even so—a teacher! For Helen! And living in a miserable little house in Ealing. And—Jim. Why Jim? Why not James, such a fine name? She had thought that, hearing it spoken for the first time at the wedding. I, James Richard, take thee, Helen Frances . . .

In fact, altogether—why Jim?

Jim because Helen loved him. Very much. She found him gentle and caring, and he gave her self-confidence, not only because he found her extremely attractive ("I always dreamt of a tall girl with dark hair and blue eyes; I never thought I'd get one") but because he found her interesting and said so frequently.

Jim was a wonderful father too; supportive over the adoption business—lots of men weren't—and terribly involved with every aspect of the girls' upbringing: being rather old-fashioned he hadn't actually felt it was his job to get up in the night or change nappies, but he discussed everything with her, giving it all the seriousness and attention to detail that he did to everything else in his life. Potty training, play-school, discipline. And he was so proud of them both: Kate as well as Juliet. Everyone wondered, Helen knew, if they felt differently about Juliet, being their own child rather than someone else's, but they both said, with absolute truth, that they didn't. They were both their children and they loved them: it was as simple as that.

By the time Kate and Juliet had arrived, Jilly was no longer a secretary; a job in the personnel department of Allders of Croydon had led to a friendship with one of the fashion buyers, who was about to open a shop of her own in Guildford; taking a tremendous chance, Caroline Norton offered her a job as deputy manageress.

"I know you don't know anything about clothes in theory," she said, "but anyone can see that you know all about them in practice. Please come."

Jilly did, and Caroline B (the B was a pretty compliment to Jilly) opened in Guildford in 1984. It was a great success with the ladies of Guildford, offering real clothes for real women, as it said on the window; elegantly simple coats and dresses, stylishly soft tweed suits, and for evening, suits with wide trousers, so kindly flattering to plump, not-so-young legs. And Jilly and Caroline offered not only elegant clothes; they offered a personal service. If a dress didn't become a client, they told her so, albeit with charm and tact; if she wanted an outfit for a particular occasion, they wouldn't rest until they had found one for her. In 1990 a local tycoon had offered to back them in a franchise operation and there were now five Caroline Bs, all immensely successful, all run with the same careful philosophy of personal service. The nearest to London was in Wimbledon; as Caroline said, they would be lost in town.

Helen loved her mother, and she was very proud of her. She knew how Jilly had struggled to bring her up successfully, but Helen had known she was something of a disappointment—too quiet, too shy, not ambitious enough. And not nearly successful enough with men. In her late teenage years, she had suffered agonies of embarrassment as her mother had organised little supper parties so that she could meet the eligible sons of her friends, and had watched Jilly's irritation as she failed to attract any of them. That was why it had been so wonderful to meet Jim. Who was nothing to do with her mother, or her mother's friends, who didn't have to be charmed or flirted with, who was just—well, just right. Calm, kind, interested in her.

Helen had never even considered going back to work (she had been a secretary); one of the many things Jim and she absolutely agreed on was that mothers should be at home to look after their children, even as they grew older.

Just the same, financially life was a struggle. There was very little money for luxuries and, as the girls grew more expensive—Kate, particularly, wanting what Jim called "label clothes," and sound systems and mobile phones—it became more of a problem. Kate had been arguing for months now to be allowed to do a Saturday job. "Sarah works at the hairdresser, she really likes it and they pay good money, I just don't see why not." Both Jim and Helen saw very clearly why not.

Jilly helped as much as she could, passing clothes on to Helen for nothing which she swore the shop couldn't sell and which Helen was too grateful for to argue about. There was nothing else Jim would accept—apart from the occasional treat—and there had been an appalling row when Jilly had offered to help pay for school fees.

"In the first place, I wouldn't take the money, and in the second, there's no question of the girls going to private schools."

Kate was at the local comprehensive; it was a very good school and she was extremely happy there. But there had been a considerable problem when Juliet had won a music scholarship at the local independent school. The head of her primary school had suggested she try for it and that she had a really good chance of getting in; Jim said that his principles and indeed his own situation would make her taking the place impossible. Helen, unusually firm, said it was a wonderful chance for Juliet and she wasn't having her deprived of it "simply because it goes against the comprehensive ideal. Sorry, Jim, but it's either Gunnersbury High School or me. If she gets this place she's going and that's that."

He was shocked into agreement.

When they got to the restaurant, Jilly was already at the table, with a huge box at her side. It proved to be a beautiful soft leather biker jacket; Kate was enraptured with it and insisted on wearing it throughout the meal. "Isn't it gorgeous?" she kept saying, stroking it and getting up to do a twirl. "Isn't it great?" Each time followed by a hug and kiss for her grandmother, and a demand that they all agreed how cool she was. Jim was painfully furious that Jilly should have given her something so expensive; Helen knew why: it made their own gift—a new mobile—seem very puny by contrast.

The girls enjoyed the meal, rather noisily spotting celebrities—Zoë Ball was there, and so was Geri Halliwell and a star from *EastEnders* who

Helen had never heard of—and when the waiter arrived with a cake and candles, and led the singing of "Happy Birthday," Kate's dark eyes filled rather unexpectedly with tears. "This is just so cool," she kept saying. "So cool . . ."

Jim managed to join in the singing, but said, as soon as the cake had been cut and handed round, that it was a bit of a waste of the cake Helen had baked at home.

"Dad," said Kate plaintively, "don't piss on my bonfire."

"Kate, don't talk like that," said Helen quite sharply, and Jilly told her not to be silly, that Kate was overexcited.

"Now let's all calm down, shall we, and enjoy our cake. Juliet dear, eat up."

"It's gorgeous," said Juliet politely and then defusing the situation nicely, "Hey, Kate, isn't that Dr. Fox?"

"Speaking of doctors," said Jilly, "I—"

"Gran!" said Kate. "Foxy's not a real doctor! He's a DJ. I thought you'd have known that."

"Take no notice, Mummy," said Helen. "Go on."

"What? Oh, yes. I have a very nice new GP. Charming girl, just arrived at the practice. I liked her enormously. So much nicer than that old bore Gunter."

"Good," said Helen politely. "You're all right, are you, Mummy?"

"Of course I'm all right," said Jilly, almost indignantly.

"Just a social call, was it?" said Jim, his voice edgy. "As she was so charming."

"Yes," said Jilly firmly, "yes, it was. Now where's that waiter? I'd like a coffee."

"Do you know," said Kate half dreamily, looking across the restaurant at a waiter bearing an ice bucket, "I've never even tasted champagne."

"Well, you must now," said Jilly. "I'll order us some."

She knew exactly what she was doing, Helen thought; Jim's last words had annoyed her and she knew she could annoy him back. She had raised her hand to call the waiter; Helen gently put it down again.

"Mummy, please don't. It's such an extravagance, and the girls have already eaten so much rich food. They'll be sick."

"We will not," said Kate. "Will we, Jools?"

"No," said Juliet slightly nervously.

"Jilly, no," said Jim. His voice was heavy, his dark eyes hard. "If you don't mind."

"Dad—"

"Oh, never mind, Kate," said Jilly quickly. "I tell you what, next time you come for the weekend, I'll get some in. How's that? Shall we set a date now?"

"All right," said Kate sulkily, "but it would be more fun now."

Helen felt a wave of rage against her mother. Deliberately setting out to annoy Jim. And what about Juliet, when did she get her chance to have a glamorous champagne-fuelled weekend with her grandmother?

"Perhaps Juliet could come some time. For a weekend," she said, aware even as she spoke how crass it sounded, and how embarrassed Juliet was.

"Of course!" said Jilly. "That would be great fun. We'll arrange it very soon. Now, has everyone had enough, and shall I get the bill?"

"Quite enough, thank you," said Jim.

Helen suddenly wanted to burst into tears.

Kate's birthday always made her emotional, just as it did Kate. She thought of Kate's mother, giving birth to her all alone, with no one to help her; she thought of the newborn Kate and the physical danger she had undoubtedly been in; and then she thought of her being abandoned, left cold and alone, in all her dreadful vulnerability, as her mother walked so determinedly away.

How could any woman do that? How? And where was she now, and on this day of all days, how much was she thinking about that tiny vulnerable baby she had so callously and ruthlessly abandoned?

A lot, Helen hoped; and she also hoped it hurt.

Chapter 5

· · · ·

It hurt. It really hurt. It was like a physical pain sometimes.

And it was so unfair. That he should belittle her and what she did. He was supposed to love her, for God's sake. He was always telling her he did. And that he needed her.

Sometimes, just sometimes, she actually thought of confronting him, telling him she couldn't stand it, that this wasn't marriage as she understood it. But she lacked the courage, that was the awful truth. And besides, he was too clever for her: he always won any argument. He should have been a barrister, Clio thought savagely, pressing the buzzer for her next patient, not a surgeon, he—

"Oh, Clio. Before I send Mrs. Cudden in, Jeremy's been on the phone. Apparently he's at home. Do you want to call him quickly?"

"Um . . ." She thought fast. If she didn't he'd be angry; if she did he'd still be angry because she couldn't talk to him properly.

"No, it's fine. Mrs. Cudden's been waiting ages. If he rings again, tell him—tell him I've been called out."

"OK."

She loved Jeremy, of course she did, and she was happy being married to him: most of the time anyway. She also—rather perversely she knew, given her professional achievements and ambitions—enjoyed running the house. She found the mechanics of housekeeping rather soothing, a contrast to her chaotic life at the practice. She liked keeping the house clean and tidy, now that the endless building work had been finished; liked keeping the fridge and food cupboards well stocked, adored cooking, enjoyed arranging flowers and putting clean linen on the beds.

Her friends teased her about it, telling her she was just a little woman at heart, an anachronism in an age where women were fleeing from such tasks, and claiming them as symbols of male tyranny. Clio didn't see any of it like that. She saw it as the means to the end of a calm, pleasing environment, where she and Jeremy could recover from the stress of their difficult professional lives and entertain their friends. And she had loved dressing the house up with curtains and carpets and lamps and pictures, and slowly filling the rooms with furniture she and Jeremy chose on long, exhaustive trips to sale rooms and antique shops.

Of course he was arrogant and demanding: he was a surgeon. Clio had spent her working life around surgeons, she knew the culture of adoration and near-reverence in which they worked, knew how they expected perfection and absolute respect in theatre and brought that attitude home with them. Jeremy did see his place at the top of the heap—at home as well as at work. She simply didn't mind. In the first place, he *was* top of the heap, and in the second, she had grown up with her fiercely supercilious father, with his huge intellect and distant manner, and it was something she accepted as the norm.

Her sisters, her beautiful and brilliant sisters, both now with doctorates—Artemis in classics at Oxford, Ariadne in chemistry at Cambridge—had always treated her as some kind of rather simple handmaiden, and indeed still did, on the rare occasions when they met. To be looking after someone who actually loved her and appreciated her was a genuine delight.

And she did love her job. Absolutely loved it. Yes, it was stressful, of course, giving patients enough time, fretting over the waiting lists, recognising the lifestyle problems that caused so much illness. But there was the great joy of getting to know her patients, being involved in their lives, knowing which ones to be brisk with, which to give extra time to. It was all so pleasingly different from hospital work where you saw people a very few times out of nowhere and then were parted from them, probably never to see them again. It was so good to become if not exactly a friend, then certainly an ongoing part of their lives, a comfort, a reassurance. Most of them were so brave and so grateful for whatever small thing she could do for them. Clio found the whole thing extremely rewarding.

What she had never realised before, when working in hospital clinics, was the extent to which the buck stopped with the GP. You were the end of the line, the contact with the patients. They relied on you. Especially the old people. She had one couple, the Morrises, of whom she was particularly fond; both in their late eighties, they were still managing to look after themselves at home together, an immaculately clean, ordered home. But they needed to take tablets and the dosage was quite complicated. If they didn't take their tablets, they became confused and went on a hideously swift downward spiral—and their one daughter, living forty or so miles away, either couldn't or wouldn't help.

Twice now Clio had received calls from the social services, who reported uneaten Meals on Wheels, and had gone round to find Mrs. Morris in her nightdress, sitting in the garden, and her husband wandering about the house trying to find the kettle. Clio had located it in the utility room, inside the washing machine. "Another day and God knows what would have happened to them," she said to Mark Salter, "but I got their medication into them, persuaded Dorothy back into the house, and called back later. They were already much more cheerful, tucking into their tea, watching *Home and Away*. Anyway, I remembered those samples of tablet dispensers a rep left and filled two of them with the right dosage for a week. I can just keep doing that."

"You're very good, Clio," said Mark. "That really is over and above the call of duty."

"Mark, think of the alternative. They'd be in a home inside a month."

"It's ridiculous," he said wearily. "The carer who goes in the morning to help them get dressed could perfectly well give them the tablets, but she's not allowed to. Bloody regulations. God, when I think of the old days, when my father ran his practice!"

"I know," said Clio soothingly. "But things have changed. Nothing we can do about it, Mark. And the Morrises are on my way here—it's not a problem."

But Jeremy was a problem. It wasn't so much that he constantly, albeit gently, belittled her work. It was that he assumed it could be pushed aside on demand. If he had an early night and she was still working, he would arrive at the surgery and send a message through that he was there and would like to take her out to dinner or the cinema, and then sit in reception, asking the receptionist loudly as each of her patients went in if that was the last one. He made an appalling fuss when she had to do her weekends on call (only one in five), and he had a genuine and complete disinterest in her patients and their problems, while expecting her to show an immense interest in his.

Things had got so bad that she had recently asked Mark if she could cut her days down to four; recognising the problem, he had agreed. She was an excellent GP; the patients loved her, especially the elderly ones, and she had the rare talent of being able to give enough time to each one to make them feel cared for, without running too terribly late on her list.

"You're too valuable to lose," he said, smiling at her. "If you can manage to do four days, I think we can accommodate that."

It had satisfied Jeremy for a while, and she actually enjoyed having the extra day in the house. But now his agitation—she could only call it that—was building up again.

There was another problem too, or at any rate a worry: one which only she knew about and which was increasing by the day. Or rather the month.

She was just packing up her things when Margaret, the receptionist, rang through again.

"Sorry, Clio, but I've got Mrs. Bradford on the phone. She says she wants a quick word."

She rather liked the glamorous Mrs. Bradford, with her sleek blond hair and her stylish clothes; she had come in a few weeks earlier to ask for some sleeping pills.

"Now please don't tell me I can manage with a hot drink and some gentle exercise before bed because I can't."

"I should," Clio said, "and it would be better for you, but we'll take it as read, shall we?"

"Do let's," said Jilly Bradford, smiling at her.

Clio had scribbled the prescription and then said impulsively, "I do love your jacket."

"Oh, how kind. Well it came from my—our shop. Do you know it? Caroline B in the High Street. The jacket's MaxMara, we carry a lot of his stuff. Although this is last season's, of course."

"It's just that I love dogtooth," said Clio, "and I've been looking for something to wear to a conference in October."

"Well, when the next collection comes in, I'll give you a call. I'll be delighted to help you pick something out. It saves so much time, I always think. Which we working women don't have."

"That would be wonderful, thank you," said Clio, and promptly forgot about it.

"Mrs. Bradford?" she said now. "What can I do for you?"

"I'm just calling as promised," Jilly Bradford's rather dated upper-crust voice came down the phone, "to tell you the new MaxMara collection has arrived. With some very nice jackets. Would you like me to put a couple by for you? I would imagine you're a ten."

"I wish I was," said Clio. "I'm a good twelve."

"Well, his sizes are on the generous side. I'm sure you'd be a ten. When would you like to come?"

"Saturday afternoon?"

"Wonderful. I shall look forward to seeing you. I won't take any more of your time now. Goodbye, Dr. Scott."

"Goodbye, Mrs. Bradford. And thank you."

Jeremy was in a foul mood when she got home: he was watching the Channel 4 news and eating bread and cheese.

"Oh darling, you shouldn't fill up on that. I've got some lovely trout for our supper."

"I couldn't wait. I've been here for hours."

"Why? I thought you had a full list."

"Just try telling the hospital managers that. Them and their bloody targets. You know as well as I do what happens. Three hips this morning and then a tricky spine fusion this afternoon. Well, that wouldn't do, would it? Only four operations in one day. Do three more hips, they said, and postpone the fusion. And then there was a shortage of nurses in theatre this afternoon, so I only got one done anyway. God, this system! Bloody interference. You know which department has just had its budget upped again? Day Surgery. And you know why? It provides a nice lot of ticks on the target sheet."

"Darling," said Clio soothingly, "I know it's outrageous, but there's nothing we can do about it, is there? Now, why don't you come and chat to me, while I do the supper?"

"I thought we might go away this weekend," he said, pouring her a glass of wine. "What do you think?"

"It sounds lovely. Yes."

"You're not on call, or anything ridiculous?"

With an effort she ignored the "ridiculous."

"No. No, it's fine. Jane Harding, the other junior partner, she's doing it, because next weekend, when I *am* on," she said bravely, thinking it wise to remind him, "her brother is coming over from the States and—"

"I thought it might be fun to go to Paris," he said, interrupting her. "Would you like that?"

"Oh, Jeremy, yes. Yes, I would. Lovely idea."

"Good. I'll get a couple of cheap flights."

Clio breathed a sigh of relief and asked him to tell her about the difficult hip operation.

She was doing her home visits when it happened. She had knocked on the door and was wondering rather irritably why a woman who was so worried about her vomiting, feverish child that she had been in tears on the phone should be so long answering her knock. She had actually seen her watching television through the window as she walked down the path. She knocked again.

The woman came to the door; she was white-faced and clearly shocked.

"Oh, Doctor. Yes. Hello. Have you heard the news?"

"What news?"

"A plane has just flown into one of the twin towers in New York. Right into it. Blown up. It's so awful. It's like watching a disaster movie. Yes, please do come in, Chris is in the front room watching it with me."

And Clio, trying to concentrate on the feverish child, while watching at the same time what was to become the most famous piece of news footage in history, shocked and terrified by what she saw, the savage explosions and great mass of dark smoke bursting into the brilliant blue New York morning, suddenly heard Jane Harding's voice talking about her brother. "He works in the World Trade Center, very high-powered . . ."

"Oh God," she said. "Oh God, poor Jane."

"Jeremy, shut up! It's only one night. I can join you on Saturday morning. I'll get a cheap flight; I hardly think they're going to be hard to come by. I can't believe we're having this conversation. Suppose it was your brother? If you have that much imagination, which it rather seems you don't."

As always, when confronted by her rare anger, he pulled back. "Sorry. Yes. Of course you're right. We'll both go on Saturday. I'm sorry. Of course you must do it."

Jane Harding's brother had been killed. Or they assumed he had been killed. Later, everyone recognised that as the worst thing, not knowing. Just because he hadn't managed to phone, because they hadn't got through to him on his mobile or at his apartment, it didn't actually mean he was dead. He might be buried in the rubble. They were getting people out alive all the time. Or he might have been rescued and be in hospital somewhere, unconscious, not able to contact his family. Or horribly injured and—it went on and on.

They had shared out the weekend between them; Mark was doing Saturday, and Graham Keir, the senior partner, Sunday.

"But we can't find anyone to do Friday," said Mark. "Sorry, Clio."

"Mark, don't say sorry. Of course I'll do it. Don't even think about it. Jeremy won't mind."

It had shocked her how much he had minded—until she tore into him.

The whole country was in shock. It was all anyone talked about. The pictures, the famous pictures, of the towers being hit, exploding, collapsing; the people phoning their loved ones from the towers to say goodbye, people standing for days at the site, waiting, praying for news, for the recovery of more bodies. There was terror in those first days; everyone afraid, asking where next? Flights were cancelled by the thousand; Clio was grateful that Jeremy wanted to postpone their trip, and told Mark she would do Saturday as well.

"Jeremy's doing some private patients on Saturday now. I might as well."

There were very few people in surgery, few call-outs. It was as if people didn't like to complain about trifling illnesses when there was so much grief in the world.

Jeremy called to say he wouldn't be back until teatime: at midday Clio found herself with nothing to do. Nothing to do and no husband. It was a dizzy prospect; she had already shopped, cooked ahead for a lunch party on Sunday, and done the flowers; she would take some time for herself and have a look round the Guildford shops. And then she remembered Jilly Bradford's phone call.

Now that would be fun.

She arrived at the shop about two; it was very quiet, like the rest of the town. Nobody was in a shopping mood; Clio felt suddenly guilty.

Jilly smiled at her and said how delighted she was to see her. "Such a dreadful business, this. I nearly didn't open today, and then I thought that was letting them win. The terrorists, I mean. Now, I've got your jackets here, and some tops I thought you might like. Shall I put you in one of the changing rooms and you can play around? And would you like a coffee?"

"That would be lovely, yes. Thank you."

What a charming woman she was; no wonder the shop did so well. And such an advertisement for her own good taste, dressed today in a simple black shift, with black tights and black low-heeled pumps; and she was so slim. Clio promptly felt plump and messy.

The jackets were both extremely nice; after a very brief struggle, she said she would take them both. "And that black top is lovely too, the plain one."

"Right. Well, look, I've got your number, and in future I'll call you whenever I get anything in I think would be you. If that's all right, of course."

"Yes, fine," said Clio. "I usually never think about clothes until I need them." And then glancing at herself in the mirror, back in her own things—sensible tweed skirt, striped shirt, and sleeveless puffa jacket—thought that it showed.

"Well, that's what we're here for," said Jilly, smiling at her, "to think of them for you. We are much more than just a shop, you know."

"Yes, I can see that. Here's my card and—"

The door opened and a girl burst in: a rather beautiful young girl, with a mass of wild fair hair, large dark eyes, and extraordinarily long legs in what were clearly carefully torn and faded jeans.

"Hi, Granny. Sorry I'm early. I couldn't stand Dad going on about terrorists any longer. He seems to think some are about to strike our street. Oh, sorry!" she said, seeing Clio standing by the till.

"It's all right, darling. I'm not terribly busy. Dr. Scott, this is my granddaughter, Kate Tarrant. Kate, this is Dr. Scott."

"Hi!" said the girl. She looked at Clio, smiled briefly, then disappeared into the back of the shop.

"Kate comes to spend the weekend with me sometimes," said Jilly, giving Clio her credit card back. "We get on rather well."

"I can see that. Does she live in Guildford?"

"No, my daughter and her husband live in Ealing."

Something struck Clio as awkward, just slightly awry, about that statement; she couldn't think what it was.

"Well, thank you again," she said, "and I hope I won't see you in the surgery. If you see what I mean."

"Of course. I don't think you will—I'm a tough old bird."

"Gran . . ." The girl had appeared again; she flashed another brief, brilliant smile at Clio. "I think I'll go and get some sandwiches. I'm starving. And you haven't got any Coke in the fridge."

"Sorry, darling. Yes, you go and get me some as well. Sandwiches, not Coke. Here's some money."

"Thanks." She was gone.

"What a pretty girl," said Clio. "She looks like you."

"How charming of you to say so," said Jilly. "But as a matter of fact—"

The door pinged: another customer. Clio smiled and picked up her bags. "I'll leave you in peace. Thank you again."

Outside in the street she stood for a moment, looking up and down the street for the girl. There had been something about her. Something slightly—well, slightly familiar. She couldn't imagine what.

•━•

People often asked Martha if there had been one single thing that had done it, had persuaded her to change her entire life, risk everything she had worked so hard for, and yes, she would say, there had: it had been walking into the mixed-sex ward of St. Philip's Hospital where Lina lay, dying quietly and uncomplainingly of inoperable cancer of the liver, deeply distressed because she had wet her bed (having requested a bedpan hours earlier), and slowly just fading away, against a background of what could only be described as squalor.

Martha had done her best, of course. She had found a nurse and demanded that the bed be changed, and when the nurse had said she had no time, had walked into the small room marked SUPPLIES and found some clean sheets, helped Lina into a chair and started changing the bed herself. A nurse told her she couldn't do that and Martha had said she *was* doing it, clearly nobody else was going to, and that was all there was to it. The staff nurse had then been summoned and she said what did Martha think she was doing? Martha told her and added, perfectly politely, that she would have thought they would be grateful for some help, adding (with truth) that she was prepared to clean the lavatory as well, that it was truly disgusting and must be spreading infection.

At which point the woman had sighed and said she knew that, and that she had been trying to find the time all day to do it.

"Surely," Martha said, "the cleaners should be doing it, not you?"

"Oh they're not allowed by their union to touch soiled dressings or human waste. There are special people to do that, but they haven't come today yet. I—" Then someone called from across the ward to say that a patient's drip had come out, and the nurse had to leave. Martha sat stroking Lina's hand gently and looking over it at the old man sitting on the next bed, his penis hanging out of his pyjamas, while a young couple, presumably relatives of some kind, sat in chairs on either side of his bed, eating burgers and arguing about what film they were going to see when they left. The picture had stayed with Martha; nothing could erase it.

She was only thankful that her own mother's surgery (a fusion in her lumbar spine) had already been accomplished privately. But that didn't help Lina—or all the other Linas.

That had been June; in August, Lina's friend told her, mopping her streaming eyes, wiping them on the duster she was using on Martha's desk, that Lina had died.

"They said it was the cancer, Miss Hartley," she said, "but I think it was that her heart just broke. She felt her family had been failed, and she couldn't bear it."

And Martha, crying too, remembering Lina's sweet, gentle face, her heroic struggle to care for her family, wondered if there was anything, anything at all, she could do to make things better, not for Lina, it was too late for that now, but for all the other people who were being failed by a country that seemed to have entirely lost its way.

She was upset all day, performing badly in meetings; later that afternoon, when her friend Richard Ashcombe called her to cancel a visit to the cinema, even that seemed a major blow. "I'm sorry, Martha, I'd completely forgotten I'm supposed to be having supper with my cousin. I can't let him down."

"Of course you can't." Absurdly, she could hear her own voice shaky, tearful once again at this latest blow.

"Martha, are you all right?"

"Yes. Yes, of course, I'm fine. Honestly. Bit of a bad day, that's all."

"I'm sorry. But I really do have to go. Of course . . ." he said slowly and she could hear him thinking. "Of course you could come too, if you liked. We don't have all that much in common. In fact conversation's sometimes quite sticky. I know he'd like you and he's a politician, so you can share all your thoughts with him."

"What thoughts?"

"Oh you know, country going to the dogs, everybody being let down."

"Do I go on about it that much?"

"Well, quite a lot. But he won't have heard it, will he? And I can just get drunk and not listen. Go on, Martha, you'd be doing me a favour."

"We-ell." It was an intriguing thought. "It might be fun. If you really don't think he'd mind?"

"Of course he wouldn't mind. He'd love it. I'm meeting him at the House of Commons. We're having a drink there. You'd like that, wouldn't you?"

"I'd love it. Thank you, Richard. But call him first and ask him, won't you? What's your cousin's name?"

"Marcus Denning."

"What—the arts minister?" said Martha.

"Shadow *junior* arts minister . . . I'll call you when I'm leaving."

She was very familiar with Denning's name; she loved opera, and was a Friend of both the Royal Opera House and the English National Opera. Denning had attended several galas in his official capacity and was famous for having a genuine desire to popularise opera. It would be interesting to meet him.

They were late arriving at the House of Commons; the traffic was so bad they paid the taxi off and walked the last quarter mile. As they put their coats and briefcases on the security conveyor belt she spotted Denning, clearly impatient, looking at his watch. Martha stepped through the security arch and the alarm promptly went off (as always); she subjected herself to a search (as always her jewellery was to blame), and then, extremely embarrassed, reached Denning before Richard, who had been asked to unpack the entire contents of his briefcase.

"I'm so sorry to do this to you," she said, "first crashing your evening and then being late. Richard did warn you, didn't he?" she added, seeing his slightly bewildered expression. "That he was going to bring me along?"

"He didn't, no. But what a pleasant surprise." He held out his hand. "And you are?"

"Martha Hartley. Richard and I work together."

"Ah. Another lawyer?"

"Yes, there are a lot of us, I'm afraid."

"Well, I'm sure we need you." He looked younger close up; she would have put him at only midforties, less daunting when not surrounded by the dignitaries of the Opera House, and dressed in a shabby suit rather than a dinner jacket. "Ah, Richard, good to see you. They're not carting you off to the Tower then? No lethal weapons in your briefcase?"

He grinned at Richard and Martha liked him.

"Not this time. Sorry to keep you waiting."

"That's perfectly all right. Shall we go through? I thought we'd go to the Pugin Room. The Strangers' Bar is packed. Lot of excitement over the Lords Reform."

"I've never really been here before," said Martha, "only very briefly anyway. I was rushed in and out in about five minutes."

"Oh really? We can do a little tour if it would amuse you."

"Oh, please, no," said Richard, "not the tour. I'm starving."

"Well, just a mini one. You know what this is." He waved his arm above his head. "Central Lobby. Chamber's through there. Lovely, isn't it, this place?"

"It's glorious," said Martha, gazing up at the great domed roof, the stained-glass windows, the huge heraldic beasts carved in stone high above her head, aware of the rich, echoing quality of the sound. You could hear history in that sound, she thought.

They set off on their tour; expecting solemnity, Martha was charmed by its acutely sociable nature.

"Now down there," Marcus said, steering her out of the lobby, "oh, hello, Hugh. Nice to see you."

"Marcus! What did you think of all that?"

"Not a lot, if you want to know. Did you speak to Duggie afterwards?"

"Yes. I'm off up there in a minute. You?"

"No. Taking this charming lady to dinner and this is my cousin, who's playing gooseberry. Come along, Martha," he said, steering her to the right. "Now, before we leave, one of the Pugin tiles on the floor is the wrong way round, can you spot it? Evening, Henry. You off? Wise man . . . Just come and look at these busts, Martha, they might amuse you; see that one of Alec Douglas-Home? They say he lost the '64 election because he wore half-moon glasses—as you see he doesn't have them on there. Right, we're back in the Commons here. You can tell when you've changed, because of the carpets: Lords red, Commons green. The Lords have a more classy sound to summon them to Divisions as well: we have a bell, and they have a tinkle. Now look, Martha, that's the library. A lot of people have died having sex there."

"Really?" she said laughing.

"So it's said. And you're not allowed to die anywhere here, as you probably know. They get you off the premises somehow. Now, in here," this is the Pugin Room. He's blamed for most of the decor and all that fancy wallpaper."

They turned left, walked into a room that was so dazzling, she literally blinked. With its glorious view of the river, the walls and ceiling covered in gilt Pugin wallpaper, and a vast chandelier hovering over the centre, it was rather like the reception area of an exceptionally grand hotel, chairs and sofas arranged in groups, and what looked like elderly retainers carrying drinks on silver trays. Marcus steered them towards a table; someone stood up.

"Marcus, hello. What did you think about all that?"

"Absolute drivel. Are we really expected to appreciate it?"

"I think we are. Can I get you a drink?"

"No, no, we're not staying long. I'm buying these young people dinner." He sat down, waved across the room at someone else. "Evening! Nice to see you."

"This is like going for a walk in my parents' village," said Martha laughing.

"This whole place is a village. Something like two thousand people work here. It has everything, a florist, post boxes, a ladies' hairdresser. And you can get a drink here twenty-four hours a day, if you know where to look. That's not too much like a village, I suppose. Or maybe it is. And it runs on gossip. What would you like?"

"White wine spritzer, please." She felt oddly at home and smiled. "I like it here. I really do!"

They ate at Patrick's, a below-ground restaurant just along the Embankment, actually called Pomegranates. "We all like it here," said Marcus, as they settled at their table. "It's fairly near the House and its other main benefit to political life is that it's just next to Dolphin Square. An awful lot of MPs live there. Used to be that mistresses were kept there—but we all have to be squeaky clean these days. Although I read the other day that politicians come even lower in the public estimation than journalists. Now that *is* an indictment."

"But you can't be surprised," said Martha. "Everyone feels let down, disillusioned. It's not just your party, of course, it's all of them."

"You're right, of course. Oh—hello, Janet. Good to see you. Can I introduce my cousin Richard Ashcombe, and his friend, Martha Hartley?"

Martha looked up at Janet Frean and as always when confronted by an absolutely familiar face belonging to a complete stranger felt as if she must know her. It was a nice face, not beautiful by any means, but attractive, with strong features; her hair, which was auburn, was carved into a bob. She was tall and very thin, with good legs and beautiful, slender hands. She smiled at Martha.

"Martha has some very interesting views," said Marcus. "You should hear them."

"I'd love to, but I can't at the moment. I'm waiting for—ah, here he is. Evening, Nick. You know Marcus Denning, of course."

"Sure. Evening, Marcus." An extremely tall, rather untidy-looking young man paused by their table, smiled vaguely at Martha and Richard, then said, "Janet, I hate to sound rude, but I've only got half an hour. Is Chad here?"

"No, but he will be in five minutes. He just called me. Will you excuse us?" she said to Marcus. "And I'd love to hear your views sometime, Miss Hartley."

Martha smiled at her, embarrassed. "You really don't have to be polite. I'm sure my views are absolutely bog-standard."

"I doubt it," Janet Frean said, smiling at her. "You don't look as if anything about you is bog-standard. What do you do? You're not in this game, are you?"

"No, she's a lawyer," said Marcus, "partner at Sayers Wesley. Very high-powered. Anyway, enjoy your meal."

"Thanks. Here's Chad now. Nick, come on, let's go to our table."

"I met him once at some event," said Martha, staring at Chad Lawrence. "I'm sure he wouldn't remember me, though. And who was the Nick person?"

"Nick Marshall. Brilliant young man. Political editor of the *Sketch*. I don't suppose you ever read it."

"Not often, no. I always read the *Sun* and the *Mail*, and that has to do for the tabloids."

"You should take a look at it—it's very good. Now, are we ready to order?"

Next morning, Martha bought the *Sketch* on her way to work. Marcus was right; it was extremely good. Less predictable than the *Mail*, more serious than the *Sun*, but still lively and intelligent. There was an article by Nicholas Marshall, which she read with huge interest. Headed IS THE

PARTY OVER?—she liked that—it was a sober assessment of the Tories and where they were in the polls.

> Despite the fact that there is much that is rotten in the state of Millbank, the Tories seem incapable of making any capital out of it. Is it really possible that, within the confines of the party, there is no one able to fight for it? One of the biggest of the Tory big beasts, now in the Lords, told me last night that if only Janet Frean (sacked from the shadow cabinet eight months ago for her over-vigorous pro-European stance) or Chad Lawrence (similarly treated as a result of his refusal to toe the party line on asylum seekers) were brought back into the front line, the opposition could rediscover some of its muscle. Which has gone very flabby.
>
> Wanted: a Rambo (or Rambette) for the Tory Party. Before it dies on its feet.

Martha didn't know quite enough about the political press to recognise the article for what it was—not just a piece of political comment but part of a painstakingly planned piece of propaganda for Lawrence and Frean—but she did feel a rush of excitement at having met what were clearly key people in an unfolding drama. An excitement which, she realised, the law had failed to deliver to her for some time now.

Just the same, if anyone had told her that less than a year later she would be the prospective parliamentary candidate for Binsmow, she would have assumed they were stark raving mad.

Chapter 6

·   ·   ·   ·   ·

"What a pair of tossers," said Kate, peering over her father's shoulder at the newspaper. "Who are they?"

"Kate, that's not a nice word."

"Sorry, Dad. Who are they?"

"That one is Kenneth Clarke. And that one is Iain Duncan Smith."

"So. Who are they?"

"Oh dear. Don't they teach you anything at that school of yours? Iain Duncan Smith has just become leader of the Tory Party."

"Why should they teach us that at school?" she said, genuinely puzzled. "What have they got to do with us?"

"Well, quite a lot in theory," said Jim, "although it's really rather unlikely. I hope so, anyway."

"Me too. I don't want anything to do with people who look like that. Is it all right for me to go to London on Saturday?"

"It depends where you're going."

"Oh . . ." Kate's voice was vague. "You know. Around. Covent Garden, that sort of thing. I'll be back before dark. Don't worry. And I won't talk to any strange drug peddlers. Or join up with any terrorists."

"Who are you going with?"

"God! What is this? I'm only going shopping. I'm going with Sarah and Bernie and a few others. Look. I'm *fifteen*. I had no idea we were still living in the dark ages."

"Kate—"

"I'm going anyway. And now I'm going to school. Is that all right? Or do you want to escort me there? Put me on reins or something?"

"Kate," said Helen, "you haven't had any breakfast—"

"I don't want any breakfast. I feel sick. See you. Juliet, you ready? Or are you having a second bowl of fibre, like the good little girl you are?"

"No, I'm ready," said Juliet, pushing back her chair, following Kate out into the hall. She had actually wanted a piece of toast, but she didn't want to be left alone with her parents after Kate had gone. Kate would accuse her of taking their side against her.

They walked down the street together, Juliet frantically checking what was in her satchel as they went.

"God, they are just so ridiculous," said Kate. "I mean, I don't know anyone who has to ask permission to go out shopping. Do you?"

"Well, no," said Juliet, "but it's not just shopping, is it? Not to Dad."

"What does that mean? You think I'm going to meet up with some boys and start smoking spliffs or something?"

"Of course not. Don't be stupid. I suppose he thinks you're going to hang around the streets, as he puts it, and meet people he doesn't know—"

"Thank God!"

"And get in with a bad lot. Oh, Kate, don't look at me like that, I'm only telling you what he thinks. I think it's stupid too, of course I do."

Kate sighed. Then she said, "It's all because of my mother, I suppose. He's afraid I'm going to turn out really badly like her. Get pregnant, end up on the streets."

"I—I suppose that might have something to do with it," said Juliet reluctantly. "It really is stupid, because he doesn't know she ended up on the streets. She might be some terribly successful person by now. He just doesn't know."

"Nor do I. None of us do." Kate's voice was heavy suddenly. "God, I wish I did. I wish I knew something about her. Just something. What she looked like—"

"Well, you do know that," said Juliet, struggling to ease her mood. "A bit. I mean, she's probably tall and slim and blond, with curly hair like yours—"

"Not necessarily. Your hair isn't like Mum's, you've got brown hair."

"Mouse, you mean," said Juliet.

"Well, it was you who said it. You're not a bit like her altogether, much more like Dad; you've got brown eyes and his sort of pale skin. I might be the same, I might be like my dad. My mother might be a tiny round little person, with grey hair in a bun." She was silent for a moment. "It's about the worst thing, you know. Not having the faintest idea what she's like. Sometimes I look at people on the bus, for instance, and I think that woman sits like I do, with her legs crossed quite high up, maybe she's my mum. I have absolutely no idea and no way of finding out. It's like be-ing—oh, I don't know. Like I didn't come from anywhere. Like I just fell to earth and Mum and Dad picked me up."

"Like Superman," said Juliet and giggled. "Sorry, Kate. I don't think it's funny. I think it's horrid for you. I don't know what I'd do. Are you still looking for her?"

"Of course. But I'm giving it a rest for a while." Her voice was suspi-ciously vague; Juliet knew that tone. It meant Kate was doing anything but giving it a rest.

"Well," she said, "If you want me to help in any way . . ."

"Thanks," said Kate, "but no thanks. Look, there are your poncey friends. I'm off. See you tonight, Jools."

It had been Sarah who'd had the idea. She'd thought about the problem, and come up with something sensible. That was the whole thing about Sarah, Kate thought. She was a real friend, always there for you, and it had been her idea to advertise in the paper.

"They all have these—what do you call them, yeah, personal ads. Why don't you try that?"

"What would I say?" Kate's voice was doubtful.

"Something like 'If you abandoned a baby at Heathrow airport in August 1986 get in touch with me, your daughter.' "

"What? And give my mobile number?"

"No! They have these box numbers; people write in. You might get some nuts calling up otherwise. You have to be careful, Kate. Lot of funny people out there."

She'd composed her ad very carefully. "Please help," it said. "I'm looking for my mother. She left me at Heathrow airport in August 1986, and I really want to find her."

The next decision was which paper. Her mother might live anywhere from Land's End to John O'Groats, so it would have to be one of the nationals. Her parents took the *Guardian* and might see it; none of the papers she liked seemed to have such columns. So it was *The Times* or the *Telegraph*. She had bought a copy of each and studied them; she couldn't imagine that anyone who had been her mother and done what she had would read papers like them—but of course she didn't know that.

Her mother might be young—well, not so young now, about thirty-something—or she might be much older. She might be married and she might not, she might be married to Kate's father and she might be married to someone else; she might have other children. That hurt more than anything, the thought that other children were with her mother, being loved and looked after by her and going shopping with her and being cooked nice food by her, knowing she was their mother, knowing where they belonged, but having no idea at all that they had a sister who could claim a place in their family, who had every right to it, more than them, actually, since she had been there first.

She had never forgotten the moment when she had first seen her birth certificate. She was ten, just beginning to find that it all really mattered, and she had stood there, staring at it, reading the words "Mother: un-known, Father: unknown," feeling more alone than she could ever imag-ine, alone and absolutely uprooted, torn out of the ground and flung down like a weed. Even in the morning she had woken up with a pain in her heart that she could actually feel, physically. And all she had wanted, ever since, was just to know who her mother was, and why she had done what she had.

Sarah's idea hadn't worked. She had called *The Times* and given them the wording—it had been so hard that, hearing her voice saying: "Please help, I'm looking for my mother," but it seemed to be going all right, and then the woman had said did she know their terms? Eleven pounds a line, plus VAT. Which came to nearly sixty pounds. Sixty! It might as well be six hundred.

Shaking, Kate rang off. Sixty quid! How was she going to get that? If only she had a Saturday job, like Sarah. Then she could earn it. She felt her eyes suddenly blurring. Whichever way she went, her path was blocked. There seemed some conspiracy to keep her from ever finding her mother.

They were sitting in a history lesson, when Sarah suddenly turned round, her face radiant.

"Kate!" she hissed. "What about the Web?" Kate frowned, her face a question mark. "You know, the Web. The Internet. Thought of looking there?"

It was actually a good idea. She would go to the library after school and see what the Web had to offer.

She typed in "missing persons" and waited; a long, long list of orga-nisations came up on the screen: "People Found," "Missing Persons Throughout the World," "Find Anyone."

Sarah was a genius. Why hadn't she thought of this before?

She went for "Find Anyone."

"Lost persons for $7.95 instantly," it said.

Her heart started to thud: $7.95 for your mother. Not bad.

Half an hour later, she left the library, filled with rage. At herself, this time. She'd been really, really dumb—again. Whatever had made her think she was going to find anything this way? It was the old problem: she didn't know enough even to start. Every site said things like "All you need is a first and last name," or "If you only have a name to go on, click here for more options." One organisation told her that if she searched by name only, she would get too many matches. Too many! How about one?

"Good luck," it said, "and enjoy your reunion with that special someone."

If only. She went home, angrier than ever.

After a while, she stopped being angry and felt the old misery and loneliness descend on her instead. It was all very well, her parents telling her how much they loved her, and Juliet saying she did, too; the fact remained that her mother, the person who had given birth to her, had thrown her aside, as casually as if she was a skirt she didn't like, just walked away from her and never came back. Not even to check she was all right.

Of course the woman would at least know she'd been found; she would have read the papers. And maybe that was enough for her. She didn't want to know if her daughter was well, or happy, or who was looking after her, or what she was like as she began to get a bit older. She had just—wiped her out. The more Kate thought about it, the worse she felt: that the person who should love her most in the world, who should care about her the most, had absolutely no interest in her at all. It was a horrible, hideous thought. It made her feel worthless. If your own mother couldn't be bothered with you, for God's sake, why should anyone else?

Of course, her mother might be going round too, looking at girls of about fifteen or sixteen, wondering if they were her daughter. She wouldn't know where to start, either. Only at least she could try the adoption agencies; she could try the missing persons lines and Web sites herself. It wouldn't be nearly so difficult for her, they wouldn't keep telling her she wasn't legally of an age to make such enquiries, or demanding impossible sums of money to advertise in the paper. She could do it easily if she wanted to.

The simple fact was that she didn't. She just didn't want to know. Bitch! Horrible, hideous, selfish cow. One thing Kate was quite certain of: if she did ever find her mother now, she would hate her. Absolutely hate her. And make very sure she knew it, too.

Chapter 7

· · · · · ·

Just as (or so some say) the real action in the House of Commons is not found in the debating chamber but in the committee rooms, corridors, and tearooms, the real business at the party political conferences is conducted not in the conference hall and on the platform but in the bars or at the myriad fringe meetings that take place all day. Rather thinly disguised as discussion groups, sponsored by high-profile but not disinterested associations, the movers and shakers of the parties and those keen to lobby them move from hotel to hotel, hall to hall, from breakfast time until quite late at night, airing and sharing their views with both the press and any interested members of the constituency parties.

There is also a lot of sex; the adrenaline-charged atmosphere, the power and intrigue on display, and the heady freedom from day-to-day restraints is, as Nick Marshall once wrote, more powerful than an ocean full of oysters. Many a worthy afternoon speech is missed for a little apolitical activity in a hotel room. Indeed, it is said that if you can remember too much about any party conference, you have missed the best of it.

That autumn at the Tory Party conference in Blackpool, a very large and glitzy fringe meeting had been held. On the penultimate evening, funded by Gideon Keeble, the billionaire retailer, it had addressed the question of the nanny state and its sinister and growing power over the family. Speakers had included the charismatic and much televised Lord Collins, professor in child psychiatry at Cambridge; TV agony aunt Victoria Raynsford; and Janet Frean, who, as well as being a prominent Tory MP, had the relevant distinction of having five children. Chad Lawrence had also attended and spoken passionately at the debate that followed. The meeting had been packed with the party faithful and it had scooped up most of the next day's best headlines.

"And people have been congratulating Janet ever since," Nick had said to Jocasta over breakfast. "It would appear she has Keeble onside. Very influential man, is our Gideon. Influential and rich. Exactly what's needed for the new party."

"It's going to happen, is it?"

"Think so. It's all looking very exciting."

Jocasta, who was nursing an appalling hangover, found it hard to care.

Nick grinned at her. "You do look—tired. I've got to go. What are you going to do?"

"I'm going back to bed." She kissed Nick goodbye rather feebly and sat sipping coffee and flicking through the pile of newspapers he had left behind. She felt terribly sick; maybe she should get back upstairs.

As she got into the lift, a girl stepped out; she was wearing an almost nonexistent dress, some very smudged makeup, and her conference pass round her neck. She had obviously had a very good night.

Jocasta found Nick at lunchtime at a café near the press office; it had been, he said, a morning of dazzling dullness. "You should have stayed with me," she said, picking at a rather tired sandwich.

"If only I could have done. I must say, my mind strayed towards you repeatedly while they all wittered on. I've just got to file one last piece and I'll come and find you when I'm done."

"What? Nick, I've been waiting for you all day!"

"Look, sweetie, I told you not to stay today. I told you it would be boring. You enjoyed the party last night. Until you flaked out on the floor, that is."

"I did not flake out on the floor! I tripped on my new heels. Can't I come to the press room with you?"

"You can, but you won't find anyone to talk to. Everyone's either doing their wrap-up jobs, or watching the final session and singing 'Land of Hope and Glory.' "

Jocasta shuddered. "I'll come."

She followed him into the press room, with its rows of desks equipped not only with computers and phones but with TV screens giving constant access to what was going on in the conference hall. She fetched a carton of coffee. God, it was disgusting; it tasted as if they had used the same grains over and over again since Sunday. Nick was already gazing intently at the screen, absolutely lost to her. Jocasta sighed. He was treating her like the little woman, told not to bother her pretty head with difficult stuff like politics, when by his own admission she'd given him at least two ideas for pieces this week. She decided to go for a walk.

She wandered round the near-desolate area leading into the main conference hall. God, she felt terrible; the *Sketch* had given a party the night before and she'd got incredibly drunk and ended up dancing simultaneously with a reporter from the *Sun*, a cameraman from Channel 4, and someone from the *Today* programme. She'd hoped Nick might see her and be jealous, but every time she looked for him he was huddled with a lot of dreary-looking men—well, they looked dreary from where she was. When she'd finally fallen—or rather tripped—one of them had come over with Nick to help her up and sit her down at the table. He had been, she seemed to remember, quite tasty, in a middle-aged sort of way; he asked her if she was all right and then smiled at her and moved away to another group. God, how embarrassing. She really must stop drinking so much. She—

"Feeling better today?"

The voice—and the smile—swam rather hazily into her consciousness. It was Chad Lawrence. Who'd made a rather good speech, she thought.

"Yes. Yes, thank you. I'm fine," she said briskly.

"Good. That was a nasty purler you took. I was afraid you might be a bit bruised this morning."

She looked at him helplessly. "Was it you who—who helped me up?"

"No, that was Gideon Keeble."

"What, as in Gideon Keeble, the Billionaire Retailing Tycoon?"

"Absolutely."

"Oh dear."

"You thanked him very charmingly. And kissed him tenderly as well."

"God!" This was getting worse. "It was just—just my heels, they were so high."

"Of course. Very pretty though. The shoes, I mean. Did you enjoy the party? Otherwise, I mean?"

"Yes, I did. Did you?"

"Yes, I suppose so. Been to a few too many this week. I'll be glad to get home."

"Me too. Not my favourite place in the world, this. Although . . ." Her voice trailed off.

Across the lobby was the horribly familiar figure of Gideon Keeble followed by a hotel lackey pushing a luggage trolley: at least four suitcases, a Gladstone bag, a flight bag, and a suit carrier, all (apart from the Gladstone which was old and leathery) predictably Louis Vuitton. How absurd! Did anyone need that much luggage for four days?

She was about to make a run for it, to say she had to go to the loo, when Chad hailed him.

"Gideon, hello! You off? I was hoping I'd catch you. You'll remember our young friend of last night. She was just telling me how enormously grateful she was for your help on the dance floor when her heel broke."

Jocasta looked distractedly up at Gideon Keeble. How could she possibly not have recognised him? God, she must have been drunk. He was very tall, about six foot five, and powerfully built, without being in the least fat. He was tanned and looked as if he spent a lot of time outdoors, and he had an energy that was almost infectious; he wasn't exactly good-looking, but he had large and brilliant blue eyes, and his dark curly hair was exactly the length Jocasta liked, a little longer than was fashionable, and just flecked with grey.

"Yes. Yes, I was," she said helplessly, "very grateful. Thank you."

"It was entirely my pleasure." He had an accent tinged with Irish and he smiled at her, a brilliant, warm smile. "Is the shoe too sick to be cured?"

"No, I don't think so. I hope not."

"Where on earth are you going with all that luggage, Gideon, you old poser?" asked Chad.

"To the States for a week or two. There's a tempting little morsel over there I've got my eye on. I'll call you when I get back."

"Fine. Look forward to it. Bye."

"Goodbye. And goodbye to you, Jocasta. May I say I enjoy your articles very much."

"You've read them?"

"Of course. I regard it as my business to read everything I can. I especially enjoyed your piece last week about that girl in the Bournemouth hotel. The one who said the only people who'd ever properly thanked her for what she'd done for them, in five years of conferences, had been Maggie and the Prescotts. That sounds a bit like a TV programme, doesn't it? Maggie and the Prescotts—someone should commission it. No, it was excellent. Your piece, I mean."

"Thank you," she said, smiling. She got a warmth and excitement that was almost sexual when people admired her work. "From you that's really praise."

"Deserved. You're a clever girl," he added. "And what a lucky man Nicholas is. I was telling him only last night, he should make an honest woman of you."

The dark blue eyes sparkled at her. He was flirting with her. How morale boosting was that? And he really was *very* attractive.

"I wish," she said, laughing. But her heart squeezed suddenly. She wondered what Nick might have said. Whether she could possibly ask . . . No, she couldn't. Anyway, she could guess. "I think he prefers me dishonest," she said, trying to sound amused.

"Then he's a fool. Girls like you don't come along too often. With both brains and beauty. I can see my driver looking extremely constipated over there. I'd better go. Farewell to you both."

"He's very nice," said Jocasta, looking after him. She felt slightly weak-kneed.

"Oh, don't be deceived," said Chad Lawrence. "That charm is hugely dangerous. And his temper is legendary. Now, let me buy you a coffee or a drink."

Jocasta was miserable and irritable when they finally got to London: Nick had spent the entire journey in a huddle with a couple of other *Sketch* writers, getting steadily drunk. She had thought she would be able to sleep her hangover off, but she couldn't; just sat there through the endless uncomfortable journey, with her eyes closed.

"Well," Nick said as they got off the train, "it seems they've made their minds up. Full steam ahead."

"Ahead where?" she said confusedly.

"The new party. They've got some funding now—Keeble has pledged a million or two, and Jackie Bragg's coming up with an obscene amount. You met her once, didn't you?"

"Oh yes," she said. "Very clever girl, Jackie."

Jackie Bragg had just floated her hugely successful brainchild on the stock exchange. Hair's to You sent a fleet of highly trained hair stylists to visit offices at any point during the day to blow-dry the tresses of female (and male) executives too busy to leave their desks. Five years ago she had been a brand manager in a small manufacturing company, with a boss who had complained that she never had time to go to the hairdresser; she was now well up the *Sunday Times* Rich List with a second project (the same but different, she was often quoted as saying) planned.

"Indeed. And both are good commercial names—essential when they go on the charm offensive. The new party, that is."

"I would have thought they'd have a name by now," said Jocasta.

"Well, they haven't. Can't hack that. If *you* can, they'll probably reward you with a damehood when they come to power. Oh, and did I tell you? Chris is persuaded it's a good idea. Chad's invited him up for a shooting weekend—you know how he loves all that country gentleman stuff even while he says they should all be strung up—and of course he and Keeble are old muckers. And—"

"Nick, this is all very fascinating, but I'm terribly tired. I think I'll just go straight home to Clapham," she said, expecting him to argue, or at least to say he would come with her; but he gave her a swift kiss on her cheek and said, "OK, sweetie, you do look done for. Call me tomorrow."

Jocasta stared at him. "Nick! I can't believe you just said that."

"Said what?"

"What you just did."

He looked at her. "Sorry, you've lost me. I thought you said you wanted to go back to Clapham."

"I did. I thought you might want to come with me. Oh, it doesn't matter." She felt like crying; crying or hitting him.

"Jocasta—"

"Nick, I trekked all the way up to Blackpool to be with you."

"That's not true," he said easily. "You had to cover the party."

"Anyone could have done it. I wangled it specially—Chris wasn't that keen. But that's not the point."

"Yes, it is. Jocasta, I'm sorry if I've upset you, but I really—"

"Oh, shut up, will you?" She wasn't sure why she was feeling quite so hostile; she just was.

He stared at her. "OK. I will. Bye."

And he walked away from her, his tall body melting into the crowd, his mobile held to his ear.

Something had to be settled, they couldn't go on like this. It had happened one too many times, his behaving as if she was just some casual girlfriend he was moderately fond of, who should be incredibly grateful if he suggested they went home together. She felt used, disregarded, undervalued. She kept hearing Gideon Keeble's words: "He should make an honest woman of you." Probably, she thought, misery making her emotionally reckless, the entire conference, the whole newspaper industry, had been watching them, thinking exactly the same. It was a humiliating thought.

Anyway, she didn't want to be made a completely honest woman. Not with a wedding ring. Not quite yet anyway. But Nick could at least make a start: commit to her, suggest they move in together.

She drifted off to sleep at about four, and got through the day somehow, expecting him to call any moment; he did, at about five thirty. "I'll be very late. Sorry. Big debate on security."

"That's absolutely fine by me," said Jocasta and put the phone down.

She spent a long and miserable evening, and another wretched night, waking on Saturday with her mind made up. She went for a walk, deliberately leaving her mobile behind. When she got back midmorning, he had called and left a message on her answering machine. "Hi. It's me. Do you want to see me? I'd like to see you."

She called his mobile; it was on message. "Yes," she said. "We need to talk."

He arrived with a bottle of red wine and some flowers that clearly came from a garage, and bent to kiss her rather cautiously.

"Hi." He handed her the flowers. "For you."

"Thank you. Would you like some coffee?"

"That'd be great." He watched her as she made the coffee in silence; then: "Jocasta, what is this all about?"

"Me, Nick. That's what it's about."

"I can see that. Do I come into it at all?"

"That's up to you. Look, would you like to tell me exactly where you think we're going?"

"Well—forwards. I thought."

"Together?"

"Obviously."

"What exactly does that mean?"

"It means I love you—"

"You do?"

"Jocasta, you know I do."

"I don't," she said. "Actually. I know you enjoy my company, I know you like having me around, I think I know you like sleeping with me. But I certainly don't know you love me. What have you ever done to make me know that? Nick, we've been together for about two and a half years and you still treat me like some new girlfriend. We've never even been on holiday together."

"Well," he said equably, "I hate the sun. You hate the countryside. What would be the point?"

"Nick, it isn't about holidays. It's about life. You know. Planning a future together. Being together all the time, not just when it's convenient. Saying, yes, Jocasta, I do want to be with you. Properly."

"I'd rather be with you improperly," he said, coming over to her, trying to kiss her.

"Don't try and charm me out of this, please, Nick. I've had enough of it. I want you to say or do something that . . . that—I want you to make a commitment to me," she said. "I want you to say—" She stopped.

"Say what?"

"You're enjoying this, aren't you?" she said, her voice rising with her misery. "Enjoying seeing me squirm, enjoying making me say things that—that—"

"Jocasta," he said and his voice was gentle suddenly, "I'm not enjoying it at all. It's making me feel very miserable seeing you so unhappy. But if you want me down on one knee, asking you to become Mrs. Marshall, I really can't do that. Not yet. I don't feel ready for it. And if I did do that, propose, just to make you happy—well I don't think it would do much good to either of us."

"But Nick, you're thirty-five. When are you going to feel ready for it?"

"I don't know," he said. "The idea simply fills me with terror. Maybe because so many of my friends have got married and then unmarried again, with enormous unhappiness. I don't feel settled enough, I don't feel well off enough, I don't feel—"

"Grown-up enough?" she said, her voice heavy with irony.

"Well—yes, yes, that's about it. Actually. I don't. I'm sorry."

Jocasta suddenly felt very tired. They were no further along than—the last time they'd had this conversation. Further back if anything.

"Jocasta," he said gently. He put his hand on her arm. "Jocasta, I'm sorry. I wish—"

She interrupted him in a haze of rage and despair. "Oh just shut the fuck up, will you? Stop saying you're sorry when I know you're not!" She was crying now, out of control, hurting dreadfully. "Go away, why don't you? Go away and—"

"But—but what for?" His voice was genuinely bemused. "What would be the point of that? We love being together. And I really do love you, Jocasta. It's very unfortunate for you that I'm an immature commitment-phobe. But I am maturing. There has to be hope. And meanwhile, why can't we go on as we are? Or—is there someone else? Is that what you're trying to tell me?"

"Of course not," she said, sniffing, reaching for the handkerchief he was holding out to her. "I wish there was." She managed a half smile.

"Well, I don't. And there's certainly no one else for me. Never could be. Not after you." He reached out tentatively, stroked her cheek. "Please, Jocasta, give me just a little more time. I'll try very hard to do some growing up. I do want to, I promise."

"Well . . ." She hesitated. He leant forward and started to kiss her, tenderly at first, then harder, his mouth working on hers. Against her will, against all common sense, something stirred deep within her, something dark and soft and treacherous. He pushed his hand under her T-shirt, began encircling one of her nipples with his thumb. She shivered in anticipation, then pulled back from him; his eyes on hers were very bright, very tender.

"I meant it," he said. "I do love you. I'm sorry if I don't make it plain enough. Now—shall we go and lie down and recover?"

But all through the sex which followed, lovely and healing as it was, Nick gentle and tender, waiting for her a long, long time as she softened, sweetened under him, coaxing her body skilfully in the way he knew best, into a mounting, brightening pleasure; even as she felt her climax gather and grow and then spread out into starry, piercing release, she felt still wary, hurt; and as she lay beside him, his hand tangling in her hair, his eyes smiling into hers, she knew that however much he said he loved her, it was not enough. And that once again she seemed to love someone more than he loved her.

Chapter 8

· · · · ·

Clio sat staring at Jeremy; she felt terribly frightened. Throw-up, shit-in-the-pants frightened. He stared at her, his face cold and distasteful. When he was in this mood, his face became mean, his eyes narrow, his lips tight. She hated it. At this very moment she hated him.

It had all begun—rather absurdly—with the Morrises. They had been found in the middle of the town, wearing their night clothes. Mrs. Morris had failed to take her pills, woke up hungry, walked down to Waitrose, and was found tucking sweets and crisps into her dressing-gown pocket; Mr. Morris had, meanwhile, gone to look for her, also in his dressing gown, and was apprehended, as the police called it, driving in the wrong direction down a one-way street, frantic with worry. The social services had been called and the pronouncement had been made that the Morrises were not coping and would have to go into a home.

"But they can't," Clio said to Mark Salter, almost in tears. "They're fine if they take their pills. I should have popped in every day, then they'd be all right."

"Clio, stop it," said Mark. "The Morrises are not your personal responsibility. I can't think of anyone who'd have done what you have."

"It's not enough though, is it?" said Clio. "The poor old souls are going to end up in some hideous place, removed from everything familiar, and they'll absolutely gallop downhill."

"Dear Clio, calm down. You don't know that."

"I know it," said Clio, "and I'm very upset. This whole system stinks. Where are they?"

"At home. The daughter's with them apparently."

"Better not visit, then. I'd want to ram her mother's pills down her fat throat."

"Clio, Clio." He twinkled at her. "That's not a nice thing to say."

"She's not a nice woman." Just as she was leaving, her phone rang; it was a friend of hers, Anna Richardson, another geriatrician, from the Royal Bayswater Hospital where Clio had been working before moving to Guildford.

"Hi, Clio, how's it going?"

"Fine, thank you. Lovely to hear from you, Anna. I'm sorry I haven't called."

"It's OK. Neither of us has that sort of time. How're things there? Still enjoying general practice?"

"Loving it. It's more—personal. You feel more in control."

Anna laughed. "You certainly can't say that of hospital life. Look, I've rung to say goodbye for a bit. Alan's been offered a job in the States. In Washington. Huge salary hike, loads of perks. So, obviously we're going."

"That's fantastic."

"I s'pose so. I'd rather stay here. But—you know. No choice really. I mean, who's got the real career? Anyway, I've decided to put mine on hold, have a baby or two."

"Really?" Clio tried to keep her voice casual; this was the third friend who had made this particular announcement in the past month. It made her feel panicky.

"Well, look, Clio, there was one other thing. Old Beaky's retiring in a year or so."

"Bless him." Donald Bryan, whose vast nose had given him his nickname, was the senior geriatrician at the Royal Bayswater and their boss. He had been much loved.

"Yes. So if you wanted to get back into the swing of things, they'll be looking for at least one person to replace me and if they promote from within to Beaky's job, two. And—well, your name did come up."

"Golly." Clio sat staring out of the window; it was a grey miserable day, and suddenly it looked quite different. Brighter. More interesting. Of course there was no question of her taking what she thought of as a proper job again, and certainly not one in London, but still—it was wonderful to know that she should be considered sufficiently good at what she did to be a possible contender for a moderately senior position. "Who mentioned me?"

"Beaky himself. And a couple of other people. If you're interested, Clio, I would say you only had to lift the phone and they'd ask you to apply. Anyway, I thought you'd want to know. Even if only for a bit of an ego boost."

"Yes. I do. Bless you!"

After Anna had rung off, Clio sat at her desk, doodling on a piece of paper, and feeling, briefly, like a different person. Not a rather unsatisfactory wife, not the family dunce, not a junior member of a general practice, but someone clever, someone sought after, someone doing well in her chosen profession. Just for a very little while she felt sleeker, more successful, oddly confident. And she would tell Jeremy; he'd be pleased for her at least. She was sure about that.

She dropped in on the Morrises on her way home; they were both subdued and frightened, and their daughter hustled her out again as fast as she could.

"They can't cope," she said, "and it's no use turning a blind eye any longer. They need to be in a home for their own sake. Now I'm sorry, but I have to get them to bed. They're very tired and being quite difficult."

She spoke of them as if they were naughty children. Clio left with a heavy heart.

She was late home: Jeremy's face was like thunder. "I thought you were going to be early tonight. We were supposed to be going to the cinema."

She had forgotten. "Jeremy, I'm really sorry. But I had a big surgery and then the Morrises, you remember, the poor old couple who—"

"Clio, I've told you before, I really can't be expected to remember details of all your patients."

"Of course not. But— Sorry," she said again. "Is it really too late? It's only seven—"

"Much too late," he said. "Can we eat soon, or shall I make a sandwich?"

"Could we go out? I hadn't planned on cooking, because of the cinema."

He hesitated, then said, "Yes, all right."

They went to the local Italian; he cheered up after a bit, telling her about a tricky knee operation he had performed that afternoon which had gone well.

"Oh, and I forgot to tell you. I've been asked to do another session at the Princess Diana."

"Jeremy, that's marvellous. I'm proud of you." She meant it; she really was.

It seemed a good moment to tell him her news. Not that it was news, of course. Just a bit of gossip really. She waited until he had filled the glasses, then said, "Anna rang me today. You remember, Anna Richardson? She and her husband are moving to Washington."

"Oh yes?"

There was a silence; clearly he wasn't finding the conversation very interesting.

"Anna told me something quite . . . nice," she said. "She said there were a couple of jobs going at the Bayswater. In geriatrics."

Suddenly she had his attention. "And?"

"And—my name had come up," she said. Isn't that nice?"

"Your name had come up? For a job in London? You're seriously considering a job in London?"

"No. Of course I'm not. I was just pleased they'd thought of me. I thought you would be too. Obviously I was wrong."

"You are. *Very* wrong. I find the whole idea absurd."

"Absurd? Why?"

"Well, that you should be thinking about your career at all."

"Why shouldn't I think about my career? It's important to me. Terribly important. I've trained for it, worked hard for it. Can't you see that I want to do well?"

"Not really," he said. "And I hope you mean it when you say you have no intention of taking a job in London."

"Of course I mean it. I just was pleased I hadn't been forgotten and that while I was there they valued me. It was nice to hear."

"Right. And what exactly do you mean by wanting to do well? I thought we had agreed that any work you did was temporary and a means to an end. I hope you won't be working at all soon. As you very well know. Now, shall we order a pudding, or shall I get the bill?"

"Get the bill."

She was silent all the way home, hurt beyond anything. And thinking this wasn't a marriage at all: or not the kind she had looked for.

She woke up the next day feeling dreadfully depressed. Apart from the row the night before, she was tired, and worried about the Morrises, who were being "assessed." It was practice conference day, when they all met in the lunch hour to discuss patients and any problems, and it was a rather depressing meeting that day. Mark had a case even more heartbreaking than the Morrises, a young woman in her thirties with severe cerebral palsy. Her parents were elderly and could cope with her no longer; she had to be moved into a home, and the only suitable one locally was full of old people.

"She'll just sit there, rotting. With carers, the parents might have managed. But—"

As Clio left the room, Mark asked her if she was all right. She managed a smile and an assurance that she was, then shut herself in the loo and had a good cry.

At four o'clock, as she was settling down to some paperwork, Jeremy phoned.

"Clio, I'm sorry. I'm going to be very late. Simmonds wants to have a meeting with me and suggested we have a meal afterwards. No idea when I'll be back. Don't wait up for me."

Angry, useless thoughts shot into her head: Why was he allowed to work late, without warning, when she was not?

Margaret came in. "I'm off to the pictures tonight with a couple of girlfriends. Any chance of your coming? You look all-in, Clio."

In a flurry of what she knew was rather short-lived courage, she said, "I'd love to. Jeremy's out, so—"

"So good," said Margaret.

They saw *Notting Hill* which was wonderfully distracting, and then went for a curry. It was really fun. Clio felt much better about everything. Even Jeremy. She ought to do this more, fuss over him and his attitude to her less. He meant no harm, he was just a bit old-fashioned. She had to keep a sense of proportion, that was all. She'd have to be a bit firmer with him.

As she turned into the drive, she tensed: Jeremy's Audi was there and the house was a blaze of light. He always did that if she was home after him, went roaring round the house looking in every room, even the attic bedrooms, just to make the point.

She swallowed hard, went in.

"Hi."

He appeared from the kitchen, scowling. "Where the hell have you been?"

"I've been—well, I've been at the cinema."

"The cinema? Who with, for God's sake? And why couldn't you have left a note? I've been worried sick."

"You could have called me," she said, "on my mobile. And I haven't been home, I stayed in the surgery working until I went out—"

"And you went to the cinema?"

"Yes. Why shouldn't I?" She faced him, angry suddenly. "You were out with your cronies. Anyway, what happened, why are you home so early?"

"Simmonds cancelled dinner. I foolishly thought you'd be pleased to see me, that we could have a nice evening together. But, as usual, you weren't here. I just don't understand you going out, when there is so much to see to here. Incidentally, that wretched cleaner didn't come again, the breakfast things were still sitting on the sink."

Something snapped in Clio. "Stop it, Jeremy! Stop it. I'm not here just to run the house, and do what you tell me. You constantly diminish my job, you have no real interest in what I do, what I'm about."

He was silent for a moment; then he said, "Clio, I've had enough of this, quite enough. I want you to stop working."

"Jeremy—"

"No, Clio, I mean it. I want you to give up your job. You say we need the money, but it seems to bring in precious little to me, once you've paid the cleaner and so on, and bought expensive clothes that you tell me you need. And I shall be getting more from my private work. So tell Salter tomorrow, please."

Clio fought to stay calm. "Jeremy, please! You're talking nonsense. And besides, what on earth would I do all day, it's not as if—"

She stopped; she had walked into a trap. He slammed it shut; she felt the steel bite into her as harshly as if it was physical.

"As if what? As if you had a baby? I was coming to that, Clio. I really think the time has come. You're not getting any younger, you're thirty-five—"

"Thirty-four," she said automatically.

"Thirty-five next birthday. You of all people should know the risks involved in leaving it too late. And I would like to have a child before I'm forty. Which doesn't leave much time. About two years, in fact."

"But, Jeremy—"

"Yes? What are you about to tell me? That you don't want one?"

"No," she said quietly, "no, I do. I'd love to have a child. But—"

"But what? Is there something you haven't told me, Clio? Something I ought to know?"

"No. No, of course not."

But there was. And he was going to have to know sooner or later. It was incredibly wrong of her not to have told him before. She stood there, staring at him, willing up the courage to say it—and failed totally.

"I agree," she said, quietly. "Yes. Yes, we should. Let's—let's try to have a baby. Before it's too late."

Chapter 9

· · · · ·

What was she doing, even thinking about it? For God's sake, was she completely mad? How had this even begun to happen, let alone managed to sweep her along on this huge, breaking wave that had left her fighting for breath, absolutely terrified—and yet desperately, wildly excited?

Actually, of course, Martha knew very well. It was a congruence of everything that mattered to her: her own ambition, an infinitesimal but dangerous boredom with the law, a sense of emptiness in her personal life; and the sheer irresistible force of four very powerful people all telling her they needed her. Just the same, it still seemed a very scary thing for her to do, to consider actually moving into politics.

It had begun—well, when and where had it actually begun? In that hospital ward with poor Lina dying? In the House of Commons that night, when she had found the atmosphere so beguiling? Or when Paul Quenell, the senior partner, had asked if she would like to become part of his team working on a new client of his, the Centre Forward Party: "It's a new political party, might interest you, breakaway from the Right—"

"Ah," she had said, "Chad Lawrence, Janet Frean, that lot," and he had been so impressed by her knowledge of them that it had given her an almost physical excitement to be so carelessly close to the corridors of power. That had been a very big factor.

She had gone to the House of Commons several times to meet them, had grown familiar with its complex geography, had listened to debates from the public gallery, had slowly begun to understand how it worked. She had got to know Chad and Janet rather well, even Jack Kirkland a little. Kirkland fascinated her, his passionate idealism, his scowling intensity, his gift for oratory, and the way, just occasionally, he would suddenly and visibly relax, start listening rather than talking, and even laughing when something amused him: a great bearlike infectious laugh. They were so hard to resist, these people, possessed of a quality she could only rather feebly call charisma, that made you want to impress and please them. And then when you did, you felt absolutely fantastic, clever and starry and— God, it was all so schoolgirly!

It was madness, total madness, and she knew it, with her life already so overstretched, her time so limited, her commitment to her work so necessarily intense. It helped that the party was officially a client, but she found herself proofreading their policy documents, suggesting likely supporters, and attending schmoozy lunches or dinners, or even—occasionally—drafting press releases on their behalf. It was partly vanity, she knew, vanity and excitement that she, Martha Hartley, had become someone in at the centre—or near the centre—of something so important, so high profile, in however modest a capacity.

But there was a serious side to it too, of course, in that she believed in them; she felt she was involved in something that could actually help the likes of Lina and her family, trapped in a cycle of deprivation. It was the kind of thing that she thought she could be proud of—and that her parents could be proud of too.

And there was also the fact that she seemed to have tumbled into her natural habitat. She loved the way politics was a world of its own, loved the villagey atmosphere of the House, the way everyone knew everyone else, the way people could be screaming at one another across the Chamber one minute and sharing a bottle of claret the next; she loved the way it ran on gossip and inside knowledge and deals and what she had once described to Marcus as a live game of chess.

They had, from time to time, suggested she think about going into it at the sharp end herself. "You're a natural, I'd say," said Chad, looking at her one evening on his return from a protracted and fruitless struggle with a local constituency. "We should parachute you in somewhere. You'd love it, I know you would."

"Don't be ridiculous," she had said, laughing. "I don't know anything about it."

"Rubbish. It's not rocket science. Common sense and energy are the main ingredients. And being moderately articulate, I suppose. All of which you are. You should think about it."

How could she not respond to that? To one of the most famous politicians of his day, telling her he would like her to join his party?

It was all extraordinarily exciting.

Martha was sitting at her desk one morning in late January when her phone rang.

"Hi," said a voice, "this is Ed Forrest. I don't suppose you remember me. You gave me a lift up to London, one night last year."

She did remember, of course: beautiful, charming Ed. "Ed," she said, "how lovely to hear from you. I thought you were in Thailand or something."

"I was. But I'm back now. And I thought I should call you. Fix a date. I said I'd buy you a drink. I felt bad, never doing it, but I kind of ran out of time. Sorry."

"Ed, it's quite all right. I haven't been harbouring a grudge against you all this time."

"I didn't think you had," he said. "You don't seem that sort of person. And anyway, I'd really like to see you again."

"Well, that's a lovely idea," she said, hesitating. But what was the harm? What on earth was the harm? "It—it would be nice," she said. "Only it will have to be—let's see—the end of the week. Like Friday."

Maybe he'd be busy. They always were busy on Fridays, people his age. It was the beginning of the weekend, it was for getting drunk, making a noise, planning the rest of the weekend.

"Friday'd be cool," he said. "Where should we go, do you think? Smiths? Or do you go there all the time?"

"Why should I?"

"I'm told lots of you city types do."

"Well, this one doesn't. But I like it there."

Now, how stupid was that, she thought, putting the phone down. When she could hardly find the time even to breathe? Yes, she should cancel it. Or postpone it anyway.

He was sitting at a table just inside the door, in the dim light and raucous noise of Smiths, and she felt a shock of pleasure just looking at him;

she had forgotten how absurdly beautiful he was. He was very tanned, and his blond hair, shorter even than she remembered, was bleached with the sun and he was wearing a suit, a dark navy suit, with a pale blue open-necked shirt. The smile, the wonderful, heart-lurching smile, was as she remembered, and the intensely blue eyes, and ridiculously long blond eyelashes.

He stood up, came forward to greet her. "Hi. You look great."

She wished she had worn something less severe than her black suit—although the white Donna Karan top she had changed into was quite sexy. "Sorry I'm late," she said, feeling suddenly foolish.

"That's OK. I thought you probably would be, doing lots of high-powered things."

"Well, I wasn't," she said and laughed. "I was waiting for a cab and discovering my phone was very low. Which is why I didn't call you."

"It's cool. It's good to see you. You look great. What do you want to drink?"

"Oh . . ." She hesitated. "White wine?"

"What do you like? Chardy?"

"Um—yes, that'd be nice." Actually, she hated Chardonnay.

He loped off and came back with two glasses and a bottle of Sauvignon. "What happened to the Chardonnay?"

"I could tell you didn't like it. So I took a flier on the Sauvignon. Am I right?"

"Absolutely right," she said. She felt suddenly almost scared. How on earth did he read her so well? Already?

Three-quarters of an hour later the bottle was empty; and to her infinite surprise she had told Ed about what he called "your life-changing changes." His response had been predictably low-key and approving—and she heard herself agreeing, as the noise and smoke level in Smiths rose, to have a meal with him.

"But I mustn't be long," she said. "I've got a lot of work to do."

"What, tonight? Why?"

"Well—because it's got to be done. Sorry, Ed. I really do have to be home by around ten."

"You must take time to eat," he said. "If you don't, you'll get ill and you won't be able to work. Anyway, we've still got lots of ground to cover."

"I know," she said, suddenly remorseful that they had hardly discussed him, apart from his travelling experiences. "I want to know about your plans."

"I'll tell you while we eat. Come on, where shall we go?" Martha considered his probable disposable income, and that he might not let her contribute.

"There's a very nice Thai place just down the road," she said, "called the Bricklayers' Arms."

"Doesn't sound very Thai."

"I know. But trust me."

"OK. I'll just go and pay for the wine."

"Can I—"

"Of course not," he said, and his blue eyes were genuinely shocked.

She smiled at him. "Thank you," she said. "It was the nicest Sauvignon I've had for a long time."

"That's good," he said. "I really wanted you to like it."

He had been for several interviews, since he got back. "And today, just today I got a second interview somewhere, and I think I got the job."

"Ed, that's great! Where?"

"With an independent television company; I want to be a researcher. And funnily enough," he said, nibbling on a rice cracker, "the first programme I'd be working on is about politics. So knowing a politician myself would be a big help."

"Ed," she said laughing, "no way am I a politician."

"No, but I bet you will be," he said. "More wine?"

It was almost midnight when they left the restaurant.

"It's been such fun," she said. "Thank you. Let me know about the job. And if you get it, I could certainly arrange for you to meet some MPs."

"You could? I'll tell them that."

He got the job; Chad Lawrence agreed to see him, and arrange a tour of the House for him. "But there's a price tag on this, Martha. You've got to join us."

"Oh, Chad, shut up."

"I won't. Why should I help you get yourself a toy boy for nothing?"

She did the tour with Ed, then said she would buy him dinner. "I owe you one."

They went to Shepherd's, where she felt like an old hand, pointing out various politicians to him, telling him morsels of gossip. Almost against her will, she heard herself agreeing to see him again.

"I'll see if they'll let you come into the office," he said. "They've been interviewing young people about politics—that would interest you, wouldn't it? You could see some of the tapes."

She spent a couple of hours there, talking to Ed's colleagues, and liked them very much—a young, aggressive, feisty lot. She was intrigued by the creative mind, the way it said "Let's try" and "Why not?" rather than "That's not possible" and "We'd have to find a precedent." She enjoyed the way they grabbed ideas out of the air and pushed them around, rather than looking at the facts and lining them neatly into shape. Ed had let her see some of the tapes of his political interviews and she was fascinated—if a little shocked—by the way they were put together, taking remarks out of context, editing out what they didn't like.

"That's really rather dishonest," she said, laughing, as they watched the rough tape of the first interview, and then the neatly clipped result.

"That's television for you," said the producer, grinning. "Let's go for a drink, shall we? Maybe we should interview you."

"Me! I thought this film was about young people."

"You are quite young," he said. "For an MP, anyway."

"I'm not an MP," she said. "I'm simply involved with this new party."

"We could say you were an MP, a new one."

"No, you couldn't," she said.

"Well, let's go for a drink anyway."

That was when she began to feel bad. She stood in a Wardour Street bar with Ed's arm round her shoulders—she liked that, it was the first time he had touched her apart from some very brief goodbye kisses—chatting to them, and they were joined by a few more of his friends, all in the same business, and they thought it was odd, the relationship: she could see that. In their early to midtwenties, most of them, how could they relate to a woman who must seem to them already nearly middle-aged? And it wasn't only her age that set her apart. They were just starting out on their careers, many of them not sure what they wanted ultimately to do, some of them still working for nothing, as runners, hoping to get proper jobs. How could they talk satisfactorily to a woman so successful that she was one of the highest earners in the country? Which they seemed to know she was. Clearly Ed had been talking about her.

She hadn't felt really bad until the cameraman left and one of them said, "Nice old buffer, isn't he?" and she had thought that actually she was probably nearer to the old buffer in age than she was to Ed and his friends. Although it didn't matter, it had made her feel vulnerable and uncertain; and she had realised, too, that this was going to happen over and over again, if she continued to see Ed.

"Are you all right?" Ed's face was concerned as he looked at Martha. They were in the Pizza Express in Covent Garden; it seemed to her to be full of twenty-year-olds.

"Yes. Yes, of course. Just a bit tired."

"Well, that's a first," he said cheerfully. "You're never tired. You told me you didn't believe in being tired—"

"That was very arrogant of me. And I can't quite believe I said it."

"You did. On our first date. I was well impressed. Have you decided what you want to eat?"

"Yes. The pollo. With no dressing."

"Frites?"

"Oh, no thank you!"

"No need to sound quite so horrified," he said. "I'm offering you a few slivers of fried potato, not a plate of cow with foot-and-mouth."

"Sorry." She smiled quickly. "I just don't—don't like chips."

"Like you don't like cream or chocolate or pastry? Or salad dressing?"

"Well, yes. Actually."

"Not because you're on some rigid eating programme?"

It wasn't a good evening; she was edgy, not at her best. Conversation flagged. At about ten thirty, she said she must go. "I have so much to do tomorrow. It's been great, Ed, honestly."

"No it hasn't," he said. "It's been crap. Anyway, I'll find you a cab."

"No need, I'll call one."

"You're very self-sufficient, aren't you?" he said, his voice rather flat. "And very in control—"

"Yes, I suppose I am. I've had to be."

"It's a pity," he said. "You should let go a bit."

"I don't think so," she said.

"Fine. Well, go on then."

"Go on what?"

"Getting the cab."

"Yes, all right."

He looked baffled, dejected. More than anything she wanted to explain, to say it was nothing to do with him, her disquiet; but the only solution was to end the whole thing, here and now. There was no future in it, in their relationship, it was a piece of absurd fantasy, vanity on her part.

"Ed," she said, and he looked at her, his blue eyes wary. "Ed, I really think—"

"It's OK," he said. "I understand. I'm not what you want, am I? I don't suit you. I shouldn't have tried, even. So—best leave it. Pity. It could have been great. Well, for me anyway . . ."

And what, she thought afterwards, what if she had just nodded, kissed him briefly on the cheek, and left? As she knew very clearly would be . . . sensible. Only she looked at him, staring down at the table, everything about him dejected, and she felt a terrible need to tell him that the fault was not his.

"I would say it was the other way round, actually. Surely you can see that. You don't need some bossy older woman, with a complicated life—"

"Oh, for fuck's sake," he said, and there was real anger in his voice, "stop presenting yourself as some dried-up old schoolmarm. When you're beautiful and clever and sexy—"

"Sexy? Oh, Ed, I don't think so," she said, managing to smile.

"Well, you think wrong. Anyway, you're hardly the one to judge, are you? That's my job."

She sat there staring at him, feeling suddenly very confused and . . . something else as well, a lick of desire, brief but horribly, dangerously strong, and it must have showed because he smiled, a slow, almost triumphant smile, and said, "Come on. Let's go and get into an ordinary cab, one I can pay for, and I'll take you home." They sat in the back of a black cab, and all the way from Soho to Docklands he kissed her, slowly, gently at first, then harder, with a skill that she would not have expected, and she felt herself whirling into a confusion of hunger and pleasure and fear and a pure, flying excitement. And when the cab finally stopped, she wanted to ask him into her flat more than anything, and she might even have done so, so badly did she want him, but he said, "I'll call you tomorrow. OK?" and she nodded, feebly, and said nothing.

As he paid off the cab, he turned to her and smiled, his beautiful, heart-wrenching smile, and said, "You're totally gorgeous, Martha. Totally. Bye now."

And he was gone, loping down the street, not looking back, exactly as he had done the night she met him, that long year ago.

And so it began: she felt sometimes, not of her own volition, as if he had worked some sleight of hand while she wasn't looking. It was ridiculous, such a totally unsuitable liaison, between this beautiful man, little more than a boy, and herself, a lot more than a girl; she didn't have time and she didn't want to get involved. But she went on and on wanting to see him. And seeing him. It was just that he made her feel so happy.

She felt uncertain a lot of the time with him. It was part of his charm. Or rather the charm of what he did to her. She was used to being absolutely certain—of who she was, what she wanted, where she was going, what she was going to do. Ed questioned all of it.

"Why?" he would say. "Why work on a Sunday, for God's sake?"

"Because there's so much to do."

"Can't it wait?"

"No, it can't. The client wants it first thing."

"And he'll leave, will he, go to some other poncey firm, if he gets it second thing?"

"No, of course not."

"Well, then. Don't go to work. Come out with me instead. We'll have fun."

Or: "Why? Why don't you eat more?"

"Because I don't want to get fat."

"Martha, you're so not fat. So not anywhere near it. Anyway, why does it matter?"

"Because I like being thin."

"But you'd still be thin, you've got a long way to go. Would you die, or something, if you went up a size?"

"No, of course not."

"Well, then. Have some frites. They're really good."

That had been the night she had first gone to bed with him; determined to resist, she had allowed him to argue himself into her bed.

"I just don't think it's a good idea."

"Why not?"

"Because—well, because this isn't a very sensible relationship."

"Relationships shouldn't be sensible. They should be good. Anyway, why isn't it sensible?"

"Well—because—oh, Ed, you know. You're twenty-three, I'm—"

"You're beautiful and interesting and I want to have sex with you. What's me being twenty-three got to do with it?"

"I don't know."

"Well, then. Let's go."

As she lay in bed and watched him undressing, looked at his beautiful boy's body, she felt a stab of terror. Suppose she was a disappointment? Almost certainly he had only known young girls. Suppose, in spite of all her care and attention, her body was beginning to look less good. Suppose— She felt taut, tense with fear, almost told him to go away, to leave her to herself.

But, "You are so beautiful," he said, sliding in beside her, pulling back the cover, studying her, "you are just so, so beautiful . . ."

And gently, slowly, very tenderly, he was somehow all over her, everywhere, kissing her breasts, stroking her stomach, moulding her buttocks. Then he was in her, infinitely gentle, desperately slow, and then, then she wanted him terribly, and she was going to meet him, rising, falling, pushing, thrusting herself on him, and the great tangled waves of need grew higher and higher, and she thought she would never get there, reach the crest. She was struggling, fighting, desperate: and then she was there and she rode it, shouting with joy, and on and on she went, for what seemed a long time, swooping and flying, and then slowly and almost reluctantly she let it go, released it, and fell down sweetly into peace.

Afterwards, lying beside him, her body finally relaxed, fractured with pleasure, more than she could ever remember, smiling at him, half surprised at herself, half delighted, she wondered how she could ever have thought it might not be a good idea.

But it did frighten her—a lot. She was frightened of giving too much of herself away, of losing her iron control on her life, of ceasing to function in her own, ordered, Martha-like way. Yes, she would think, as she lay restless and anxious in the small hours, she'd enjoy it for just a few weeks and then end it, before she made a fool of herself, before her life was too disrupted. He must see it couldn't go on forever, that he really needed someone much nearer to his own age. As she did.

But she wouldn't do it just yet. She was too happy.

It was absurd, how well they got on. How easily they talked, how much they managed to enjoy the same things, how seldom it seemed to matter that she was ten years older than he was. She even shared her smaller insecurities with him; she had never done that before.

"I hate my nose. It's too big. Too much."

"It's a fine nose. You can smell with it, can't you? It lets the bogeys out."

"My boobs are so pathetic."

"They are not pathetic."

"They are. They're so small."

"They're not too small to kiss. They give your bra something to do."

The sex became more wonderful as she became less afraid. He was all the things she might have expected, inventive, tireless, sensuous, but others that she had not: tender, careful, infinitely patient. He would spend a long time arousing her, kissing, talking, easing her into excitement; she told him how lovely that was, how much she appreciated it.

"What about all your other lovers?" he said, grinning. "Didn't they do that for you?"

"Ed, I haven't had many other lovers," she said truthfully and then regretted it. She tried not to do that: to talk about anything personal. Apart from him, apart from them.

"Why not?"

"I—just haven't. Didn't want to. Didn't—"

"Have time?"

"Well, obviously," she said, laughing, glad to be able to turn it into a joke.

"Did you—love anyone? Ever?"

"Once, yes, I did."

"And?"

"And it ended."

"Why?"

"He was married," she said quickly, "and I don't want to talk about it."

"OK." He always respected that if she spelt it out.

Martha was happier than she could ever remember, and knowing that it couldn't last made it sweeter still.

For just three weeks, she felt very, very happy.

And then it was Valentine's Day.

It started out quite well: A posy of red roses the night before, some sex at midnight—"I was hoping I could make you come as the clock struck, but I think I failed, let's see, yes, it's 12:13, damn"—and he rang her just before her six o'clock alarm call, to say Happy Valentine's Day: "That was the hardest part, waking up before you."

They were going out to dinner at the Pont de la Tour—her treat, she said—and had agreed to meet at eight, but at seven thirty he called and said he'd been held up doing some important editing and would she come down to Soho instead. Slightly irritated—while reminding herself this was what she did to him all the time—she cancelled the table and got a cab to a Thai restaurant in Old Compton Street, which he said would remind them both of their travels. He wasn't there when she arrived, but a table had been booked and there was a bottle of white wine on ice beside it; she sat down, ordered some water instead, and waited. For twenty minutes she waited, and there was no phone call, no sign of him; she was about to walk out when one of the boys who worked with him came in, breathless, and said Ed would be just another ten minutes, his phone had died, he was really sorry and could she please hang on? Martha thanked him for coming, but after fifteen minutes, she couldn't stand it any longer, got up, and stalked round to Wardour Street to the building where he worked. She pushed the entry-phone bell, and announced herself.

"Come on up," said a voice and she went up the rather scruffy stairs and into the minuscule space that called itself reception.

There was nobody there; she had just started walking along the corridor when she heard a voice coming out of one of the offices. And heard her name.

"She was in a right state, Ms. Martha was." It was the boy who had come round to the restaurant. "Don't rate his chances much tonight. She practically smacked my hand just now. Not pleased."

"Yeah? Maybe that's how their relationship works—maybe she dresses up in leather and whips him."

"Nah. Anyway, it's not a relationship, not really. How could it be? I reckon, now he's won his bet, it'll be all over in next to no time . . ."

Martha took a deep breath, walked on, and pushed open the door of the editing room. Ed sat staring at a screen, scrolling images backwards and forwards.

"Fuck off," he said without looking round. "Can't you see I'm busy?"

"Yes," she said, "actually. I can. And I won't be interrupting you any longer, Ed, not tonight, not ever. I'm so glad I helped you win your bet. Now why don't you fuck off yourself."

She walked out of the building, got into a taxi, and went back to her apartment. And refused to answer any of the twenty-two calls he made before he gave up and, she imagined, shrugged his shoulders, and went out to have fun with some people his own age.

Chapter 10

· · · ·

"Shall we get a Chinese? Mum's left me some money."

"You're so lucky, Sarah," said Kate wistfully. "No one nagging at you all the time to do your homework and tidy your room, or turn your music down. And you can eat whenever you like. We have to sit down every night, all four of us round the table, and make polite conversation, it's gross. Dad calls it communicating. God! He doesn't know what the word means."

"Yeah, well, it's all right here in some ways," said Sarah. "Sometimes it's not so good. Like I have to look after the little ones a lot. Mum's never here, not in the evenings."

"Where does she go?"

"Oh—out. After she's finished at the pub. Drinking. Clubbing."

"Clubbing! At her age?"

"I know. It's pathetic. And then she stays over at Jerry's place quite often."

"What, the guy with the motorbike?"

"Yeah, he's her boyfriend. Didn't you realise?"

"Not really." Kate digested this in silence. "Do you think they—they—"

"Yeah, course," said Sarah. "What else do you think they do?"

"I don't know," said Kate. She looked at Sarah in silence for a moment, then: "You haven't yet, have you?"

"Course not! I'm thinking of it, though."

"With Darren?"

"Yeah, he's so fit."

"But—but what's the point? Really?"

"The point is I want to," said Sarah. "At least, I think so. I mean, half the class has. I'm beginning to feel like an alien. Aren't you?"

"No," said Kate firmly. "I'm not."

"Not even if you finally landed Nat Tucker?"

"No way!" Nat Tucker had been in the year above them and the object of a great many girls' desire; he was tall, dark, and although only moderately good-looking and at times even slightly spotty, he was extremely sexy. He had left school and was working as an apprentice at his father's garage and had consequently acquired a car which he drove round the neighbourhood, stereo at full volume, one arm dangling out of the window, nonchalantly holding a cigarette. He had twice told Kate that he was going to take her out; so far nothing had happened.

"S'pose you got pregnant with Darren. Then what'd you do?"

"I wouldn't," said Sarah. "I'd make him wear something." She looked at Kate. "It's because of your mum, isn't it? Your *real* mum? You're afraid of the same thing happening to you."

"Course not," said Kate. "I'm just not that stupid. Now listen, I've got a new idea."

She had seen an ad in the local paper. "Private Detective Agency," it had said, "Company Searches, Matrimonial, Missing Persons Etc. Discreet and Confidential." And then the magic words: "No Find, No Fee."

Well, it was worth a try. And if she did find her mother, then *she* could pay the bill. Bitch. It would be the least she could do. Shaking slightly, she had called the agency; a bright and breezy woman answered the phone.

"Yes?"

"I—want to speak to someone about finding someone. Please."

"Ye-es. Can you tell me a little more? Is this a relative?"

"Yes. Yes, it is. I want to—want to find—my—" She stopped. God, this was always so hard. "My mother," she said firmly.

"I see." The voice was reassuringly calm. "Well, we'll do our very best. But before we can go any further, I shall have to take a few details."

"I—I don't have a name. Of any kind. So—"

"Well, that does make it more difficult, but not impossible. We have solved similar cases."

It was raining; a grey and wretched day. To Kate it suddenly seemed filled with sunshine.

"Could you give us any idea of location, where she might be?" A few clouds gathered.

"No. None at all, I'm afraid."

"Well, do you have a starting point? Like where you were born? And when?"

"Oh yes." This was easy. Gloriously easy. "I was born at Heathrow airport. On August the fifteenth, 1986."

A long silence, then: "Actually at the airport?"

"Well, yes. And then she—well, I—that is, I was found—a bit later that day."

"I think," said the voice, "you really should come in and see us. We obviously need to discuss this very carefully."

Sarah offered to go with her, but Kate thought she should go alone. "It looks more . . . more grown-up."

She went after school next day. The offices were over a jewellery shop: quite flashy, not seedy as Kate had expected, and Mr. Graham was not the sad old man she had expected either. He was dapper, quite good-looking, well-spoken. He was fairly old, she thought, although not as old as her parents, probably about forty. He gave her a horrible cup of coffee and told her to tell him what she wanted.

After about five minutes he held up his hand. "Now look, dear. We could just possibly find her, find your mother—"

"You could? Oh my God!" He said all sorts of encouraging things: that they knew where she was born, the hospital she was taken to, that trails could be picked up long after they'd seemed to go cold. It was like some wonderful fairy story. And then came the bad bit: that they couldn't possibly do it for no fee. That it was going to be a long haul, a big invest-ment of their time. He'd want at least £300 on account.

She felt sick: the tantalisingly bright vision, of her mother delivered to her, fading slowly.

"Look," said Richard Graham, who was not an unkind man, "you speak to your mum and dad. The ones who adopted you. See if they can help. And then tell them to come back to me."

There was no way her parents would part with £300. Not for this. They would tell her it was all very dodgy, warn her it could run into much more money, and that someone like the National Organisation for the Counselling of Adoptees and Parents would help her for nothing, when she was eighteen.

When she was eighteen. Years away. And even then they'd say all the usual things, like did she really want to, and was it a good idea, and what about counselling first? And they were very hard up at the moment, any-way. They kept saying so. She felt totally miserable; it was as if she had been told her mother was just round the corner and that, if she hurried, she would find her there. Only someone had anchored her to the street, so she couldn't hurry. It wasn't fair! It just wasn't fair!

And then she stood stock-still, right in the middle of the pavement, felt herself getting quite hot—her grandmother could afford £300. There was no doubt about that. And she'd be more sympathetic, less fussy too. She might even go and see Mr. Graham with her. She'd think it was ex-citing, a bit of an adventure.

The more Kate thought about it, the better an idea it seemed. She was due to go and stay with Granny next weekend; she would ask her then. Maybe, just maybe, she really was getting a little bit nearer.

•◆•

When Martha left the office late on Wednesday evening, it was raining. Dismal, cold, wind-driven rain. God, she hated February. She walked down the steps towards her waiting cab and then noticed that a couple of people in front of her were pointing at something just out of sight and laughing. As she reached the bottom step she saw why: a six-foot-high bright yellow chicken was walking towards her. Very elaborate, it was, with a proper chicken body, a long rather ostrichlike neck, and sturdy legs above its splayed chicken feet. It had started to skip now, and it was holding an envelope in its beak. Even in her cold, wet misery she had to smile, then giggle, it was so absurd.

"Miss Martha Hartley?" it said. Its voice was high, drag-style high, and very American. "Letter for you. Special delivery."

It was a huge yellow plastic envelope bearing the words "Chicken Post: We Beat the Pigeons to It," with a large bunch of yellow feathers fixed where a stamp might be.

"I'm sorry," said Martha, trying very hard to look severe. "I don't really want anything."

"You want this, believe me," the chicken said, dropping the letter at her feet and skipping off down the road away from her. "Good news in there, I can tell you," it called over its shoulder, with a flap of its wings.

Martha picked it up, looked rather awkwardly at the people around her, and got into her cab.

"You get all sorts round here, don't you?" said the driver.

Afterwards, she couldn't believe that she hadn't thought it might be from Ed. If she had, she would have dropped it down the nearest drain. As it was, she opened the envelope, found another inside, and then another inside that, and hadn't even opened the final bright yellow envelope by the time she reached her apartment; she was changing by then, running her bath.

She started reading the chicken's letter and recognised Ed's appalling writing.

"Stop!" it said. "Don't throw it away. Read this. Please, please, please read it." Martha, wearing nothing but a pair of silk knickers, her heart thumping uncomfortably hard, read it.

OK, you were a bet. Getting you into bed was a bet. But before I knew you, before our first date. I can produce witnesses. Hopefully you're still reading.

I just want to tell you a few things.

1. You're fantastic.

2. I feel like a complete load of shit.

3. I wouldn't have hurt you for anything.

4. I miss you.

5. *It's totally horrible without you.*
6. *I think you're quite right never to eat more than once a day.*
7. *Nobody should ever go away for more than a week at a time.*
8. *Everybody should work at least twelve hours a day and on Sundays.*
9. *Nobody should have sex when they've got a meeting in the morning.*
10. *Your nose is not too big.*
11. *Your boobs are not too small.*
12. *I want you back.*

Ed. X

Her doorbell rang.

"Who is it?"

"It's me. The chicken. Can I come up?"

And reluctantly smiling she pressed the entry phone.

"It was Mum's idea," he said, as they sat on her sofa, his arm round her; she was still stiff, edgy, ready to be hurt.

"Your mother's? Ed, you didn't tell her?"

"Course not. Well, not that it was you. But that I'd upset someone, couldn't get her to talk to me even. She said Dad could always get round her, however angry she was with him, if he made her laugh. She said once she'd laughed, she'd had it, because she'd let go a bit. I'd been out there hours, waiting in my car. Got a lot of funny looks. But driving there was the worst. Every time I stopped at traffic lights, people started pointing at me and laughing. And then I wanted to pee and I couldn't. Just had to hang on. Once you'd gone, I ripped the whole kit off, rushed into a doorway. I was afraid of peeing on your feet," he added, "ruining your Jacky Choos."

"Jimmy Choos," she said automatically.

"Sorry. It's a good thing I've got you back, correcting my mistakes."

At which Martha burst into tears.

"Don't you see?" she said, wiping her eyes. "That was why it hurt so much. It was exactly what I was afraid of, that first night I met your friends, here was me, crusty old battle-axe, bossing you about, telling you what to do, laying down the law, and you, you—"

"Me what?" he said tenderly. "Me, the complete idiot. I don't know nothing from nothing."

"You just don't get it, do you? That's the whole point. That's how I make you feel. And I hate it. I hate myself being that person."

"Look," he said, "I'll be the judge of how I feel and whether I like it. OK, you're a bossy old bag. I don't mind—I find it rather sexy, actually. I specially like it when you stop being bossy. When"—he looked at her thoughtfully—"when we're in bed. You're very different in bed, you know, Martha. You get all—biddable. You want to please me. It's sweet. Very, very sweet."

"Oh," she said.

"And you know something else? Here you are, this hyper-controlling, brilliantly clever woman, running the world, knowing more than I ever will, and the whole of the British legal system cowering before you . . . And you know how I feel?"

"No."

"I feel really proud. Proud you want to be with me. Proud you want me. It's gorgeous."

Martha felt her eyes fill with tears. She sat digesting all this for a long time in silence. Then she smiled at him.

"So am I forgiven?" he said.

"Yes. You are. Totally. Thank you."

"It's OK. I'll leave now. Leave you in peace."

"Oh," she said. She felt rather surprised, and discomfited.

"I think it would be best," he said. "Really."

"No," she said, "no, it wouldn't. I'd like you to stay." She wasn't used to asking for anything from him. It was difficult. "Please, Ed, please stay—I don't want you to go away again."

"You'll be telling me you need me next," he said, and very slowly and gently started to undo her bathrobe. "Now," he said, minutes later, "what are those incredibly voluptuous things I see there? Between your neck and your waist. Can they be breasts? And please may I kiss them?"

Chapter 11

The Centre Forward Party had actually been launched, at the Connaught Rooms, the same location that the Social Democratic Party had used twenty years previously. There was no hidden agenda in this; it was simply central, large enough, famous enough, and splendid enough. The KFL trio, as they came swiftly to be known, who had made it happen and who had equal billing—"until we're elected"—were Jack Kirkland, Janet Frean, and Chad Lawrence.

They boasted twenty-one backbenchers, most of whose constituencies had agreed to let them stand under their new colours until the next election. Chad Lawrence's constituency was one of the few to force a by-election and he had won easily.

Their timing was perfect: with their slogan of "People First, Politics Second," they had swept a rather tacky board and for a moment in history, at least, had everything going their way. Their timing was not just careful but lucky. Infighting and despair had swept the Tory Party, and fresh horror stories about hospitals, schools, and crime had beset New Labour.

And the Queen Mother's funeral had sparked a wave of patriotism; people were in the mood for something uplifting and new. In a new political party, Kirkland said, they just might feel they had got it.

Nobody could have asked for more publicity. Every notable TV and radio programme featured the launch, and three newspapers had come down heavily on their side; others were more sceptical, but still welcomed what everyone was calling a fresh breeze in politics. The name was a huge success and the sketch writers had a field day, comparing the first press conference variously to a photo call for the World Cup and to the lineup of the runners in the Grand National.

There was much purplish prose about months of plotting in smart houses in Pimlico, dark corridors and underground committee rooms in Portcullis House; it all sounded rather easy and far removed from the reality, the all-night sessions in various flats and restaurants, the endless patient planning, the ongoing struggle to get people onside, the heroic battles to enthuse the constituency party workers.

There had been some very nasty stories planted about the three of them and there were also a great many unfounded rumours about who was leaving which party for the new one. All the main protagonists, Kirkland, Frean, and Lawrence, were on the front pages and many of the inside ones as well.

All had attractive families, wheeled out, smiling dutifully, for photo opportunities; Gideon Keeble said that he was proud to be involved and so did millionairess hairdresser Jackie Bragg, who said that she knew a good idea when she saw it, and she was proud to be part of this one. There was an interview with Keeble in *The Times*, complete with a photograph of him in front of his Irish mansion flanked by two Irish setters, and a quote that what you needed, in both politics and the press, was above all courage; and one with Bragg in the *Mail*, which plugged her company Hair's to You rather heavily (a condition laid down by her, in return for a photo shoot in her house), but in which she said that for something to succeed in today's world, it had above all to be sexy, and the Centre Forward Party was certainly that. The city had analysed the fortunes of Keeble, Bragg, and other big backers, and the extent to which they had been prepared to put their money where their mouths were; there was also much talk of anonymous donors.

Wherever the money had come from, it had come: to the tune of twenty million pounds. Quite a large percentage of this had come from private individuals, more than fifty thousand of them, who had pledged sums ranging from twenty-five pounds to a thousand on their credit cards. Chad Lawrence said repeatedly in interviews that this said more about the popularity of their cause than anything. It was observed by more than one commentator that this was a team which included people outside the world of politics, who were businesslike and successful in their own lives and had a better than average chance of actually getting things done. Many of the people tasked with setting up the party on their own patch were still doing the day job, and came with no personal experience in politics; this was a big factor in the fresh thinking. And this group, of course, included Martha Hartley.

On Friday, April 19, a very big party was thrown in Centre Forward House, a new building in Admiralty Row. This was partly a thank-you to all the workers, partly a further PR initiative. Apart from the politicians and the backers, a handful of city men and as many celebrities as the combined address books and e-mail directories of the core team could muster were invited, together with every journalist from the world of print and radio and television. The food was good, the wine excellent, and the atmosphere heady. If you hadn't been invited and were an obvious contender, you hot-footed it out of town.

Jocasta Forbes was there; she would have been there anyway, brought by her boyfriend, but her editor (who was also present) had briefed her to write a big piece about it for the gossip column the next day. "And find a few unusual people. I don't want to read about Hugh Grant or the Frosts, God help me."

Several people had remarked that Jocasta was looking less dazzling lately; she had lost weight and had a weariness about her. But her stories were better than ever; that day alone she'd had two, one about a woman who was suing her credit card company—"If people can sue the tobacco people, why not, they shouldn't make it so easy for us to borrow"—and another about a scientist who had successfully cloned his own cat and was offering his services to the owners of elderly moggies on the Internet.

She did look dazzling that night, however, dressed in a very short black leather skirt and jacket and a sequinned top which showed most of her bosom and quite a lot of her tummy. She arrived with Nick, but promptly left his side and, inside an hour, had enough quotes to fill six columns. She relaxed, drained a glass of champagne, took another, and began to wander round the room. Nick was doing his political groupie number with Janet Frean, and Chris Pollock was locked in a fierce argument with Carol Sarler of the *Daily Express*.

"Well, if it isn't my favourite reporter. How very, very lovely you look this evening. I've been hoping against hope that you'd be here."

It was Gideon Keeble, smiling down at her, looking wonderful as always, holding a bottle of champagne in his hand.

"Hello, Mr. Keeble," she said rather uncertainly, allowing him to fill her glass. "There are waiters to do that, you know."

"I do know, but this is such an excellent way of extricating myself from boring people and involving myself with interesting and beautiful ones, such as yourself. And please don't call me Mr. Keeble, it makes me feel most dreadfully old. Gideon, please. And where is your charming boyfriend?"

"God knows," said Jocasta, "but wherever he is, he's talking. And not in the least concerned with me."

She didn't mean to sound edgy, but she did. Gideon Keeble's eyes met hers.

"What a foolish young man he is. I hope he's heeded my advice now, and put a ring on your finger."

"Not quite," said Jocasta determinedly smiling, "but if he had, one thing is quite certain, I wouldn't like it. His taste in jewellery is execrable."

"Well, that is a serious shortcoming in a young man. I pride myself on my own. Jewellery is like perfume—it should complement the wearer's style."

"And what would you think my style was?"

"Well, now, let me see." His brilliant blue eyes were on her, half serious, half not. "I think you are a diamond girl. Glittering and brilliant. But—not big diamonds. Nothing vulgar. Small, intense ones. With white gold."

"It sounds wonderful," said Jocasta, "but Nick isn't in the diamond league. Sadly."

"I wasn't thinking of Nick," he said. "I was thinking of you. I would like to settle some diamonds on you here"—he touched one ear gently—"and a few more, let me see, yes, there." And he picked up her hand and settled it in the valley of her breasts. It was an oddly erotic gesture, far more so than if he had touched her himself.

There was a silence, then she said, briskly careless, "Well, that would be lovely. Very lovely. Now—perhaps you could tell me about a few more of the people who are here. And going to be here. I am half on duty, you see."

"What a shame. I was hoping to spend quite a bit of time with you."

"You can, if you like. Just take me round and introduce me to a few importantly famous people. Or famously important, whichever you prefer."

"Very well. Do you know Dick Aoki, chair of the Jap-Manhat bank, as it is rather disrespectfully known?"

"No. What on earth has be got to do with a new British political party?"

"Nothing. Yet. Come along. I'll introduce you."

She liked Aoki; half Japanese, half American, he was amusing and self-deprecating.

"I'm buying a house in Wiltshire," he said. "Do you think the English country-house set will accept me?"

"Of course," she said. "If you spent enough money entertaining them. They're all tarts really, that lot."

"Oh really? An interesting view. I fear they might not. But it is a very beautiful house and if I am forced to live there in total isolation, I will not mind. You've seen Gideon's house in Cork, I presume."

"No," she said, "no, I haven't."

"What a dreadful shame. Gideon, you should take her there. They would suit each other."

Gideon looked at her consideringly.

"You're right. I would never have thought of it. Very well, Jocasta, you shall come as soon as I can arrange it. Would you like that? You must bring Nick, of course. I am not looking to compromise you."

"I'd love to come," she said. She smiled at him and he smiled back, holding her eyes for just slightly too long. Why wasn't Nick around, noticing this?

"Now let me find you some more copy. Ah, there's a nice story over there . . ." He introduced her to an American film star who looked like a blond Richard Gere, who "happened to be in town"; an Irish racehorse owner, en route to Dubai, whom he described as acquisition-bound; and several English bankers.

"Now, who next?" he said, his eyes scanning the room.

"Gideon, there's no need for any more," she said, laughing. "You've done brilliantly."

"Good. I'm delighted to hear it. Now, what are you and Nick doing after the party? I'm taking a few people out to dinner, would you like to join us?"

She certainly would, she thought happily. Without Nick if she could possibly arrange it.

Martha Hartley arrived at the party very late. She had been delayed by a call from Ed, checking on the arrangements for the weekend. He had been upset that she hadn't been able to take him to the party: so upset that she had thought at first he was putting it on.

"I bet you'd be able to take one of those important old guys you know," he said. "I bet it's only because it's me. I'm not quite up to standard."

"Ed, that is so not true. Invitations are like gold dust. I couldn't take you if you were—well, Prince William."

"Now, why do I find that hard to believe?" he said.

She sighed. "Sorry, bad example. But some of the partners are dying to come and can't, honestly."

There was a silence, then: "OK." But he clearly wasn't convinced. Matters weren't improved by her being unable to see him for more than a week; she genuinely was too busy. He had become very cross and even sulky about it. Sulking was one of the few things he did that reminded her how young he was. Only the promise of a whole weekend spent in his company had mollified him.

"And you'd better not shave so much as five minutes off it."

She promised she wouldn't.

Her main concern at that moment, however, was whether she was dressed appropriately. She had chosen a black crepe Armani trouser suit, very simple, lent a certain pizzazz by the addition of some very over-the-top diamanté drop earrings. Her brown hair in its sleek swinging bob was caught back on one side by a matching clip, and her new Jimmy Choos—perilously high, with diamanté ankle straps—made her feel sexy and daring.

When she arrived, the room was so thick with people that movement seemed impossible. There must have been at least three hundred people. She spotted Marcus and went over to him.

"Hi, Marcus. Sorry I'm late."

"I'd say it doesn't matter, but it does."

"Oh, God, why?" She had a vision of being asked to say a few words, talk to a journalist, check a legal document.

He smiled, his plump, twinkly smile.

"Because you look so lovely. The room is about a hundred percent better for your arrival. Now, do you see anyone you know—"

"It's hard. Oh, yes—Jackie Bragg. I'll go and talk to her."

Jackie was in high spirits. "I just met a guy from Japan who thought I should open Hair's to You in Tokyo."

"I agree with him. Absolutely."

"Good. Hurry up and get onside and we'll plan it together."

Martha laughed. "Jackie, you'll do much better without me. Lawyers tend to put the brakes on rather than the accelerator. You wouldn't have started Hair's to You yet if I'd been on your board."

"Well, maybe. You know, Martha, you really should think of having your hair shorter. It would suit you. And a bit of colour—"

"Jackie! One of the three a.m. girls wants to interview you about life in the fast lane. OK? I know how much experience of that you've got." It was Chad. "Oh, hello, Martha. Glad you made it. You look stunning, you really do. I'll be back in a minute. Jackie, follow me."

She didn't expect him back; she started wandering round the room, surprised by how few people she knew. Jack Kirkland waved at her, but he was deeply embroiled in conversation with a BBC dignitary, and a couple of people from the ad agency said hello and moved swiftly on. She was trying to look busy, sipping her glass of champagne, when she heard a familiar voice.

"Martha. Hi. Nice to see you. You look great."

It was Nick Marshall. She had met him a couple of times now, but had never talked to him for more than a minute or so—like her, he was terminally in a hurry. But she had always liked what she saw, the long lean body, the interested, interesting face.

"This has been quite a day," she said. "You guys have all done a very good job for us. *Them*," she corrected herself hastily.

"Martha, my lovely girl, hello." Gideon Keeble gave her a giant hug. "My God, you look wonderful. This room is full of beauty. We poor lowly males can only look and wonder at you."

"Gideon, you do talk nonsense—but it's very nice nonsense. Thank you."

"Gideon." It was Marcus, puffing slightly, pink in the face from champagne and the heat. "Quentin Letts from the *Mail* wants a chat. Would you mind?"

"I would not. Martha, my darling, I'll see you later. And Marcus, you stay here and look after this beautiful creature."

"I will," said Marcus. "Bit of bad news just now, I'm afraid. We've lost one of our most fervent supporters, out in the wilds of Suffolk, heart attack, poor chap. He'll need to retire."

"Oh," she said, "you mean Norman Brampton."

"Yes, that's right. How do you know about him?"

"My parents live in his constituency. He practically dandled me on his knee. My father, I'm sure I've told you, is the vicar there, knows him very well."

"I see." There was a long silence, while he stared at her.

"Marcus, whatever is it? Have I got spinach between my teeth or something?"

"No, no. I was just thinking about something. Now look, would you mind if I asked you to chat to a couple of constituency workers? They're a bit lost here, and I don't want them feeling we don't care about them."

"Of course I don't mind," she said.

She was saved from too long a stint by Chad, who took her arm and drew her away.

"I wonder, could we have a word afterwards?"

"Could it be now? I've got to leave early, I'm afraid."

"What on earth for?"

"Let's just say a bit of arm-twisting. Client business. I'm sorry, Chad, but it's terribly important."

"You never stop, do you? You ought to get a different job, one that allows you a bit of leisure."

"What, like politics, you mean?" she said, laughing. "Yeah, right. And spend my evenings shouting in the Chamber instead."

"Not every evening. Martha, I'm serious. We would so much like to have you on board. We really want you to take on a constituency. Think about it."

"I *have* thought about it. In fact I've finished thinking about it. Sorry. Look, I have really got to go. Back to the day job. Or rather night."

She reached up to give him a kiss; and over his shoulder, she saw the room as if she had only just arrived, saw the people in it as if she had never seen them before, powerful, brilliant people, all involved in something really important, something she already felt a little a part of; and she felt something shift in her head. And he sensed it; brilliant tactician that he was, and he moved in on her.

"Well, look, could we talk in the morning? Meet maybe for brunch?"

"Yes, maybe," she said, slowly, "but I've got a lunch appointment."

"Client business?"

"No," she said, "personal."

She was meeting Ed, persuaded by him tonight.

He gave her a quick kiss. "Wonderful. Joe Allen at eleven, then?"

"Fine."

He left her. She chose not to see Marcus waving at her across the room, because she could afford no more delay.

She had no idea, no idea at all that he had wanted to introduce her to Nick Marshall's girlfriend, who was a journalist on the *Sketch*. Or that the girlfriend had been at the party at all: or indeed that Jocasta Forbes was moving, albeit on the outer edges, in the same orbit as herself.

Jeremy was working late, the night of the launch. Clio sat watching the TV news, trying to distract herself, watching them all being interviewed endlessly. She envied the woman, what was her name? Frean. Janet Frean. Her husband hadn't told *her* to stop working when she had a baby. She had five, for God's sake. Even Clio felt that was going a bit far. Her children couldn't get a lot of mothering that way. But at least she had children.

Clio was depressed; she was dreading leaving the practice and her patients. The Morrises were now in a home, despite all her efforts, and she suspected the staff of overdoing the sedatives. They were subdued and silent when she visited them, not the bright, eccentric pair she had first met. Mark Salter's patient, Josie Griggs, the girl with cerebral palsy, was in the same home. It hurt Clio even to look at her. She was in the day-room, staring hopelessly at the television. She was the youngest person in the home by forty years. It was hideous.

The interview with Janet Frean ended and Clio got up to make herself a cup of tea. A new wave of depression hit her; her period had started that morning and the cramps were unusually bad. Jeremy didn't know yet. God, this was a nightmare; she had to tell him, absolutely had to. But how could she? Now? When every month, every period, made it worse. Worse and more impossible. Why, in the name of God, hadn't she done it before?

But no use going down that road, Clio. And somehow, now, it really was too late. She just had to hope: hope and pray. At least nobody, nobody at all could possibly know about it. Except of course for that gynaecologist. All the gynaecologists.

Thank God for medical ethics.

·   ·   ·

Jocasta went to dinner with Gideon Keeble. At Langan's. Not alone of course. With about a dozen other people. Only they hadn't included Nick. And she had been sitting next to Gideon.

Chad was there, and so was Mrs. Chad. She'd never met her before, just seen her in lots of gossip columns. Abigail Lawrence. Tall, dark, beautiful, very cool, very composed.

Marcus was there, and his wife, a lovely, warm, bubbly woman, who obviously adored him. She'd had an engrossing conversation with her about universities—their eldest child was doing her application forms—and after that they were friends for life. Jack Kirkland stayed only for a drink. He looked exhausted.

"Is there a Mrs. Kirkland?" she asked Gideon, and he said, "No longer, sadly. Brilliant woman, they met at Cambridge. She said she couldn't compete with his mistress—"

"His mistress?"

"Yes. Well, there have been two. First the Tory Party, and now the Centre Forward."

Jackie Bragg was there, with her new husband, much older than she was. He was her financial adviser.

"He liked the company so much he married it," said Gideon, laughing, "and now he treats it rather like a train set."

"And what about you, Gideon," she said. "Do you have many expensive toys to play with?"

"Oh, a great many," he said smiling at her, deliberately obtuse. "I have my cars—" He had a fleet of vintage racing cars which he put on show once a year for charity and which he occasionally drove at Irish rallies.

"I'd love to see them," she said, and meant it. "I love old cars. My grandfather had a wonderful collection, but my father sold them all. Terrible thing to do."

"Not for me," said Gideon. "I bought a couple of them."

"Really? I had no idea. Which ones?"

"The Phantom Rolls and the Allard. That was a wonderful auction. I never could understand how your father could have let them go. They have souls, those cars."

"Yes, well, my father doesn't care about anything, except money," said Jocasta, "and he wouldn't recognise a soul if he tripped over it in the street. Sorry. We're not very good friends, my father and I."

"No, so I gathered."

"Who from?" she said curiously.

"Oh, a few people who've been talking about you."

"And why should anyone have been talking to you about me?"

"I invited them to," he said, and her head and her heart lurched in unison.

"Why?" she asked.

"I find you extremely interesting. As well as beautiful. I wanted to know more about you. Now tell me, is it true, has your brother really left his clever wife?"

"Not exactly. She threw him out. Rather sensibly. And says she's going to divorce him."

"Why was that so sensible?"

"Because he got caught playing away just once too often. I'd rather not talk about it, if you don't mind."

"Of course. I'm sorry. Now come along, you're not eating. I'm sure your mother told you to finish everything on your plate."

"My mother certainly didn't. We ate most of our meals in the nursery. But my nanny did. And you—were you trained to eat up?"

"I grew up in a rather crowded environment in Dublin. There were nine of us, and we ate in two shifts. It certainly taught me to eat quickly. And to finish everything on my plate. Which was not always quite enough."

He sounded not remotely bitter, or as if he was playing on her sympathy; quite cheerful in fact. He smiled at her again.

"Now, I am neglecting the charming lady on my left. But I shall come back to you later. Eat your greens."

It had gone on like that, a series of brief, seductive conversations, and gradually the table thinned out; and finally there was only herself, the Lawrences, and the Dennings. And Gideon. They relaxed into chat, gossip, swapping anecdotes about the party. Gideon said several times what a shame Nick wasn't with them, wouldn't she like to call him again. She said untruthfully that she had, when she went to the ladies'.

"Perhaps he ran away with Martha," said Marcus, laughing. "They disappeared at about the same time."

"Martha? Martha who?"

"Martha Hartley. Lovely girl. Lawyer. She's been doing a bit for us."

"Martha Hartley is working for the Centre Forward Party?" said Jocasta. "How extraordinary. Nick never mentioned it."

"Why, do you know her?"

"I met her once. Long ago. When we were just kids. How on earth did she get mixed up with you lot?"

"Her firm acts for us," said Marcus. "Charming girl. Very bright. And very attractive, too."

"And is she, you know, married or anything?"

"I haven't heard anything of it. Since she, like all those lawyers, works round the clock, at least seven days a week, I think I would be rather sorry for him."

"Oh Marcus, that is such an old-fashioned attitude," said Jocasta. "Slippers by the hearth and nicely ironed shirts are history. You're showing your age big-time."

"Then I think I should show my own by agreeing with Marcus," said Gideon, his eyes smiling at her. "And when you are sitting next to an old man like me, you should be careful what you say."

She turned and looked at him.

"You're special," she said. "I couldn't think of you as any age. Not young, not old. Just—just you."

"Well," he said, "I'm glad to hear that. And very prettily put, if I may say so. Now, does anyone want another brandy or shall I ask for the bill?"

He drove her home; he said he couldn't possibly entrust her to a taxi.

His car, brought to the front of Langan's by the doorman, was glorious: a prewar Mercedes in gleaming black, with spoked wheels and a running board. She had expected a driver, but there was none. Gideon said he didn't like being driven, he preferred to remain in control. "And besides, I wouldn't trust this car to many people."

She climbed in, looked round her.

"This is gorgeous."

"Thank you. Now, where do we go?"

"Clapham, please."

God, this was amazing. Alone with him, in this incredible car. And when they got there, then what? Did she ask him in? Did he want her to ask him in? Was this a huge pass, or just a kind man giving her a lift?

He chatted easily all the way, asking her about the *Sketch*, what she thought of it, how she got on with Pollock, her personal ambitions, whether she thought they would be fulfilled.

They finally reached her street and she realised they hadn't talked about him at all and said so.

He said, "I would much rather talk about you."

"But I must seem so self-centred."

"Now that is nonsense. I encouraged you."

"Well, thank you. And for the lift. And for dinner, of course. I . . ." She hesitated. No, she'd ask him. What harm could it do? "Would— would you like to come in for—for a nightcap?"

"Oh, now that would be very dangerous, don't you think?" he said and his face was serious. "I would think that not very sensible at all. You are far too beautiful and far too beguiling to be in a room alone with me, Jocasta. Unless, of course, a few things were different. In which case I would like it beyond anything. Obviously."

"I . . . suppose so," she said. "Yes. But—" She stopped, looking at him rather helplessly. What could she say that wouldn't appear brazen, or duplicitous, or any number of other unattractive things?

"Anyway, it's late and you are very tired." He leant forward, kissed her very gently on the mouth. "Now off you go. Sleep well. And tell young Nick that I think he is the luckiest young man in Christendom. Good night. Sweet dreams."

She watched him drive down the street in the absurdly beautiful car and wished, passionately, that she had still been in it with him.

Next morning she felt terrible; not only hungover but terribly guilty. She should at least have told Nick. Have called him. He would certainly have called her. Probably lots of times. She made herself some weak tea, then propped herself up on her pillows and forced herself to listen to her messages.

"Jocasta! Hello sweet pea, where are you? I'm in the press room. I'll wait till I hear from you." OK. That was one. "Mrs. Cook, hi. I'm going down to Shepherd's. Chris has booked a big table. Come and join us." Two. "Jocasta, where the hell are you? It's eleven o'clock and I'm at Shepherd's. Ring me." Three. "Jocasta, ring me. Please. I don't know where you are, but I'm worried about you." Four. "Jocasta, it's almost one. I'm going home to Hampstead. I heard you'd gone off with Gideon and some other people. Thanks for letting me know. Perhaps you'd call me in the morning." Now that had been wrong. To let him worry about her. She should have called him. Tentatively, almost nervously she dialled his number: mercifully it was on message.

"Hi, Nick, it's me. I'm fine, sorry about last night. I got caught up in Gideon's party and he said he'd left a message for you. They obviously didn't deliver it. Sorry you were worried. I was fine. Speak later."

That might, just might, do it. He might believe that. And if he didn't—tough. Two people could play at noncommitment.

Still, this morning her mind, sobered and uncertain, was exercised with three things: Whether she had just been foolishly flattered by Gideon the night before, or had he had something more serious in mind. How cross Nick was going to be with her and how much it mattered. And—rather more mildly—what Martha Hartley might be like now, what she was doing, and whether it would be worth seeking her out for their very long-postponed reunion.

"No," Martha kept saying. "No, no, no."

"But why not?"

"I couldn't possibly do it. That's the main reason. And I don't have time. That's another main reason."

She sat looking at them. When she arrived at Joe Allen, Marcus was there as well. That was a shock.

"Being an MP doesn't take that much time," said Chad, "especially if you're not in government. Which we just possibly may not be."

"Chad, please! I work six days a week as it is. I was working until the small hours this morning."

"Oh, all right. Well, maybe you could cut it down to five. Or work locally instead."

"I don't want to work locally instead. I love what I do."

"Do you? Do you really?" said Marcus. "You told me the other day you were falling out of love with it."

"I know. But I didn't mean it." She felt as if she was falling into a deep, deep hole. She felt panicked, terrified.

"Look, Martha, you would almost definitely be selected," said Chad.

"You're a dream candidate. Local girl, well-known family, young, dynamic—"

"Female," said Marcus.

"Well spotted."

"And is this what's known as parachuting in?"

"It is. But us being a new party and squeaky clean, it would not be good to appear to be doing anything so manipulative. We would stress that you were only one of a field—a very level playing field. Only of course it wouldn't be."

Chad smiled at her again. "How does it all sound?"

"I keep telling you, not what I want. Anyway, I don't understand, Norman Brampton's a Tory."

"A disillusioned one. He'd already signed up to our policies, and persuaded a goodly quotient of his constituency committee to do the same."

"Maybe one day. Not now. I've got no political background—"

"You have now. And she did six months on the Citizens Advice Bureau you know, Chad," said Marcus.

"Oh God," said Chad, "you really are made in heaven. *Please*, Martha. At least think about it. I know you'd do it well. And I know you'd love it."

She was silent: thinking. Thinking properly, for the first time, of what it would mean. Could mean.

A new life. A new purpose to it. A chance to do something, to make a difference. A stab at real achievement, a grasp at real power, real success. She had seen enough of politicians now to know she possibly did have what it took.

Chad saw her hesitation, saw her thinking, and said, quietly, "We're being unfair. Rushing you, pushing you. Think about it, for a day or two. If you're even of half a mind, give me a call, and I'll sound Norman Brampton out."

"And then what?"

"Then you can slap in your CV and he would 'advise,' in quotes, the disillusioned local Tory Party members to adopt you. And with your particular presentational skills, I think you'd walk it. Martha, you're in with a flying chance. It's God-given."

"Do you really think God has any interest in politics?" said Martha with a feeble smile.

"Of course He has," said Marcus briskly. "Immense. And just think, you'd have Him on your side, your dad being the vicar and all. Anyway, Chad's right. We shouldn't be rushing you like this. You go home and think about it. And take your time."

"Yes," said Chad, "any time before Monday morning would do."

Ed was waiting at the table for her, sitting outside in the April sunshine. As always her heart lurched.

He had a bottle of white wine in an ice bucket by the table, and a plate of nibbles.

"Sorry I'm late," she said, kissing him briefly.

"That's all right. How was the party?"

"Oh, great. I didn't stay for long. Had to get back for a meeting."

"No! Not a meeting!"

He seemed slightly subdued, less good-natured than usual.

"Are you all right?" she said, taking his hand.

"Yes I'm fine, thanks. Do you want to eat?"

"No, thank you. I've just had brunch."

"Oh really. With . . . ?"

"Marcus Denning and Chad Lawrence. I'll tell you why later. Bit of a—a dilemma."

He didn't ask what it was about; she was surprised.

"Well, I'd like to eat," he said, slightly truculent.

"Of course. You go ahead. I'll just watch."

"You know it's really fun, eating on your own," he said suddenly, "being watched. It makes everything taste much nicer."

"Ed, I'm sorry. But I couldn't eat any more."

"No, of course not. You must have had—God, what? A croissant? With some honey on it. No, probably not honey. Just the croissant and some black coffee on the side. I asked you for lunch, Martha. I haven't seen you for ten days."

"I'm sorry," she said, realising he was genuinely upset. "Let's share a big Caesar salad. I'd like that."

"Whatever you want."

"Ed, what's the matter?"

"I told you, nothing. I—nothing."

He ordered the salad and a big bowl of frites; she picked at them carefully. He seemed happier after a while.

"So, what have you been doing?" she asked.

"Not a lot. Going to work, getting pissed in the pub, you know, that sort of thing. Tell me about the party."

"Oh, pretty exciting. Everybody was there, Ed—Jeremy Paxman, both the Dimblebys, Greg Dyke—you'd have enjoyed it."

"Pity I couldn't have come, then," he said.

"Yes, it was," she said, realising suddenly she was being tactless. "Although I wasn't there long. Had to leave and persuade some whiz-kid tax lawyer to join our team. And then go back to see Paul Quenell—"

"What would we all do without you, Martha?" he said, and his tone was almost hostile. She stared at him. Something passed between them, something that hadn't been there before. Irritation, resentment, and impatience: real life, she thought. Maybe the honeymoon was over. She felt a flash of panic.

"Come on," she said, covering his hand with hers, "please tell me what the matter is."

"It's nothing," he said after a bit and smiled at her, and suddenly he was Ed again, the Ed she knew and loved. "Sorry. Got out of bed the wrong side. Tell me about your dilemma. Then maybe we could go for a movie."

"Wonderful. Yes, well, it is all a bit peculiar. I really would like to know what you think."

He was surprisingly interested in the idea. He couldn't see why she thought it was so ridiculous.

"Yeah," he said, "why not? You've been talking about it long enough. Sort of. And you'd be good at it. And it would mean you could actually do something about the things you're always going on about."

"Like what?"

"Well, like your friend. The one you were so upset about, the one who died in hospital. And lots of politicians are lawyers, aren't they? Tony Blair and Ken Clarke and Michael Howard—see, I've been mugging up on all these guys."

Of course, it was true. There were endless ex-barristers and QCs in Parliament. She supposed it was because speaking in public came so naturally to them—that and the huge confidence that they all seemed to have imbibed with their mother's milk. That she certainly didn't have: the only confidence within Martha Hartley had come from a sense of achievement at her own success, the order and sense of purpose she had brought to her own life. Which she would lose if she started again . . .

"I couldn't do it," she said finally. "I really couldn't. And it would mean leaving Wesley's. Come on, let's go to the movies."

"Right. And then can we go to bed afterwards?"

"Oh, I should think so," she said, leaning forward, giving him a kiss.

·•·

"Perhaps you should get yourself checked out," said Jeremy.

"What do you mean?" She was surprised to hear her voice sounding so normal: calm and almost surprised.

"I mean checked out. Gynaecologically."

"What on earth for? More salad?"

"No thanks. You know what for. Three months and you're not pregnant. Maybe there's something wrong."

"Jeremy, three months is nothing. And I was on the pill, don't forget. I think it would be surprising if I was pregnant."

"Yes. Yes, I suppose so. Well, we'll give it a bit longer."

"Anyway, it's fun trying," she said and managed to smile at him. "Now, shall we go for a walk? I feel I need some exercise."

"OK. Good idea. We could go up on the Hog's Back."

They walked along in silence for a while, then she said, "You know, I'd like to get a puppy."

"A puppy? What on earth for?"

"I've always liked dogs. And it would be company for me when I leave the practice."

"I'm not too keen on dogs," he said. His tone was dismissive.

"I wasn't actually thinking of you. I said it would be company for me."

"Don't start that. Implying you're going to be lonely and bored. That you're dreading giving up your job."

"Well, I am," she said, reasonably. "And I don't think it's necessary, but I've agreed to do it, to make you happy, and I don't see why I shouldn't have—"

"I think you should be happy to be spending more time at home, our home, not always rushing in exhausted."

"I am not always rushing in exhausted."

"Besides, you're more likely to get pregnant if you're less tired, if you're calmer—"

"Jeremy, that is absolute crap. The world is full of frantically busy, exhausted women getting pregnant. Anyway, I don't want to talk about it. It's so unimportant."

"What? That you're failing to get pregnant?"

"Oh, Jeremy! For God's sake can we please stop this? *Please*. Otherwise I'd like to go straight home."

"All right," he said. "What would you like to talk about instead? The weather?"

"No," she said, "our holiday. I want to go to the Scottish Highlands. I've never been. What would you think about that?"

• ◆ •

"Well, I'm not sure," said Jilly. She looked at Kate and smiled gently. "I can see this is terribly tempting, darling. I can see how much you want to find your mother."

"I don't even exactly want to," said Kate. "I know I'll hate her."

"Why are you so sure about that?"

"Granny! She has to be horrible. Doing what she did. But I just feel I've got to. Until I do I can't settle. I feel I don't know . . . well—"

"Who you are?"

"No. Who I might become. I mean Sarah, my friend—you can see she's turning into her mum. And Juliet's turning into *our* mum, she's, like, so nice and hardworking and—and annoying. Sorry, I know Mum's your daughter, but she *is* annoying. Well, isn't she?"

"Just occasionally," said Jilly carefully.

"So what am I going to turn into? Someone awful and . . . and irresponsible? Like my birth mother, who didn't care, just left me in a cupboard?"

"Kate, she must have been absolutely desperate. It's hard to imagine what she went through. What she's still going through. I'm sure she thinks about you every day."

"Yeah? So why doesn't she come and find me? That wouldn't be very difficult."

Jilly was silent, then she said, "Well, I tell you what, Kate. I might go and see this man. On my own. I don't mind how angry your parents are with me, but I don't want them feeling I'm driving a wedge between you and them. All right? Now, what film are we going to see?"

• •— •

"So—you think I should do it?" Martha said.

"Yeah, I do. Want some of this one? Very spicy, be careful."

They were sitting at her small dining table, looking over the lights of London, eating a Thai meal that she'd had delivered.

"Ed! Is that it?"

"I'd say so, yes."

"But we've hardly discussed it."

"God," he said, pushing his plate aside, folding his hands neatly in an exaggerated pantomime, fixing his eyes on hers, "so sorry. Right. From the top. Let's go through it again. There's nothing to discuss, Martha. I think it's a good idea. OK?"

She felt rather confused. She had wanted a full-blown, careful dissection of the whole thing, the risks, the advantages, her ability to cope with it. "Well, if that's really what you think—"

"Of course it's what I think! I'm finding it a tiny bit tedious, to tell you the truth."

"I'm sorry," she said, slightly indignant. "What would you like to talk about instead? You?"

"Well, it might make a change," he said.

She stared at him. "That's not fair!"

"It's perfectly fair. I hadn't seen you for almost a fortnight, and how long before we got onto you? Roughly sixty seconds. Telling me about the fucking party, about how wonderful it had been, about how you had to leave early to go back to a meeting and then suddenly remembering me and asking me politely what I'd been doing. And then back to you again, and what did I think about this thing with Chad or whatever his name is, should you do it, on and on. Somehow, you know, I don't think you ever will. You'd have to make time for it. Spare it some of your precious energy, interrupt your sacred routine. You should try thinking about something other than yourself for a bit, Martha. It might even be interesting for you."

She felt as if he had hit her.

"I mean, look at us, eating this—this fucking neat and tidy meal, with the telly turned off because you don't like eating when it's on, even though I do, and you picking at it like some kind of dainty vulture. It's all so fucking *ordered*. I tell you, Martha, if you'd started stuffing your face and talking with your mouth full, I just might still be sitting and debating your future. I do have a life, you know," he said. "I do have my own problems."

"Like what?" she said. She felt quite shocked; she had never seen him like this.

"Oh, doesn't matter."

"No, tell me."

"Look, Martha," he said, "I might have wanted to talk about it earlier. I don't now. I'm not in the mood. OK? Now for God's sake eat something. And actually, I think I'd better go. I've got work to do tomorrow. You're not the only one with extra hours to put in."

He stood, picked up his jacket from the sofa, bent and kissed her briefly. "Cheers. See you in a bit."

The door slammed. He was gone. And Martha was left staring out the window, not sure how she felt, just slowly and very carefully, rather as if she had still been eating her Thai meal, picking over what he had said, painstakingly putting it into neat rows and piles and trying to digest it.

⟶•⟵

"Right. Here we are . . ." Jilly pulled up in front of her house; it was raining. "Now you bring the food, darling, and I'll go ahead and open the door. Only be careful, because the path gets very slippery."

Kate watched her walking up the path in her high heels. She had heard that accidents seemed to put things in slow motion and had never believed it; but she watched her grandmother turn to check she was following safely, then very, very slowly and gracefully, turn almost in a pirouette and skid sideways, her skirt floating up and then down again, settling round her in a sort of blanket as she fell, equally slowly, onto the ground. And lie there, absolutely still.

Jocasta switched her mobile off and smiled at Josh.

"Sorry about that."

She wasn't quite sure what she felt. Guilty? A bit. Worried? She supposed so. And—what else? Well, you know what else, Jocasta? You're excited. Very, very excited.

She was having supper with Josh: a rather subdued Josh, because it was his birthday and she had felt she couldn't leave him all alone. Nick had refused to come; he was still angry about her disappearance the night before.

"It'd have been nice if you'd tried a bit harder to contact me. I was actually worried about you, Jocasta."

She'd told him she couldn't count the number of times he hadn't contacted her under similar circumstances, and he'd said OK, fair enough and let's not go down that road, but he really couldn't face supper with Josh.

"But he's so lonely, Nick."

"I expect he is. Stupid bugger. Would that be his third birthday? Or maybe even his fourth?"

"Well—I know. But I can't help feeling sorry for him. Living all alone in that beastly flat—"

"What, that little hovel in Chelsea, you mean?"

"Oh Nick, shut up. Don't you have any human feelings?"

"Yes, for Beatrice. Anyway, I've just got an exclusive interview with Iain Duncan Smith, comments on the new party and the future of his own as he sees it. The Sunday paper wants it first thing in the morning."

"Fine. Absolutely fine. Don't you worry about me."

"I'll call you in the morning."

"And what were you thinking we might do tomorrow? Read your piece? Read everyone else's? And then read yours again, and say how much better it is than theirs?"

"Jocasta, don't be childish. I'll call you in the morning. I'm having lunch with David Owen, but apart from that I'm free."

"Wow," she said, "that does sound marvellous—Sunday evening, *maybe*, after you've finished that piece. Don't bother, Nick!" She rang off, knowing she had to an extent picked a quarrel with him, and knowing very well why. Picking quarrels was one of her talents. So Nick said.

That was when she started wondering how she felt.

And now she was really wondering. It had been Gideon Keeble on her mobile. Would she and Nick like to come to lunch with him the next day?

"Nick isn't free," she said, her head already fizzing with excitement. "So—"

"So," he said, and there was a long silence. "So what about you? If you'd like to risk a boring Sunday with an old man, you're very welcome. It's up to you."

"I'd love it," she said. "Thank you."

"Excellent. How do you feel about the Waterside Inn?"

"I feel very warmly about it," she said. It was good that: far less compromising. Not that she cared about being compromised. Not in the least.

"Good. I'll pick you up at—what? Eleven thirty?"

"Great. I'll be ready. Bye, Gideon."

Actually, she felt guilty, she realised, as she pushed calamari round her plate, very guilty indeed . . .

•━•━•

"I must ask you to switch your phone off at once."

The voice rapped across the waiting room: a bored, harsh voice.

"But I want to call my mum. That's my gran in there." She indicated the cubicle where Jilly lay. "My mum needs to know."

"Well, you must use the public call box. Mobiles interfere with hospital equipment. You can see the notice there."

"So where do I find a public call box?"

"There's one in the main hospital entrance."

"Yeah, and it's not working. I've tried it. Any other suggestions?"

Everyone was looking at her now: a packed Casualty Department. White-faced young families with babies; small children crying; one vomiting constantly into a plastic sandwich box; a drunk with a bleeding head, several more drunks lolling against the wall; a pitifully young Asian girl, visibly pregnant, holding her husband's hand; at least three elderly couples; a couple of middle-aged men, one with his foot roughly bandaged: a sad wave of misery and pain and anxiety washed up on a hostile shore, waiting with painful patience, occasionally going up to the desk to ask how much longer it would be, only to be sent back again to sit down and wait some more. They all welcomed the diversion of the small drama.

"There's no need to be rude," said the woman behind the desk.

"I wasn't being rude. I was asking for another suggestion. Since that one was totally unhelpful."

Misery and anxiety were making Kate feel worse by the minute; she had expected comfort, attention, a swift resolution of her grandmother's troubles, had thought to see her safely tucked up in a warm hospital bed, her pain dealt with efficiently and fast. Instead she had been lying on a trolley in a cubicle for almost two hours, ever since the ambulance which had come after forty long minutes had delivered them here, waiting to be taken to X-ray, with no discernible improvement in her condition whatsoever. A doctor had examined her, said it might be a broken hip or a fractured pelvis; he could do nothing until she had been x-rayed.

She was still in her rain-soaked clothes, shivering violently, despite a nurse having promised three times to get her something warmer. Kate had offered to take her to X-ray herself, since no porter was forthcoming; they had looked at her as if she had suggested she should do a strip in the middle of Casualty.

"A porter has to do it, she can't be moved off that bed."

"I could push it."

"I expect you could," said a nurse, pulling the curtains round her grandmother, "but you don't know where to go."

"You could tell me," said Kate.

"I could," she said wearily. "But I still couldn't let you do it. I'm sorry. The porter shouldn't be long."

She looked exhausted; she seemed at least kinder than the others, said she would go and find Jilly another blanket.

She hadn't.

Jilly was finally x-rayed at 1:00 a.m.; her pelvis was fractured, but her hip wasn't broken.

"So there's no need to operate," said the doctor, summoned back to her cubicle. "The pelvis will heal itself, given time. Now then, I think as she has possible concussion, and in view of her age, we'll get her up into a ward, settle her down for the night, sort out some pain relief."

"She's terribly cold," said Kate, "she keeps shivering."

"That's shock," he said. The nurse, standing beside him, nodded sagely. The minute a doctor appeared, there seemed to be plenty of nurses; the rest of the time there were none to be seen. They'd even managed to get her out of her wet clothes.

The doctor patted Jilly's blanket condescendingly. "Poor old soul. What name is it—oh yes, Jillian. Soon have you nicely tucked up, Jillian."

"My name," said Jilly, and her voice was steadier suddenly, "is Mrs. Bradford. That is how I wish to be addressed."

The doctor and the nurse exchanged glances.

When Helen and Jim arrived it was two in the morning; Kate had finally gone outside and called them, after the doctor had left.

"Where is she?" said Helen. "Is she in bed?"

"No," said Kate, "she's on a trolley. They're totally useless. She was freezing to death until I made them get a blanket. She's had nothing, except for the cup of tea I got her. No painkillers, nothing. Stupid tossers!" she added loudly.

"Kate, dear, don't talk like that," said Helen. "Er—do you think I could go and see my mother?" she asked the woman behind the desk rather tentatively.

"Of course you can," said Kate. "Don't ask anything, they only know how to say no."

An old woman with no teeth cackled loudly.

"She's a right one, isn't she?" she said to Helen. "She's put 'em all to rights round here. More guts than all the rest of us put together. You should be proud of her."

Helen smiled rather nervously and followed Kate to Jilly's cubicle.

Kate woke up with a start; her head was in her mother's lap. She was asleep, too, her head on Jim's shoulder. Daylight was coming in through the dingy net curtains. Kate looked at her watch; it was half past six.

She sat up, walked over to the cubicle; please, please let her be gone.

She wasn't; she was still there, wide awake, feverish.

"Kate! Oh, how nice to see you. I thought you'd all gone."

"Of course we haven't gone. Oh Gran, I'm so sorry. How is it now?"

"Painful," said Jilly, "terribly painful. Could you ask again for painkillers? I can't stand it much longer. And Kate, darling, could you get me another cup of tea? Or even a glass of water?"

By ten o'clock, still no bed had been found. Kate slumped in Casualty, biting her nails. This was unbelievable. She was exhausted: How on earth did her grandmother feel? She walked round the room, her arms folded, trying not to scream. Her mother was standing anxiously by the cubicle; her father had gone for what he called a little walk. He hated hospitals.

Someone had left a newspaper behind; she picked it up idly. It was the *Sketch*. There was a big article on the inside page, about an old lady who'd been on a hospital trolley without food or water for twelve hours and had died. It was a disgrace, the *Sketch* said, that such things happened in a country that had pioneered the National Health Service; the old woman's daughter was saying she would sue the hospital, the doctor, and the NHS.

At least they had some guts, Kate thought, they didn't just sit around saying yes doctor, no doctor, three bags full doctor.

God, this was awful. What could she do? Who would help? And then she remembered her grandmother's nice doctor. The one who'd come into the shop that day. Surely she would be able to do something. She went into the cubicle; Jilly was dozing restlessly.

"Granny?"

"Yes?" She woke up at once.

"Granny, what's the name of your doctor? The lady who came into the shop that day?"

"Oh, Dr. Scott. Yes. Nice girl."

"Do you have her number? I thought I'd ring her. See if she can help."

"It's in my address book. In my bag." Her voice was slightly slurred. "But darling, she won't come on a Sunday. And what could she do?"

Kate shrugged. "Dunno. But it's worth a try."

She went outside and rang the surgery number. A robot answered.

"The surgery is closed. You have a choice. If it is a real emergency, you should go to the Casualty Department at the Duke of Kent Hospital. If it is a minor problem, call the NHS direct help line. Or stay on the line to be connected to our duty doctor who can advise you further."

Kate stayed on the line. Please, please God, let it be her. Let it be Dr. Scott.

Chapter 12

. . . . .

Somewhere in the long wakeful hours (however could they be called small?) she had made the decision. She called Chad early and said she would do it. Well, begin to do it. Go along with them, just a little way at first, see what happened, try and judge whether it was even possible. Take a week's leave—once the big presentation was over—and really give it her best shot.

Chad had been very surprised; delighted, excited even, but still surprised.

"All I'm saying," she warned him, "is that I'll go down there with you. Talk to the constituency people, to Norman Brampton. All right?"

"All right. Martha, that's fantastic. I know we can make it work. Absolutely know it."

"You don't," she said. "But at least this way you'll know if you can't." She sounded odd. She could hear it herself.

Marcus was pleased and extremely surprised also. "Wonder what persuaded her?" he said when Chad called.

"God knows. Let's just be thankful. And put some arrangements in place before she changes her mind."

Chad had invited Jack Kirkland and Janet Frean for a working lunch at his London flat, to discuss policy. The next day, Chad said, they would—hopefully—stop being front-page celebrities and instead become working politicians again. The electorate was a bit tired of celebrities; it wanted the country in the hands of sensible, grown-up people.

The immediate challenge was persuading as many MPs as possible to join them; there was also the need to establish local councillors where humanly possible.

It was going to be tough, but a few gains would grab all the headlines and put them on a roll. The more success they had, the better the publicity; the better the publicity, the greater the chance of success. At the same time, they were embarking on a heavy programme of public round-the-country speeches. Jack would be taking on the home counties and London,

Janet the Midlands, Chad the North. "But then on Saturday I'll come down south, head for East Anglia, starting with Binsmow in Suffolk, with our lovely young putative candidate, and see what I can do there. Best I go personally, for several reasons, not least that I've had several conversations with Norman Brampton already."

"Which lovely young putative candidate?" asked Kirkland. His voice was slightly edgy.

"Martha Hartley."

"Good Lord!" He had wagered Chad that Martha would say no.

"Yes, indeed. So you owe me a hundred pounds, I think."

"It's extraordinary. Maybe she really is out of love with the law."

"Maybe. Maybe she does think she'll enjoy it," said Chad.

"Maybe she's just a bit starstruck," said Janet. "It's hard to imagine the slog of the thing until you've done it."

They agreed it was probably a combination of all those things.

⚬—⚬—⚬

Clio arrived just after two. "I'm sorry I've been so long," she said rushing into Casualty. "I was on endless calls this morning. It's Kate, isn't it?"

"Yes," said Kate. She looked exhausted, Clio thought. Her wild hair was straggling round her white tear-stained face, her eyes were dark and heavy, and she also looked rather grubby.

"How is your grandmother? And where is she?"

"In something called HDU," said Kate and burst into tears.

"Oh no! Look, I'll go and find out— Oh, hello. You must be Kate's mother."

"That's right. It's very good of you to come, Dr. Scott." Helen looked and sounded tired. "We need some help. My mother's just been rushed off to HDU and then we had a bit of an upset. Kate started shouting at a nurse."

"I wouldn't worry," said Clio, "they're quite used to it. But why is she in HDU?"

"Something about a clot. She was having pains in her legs, said she didn't like to complain and then suddenly had quite bad chest pains. Oh dear. It's all such a nightmare."

"I'll go and see what I can find out," said Clio patting her hand. "Try not to worry too much."

Some insistent questioning of the duty doctor revealed that not only did Jilly have a deep-vein thrombosis—arguably caused by the long period on the trolley—but it had moved upwards and part of it had lodged in her pulmonary artery. Clio returned to Helen and Kate, and broke the news as gently as she could.

"I know it's terribly worrying for you. But she's getting the best possible care now. She's on intravenous heparin which is a wonderful drug, and the doctor will keep you informed—he's promised to come down as soon as he knows any more. I'm afraid they wouldn't let me see her, but she's basically fit, and she should be fine. She's such a—such a splendid woman," she added, flailing around rather wildly for things to say, cheerful, positive things. "So smart and attractive. I love her shop."

When Clio left, Kate was talking to some young man who'd walked into Casualty who obviously wasn't a patient. Maybe he'd come to collect someone. He was clearly taken with Kate—not surprisingly. She was very attractive, even with her dirty face. But who did she remind her of? Who, who?

Clio thought of herself at sixteen: tubby, plain, anxious, pushed about by her sisters, totally devoid of self-confidence. She could never have done what Kate had done, battled with bureaucracy, questioned authority. She could hardly do it now, for God's sake; she couldn't even stand up to her own husband.

•◆•

"You remind me of my mother," said Gideon Keeble. "She was the great love of my life," he added, smiling, "although I don't suppose you would quite regard that as a compliment. But you would have loved her. And she would have loved you."

"When did she die?"

"Five and a half years ago. She did very well, she was eighty-five."

"Eighty-five!"

That was quite old. Too old, she felt, to be Gideon's mother. He read her thoughts.

"I was her last but one child. She was almost forty when I was born. Let me put you out of your misery. I'm fifty-one. Not quite Methuselah."

"I told you, Gideon, you seem absolutely ageless to me."

"Well, I should be thankful for that."

It was true; sitting there, smiling, in the sunshine, his blue eyes boring into hers, he was no age at all, just a powerfully attractive man.

"And how am I like your mother?"

"Oh, well now, she was clever. And tough."

"How do you know I'm either of those things?"

"You couldn't do the job you do if you weren't. And then you're both charming. And loving."

"And how do you know I'm loving?"

"I . . . sense it," he said, and it was one of the most erotic things that had ever been said to her. "Now," he added, "what would you like to talk about?"

"You," she said. "Please. Tell me about you."

She knew a lot of it, of course: the rise from a childhood spent in considerable poverty to a fortune that was now counted in billions rather than millions, from a first job as a messenger and a second as a salesman for a small Dublin menswear store, to the ownership of a worldwide retail organisation. There had been titanic struggles for the control of other companies, famous bidding wars, even more famous deals. He owned fashion chains in Europe, America, and Australia; and large furniture warehouses, operating largely in out-of-town shopping centres. He also had a chain of small exclusive stores selling what he called couture for the home. He had recently branched into hotels—"boutique hotels, you'll have heard of them no doubt"—foodie shops, and delis cashing in on the fashion for what he called smart food, and a worldwide chain of coffee shops. A great deal of his wealth inevitably came from real estate, shop frontage on some of the world's most famous streets.

Along the way were casualties, namely three marriages, and—on one famous occasion—almost himself. A massive heart attack, three years ago, had left him half dead, but absolutely opposed to doing what he was told and taking life more quietly.

"What would I do with a quiet life? I would get very noisy indeed, noisy and troublesome."

He worked as hard as ever now, he said, but with the important difference that he took care of himself. "I don't smoke, hardly drink. I swim two miles a day, which is excessively boring, but I do it."

"Wherever do you do that?" she said.

"Oh, well now, in my house in London I have one of those very clever little pools that sets up a current against you and each length measures about half a mile; in the country I have a bigger one, rather vulgar but none the worse for that, and in Ireland, unless the weather is absolutely frightful, I swim in my lake."

"Oh my God," said Jocasta.

"Yes, I do call on Him quite often as I plunge in. But it is truly wonderful once you get going. I shall make you sample it."

"Then I shan't come!"

"In which case, I promise not to make you sample it. Anyway, for all those reasons I am now as fit as the proverbial flea. A rather large one, it has to be said. Look, shall we forget about the food, since you are so clearly not enjoying it, and take their very splendid boat trip instead? And after that I am afraid I shall have to start heading back to London. I have to catch a plane to Australia very early in the morning and I have a great deal of work to do first."

She arrived home feeling drunk: not with wine, of which she'd had very little, but with him. He had hardly touched her, except to kiss her as he picked her up and again as they parted, to hand her into the boat and to help her into her jacket; but she felt disturbed by him nonetheless. Much of it, she knew very well, was the dizzy pleasure of being with someone so famous and powerful, of him finding her desirable and interesting. It made her feel soothed and comforted, made Nick's rejection just a little less painful.

"It has been very lovely," he said, smiling at her across the considerable width of the car. "I don't know when I enjoyed a day so much. Would you like to do it again? Well, perhaps not an absolute repetition, but— well, I'm sure we can find something similar."

"Yes," she said, reckless with the excitement of it, "I would love that. I really would."

"Then speak to Nick," he said, "and when you have done that, let me know."

·◆·

"Dr. Scott? It's Kate."

"Oh—hi, Kate." She looked across the room at Jeremy; he was deep in the motoring section of the *Sunday Telegraph*. "Any news?"

"Not really. The clot thing's quite serious. She's really ill and they won't let me see her. They said Mum could, but not me. What's going on, do you think?"

"I don't know, Kate. But I expect she's been sedated, and they think too many visitors are a bad idea. When she's better, you'll be able to, I'm sure."

"OK." She sounded childlike, near to tears.

Clio looked at Jeremy again; he was waving at her, tapping his watch. "Look, I've got to go now, I'm so sorry. Let me know how she's doing. And if you're really still worried, I'll try and come back, get some more news. All right?"

"Yeah, OK. Thanks. Bye."

There was a click as she hung up. She had failed her, Clio thought, she should have offered to go back anyway, only there really was nothing she could do. And what on earth would she say to Jeremy?

In fact, she didn't have to say anything to Jeremy for quite a while; he was called in to the Duke of Kent Hospital himself to operate on one of his private patients who had fallen and broken her hip. Clio prayed that no one would mention her presence there a few hours earlier because she hadn't told him . . .

•-•-

"So, how was lunch with the billionaire retailer?" Nick's voice was light, teasing; it annoyed her.

"Fine," she said, slightly coolly.

"Where did you go?"

"The Waterside Inn."

"Well, get you. Wish I were a billionaire retailer. I'd like to have taken you there."

"You could have done. Actually."

"Jocasta, don't be difficult. I'm trying to make amends."

"Sorry. How was David Owen?"

"He was charming. Very helpful. Now, I'd like to come and see you. If that's all right."

"Well . . ." Did she really want to see him? She felt unsettled by her day. If he came round, they'd have another row. She knew it. Nick would be full of political gossip and professional chitchat. She wanted more of Gideon Keeble, flattering her, telling her how beguiling she was . . .

"Well, the thing is," she said, playing for time, "I—"

Her mobile leapt into life: she looked at it, wondering if it was Gideon, if it could possibly be Gideon, wondering what she could say to Nick if it was.

It wasn't Gideon. It was the news editor at the *Sketch*. "Hold on, Nick," she said, "it's the news desk, sorry."

"Jocasta? Trolley tragedy. Duke of Kent Hospital, Guildford. Agency bloke already there, with photographer. Quick as you can."

Derek Bateson felt rather pleased with himself. He had only been working as a stringer for the North Surrey News Agency for three months and this was his third big story. Of course this one didn't compete with the one in January where someone had been on a trolley for three days, covered in blood; but it wasn't bad, given that this old lady was so ill.

"Derek Bateson? Hi!" A slightly breathless voice sounded behind him. Derek turned; an amazing-looking girl was smiling at him, holding out her hand. She was very tall, and she had all this blond hair, and legs that seemed to start at her shoulders, and the most brilliant blue eyes.

"I'm Jocasta," she said, "from the *Sketch*. So tell me what's happened."

"Well, this woman, Jilly Bradford, slipped last night, broke her pelvis, the usual after that, long wait for ambulance, the granddaughter was with her, then all night on a trolley, nothing happening, apart from an X-ray, then around lunchtime her leg got really painful, and she's got a pulmonary embolism. She's in Intensive Care and apparently it's touch and go."

"Poor lady! And relatives? Any here?"

"Her daughter. Nice sort of woman, very quiet, and the granddaughter—now she's a live wire. She tore them all off a strip earlier, for not doing anything, and she's been trouble all night according to some old biddy who's been here nearly as long."

"Well done her. So, who can I talk to?"

"I'd say start with her but her mum's taken her off to her grandma's house for a shower and that. They're not allowed to see the old lady for a bit."

"Well, she'll be back soon I expect. What about the duty doctor?"

"He's over there. But it's not the one who was on last night."

"I'll have a word with him. Thanks, Derek. Is your photographer around? Just in case we need him."

"In the pub. But we can get him anytime."

"Great."

God, she was gorgeous. Maybe she'd like a drink later on.

"So where exactly is Mrs. Bradford now?"

"In HDU." The doctor looked at Jocasta coldly. He was very thin, with huge bony hands and a long bony nose, and a crop of spots on his chin. She wondered how old he was; probably younger than her. Like policemen, doctors were getting younger.

"I imagine you won't suggest interviewing her there," he said. This was clearly intended as cutting irony.

"I'd love to." She smiled at him. "But I can see that's not at all practical. Maybe a little later on."

"I can assure you that you won't be seeing her at any point, later or sooner."

"Well, that will be up to her, won't it? Who was on duty last night?"

"I don't have to answer that question."

"No, of course you don't. Thank you so much, you've been terribly helpful."

She looked around: a very young girl was tidying up a bed in one of the cubicles. She looked much more promising. Jocasta waited until the doctor had disappeared into another cubicle and drawn the curtain, then went over to the nurse.

She was very forthcoming. Yes, Mrs. Bradford had been brought in at about nine. "Poor lady. With her granddaughter. She was in awful pain, soaked through from the rain. She was seen quite quickly by a doctor. And then sent down to X-ray. I mean, it wasn't as if she was ignored or anything."

"Of course not. It must be so difficult, especially on a Saturday night. Lot of drunks and so on, I expect."

"Yes. And drugs and that. And we get a lot of abuse, you know, and we really are doing our best."

"I'm sure. And no thanks either, I don't suppose. Now, after she'd been seen, what happened?"

"I don't really know. I was very busy. We had a couple of overdoses, that's always a nightmare. A girl having a miscarriage, which was awful. Everyone was completely overstretched. I went off duty at breakfast time. But apparently the granddaughter phoned Mrs. Bradford's GP and she came to see if she could help. That set the cat among the pigeons—they don't like that, and you can see why."

"Of course. But it was nice of her to come. Do you know her name?"

"Who, the GP? I don't, sorry. But she went down to X-ray, they might just know."

"Well thank you . . ." She peered at the nurse's badge. "Thank you, Sue. You've been really kind."

Jocasta had learnt long ago that you could walk about unquestioned in a great many places where you had no business to be, providing you proceeded fast and confidently, smiling at anyone you passed, and were carrying a file of papers. She took off her jacket, filched a brown file from a trolley (first emptying it of the papers inside in case they were, literally, life and death), tucked the *Sunday Times* inside it, and followed the signs to X-ray.

The X-ray Department looked like a scene from a documentary on the plight of the NHS. Dingy, dimly lit, with two depressed fish swimming round a tank, a pile of broken toys on the floor, and year-old magazines on a low table, it housed several people staring listlessly in front of them.

Jocasta went over to the desk.

"Hi. I wonder if you can help me. There was a Mrs. Bradford here last night; she'd fractured her pelvis. Her GP was with her, and I need the GP's name."

The woman looked terminally bored, leafed through some papers. "Who's it for, Admin?"

"Yes, that's right."

"Mrs. Jillian Bradford—GP's down here as Dr. Scott."

"And do you have the number?"

"Only the group practice number. It's Guildford." She looked at Jocasta. "I thought you were from Admin. They've got all the practice numbers up there."

"I know, but they're closed. I'm just doing a bit of overtime, catching up on records."

"Oh, right. Well, it's Guildford 78640." She looked at Jocasta again. "You're not the press, are you?"

"I wish. Might be a bit more excitement in my life."

"Only we've all just been told not to speak to the press. Order from on high. And it was to do with this Mrs. Bradford."

"Really? Wonder why."

"Some cock-up, apparently. She was left too long, got a clot on her leg—we had her down again for a venography this morning."

"Did you see her yourself?"

"Couldn't say—it's all a blur, this point in the day. One patient is just like another . . ."

Derek Bateson was still in Casualty when she got back.

"Has the granddaughter come back?"

"Not yet. I've got her mobile number, though. Do you want that?"

"Oh—yes, please!"

Stupid twit. Why couldn't he have told her that, saved her all that nonsense in X-ray. Except she had got a useful quote out of it.

"Hello. Who is this?"

It was a young, wary voice.

"Oh, hello. I presume that's Kate. My name is Jocasta Forbes from the *Sketch* newspaper. I'm so sorry about your grandmother—"

"Is there any news about her?"

"Not yet. I really want to talk to her GP, the one who came today. Derek, who you've been talking to, said you might have the number."

"Yeah, I do. But— What, Mum, for God's sake? It's just someone from the newspaper, she—" A pause, then she said, clearly cross, "My mum wants to talk to you."

A pleasant, worried voice came on the phone.

"Hello. Look, if you don't mind, I think we don't want to get involved with the press. Sorry."

"That's all right. I can imagine you must feel dreadful, I'm so sorry about your mother."

"Yes, it has been a dreadful day. We're just on our way back there now."

"I see. Well, I don't want to upset you any further. The only thing is—"

"I'm sorry," said Helen. "I really would rather not talk about it."

Clio was trying to concentrate on a programme about wildlife when the phone rang.

"Hello?"

"Hello. Is that Dr. Scott?"

"Ye-es."

"Hi. Dr. Scott, I'm so sorry to bother you at home. My name is Jocasta Forbes. I write for the *Sketch*—"

It was at moments like this, Clio thought, that the earth really moved: moments of shock, of strangeness, even of fear, rocking you dizzily about.

"Did you say Jocasta?" she said finally, hearing her own voice shaky, odd. "Jocasta Forbes?"

"I did, yes. Why?"

"Oh my God!" said Clio and she had to sit down suddenly. "I can't believe it. Jocasta Forbes. So you made it, you did what you said!"

"I'm really sorry, but— Have we met or something?"

"Jocasta, it's Clio. Clio Scott. Well, Clio Graves, actually. Thailand, eighteen years ago. How amazing. How absolutely amazing!"

"Clio! Oh, my God. How are you? How extraordinary—"

"Totally extraordinary. All those clichés about small worlds are so true. God, it's so weird. But why are you calling me now? And how did you get my number?"

"I'm doing a story about one of your patients. Mrs. Bradford."

"A story! Why is it a story?"

"Well, as I understand it, she was on a trolley for a long time and now she's quite ill. In the HDU. Tabloids like these stories. I've been at the hospital, but her granddaughter—"

"Kate Tarrant?"

"Yes. Haven't met her yet, but she gave me your number. She sounds like quite a girl. Anyway, that's not very important. Oh, Clio, I'd so love to see you! Why on earth didn't we do what we agreed and meet when we got home again all those years ago? Could I come round, do you think?"

"Um . . . hold on a minute, Jocasta, could you? My husband's just come in."

"Your husband! How very grown-up of you. Look, ring me back in five minutes. Number's—got a pencil? Right—"

Jeremy came in, tired and irritable. "Chaos there, some woman's got a pulmonary embolism, supposed to have been left on a trolley, press involved, dreadful nonsense."

"And . . . how is she?"

"God, Clio, I don't know. Can we have that soup now?"

"Yes. Yes, of course. It's on the stove. Only, well, Jeremy, I'm terribly sorry, but I've got to go out again. The child with meningitis this morning—the mother's still very worried. So—"

"Dear God, I'll be glad when all this nonsense is over. All right. Don't be long, will you? This has been a dreadful Sunday."

"Of course. I mean of course not. But I might be a bit of a while. Sorry."

"What's this rubbish?" He was pouring himself a scotch, staring at the television, already engrossed in a programme.

Clio left the house quietly, drove down the lane, stopped, and phoned Jocasta.

"Hi. It's me. Look, I don't want to come to the hospital. Medical conventions and all that. Could we meet at the pub just down the road from the hospital? It's called the Dog and Fox. Saloon bar."

"Sure. Can't wait."

Clio saw Jocasta immediately as she hurried into the pub. She was sitting at a table by the window, smoking, reading something; she had a bottle of wine and two glasses in front of her. She looked up, saw her, and smiled, then stood up, pushed her mane of hair back, and came towards her—and in that moment Clio knew exactly who it was that Kate Tarrant had reminded her of.

"There's not a lot more news, I'm afraid." Staff Nurse Campbell smiled with officious patience at Helen and Kate. "Your mother is still in HDU—the High Dependency Unit—receiving the very best, most technologically advanced care available, on a virtually one-to-one basis. Believe me, she is in the very best place."

"It might be the best place now," said Kate. "But if you'd looked after her properly in the beginning, she wouldn't need all that, would she? If she hadn't been lying in the gutter for hours and then on that trolley all night and half today she wouldn't have to be given all that crap."

"Kate! I'm sorry," Helen said apologetically to Nurse Campbell, "she's very upset."

"I daresay." The look Nurse Campbell gave Kate would have terrified a slightly frailer spirit. "Well, I think the best thing would be for you to go home and come back in the morning. Your mother isn't really aware of very much at the moment and if she was . . . If she was, I don't think this young lady's attitude would help. She needs peace and quiet, not aggravation."

"Oh and she's had that, has she?" asked Kate. "I don't remember much peace and quiet down in that cruddy Casualty all last night, people throwing up and shouting and shitting themselves in that filthy toilet!"

"Kate, please! Be quiet! I do apologise," said Helen.

"Oh don't worry, Mrs. Tarrant. We get used to hysteria, I do assure you. Now I would advise you very strongly to go home."

"Is there nowhere we could wait here?" asked Helen humbly. "We live quite a way away, you see."

"There is a relatives' room," said Nurse Campbell reluctantly. "On the ground floor. But it's not very comfortable."

"I wonder how we knew that," said Kate. "Come on, Mum, let's go."

Helen followed Kate down the corridor, too weary and anxious to reprimand her further.

"I could sit here forever," said Jocasta stubbing out her cigarette. "We haven't even started on our travels, have we? Just tell me one thing—did you stick to your plan? End up where you thought and so on?"

"No, I didn't. Not really. I often wonder what Martha's doing."

"I heard something about her the other day. Right out of the blue. She's in politics, I was told. Well, on the edge. In with this new party, apparently. I was going to try and track her down as well. Oh, dear, I must go."

"What—what exactly are you going to write?" asked Clio.

"Oh, you know. Lots of sob stuff. And shock-horror, NHS fails again. Yet another old lady left on a trolley."

"Jocasta, she's hardly an old lady," said Clio. "She's a rather glamorous sixty."

"She is? God, I wish I could meet her. Do you think I could?"

"Absolutely not, if she's in the HDU."

"Have you met the daughter?"

"Yes. She's very nice indeed. The granddaughter . . ." She hesitated; she was still—absurdly she knew, for what reason for it could there possibly be?—slightly bothered by the resemblance between Kate and Jocasta. "She's a tough little nut."

"Yes, so I gathered. Maybe I could find her at least."

"Maybe. Yes, it would be interesting for you." She would be interested herself. Would Jocasta see the likeness between them? Probably not. There were after all only so many variations that could be worked on two eyes, a nose, and a mouth. The tumble of a billion genes was bound to yield some duplication.

Her stomach lurched. She looked at Jocasta, said hesitantly, "Jocasta, I know it's your job and everything, but, well, do you think it's going to do any good? Writing this story, putting the names of these nice people all over the paper?"

"Oh Clio!" Jocasta shook her head sorrowfully. "I'm not about doing good. I'm about doing a good job. It's what I'm paid for. I'm sorry. I hope it's not going to strike our friendship down at the first hurdle, but I really, really do have to write it."

"Yes. Yes, I see." She couldn't really. "But it will make things much worse for poor Mrs. Bradford—the hospital will hate it, I can tell you that. And, well, my husband would absolutely kill me if his name got into it. Or mine."

"Why should his name get into it?"

"He's one of the consultants there. Quite an important one."

"OK. So why should he kill you? It won't be your fault."

"He'd think it was. If he knew I knew you—"

"Well he won't, don't fret about that. I won't use either of your names. They don't improve the story and it's the system we're on about, not the people. Now look, where might I find a white coat? You'd be amazed how far I've got in the past with one on. Practically into the operating theatre."

"Jocasta, that's so terrible."

"Not at all. You haven't got one, have you?"

"No, I have not," said Clio untruthfully.

"Doesn't matter, I'll find the hospital laundry. I've done that a few times. Call me in a day or two. Here's my card, phone number, e-mail address and everything. And I should warn you, the other rats will be down tomorrow."

"What other rats?"

"The other papers."

"Oh God, Jocasta, do you have to—"

"Yes, I do. Sorry." She leant forward and kissed Clio. "I'm so glad I found you. Don't worry about the story. Tomorrow's fish-and-chip wrapping, you know." She always said that; it was doubly untrue, now that fish-and-chips were wrapped in hygienic white paper, and every story was available to be read afresh on the Internet at the press of a button or two. But it still comforted people.

Helen was dozing fitfully in the shabby discomfort of the visitors' room and Kate was reading old copies of *Hello!* when a doctor walked in.

She didn't look much like a doctor, apart from her white coat. She was very young and pretty, and she smiled at Kate and put her fingers on her lips.

"Kate?" she whispered.

"Yes. What is it, is Gran—?"

Jocasta jerked her head towards the door; Kate got up gingerly and followed her out into the corridor.

"As far as I know your gran's just about the same. But I'm not actually a doctor. I'm Jocasta from the *Sketch*. We talked earlier." She smiled at Kate. She looked exhausted, poor little thing; it must have been a terrible ordeal for her. "How're you doing?"

"Pretty worried. They just won't tell us anything and I want to see Granny and they won't let me."

"Well, we'll go up there in a minute, shall we? See what we can find out. I don't know how far Dr. Jocasta will get, but we might make first base. Are you hungry? I've got some crisps outside."

"Oh yes, please. I'm starving. How did you get this far? They said the outside doors were all locked now."

"Casualty's always open. I just walked in."

She was great, Kate thought, wolfing down the crisps gratefully minutes later, really, really great. She liked her a lot.

Chapter 13

She could hear the shock in their voices. Of all the things she had done that they found difficult to understand, this clearly topped the list.

"But, dear," her mother said, "of course we would be very pleased. And proud. But—why? I thought you loved your job."

"I do. I do love it. And in any case, I wouldn't be thinking of leaving it until I get selected. Which I almost certainly won't. But, well, just lately I've found it a bit less satisfying. And I'm intrigued by this as a . . . challenge." She needed a challenge. She needed something. If she couldn't have Ed.

"But you don't know anything about politics."

"I didn't. But I've been working for this party, doing bits of legal work and so on, for a while. And I like what I see of it. Well, some of it anyway. Honestly, I'm almost as surprised as you are that they've asked me. And I'm as sure as I'm sitting here that I won't even be short-listed. Let alone adopted as the local party candidate. So it's all a bit of a farce, really. But I've said I'll give it a go."

Only because of what Ed had said, really. Only because of the expression on his face when he left, which had looked like dislike.

After she had rung off, she decided to allow herself another, proper cry. It seemed to help with the pain: briefly.

．◆．

"Oh, what fun! This is doing me much more good than all that awful stuff they keep pumping into me. There! How do I look?"

"Mummy, I'm not sure about this," said Helen.

She sounded as exhausted as she looked; Jilly, on the other hand, was rosy and brilliant-eyed, lying back on her pillows, fluffing up her hair and contemplating herself in her small mirror. Anyone studying them would have thought it was Helen and not her mother who had almost died four days earlier.

"Not sure about what, darling?"

"You seeing this girl again. She's caused so much trouble—"

"Not for me she hasn't," said Jilly briskly. "If it hadn't been for her, I would never have seen you the other night. Or Kate. And then being able to tell her exactly how ghastly it was, and reading about it the next day— or was it the next, I'm rather confused now . . ."

"It was yesterday, that bit of the story," said Helen.

"Oh, yes. Well, it did feel like revenge, of a sort. On those stupid people in Casualty, and that dreadful staff nurse up here. All so pleased with themselves, so unconcerned about everyone's suffering. And then it's splendid that they've put me in this nice little room, isn't it? So thoughtful."

Helen was silent; her mother had been put in a side ward at the express instructions of one of the senior consultants, Mr. Graves, under whose care she was, and who had been incandescent with rage at the story in the *Sketch* on Monday morning and the descent of at least a dozen other journalists and photographers on what he called his hospital. It had been a mistake, that, leading as it had to a seventy-two-point headline in the *Sun* reading THEY'RE OUR HOSPITALS, ACTUALLY, MR. GRAVES.

Jocasta had visited a rather frail but animated Jilly in her room at about noon on Monday; the rest of the press had been kept out, but as the new best friend of Jilly Bradford's granddaughter, there had been no such control over her, and in any case, with her unruly hair tucked neatly under a baseball cap, nobody recognised her as the young woman masquerading as a doctor who had caused such trouble the night before, walking into HDU to check on Mrs. Bradford's progress and, having ascertained it was satisfactory, telling the agency nurse in charge that she thought seeing her daughter and granddaughter for a minute or two would do her good.

A real doctor had arrived very shortly afterwards, Jocasta had been thrown out, and the nurse had been most severely reprimanded, but had defended herself, saying that she could hardly be expected to know every houseman walking about the hospital, and adding that if this was the National Health in England, she couldn't wait to get back to her own hospital in South Africa.

This had been reported back to Jocasta, who had passed it on to her readers, along with the quote from a girl in the X-ray Department that one patient seemed much like another, and another from a nurse in Casualty that it was impossible to look after people properly, so understaffed were they, and it simply wasn't right.

"How much longer are we going to have to put up with this sort of thing?" her emotive article had ended.

In a health service that used to be the envy of the world? How many more patients are going to die, how many more old ladies are to be left alone and frightened, and in the case of Jilly Bradford, soaked to the skin after lying in the rain for hours waiting for an ambulance? And then denied such basic comforts as a warm bed and a cup of tea? How much longer do we all have to wait before someone takes the NHS in hand?

Apart from finding herself described as an old lady, Jilly was entranced by the article and her starring role in it.

"I'm sorry about that," Jocasta said to Kate, who reported it, giggling. "But we'll get a nice picture of her in a day or so when she's looking a bit better, and show everyone that she isn't really an old lady at all."

Clio had crept out early on the Monday morning to buy the *Sketch*, had sat in her car reading it, her heart in her mouth, absolutely horrified by almost every word. Jocasta had kept her promise, there was no mention of her by name, or even by reference, as Mrs. Bradford's GP, but the opprobrium she had heaped on the hospital, the out-of-context quotes from various departments—it all made her feel very sick.

She had managed somehow to chat normally over breakfast with Jeremy, saw him off to the hospital with a sigh of huge relief, and got ready for work herself; maybe that would be the end of it. But it wasn't; two copies of the *Sketch* were being fought over in the surgery, and the receptionist wanted to know if the paper had approached her.

"Why should they, for goodness' sake?" asked Clio.

"Well, you *are* Mrs. Bradford's GP—and I bet they get onto your husband. He's the consultant orthopod there."

"Well," she said, reluctantly, "I suppose so. But—"

"Clio," said Mark Salter, "if there's a follow-up on this, someone's bound to want to talk to Jeremy. I'm surprised the girl who wrote this piece didn't try herself."

"She obviously didn't think it was very important," said Clio coolly, blissfully unaware that at that very moment, a reporter from the *Daily Express* and another from the *Sun* were standing in front of Jeremy, demanding a quote, even as he ordered them out. That was when he had made the unfortunate remark about it being *his* hospital.

An hour later the papers caught up with her; there were several phone calls, followed by a visit from three reporters and two photographers, who sat in the surgery reception for hours: Did she, as Mrs. Bradford's GP, have anything to say about the conditions at the Duke of Kent Hospital, and how had it been possible for an old lady to be treated, or rather not treated, in such a way? While she was stalling helplessly, feeling like a rat in a trap, Jocasta phoned; angry with her as she was, Clio accepted her advice to give them a quote.

She cobbled something together about the Health Service struggling under enormous pressure and everyone doing their utmost to cope, and that she greatly regretted what had happened to Mrs. Bradford, "But the GP's role is quite separate from that of the hospital's and I cannot possibly comment on what happened to her while she was not in my direct care."

She sent this out via Margaret, neatly typed on her computer, refusing to see anyone personally. Her quote was sufficiently dull to persuade the reporters that they were wasting their time and to send them back to the much greater excitement of the hospital.

Both her sisters phoned, intrigued by the fracas and the way in which Jeremy had been vilified. Ariadne, who loathed him, was clearly hugely amused. Several friends in the medical profession called to sympathise.

All the papers covered the story on Tuesday; the *Sketch* was still winning the race by a head, with a brief personal interview given by Mrs. Bradford "in a frail whisper" to Jocasta Forbes, relating all that she had endured, and paying tribute to her granddaughter Kate, who had gone into battle so manfully for her, and, indeed, to Miss Forbes herself who had managed to help her daughter to visit her in the HDU when she felt desperate for reassurance and personal contact.

"I would say it was at that moment that I began to turn the corner."

The reporters were all desperate to get a shot of Kate, who had become very much the heroine of the hour, and she was desperate to be allowed to talk to them, but Helen refused point-blank. Jocasta, her sympathies torn between the two of them, managed to smuggle them out of the hospital that evening by a back door; but her car was spotted and a rather blurry picture of Kate, sitting in the backseat and smiling delightedly, appeared in a great many papers next day.

By Wednesday it was all dying down, apart from a paragraph in Lynda Lee-Potter's column in the *Daily Mail*, blaming the whole affair on the demise of the matron and the fact that nurses were no longer trained on the wards.

"Right, now this is for tomorrow's paper," said Jocasta. "I promise you that after this I'll be leaving you in peace."

"Oh, please don't," said Kate. "I'll really miss you. It's been great."

"Hardly great," said Helen slightly coldly. She found Kate's adoration of Jocasta irritating and misplaced; as far as she could see, Jocasta had caused them a great deal of trouble. Of course she had managed to smuggle her in to see her mother that night; and Jilly, once she was out of danger, had hugely enjoyed herself. Her pelvis was still painful, but she was displaying, as always, her robust constitution, had recovered from the surgery very fast and was eating well, even demanding wine with her meals.

"I'm afraid only the private patients get that, darlin'," said the large Jamaican lady who brought her food round, "and you're not one of them, even if you are in this very nice room."

She was to be allowed out at the weekend, but not to her own home; she was going—with extreme reluctance—to stay with Helen for a week or two. Kate was thrilled.

"We can have a great time. I'll be chief nurse, and bring you all the champagne you want, and I'll get you loads of videos and stuff."

"Oh Kate," said Jilly, patting her arm, smiling at her affectionately, "what would I have done without you? Died, I should think. Now, Jocasta dear, I've done my best with my hair and Kate's fetched me this pretty bed jacket—will that do?"

"It's gorgeous," said Jocasta and indeed it was, palest pink, edged with swansdown.

Kate looked at Jocasta and smiled. "You don't think I could be in one of the pictures, do you?"

"Well—"

"Kate!" said Helen. "That's out of the question."

"Why? Gran just said I'd saved her life. I don't see why I shouldn't. It would be so great. I might even be discovered by some model agency."

This was her current ambition: to be a supermodel. She had confided it to Jocasta, who had actually thought she could be very successful but hadn't said so. She knew too much about the dark drug-fuelled world of some of the fashion industry, and wouldn't have encouraged Kate into it.

"I really don't see why she shouldn't be in the photographs," said Jilly. "She saved my life, it's perfectly true. I'd like it very much. Jocasta, what do you think?"

"I think it would be lovely," said Jocasta carefully.

"Mum! Please!"

"I do think it would be very nice to have Kate in the picture, Mrs. Tarrant," said Jocasta, suddenly firm. "She's so much part of the story. So let's just get on with it, shall we?" There were certain times when you could bulldoze people into what you wanted, when their resistance suddenly lowered. She had felt Helen's go then. "I'll get the photographer in straightaway. Kate, go and comb your hair. You don't want to meet the press looking less than your best."

Kate giggled.

The photographer set up his camera. "This'll make a great shot," he said to Jocasta, while Jilly fussed over her hair for the umpteenth time and Kate settled on the bed beside her, putting her arm round her grandmother's shoulder. "Probably get the front page."

"Hope so. But get on with it—the mother's not happy, and I don't want to upset her."

"The kid's gorgeous. And you know something? She looks a bit like you."

"God, I wish," said Jocasta.

"Those should be lovely," said Jocasta, smiling at them when he had gone. "You both looked very glamorous."

"Well, thank you," said Jilly. "I doubt it, rather. It's when one is unwell that the years show."

"I promise, they don't show on you. And Kate's wrinkles didn't look too bad either. You both looked great. She really does look a lot like you."

"Well, it would be nice to think so," said Jilly, "but unfortunately that's quite impossible."

"Really? Why?"

"Well, you see—"

"Mummy," said Helen, and her voice was very cold, "not now."

Kate was staring at her mother; then she looked at Jocasta and smiled at her quickly.

"I'll come and see you off."

"Fine," said Jocasta. "Goodbye, Mrs. Bradford, I'm so glad you're recovering so well."

"Thank you, my dear. And thank you for all your help. I'm sure you've helped a great many other people, indirectly. And if ever you're in Guildford, come and find my shop. Caroline B, in the High Street."

Kate was going to miss Jocasta; she really liked her so much. She wasn't scared of anyone, just went for it and got what she wanted.

"Will you just be writing about Granny?" she asked. "To go with that picture?"

"Oh no," said Jocasta, "we need to remind them of the whole story. Four days, which is what it will be, between this picture and the last, is a very long time in newspapers. So I'll certainly be mentioning you and all you did."

"Great! Thanks for persuading Mum. Um . . . could you do one more thing? Put my whole name in. There are so many Kates, it's really boring."

"OK," said Jocasta smiling. "What is your whole name?"

"Kate Bianca Tarrant."

"That's a pretty name. Bianca, I mean."

"Yeah. When I'm older I'm thinking I might call myself that. Your job must be so fun," said Kate wistfully. "Maybe I could be a reporter, instead of a model."

"It is fun. And you do get to meet a whole lot of people you never would normally. And hear some incredible things. But there's a lot of dogsbody work, as there is in everything. I actually think," she said looking at Kate consideringly, "you'd be rather good at it."

"Cool! Well that's what I'll do, then. Could you get me a job?"

Jocasta laughed.

"Not at the moment. You're a bit young. And these days, they want you to have a degree."

"Degree! No thanks. I can hardly face A levels."

"Well, it's up to you. Tell you what, we do sometimes take on people for work experience. Maybe this summer holidays, if you wanted, I could get you a week. Not necessarily with me. Maybe even in the fashion department."

"Oh wow, yeah! That'd be great. Don't forget, will you?"

"I don't suppose you'll let me," said Jocasta. "Here, take my card. All my numbers and my e-mail address. Is that any good to you?"

"Yeah, Dad's got a computer. Thanks, Jocasta. I'm going to miss you."

"Me too."

"Sorry about Mum, just then. I don't know what's the matter with her. Honestly, she's so weird—usually she tells everyone. It was because I'm adopted."

"Oh, are you?" said Jocasta. She didn't appear surprised, Kate noticed, just politely interested.

"Yeah."

"You all seem very close anyway."

"I s'pose we are, really. To be honest, I get on with Gran best. She's such fun. My dad's all right, but even stricter than my mum, and then I've got a little sister who's just Little Miss Perfect, all clever and hardworking, with a scholarship to some posh school for her music."

"Is she adopted too?"

"No, she's theirs. She was born after they adopted me."

"And . . . how do you feel about being adopted?" said Jocasta. "Sorry, do you hate talking about it?"

"Course not. It's cool."

"Do you know anything about your—your birth mother? Would you like to meet her one day?"

"No," said Kate firmly. "I mean, what would be the point? After what she did to me."

"And what exactly did she do to you? Did she hand you over when you were a baby, or— Sorry," she said again, "is this upsetting you?"

"Course not," said Kate. "Yes, that's right. Well, I was still a baby anyway."

She was beginning to wish she hadn't embarked on this. She certainly wasn't about to tell Jocasta, cool, clever, successful Jocasta, all the shameful, painful facts, about being abandoned like a piece of rubbish in a cleaning cupboard. "She was a—a student," she improvised wildly, "from—from Ireland. She was a Catholic, so she couldn't possibly have had an abortion. But she loved me and she wanted to know I was in a good home. In fact, she wouldn't let me go to the first people who wanted me, she waited till my mum and dad turned up and she was really satisfied they'd look after me properly. All right?"

She felt aggressive now, and angry, as if Jocasta had dragged the information out of her in the first place. She turned away, looked across the car park. Suddenly she felt an arm round her shoulders.

"Kate. It's OK. Calm down. I didn't think anything bad about your mother at all. Not for a moment. She must have been very special to have you. And very brave to have let go of you for your own sake. Very brave indeed. Now look, it's been fun getting to know you. Don't forget about the work experience, will you? Give me a call when you feel you're ready. Or even if you just want to go out to lunch or something. I hate to think I'm never going to see you again, I really do."

She probably didn't mean it, Kate thought, watching the black Golf zoom out of the car park; and they'd probably never meet again. Why should they, after all?

"Jocasta, you all right?"

It was Chris Pollock; he had called her in to congratulate her on the story.

"Yes. Yes, I'm fine. Thank you."

"You seem a bit . . . distracted."

"Oh, I'm a bit tired, I guess."

"Reporters aren't allowed to get tired. I've got a real beauty for you this afternoon. Some poor cow's had a baby in Holloway, while shackled to the delivery bed. Her mum's just phoned, wants to talk to us. Right up your street. She lives in Dalston—news desk has the address. Now, are you really OK? I don't want this story messed up."

"You're such a gentleman, Chris. Don't worry. It won't be."

She did feel tired: terribly tired. And depressed. Nick hadn't called. And she had missed him. In spite of his refusal to do what she asked, to commit himself to her, in spite of the heady excitement—fading now—of the lunch with Gideon.

So much about him was right for her: he understood her, knew her completely, admired what she did. But in one way he failed her. One huge way. He might tell her he loved her, but what he did made her doubt it. And there was nothing, nothing at all, she could do about it. It made her very sad.

DALSTON 1 MILE, said a sign. Forget Nick. She had more important things to think about.

She got home very late that night; Nick was waiting at her house.

"I wanted to see you," he said, giving her a kiss. "Am I forgiven?"

In that moment, in her weariness, she was only pleased to see him: everything else was wiped out. "You're forgiven," she said, going into his arms.

"I'm really working hard on myself—"

"Nick, let's not even talk about it. I'm just glad you're here."

"That's nice, very nice. I'm glad I'm here too. And you don't have any retailing billionaires hidden anywhere?"

So he had noticed. Had even—possibly—minded.

"Not one."

"I'm pleased to hear it. He's just a tad too attractive, to my way of thinking."

"Is he?" she asked, her eyes very wide. "I hadn't really noticed. He's just—"

"I know. An ordinary old billionaire. You look all in, sweet pea."

"I feel it. I've had an awful day. Well, not awful. But upsetting."

"What, steely old Jocasta, aka Lois Lane, upset? Here, have a glass of wine. I've left you just about enough."

"I know. But . . . well, anyway, this poor woman, she had a baby in prison. She was actually in chains, Nick, while she was having it. And it was an awful birth, went on for hours and hours and in the end they had to— Well, I won't go into detail. But her mother did. I've got it all on tape. She was screaming and screaming for help. And the baby practically died. I just didn't know how to sit there, how to go on listening. I actually had to ask to go to her bathroom and I was sick. And then I had to write it and something was wrong with my e-mail connection, so I had to phone it in."

"Poor baby. *You*, I mean. Come on, drink that all down. And then I'm going to take you out to dinner. All right?"

"All right," said Jocasta. "But first I'm going to pull that tape out of its cassette and shred it. And don't let me even near the paper in the morning to read the story. OK?"

"OK. I love you. And I'm sorry again, about—well everything."

She stared at him. He so seldom said he was sorry. It was even rarer than his telling her he loved her. Her day and its traumas promptly faded into near-nothingness.

"I love you too," she said. "And I'm sorry too. Let's not go out to dinner."

"Let's not."

•◆•

It had come without warning. Friday, the fateful Friday, had been the most beautiful day, windy and sun-dappled; although it was her last day at the practice, Clio felt oddly happy. It might not be so bad. She did after all enjoy being at home. And it would give her a chance to—well, see if she could sort things out, she'd have some time. All might not be lost. And Jeremy would be better tempered and happier. Which would help a lot. She did still love Jeremy. She did. She knew she did.

At lunchtime, on a whim, she called him. She'd had her farewell drinks at the surgery the night before—Mark was away on that Friday on a course and he had wanted to be there.

"We'll miss you so much, Clio," he had said, handing over a big scented candle and a box of chocolates. "And this comes with all our love. You've been the most marvellous member of the team, and we're as fortunate as your patients. God knows how we're going to replace you. Well, we're not. As you know. Series of locums, right up till the end of June. Still, no doubt the practice loss will be your gain. And Jeremy's, of course."

Clio, eyes filled with tears, said she wasn't sure that either of those statements was correct, and said how much she would miss them too. In the end it had all been quite jolly, but she had felt very tearful again at bedtime (which she managed to conceal from Jeremy) and fate had managed to send her not one but three of her very worst patients that morning. It would be quite nice to be rid of them, at least. And then in the afternoon she was on call, and was planning to drop in on the Morrises and Josie Griggs at the Laurels, to make sure they were doing as well as they could possibly be; so there would be no painful last departure from the practice.

Jeremy agreed to lunch. "It would be good to get out for an hour or so. One o'clock all right with you?"

"Of course. Order me a chilli jacket if you get there first."

"Fine. Look forward to it. Thanks."

She drove towards the pub singing. She could do a lot of this sort of thing in the future, make him happier. And that in turn would make her happier.

Clio got to the pub first; Jeremy walked in at about one fifteen, looking harassed. She waved at him.

"I've got you a drink. Virgin Mary!"

"Thanks. But I'll have to just have a sandwich—they've added to my list."

"Oh no. Poor you. OK, I'll go and change the order."

"I'll come with you. I want more ice in this."

It was the unofficial hospital local. Several people recognised them, said hello. Clio noticed that a couple of them looked at Jeremy rather oddly. She supposed it must have been the article; they hadn't been out since. She prayed no one would mention it and wished fervently she hadn't suggested this, of all pubs.

Jeremy went off to the gents'; Clio returned to their table. A large woman had perched herself at the corner of it, on a stool she had dragged over from the other side of the bar.

"You don't mind, do you? There's nowhere else to sit."

"Well, not really," said Clio, knowing that Jeremy would be furious, "but—"

He came back, glared at the woman.

"This is our table. Sorry."

"Well, I'm sorry too, but there's nowhere else and I wasn't aware tables in pubs could be exclusively booked," she said, and then stared at him rather intently. "I don't know you, do I?"

"Absolutely not," said Jeremy. He turned his glare on Clio. "You should have kept the table. Can't we find another?"

The woman sighed and got out a crumpled paperback. "Please don't worry," she said, with heavy irony. "I won't disturb you."

Maurice Trent, the landlord, appeared with their food. "Here we are then. Sorry to have kept you. Nice to see you both. What a to-do this week, eh? Paparazzi all over the place, load of rubbish all of it. That girl you were talking to on Sunday, Dr. Scott, she was one of them, wasn't she? Nice, she seemed, not the sort you'd expect on a paper like that."

Clio had often read of bowels turning to water and had scoffed at it; she knew suddenly exactly what it meant.

"What girl was that?" said Jeremy, his expression ice-hard.

"Oh, just one of the reporters," said Maurice. "First one down, I think. Yes, all right, all right," he called to the barmaid who was gesticulating at him. "Coming. You can't get the help these days, I tell you that. Enjoy your meal."

Jeremy stared at Clio. "You were talking to one of the reporters? On Sunday? And you didn't mention it?"

"No. I mean yes. Well, not because she was a reporter. Honestly, Jeremy, I promise you. She just turned up out of the blue. I mean, she *is* a reporter, but we—we went travelling together years ago, when we were both eighteen. I hadn't seen her since. I—"

"And she just turned up, on your doorstep, at precisely the right moment. How very convenient for her."

"Yes, well she rang me because I was Mrs. Bradford's GP, and then she recognised my name, you know how these things happen, what a small world it is—"

"No, I don't. Actually. As far as I can remember, you sneaked out of the house, under the pretence of making some house calls. And came to meet her here, and—"

"Jeremy, please be quiet. Everyone's looking." He turned round; it was true, half the bar was staring at them. He stood up. "We can discuss this later. Perhaps you'd be kind enough to settle the bill."

"Yes. Of course. But Jeremy—"

He was gone. The fat woman looked up from her paperback.

"I've just realised why he looks familiar," she said. "He's the one in the *Sun*, isn't he? The one who said—"

Clio half ran to the bar, flung a twenty-pound note at the bemused Maurice Trent, and went out into the car park. Jeremy's car had gone.

◄-►

"Martha?"

"Yes. Yes, it is. Hi, Ed."

She had literally dreamt of this, imagined it so often over the past few days, while the phone so determinedly rang, delivering unwelcome other people to her, bleeped her endlessly with text messages from other equally unwelcome people, while e-mails leapt relentlessly onto her screen from nobody she wished to hear from: so that now, when it was really him, she wasn't surprised at all. Just terrified.

Her voice didn't sound terrified; it sounded its brisk, orderly self.

"I . . . I'm sorry about the other night," he said. "I said some pretty bad things."

"Justified, most of them, I'd say." Less orderly, the voice, then. Shaky, out of breath.

"Even if they were . . . I shouldn't have said them."

"Well, they did some good," she said, "or maybe they did. I've—" No, she mustn't say that. Start talking about herself, her career. "I've done a lot of thinking," she said.

"Oh. Well, I didn't want to leave it like that. That's all. I wanted us to stay—stay friends at least."

"Of course." God, this hurt worse than she could have believed.

"Yes. So—sorry."

"Ed, it's OK." She struggled to sound light-hearted. "I forgive you."

A long silence, then: "Great," he said, "I'm glad. Maybe—"

"Yes?" Don't sound hopeful, Martha, for God's sake.

"Maybe we could have a drink one night."

"Yes. Let's. Call me. Or I'll call you."

"Fine. Right, well—well, cheers. See you later."

If only those words could have had their real meaning: if only she *could* see him later, see him smile, feel his lips brush her hair, take his hand, kiss him, hold him, lie down with him, have him . . .

"Bye Ed," she said. Very cool, very controlled again. Martha, again, in fact. Only Martha had never hurt like this before. Well, not quite like this.

Thank God, she was so busy. How could she have coped with this misery if she wasn't?

Jocasta was walking into a bar when her phone rang.

"Is that Jocasta? This is Jilly. Jilly Bradford."

"Oh, hi, Mrs. Bradford. How are you? Nice to hear from you."

"I'm very much better, thank you. Bored to death, of course. They won't let me out of here until I can manage the stairs, and even then I can't go home, I've got to stay with my daughter. Of course I'm fond of them all, but I want to be in my own home. Anyway, I just wanted to thank you for putting that nice photograph in the paper. It was very flattering, and it will certainly disabuse everyone of the notion that I'm some senile old woman. Kate bought about six copies. She's the heroine of the hour at school, of course. Very indignant that your name wasn't on it, though."

Jocasta laughed. "That often happens in a follow-up like this one. She's so great, your granddaughter. I think she'll do very well in life."

"I think so, too. I hope so, anyway. She deserves to."

There is a sensation that every good reporter knows: a kind of creeping excitement, a thud of recognition at something forming itself just out of reach, something worth pursuing: Jocasta felt it then.

"She was telling me all about being adopted," she said.

"Was she? She obviously sensed a kindred spirit. She doesn't normally like talking about it."

"Oh really? No, she was very open with me, brought the subject up herself, in fact."

"Extraordinary story, isn't it?"

"Well, not that extraordinary. Except that these days most girls don't give their babies up; they keep them and raise them on their own."

"I didn't mean that. I meant her being found in that way, at the airport. Didn't she tell you that bit?"

"Well—well, not in any detail, no." Careful, Jocasta, careful . . .

"Oh, I see. But she told you the rest? It's so hard for her. She feels it very keenly, poor little thing. Being just abandoned like that."

"Yes, it must be . . . hard."

Her phone bleeped warningly. Shit. If it ran out of power now, she'd scream.

"Terribly hard. She wants to find her, of course, but I think—"

Another bleep.

"Mrs. Bradford, I'm going to have to ring you back. My phone's dying on me. If you—"

"Oh, my dear, no need. I just wanted to say thank you. Come and see me when I get home to Guildford; I'll tell Kate to organise it. Or we could have a jolly lunch in town. That would probably suit you better. Good-bye and—"

The phone died. Jocasta wanted to throw it on the ground and jump up and down on it. It was her own fault, of course, totally her own fault; she'd known it was low; she should have done it that evening before she left, but—well.

Now what should she do? She could hardly ring Jilly back, on a public hospital phone, and say, "Now, about Kate and her adoption, do go on . . ."

The moment had been lost. And it was her own fault.

•-•-

Jeremy came in at about eight, the taut fury, which Clio had grown to dread, set on his face. She smiled awkwardly, said, "Jeremy, hello. You must be hungry. I've got some very nice jugged hare if you'd—"

"Please don't try that," he said.

"Try what?"

"Pretending everything's normal. It simply makes it worse."

"Jeremy, I wish you'd let me explain. I didn't say anything about the hospital or Mrs. Bradford to Jocasta."

"I thought you met her in the pub."

"I did. But only to talk about old times."

"Which you couldn't have done in the house? You had to sneak off without explaining she was an old friend?"

"Well, yes. I thought you'd be suspicious, that you wouldn't believe me. I knew you wouldn't listen, that you wouldn't let me go." She was beginning to feel angry herself.

"I wouldn't let you go! Is that how you see me? As some kind of tyrant? I find that immensely insulting."

"Well, it isn't meant to be. I'm just trying to explain how it happened, why I did what I did."

"And then you sat with her in the pub, this reporter friend of yours, and didn't even discuss the wretched Bradford woman? You expect me to believe that?"

"Yes! In fact I actually asked her not to write the story and certainly not to implicate you or me in it."

"And that was very successful, wasn't it?"

"Actually, yes. If you read the piece you'll see she made no mention of either of us. I could get it if you like—"

"You actually expect me to read that drivel?"

"Oh shut up," said Clio wearily, surprising herself.

He was clearly surprised too; she so seldom went on the offensive.

"I just can't get over your deceiving me like that," he said, changing tack. "It was so unnecessary."

"Maybe if you weren't such a bully, if you didn't treat me like some kind of inferior—"

"That's a filthy thing to say!"

"But it's true. You *do* bully me. You don't respect what I do, you've made me give up a job I absolutely love, you're dismissive of almost everything I say, you're always in a bad temper—well, not always," she added, anxious, even in her rage and misery, to be accurate, "but very often. You won't allow me to do anything on my own, you blame me for everything that goes wrong in our lives, even the simplest thing, like someone sitting at our table in the pub. Can you wonder I didn't ask you if I could invite an old friend round for a chat? I think it's time you took a proper look at yourself, Jeremy, I really do."

He said nothing, just stood staring at her in silence for several moments; then he turned and went upstairs to their room. She followed him; he had pulled out a suitcase and was putting things in it.

"What are you doing?" she asked. She was frightened now.

"I'm packing. I would have thought that was perfectly evident."

"To go—where?"

"I'm not sure. But there clearly is no room for me here. I have nothing to contribute to our marriage. So I think it's better I go."

"Jeremy, don't be stupid. Please!" She could hear the panic in her voice.

"I see nothing stupid in it. You're obviously much better on your own. Doing your job, which clearly means much more to you than I do. It made me feel quite ill listening to you last night, telling me how sorry everyone was, how they hadn't replaced you yet, how much they were going to miss you. My God, how are the sick folk of Guildford going to get on without you, Clio? Could you move, please, I want to get at my shirts."

"Fuck your shirts," she said in a quiet voice, "and fuck you. And how dare you diminish my work like that."

"You never even consulted me over taking that job in the first place," he said. "I had something altogether different in mind, not a part-time wife, obsessed with her career. I had hoped we would have had children by now, but I've been denied those. I wonder if you're trying to cheat me there, as well. I wouldn't put anything past you, Clio."

"You bastard!" she said, tears smarting at the back of her eyes, a lurch of dreadful pain somewhere deep inside her. "You absolute bastard. How dare you, how dare you say that!" Then suddenly everything shifted and she felt very strong, and she looked at him, in all his arrogant self-pity and cruelty, and knew she couldn't stand another day, another hour of him. "Don't bother packing any more, Jeremy, I'm going myself. I don't want to spend another night in this house, where we could have been so happy and where you have managed to make us so miserable. I want to get out of it, and out of this marriage. It's a travesty. I hate it."

And without taking any more than her bag and her car keys, she walked out of the house, got into her car, and drove away from him and their brief, disastrous marriage.

Chapter 14

· · · · ·

She had tried to shrug it off; to tell herself it wasn't that important, but she knew it was. An abandoned baby was a fantastically exciting story. Especially an abandoned baby who had grown up into the most beautiful girl, a troublesome, beautiful girl, who wanted to find the woman who had abandoned her.

It was an absolutely wonderful story. It made her feel quite sick, so wonderful was it.

Only—and this was where the occasional struggle Jocasta had with herself began—this could really hurt Kate: damage her dreadfully. The mother might not turn up at all and break Kate's heart. Or she might be absolutely wonderful, claim Kate, and break the Tarrants' hearts. Or she might be an absolute horror. How much better for everyone if Jocasta forgot about it, let them be. She knew too well the demons released from Pandora's box by tabloid newspapers, by any newspaper, indeed; she saw it all the time.

Jocasta thought suddenly of Clio and how she was coping with the aftermath of the story; Clio and her dreadful, arrogant husband. How did a sweet, clever girl like her come to be married to such a creature? She hoped she hadn't caused any trouble between them. She might call her and see if she was all right. And then—Kate? She could talk to her direct; make the excuse of the work experience in the summer. She could get her to talk, she knew she could. Especially now she knew the sort of things she should ask her. And then not take it any further if it seemed really wrong. Yes, that's what she could do; she told herself that, very firmly, while knowing it was almost certainly a lie. But she had to get the story; she just had to.

•—•

Martha was listening to her own voice when her mobile rang, listening to herself making her presentation on her tape recorder, making notes of minor adjustments and at the same time carefully sorting through the contents of her briefcase. Chad again, she thought, it could only be him. And decided not to answer it. She was extremely tired of his endless phone calls. Working with him had become a lot less attractive this week. There was something of the old woman about him, very much at odds with his brusque manner and svelte appearance.

She had finished her notes and was sitting on her bed, leafing through the political pages in the papers, when her landline rang. Bloody man, she thought, walking through into the living room, this was not what she needed.

"Chad," she said, snatching it up, "please—"

"Martha, dear, it's Mum. Your father and I just wanted to wish you well for tomorrow."

"Thanks, Mum," said Martha, "that's very sweet of you."

"I know you'll do well, dear. Everyone is so excited about it, about your going into politics. Anyway good luck, and mind you get a good night's sleep."

"I will. I'm in bed now as a matter of fact. Thank you for calling."

She put the phone down and realised the message light was blinking. Someone had called before and she hadn't noticed. Also Chad, no doubt. Well, she'd better check. Bloody bore he was. She'd have to say something if—

"Martha, hi. This is Ed. I—I hoped we could talk. I'll try your mobile."

"Oh my God!" she said aloud, and went back to bed, dialled his number, shaking violently; it was answered at once. "Hi, Ed. It's me. Sorry, I didn't realise you'd rung."

"That's OK."

"Um—what can I do for you?"

"I—" There was a long silence, then: "I just wanted to wish you luck. For tomorrow."

"Ed, who on earth told you?"

"Mum. She called this evening, said did I know you were going to be the new MP for Binsmow."

Martha started to laugh. "Oh God," she said, "mothers!"

"Yeah, well. You should have told me."

"Why?"

"Well, because of what I said. It was obviously unjust. I'm sorry, Martha. Sorry I said all those things. I was totally out of order. I can see that now." There was a silence, then he said, "I've missed you so much. I thought I could do without you—but I can't."

"Ed," said Martha, "I *am* self-obsessed. I *am* a control freak. But I'm trying very hard not to be. If you hadn't said—what you did, I'd have said no to Chad. Now then, I've got an important meeting tomorrow. I've got an early start—"

"Yeah, OK," he said, "sorry. I just wanted to—"

"But even so, why don't you come round? We can discuss my presentation. Among other things."

Well, she thought, switching off her mobile, at least she'd be in bed early.

She drove down the M11 on Saturday morning, feeling extremely nervous. She had woken at six, leaving Ed fast asleep, gone to the gym and then suddenly realised a Mercedes convertible wasn't exactly a tactful vehicle to arrive in. She wished she'd thought of it earlier. She would just have to dump the Merc in the car park of the Coach and Horses and use Chad's car instead.

She ran over her ten-minute presentation speech again and again and rehearsed answers to imagined questions. Certain rather insistent images and memories kept disturbing her concentration; she tried to ignore them. Even Ed telling her it was the best sex he had ever had; and falling asleep hearing him say— No, she would allow herself to replay this one at least, she thought, smiling foolishly at the memory.

"I really, really love you," he had said. "I know I do. I wasn't sure before." That had been the best. She would pick it all over and enjoy it properly later.

She felt fantastic: energetic, alive, and smoothly, sleekly happy. She was wearing a pair of leather trousers and an extremely expensive Joseph sweater for the journey, but on a hanger in the car was more modest stuff, a navy suit from Hobbs, and a pale pink top with a slash neckline; she wore a little makeup, no nail polish, and her shoes and bag were from L.K. Bennett, rather than the more exclusive shelves of Gucci. She changed at the service station about ten miles before Binsmow.

When she got to the Coach and Horses, Chad was already there, drinking orange juice; he stood up and gave her a kiss. "Like the outfit. Very good. You look straight out of central casting for a prospective near-Tory candidate. Want anything?"

"Not to eat; maybe a tonic water. I feel terribly nervous."

"That's good. You'll perform better. Very valuable things, nerves. Get the adrenaline pumping."

"And when did you last feel nervous?"

"Oh—day before yesterday," he said, surprising her. "I often think I'm going to throw up whenever I have to speak in the House." She felt strangely comforted. "I hope you had a good night last night."

"Very, very good," she said, and felt herself flush as a particularly vivid memory hit her; surely a prospective candidate should not, a few hours before her presentation, be lying over her beautiful young lover, head flung back, body arched, invaded with sweet sweeping pleasure, and calling out with the raw, joyful noise of sex. But: "Yes, it was excellent."

"Good. Now any points you'd like to run through?"

"Well, I don't think so. I've mugged up on the town and everything and I just had a look at a proposed bypass site. It would do dreadful things, Chad. I'm sure I could get very worked up about that."

"Well, be careful," he said, "you mustn't assume that they'll see it in quite the same way. A lot of these schemes may cut through hallowed woods and so on, but they relieve noise and pollution in residential areas. Just feel your way. Now do you want to run through your presentation with me?"

"I think I'd better," she said and handed him her notes.

A jolly red-faced young man called Colin Black, dressed in a tweed suit and extremely well-shined shoes, arrived. He would be her agent, advise her on local matters, help at election time. He had been a Tory agent, become disillusioned, and "Come out to bat for you lot," he said, grinning his rosy grin. He turned out to be a rather well-heeled farmer with a background in student politics. Martha liked him.

"Sorry we couldn't have met before," he said. "All been a bit of a rush. Look, they're ready for you, looking forward to meeting you. They're mustard-keen on the new party, even though they only represent about a third of the old committee. They've seen the three others already. Only one of them should cause you any concern. Young chap. Teacher. The other's a woman, very good, very sound, but a bit of a wild card. Comes from the north." Clearly coming from the north was tantamount to coming from Sodom and Gomorrah. "Anyway, nothing more for me to say except good luck. Chad will have briefed you on the form, no doubt."

Martha said he had, but added tactfully that she'd be grateful for any further advice. "Best I can give you is have as few notes as possible; speak from the heart. They can see through anything else."

"I won't have any notes," said Martha. "It's all in my head."

"Jolly good. Well, best go. Good luck."

On the way her phone bleeped: it was a text from Ed. "Good luck. I love you xxx."

They arrived at two thirty at a large building in the old Market Square, where Martha had gone with her mother every Saturday morning to buy fresh fruit and vegetables, and went upstairs to a large room, where a rather tired-looking middle-aged woman was pulling chairs into a semi-circle. Chad offered to help her. She was clearly dazzled by his presence.

When Martha offered to help as well, she seemed rather disdainful and said she could get the small table out for her notes if she liked.

The room filled up quite quickly with an equal number of men and women. They were mostly middle-aged, friendly in a rather distant way, smiled at her briefly and then carried on talking to one another. Only one very imposing woman even talked to Chad. They were clearly both being put in their place.

At three o'clock exactly, the imposing woman, who proved to be Geraldine Curtis, the chairman, clapped her hands and said would everyone take their places; they all sat down in the semicircle, with Martha placed at her small table in the middle. She felt rather like the boy in the "When did you last see your father?" painting. Chad indicated to her to sit down, then stood beside her, smiled his brilliant smile, and made a brief speech thanking them for giving the party a chance, outlined their general policy, and said he was confident that, with the backing of people like the residents of Binsmow, they could radically cut Tony Blair's majority at the next election. They continued to sit looking stone-faced.

And then it was Martha's turn. She started fairly confidently, she played the local card, threw in a couple of childhood reminiscences—the market shopping, the grammar school, and picnicking in the meadows on the edge of the town—hoping for some kind of reaction she could build on. She got none. They just sat and listened to her, fairly expressionless; they didn't smile, nor did they frown. She had decided to be honest—no point pretending a lifelong passion for politics—simply said that she had felt her interest in the subject growing over the past year, along with her association with the Centre Forward Party. She said she had done some Citizens Advice work in Binsmow, and had some practical experience of people's problems and how to solve them. She referred to Lina and her distress over the sink estates and poor schools that she and others like her had to endure, and said that had been the turning point that had led her into politics.

She said how much she liked the Centre Forward philosophy of people before politics, that she felt that a revived sense of community could help solve many problems in society, and promised to run a fortnightly free legal advice service if she was selected.

Still no reaction: increasing panic. What on earth was she doing here? The toughest argument in court was easier than this. Well, no way back now. Just keep going, Martha.

Somehow she got to the end of her speech: "I would dearly love to work for the people of Binsmow and to give back something of what they gave me."

When she had finished and sat down, there was a silence in the room; it was unnerving. She hadn't expected applause, but she had hoped for some reaction, some questions. Everyone looked down at the pads of paper on which they were scribbling notes.

I was a disaster, she thought miserably, and looked at Chad; he winked at her.

"Right," he said, "well, I think you know a little about Martha and her—and *our*—philosophies now. Would you like to ask her some questions, find out some more?"

There were several. Would she move down to Binsmow? Did she, as a single and clearly well-off young woman, really understand the financial pressures and problems faced by families? If she did marry and had a family, would she see herself continuing as an MP? What had drawn her to the Centre Forward Party, what had she against the traditional Tories? (Careful on this one, Chad had said, there are sure to be at least a couple of doubters on the committee who will be opposed to you on principle: don't knock the others, just say you feel instinctively, as a young, ambitious person, that this is the party for you.) What were her views on primary education? How would she go about re-creating the sense of community she spoke so emotively of? What did she think about the bypass? At this point, Geraldine Curtis clearly felt the questions were becoming too specific and she rose rather majestically and clapped her hands.

"I think that will do for now. I wonder if we could have tea, Betty, and then we can talk to Miss Hartley more informally? I would personally love to hear about her childhood in Binsmow and her education at the grammar school."

Betty, the downtrodden placer of chairs, disappeared into the back of the hall, followed by a couple more members; they returned with a trolley laden with cups of tea, and plates of biscuits. Martha decided that this was the one time in her life when calories wouldn't count, except in her favour, and ate several biscuits. They were all very soggy. She stood there, smiling endlessly, answering questions, charming the men with ease and the women, particularly the younger ones, with more difficulty, expressing huge interest in housing schemes, playgroups, the possibility of a local radio station, youth clubs, and realised, with a sudden thud of excitement, that everything Chad had said was true, that it really wasn't rocket science and that she could—if they gave her the chance—probably do it. And she realised she wanted that chance—very, very badly.

·•·

The worst thing, Clio thought, was the feeling she had nowhere to go. That she was, temporarily in any case, homeless. After some thought, she had driven herself to a motel on the edge of the town and booked herself in for the night. Settling herself into the anonymity of her small beige cell, she had felt it was extraordinarily suited to her situation, a place with no past and no future, only the present. To her great surprise, she slept for a few hours, and woke at six, with a sense of dreadful panic and loneliness.

Now what?

She realised that she had very few close friends. Actually, she had *no* close friends. Not anymore. Couples, yes, halves of couples, even, but only on a rather superficial level. Jeremy had most effectively driven a wedge between her and her previous girlfriends, expressing first hurt and later irritation if she wanted to spend time with them rather than with him. And she had never had a soul-baring kind of friendship with anyone; she supposed it was all to do with her emotionally starved childhood, her sense of failure, her comparison of herself with her brilliant sisters. She could certainly never go to them for help; her major ambition, from the moment she left to go travelling on that fateful August day, had been to show them that she could manage on her own. She would starve to death before admitting she had failed. Her father, too, would never be a source of comfort or strength; he had always made it clear that she was a worry to him, more demanding and distracting than her sisters, and clearly destined to be less successful. She was simply an anxiety that he didn't want.

What she couldn't understand was that she didn't feel more unhappy. Scared, yes; lonely, yes; and desperately worried, yes. But not actually unhappy. She supposed that would come; she was still anaesthetised by shock.

She got into her car and drove—for some reason—along the A3 towards London. It seemed as good a route as any. She felt a need for coffee and turned her car into a Little Chef; the coffee was good and she suddenly wanted some toast as well. She was biting into the second slice when her mobile rang.

Jeremy? Worrying about her, wondering where she was?

"Clio? Hi, it's Jocasta. I just wondered how you were, hoped that story hadn't done you too much damage."

"Oh," said Clio lightly, and was astonished to find she could be honest, indeed wanted to be, "not really. I've left my husband, as a result, don't have a home anymore, that sort of thing. But don't worry about it, Jocasta, not your fault."

"Oh my God! You *are* joking, aren't you?"

"No, actually. I'm in a Little Chef on the A3 with no home, and nowhere to go, and only the clothes I'm standing up in. Oh, and no job, either."

"My God! Oh, Clio, I'm so, so sorry. And how inadequate is that? Jesus. What happened, was it really my fault?"

"No, not really," said Clio with a sigh. "I mean, you might have been the catalyst—well, the story might—but it was all there, really."

"What was all there?"

"I don't want to talk about it, Jocasta. Sorry."

And then her calm and her bravado suddenly left her and she started to cry, huge heavy sobs; the three other people in the Little Chef stared at her. She cut Jocasta off and fled to the ladies', where she shut herself in one of the stalls and sat on the loo, her head buried in her arms, weeping endlessly.

Every so often, her phone rang; she ignored it. After about half an hour, she couldn't cry any longer; she felt strangely calm. She washed her face, combed her hair, and walked as nonchalantly as she could manage back to the restaurant, where she paid her bill and then went out to the car.

•◆•

"She was marvellous. Really marvellous." Chad smiled at Grace Hartley. They were, inevitably, in the vicarage drawing room, using the best china, with enough cakes on the tiered wooden cake stand to feed the entire Centre Forward Party. "Thank you so much, Mrs. Hartley, that lemon cake looks wonderful. Go on, Martha, have a piece."

"Martha never eats anything," said Grace with a sigh, "and certainly not cakes."

"She was tucking into the committee's biscuits. Weren't you, Martha?"

"Well, I thought I should."

"And so you should eat your mother's lemon cake. Go on."

Martha held her plate out resignedly; she could see that politics could make her fat.

Chad was saying how well she'd done, even better than he'd hoped, that they wouldn't know for a while, probably not for a week, "Just to show us at Westminster who's really in charge."

His phone rang and they all jumped. He went out of the room, closing the door. It was obviously someone from the committee: so swift a decision must mean bad news, Martha thought miserably. It felt very bad. She had failed at something important. Something she really wanted. And very publicly. Everyone would be so disappointed in her. She was even more disappointed in herself. It was going to take a long time to—

The door opened; Chad was smiling. "Well," he said, "very good news. That was Norman Brampton. It's unofficial but—Martha, they want you! Geraldine Curtis called him. They were very impressed indeed. They accept your inexperience, but they feel you'll appeal to young people, which is important to us. And there's the local card, of course, which you played so well."

"Oh my God!" said Martha. She felt extraordinary. In that moment she could have flown. She felt completely inviolate. She hadn't failed. Hadn't made a fool of herself. She'd done it. She had succeeded. She—

"Oh, that's wonderful, darling," said Grace. "Well done. Let me give you a kiss."

"Marvellous," said Peter Hartley. "What a clever girl you are. It's absolutely wonderful. We're so proud of you, Martha. And how lovely it will be to have you down here—"

"Now, you must keep this under your collective hats," said Chad. "Norman really shouldn't have told me. But he was quite certain—you've definitely done it!"

She went back to the pub with Chad to collect her car and realised that it was practically out of petrol; she'd fill it up on her way back to her parents', maybe even go for a little drive. She needed to unwind.

There was something wrong with one of the pumps; it required a lot of jiggling about to get the petrol running and then it suddenly spurted out. Damn! That wouldn't do her suit any good. And she was going to be wearing it a lot, it seemed. She finished filling the car, paid for the petrol, and then went to the lavatory to wash her hands.

It was predictably filthy, paper towels and some fag ends littered the floor, there was an oily rag in the washbasin, and a tabloid newspaper balanced on top of the hand dryer. As she switched the dryer on, the paper slithered onto the floor. Martha, deciding it was in its rightful place, was about to unlock the door to leave when her mobile rang; as she fumbled for it in her bag, one of the neat leather gloves that she had brought to complete her new persona fell onto the floor.

She swore, checked her mobile—it was Ed, wanting to know how she had got on—and bent down to pick up the glove. And there it was: the photograph. A very ordinary photograph, really, taking up about a quarter of the page; it showed a middle-aged woman, apparently in a hospital bed, and a young girl. The woman was dressed in a bed jacket and some rather incongruously large pearl earrings. The girl, who had a great deal of curly blond hair, was wearing a denim jacket and several studs in one of her ears. She had an arm round the woman's shoulders, and was smiling radiantly at the camera.

WHAT KATY DID, said the caption.

And Martha, crouching there on the floor, strangely compelled to read on, discovered precisely what Katy had done, which was care for her "beloved grandmother" as she became desperately ill, after spending twenty hours in Casualty on a hospital trolley.

But there was a very happy ending. Mrs. Jilly Bradford is now recovering fast and has nothing but praise for her granddaughter's courage, as she battled with NHS staff to secure attention and treatment for her. Fifteen-year-old Kate Bianca—as she likes to be known—has ambitions to be a model. Why not a career in hospital management, Kate?

Martha leant over the filthy lavatory bowl and was violently sick.

Chapter 15

"Of course I won't tell anyone. Of course. My dear, if you knew how many confidences I have kept over the years, you wouldn't even ask. But look—do you have anywhere to go?"

"Oh . . . yes." Clio wasn't going to tell Barbara Salter, so orderly, so nice, that she had nothing of the sort, no refuge of any kind; it was too humiliating. "I'm on my way to friends in London now. But, well, thank you so much for listening to me."

"I'm only sorry I couldn't do more. I'll get Mark to call you as soon as he gets in. On your mobile, yes? Try not to worry, my dear. These things often blow over. It's all part of the fun and games of being married."

"Yes, well maybe."

As if Barbara and Mark could possibly have had arguments over anything more serious than his tea being too strong. Everyone at the surgery hated making it for him.

"Yes," she said again, trying to sound more cheerful, "yes, I expect it is."

She had been surprised to find herself calling Mark; it was just that out of the panic and loneliness that had taken her over, she had suddenly realised that her work, her job, was the one stable thing that she could cling to and find comfort in. And yes, she had left the practice, but they had no replacement for her, only a locum for a couple of weeks and then another one, and neither had really pleased Mark at all. So maybe, just maybe, he would allow her back.

She had spent the second night in another anonymous motel-style place by the river in Battersea. When she got up to her room, she found herself with a breathtaking view of the river, and when she opened the window, she could hear tugs hooting and seagulls crying, and it was like stepping into another country. She had happened upon it completely by chance, driving listlessly into London, but it had seemed a happy accident. She wondered if Jeremy would ever phone her and see if she was all right; after a while, she got into bed and then lay awake fearful and tearful. In the morning she phoned Jeremy, simply to say she was all right. There was no answer except the answering machine. "It's me, Clio," she said, and then stopped, for what could she say? "I hope you're not worried" or "I'm fine, don't try and find me"? He was so clearly not worried, had no intention of trying to find her . . . She fell foolishly silent and then just said, "I'm fine," and rang off.

She put the phone down and felt the tears welling again. It was at this point that her mobile rang and she answered it without checking: it was Jocasta. Yet again.

Clio stood on the doorstep, looking at Jocasta's pretty little house and trying to pluck up the courage to ring the bell. What on earth was she doing here, at the worst hour of her life, paying a call on someone who was virtually a stranger? It made her feel more pathetic than ever. It was just that at this precise moment, in her acute loneliness, Jocasta had called. And had been so kind, so friendly, so genuinely concerned, it suddenly seemed quite a good idea.

She was considering running away when the door opened and a very tall, thin man dressed in running gear appeared, smiled at her and said, "You must be Clio. Go along in. I'm going for a run, so you and Jocasta can enjoy some girly talk. I'm Nick," he added, holding out a bony hand. "Nick Marshall. Friend of Jocasta's. See you later."

Clio smiled up at him. "Thank you," she said, and then worried that it might sound rude, to be thanking someone for going away from their own house. Or their girlfriend's house.

"Cheers then." He was gone, a long, loping figure.

"Clio, come on in," said Jocasta's voice, and she was not only in the house but held in Jocasta's arms, and she was crying again, and Jocasta was stroking her hair, and talking meaningless, soothing nonsense and then leading her into a warm, chaotic kitchen where she sat her down and placed a large mug of coffee in front of her and Clio stared at her and thought, as she had thought so long ago, what an amazingly nice person she was, and wished she hadn't let her go.

⚬⚬

Chad would have been proud of her next day, Martha thought, half impressed, half ashamed of herself; after her feverish, fretful night, she got up early, took Bella the elderly Labrador for a walk (knowing she would meet other dog walkers she might be able to talk to about her political plans), and then attended family communion and the coffee-and-biscuits get-together in the vestry afterwards: saying that yes, it was true, she was hoping to be adopted as the local candidate for the Centre Forward Party, that she did indeed have the support of Norman Brampton, adding that she would be around all week, apart from Monday, that if anyone wanted to talk to her about it further, she would be at the vicarage, and she actually had some leaflets about the new party if they were interested. After that, she went to see Norman Brampton, who was clearly bored while his wife fussed around him.

"Give anything to be in your shoes," he said, "going mad here. Anyway, I'm delighted with what's happened—you'd certainly have been my choice and you've obviously impressed them no end. And what's Jack Kirkland like? I always admired him, but he keeps one at arm's length rather, doesn't he?"

"He's a bit of an enigma, actually," said Martha. "He seems so forbidding and stern, but in fact he's extremely kind and thoughtful. He's wonderful in the Chamber—"

"I see you've picked up all the jargon," he said, smiling at her. "Well done. Now, how about another coffee, while we discuss the next year or so?"

And so the day went on; Martha went home and managed to eat quite a lot of the lunch her mother had cooked—she must have put on pounds this weekend—and helped her clear away against a backdrop of Binsmow gossip. She took her for a drive out to the meadows and walked slowly along the tow path with Bella and then home again, where she helped her father sort out some flyers for a concert at the church in early June. And all the time doing what she had done all her life, suppressing the fear, denying the memory, struggling to control the uncontrollable.

She had sat for a long time the evening before, in a lay-by, staring at the photograph, reading and rereading the caption, calming herself by sheer willpower. Of course she was being absurd. Hysterical. The country was filled with thousands—millions—of fifteen-year-old girls. Several hundred of them undoubtedly called Bianca. It wasn't that unusual a name now. Anyway, this one, the one with the beloved grandmother (would you be that close to an adoptive grandmother?—surely not) wasn't called Bianca, she was called Kate. Bianca was just a middle name, an afterthought. And what if she did have that hair? Millions of them had that hair, that long, wild hair. Blond hair. Probably carefully lightened by the newspaper to make her look more glamorous. And she was only fifteen. No—nearly sixteen. They would have said that if she was. In fact, Kate Bianca would have said she was *six*teen. All girls of that age wanted to be thought older than they were. No, the whole thing was ridiculous.

And she put the paper in a rubbish bin, very carefully and deliberately, and texted Ed—she didn't dare speak to him just yet—then drove slowly home where she sat and watched television with her mother, while her father wrote his sermon.

First *Blind Date*, then *Casualty*, and then a murder mystery, an endless stream of mind-numbing rubbish. Only it didn't numb her mind quite enough; when she went up to bed it was still throbbing feverishly.

There was a text from Ed. "All hail to the new PM," it said. "Love you. Ed xx." It made her feel suddenly, wonderfully better.

But not for long . . .

She stood at the window, staring out at the starry sky, wishing the night away. It would be better in the morning; everything was always better in the morning. And how often had she told herself that, almost sixteen years ago?

‹•›

"I cannot believe this is still going on. Haven't people got anything better to think about?"

"What's still going on, dear?"

"Look for yourself. Half a page nearly. What's this garbage doing here anyway?"

Jim passed a crumpled copy of the *News on Sunday* across the supper table to Helen.

IS THE NHS RIGHT OFF ITS TROLLEY? it said right across one of the inside pages.

"That's clever," said Kate, craning her neck to read it. And then as her father frowned at her: "Sorry, Dad. It's Sarah's. She brought it round because there was a story about Robbie in it."

"Robbie who?"

"Dad! Get with the programme. Robbie Williams."

"Oh, I rather like him," said Jilly. "Though I preferred him when he was in Take That. We always loved them, didn't we, Kate?"

"Yes, we did," said Kate. She shot an expression of triumph at her father.

"Anyway, Jim, why shouldn't people read about him if they want to?" said Jilly.

"Gran, it's not about him. It's about *you*!"

"Me! Oh, how exciting. Is there a picture?"

"There is no picture," said Jim heavily.

"Well, I'd still like to read it. Helen, after you, dear—thank you. Good heavens! Listen to this, Kate: 'In the week that has followed the latest hospital scandal, and a neglected elderly patient . . . nearly died on a hospital trolley . . . 57 percent of voters now think the NHS is in a worse state than it was when New Labour came to power in 1997. Will Mrs. Bradford and others continue to nearly lose their lives, as Tony Blair continues to play his guitar, while the NHS burns?' "

"What does that mean?" asked Kate.

"It refers to Nero," said Juliet. "You know, fiddling while Rome burnt."

"Well obviously, Miss Smartarse, I don't know," said Kate. "It must be so wonderful to be so clever!"

"Kate," said Helen, "Juliet was simply answering your question. Now apologise. Please."

"Sorry," said Kate in the flat, automatic tone she always used when asked to apologise.

"It's not very clever to display ignorance, you know," said Jim. "You've had a perfectly good education and that is a basic piece of knowledge."

"Oh for God's sake!" said Kate. "I'm going upstairs."

"You are not. It's your turn to clear away."

"Oh, for f— OK, OK, don't say any more." She got up, started packing the dishwasher very noisily, cramming two plates into the space designed for one, pulling bowls away from people before they were empty.

"Kate, stop that at once," said Jim sharply.

"You told me to clear away. Make your bloody mind up."

"Kate! How dare you speak to me like that! Go to your room."

"It'll be a pleasure. And then Little Miss Mealy Mouth can do it all nicely and you can sit and admire her—"

"Kate, you are not to speak of your sister like that."

"I'll speak about her how I like. Anyway, she's not my sister, thank God. Not really."

"Kate!"

"I think I'll just go into the other room," said Jilly, "watch *Monarch of the Glen*, it's so marvellous—"

"She's upset again," said Helen, when she and Jim were finally on their own. Kate had apologised to Juliet and stormed upstairs, and Juliet had been comforted and was doing her piano practice. "I don't know why. I mean, I do know it's about her mother, but quite why at this point I—"

"I'm getting very tired of that as an excuse," said Jim. "She can't be allowed to behave exactly how she chooses, simply because she's had some trauma in her life. We've all had our troubles—"

"Jim, I don't think anything you've had to endure could compare with what Kate has been through." Jilly's voice came from the doorway. "I'm sorry to interfere—and I agree she was very naughty and rude this evening—but knowing she was abandoned by a mother who apparently had no interest in whether she lived or died is a dreadful thing."

"Mummy, please don't—" said Helen, but it was too late. Jim had stormed out of the kitchen and into the sitting room, and the sweet tinkling of Susan Hampshire's voice had been replaced by the harsh tones of Taggart.

‹•›

"Are you sure you're going to be all right?" Jocasta looked at Clio thoughtfully.

"Of course. I'll go to these friends in Guildford, and they'll put me up for a few days while I sort myself out."

"You've spoken to them, have you?"

"Of course."

It was not a complete lie; Mark Salter had called her and in his sweet, tactful way had said there was no need for explanations, Barbara had told him all he needed to know, and that nothing would make him happier than to have her back in the practice, but that he would have to honour his fortnight's commitment to the first locum. "I'm only sorry the circumstances are so unhappy for you."

She'd had that conversation in Jocasta's bedroom, having explained it was rather delicate; Jocasta had clearly assumed it was Jeremy, and had made a second jug of coffee. Nick had returned by then and was smiling dutifully at her. Clio had suddenly felt appalling, a burden on a lot of perfectly nice people who were trying to have a normal, peaceful Sunday.

"I must go," she said. "Honestly, I can't take up any more of your time."

"Of course you mustn't go," said Jocasta, "you're staying right there. We're not doing anything, are we, Nick?" and, "No," he had said, after the most momentary of pauses, "no, nothing. In fact I've got to get back to my place and write a piece for tomorrow's paper—Chris called while I was out running."

"Well, there you are," said Jocasta. "Think how lonely and lost I'd be without you, Clio. It happens all the time, you know, I get abandoned just like that."

Clio excused herself and went to the lavatory so that they could communicate in peace; when she came back, Nick was in the shower.

"I'm sure you think he made that up," said Jocasta, grinning at her, "but he didn't. Anyway, we can have a nice day together."

Clio was feeling too lonely and dispirited to protest any further.

She tried not to tell her too much; it seemed absurdly disloyal to discuss a marriage—albeit a failed one—with someone who was not a close friend, but Jocasta was dangerously easy to talk to. She sat quietly most of the time, only speaking when a silence became too long, and then in the most minimal terms—"And then?" or "So you?"

Clio tried to ignore the prompts, but as the silences grew, it became very difficult, and later, eased into greater intimacy by a good deal of wine, she told Jocasta this. She laughed.

"It's one of the first things you learn, the pressure of the silence. Carol Sarler, she's the *Daily Express* columnist, you know, unutterably brilliant, she told me that she once sat for nearly two minutes in complete silence waiting for an interviewee to answer one of her more difficult questions. And he did. In the end, everyone does. Or walks out. But I try not to practise it in my personal life. Sorry, Clio."

"It's all right," said Clio. "I'm sure it's done me good. In a way it's better than some mutual friend who'll feel they're taking sides."

"Hope so. It does sound like you've done the right thing. Maybe a bit rash actually walking out, but—"

"Jocasta, if I hadn't walked out, he'd have talked me round. He's a brilliant tactician. You've no idea how often I've gone into arguments knowing I'm right, absolutely knowing it, and ended up sobbing and asking him to forgive me."

Jocasta said nothing.

"So—I'm glad, really. But it's been very drastic. I wouldn't like to re-live this weekend."

"How many times has he called you?"

A very long silence, then Clio said, not looking at her, "He hasn't. Not once."

"Clio," said Jocasta, refilling her glass yet again, "you have done absolutely the right thing. I know I shouldn't say that, but it has to be true. And at least you haven't had any children."

"No," said Clio. And burst into tears again. This time she resisted the silence.

"I think you should stay here tonight," Jocasta said.

"Jocasta, I can't. And what would Nick say?"

Jocasta stared at her. "I don't give a shit what Nick says. This is my house, my life. It's nothing to do with Nick. This is not the 1950s. And we haven't even started on Martha yet."

"Martha! Have you seen her?"

"Not exactly, but our paths may cross. She wants to be an MP, according to Nick. He's met her. Says she's rather important and successful."

"Well, she did seem very ambitious, even then. Funny thing, ambition, isn't it? It seems to be in people's genes. How about you, are your ambition genes powerful?"

"Pretty powerful. Yours?"

"More than I thought," said Clio slowly. "I mean, when I first married Jeremy, I thought I'd want to give it all up, but I didn't. I really minded leaving my job at the hospital—"

"What did you do?"

"I was a junior consultant. In geriatrics. I know it sounds rather dreary, but it isn't, it's fascinating and lovely and very rewarding. And then I really enjoyed general practice. I was so miserable the day I left. It wasn't just because it coincided with the end of my marriage."

"So, now what?"

"Well, for the time being I can go back."

"And long-term?"

"I don't know. Funnily enough, just a few weeks ago I heard from a colleague that there are a couple of new jobs in my old department. And they wanted me to apply. Of course it was out of the question, Jeremy was furious at the very idea . . ."

There was a silence while Jocasta clearly struggled not to comment on Jeremy and his behaviour; then she said, "But now—why not?"

"I don't think I've got the stomach for it at the moment. I'm feeling a bit fragile, to put it mildly."

"Of course you are. But you won't always. And it could be just what you need. New challenge, all that. It might not be the best thing, going back to Guildford, where Jeremy is. Look, why don't you call those people and tell them you're not coming tonight? We've got too much to talk about, and— Clio!" She had obviously read her face. "You weren't going there anyway, were you?"

"Not . . . exactly," said Clio, "no. But—"

"Right. You're staying. Another bottle of wine, I think. I wish you smoked, Clio—you make me feel so corrupt."

She fetched a bottle of wine, opened it, and poured Clio a glass. "Cheers. Again. It's lovely to see you. Even under such unhappy circumstances. Now—" There was a loud ring at the door. "Shit," said Jocasta. "Excuse me a minute."

Clio took a large slug of wine, not really wanting to see anyone either, half listening to Jocasta greeting someone, then speaking rather quietly (obviously telling whoever it was she had an awkward visitor), and then finally walking in and saying, "Clio, look who's turned up—Josh!"

And there he was, standing in front of her, not greatly changed, much as she remembered him indeed, only there was rather more of him, all blond hair and blue eyes and wide, white-teethed grin, the cause—albeit indirect—of so many of her troubles. And now what should she do?

Chapter 16

· · · ·

"Hi, Martha! Blast from the past. Don't you dare say you don't remember me!" For the second time in forty-eight hours Martha felt time jerk to a standstill. She knew that voice so well; that musical, slightly low-pitched voice. The last time she had heard it, it had been calling her name across the crowded station in Bangkok. She felt the heat again, the suffocating humid heat, and she could hear the noise, that strange, unmistakable blend of foreign babble, slurring Anglo-American, and the relentless pumping of pop music; and she felt her panic again, saw herself hurrying away, pretending she hadn't heard or seen Jocasta, slipping into a tiny narrow street and taking refuge in the chaos of the stalls.

"Martha? It is you, isn't it? Chad Lawrence gave me your number. It's Jocasta. Jocasta Forbes."

"No, of course not. I mean, of course I remember you. It's very good to hear from you." She could hear her own voice, astonishingly normal, pleasant, friendly, but no more.

"I'd love to see you, Martha. You know, this weekend, it's really weird, I've been with Clio."

"Clio Scott?" This was getting worse by the minute.

"Yes. Bit of a long story how, big coincidence, I won't bore you with it. Anyway, Chad tells me you're joining them."

"Well, only thinking of it."

"Really? I heard prospective candidate for your hometown."

"No! Not yet anyway. I'm only a little way along the road. I'm sure it won't happen. Look, it's a bit difficult to talk just now."

"Exactly why I'm calling. To try and fix a meeting. Chad called me because he said he thought I might write an article about you for the paper." God. Dear God. What might she ask, what?

"In the paper?"

"Yes. The *Sketch*, I write for it. I thought Chad had told you." Pull yourself together, Martha, she must think you're a complete idiot. "So what about it? It would really raise your profile, you know."

"I'm not sure I want it raised," she said, and her voice now was really cool.

There was a silence, and then Jocasta said, her own voice changed, "Well, if you're going into politics you'd better get used to the idea. You can't run with a low one, I'll tell you that. Anyway, here's my mobile number. Give me a call if you want to meet. When you want to do the piece."

"The piece?"

"The article."

"Oh. Oh, yes. Well, honestly, Jocasta, I don't think so. Sorry."

"Fine. Absolutely fine. Bye now."

"Goodbye, Jocasta. And thanks for calling."

"Silly bitch," said Jocasta aloud as she put the phone down.

• ◆ •

"I . . . wondered what your plans were."

Jeremy's voice was as she had never heard it; almost diffident, just short of nervous. Clio was standing looking at the shampoo range in Boots; she was so surprised she practically dropped the basket.

"Well, I'm not absolutely sure, to be honest."

"Where—where are you living?"

"In a flat in Guildford. Or I'm about to be. At the end of the week. I just signed the agreement this morning. Meanwhile I'm staying with the Salters."

"The Salters! You've told them about—about what's happened?"

"That I've left you? Well, yes. I had to really. But look, Jeremy, I'm in Boots—not the place to have a conversation like this. If you really want to talk to me, we'd better meet." She felt cool and in control.

"Yes. I think we should. Would you like to come to the house?"

"I'd rather not. A pub?"

"Of course. What about the one at Thursley? About six?"

"What, tonight? No, I can't do tonight. Sorry." She could, of course, but . . .

"Oh. Well, tomorrow, then? Maybe nearer seven, I've got a long list."

Clio switched off her mobile and went to join the queue at the checkout; her mood of confidence and pleasure had been very short-lived. Still—it had been a beginning.

"Do you have a Boots card?" said the girl.

"Oh, no. No, I don't."

"Pity." She was very friendly. "You've got an awful lot of stuff here. You going on holiday or something?"

"No," said Clio, "just restocking." Restocking her life. It was a rather good phrase, she thought. Her spirits seesawed up again.

•◆•

"Jocasta, hi. I just wanted to say thanks for last night."

"That's OK. Anytime you need a square meal. But Josh, you've got to get your life sorted out."

"I know, I know. It's not a lot of fun without Beatrice, and I'm missing those children horribly."

"I expect you are. Still—" Her voice softened. "I don't suppose she means it about divorce. She's just trying to teach you a lesson."

"'Fraid not. She's seen a solicitor."

"Oh God, Josh, I'm so sorry. You didn't say that last night."

"Well, I didn't want to, in front of Clio."

"She's so sweet, isn't she? I really like her. But she seemed a bit . . . awkward with you, I thought. Josh, is there something I should know? About you and her? You didn't, well, sleep with her, did you? While we were all travelling?"

"Of course I didn't!" He sounded so genuinely indignant that Jocasta believed him.

"Sorry. She just seemed a bit thrown. I wondered, that's all."

"Jocasta, nothing happened between Clio and me. OK?"

•◆•

Martha was trying to do some work when the phone rang again. It was Chad.

"Martha, what do you think you're playing at?" he said, his voice clipped and harsh.

"What do you mean?"

"Turning down what would have been a very big article in the *Sketch*? Are you mad? It could have won you hundreds, possibly even thousands of votes. I would advise you very strongly to see Jocasta Forbes. It's the opportunity of a political lifetime. Well, at your stage, anyway."

"Yes, but—"

"Martha, just do it. She's not going to say anything unpleasant about you. Even if she does, it won't do you any harm. It's exposure. But why should she? It's such a charming story, all of it. Binsmow childhood, going travelling together, and then your dizzy rise in the law, the cleaner dying, converting you to politics . . . It's so good it sounds as if we made it up. If you get selected, you are to call Jocasta immediately. And eat a little humble pie when you do so—she was quite sniffy about it all."

Martha was silent.

"Look," he said, as if he were talking to a young child, "Martha, either you do this thing, or you don't. Politics is a high-profile profession. I thought you'd have realised that by now."

"I'm beginning to," she said, "and actually, Chad—" Maybe she could get out of this, even now.

"Hold on a minute," he said, "my other line's going."

She sat waiting. Why had she got into this, why hadn't she thought about it properly? She was such a fool, such an absolute fool . . .

"Yes, what was that?"

"I . . . well, I was just wondering if . . . if . . ." Go on, Martha, say it, get it over, it's only a sentence, a few words, then you'll be safe again.

"Martha, what is it? I'm very busy."

"If I could change my mind."

There was a long silence; when he spoke, his voice was absolutely incredulous.

"Change your mind? What, stand down again?"

"Well . . . yes."

"Martha, what the *fuck* is the matter with you?" She was shocked; she had never heard him swear.

"Nothing. I've just been thinking and—"

"You've been thinking! A little late, I have to say. Don't you realise the amount of effort that's been put into this for you? That Jack Kirkland's written to the constituency himself? That I've given up a lot of time for you? That Norman Brampton has been working his tail off, making phone calls, probably incurring another heart attack? How dare you start playing games like some silly tart! I'm beginning to think we've made an appalling mistake."

She was silent, wondering if she dared push on, wondering which fear was greater.

"Look," he said, "I've got to go. You'd better pull yourself together, Martha, and pretty damn quick. Make your mind up, one way or another." He rang off abruptly.

A little later her phone rang yet again. It was Janet Frean. "Hello, Martha. I just called to congratulate you. You really have done awfully well. It's hard enough when you've spent years in the business. I should know."

"Thank you, Janet. Look—"

"We really need you, you know. People like you. You're going to be the backbone of the party. I mean it. And we so need women, and especially young successful women like you. Now, I gather you're feeling a bit wobbly. It's completely natural—anyone would. I remember going into mega panic mode more than once. It's pretty terrifying. But you'll feel better again soon. Honestly."

"Janet, I—"

"Look, if I could make a suggestion, what about a media course? They're so worthwhile, they teach you presentation, how to deal with both radio and television, how to get your points across, even what to wear. I'll give you the name and number of the one I did. And don't let Chad bully you. Any worries, come to me with them. All right?"

As if, Janet, as if.

And then there was an e-mail. From Jack Kirkland. "Hello, Martha. Just to say congratulations. Very well done. I knew you could do it. All we need is about a hundred more of you. Don't fail us now. We need you. Jack."

"Oh God," said Martha, and buried her head in her hands. And then Chad called again.

"Darling, I'm sorry I bawled you out. It's natural you should be nervous. Absolutely natural. But you're doing so well. And we're all behind you. All right?"

"Yes, Chad."

"Good girl. And call Jocasta back, will you? Soon as you can."

God, thought Martha wearily, he's got a hide like a whole herd of rhinos. "Yes, Chad," she said again.

"Oh, and Janet called me, said she'd suggested a media course for you.

Excellent idea, should have thought of it myself. I'll get HO to book it for you. It'll help you a lot. Right, well I'll leave you to make that call."

"Yes, Chad."

She seemed to be stuck with it; she couldn't fight this lot. And when she got back to her flat that night, her father had written to her; she recognised his beautiful handwriting. She stood there, reading, tears in her eyes.

> . . . *People keep coming up to us, saying how much they hope you'll be selected, and how proud of you we must be. Which we are, my darling, so very proud. And we're being extremely discreet, of course. We both send you very much love. See you in a day or two.*

How could she turn her back on that, tell them she wasn't going to do it after all?

And after all, she thought, her panic receding again, why should she? She had this great new opportunity; she had wanted it so much. She couldn't throw it away. Not now.

Millions of girls, millions of girls . . .

Jack Kirkland smiled at Janet across his desk, gestured to her to sit down. "Thanks for sparing the time. I just wanted to run something past you."

"Oh yes?"

"We seem to have got young Martha back on the rails. I really wouldn't want to lose her. It's not so much herself that's valuable to us—God knows how she'll turn out—it's what she represents, youth, a corner in the professional business world, a—"

"Jack, I'm sorry, but if you just want to talk about Martha Hartley, I have to be in a committee room in ten minutes—"

"No, no, of course not. Sorry, Janet. No, I think we've got Eliot Griers on board."

"Oh, really?" Eliot Griers was the Conservative member for Surrey North; he was deceptively soft-spoken, savage in debate, and had been promised a position in the shadow cabinet by Iain Duncan Smith, which had never materialised.

"Yes. He's confident he can talk his constituency party round. Enough of it anyway. How would you feel about that? Personally I'd be delighted. High profile, very clever, he's more of what we need."

"Well, obviously I'd be extremely pleased. He's very clever, no doubt about that. Surprised though. Last time I spoke to him, he went on and on about how courageous we were, seemed in no mind to join us."

"That was before he didn't get his shadow cabinet post. He's very bitter about that. Of course he'd want a seat on the top table, so to speak. He'd be coming in very much at our level. A spokesman for the party in a big way. We'd make a big song and dance about him."

There was an almost unnoticeable pause. Then: "So why are you asking me?"

"Well, he'd be very visible. I wouldn't want you to feel in any way sidelined."

Janet stood up, pushed her chair back rather vehemently. Her eyes looked dark and almost angry.

"Jack, I would hope I'm above such things. What I care about, above all, is the party and its success. I am not in this thing for personal gain. Women mostly aren't, you know. They have other concerns."

"So you say, all of you. I'd personally beg leave to doubt it. I've always regarded you as pretty ambitious, Janet."

"Of course I'm ambitious. But if you think I'm looking for the top job in any party, you'd be wrong. I do have another life, you know. I'm not married to Westminster."

This was a slightly cheap jibe, given Kirkland's failed marriage. He flushed. "Good," he said. "As long as you don't have a problem with Griers. I was only clearing the deck, so to speak."

"Yes, and I appreciate it. Sorry, Jack. No, Griers would be nothing but good news." She hesitated, then said, "His marriage is all right now, is it?"

"Oh, that stuff years ago? Gossip, Janet, nothing more. I've spoken to Caroline, lovely girl, she's right behind him in every way. And like you, he's got a very attractive family, always a help."

"Well, he seems just about perfect then," said Janet. "Thanks, Jack. I really appreciate your . . . thoughtfulness. I'd be more than happy to have Eliot Griers on board."

Several people serving on the Joint Committee on Human Rights with Janet Frean that day remarked that she didn't seem in the best of tempers.

. . .

"You're a star," Ed said, "an absolute star. I'm so proud of you."

She'd been afraid of seeing him after the weekend, afraid he might sense there was something wrong, something worrying her. He read her so well.

"Ed, don't. I've got such a long way to go. I may never get elected at all, I—"

"I know all that," he said. "I'm just proud of you for having a go."

"I wouldn't have without you," she said. "I'd still be dithering."

"Nah. You'd have done it anyway. I know you." He smiled at her, raised his glass. "Or I'm beginning to. To the Right Honorable Martha. Long may she reign."

It was a perfect May evening; the light brilliant, the air cool and clear, drenched with a recent shower. They were sitting on Martha's balcony, drinking some champagne Ed had brought round.

"Are you all right?" he said suddenly. "You seem a bit edgy."

"Oh—oh, I'm all right. I was a bit . . . worried about something."

"Not any longer?"

"I don't seem to be, no," she said, half surprised.

"Well, that's being with me. Cure for any amount of worry, I am. Give us a kiss. And now look at that, will you? Rainbow."

And indeed there was, glancing down from a newly black sky onto the shimmering buildings across the river.

"Well, that should do it, even if I don't. Melt your troubles away like sherbet lemons or whatever it is."

"Lemon drops. Oh Ed—how did I ever manage without you?"

"I have absolutely no idea," he said complacently. "You know what I was just thinking? I've never been to bed with a politician. Could you put it in your manifesto, do you think? Sex for the masses?"

"Certainly not," she said, "just the chosen few."

"Well, here's the first of the few. All ready and waiting."

And as she took the hand he held out and followed him inside, laughing, she thought that he would never agree to her giving up politics again, either.

• 204 •

Clio looked at Jeremy as he put a white wine spritzer down in front of her; he was pale and seemed very tired. He smiled at her almost nervously and said, "Well, how are you?"

"I'm . . . fine. Considering."

"Good. Is it all right at the Salters'? What did you tell them? About us?"

She looked at him; he was sweating slightly. She was surprised. Why should he care so much? She supposed it was all part of his arrogance, not wishing to appear in any way less than perfect.

"I told them we'd separated. I had to. Why else should I need somewhere to stay? And my job back."

"Your job back?"

"Well, yes. I have to live, Jeremy. I'm not the sort to demand huge alimony payments. And anyway, I love my job. There seems no reason to give it up now."

"You decided that? Without consulting me?"

"Why should I consult you? You made it perfectly clear our marriage was over. I don't see what it has to do with you."

"I was . . . upset," he said. "And I—I'd like you to reconsider. Well, both of us to reconsider."

"What do you mean?"

"That we should—should try again." She stared at him; this was the last thing she had expected. "Clio, I was very hasty. I said a lot of harsh things and I really don't want to live without you. I don't want our marriage to end."

"Jeremy, on what basis? I mean, do I still have to give up my job?"

"No," he said quietly, after a long pause, "no, you don't. That was . . . unreasonable of me. I can't face life without you, Clio. I came to see very quickly that I . . . well, I do still love you. I want you back. I really do." He waited, as she stared at him. "What do you say?"

"I—I'm not sure," she said. "I mean it was a bit of a shock, all that. But—you mean I can go on working and everything?"

"Yes, you can."

It was tempting. So very tempting. The thought of living alone, of making her own way again, might be attractive in theory, but in practice it was scary. She was used to being married, to living with someone, considering them. And he had made several huge concessions. She had never heard him apologise before. To anyone. Clearly he had missed her considerably.

Even allowing for the fact he would have found it so hard to admit to his colleagues and their mutual friends that their marriage was a failure, this was pretty astonishing stuff.

"Well," she said again, "as long as I could work . . ."

"You can work, Clio. I promise." He stopped and looked at her. "Of course I would hope it wouldn't be for long. That we should be having children pretty soon. I mean, that is a given, as far as I'm concerned. And you too, I'm sure."

Clio knew the moment had come, that she couldn't go on any longer, deceiving him, when he had made such huge concessions to her.

"Jeremy," she said, "Jeremy, I'm afraid that isn't going to happen. Or almost certainly isn't going to happen."

He stared at her, his face absolutely puzzled.

She took a deep breath.

"I've got something to tell you, Jeremy, something I should have told you a long time ago. Should we talk here, or would you like to go back to the house?"

"Let's talk here," he said. His face was expressionless.

Clio moved to sit beside him. She took his hand and, feeling sorry for him, as she had never thought to be again, her voice surprisingly steady, she began to tell him.

Chapter 17

· · · ·

She hadn't seen Ed for almost a week. He'd been filming out of London and she'd missed him horribly. He'd called her a couple of times, but rather briefly, saying he was frantic. It had been unnerving—she felt eighteen again. Had he gone off her? Had he found someone younger or prettier, someone with curly hair and a small nose? Probably. She wanted to see him, talk to him, be with him, have him. She really, really wanted to have him. Maybe she never would again, maybe that had been the last time . . .

Her phone rang.

"I just wondered if you could give me a lift to Suffolk this weekend, Miss Hartley. I ought to visit my mum and my car's completely fucked up."

"I hope you don't use that sort of language in front of your mother."

"Of course I don't. Also, I have this girlfriend down there I really want to see. She's the most fantastic lay and I've been missing her a lot."

"Well, I'll have to look at my diary. Let's see . . . Yes, I think I could just about fit you in. Now I do warn you, Ed, I'm horribly busy. I've got to see the Centre Forward people, I've got to do an interview with the local paper, and Norman Brampton has asked my parents and me to supper on Saturday evening. I'm sorry—"

"That's OK. I could come along, say I was your secretary. Hold your microphone while you address your adoring public."

"Yes, that's a really good idea."

"Or I could gate-crash the wild evening at the Bramptons'. That sounds really cool. We might even be able to sneak upstairs after the dessert."

"Yes, that's an excellent notion too."

"Or how about we leave early on Friday and spend the night at some luxury hotel off the M11? We could have dinner on the way."

"Now that is clever. You're on."

"That's my girl. You're really living dangerously these days, aren't you?"

If only he knew how dangerously. Or rather, if only he never would.

Tension, trauma, the delight of finally being with Ed again had made her overexcited; she came swiftly, heard herself shouting as she did so, as the bolts of pleasure shot into her, bright, dazzling, ferocious. Later, it was softer, sweeter, and very slow; and after that, she lay curled against him, her arm across him, and told him how happy he made her.

She woke to find him shaking her, saying, "There, there, it's OK, shush, shush. You had a bad dream," he said, as she stared at him. "You were crying, talking in your sleep—"

"Talking? What did I say?" she asked sharply, terrified.

"Oh, just a lot of nonsense. Nothing that made any kind of sense."

"Yes, but what?"

"Just a lot of words," he said, folding her into his arms again, "rubbishy words. Go back to sleep."

But she was too afraid for that, and lay awake until dawn, watching him and wondering whatever he would do or say, if he knew.

She felt much better in the morning. She bought a pile of papers and they sat reading them over breakfast, Martha drinking orange juice and coffee, Ed eating what the place called a full English. He kept offering her bits of it, feeding her mushrooms and tiny slivers of bacon on his fork.

"I'll have you overweight in no time," he said, grinning. "Tell you what you did say last night. When you were asleep."

Terror hit her. "What?" she said. "What did I say?"

"You said, 'Treacle tart,' " he said, "and then you said, 'Chips, please.' Pretty incriminating stuff, wouldn't you say?"

"Oh shut up," said Martha, and threw a bread roll at him.

They parted at the Coach and Horses, where she was meeting Colin Black; he said he'd call her at her parents' house in the morning.

•—•

Clio sat on her new beanbag in her new sitting room and stared at her new television. She couldn't, at this precise moment, quite think why she had got it; it was only Jeremy who had watched TV, but when she had bought the stereo, the young man had said they had special offers on televisions and she had suddenly thought that, actually, she would be on her own a lot and she wouldn't be getting Jeremy's supper or catching up on paperwork or returning phone calls, which were all the things she did while he watched it, because she'd have time to do that whenever she wanted, and maybe she'd even be rather bored sometimes, and a television might be a good idea.

She looked up at the bare windows and at the blinds still in their Habitat bags, then she wandered into the kitchen, put on her new kettle, made herself a cup of coffee in one of her new mugs, and wondered however she was going to survive her new life.

He had taken it quite well, really. He had listened to her quietly and politely and at the end they had agreed that the only thing was to part. He wanted a chance at least of having children, and clearly, with Clio, it was very unlikely. And she was (equally clearly) not quite the person he had thought; although the deception had initially been very minimal, almost nonexistent, it had grown disproportionately fast, in the end becoming so tragically huge that he could not contemplate trying to cope with it.

Chlamydia. It was rather a pretty word. It could almost be a girl's name. It certainly didn't sound like the name of an ugly, loathsome disease. A disease that appeared to have rendered her totally infertile.

Of course she didn't know if it had. There was still hope. But the two last gynaecologists had both expressed grave doubts. Her fallopian tubes appeared completely blocked. And it was absolutely her own fault. She had slept with several men she had hardly known, and had contracted, in blithe ignorance, this awful, symptomless, unsuspected thing that had come back to haunt her when it was—probably—far too late to do anything about it. One of the things she most longed for, motherhood, was to be denied her: all as a result of some foolish, irresponsible behaviour when she was eighteen years old.

It was on the trip to the island that it started. The dreadful need to know that men—any man—could want her, find her sexually attractive.

She hadn't expected sex to matter so much. She had just thought it would be a wonderful trip, meeting lots of people, seeing fantastic places; it hadn't struck her that with hundreds, thousands of young people wandering untrammelled by any kind of discipline all over the world, pleasure of every kind must include sex in a big way. No one had thought to say, "Now look, Clio, everyone will be having sex all around you, all the time." Or even tell her that she was very unlikely to return a virgin. Why should they? She had grown up in an extraordinarily uncommunicative family, repressed by her father, suppressed by her sisters, made to feel less pretty, less clever, less interesting than she actually was. She had gone to an all-girls' school, and had never developed much of a social life, largely because she was shy and overweight and, when she did go to parties, would find herself bypassed for the other sorts of girls, the skinny, confident ones who knew exactly how to exploit their own attractions. After a few miserable experiences of standing in corners, talking to other dull girls, it became easier just to say she wouldn't go. Of course her sisters had made even that worse, had commented on her weight and the fact that she didn't seem to go out much, and told her she should learn to deal with her shyness, not give in to it.

"It's a form of arrogance," Artemis had said once, "thinking everyone's going to be looking at you," and Ariadne had said yes, quite right and why should they, for heaven's sake. "Just forget about yourself for once, Clio, think of other people instead."

That had been bad enough; it was worse when they tried to be kind and help her with her hair and makeup and suggest diets; none of their advice ever did any good. She'd had one boyfriend in her last term at school; she hadn't even liked him, but he was someone to go to the cinema with and to take to the end-of-term dance. He had kissed her a couple of times, which she had found revolting, but nothing worse than that; the best thing he had done for her was tell her she was pretty, and she had liked his best friend a lot, which had goaded her into dieting, so that by the time she actually set off on her travels she had lost about a stone, and although comparing herself with the other two she felt she was the size of a house—she took a size fourteen and they clearly took tens—she knew she did look much better. Almost pretty in fact.

And because the Thai food was the opposite of fattening, she had lost another half stone by the end of the second week on Koh Samui. She caught sight of herself in a cracked mirror in someone's hut one morning and thought she was almost not fat anymore; her hair had gone lighter with the sun, and she was brown and—well, she began to feel just a little bit self-confident, less apologetic about her appearance at least.

Although that was a long way from being sexy.

It was only when she went to Koh Phangan, for one of the full-moon parties that everyone had told her were so wonderful, that she had felt hopelessly, helplessly virginal. She had watched them in the darkness, against the background of the throbbing music, all the wonderful skinny brown bodies, enjoying one another, and although she had started talking to a very sweet boy, who was obviously also a virgin, and they had kissed a bit, nothing else had happened and he had fallen asleep on the sand after smoking a lot of dope. Clio was still at the stage of refusing dope—there were all sorts of scary warnings that the Thai police were at the parties undercover, offering spliffs and then arresting people who took them—but she had gone on drinking rather a lot. And in the end she had felt so wretched and sick that she had gone back to the hut and lain on her bed all alone, wondering if she might go on to Sydney much sooner than she had planned.

And had gone back rather miserably to the relative homeliness of Koh Samui.

Then something wonderful happened. The next morning, as she drank some very nasty coffee on the veranda of the hut, Josh suddenly appeared. Gorgeous, sexy, charming Josh.

He had been up in the far north. It was amazing, he said, he'd done a three-day trip walking through the jungle—"It was uphill mostly, miles and miles, eight hours a day, and incredibly hot and humid, I was practically hallucinating about a shower and my bed." He had done a four-hour boat trip to an elephant village, where they stayed for several days. "But it was getting a bit like hard work, so I decided to come down here."

Clio offered him some of the disgusting coffee and they sat on the beach and he went on talking about his trip.

"They're really poor up there; they live in these little huts, off the ground, with animals living underneath them. They wear proper tribal gear, with wonderful headdresses and then Snoopy T-shirts underneath that the tourists have given them. You'd have loved it, Clio."

She knew why he said that and it hurt: because he saw her as a swot, not the sort of sexy girl who pulled a different bloke every night. But she managed to smile, and say it sounded wonderful.

"It is," he said with a grin. "You feel you're in another century as well as another place. There's no contraception, of course, so there are absolutely loads of children. The poverty's dreadful and quite little girls are sent south and sold into prostitution. Very sad."

He said he'd been a great novelty there, being blond, and that the whole village had been summoned to stare at him. "They sat and stroked my arms, because I'm so hairy."

"I'd love to go," she said, and then, because it would give her an excuse to leave the beach, she said she was thinking of moving on and she might make her way up there.

"Oh, but you mustn't go on your own," he said. "It's much more dangerous up there, you must go with a guide, pay for your food and accommodation in advance. You do that in Bangkok, it's quite easy. Now, you in touch with the others?"

"No. Jocasta left weeks ago to go north—I'm surprised you didn't bump into each other—and Martha left about a fortnight ago. To go to Phuket, I think."

"So you're on your own?"

"Well, no, not really. I'm staying here with two other girls and a bloke."

"Do you know anywhere I could sleep?"

"In my bungalow," she said and then thought he might think she was trying to pull him and flushed. "The thing is, there are four of us, and one is moving on today. We could go and ask the guy who runs the place."

"Cool. Well, if you don't mind. I'm going to check a few things out."

He came back quite quickly; she was sitting chatting to a couple of the little Thai boys who swept the beach and put out the loungers, enjoying their sweet friendliness, their pride in earning some money for their families.

"Well, apparently Ang Thong is a must. Why don't you come too? It's a day trip; boat goes from Na Thon, at eight thirty." He had looked at her rather consideringly with his amazing blue eyes and suddenly grinned and said, "You look great, Clio. Being here obviously suits you."

Clio didn't eat anything for the rest of the day, in case her flattening stomach redeveloped a bulge.

She felt distinctly nervous but hugely excited next day, joining Josh and half a dozen friends he'd made the night before. It was a stunning morning, clear and blue, as they moved out of the harbour towards the archipelago of Ang Thong. The boat served the usual disgusting coffee and some rather nice cakes for breakfast and, after a bit, Josh and most of his new friends fell asleep, stretched out on the hard benches in the sun. Clio stayed carefully under the tarpaulin; she burnt easily, in spite of her dark hair.

After about half an hour, Josh woke up, saw her sitting alone, and patted the bench next to him. "Here," he said. "Come and sit with me."

And she had, her head swimming with excitement, sat down next to him and he'd grinned at her and put his arm round her and passed her his beer to share. He liked her! Josh Forbes, the gorgeous, *gorgeous* Josh liked her. Fancied her. She could feel it. And somehow it didn't matter when another girl arrived and sat the other side of him and he put his other arm round her, because for the first time in her life she felt good about herself, and she knew that really he liked her best.

The boat had reached the mass of islands now, was making its way between them, some of them quite large and lush, others little more than huge rocks carved into incredible shapes by the sea. They saw dolphins playing, and above them clouds of seabirds crying in the wind; and nearer to shore gazed down at rainbow-coloured fish through the incredibly clear water above the coral reef. It was an extraordinary journey.

They anchored off the biggest of the islands, and transferred to a longtail boat to take them in to shore. They jumped out into water knee-deep and, even by Thai standards, warm—"Too hot to swim in," Clio said to Josh—and the boat's captain pointed them in the direction of the island's greatest challenge, a steep 500-metre climb in a hollow behind the beach.

"Very hard," he said. "Not danger, but hard."

"Right," Josh said. "I'm off. Who's coming with me?"

Clio was—and to her slight disappointment, all the others too.

It was an incredibly tough climb through hard scrub and awkward boulders, up and up, sheltered to an extent from the sun, but not the heat, by the trees. They began light-heartedly, larking about, became tired and hot and increasingly silent. Two of the girls gave up, started slithering down, laughing again, telling them they were mad. Clio, directly behind Josh now, less fit than they were, knew she would rather die than give in.

As she struggled on, feeling her salty sweat stinging her eyes, her muscles straining, everything hurting, dying seemed quite likely.

But she made it, emerged from the darkness of the trees into brilliant blue light and up the last few metres to the summit; and then stood there, weariness set aside. It was as if she was flying above the islands, spread below and beyond her, jagged shapes, rimmed with white sand, carved out of the blue, mystically beautiful. Even Josh seemed moved by it, stood there, gazing at it in silence, and then smiled at her rather slowly without speaking. Clio wished she wasn't quite so drenched in sweat.

She had expected the descent to be easy but it wasn't, and she was tired, dreadfully tired. As she neared the bottom, she began to feel dizzy and sick, the sun seemed horribly dazzling and she found it hard to find footholds; twice she slipped. Josh was ahead, and she was thankful; she didn't want him thinking she was pathetic.

There was a stretch of grass at the bottom of the steps; Clio just reached it, collapsed onto it, under a palm tree, her legs completely without strength. She sat, her head buried in her arms, feeling faint and dreadfully thirsty; she knew she had to get back to the boat within a few minutes, everyone else had gone, but she literally couldn't walk. Nor did she care.

"You OK?" It was Josh's voice, clearly anxious.

"Yes, I'm fine. Thanks."

"You don't look it. You look awful. Quite green."

"I'm OK." She struggled to stand up and couldn't.

"Clio, you're not. You're dehydrated. Stay there, I'll get some stuff for you."

He was back in minutes, carrying not only water but crisps ("You need salt") and cola ("You need sugar"), and stood over her while she consumed them. Their captain waved to them to hurry; Josh shouted that he had to wait, gesturing to Clio lying on the ground; everyone stared. She could imagine them getting impatient, scornful of her, and worst of all, amused.

Gradually she felt her strength return and managed to stagger to the boat, leaning on Josh's arm, and felt self-conscious, sitting in the longboat, smiling feebly at people.

"Right," said Josh, handing her up the ladder into the other boat, "there you go. OK now?"

"Yes, I'm fine," she said. "Thank you. Sorry."

"Don't be silly. You did well." He grinned at her.

She had expected him to leave her then, but he sat by her while they ate the lunch, and the others came over to them and chatted, asked her if she was all right. She felt wonderful; she could have laughed for joy, sitting there, with Josh at her side looking after her, sharing his bottle of beer.

They stopped again later, on a much smaller island called Mae Koh, where another wonder awaited them—"And another climb, great!" said Josh—but this one was easy, leading through a narrow gorge and suddenly arriving at an extraordinary green-blue lake far, far below, entirely circled by cliffs, and filled with fresh seawater by way of an underground tunnel. It had a magical quality. Clio half expected some exotic sea creature to rise from it in greeting, and said so; two of the girls looked at her and then each other and raised their eyebrows; she felt incredibly foolish, until Josh said, "Or even a mermaid," and again she felt fantastically happy.

They snorkelled and then sat on the beach in the sun; one of the girls passed round a spliff and this time Clio took it—it was obviously so boring not to, and she inhaled, felt an easy warmth, a heady spinning of her senses. The girl wandered off down the beach, her small, perfect bottom moving very gently from side to side.

"She's nice," said Clio, looking enviously at the bottom.

"She's OK," Josh said, beginning to roll another spliff, "not as nice as you," and gave her a kiss on the top of her head. They smoked together for a few minutes, Clio feeling increasingly wonderful. And then he said that she was burning. "Why don't we move round there, into that sort of cave thing, you'll be sheltered there."

That had done it, really. She had known this was it, now, here, at last: a man wanted her and she wanted him. She was suddenly sexy and confident and they were away from the others at his instigation, so surely he felt the same too. She turned to him and pulled his head down to hers and kissed him on the mouth. She could feel him first hesitate, and then respond; he was a very good kisser, she thought confusedly, a lot better than anyone who had ever kissed her before.

She found she was experiencing a lot of strange things, strange sensations. There seemed to be some link between her mouth and a place deep within her, a dark, sweetly soft place, that moved every time he kissed her, and her heart was racing. She felt warm and relaxed and excited all at the same time, and she could feel a longing that was exactly like hunger—or was it thirst? Somehow the two fused together—to have Josh there, meeting the place—and she turned on her back and tried to pull him onto her.

"Hey, now," he said, very gently. "Careful, Clio."

But she was beyond being careful, beyond sense, beyond caution or anything, she just wanted him; she could feel his penis stiffening against her, and he was kissing her again, but very gently, and she tried desperately with her free hand, the one that was not holding his head to hers, to pull off her bikini pants.

She thought he would go on kissing her, but he had stopped. Maybe he was going to take his shorts off; she lay back, breathing heavily, looking at him, then pulling his head down again, pushing her tongue into his mouth, wondering how to find his penis, urge it into her, and all the time this fierce, strange, violent sensation: but then, suddenly, it was different. He was resisting her, pulling his head back slightly, and he said, "Clio, not now, not just now. Calm down." And then he stopped and gave her a half smile, and even through the booze and the dope and her own ignorance, she knew. He didn't want her—not now, not ever. She was being rejected, turned away as she always was, as she always had been. She felt fat again, naïve, uncool, and looking over his shoulder she saw the girl, the other girl watching them from the other side of the rocks, a half-amused look on her face. Hot with shame and misery, she turned away from Josh, pulled up her pants, and ran fast, as fast as she could, down to the sea and into it, careless of the coral hurting her feet, and if she'd had the courage she would have walked on and on until she could be seen no more, but it was no good, she couldn't do that, and finally, she turned and looked for him on the beach, but he had gone and was walking towards the long queue forming to get back to the boat.

They were on their way back; Josh was standing with a group of friends at the bows of the boat; he saw her looking at him, waved awkwardly, and then turned away, staring out to sea. A girl joined him, put her arm round his waist, pushed her hand into the pocket of his trunks, and it physically hurt Clio to see them, it was like a twisting wound in her stomach. The journey back seemed endless.

That night, as they all sat on the beach, Clio desperate for an excuse to go inside to bed, still watching the group miserably, expelled from it by her own foolishness, it happened. A boy—quite a nice-looking boy— asked if he could join her, offered her some drink, and after a little while started to kiss her and stroke her breasts, and then to push his hands down into her pants, probing into her pubic hair and further still; and after only a very little time, she was leading him into their hut, giggling deliberately loud, making sure that Josh was watching. Already a little of her humiliation and sense of worthlessness had gone.

It was not a good experience; the boy was inside her swiftly, far too swiftly, and it hurt dreadfully, but she felt healed and restored and less humiliated, all at the same time, and she hoped against all hope that Josh might realise someone did want her, and assume that he had been alone on the beach and on the boat, and even in the whole of Thailand, in being foolish enough to reject her.

Over the next few months, she slept with a great many boys, some of them extremely good-looking and sexy, some of them less so; sometimes she enjoyed it and sometimes she didn't. The important thing seemed to be that she could persuade them to want her. She had become, she supposed, that much-despised creature, a slag, and she also supposed she should despise herself, but she didn't; she felt very little about herself at all. She was simply running away from the plump, dull, innocent person she had been and was so afraid of; and every time she had sex with someone, that person was further away from her.

A new Clio came home, the old one left behind in the sun and the islands or perhaps in the hill villages of the north, or even the glittering os-tentation of Singapore: a slim, even thin Clio, with sun-streaked hair and a deep tan, a Clio who could attract men quite easily, but who was still anxious, still eager to please, still very far from sexually confident.

And the new Clio did not know, had not even considered, that she might carry a legacy from those dangerously careless days, which would damage her for the rest of her life.

·•·

"I wondered . . . I wondered if we could meet." It was Kate's unmistak-able little voice, rather shakier than usual. Clearly she was nervous. "Have lunch or something, like you said."

"Of course." Jocasta smiled into the phone. "It would be lovely. When did you have in mind?"

"Well, Saturdays are best. Because of school."

"I can't do today. Next week? Where would you like to go?"

"Oh, I don't mind really."

"Shall we say the Bluebird? In the King's Road? It's really fun there, specially on Saturday."

"I'm not sure. Is it very expensive?"

Jocasta's heart turned over. What a baby Kate was. How could she be even thinking about—? Well, she wasn't. Of course she wasn't.

"Kate, this is on me. I suggested it, didn't I? Do you know where it is? Right down the end, near World's End."

"I think so, yes. I'll find it anyway."

"Good girl. Oh, Kate—" Jocasta, don't. Don't do it . . .

"Yeah, what?"

"When's your birthday?"

"August the fifteenth. Why do you want to know?"

"I was just thinking about your work experience, you know. OK. See you on Saturday. How's your gran?"

"She's fine, thanks. Bye, Jocasta."

Jocasta put down the phone and sat staring at it for quite a long time; then very, very slowly, as if someone was physically holding her back, she called up the *Sketch* archive site on her computer and typed in August 15, 1986.

Chapter 18

· · · · ·

Carla Giannini was one of the great tabloid fashion editors. She understood precisely what fashion meant to tabloid readers: not so much silhouettes and hem lengths and fabric and cut, but sex. She ignored the collections and the couture designers; using upmarket photographers, she had them shoot sharp trouser suits and dresses from Zara, Topshop, and Oasis, shoes from Office; jeans and knitwear from the Gap, on young, long-legged, bosomy models, who preened themselves on her pages, saucer-eyed and sexy.

Carla was herself a beauty, dark-eyed and slightly heavy-featured, in the style of a young Sophia Loren, the child of an English aristocrat mother and an Italian car mechanic father. It was, against all odds, a very happy marriage, lived against the background of industrial Milan; but at seventeen, Carla had left home and moved to London and a new life—she hoped—as a model. She established herself quite quickly as an underwear model, which she hated, but she made enough money to do an evening course and became a sought-after makeup artist. She didn't like that much either, but she made a lot of very good contacts in the business and from there managed to move into what she realised she really wanted to do: fashion journalism. After a few years establishing herself on women's magazines, she finally found her true home—newspapers. Chris Pollock installed her in an office at the *Sketch* on her thirty-ninth birthday.

Carla's office was just off the newsroom, and Jocasta's desk was nearest to it. They were not exactly friends, but they fed each other cigarettes and quite often compared their extraordinarily different problems at the end of the day in the nearest wine bar, and occasionally Carla invited Jocasta to go with her to health farms like Ragdale Hall and Champneys, whose press agents invited journalists for the weekend in the hope that they would write about them or, better still, use them in photographs.

Carla's major problem was finding girls to photograph; she liked real girls, not quite off the street, but singers, actresses, designers, anyone with more of a story to them than their statistics and their model books. She used friends, daughters of friends, her boyfriends' sisters, even her own sisters; she had tried to persuade Jocasta to model for her, with a complete lack of success. Jocasta said she was too old for it and that it was so much the sort of thing she hated. "And I don't think Chris would like it."

"Of course he would," said Carla briskly. "You know how he loves the whole personality thing. You have such a great look, Jocasta, and for God's sake, Elle is pushing forty, Naomi's no spring chicken, and look at Jerry Hall!"

"I know," said Jocasta, "but the big difference between them and me is they all really care about how they look and know how to make the most of themselves. I don't. I mean, I can't even remember when I last more any makeup, apart from on my eyes."

"Yes, and that's a story in itself," said Carla and sighed. "Well, I'll just keep nagging on."

She was walking past the Bluebird Café at lunchtime one Saturday when she saw Jocasta sitting at a table, talking earnestly to one of the most beautiful young girls she had seen for a very long time.

•◆•

Anna Richardson called Clio again.

"We're off tomorrow. Look, do think about applying for that job at the Bayswater. They asked me if I'd mentioned it. They really want you."

Clio said she would think about it. Hard. And poured herself a glass of wine to celebrate. At least somebody wanted her. And not just any old place but one of the best teaching hospitals in London. It made her feel quite different. Happier. Sleeker. Less of a disaster.

After drinking another glass of wine, she sat down at the table and starting drafting a letter.

•◆•

Martha had told Paul Quenell about her new life. She felt she must. He had been surprisingly sympathetic and very interested; and far from saying she must resign, that her work for Wesley's was sure to suffer, he told her that as long as it only encroached on her life at weekends, then it was fine by him.

"Although I suppose if you get elected, you'll be leaving."

"Well, yes. But I won't be elected, I'm sure."

"I certainly hope not," said Paul, and then he smiled at her. "I wonder if I could sue them for enticement?"

He was a tall, stylish man, very slim, with thick grey curly hair and a rather ascetic face; his smile, which rarely came, was a minimal affair. He was forty-five years old, divorced, without children; that was the sum total of what anybody knew about his personal life.

"I don't think so," said Martha very seriously.

"What a waste," he said. "If you go, I mean. But I'm full of admiration for you. Well done. I thought of going into politics myself once, you know."

"Really? Why didn't you?"

"Mostly because I couldn't face the considerable loss of income. Anyway"—he walked over to the fridge set into one of the tall cupboards that lined his walls—"I think your success thus far should be celebrated. Champagne?" She was so astonished by the whole encounter that she could hardly swallow the glass of extraordinarily good Krug that he poured for her.

●●●

"No," said Jocasta. "No, no, no, Carla. You can't. You are not even to try to, OK?"

"But Jocasta, why not? She's *gorgeous*. Beautiful. Please. I'll take you to Babington House for the weekend. I'll buy you dinner at Daphne's. I'll let you borrow my Chanel jacket—"

"No," said Jocasta.

"But I'm not going to sell her into white slavery, for God's sake. I'm just going to put some clothes on her and take some pictures. Who is she, anyway?"

"I'm not going to tell you. She's just a girl I've met."

"She seemed rather young to be a friend."

"Don't be so rude," said Jocasta.

"Well, darling, it's you who's always going on about your wrinkles. Actually, she looked a bit like you—she could have been your younger sister."

"Yeah, right," said Jocasta, and then: "Funny, Sim said that as well. Oh shit." She stared at Carla and prayed she hadn't taken in what she had said. Her prayers were not answered.

"Sim? Sim Jenkins the staff photographer? Jocasta, has this girl got anything to do with that story about the old woman on the hospital trolley? She's not the granddaughter, is she?"

"No," said Jocasta firmly.

"I'm sure she is." Carla's vast brown eyes were amused.

"Yes, all right, she is. But her parents are very protective of her, they didn't want her even in that shot, and anyway, she's not sixteen yet."

"Why are they so against it?"

"I suppose they mistrust newspapers. Quite right too. He's a teacher and she's a full-time mum, they're real innocents abroad. So you are not to do anything, Carla. Absolutely not to. We're talking important things like people's lives here. Not just some cruddy fashion pages."

"I don't do cruddy pages," said Carla with dignity.

"Anyway, I must go," said Jocasta, standing up, pulling her tape recorder out of her drawer. "I've got to interview this girl—woman—I used to know. Well, I didn't know her really; I travelled with her for a few days when we were eighteen."

She was feeling edgy, nervous; she told herself it was because this interview was important, but she knew it was nothing of the sort. Gideon Keeble had phoned her that morning, asked her if she would like to take him up on his invitation to stay with him in Ireland.

"I'm here for a few days and my doctor has told me to rest."

"Gideon, you're not ill, are you?"

"No, no, just a little tired. Now I'm not compromising you, of course. It's the pair of you I'm after, you and your lovely boyfriend."

"You sound much more Irish than usual," she said laughing. "Is that how you talk when you're over there?"

"Maybe. What do you say? Could you consider it, even? Just a few days, around this weekend."

Jocasta considered it. The very idea of spending any time at all in Ireland, under the same roof as Gideon Keeble, excited her. That he wanted to spend time with her—and Nick, of course—was amazingly flattering. And she did find Gideon horribly attractive. It wasn't just the aura that all powerful men trail around with them—when he looked at her, with those amazing blue eyes of his, she wanted to get into bed with him. At once. Without further ado. And she was sure he recognised it.

God, she wanted to go, wanted to say yes. But Nick was away. For the weekend. So what should she do? And more important, what should she say?

"Nick's away for the weekend," she said. Leaving it up to him.

"Then," he said, and she could feel him refusing to do it for her, "Jocasta, it is entirely up to you. But I would love to see you."

And knowing with absolute certainty that if she went, she would never see Nick again, and summoning up every shred of willpower (weakened considerably by the image of Gideon, the sound of his voice), she said, very quickly and before she could change her mind, that she thought it would be better not.

"A pity," he said. "But you know, I have to tell you, Jocasta, that I am encouraged by your refusal."

"Why?" she said laughing.

"Well, if you had said you would come, I would have assumed you saw me as a nice old gentleman who would not disturb your relationship or trouble you in any way. And I think we both suspect that is not the case. Goodbye, Jocasta. Thank you for considering it."

She put the phone down and had to take several deep breaths before she could even stand up.

·••·

"I told her. I told her everything. And she's going to see what she can do. She was great."

"Told you."

It had been Sarah's idea: for Kate to talk to Jocasta, tell her everything, get her to write about it, so that her mother could get in touch with her. Since the detective agency idea had never got off the ground. "And do your mum and dad know?"

Kate looked discomfited. "No. Jocasta did say I should talk to them some more. She said she wouldn't like to do anything until she was sure they were happy."

"Oh I wouldn't take any notice of that," said Sarah. "She's a journalist and they'll do anything for a good story. Honestly, Kate, if she wants to write about you, she will. She won't wait for you to ask your mum."

"I . . . think she will," said Kate. Her heart was beating a little faster than usual.

"Kate, she won't. Anyway, what's it matter? I thought that's why you told her in the first place."

"Yes, it was. But, well, in the end, I think I would want to talk to Mum about it. It would be awful not to. She'd be really upset. Jocasta said that as well," she added.

"But, Kate, that's the whole point, isn't it? Your mum would never agree."

"She might," said Kate. She was beginning to wish she had never had the conversation with Jocasta. "Anyway," she said, slightly aggressively, "she said she wouldn't do anything in a hurry."

"I thought you were in a hurry."

"Oh for God's sake!" Kate was getting irritable. "Look, it's up to Jocasta, OK? Not my parents."

"That's what I just said. Course it is. Crikey, Kate! Do you realise, you might even find out who your real father is, as well?"

"Yes," said Kate, "I thought of that. How he must be a complete arsehole."

"Most men are," said Sarah knowledgeably.

"Hi." Kate, waiting for her bus, looked up from her *Heat* magazine. Nat Tucker stood in front of her. He had his black hair cut very short and was wearing baggy combats and a white sleeveless T-shirt. He looked fantastic. Why did it have to be today, here, with her in her school uniform? Thank God she'd taken her tie off.

"Hi," she said, pulling her headphones out of her ears.

"You all right?" he said.

"Yeah. Yeah, cool thanks."

"Still at school?"

"Yeah. Doing my exams, aren't I?"

"S'pose so. Want a lift home?"

She swallowed hard, simply to delay her answer, not sound too eager. "Well, maybe. Yeah. Thanks."

"Car's round here." He jerked his elbow in the direction of a side road, started walking. Kate followed him. This was amazing. A-mazing.

"You've got a new car," she said, looking at it admiringly.

"Yeah. It's a Citroën. Citroën Sax Bomb."

"Great," said Kate carefully.

"My dad got it into the workshop, let me do it up. Like the spoiler?"

"Course."

"I lowered the suspension seventy mill all round. Looks better, don't it?"

"Yeah."

"It'll be lower when I've finished with it. It does hundred and eleven," he said, with an attempt at nonchalance. "I upgraded the ignition and that. And the sound's great."

"So—your dad let you have it for nothing?"

"No," he said indignantly, "I have to work for him, don't I? Well, get in. Here, give us your bag."

He threw her school bag into the boot, and got in beside her, switched on the stereo. The street was filled with the thumping, punching rhythms of So Solid Crew. He started the engine, pulled away with a loud screech, dangerously close to the kerb. A middle-aged woman jumped back, scowling at him, shouted something; he grinned widely at Kate.

"Can't see for looking, can they, those grannies. So, what you going to do next? After the exams I mean?"

"Oh, don't know. Go to college I suppose."

"What?" His voice was incredulous. "You get out of school and go straight back in again?"

"Yes. I want to do A levels."

"Yeah? What for?"

"Well . . . to go to uni."

"What for?" he said, clearly genuinely puzzled. "I haven't got any GCSEs even, and I got a good job, plenty of dosh."

"Yeah, but Nat, I can't go and work for my dad like you. I want to work for a newspaper or a magazine, something like that."

"What, as a model or something?"

"No. A writer. Why should I be a model?" she said, stretching out her legs, surreptitiously easing her skirt a little higher.

"Well you've got the looks and that. Make a lot of money that way, you could." Kate was silent; this was beyond her wildest dreams. "Where d'you want to go?" he asked.

"Franklin Avenue, please."

"How's Sarah?" he said.

"She's OK." He nodded. That's why he wanted to talk to me, she thought, he wants to know about Sarah. Sarah was more his type: dark, small, loud. Kate tried to be as lippy with boys as Sarah was, but she never could quite manage it.

"She still at school?"

"Yeah. Then she's going to go full-time at the salon. The one where she's a Saturday girl."

"What, she's going to be a hairdresser?" he asked and his face was incredulous, as if Kate had said Sarah was planning on entering a convent. "How sad is that?"

"What's sad about hairdressing?" said Kate defensively. "She likes it."

"It's a sad job," he said, "running around old women all day, asking them if what they've done is all right, would they like a magazine to read, all that crap. My mum's one and I used to go and see her after school when I was younger. Awful job."

"Sarah likes it. She gets good tips."

"Yeah?" He didn't seem very interested in Sarah anymore. Kate's heart lifted; maybe he'd just been making polite conversation. Not that it was really his style.

"Well, here we are," he said, turning into her road, pulling up with a screech of brakes. He left the stereo running; she could see her grandmother looking out of the window. God. Suppose she came out, asked to be introduced to him.

"I must go," she said. "Thanks for the lift."

"Want to come out Saturday?" he asked. He was looking at her legs as she swung them sideways out of the car.

"With you?" she said. And then realised how stupid she must sound.

"Yeah. Clubbing over Brixton."

Kate felt herself starting to blush with excitement. This was unbelievable. Nat Tucker was asking her out.

She managed to wait a moment, then said, "Yeah, thanks." Her voice sounded astonishingly level.

"I'll pick you up. Nine-ish. OK?"

"Yeah. OK."

The effort of keeping her face expressionless, her voice level and disinterested, was so immense she found it hard to breathe. She was halfway up the path when he called her.

"Don't you want yer bag?"

"Oh. Oh yeah. Thanks."

He got out of the car, pulled it out of the boot, slung it over the gate. "Cheers. See you later."

Kate was incapable of further speech.

•◆•

"Martha? Hi, I'm Jocasta."

"I think I'd have known that," said Martha. She smiled, a charming, courteous smile. "You look just the same. Do come in."

"I'm afraid I don't look just the same." Jocasta walked into the apartment. It was quite simply stunning. A mass of ash-blond wood flooring, white walls, huge windows, and a minimal amount of black-and-chrome furniture. "This is gorgeous," she said.

"Thank you. I like it. And it's near to my work."

Martha was gorgeous too, in a cool, careful way. Very slim, wearing dark grey trousers and a cream silk shirt; her skin was creamy too, and almost makeup-less, with just some eye shadow and mascara and a beige-brown lipstick. Her hair, brown, straight, shining hair, streaked with ash, was cut into a neat, sleek bob.

"Which is where?" Jocasta asked. "Your work, I mean?"

"Oh, just over there." Martha waved rather vaguely down at the world below her.

"Yes, but what's it called, what do you exactly do?"

"I'm a partner with a city law firm. At the moment." She ignored the request for the name.

"Oh, OK. Fun?"

"Not exactly fun. I like it though. Can I offer you a coffee or something?"

"Yes, that'd be great."

"Fine. Just excuse me a moment. Make yourself at home. Do you need a table or anything to write on?"

"No, thanks, it's fine."

She disappeared. Snooty cow, thought Jocasta; and thought of that other Martha, slightly nervous, eager to be friends, mildly defensive about her background. She had been so polite, so eager to please. What had changed her so much? Clio had hardly changed at all.

And she had been fun. Undoubtedly fun. The very first night in

· 226 ·

Bangkok, they'd huddled together in one bed, the three of them, screaming at the cockroaches that had appeared when they put the light on, and then she'd pulled a bottle of wine from her bag and they'd shared it, drinking from the bottle, giggling and shaking at the same time.

"Right. Here we are." She appeared again, with a dark wooden tray, set with white cups, a cafetiere, milk jug, a bowl of both brown and white sugar lumps. Jocasta almost expected her to put a bill down on the table in front of her. She was very still, Jocasta noticed, still and totally self-controlled. She was also, clearly, very nervous. It seemed strange, when she was so patently self-confident. Well, that was what interviews were all about. Finding out.

"Tell me," Martha said, "what's your brother doing? Is he a barrister?"

"God no," said Jocasta, "much too much like hard work. He works for the family company. He's married—just about. Got two little girls." She smiled at Martha. "So you went to Bristol Uni, did you?"

"Yes, I did."

"And did you like it?"

"Yes, very much. Look, is this part of the interview? Because I did say—"

"Martha," said Jocasta as patiently as she could, "I'm just playing catch-up. I'll tell you all about me if you like. And Clio."

Martha visibly seized on this. "How is Clio?"

"Not very happy," said Jocasta. "She's getting divorced. She's doing well at her job, though."

"That's so sad. About her divorce I mean. Have you met the husband?"

"No. He sounds like an arsehole." She smiled expansively at Martha. "He's a surgeon. Arrogant. Totally up himself. She's better off without him. Mind you, I did upset him."

"I thought you hadn't met him?"

"I didn't. But I wrote about his hospital. Long story. Anyway, he didn't like it."

"I don't suppose he did," said Martha. She picked up her cup of black coffee. Her hand was shaking slightly, Jocasta noticed. Her small, beautifully manicured hand.

"But she's just the same, dear little Clio—remember how we started calling her that, on the second day in Bangkok?"

"No, I don't think I do," said Martha. She was clearly going to block any attempt at reminiscence.

"Anyway, did you do what you said, do Oz, and end up in New York?"

"You have an amazing memory," said Martha, and there was a silence. Then she said, "Oz, certainly. I didn't see much of the States. Look, Jocasta, I don't want to be rude, but I don't have an awful lot of time. So maybe we should start."

"Of course. Fine. Let's start with a few basic facts: your age, what you do, how you got drawn into politics, all that stuff. Then we can do some details. It's a very good story, I think."

She watched Martha slowly relaxing, growing in confidence as she took control, presented what was obviously a carefully rehearsed story. And it was a good one, from a spin point of view: the death of the office cleaner, her longing to do something to help, to change things, her growing involvement with Centre Forward, her returning to her roots.

Jocasta listened politely, asking questions about Centre Forward, about the number of MPs they had, how many they hoped to field for the general election; went on to some incredibly boring stuff about the election process. And then began to move, very stealthily, in. What she had so far wasn't going to make her the next Lynda Lee-Potter.

"You're obviously doing awfully well at your firm," she said. "Won't you miss it?"

"Yes, but I think it'll be worth it if I can make a difference, even quite a small one."

"I meant the trappings?"

"I'm sorry?"

"Well, this flat obviously didn't come cheap. And you clearly like nice clothes—I know a pair of Jimmy Choos when I see them. And a Gucci bag, come to that."

"Jocasta, I don't think this is relevant." She was looking edgy again, fiddling with one of her earrings.

"Of course it is. You must care an awful lot to give it all up. I think that's great."

"Well"—she relaxed a little—"as I told you, it'd be nice to be able to make a difference. And Gucci bags don't exactly melt, do they? I just won't be able to have the latest models anymore. If I get in, that is."

"You'll be doing a lot of driving up and down to Suffolk, won't you?"

"Quite a bit. Every weekend."

"And what about your personal life?"

"My what?" She had flushed scarlet. "Jocasta—"

"You'll be moving down to Binsmow. I just thought if there's a man in your life, he might not like that. It's a pretty radical step. Or does he live down there?"

"No. I mean, I don't have a man in my life. Not—not an important one. Just a few good friends."

"That's lucky. Or maybe it isn't."

"I'm sorry, I don't know what you mean—"

"I mean, it may be lucky for your political plans, but wouldn't you like to have someone?"

"I really don't want to comment on that."

"Oh, OK. Well, from what you've seen of it, is politics really very sexy?"

"I don't quite know what you mean—"

"Oh, Martha, come on, all that power, all those secrets, husbands living away from home, nubile secretaries and researchers at every corner. I find it very sexy, and I'm only on the edges of it!"

"Perhaps that's why," said Martha coolly. "I can only tell you I have no personal experience of that kind of thing."

Jocasta gave up. "I remember you being rather shy. When we first met. So how different are you today from the young Martha? The one I went travelling with?"

"Jocasta," said Martha, "I don't want to go into all that."

"But why not? I really don't understand. It's such a sweet story. Three little girls from school, meeting by chance, setting off round the world, and then meeting up again all these years later, all of us quite successful—no, it's too good not to use, Martha."

"I don't want it used."

"Honestly, I'm sorry, but there's no reason not to. It's not unsavoury or anything, it just makes you sound more colourful and interesting."

"Look, I said right at the beginning I didn't want this to be a personal article."

"Did you do a lot of drugs or something?" said Jocasta. She was growing curious now. "Because naturally I wouldn't mention anything like that."

"Of course I didn't do a lot of drugs!"

"Well, I did," Jocasta said cheerfully. "And I got ill as well. Horribly ill. Dengue fever. You never had anything like that? Never had to go to one of their hospitals?"

"No. I—I didn't stay long in Thailand at all, I went off to Sydney."

"When was that?"

"What?"

"I said when did you go to Sydney? Don't look so scared, I just wondered. I was there in the January."

"I'm really not very sure. It's so long ago. Jocasta—"

"And then did you go up to Cairns? And the rain forest?"

"Yes, for a bit. It was wonderful."

"And you really didn't feel that year changed you much? It didn't affect what you might now call your political philosophy?"

"No," said Martha firmly, "no, it didn't. I'm afraid I really do have to go in a minute, Jocasta—"

"So what is your political philosophy? Could you encapsulate it for me?"

She was caught unawares by this sudden return to safe ground. "Well, yes. It's that people, all people, ought to be given a chance. Lots of chances. Good education, decent health care, reasonable living conditions. No one should be written off, abandoned to his or her fate."

"That's really nice," said Jocasta, smiling at her sweetly. "I like that. Thank you so much, Martha, you've been great. I can do a nice piece about this and I'm sure Chad will be very pleased."

"Can I—can I see the piece? Before it's published?"

"I'm sorry, we can't do that. The editor doesn't allow it."

"Why not?"

"Well, just think about it. If everyone we wrote about every day had to read their copy, and maybe change it, then it had to be rejigged and shown to them again, we'd never get the paper to bed at all."

"I would have thought this was slightly different," said Martha, her voice very crisp now. "It's not a news story, it doesn't have to be rushed to . . . to bed as you call it."

"You're wrong there, I'm afraid. This is scheduled for the Saturday magazine section, and that goes to press tomorrow. Sorry."

"Jocasta, I really would like to read it," said Martha and there was an underlying anxiety in her voice. "You could e-mail it to me and I'd e-mail it right back."

"Honestly. It would be more than my job was worth. You can ask Nick, if you don't believe me."

"I think it's rather different in his case. He's writing about politicians, news stories—"

"Well, you're a politician. Surely. And this is a news story. You've only just been elected—"

"Selected," said Martha. "You see, it's so important to get these things right. Please, Jocasta."

Why was she so worried? It was odd. Jocasta raked back over the interview; she hadn't said anything that could be remotely misconstrued. She'd been minimal with most of her information. In fact, it was going to be a pretty dull piece. She actually felt rather worried about it.

"I can only tell you," she said, "that you have absolutely nothing to worry about. You've been the soul of discretion, Martha—you're going to come out of this squeaky clean."

"I don't know why you should say that," she said and there was a spot of high colour on her cheeks now. "Why on earth shouldn't I come out squeaky clean, as you put it? Are you implying—" She stopped, visibly took a deep breath. "I hope you're not going to imply the reverse."

"Of course I'm not! Calm down."

"I'm perfectly calm. Sorry. It's just that you—well, this is a new game for me."

"Of course. But—"

Martha's mobile rang; she answered it at once. "Hi," she said, her face immobile. "Yes, I know, but I've been very busy. What? No, I'm looking forward to it. Yes, about eight. I can't talk now. I'll see you later. Sorry, Jocasta," she said.

"That's OK. Martha, when did you get back?"

"When did I get back? Where from?"

"From travelling," said Jocasta patiently. "I just wondered if you did anything between getting back and going to uni."

"Of course not," said Martha and she suddenly sounded almost angry. "How could I have? There was no time."

"But—"

"Excuse me," she said suddenly, "I've just remembered something." She stood up and walked, very quickly, out of the room—and that was what did it for Jocasta. Turned over the memory: one that she had long ago decided was not a memory at all, but a mistake, a case of totally mistaken identity, made as she was pushed and jostled in a swarming, stinking street. She sat and turned it over, that memory, reviving it, breathing life into it and waiting for Martha to return.

She was quite a long time; Jocasta heard the loo flush, and then a tap running. When Martha came back in, she had renewed her lipstick, and clearly resprayed her perfume.

"Sorry about that," she said. "I just remembered I had to check an e-mail."

"That's all right," said Jocasta. "Well, I must go. And I promise you faithfully the article will be nothing but positive about you. You and the party."

"Thank you. Right. Well, I'll have to trust you."

"Yes, you will. Now, what we must have is a nice picture of you. Chad gave me the one that was on your leaflet, but it looked a bit dire to me. Would you mind if we took one? It wouldn't take a minute to do—our chaps are really quick. Someone could come to your office even—"

"Absolutely not. I have back-to-back meetings for the next two days."

"Oh, all right," said Jocasta with a sigh, "we'll use the one Chad gave me. Well, bye, Martha. And we must have a threesome one evening, you and me and Clio. Such a shame we all lost touch. We've missed so much out of one another's lives. Still—we've found each other now." She walked to the door, picked up her jacket, and smiled at Martha. "Please don't worry about the piece."

She saw her relax. "I won't," she said, and smiled back. For the first time she looked more friendly, less aggressive. Jocasta took a deep breath. This was the moment.

"I just remembered something," she said. "Off the record—don't look so scared. You didn't go back to Bangkok, did you? That year? In—let me see—yes, in late June?"

The smile went completely. Martha looked—what did she look? Angry? Frightened? No, worse than that, terrified. Trapped. As she had looked that day. And then angry.

"Go back? Of course not. I told you, I went to the States—I went home from there—"

"I must have been mistaken then," said Jocasta, her voice at its sweetest. "I thought it was unlikely. But I thought I saw you there. I went back

· 232 ·

that way, you see. It was outside the station, Bangkok station. I called your name. Quite loudly, but whoever it was just walked away, disappeared."

"Well, I expect she did," said Martha. "If her name wasn't Martha."

Of course it had been Martha. Jocasta knew in that moment as certainly as she knew anything. And Martha knew she knew.

So why was she lying about it?

Chapter 19
. . . . .

Kate couldn't ever remember being so angry. How could they do this to her, how dare they? The most important thing in her whole life and they were wrecking it for her.

"I just don't believe this," she kept saying, "I just don't believe you're doing this to me."

"We're not doing anything to you, Kate," Helen said, "except trying to look after you."

"Oh right. So you do that by not letting me go out for a few hours with my friends?"

"Kate, we're not talking about your going out for a few hours with your friends," said Jim. "You've just told us you're going to a club in one of the most crime-ridden neighbourhoods in London with some layabout—"

"Jim," said Helen warningly. But it was too late.

"He is not a layabout!" shouted Kate. "He works for a living. You know? Earns money, does a job. That sort of thing. And what do you know about Brixton?"

"It's very—very rough," said Helen.

"What you mean is it's got a lot of black people there. You don't know any more about it than that. You're racist, as well as everything else."

"Kate!"

"The whole point about clubs in Brixton is they're cool. Sarah's been there lots of times. Dad, what do you think's going to happen to me, for God's sake? That I'll take some Ecstasy and die? That I'll be beaten up? End up on the streets? I'm going with Nat. He'll look after me."

"No," said Jim. "You are not going with anybody, and that's my last word."

Kate glared at him, then said, "I cannot believe you are so pathetically ignorant," and left the room. Very shortly the familiar thud of her music filled the house.

Jim looked at Helen. "You do agree with me, don't you?" he said.

"Of course I do. It's a terrible place, soaring crime rate—and she's still a child. Oh, hello, Mummy."

"What was that all about?"

"Kate wants to go clubbing in Brixton," said Helen reluctantly.

She knew what her mother's reaction would be. "Oh really? And you won't let her, I suppose?"

"Of course not."

Jilly sighed, put down the silver-topped cane she had taken to using, rather than a walking stick, and sat down.

"My mother forbade me to go to a club called the Blue Angel. It was considered very racy in its day—there was a wonderful black pianist there called Hutch who was supposed to have had an affair with the Duchess of Kent. Anyway, I went there about a year later and of course it was really quite all right, and I had a wonderful time. All that happened was that I decided my mother was rather foolish and lost some of my respect for her."

"Mummy, I don't think clubs in Brixton quite compare with the Blue Angel. It's you who's being foolish."

"These things are all relative. Anyway, who does she want to go with?"

"Some dreadful boy who's going to drive her there in his car."

"Not the one who brought her home from school the other day?" said Jilly. "He's frightfully good-looking. I can see why she wants to go out with him. I'd go myself if I could. Maybe that would be the answer," she added, "I could chaperone her. It would be fun!"

"Oh, Mummy, really!" said Helen wearily. Her mother was going home in a few days' time and she couldn't help looking forward to it.

Jilly heard Kate come downstairs when everyone else had gone to bed. She heaved herself out of her bed in the dining room and went into the kitchen; Kate was making a cup of tea.

"Hello, darling. Make one for me, would you? I'm sorry about your date with your young man."

Kate turned a swollen face to her. "Oh Gran," she said, "what am I going to tell him? That's the worst thing, thinking of something that doesn't sound totally sad."

"Maybe I can help," said Jilly. "I've always been very good at lies."

They came up with the best they could manage: that Jilly was going home that weekend and Helen had insisted Kate went too, to look after her. Kate rang Nat and struggled with this, but she could tell he wasn't impressed.

"Can't you tell them you won't? That you're coming out with me?"

"Not really," said Kate sadly.

"OK. Fine. See you around." His phone went dead. Kate went upstairs and cried.

She was walking down the street with Bernie next day, when there was a screaming of brakes and thumping of music; it was Nat in his Sax Bomb.

"Hi," he said.

"Hi."

"You want to come out Sat'dy, then, Bern?"

"I might. Where you going?"

"Brixton."

"Yeah. OK. Cool."

"Cheers. See you later."

He ignored Kate. The effort of looking disinterested was so great, she felt it as a physical pain. Especially when Bernie got out her mobile and rang about a dozen people and told them. How was she ever going to live this down? Everybody, absolutely everybody, would think she was so sad.

•◆•

Chris Pollock came storming across the newsroom and threw Jocasta's copy onto her desk.

"What the fuck do you think this is? If it's your idea of a profile, Jocasta, you'd better go and find another paper to put it in. I'm not printing this crap. It's dull, it's uninformative, it's got no life—"

"Bit like the subject," said Jocasta under her breath.

"What's that?"

"Nothing. No. I'm sorry, Chris. I didn't think much of it myself. To be honest."

"Well, what the fuck did you turn it in for then? And this picture. I mean, give me strength! I'm not running this unless you can get more out of her, or give it a decent angle. Preferably both. Anyway, I can't waste any more time on it now, I've got to fill the fucking space somehow. Jesus wept!"

He walked off, shouting across the room at the picture desk as he went; Carla came out of her office.

"What was that about?"

Jocasta told her; Carla looked at her thoughtfully.

"Show me the picture."

"Here. She's about a thousand times better looking than that. Great figure too."

"Well, darling, we're looking at the answer, aren't we? She can be my fashion feature next week. It's a great story. We can dress her for her new life. Then your copy won't matter."

"Thanks," said Jocasta.

"No, honestly, darling, it's a great idea. Let me talk to Chris, then you can ring the bitch."

"I don't know that she'll agree," said Jocasta.

"Of course she will. It's what she wants, from everything you've told me about her. Publicity without pain."

Carla was right. It was exactly what Martha wanted. It was safer, less intrusive. And it would give her a chance, maybe, to see the copy. Jocasta sounded nervous, anxious even for her to agree. That would give her a lever too.

"Yes, I think that would be all right. I'd quite like that, I think, as long as it could be done at the end of the day."

"Oh, Martha, I'm sure it could." Jocasta's voice was light with relief.

"Especially if it meant I could maybe see the copy. I mean clearly, there's time now."

"Well—yes. Yes, I'm sure you could. See my draft anyway. Right. I'll tell Carla and she'll probably contact you direct. She's called Carla Giannini—she's really nice. Thank you so much, Martha."

"And then he said"—Jocasta paused, refilled her glass for the third time in twenty minutes—"I'd better find another paper to put the story in. I mean, it wasn't that bad. I can't believe it. My big chance and I've bloody well blown it. It's not fair, it really isn't. Well, is it? Nick?"

"I don't think you can say it's not fair. The thing is, sweetie, you turned in a bad piece. By your own admission."

"It wasn't bad," said Jocasta. "It just wasn't great."

"And that's no good. You write a big piece, it has to be great. Simple as that."

"Thanks," said Jocasta, glaring at him. "I thought I might get a bit of comfort and . . . and reassurance from you, not a lecture on journalistic standards. You're supposed to be on my side, or so I thought—"

"I *am* on your side. That's not the same thing as trying to discuss the situation properly."

"Oh really? You could have fooled me. I've been waiting around for days to see you, and you were away for the weekend with your bloody mother—again. Two weekends in a row you've been up there."

"For two good reasons. Rupert's birthday and then Mummy and Pa's anniversary. Anyway, you were invited. And actually, I found it quite difficult, explaining why you couldn't come for a second time."

So this was what she got for turning down a weekend with Gideon Keeble, resisting the temptation of a lifetime.

"Oh, well, I'm so sorry, Nick. Sorry I make your life difficult. It's just that sitting around in a freezing dining room, while everyone talks about the hunt ball and who's going salmon fishing, isn't quite my idea of fun."

"Jocasta, you're being very unpleasant. It's not like you."

"I feel unpleasant. You're not being very nice either, saying I shouldn't file lousy pieces."

"I said nothing of the sort. Don't be so absurd."

"Oh for God's sake," said Jocasta, "why don't you just go away? Back to Mummy, maybe. I'm sure you'd rather!"

"Jocasta, please." He smiled at her. "You're being so ridiculous. Come here, let me give you a hug."

"I don't want a hug," she said, and to her horror, she started to cry. "I want you to support me properly. I want you to be there for me, when I need you."

"I *am* there for you."

"Nick, you so are not! You just go on your own sweet way, doing exactly what you please, working all the hours of the day and night, seeing your friends, going home to Mummy, and coming round here when you feel in need of a fuck!"

"That's a filthy thing to say!"

"It's true. And I'm sick of it. If you really cared about me, you'd have made some sort of commitment by now—"

"Oh, so that's what this is all about. The fact I haven't gone down on one knee and put a ring on your finger."

"No. Not entirely. But—"

"Jocasta, I've told you over and over again. I'm sorry. I would if I could. But I don't feel—"

"You don't feel ready. And when do you think you might? When you're forty? Fifty? I'm absolutely sick of the whole thing, Nick, I really am. I feel so . . . so unimportant to you."

"Well, I'm sorry to hear that," he said, picking up his car keys.

"Where are you going?"

"I'm going home. I'm not going to listen to any more of this."

"Good!"

And he walked out, not slamming the door, as she would have done, but shutting it very slowly and carefully behind him. Jocasta picked up a heavy glass ashtray and hurled it at the door. It gouged out a chunk of wood before falling onto the tiled floor and shattering. She was standing there, staring at it, when her mobile rang. She looked to see who it was: Chris Pollock. Now what had she done?

"Jocasta? I want you on a plane to Dublin. Tonight if you can manage it. Gideon Keeble's daughter's run away from school with a rock star. You know Keeble. Don't come back till you've got the full story, OK? I don't want a repetition of that fuck-up with Martha whatshername."

"There won't be," said Jocasta.

•→•

It was one of the longest days she could ever remember. And the most miserable. Almost worse than when they'd first said she couldn't go.

It never stopped all day: Bernie going on and on about what a great time she'd had with Nat, how he'd driven her to Brixton in the Sax Bomb, how he'd looked so fit in his combats and vest, how he could really dance, and how they'd been there till five in the morning and then—at this point the story was repeated in a whisper into various ears, amidst wild shrieks and giggles. Even Sarah couldn't resist it, although she tried for a while for Kate's sake. "Sorry," she said to Kate afterwards. Kate shrugged and said she couldn't care less, and Bernie was welcome to him as far as she was concerned. By the time she got home she was beside herself with rage and resentment; even her grandmother's tactful questioning infuriated her.

"They all had a great time, Gran, and I didn't, OK?"

She went up to her room, turned on the radio, and lay down on her bed. It was so unfair. So totally unfair. Everything was shit. He'd never ask her out again, not now. She was branded as a poor sad creature still under the thumb of her parents. She hated everyone. She hated her parents, she hated Juliet, even now earnestly practising her violin, she even nearly hated her grandmother, fussing about, talking in her posh voice, pretending she understood, telling her about some crap place she hadn't been allowed to visit when she was what she called a girl.

Nobody was on her side, even Sarah was deserting her now, and she was no nearer finding her mother. And Jocasta seemed to have forgotten about her; it was two weeks since they'd had lunch and she hadn't heard a word.

Suddenly angry with Jocasta as well, she decided to ring her. She shouldn't have agreed to see her if she wasn't going to help. She dialled Jocasta's mobile. It seemed to be switched off. Funny, she'd told Kate it was her most precious possession, that she couldn't do her job without it; maybe it was out of range. Or maybe she was at the paper. She could try there.

Endless ringing; on and on it went without being answered. Obviously she was away on a story. Bloody typical, Kate thought, just her luck. She was about to ring off, when a voice said, "Hello, Jocasta's phone."

"Oh, hi," said Kate, nervous suddenly. "Is . . . is she there?"

"No, I'm sorry. She's away for a few days." It was a nice voice, slightly foreign, quite deep.

"Oh. OK. Well, sorry to bother you."

"Can I take a message?"

"Um . . . no. No, it's OK. I'll ring again. Could you tell her Kate rang."

"Kate? Is that Kate Moss?"

"I wish," said Kate.

"Sorry. You sound a bit like her. Well, like her when she was younger anyway. So, Kate who?"

"Kate Tarrant."

There was a brief but quite noticeable silence, then the voice said, "The girl with the granny? At the hospital?"

"Yeah."

"How is your grandmother now?"

"Oh, she's fine, thanks."

"Good. Yes, I think I saw you the other day, having lunch with Jocasta at the Bluebird. Would that have been you? Long blond hair?"

"Yes, that's me," said Kate.

Then the voice said, "You know, I wanted to meet you. I told Jocasta I thought you could perhaps be in one of my fashion features. My name is Carla Giannini, I'm the fashion editor of the *Sketch*."

"You did?" Kate's heart began to pound. "Do you really think that?"

"I think you might photograph very well. I couldn't say, until I've done a few test shots. But I think it's more than possible. You should come in and see me one day. It would be nice to meet you, anyway, such a brave young girl, taking on the NHS single-handed!" She laughed, a throaty, husky laugh. Kate felt dizzy.

"Do you mean that? That I should come and see you?"

"Of course. Look, think about it and give me a ring. Maybe tomorrow? I'll give you my direct line."

Wow. WOW! Cool, or what? God. That would change Nat's mind about her being sad. A model. In the newspapers. Wow. Oh—my—God.

Kate called Sarah.

"I've got to go somewhere tomorrow. After school. I don't want to tell my mum. Will you say I'm with you, if she calls?"

"Course. Where are you going?"

"I'll tell you about it when I get back, OK?"

"Cool. See you later."

Kate went downstairs singing.

Carla put the phone down and smiled. Good. Very good. She had no doubt Kate would be in to see her. Jocasta wouldn't like it, but that was too bad. She had no claim on Kate. And Carla had pages to fill.

She'd actually quite enjoyed doing the shoot with Martha Hartley. She hadn't been nearly as bad as Jocasta had made out. A bit . . . reserved.

But she was a lawyer. And she was certainly very attractive, and she wore the clothes—a suit, a jacket, and an evening dress all from Zara—very well. Jocasta not being there had obviously helped; far from being bothered by her absence, Carla had been relieved. It was always easier with these shoots if she could have the subject to herself. As she would have Kate, with luck. Jocasta had called to say she was going to be away for at least two more days.

Half an hour later, as Carla had known she would, Kate called her. Would it be all right if she came in after school the next day—"I could be there about five, five thirty."

Carla said that would be perfectly all right and put in a call to Marc Jones, a sexy young photographer she had used for the first time the week before, to ask him to come in to do some test shots of Kate.

◆─◆

Jocasta stood at the gates of Gideon Keeble's glorious house and waited, along with roughly two dozen other reporters, a large clutch of photographers, cameramen, and the policeman who was on duty. She had been waiting for some time now, about twelve hours; it was the first crucial thing you learnt as a reporter (or a photographer) to do. Nobody exactly enjoyed it, but nobody minded either; there was great camaraderie, time passed, people shared cigarettes and chocolate and swapped reminiscences and such scraps of news as they possessed. Generosity was, in fact, the name of the game, unless someone actually managed to get a huge scoop or an exclusive. That was not expected to be shared.

Dungarven House was on the top of a hill; every so often, someone would go up to the locked gates and peer through them, which was fairly fruitless, since the drive curved away to the right of the two lodges, and there was nothing to be seen except a tall beech hedge and, to the left of it, a thick wood. Gideon Keeble was certainly inside; he had been driven in the night before, looking very grim, and the gates had not been opened since. A local reporter had assured them there was no other vehicle access to the estate and an enterprising reporter, unwilling to accept his word, had skirted the entire area by bicycle, and reported only several small gates in the twelve-foot wall that surrounded it, which were locked with huge padlocks, with nothing more than rough tracks leading up to them. The southernmost tip of the estate was bounded by the famous lake, which was impassable from the other side, except by boat. Dungarven House was almost a fortress.

Of course Mr. Keeble might have sailed across the lake, but had he done so, he would have a long walk to any road. Their radios told them hourly that Fionnuala Keeble, the beautiful fifteen-year-old daughter of retailing billionaire Gideon Keeble, had run away from her convent school with rock musician Zebedee and still had not been found. Police were watching ports and airports but there had been no sightings of her, so it was presumed she must still be in the country. Her mother, now Lady Carlingford, was on her way back from Barbados where she lived and was not available for comment. It was generally agreed that if Fionnuala was found, she would be returned to her father at Dungarven House.

Jocasta spent quite a few of those twelve hours trying to get hold of Gideon's private number; but the charming, easy, hospitable Gideon Keeble, who had called her direct on her mobile, had done so from a number which told her politely now that Mr. Keeble was not available and to try later; there was no facility even to leave a message. The same applied to all his office numbers. His e-mail address was equally elusive; the one everyone had was at his London office and although she had sent what she thought was an irresistible appeal, it had yielded nothing. Well, she didn't blame him. She'd felt pretty shitty even asking.

She returned every so often to her hire car, which was parked a quarter of a mile or so down the lane, to check her e-mails, and as darkness fell on the Cork countryside, and the shadows of the great trees surrounding Dungarven House deepened, could only try to imagine what fear and anger Gideon Keeble must be experiencing over the disappearance of his beloved only daughter.

She looked at her screen as she typed her thoughts and sighed. That wasn't going to redeem her in Chris Pollock's eyes. Give me a break, she said, looking up at the half-moon in the soft dusk sky, please, please give me a break.

She pulled a second sweater on; it was getting very chilly. Most of them had agreed that they would give things until ten and then go and book into the pub. Jocasta was unwilling to do that. With the run of bad luck she seemed to be having, Fionnuala and Zebedee would arrive naked, astride a white horse, the minute she'd left the gates. She had already decided to sleep in her car.

God, she wanted to pee. She'd have to go and find a bush—again. She shouldn't have drunk all that coffee. She struck out to the right of the lane, and made her way across the rough moorland into a small hollow; it was safer down here, away from the good-naturedly ribald comments from the others.

She stood up gingerly, pulling up her trousers; she really was getting terribly cold. Maybe she should go for another walk, get her circulation going. If she walked down the lane she wasn't going to miss a car. She set out briskly, and after about ten minutes she saw a tiny pinprick of light coming towards her. It was fairly steady, not the up-and-down movement of a walker's torch. And certainly not a car. There was complete silence. So what—oh, of course! It was a bicycle. Someone was cycling up the hill. A farmworker perhaps, from the estate. But why should he be coming up at this hour? She waited, almost holding her breath, and the light suddenly swerved off the lane and disappeared. Or rather went off to the right. Its rear light bounced up and down now, but proceeded quite steadily; it must be a track of sorts. Jocasta decided to follow. It was probably a wild goose chase, but— And then there was a muffled cry and a curse and the light went out.

Jocasta walked cautiously over to the dark heap that the bike and its rider had become.

"Hello?" she said. "You all right?"

There was silence.

"I said hello. Anyone there?"

Nothing.

She was right up to the heap now; it took shape; it was a boy of about fifteen, sitting on the ground, rubbing his ankle. He had a canvas bag beside him.

"Are you all right?" she said again.

"Sure I'm all right." The accent was strong.

"Good. I thought you might have hurt yourself. Bit of a bad place to fall off your bike."

He tried to stand up and winced. "Fock," he said. "Focking Mary and Joseph."

"You've hurt yourself. Want me to look?"

He shook his head.

"Funny night for a bike ride," she said.

No reply.

"You on your way up to the big house?"

"I am not. Making my way home."

"Which is where?"

"Down there." He pointed down into the darkness.

"Strange, you seemed to be going in the opposite direction," she said. "Anyway, you won't get home in that state. Would you like me to drive you?"

"No thanks." He stared at her. "You one of those reporters?"

"Yup."

He hesitated. "You won't write about me, will you?" he said.

"I might," said Jocasta coolly. "Depends."

"On what?"

"Let me have a look at your ankle."

He scowled at her, then pushed his foot towards her.

She felt it gingerly, then very gently and slowly moved it. It didn't seem to be broken.

"I think it's just a bad sprain. You got a torch?"

"Only on the bike."

"OK. Let's just—" She pulled the light off the bike, shone it on his ankle. It was already swelling. "Are you sure you wouldn't like me to take you home?"

"No, I'll be fine. It's downhill to the village all the way, I can just sit on the bike."

"Pity." She looked at him consideringly. "Quite a good night for poaching, isn't it? Not much of a moon, just enough light."

"I am not going poachin'!"

"Oh really? Well, you certainly aren't any longer," said Jocasta. "I think you'd better let me take you home. And I swear I won't tell anyone, anyone at all."

"You won't?" His eyes in the half-light shone wide with fear. "Me mother would take a belt to me."

"Quite right, too. And your father, I daresay."

"Me father has passed on. There's just me and me mother. And the little ones."

"How many little ones?"

"Five. I'm the eldest."

"I see. So the odd trout or hare must be a big help. Now look—I'll just drop you at your house, no one will know. I swear."

He looked down at his ankle. "OK," he said finally. And then, reluctantly: "Thanks."

"That's OK. One thing in return. How do you get into the grounds? You must know a way."

"I don't."

"Of course you do," said Jocasta briskly, "don't be silly."

There was a long silence; then the boy said, "Follow this track right up to the wall. Follow round to your right. Few hundred yards along, there's a big tree. One of the branches hangs over the wall."

"Bit of a drop, isn't it?" said Jocasta thoughtfully. "That wall's twelve, maybe fifteen feet high. And then how do you get out again?"

"I'm not telling you any more," he said. "I thought you just wanted to get in."

She thought for a moment. It was quite true; she would find her own way out somehow.

"Right," she said standing up, holding out her hand to pull him up. "Let's get going."

Twenty minutes later, she was back. She parked her car quite a lot further down the hill. She didn't want any of the others getting on her trail. She pulled the torch out of the car, slung her rucksack onto her back, and then shut the car door very quietly. She pulled up the hood of her sweatshirt and started walking up the lane again, on the grass verge, looking out for the track. She'd better not get on the wrong one. Getting lost was all she needed.

Right. Here was the wall. To the right, he had said, a few hundred yards . . . Tree, tree, where was the bloody tree?

There! Right there, just in a curve of the wall. Not too bad to climb, either, until she was level with the top of the wall, standing on a very strong branch with a helpfully placed parallel one to hold on to.

Then it got worse. She could step onto the wall quite easily, but she then had to get down on the other side. And it was a good twelve-foot jump: onto grass to be sure, but nonetheless it looked like a long way down.

And there was absolutely no sign of the house; she had no real idea of the direction she should walk in. A mental calculation told her about ten o'clock from where she landed, but that was pure guesswork.

Shit, shit. She should have bought a map of some kind. And suppose Keeble had dogs roaming the grounds, or even an armed guard as it was rumoured the Barclay twins did?

"Oh for fuck's sake," she said aloud, unhitched her rucksack, threw it down, and then, wondering in the slow motion of fear if this would be the last thing she ever did, jumped after it.

Chapter 20

. . . . .

Right. She'd made it. She hadn't broken her leg; there were no dogs savaging her or guards standing over her with rifles. She hadn't even lost her rucksack. She was safely inside the grounds of Dungarven House and all she had to do now was find the house. She hitched her rucksack onto her back, and following her hunch, set out in what she thought was the right direction.

With the moonlight and the light from her torch she could see quite easily. She came out of the thicket and looked around her—no sign of a house. Never mind. She'd find it. She'd done brilliantly so far. Chris Pollock would be proud of her. As for Nick—she hadn't given Nick a thought, she realised, for hours. Good!

Suddenly she heard a dog barking. So he did have guard dogs. But the sound didn't move. It stayed. Which could only mean that it either was tied up somewhere or was inside the house. She would follow the sound.

She wondered as she walked, slowly and carefully, keeping her torch shining low on the ground, what Fionnuala was like. She had looked her up in the cuttings: her mother, Aisling, Gideon's second wife, had married Michael Carlingford a couple of years ago and spent half her time in Barbados, half in London. The divorce had been unpleasant and noisy and Fionnuala had obviously been shipped off to boarding school, so as to be the least possible bother to her parents. Jocasta knew what *that* felt like. If she'd had the chance to run off with a rock star, she would have done so, just to cause them the maximum trouble and embarrassment.

One of the few pieces of information available on Fionnuala was that she was a fine rider, and expensive horseflesh had been placed at her disposal almost from the moment she had been able to sit up. She rode in the occasional one-day event, and hunted from time to time, and those were the only occasions that yielded any photographs. Rather unsatisfactory ones for the gossip columns, of a rigid, unsmiling little face under her riding hat.

On the two occasions Jocasta had talked to him at any length, Gideon Keeble had not mentioned her; indeed, she would not have known he had a child. Another similarity between herself and Fionnuala.

The barking was getting louder; she was walking up a slight incline now into a group of trees—and through them she could see a light. Several lights, in fact. As she stepped out of the trees, yes, there it was. A large house, but not a huge one. She stayed close to the trees, worked her way towards the back of it: and as she did so, saw a great incline falling down again from the house itself, and below that a shimmer of light. The lake. Moonlight reflected in the lake.

Jocasta looked up at the sky, clear as it never was in the city, studded with myriad stars, and she would have stood there for a long time, just drinking it in, had not the dog started barking again, and, using the sound as a guide, she began to walk towards the house.

•◆•

"You sound absolutely terrible, love."

"I feel absolutely terrible. I don't think I can stand it much longer."

It was so unlike Helen to complain that there was a silence; everyone stopped what they were doing and stared at her.

Helen did feel appalling. She'd had bronchitis after Christmas, just as she did every year, but it appeared to have reignited; over the past few weeks, she had coughed repeatedly, night after night, went short of sleep, had a constant headache. "Have you been taking your antibiotics?" asked Jim severely.

"Yes. Of course. He might as well have told me to eat sugar lumps."

"Might have been better, love. You're skin and bone. It's all this worry, I'm sure. Your mother, the publicity, all that. It's been a big strain on you. I'm sure you'll feel better soon."

"Dad!" said Juliet. "Is that the best you can do? Poor Mum. You ought to—well, what about taking her away for a few days? See she has a bit of sunshine."

"Juliet," said Jim, "you sound like your sister. Where do you suggest I take her, the south of France or something?"

"Yes. Why not? It'd be lovely down there now."

"I daresay it would. And my name's Midas. Do you realise what it would cost just to get down there?"

"Forty-five pounds each," said Juliet firmly. "Look, it says so here in the newspaper: easyJet to Nice, forty-five pounds."

"Catch me on one of those things," said Jim, "tied together with bits of string."

"Oh Dad, honestly. Charlotte Smith's parents did it last week, and they're (a) not rich and (b) not exactly reckless," said Kate.

"It does sound a lovely idea, Jim," said Helen. "And a bit of sun would be so nice."

They all stared at her; she so seldom asked for anything for herself.

"And it's half term next week," said Juliet. "Go on, Dad, give poor Mum a break."

"And who's going to look after you two?"

"We could go to Gran. Or she could come here."

"Yes, or I could go to Charlotte," said Juliet. "Oh go on, Dad. Live dangerously."

Helen giggled, which triggered a spasm of coughing.

Jim looked at her, then at Juliet. Then he said, "I'll look into it. Give me that paper. I might look on the Web as well."

❖

Jocasta found herself at the back of the house. It was very beautiful indeed, classic Georgian, with wonderful tall windows also reflecting the moonlight, and a terrace running its full length. Jocasta walked towards the terrace, wondering for the first time what on earth she was going to do next. Did she knock on the door, tell the elderly retainer who would surely answer it that she had come to see Mr. Keeble? Did she try to get into the house—she remembered Gideon himself telling her doors in rural Ireland were never locked—or did she stand peering through the windows, rather like Peter Pan, observing the household as it went about its business?

She suddenly felt almost embarrassed. She walked quietly along the terrace, looking into a series of rooms: a drawing room dimly lit: what appeared to be a library, in semidarkness, the walls lined with books; a couple more rooms in total darkness; and then—then what was obviously a study. The light in there was quite bright. Very traditional, it too was book-lined, two leather chairs either side of a fireplace and a huge wooden desk—housing incongruously a large computer, a laptop, a fax machine, several telephones. And as she watched, Gideon came into the room, talking into a mobile; he sat down at the desk, and suddenly switched it off and sat staring at it as if he had never seen anything like it before. Then he put it down, very slowly and gently, on the desk, and almost as if he was rehearsing for a play, he folded his arms on the desk and buried his great head in them.

Jocasta watched him, paralysed, feeling like the worst kind of voyeur, probing into an intensely private grief. How could she have done this, how could she have broken into this self-contained world where Gideon felt himself safe? Better to return to London with no story, a failure, than confront him with her crass curiosity, her crude questioning.

She was actually contemplating stealing away, when a door further along the terrace opened and an Irish setter puppy, about six months old, bounded up to her, leapt up and licked her face, as if she was a long-lost member of its own family. It was followed by an older dog, its mother, she guessed, barking too, almost sternly, and after that she heard a woman's voice calling their names: "Sheba! Pebble! Will you come along back in at once, and stop that noise!"

The noise ceased briefly as the puppy continued to greet her ecstatically, and then started again. After a moment or two, as she patted and stroked and tried to hush the dogs, she saw Gideon stand up and walk to the door, clearly calling someone, and then he disappeared. As she stood petrified, both dogs now barking loudly and relentlessly, he came out through the side door. He was carrying a flashlight, which he shone around the lawns and then along the terrace in a great wide beam. She stood there, frozen like a rabbit in the headlights of a car, braced for abuse, for fury, for outrage, watching him walking towards her, very slowly. But as he reached her, he said, in tones of absolute good nature, as if she had just wandered into a restaurant or an airport lounge or some other very public place where he happened to be, "Why, Jocasta—what a pleasant surprise. You decided to come after all."

•◆•

"And you found her where?"

"In a restaurant."

"Jesus. I can't believe nobody got there first."

It was late in the evening; Marc Jones had just returned with the test shots of Kate. Carla was waiting for him with a bottle of wine.

"I know. It was just lucky," she said modestly. "So, how are the shots?"

"Sensational."

He flung a sheet of black-and-white contacts down on the desk. Carla pulled a magnifier out of her desk and bent over them. They were remarkable. Despite having been in the studio herself when they were taken, she saw something else now, something that had not been there, the strange alchemy between subject and lens that occasionally takes place, an extra dimension, almost another person indeed. A stroppy, nervous schoolgirl had walked into the studio; and there in front of them now was a gangly, wild-haired beauty, with an absolute knowledge of her own sexuality and how to confront the camera with it.

"Very, very lovely. Got any colour?"

"Yeah, I'll put them on the light box. They're great, too. It's the dark eyes and the fair hair. When are you going to use her?"

"Next week, probably. I'll go and see Chris in a minute, see what he thinks."

"Great." He grinned. "Just give me a date. What's the fashion story?"

"I thought we'd let Kate choose her own. I'll take her to Topshop, Miss Selfridge, Kookai, and let her loose. That street-fashion thing is a story in itself."

"Fine. When do you want to do it?"

"Soon as possible. I'll let you know. I'll have to speak to the parents, of course. She's not sixteen yet. But it should be OK. I can't think why not."

"Would you let your daughter loose in the fashion business?"

"I don't have a daughter," said Carla briefly.

She went to see Chris Pollock with Kate's pictures.

Kate was still high on her session in the studio, being flirted with by Marc Jones—God he'd fancied himself—and chatted up, that was the only word for it, by Carla Giannini. She'd really liked her, she was so warm and funny and appreciative of her rather crappy efforts. At least Kate felt they must be crappy, although she had somehow known what to do in front of the camera, known how to move a bit between shots, especially as the session went on, and she had felt increasingly confident, had started pushing her hair about and moving her hips a bit, pulling off her denim jacket and letting it dangle from her fingers. Carla had told her she was a natural.

It all seemed a bit of a dream now, back at home, standing in the kitchen, pouring herself a Coke, waiting to be told it was time she went to bed, asked if she had done all her homework. If only they knew! They'd be so amazed, shocked even, tell her what a dangerous world she was getting into. Only her grandmother would appreciate the excitement and importance of it all. It would be quite fun to tell her, actually.

Jim had managed to book a week in a three-star hotel near Nice. Helen was torn between excitement and guilt and worry at leaving Kate at such an important time in her life.

"If you fail these exams, you won't get a second chance, you know. You need good grades for Richmond, and—"

"Honestly, Mum, I'll study. I swear. Even if Gran lets me off, Juliet won't, she'll probably call the hotel and tell you if I stop for more than five minutes."

"I won't!" said Juliet indignantly. "Anyway, I'm doing that music course, don't forget. You can bunk off as much as you like."

•◆•

Martha pounded the running machine, sweat pouring off her; her legs throbbed, her lungs felt close to explosion. She was exhausted; she had another five minutes to go of this; she'd never last. Only—of course she would because that's what she had decided. It was as simple as that.

She could do so much with that will. The demons that had attacked her in all their horror as she knelt in that filthy lavatory, vomiting into the disgusting bowl, that had hung, obscenely threatening, above her bed during the long night that followed, had left her again, banished almost entirely. Almost.

She had finished. Target achieved. She stepped off the running machine, staggered to the shower. Now she could go back to her apartment, have an herbal tea, sort out her clothes for the morning, listen to some music, and do some background reading for a meeting. She'd told Ed she couldn't see him. Not tonight. Tomorrow they had a date though. It was their four-month anniversary. Four months since they'd first gone out. Four months of being astonishingly happy.

Happiness was not an entirely familiar condition to Martha. She knew about achievement, about meeting her own standards. She knew about success. She knew about pleasure, about the joys of having the home, the car, the clothes she wanted. But happiness: happiness was something else. Happiness was unexpected and uncontrollable. Happiness was sweet and swift and induced by the simplest things: a phone call, a silly joke, an appreciation for something small but important. Happiness was an entirely new set of values.

Ed had taught her all that as he had led her into love. She did love him; she knew that. She had resisted it for a long time, that knowledge. She was frightened of love. It scared her. She hadn't yet told Ed she loved him. It was risking too much, giving too much away.

Her first tentative courtship of her own constituency was proving as satisfying to her as she had hoped. Local politics might well be dull, but it was also a genuine opportunity to help the underdog, and to give people a voice. Her first legal advice clinic, held at her father's parish hall, had been a revelation; the terrible impotence of ordinary people when confronted by even the smallest threat to their lives—noisy neighbours, a cowboy builder, an overlarge bill sent in error—shocked her.

Accustomed to working for the rich and powerful, to dealing with vast meaningless sums of money, she felt a surge of power herself as she promised to write to the electricity company for one old lady, who was terrified, as she put it, of upsetting them, about her charges.

But it was above all—and this was what she found most exciting—a fight for hearts and minds. She was battling not only for them but also for herself, to persuade them to give her power to help them more.

The article she had been so fearful of had become a bland fashion feature, with the copy—over which she'd had final approval—little more than an extended caption, gratifyingly generous about her political career and pleasingly flattering about the Centre Forward Party. Chad would be very pleased. She had liked the pictures too. Martha was not vain; her appearance was simply one of her assets, one that she used and worked hard to improve, but no more than that. Nonetheless, the publication across a double-page spread in a national newspaper of three extremely flattering photographs of herself, wearing very nice clothes, was quite a pleasing prospect.

•◦•

Clio had decided to write to her family; she had after all left her husband, ended her marriage, there was a certain obligation to inform them, though she had very little expectation of hearing from any of them.

She was quite surprised, therefore, to hear Artemis's cool clipped tones on her answerphone on Thursday evening: "Clio. We should talk. Give me a call."

No expression of sympathy or even interest, just: "We should talk." And why should that hurt? When it was more than she had expected.

Artemis was briskly sympathetic about the divorce. She asked if Clio was all right and said that all men were fools, clearly assuming that there was someone else and Jeremy had walked out on her without warning. "No," said Clio, "actually, no. I told you, it was just a basic incompatibility."

"Hardly worth ending a marriage for, in my opinion," said Artemis. "Lucien and I could be said to be fairly incompatible, but we've worked out a modus operandi over the years. Of course we have the children to think of, so it's rather different. I'm surprised you haven't had a child by now, Clio. It was certainly something Jeremy was hoping for in the very near future, I do know that. He told me at your wedding."

"Yes, well, I haven't," said Clio, wondering how anything could hurt quite so much.

"Well, it's too late now. What a pity. I must say I rather liked Jeremy. You're all right, are you, living on your own?"

"Actually," said Clio firmly, "I rather like it."

"Oh really? I suppose it's just as well. Anyway, I told Father I'd call you—he was a little worried. I said I was sure you'd be quite all right—you're so self-sufficient. Ariadne said she'd write. Let us know if there's anything we can do, won't you?"

Ariadne did write: a supposedly consoling letter, saying she had never liked Jeremy—which irritated Clio profoundly—and telling her she should come to stay whenever she wanted.

"Only not in term time, of course."

And that was the end of the matter for all three of them. No wonder she felt so alone, Clio thought bitterly. But she had written to Beaky, who had expressed great delight at her interest in the job and invited her to lunch with him.

·◆·

"Happy anniversary. I got you a present."

"Oh, Ed. We said we wouldn't."

"Yeah, I know. But don't feel bad about not getting me anything. It's really stupid."

"Well, actually," she said, "I did. And it's pretty stupid too."

"Go on then. You first. Open it."

It was a book called *Tantric Yoga for Beginners*.

"I hope you're not suggesting I try this," she said, giggling.

"Absolutely I am. There's a chapter on sex. It says you can keep going for six hours. How about that?"

"Sounds a bit tiring. What's wrong with what we're doing now?"

"Nothing. It's great. I just liked this idea even better. That'd have her late for meetings, I thought."

"Yes. Well, I promise to read it. Now open yours."

"Hey," he said smiling, "that's really cute. I love it." It was a framed picture of the two of them, sheets pulled up to their chins, sitting in Martha's bed; she had used the remote setting on her camera to take it. "I remember that night," he added.

"Of course you don't."

"Of course I do. You know why? It was a big first. You didn't hang your clothes up neatly before you got into bed. Just left them on the floor."

"You're making it up," said Martha, laughing.

"I'm not. How could I forget that? I thought: She's more bothered about having sex with me than hanging up her Armani jacket. I must be some stud."

They were having the long-postponed dinner at the Pont de la Tour.

"It should have unhappy memories, I know," she had said, "but I thought I should lay the ghost. And it's so near my flat and it's lovely."

After dinner they walked along Butler's Wharf holding hands. He had been slightly quiet for the last half hour; she asked him if anything was the matter.

"Not . . . exactly."

"How about inexactly?"

"I didn't want to tell you tonight." Her heart felt as if something was squeezing it—very hard. "But, well, I've been offered a new job."

"Ed, that's great. What's wrong with that?"

"Not a lot. More money, much the same sort of thing, bit more responsibility."

"Well—take it."

"I—that is—it's in Edinburgh. Working for the Beeb."

"Edinburgh!"

"Yes. Very buzzy city, Edinburgh, these days. They even have a Harvey Nichols, my spies tell me. So, what do you think?"

"Well," she said briskly bright, "I think of course you must take it."

"You do?"

"Of course. Why ever shouldn't you?" She wouldn't mind; it would be fine. She could see him quite often. Not very often. But—enough.

"I can think of one very good reason."

"What's that?"

"It's called Martha."

"Ed, you can't give up a really good opportunity for me. Anyway, we could still see each other." When, though? Not evenings. Not many weekends, either. Given her work in Binsmow. Building up now. Her Saturday legal clinics. So she'd only see him . . . very occasionally.

"Well, I could. I thought I would. Actually. Give it up. But if you really think so. I mean, it would be great."

"Right, well that's settled then. Of course you must take it. We can have wonderful weekends, now and again, and you . . . you . . ." Her voice trailed off.

"I what?"

"You'll do so well, Ed. It's such a thing, working for the Beeb. You'd be set up for life."

"Yes. Good. Thanks, Martha. You're so—so grown-up." He smiled at her, just a bit too brightly.

"I should be. At my age. Let's go back now, shall we? I'm getting cold." She'd feel better about it later, when she got used to the idea. She was the last person to cling to someone, the first to know how important taking opportunities was.

Bloody Pont de la Tour. It was jinxed for them.

"That was great," he said sleepily. "Night, Martha."

"Night, Ed."

It hadn't been: not great. It was as if it had all been slightly out of focus. Nothing sharp enough.

The pleasure dulled—just a bit.

She lay there, thinking about him being in Edinburgh, how far away it was, how with the best will in the world, they would drift apart, the sweet dizzy closeness lost.

She got up and wandered into the sitting room, stood at the window, staring at the lights, thinking how far away he would seem, how lonely she would be. She felt a stab of pure misery, sat down, huddled in her bathrobe, fighting it down. Well, she would get over it. She'd been perfectly all right before she met him. Absolutely all right. She just wasn't a dependent sort of person. She had a horror of it.

And it was difficult, conducting a love affair with her life as it was; she was aware that she was fighting for time, pushing back boundaries. Mostly at the expense of sleep. She'd get a bit more of that, at least. But—

Damn, now she was going to cry. Shit. Ed mustn't hear her, mustn't know. He was obviously so keen to go, to take the job . . .

She got up, went to the loo and sat on the seat, wiping her eyes and blowing her nose. That was better—she could do this, for God's sake.

The door opened; Ed came in.

"Sorry," he said. "Just wanted a pee."

"That's OK," she said. "I'm just leaving."

"You OK?" he said.

"Yes, I'm fine. Of course."

He switched the light on, looked at her. "Martha, you're crying. What is it?"

"I don't want you to go," she said, and her voice was hopeless with misery. She felt appalled that she could give so much of herself away. "I'm sorry, I'm so sorry, Ed. I'll be all right in the morning."

"You don't want me to go?" he said, and his voice was very quiet, very gentle.

"No. Well, obviously not, I mean I've got used to us being together, so it's a bit of a shock, but I'll be all right. Sorry, Ed, sorry . . ."

"You're actually saying you don't want me to go?"

"Yes. Yes, I am. I know it's wrong, but—"

"It's not wrong," he said. "It's terribly, terribly right. God almighty, Martha, I've spent the last four months trying to tell myself that you really do care about me and now I know you do. Of course I won't go, you silly moo. I don't want to leave you, either. I want to stay here with you. Even in spite of your gigantic nose. And your pathetic tits. I wanted you to tell me not to go. More than anything I can ever remember."

"Oh, Ed." She looked up at him and suddenly it was an explosion in her head, and she had to say it, had to tell him.

"I—well, the thing is, I—I—"

"Come on. Spit it out. You what?"

"I love you," she said, and her voice was almost desperate with both anxiety and the effort of saying it.

"You do? Say it again."

"I love you," she said, and he bent down and gave her a kiss and then started to laugh.

"This is one hell of a place for a love scene," he said. "I love you, too. And now, if you could just shift your very well-toned little arse, I'd like to have my pee."

•—◆—•

"I'm so sorry," said Jocasta, "so terribly sorry."

She was sitting in what Gideon called the playroom; it was a rather grown-up playroom, with two huge sofas, a large television, a music system with two tall speakers and three stacks of CDs, a low table covered with what catalogues call executive toys, the walls lined with books. There was a huge fire burning in the stone fireplace, the lights were low and soothing. A large painting hung on one wall, of a beautiful blond woman in a black low-cut evening dress, the second Mrs. Keeble. Fionnuala's mother.

"And what are you sorry for," Gideon said, "exactly?"

He smiled at her; a formal smile that didn't reach his eyes.

"I'm sorry about being here. I feel so—so awful."

"Oh, that's perfectly all right," he said. "You are doing your job and I have to admire your initiative. You must tell me where you made your break-in, though. I didn't realise it was so easy."

"It wasn't easy!" said Jocasta, mildly indignant. "It was very difficult. I had to climb a huge tree and then jump down that massive wall—"

"Now, I hope you are not looking for sympathy," he said. "That would really seem a little unreasonable of you."

"No, of course not," she said. "Sorry, Gideon. Again."

"Don't keep saying you are sorry," he said. She found his expression hard to read: it was not his usual benign smile, but neither was it at all hostile; it was simply detached. "But I don't know how much I can offer you in the way of a story. We are all very quiet here. As you see."

"Yes, of course. Well, don't worry about it," she said and then thought how absurd she must sound. "I'm so sorry about your daughter, Gideon. About Fionnuala. You must be terribly upset."

"I'm not in the least upset," he said. "It takes more than a naughty daughter to have any effect on me."

She was reminded, once again, of her own father; he would have dismissed the whole thing thus as a naughty, childish prank, no more, not a desperate cry for help, not concerned for the danger of the situation. She began to like him less.

"You . . . haven't heard from her?"

"Now, would I be telling you if I had?" He smiled again, the same polite, detached smile.

"No, of course not."

This was a nightmare. What was she going to do? He sat, drumming his fingers gently on the arm of the sofa, apparently relaxed.

"You're all right, are you?" she said. "I mean, you said you hadn't been well."

"I think I said the doctors said I needed a rest. Which I am not getting at the moment, of course. Now it might be a good idea," he added, "if you gave me your mobile. I'm sorry if I appear discourteous, but I really would prefer you not filing any stories just at the moment."

Jocasta flushed. "Of course," she said. There seemed little else that she could say. She pulled her mobile from her rucksack and handed it to him.

"Thank you. Now if you will excuse me, Jocasta, I have work to do. Do let Mrs. Mitchell know if you want coffee. You know where she is, just along the corridor."

"Yes, of course," she said. "Thank you."

Should she make a run for it? For the front gates, climb over, forget her scoop? Anything would be better than this.

And then she heard it: first the distant whirring, then the increased beating of helicopter blades, cutting through the silence.

Gideon stood up, white suddenly, his face very drawn. He looked out of the window onto the lawn behind the house; Jocasta stood up too, and in the sudden brilliant light that flooded the area, watched the helicopter land, saw the pilot jump down, and then shortly after, a slight figure wearing trousers and some kind of large jacket follow him and run under the spinning blades towards the house. It must be Fionnuala. Returned to her father.

Gideon didn't move, just stood there, staring out. As the figure reached the terrace, she stood still herself, looking up at the house, and then began walking swiftly towards the side door. Not Fionnuala, but her mother, Aisling. Mrs. Mitchell appeared on the terrace, and walked towards her; they stood together for a moment or two, then walked back towards the house. Finally Jocasta couldn't bear it any longer.

"Aren't you—aren't you going to go and meet her?" she said, and Gideon gave a great sigh, almost visibly shook himself, and then walked silently and very slowly out of the room.

For want of anything else to do, Jocasta stayed exactly where she was, shamefully aware that she was writing the most important article of her life, inside her head.

Chapter 21

. . . . .

DRESSED FOR SUCCESS it said, right across the centre spread. IS MARTHA HARTLEY THE FUTURE FACE OF POLITICS?

And then under the headline, several extremely nice photographs of the future face. And figure.

She did look absolutely wonderful, Clio thought.

Sleek and self-assured, and sounded it too. Talking about her new career, her view on politics, her life in general, in absolutely clear, concise terms. Clio tried to remember those qualities in the rather nervy girl she had last seen on Koh Samui—and completely failed. How did anyone change that much? She certainly hadn't, and neither had Jocasta, not really. Obviously Martha's life had been very confidence-building. Well lucky her.

There was a lot of stuff about the Centre Forward Party too, about how it was the party of the future, for young professional people like herself, while still adhering to all the true Tory values. Very neatly and succinctly expressed.

Clio looked to see who had written the words beside the photographs; she expected to see Jocasta's name, but it was someone called Carla Giannini, the fashion editor. She wondered what had happened. Maybe she should call Jocasta. It would be good to talk to her anyway; but Jocasta's phone seemed to be switched off.

◆

Martha and Ed had studied the article in bed that morning. Martha had been quite pleased with the pictures but furious about the mention of her car and her salary. "What right does the bitch have to put that in? I told her there was to be nothing personal. It wasn't in the final copy I read. God, it's outrageous. I've a good mind to call the editor and complain!"

Ed leant forward and took her face between his hands.

"Martha," he said, between kisses, "you look utterly, utterly gorgeous, almost as gorgeous as you do without any clothes on. Now if they had shown that, you might have something to complain about. You're successful, for fuck's sake. What's wrong with that?"

"A lot," said Martha. "People won't like this, Ed, they'll think I have no idea what ordinary life is like, they'll be suspicious of me, and they'll—"

"Oh just shut up," he said, pulling the paper away from her, pushing her back on the pillows, bending to kiss her on the stomach, the thighs, his tongue lingering tantalisingly on her pubic hair, probing it. "Anyway, I've got a complaint about it, too. You haven't even mentioned your amazing stud of a boyfriend. Why not? Why does the Merc get bigger billing than I do?"

She stared at him, thinking he was serious, started to say, "But Ed—" and then saw his grin, smiled reluctantly herself.

"Now look," he said, sitting up again, "I know you've got to go to Binsmow today, and I know you've got to leave quite soon. Two questions: Can I come too? And can we have a fuck before you go?"

"You certainly can't come too," said Martha firmly. "Your mother might start to put two and two together. This is serious stuff; I've got a school fair and two church concerts to go to, as well as my legal clinic. I can't be distracted by you. And no, we can't have a fuck before I go—I'm late already. I seem to remember plenty of that in the last four or five hours. And it was lovely, thank you very much."

"Well, I don't know," he said. "There's still time for me to accept that job in Edinburgh, you know . . ."

"Ed," said Martha, very serious suddenly, "if you really want it, then you must take it. We'll get by."

"I don't. I don't want us getting by. I'm still reeling at the Right Honorable Hartley admitting to needing me."

It had been a very big admission she had made to him, she thought, stepping into the shower. It frightened her in a way. What price control, now? She hoped it would be all right.

❖

Kate had been looking at the pictures of Martha on and off all day. If her pictures were anything like as good as that, it would be awesome. She'd have the last laugh then, all right. And it would be this space—Carla had said when she called that she'd like her to be in the Saturday paper.

"Next Saturday, if possible. Are there any days you could get away from school early? Say by lunchtime."

"Any day," Kate had said. "It's half term."

"Wonderful! Then how about Tuesday? And we could go on Monday and pick out some things you like for the pictures. I thought I'd let you choose your own. Oh, and Kate, do bring one of your parents along with you to the session—I wouldn't want them worried in any way about all this."

"They're away," said Kate, "for a week."

"Oh, I see," said Carla, thinking that there must indeed be a God. "Well, is there anyone else, an elder sister, perhaps?"

"I could bring my gran," said Kate. "She's looking after my sister and me next week. She's got a clothes shop and she's really cool. She'd love to come."

"Fine. Tell her to call me if she has any queries."

Kate hadn't spoken to Jilly yet; she'd been waiting for the right moment. Maybe this evening—that would be a good time. Juliet was playing in some crap concert and they didn't have to go, thank God. It would be the perfect time to tell Jilly all about it and show her the paper and everything, so she could see how important it was. God, it was exciting!

•-•-•

Janet Frean read the piece about Martha Hartley. She didn't normally take the *Sketch* but a very excited Jack Kirkland had faxed her a copy of the spread. He called her half an hour later.

"Didn't she do well? Got all the points across. Very professional, I thought. Considering it's her first exposure to the press."

"Indeed," said Janet. "And yes, she does look extremely nice. Pity she talked about her personal dresser: could alienate a few people. But she'll learn. And it's only a detail."

"What's so great about her," said Jack, "is that she's young and successful herself. Out in the real world. Not much of that in politics today. I think she's a real find."

"Indeed," said Janet. "Jack, you must excuse me, I've got a line of people waiting for their breakfast here."

Bob Frean, who was serving up the family breakfast, wondered what the loud crash was that emanated from her study downstairs and sent Lucy, the fourteen-year-old, to find out. Lucy came back grinning.

"She's fine," she said. "In one of her strops, that's all. Threw a paper-weight right across the room. She says she doesn't want any breakfast."

"Fine by me," said Bob.

•-•-•

Nick read the piece about Martha Hartley with only mild interest. He had liked her when he'd met her; he thought she came across as less engaging in this piece. He was still slightly baffled as to how Jocasta had such trouble getting a story out of her—there was obviously more to them and their relationship than Jocasta was telling. The most likely explanation was that they'd been fighting over some man, Jocasta had won, and Martha had never forgiven her. Or something like that. Well, if push came to shove, most men would choose Jocasta, he thought miserably. He was missing her terribly.

He knew she'd been sent to Ireland, on the Keeble story, but she seemed to have disappeared into thin air. He'd asked Chris Pollock if he'd heard from her, and he said he hadn't since she'd filed her copy two days earlier.

"Bloody useless it was too. I don't know what's the matter with the girl. She seems to have completely lost it. If you do speak to her, Nick, tell her she's in danger of finding herself without a job if she doesn't file soon."

Nick was sure Jocasta hadn't lost it, that she had found someone, somewhere, who knew something and was even now probably writing her story, beating the opposition with some extraordinary exclusive. He knew Chris felt the same, that there was no real question of Jocasta losing her job. One of Chris's strengths as an editor was the trust he placed in his writers and reporters, his willingness to support them.

•-•-•

"Darling, it's terribly exciting!" Jilly looked at Kate's flushed face, looked down at the newspaper with the pictures of Martha again. "And I can see it would be lovely for you, but, well, I really don't know what your parents would say. I think maybe you should wait until they get back—"

"Oh no!" said Kate, who knew very well what her parents would say. "Granny, it can't wait. She said herself it was really important we did it this week, that otherwise it wouldn't be for ages, and anyway, then I'll be doing my exams, so God—I mean, goodness knows when it could be. They'd probably forget about me altogether. Oh, please, Granny, please say yes! It's such a brilliant chance for me. And honestly this woman's so nice, and she wants you to come with me. She says to call her with any questions you've got."

"Oh, well, that's a little different," said Jilly. "She's obviously a nice, responsible woman. Yes, I'll ring her on Monday, Kate, and have a chat with her."

"You could ring her today," said Kate. "She gave me her mobile number, said any time. She needs to know as soon as possible, so she can make the arrangements with the photographer and all that."

"But it's Saturday, Kate, surely she won't want to be bothered with work—"

"Gran, please. *Please*. She can always say she'll ring you back."

"Oh, very well," said Jilly, "but only if you go upstairs immediately afterwards and do at least two hours' study. And then I'll test you on it. And don't call me Gran—you know I don't like it."

"Sorry, Granny. And of course I'll work now. Of *course*," said Kate earnestly.

Carla Giannini did seem to be an extremely nice woman: clearly interested in and concerned for Kate and her future.

"I really think she has the makings of a model," she said. "If you like, I'll send over the test shots we did of her. Apart from her figure, which is wonderful—so rare you get the height with the narrow build—she has an absolutely unique quality, vulnerable and self-confident at the same time. And she has a real flair for wearing the clothes. And Mrs. Bradford—"

"Oh, do please call me Jilly."

"Thank you. You're obviously a very young grandmother. Well, I know what you look like, of course, from that photograph in the paper with Kate."

"That was very unflattering, I'm afraid," said Jilly.

"Nonsense. You looked great. Anyway, what I was going to say, Jilly, is that the *Sketch* is a very respectable paper. I'll send you a few back copies of my pages, together with the photographs of Kate," said Carla.

"That would be kind. But is there really that much hurry? My daughter and her husband are away, as you know, and I would really like to get their permission for this. It's rather a big decision for me to take and—"

"I can see that of course," said Carla, instantly sympathetic, "but next Saturday really would be ideal. I have girls booked for the next three or four weeks, so it would mean going forward a long way. When, as I understand it, she'll be doing her exams. I don't want to interfere with those in any way, of course."

"That's very understanding of you." Jilly liked her more and more.

"So I would have a problem if I had to pull Kate out now. Would it be possible for you to e-mail your daughter, or speak to her on the phone?"

"I might be able to speak to her, yes."

"Wonderful. But . . ." Carla hesitated. "I will need to know almost at once. I'm afraid Kate did lead me to understand that it would be all right."

"Yes, she shouldn't have, of course, naughty girl," said Jilly. "But—"

"I know. Of course I understand. It's so exciting for her, such a big opportunity—she's certainly not going to want to risk her parents saying no. But I really can't see why they should. I mean, I would absolutely insist on your being at the session, and if there's anything you're unhappy about, you have only to say—"

"Yes, and I'll explain all that to my daughter," said Jilly, "but . . ." It seemed so dreadful to risk depriving Kate of what was clearly an extraordinary opportunity. "Look, I'll try and get hold of my daughter in the morning, or even this evening. And I'll ring you straight back. I mean, I have no reservations at all, I know what your business is like—"

"Yes, Kate told me you had a shop. Which designers do you buy?"

"Oh, the usuals, Nicole Farhi, Gerard Darel, MaxMara. Of course I'm limited by my clientele, naturally. The Guildford housewife isn't exactly a trendsetter."

"Of course not. How clever of you to know her so well. And those are all wonderful names. It's obviously a very good shop. If I possibly can I'll mention it in the article."

"What, by name?" said Jilly. She thought of how much she'd been worrying about the shop in her absence, and the difference even a sixteenth-page ad in the Guildford paper made.

"Of course. Otherwise what would be the point? And it all makes for more interesting copy. In fact, it's a very nice line, her inheriting your fashion sense, as she clearly does."

"Yes, possibly," said Jilly. This was not the moment to elaborate on Kate's origins. "Carla, that would be simply marvellous. Thank you so much. Now I'll get back to you as soon as I can."

"Thank you, Jilly. It really does have to be tomorrow at the latest, I'm afraid. It's such a marvellous thing for a fashion editor to discover a model, you know. So thrilling. And I have a really strong feeling about Kate."

Carla smiled into the phone as she put it down. It would be all right. Nothing like a bit of time pressure to make people anxious, make them agree to what you wanted. And she had to get this settled before Jocasta returned. She was so oddly defensive about Kate.

•-•-•

Chris Pollock was becoming seriously anxious about Jocasta. It was very unlike her, this silence. He hoped nothing had happened to her. He was beginning to worry more about that than the loss of the Keeble story. Where the fuck was she? And why hadn't she been in touch? Not even a text message from her since Friday night and now it was Sunday morning.

He rang Nick's number; a rather slurry voice answered.

"Nick Marshall . . ."

"Nick. It's Chris. Any news from Jocasta?"

"Nope. Not a dickey bird."

"Shit. Where *is* the bloody girl, Nick?"

"I don't know. I wish I did. Mind you, I'm hardly going to be the first to know. We had a bust-up last week."

"Oh really? Nothing serious, I hope."

"Chris, who knows what's serious to a woman. I certainly don't. I could ask Josh. Her brother. They're pretty close. In a funny way."

"Thanks, Nick. And call me back, yeah?"

Josh was clearly very distracted when Nick rang.

"Got the kids here, Nick. Bit hectic. Just going to take them out to lunch, and— Oh God, hang on, one of them's just spilt her drink all over the other."

A lot of wailing and shouting came down the line, with Josh distractedly saying things like "No, Harry, don't do that" and "Come on, Charlie, stop crying" and "Now play nicely together just for a minute, while Daddy talks on the phone."

"Sorry, Josh. Bad moment," Nick said when Josh came back on. "I just wondered if you'd heard from Jocasta over the past couple of days."

"Jocasta? No. Nothing. Why, where's she supposed to be?"

"Well, she's supposed to be in Ireland, doing a story. But there's been no news from her at all."

"Oh, I shouldn't worry," said Josh, "she's pretty good at looking after herself. Look, Nick, I've got to go. If I do hear anything I'll let you know, OK?"

"OK," said Nick, and put the phone down. Where was the bloody girl? Just where was she? And what the hell was she doing?

◆

Jilly didn't sleep well. She should never have even half agreed to this business with Kate. Not without checking with Helen. She had led Carla to assume it was more or less a certainty. And she knew what Helen would say. That she had left her in charge of the girls, and had trusted her to see they were all right, and that agreeing to Kate being photographed by a national newspaper was not within those terms.

But what harm could it possibly do? The child would look absolutely beautiful and it really was a wonderful opportunity for her; she had studied with great care the pictures that Carla had sent over by messenger, and Kate did look glorious. Clearly, if she wanted to, she could become a professional model. And this was the kind of opportunity that didn't come along more than once in a lifetime. Just the same . . .

"Oh dear," she said aloud.

"Is anything the matter, Granny?" It was Juliet.

"No, darling. Not really. I was just . . . just thinking about Kate, as a matter of fact."

"About Kate? What's she done now? Hey, what are these?" She picked up the pictures of Kate. "God, she looks amazing. Who did them?"

"A professional photographer on a newspaper," said Jilly. "They are very good, aren't they?"

"Fantastic!" said Juliet. "Are they going to publish them? How exciting. I wish she'd told me."

"She hasn't told anyone," said Jilly, "not even your parents. And no, they're not going to publish these, but they want to do some more, as a fashion feature for next week's paper. But I'm not sure about it."

"Why ever not?" said Juliet. "It'd be lovely for her. Specially at the moment, when she's so gutted over Nat and everything."

"And what do you think your parents would say?"

"Probably try and stop her—they're parents, aren't they? But I'm sure once they were published, they'd just be proud. And it would be too late anyway. Oh, hi, Kate, I've just seen these pictures. They're amazing—and Granny says they want to use some more in the paper next week. How exciting!"

"Yeah, well—"

"You must do it, Kate. Granny says you're worried about Mum and Dad, what they'd say, but like I was saying to Granny, if you did it, and the first they knew you were in the paper, they'd just be proud of you, I'm sure. I mean, you could ask them first, I suppose," she added, "but they'd only say no. And then the chance'd be gone. Or could you do it later?"

"No," said Kate quickly. "It's this week or never, Carla says."

"Who's Carla?"

"The fashion editor. She's really nice, isn't she, Granny?"

"Charming," said Jilly. "And she insists I come to the photographic session."

"Well, it *must* be totally respectable. Not even Dad could complain about that. Oh, just do it, Kate! Honestly, what harm could it do?"

"Absolutely none," said Jilly. "Good advice, Juliet. Thank you. But of course I must tell them."

She called the hotel. A sullen French voice told her, with an almost audible shrug, that Mr. and Mrs. Tarrant were out and that she could leave a message if she liked. Jilly left a message and spent the rest of the day assuring herself that if the sensible and extremely mature Juliet thought it was all right, then it probably was.

Helen phoned that evening: they were having a wonderful time, the hotel was nice, the weather was beautiful, and Jim was taking her out to dinner at some very pretty restaurant down the road.

"I just lay by the pool all afternoon and felt so relaxed. And do you know, I'm coughing less already."

"I'm so glad, darling. You didn't get my message?"

"No," said Helen, "they're not too good about things like that here. Is anything wrong?"

"No, no," said Jilly hastily. "Of course not. No, I just . . . well, I'm so glad, darling. That's wonderful. And you mustn't worry about us, we're fine, and Kate is working really hard."

"I'm not worrying, Mummy, not in the least. I feel marvellous. I'm pleased about Kate, though. Now, they're both being nice to you, are they?"

"Absolutely sweet. Helen, there's just—"

"Oh, dear, Jim's making faces, says we'll lose our table. Thank you once more. I'll ring again in a day or two."

"Yes, but—"

"Mummy, I must go. Sorry. Love to the girls."

Well, thought Jilly, she'd done her best. It wasn't her fault if Helen didn't have time to discuss things with her.

She called Carla Giannini and told her she hadn't been able to ask her daughter about Kate. "But I do feel quite happy about it myself."

"Good. I'm so delighted. Now, would you like to come shopping with us tomorrow, picking out the clothes for Kate to wear? You would obviously be a great asset. And you could make sure they were all quite . . . suitable."

"Oh, I don't think so," said Jilly. "I still get rather tired. And you'll have more fun without me."

"I'm not so sure about that. Well, till Tuesday, then."

•—•

Chris Pollock was in his office late that Sunday night when the call came.

"Hi, Chris. It's me, Jocasta."

"Jocasta, where the fuck have you been? And what do you think you're playing at? And where's the fucking story?"

"I've been here. In Ireland. In Gideon's house."

"In Gideon Keeble's house? My God, Jocasta, that must be some story. You've been there all this time?"

"Yes. And I'm really sorry, Chris, but there isn't going to be a story. Not from me anyway. Well, you can say she's safely home again, but that's all. And the other thing is, Chris, and I'm truly sorry about this too, but I'm afraid I'm going to give in my notice."

She had been quite frightened, that first evening. Sitting there, trapped in the vast house, living out this extraordinary adventure, with no idea what she should do; just waiting, waiting for time to pass: it had been much scarier than any other job she could remember.

She had drunk a cup of tea that Mrs. Mitchell had brought her and wolfed down the biscuits that had accompanied it on the tray, had begun to study the books that lined the walls—wonderful books, some of them, first editions of Dickens, or Trollope, or Defoe, beautifully illustrated volumes of things like *The Arabian Nights* and *Grimm's Fairy Tales*, and Kate Greenaway, the pages tipped, rather than bound in, all the poets, complete sets of encyclopaedias, of catalogues of art sales, books about vintage cars, books about racing, books about paintings. And interspersed with them, in glorious carelessness of their value, paperbacks by the hundred; he liked all the popular stuff, John Grisham and Patricia Cornwell and Stephen King and Maeve Binchy—well, he would of course, she was Irish—and Jilly Cooper. She picked the latest Grisham off the shelves and set it down on the arm of the sofa, then moved on to the stack of CDs on the other side. Very catholic, his musical taste as well: ranging from church choral music, through Mozart, and Mahler, into jazz, swing, and to the present, to Bruce Springsteen, Bob Dylan, and "My God, Leonard Cohen," she said aloud.

"And what is so surprising about that?" she heard Gideon's voice asking her and she swung round and smiled at him and said, "I absolutely love him. He's so—so wonderfully dismal. Not many people do. We're in a very small minority, you and I."

"Sondheim?" he asked.

"Adore him."

"Opera?"

"Don't get it."

"Bob Marley?"

"Of course."

"Well," he said, "we are clearly made for each other. Musically, if in no other way."

She looked at him nervously. He wasn't smiling.

"I have come to see if you would like a bed for the night. We have a few to spare."

"Well, I am tired. But what's the alternative?"

"There isn't one," he said. "I'm not going to let you out yet. I'm sorry."

"It's all right. I can see you can't."

She accepted with absolute equanimity his low opinion of her. She had broken into his house in order to steal something of infinite importance and delicacy, his relationship with his runaway daughter, and she had no right to feel even remotely indignant.

"Very well, then. And in the morning, we can perhaps agree on some strategy. But not yet. Things are too . . . too delicate. Too difficult. I will tell Mrs. Mitchell to show you to your room. Good night, Jocasta. I hope you sleep well. And I hope you will forgive me—I have disconnected the landlines. So there would be no point your trying to make any calls."

"Fine," she said.

The room was on the second floor, high-ceilinged, shuttered, and very cold, with an exquisite fireplace (devoid of a fire), and a surprisingly high, hard bed. The bathroom was next door: even colder, with an enormous bath and a thronelike loo. Mrs. Mitchell, who clearly thought Jocasta a trollop, ushered her in, asked her if there was anything she might be wanting, and left again very swiftly. Jocasta undressed with great speed, fell into bed, and went straight to sleep.

She awoke literally shivering; it was six o'clock. She got out of bed, folded back the shutters, and realised why: the windows were wide open. Expecting a wonderful view, she could see only thick grey mist, and it was raining. She shut the windows, pulled her clothes on—she wasn't risking that icebox of a bathroom and, good reporter that she was, she had things like clean knickers and a toothbrush in her rucksack—and went stealthily along the corridor, down the stairs, and managed to find her way to the kitchen. No one was about, not even the dogs.

The kitchen was vast, and warmer than the rest of the house, thanks to an extremely elderly looking cream-colored Aga. The floor was slate, the walls whitewashed, and there were the inevitable shutters at the window. It looked a little like a photograph in *Interiors*, except that it was devoid of the bunches of dried flowers, pots of herbs, copper pans, and Shaker-style furniture that would have given it page appeal. It was devoid of anything, in fact, apart from a very large scrubbed table and three chairs, one of which was broken. Jocasta thought of the leather sofas and complex music systems in the playroom and the study, the fine furniture she had glimpsed through what was obviously the drawing-room door as Mrs. Mitchell led her upstairs, and felt almost sorry for her. Almost.

She filled the vast kettle that sat on the Aga, managed to find a slightly chipped mug, took some milk out of the 1950s-style fridge, and went to the back door. She looked along the terrace; it was so drenched in mist she couldn't even see the end of it, and the rain was growing heavier. Well this was no moment for exploring, trying to find a tradesman's entrance, or exit, or even a path round the grounds. She went back inside, walked back along the corridor, into the playroom. That, too, was cold. And it was May! God, this was going to make a good story. No wonder Aisling had searched for lovers in warmer climates!

There was a phone ringing, quite persistently. Did that mean he had reconnected the landline? Now that was worth investigating. At least she could make a quick call to Chris. She went out of the playroom, followed the sound down the corridor; she had passed three doors before she reached it. Of course! This was his study. She looked up and down the corridor, then slipped inside the room and closed the door. Odd, surely he had an extension by his bed. Would he really not be hearing it? She waited for four more rings, and then picked it up, waited. Silence.

"Hello," she said cautiously, "Mr. Keeble's residence."

"Who's that?" The voice was young, light, cautious. Fionnuala? Could be. "Mummy? It's Fionnuala."

Fionnuala. Jocasta Forbes, this really is the scoop of your career.

"No. Shall I get her for you?"

"Who is that?"

"A friend of your father's. Shall I get him?"

"No thanks."

Gideon's voice cut in, saying, "Hello? Hello?"—and then the phone went dead.

She stood there, still holding the receiver, feeling oddly frightened. She was just putting the phone down, wondering why she wasn't doing it more quickly, when the door opened and Gideon came in, wearing nothing but a white towelling robe; he was barefoot, his hair wild, his face white, his eyes black with fury.

"What the hell are you doing in here?" he demanded, and for a moment she thought he was going to hit her. "How dare you? Get out. Just get the fuck out. Now!"

It was the first time she had ever seen him other than relaxed, easy, charming; it was an alarming transformation. So this was the famous temper. She stood her ground.

"I *was* going. I wish I could go further. Unfortunately I seem to be a prisoner here."

"And what do you expect? Breaking into my home, prying into my most personal life. What do you think you're doing?"

"As you said last night," said Jocasta, calm now, astonished at the extent of it, "I'm doing my job. Which does consist, unfortunately, of prying into people's most personal lives. I'm sorry, Gideon, very sorry, and I'm actually not enjoying it. Any of it."

"I had thought better of you," he said, and his tone was full of deep contempt.

"Oh really? And why should that be? I seem to remember your congratulating me on some of my stories when we met at the Tory conference last autumn. What's changed, Gideon? I'd really like to know."

He stared at her for a moment, and then said, still icily hostile, "So, who was that?"

"It was your daughter."

"And what did she say?"

"Not a lot. She asked who I was. I said I was a friend of yours. I offered to fetch you."

"And?"

"And she said . . ." She hesitated. "She said, 'No thanks.' And rang off. Sorry, Gideon."

His face changed; just for a moment, she caught him off guard, saw that she had hurt him, saw how much.

"Well, thank you for that, Jocasta. Depriving me of a chance to speak to my daughter."

"Gideon, I didn't deprive you. She didn't want to. Don't shoot the messenger."

"And what in the name of sweet fuck were you doing answering my phone?"

"It was ringing," she said. "No one else was. I assumed you and your wife must have left again."

"I was in the shower. My wife—or more accurately my ex-wife—was no doubt on her own telephone. Speaking to her very unpleasant husband. Anyway, Fionnuala has been found, by the police. At Belfast airport. Mr. Zebedee is in police custody, although as Fionnuala is swearing he hasn't touched her, I doubt if he will remain there for long. So very soon you can go and write your wonderful story. What a lot of colourful detail it will have. Now just get out of here, will you. Right out."

"Yes, all right."

She turned, just as she reached the door, to look at him. He was slumped at his desk, staring at the phone; she saw him dash his hand across his eyes. "Gideon," she said, very tentatively.

"I said get out," he said, and half rose towards her, his expression intensely angry.

She stood her ground. "I am so sorry," she said again.

"For what?" he said and sat down heavily. "Just what are you sorry for? Breaking into my house? Planning to trade on my good nature? Which, as you are discovering, is rather less good than you thought. I'm afraid I find your remorse rather hard to believe, Jocasta."

"I expect you do. But I'm also . . . so sorry for you."

"Well, you have a strange way of showing that," he said. "I thought you were a friend, at the very least."

"I thought so too. I never will be now, will I?"

"Absolutely you will not. No doubt Mr. Pollock said to you, 'You know him. You can get into his house. You can make him talk.' Or words to that effect. Am I right?"

"Yes. You are, I'm afraid."

"And you thought something along the lines of, Well, yes, I can. He fancies me. I can get him to talk. Didn't you?"

"Yes, Gideon, I suppose I did. And I'm ashamed of myself."

"It's such a pity," he said. "I liked you so much, Jocasta. And, yes, I did fancy you. Who wouldn't? I was even foolish enough to think— Well, yes, that was very foolish."

"No," she said quietly, knowing what he meant. "It wasn't foolish at all."

Just for a second his expression softened, then: "Well, I hardly think that makes your behaviour seem any better. Rather worse, in fact. It really hurts to think you were willing to trade on my admiration, purely in order to advance your career, to take on a situation so painful to me, and so intimate, simply to have a few more cuttings on file."

She remained silent.

"Oh, this is ridiculous," he said suddenly. "I have no real interest in explaining to you just why I am so angry. If you can't see it for yourself, then what would be the point?"

"Of course I can see it," she said. "And I feel absolutely . . . wretched."

"I suppose that is something," he said and gave a look of such withering dislike she felt sick. "Now I really would rather you left me alone. I have a great deal to do."

He turned away from her, and she saw him shake his head quickly, as if he were trying to rid himself of her and thoughts of her.

Jocasta looked at him, and was reminded of countless similar incidents, when her father had ordered her from his presence, had made it plain he wanted none of her, and she felt a rush of courage, and knew what she should say to him.

"Gideon, there are other things I'm sorry about."

"And they are?"

"Fionnuala," she said quietly. "I feel very sorry about her. And for her."

"And what do you know about it? What right do you have to feel sorry for her? I think you should stop this, Jocasta. I am in no mood for ignorant comments."

"It's not so ignorant," she said. "I know something of what Fionnuala feels. Not exactly, of course, but I know how it is to be her."

"I don't think you do," he said. But his face had changed; he was clearly ready to listen.

"Of course I do. I also have a father who I hardly ever saw. Who seemed to have no interest in me. Except when I did bad things, of course."

"Be careful, Jocasta," he said, "be very careful."

"I can't, Gideon, if being careful means not telling you what seems to me so obvious. What might help. My father was empire-building, making money, moving round the world. There wasn't any room for me. Little girls don't belong on business trips. God, how many times was I told that!"

"I'm sorry you had such an unhappy childhood, Jocasta. You must write about it someday."

"Oh shut up!" she said and, horrified, found herself on the edge of tears. "Look, don't you see, you have a daughter who doesn't know you. Who probably thinks you don't care about her. Who has no happy memories of you, except maybe the occasional week here and there, who feels your business is much more important to you than she is. Can't you see how much that hurts? Can't you see it makes her want to do anything—anything at all—to make you take notice of her?"

"Oh please," he said, "spare me the pop psychology."

"The thing about pop psychology is that it has quite a lot of truth in it. And common sense."

"Well," he said, "at least I acknowledge my daughter. Your father seems to deny your very existence. You'll be telling me next he abused you. That seems to be a prerequisite for most successful young people of today. Perhaps you could work that into this piece, Jocasta. Make it even more moving and dramatic."

"You bastard!" she said and then the tears did come, strong, choking tears, and the memories with them, crashing in on her, horrible, miserable memories. She turned and ran out of the room, found the playroom, rushed in, slammed the door, sat on the sofa, her arms folded across her stomach, bending over them as if in physical pain, sobbing helplessly.

She heard the door open, turned, and saw him standing there, just staring at her, with an expression on his face that was somehow close to fear.

"I'm sorry," he said. "I shouldn't have said that. Please forgive me."

She said nothing, continued to sob; he sat down beside her, put his arm round her shoulders, tentatively. She shook it off.

"Did he? Is that what he did?"

"No," she said, shaking her head. "Of course not. Well, not sexually. I never quite know what abuse is," she added with a watery smile. "I mean, does it have to be sexual? Or even physical? It's such a hazy area. Ironic, isn't it, and me a tabloid journalist."

"It is indeed. I would personally define it as something permanently damaging. Which I am clearly guilty of. In your court at any rate."

"I don't think you are," she said slowly. "My father was cruel, terribly cruel, and I know you're not. I'm not comparing the two of you, just our situations, Fionnuala's and mine."

"I think I deserve a few lashes. I have clearly made what is known here as a complete dog's dick of fatherhood."

In spite of herself, she giggled.

"That's better. Do you want to talk about your father? It might help. It might even help me. You never know."

"You don't want to hear about my relationship with my father."

"I have nothing else to do at the moment. And it might be relevant. As you say."

"He just—bullied me," she said, "right from the beginning. Not physically, he never hit me once, but he mocked me, put me down, diminished me. He humiliated me in front of people, said, 'Oh, it's kinder to ignore her, she's only got half a brain' when they tried to talk to me, and then laughed and said it was only a joke. And there was endless comparison with Josh, even when I rode better, did everything better. 'Why can't you be more like your brother?' he'd say. God, that'll be engraved on my heart. And he made a big thing of planning treats and then cancelling them at the very last minute, and holidays, and ignoring my birthday, things like that. I tried and tried to please him but it never worked. I can never remember him saying anything kind to me, or even smiling at me. Then, when I was about seven, I changed, started standing up to him, arguing with him, and that made it worse, made him terribly angry. Josh never did that, he just went along with it all."

"And you've no idea why he disliked you?"

"Some drunken old uncle of ours told Josh our mother had trapped him into marrying her, got pregnant on purpose. He certainly hated her. Which is probably why he hated me, if the story's true. I've often thought he'd planned to have the son and then leave her, and I was a daughter and he was stuck with her, waiting for the boy. The minute Josh was born, almost, he left her."

"He could have got the son from someone else, surely?"

"Yes, I know but— Oh, he's just a bit mad, I think." She sighed and then, wiping her nose with the back of her hand, said, "Do you have a hanky?"

"Of course," he said, and rummaged in the pocket of his bathrobe. "Here, and in fact, here is another."

"Thank you." She took one, blew her nose on it, then looked at him and managed a weak smile.

"I'm sorry," she said. "I never in a million years meant you were like my father."

"Well, that is a relief," he said, "considering how much you dislike him. Would you like a good strong cup of tea? With a lot of sugar. My mother's remedy for everything."

"No, thank you." She was silent, then: "I was just thinking earlier, how you once said I reminded you of your mother. And that you would never say that now."

"On the contrary. She, too, was very brave. Like a little lion. She is the only other person who has dared to tell me those things."

"What things?"

"About how I treated Fionnuala. She said I neglected her, tried to win her over with material things. Of course I ignored her. As one does with one's mother. But yes, I did say you were like her. I remember saying it. And I meant it. It was true."

"Oh," she said, and wondered how much of the conversation he actually remembered, the qualities he had attributed to her.

"Well," she said, with a sigh, "I still have behaved horribly. I should never have come. And I certainly shouldn't have said all those things to you. It was nothing to do with me."

"I daresay it was good for me," he said. "One of the things about being an important person"—he smiled at her, to show that this much, at least, was intended as a joke—"is that very few people are brave enough to tell you the facts of life. The real ones, that is. And you live in a rather comfortable little bubble, thinking how clever you are and how right about everything. So you've possibly done me a great service, Miss Jocasta Forbes. And Fionnuala, too. Now I must go, if you will forgive me. Aisling is going down to collect her and bring her back here. So that we can speak, with a capital S, to her together, find out what's actually happened. And then, I suppose, Aisling will take her back to that horrible island she lives on. The half term is nearly over, and she's leaving that school anyway, in a few weeks."

"Does Fionnuala think Barbados horrible?"

"I really don't know. I think she has quite a nice time there. She's learning to play polo—Aisling is friendly with the Kidds."

"I see. Well, you'd better go. You can't arrive at a police station dressed like that."

"Oh I'm not going," he said. "She has made it very plain she doesn't want me there. She hates me; she told me that last night and would no doubt have done again this morning, had you not intercepted her. She'll probably spit in my face if I turn up."

"Gideon!" said Jocasta. "You haven't taken in a word of what we've said, your mother and I. Go, for God's sake. If she spits in your face, at least while she's doing it she'll know you could be bothered to come."

He was silent for a while, staring out at the mist. Then: "I don't know if I should," he said.

"Oh get a grip," said Jocasta, and she was smiling at him now. "Go on. Go and get your clothes on."

He came back in ten minutes; he was wearing one of his perfectly cut tweed suits, under a long Barbour. He looked very stylish: a caricature of a country gentleman. "I've shaved as well," he said, "the better to receive the spittle."

"Good. I promise you it'll be worth it. Is she really coming back here?"

"Oh yes."

"Good. Then I might meet her."

"Jocasta, you must go. I can't detain you any longer. People will be worried about you. And you have a story to write. I'll tell Mrs. Mitchell to take you, when she goes down to the village. I'm sure your car will still be there." He bent down, kissed her briefly on the top of her head. "Go a little easy on me," he said. "If you can."

It was late afternoon when they came back. Jocasta was watching from her bedroom window. The clouds were finally breaking up and a washed-out sun was gleaming through them. The landscape eased into colour, the black-and-grey of the trees and mist turning slowly green again. The drenched grass gave way a little as the helicopter landed; Gideon got out, then Aisling, and then he turned and reached up his hand to the top of the steps. A girl got out: slight, dark-haired, dressed in jeans and a leather jacket. That was all Jocasta could see: except the way she shook her father's hand off and then stalked ahead of him towards the house, after her mother. She was hunched into her clothes, hands in her pockets.

Two hours passed; there was the sound of shouting, first from the ground floor, then outside on the terrace; mostly indistinguishable words, occasionally the predictable phrases, slung out like stones: "What do you expect?" "After all we've done." "How could you be so stupid?" "You've ruined my life!" "I hate you both."

Then slamming doors, pounding footsteps, up the stairs and along the corridor. And then more slamming doors. Gideon walked out, across the drenched grass, his head bent, down out of sight towards the lake. A solitary, wretched figure. Jocasta observed it all, phrases drifting into her head; it was a perfect story, with every possible element in it: not merely love, lust, and lawlessness, but riches, power, beauty, and wilful youth. Even, should she care to mention it, her own incarceration.

And then she saw them, walking back across the lawn, Aisling and Fionnuala with Gideon following behind them; the helicopter blades began to spin, and the mother and daughter ran under the wind, climbed into it. Slowly it lifted, tilting dangerously, then began to climb. All that could be seen was a small white circle in the window, Fionnuala's face looking down. Gideon waved—please, please, Jocasta thought, wave back, please—but the circle did not move and there was no sign of any response. He turned and walked back towards the house, looking as if he was the last person in the world.

Jocasta turned also, and for the first time since early that morning, left her room.

He was in the study, as she had known he would be, staring at his laptop screen, his huge hands moving with odd deftness over the keyboard. She tapped on the door.

"Not now, Mrs. Mitchell," he said.

"It's not Mrs. Mitchell. It's me."

He swung round; his face ashen with strain, his eyes red-rimmed.

"Why haven't you gone?" he asked, and his voice was expressionless.

"Mrs. Mitchell didn't want to take me."

"Well, she should have done. I'll call her now."

"Do you have to? Can't I stay a bit longer?"

"I'd rather you didn't. I'm sorry, Jocasta, but I'm terribly tired and—"

"How did it go?"

"What?"

"I said how did it go?"

"Not well," he said, "not well at all . . . But I really don't want to discuss it. You must have quite enough for your piece. Especially if you've been here all day." He looked at her and said, "Are you sure Mrs. Mitchell refused to take you? That you haven't just stayed here, gathering material all this time? Because—"

"Gathering material for what, Gideon?" she said, and carefully made her voice childlike and innocent.

"Your story," he said, "that's what. Your bloody, undoubtedly brilliant, story. Are you happy with it now, Jocasta? I expect you are."

"Very happy," she said, "and it is undoubtedly brilliant."

"Perhaps it will even win you an award. I hope you're not going to ask if you can file it from here. There are limits, you know, even to my good nature."

"Of course," she said, "I realise that. And there are limits even to my ruthlessness. Actually."

"Well, good for you," he said, and half rose. "I'll go and find Mrs. Mitchell."

"Yes, thank you. But, well, you see, Gideon—"

"Yes?"

"It isn't ready to be filed. It hasn't been written. Except in my head."

"Well, you'd better get on with it," he said, "or it'll be late. And all those exclusives will be wasted."

"I'm not going to write it. I'm not going to file it. There is no story as far as I'm concerned. OK?"

"What?" he said, staring at her, sitting down heavily. "What did you say?"

"I didn't realise you were that decrepit," she said, smiling at him, moving slowly across the room towards him. "I didn't realise your hearing was faulty. I said"—and she was quite near him now—"I said, can you hear me all right now, Gideon, there is no story. Not from me, anyway."

"I don't understand."

"Then your brain must be failing as well. And your animal instincts, come to that. I can't do that to you, Gideon, I just can't. I care about you too much. It's perfectly simple. Now you'd better get that"—she gestured towards his ringing phone—"it might be important. I'll leave you in peace. I'll be in the playroom, if you want me."

A few minutes later he came in; he sat down beside her, and studied her as if he had never seen her before. Then he reached out his hand and pushed back her hair, leant forward and kissed her, very gently on the cheek.

"Thank you," he said.

"That's all right. Honestly."

"It's more than all right, Jocasta. Much more than all right. I can imagine what that cost you."

"Not as much as you might think."

"Oh really? I'm surprised."

"Then you don't know me very well, do you?" she said. "Not yet, anyway. Who was that on the phone?"

"It was—it was Fionnuala."

"Oh really? And what did she say?"

"She said— Do you really want to know?"

"Of course I do."

"Well, it wasn't much. She just said"—and he had clearly been playing and replaying it over and over in his head and there was a slight shake in his voice—"she just said, 'Hi Dad. Thanks for coming today.' "

"That sounds like quite a lot to me," said Jocasta. "Not easy for her, that. Now, I wonder if I could go for a walk? I've been shut indoors all day. And—"

"I would say that was absolutely your own fault," he said, and he kissed her then, very softly, on the mouth, leant back and smiled at her. "And I wonder if you would allow me to join you? I think we have rather a lot to talk about."

"I do, too," said Jocasta.

Chapter 22

· · ·

Nick was walking along the Burma Road, as the Westminster press corridor was known ("Because everyone ends up there," he had explained to a breathlessly interested Jocasta what seemed a lifetime ago), when his phone rang. He looked at the number, it was her. She had finally deigned to contact him. He had heard from Pollock, a white-faced, raging Pollock, who clearly felt some of the blame must be due to Nick, as the person closest to her, not only that she had failed to deliver what would have been the most brilliant piece but that she was leaving the paper.

"As from now. And she'd better not show so much as an inch of her arse in this place ever again. It's so unlike her, so unprofessional. I suppose you know what it's all about?"

"Of course I don't," said Nick. "I don't know anything at all. I've been trying to contact her, but her phone's been switched off."

"Yeah? What's the silly bitch up to over there, then?"

"I honestly don't know," said Nick, "and I'm trying not to even consider the possibilities."

"Do you think she's with Keeble?"

"I . . . suppose it might be a possibility," said Nick, and just saying the words was like pulling teeth.

And he thought that, actually, it might be something to do with him, for if he had asked her to marry him, even at some fairly distant date, she would be filing a story right now, and Gideon Keeble would not have earned a second of her consideration. But, even in his misery, he thought still that he couldn't have done it.

And now here she was, on his mobile, several days after disappearing, several days of not caring for his anxiety, his concern.

"Yes?" he said shortly.

"Nick? Did—Chris tell you?"

"He did. I have to say I'd have expected to be your first port of call, Jocasta."

"Sorry, Nick, but I had to tell Chris about the story. And then, well, I wanted to think."

"What about?"

"About what I was going to say to you."

"And it didn't even occur to you that I might have been worried out of my mind? So what are you going to say? What are your plans? Perhaps you'd be good enough to share them with me."

"I'm going to stay here for a few more days."

"Am I to infer you're there with Gideon Keeble? I mean actually *with* him? In his—" He stopped. He couldn't bring himself to say the word "bed," it hurt too much. "In his house?"

"Well, yes. I am. Obviously. And I couldn't do the story because of—of Gideon."

"But the story was *about* Gideon. You might just have realised that before you left."

"Yes, I did. But I didn't care then."

"What, so in forty-eight hours from not caring about him at all, you cared so much that you've thrown your entire career away?"

"It's a bit more complicated than that," she said. "It wasn't just about Gideon. I did realise what harm I could do to them all. By writing the story."

"Oh, please!" he said. "You've developed a social conscience—is that what you're saying?"

"Sort of, yes, only it was about Gideon as well. That was what made me realise. I suppose."

"How touching!"

She was silent. Then: "Sorry, Nick. I'm very sorry."

"Jocasta, how can you turn your back on us? How can you throw away a long and very happy relationship just like that? On a whim."

"It wasn't just on a whim. It absolutely wasn't."

"Oh really? So you'd been planning it for some time, had you?"

"I suppose so. In a way. Without realising it."

"Oh, for fuck's sake! I've never heard such drivel."

"It's not drivel!" she said. "And if you thought for just a little while, you'd realise why it happened."

"Dare I assume this has something to do with my refusing to trail down the altar after you?"

"Actually," she said, "I'd be trailing after you. You obviously haven't been to many weddings, Nick. But yes, just something. In a way."

"How fucking pathetic," he said, and cut her off.

Jocasta went to find Gideon. It was a glorious day, blue and green and golden, the kind Ireland did best. She lifted her head to the sun and it felt warm and welcoming. She found Gideon walking towards the stables.

"Hi," she said, and tucked her hand into his back pocket.

"Hello, my darling. Did you do it?"

"Yes, I did."

"And? You've been crying."

"Yes, well, I feel bad and sad. It was—I mean, it's been a long time, Nick and me. It's hard to just end it. Even though I knew it was over before—well before—you. But I'm fine. I know I did the right thing. And it made me realise how much I actually do love you."

"I'm very happy about that. And I love you very badly."

"You can't love someone badly, Gideon."

"I can. As in, 'I want that very badly.' "

"Oh, all right. I love you very badly too. And want you very badly."

"That's nice to know."

How exactly had it come to this so quickly and with such astonishing ease? It had been like a film, moving the story forward in a series of short sequences, all intercut, with no dialogue, just wonderful emotive music. There had been the walk down to the lake, the two of them together, walking apart at first and then gradually moving closer together, until his arm was round her shoulders, hers round his waist; there had been the kiss, tender, not passionate, by the lake; there had been dinner, served by Mrs. Mitchell in the grand dining room; there had been his taking her hand and leading her upstairs, only to bid her good night on the second-floor landing, very properly; there had been her lying awake, staring into the darkness (and she supposed further intercutting of a shot of him also lying awake), and then her padding along the corridor, in search of him, opening several doors, the moonlight shafting most obligingly through the vast window at the top of the stairs; and then hearing someone behind her on the landing and turning in panic to see him smiling at her; and of course the sex scene, wonderfully passionate (the music rising to a crescendo here); and finally, before the film returned to proper time and words and all that sort of thing, them lying in bed together, smiling at each other, with the sun streaming in the window.

It was all slightly over the top, glorious setting, dashing hero, marvellous trappings—horses, servants, the incredible cars, he had actually allowed her to drive the Bugatti—but extremely wonderful just the same.

"I keep thinking I'm going to wake up," she said to Gideon, "find it's all a dream."

"Well, you're not," he said, "this is real life. Although I should have tried to seduce you much earlier."

"You did try. I think," said Jocasta. "But in a horribly gentlemanly way. Always including Nick in your invitations. I mean, really! No wonder progress was slow."

"I'm a patient fellow. I saw you, dancing in that ridiculous way at the conference, Jocasta, and I wanted you. And I knew that sooner or later I'd have to have you. It was as simple as that. I've just been waiting for the opportunity. My only fear was that Nicholas would have made an honest woman of you in the meantime."

"He was never going to," said Jocasta, "and until yesterday, I thought it mattered. Now I know it doesn't. Not in the very least."

And it didn't.

"Fionnuala wants a new horse," he said, as they walked back into the house. "A polo pony, actually."

"How do you know?"

"She texted me."

"That's good, that she's texting you. What did it say? Or would you rather I didn't see it?"

"Of course not. Here you are."

He passed her his phone; she looked at it.

"Hi Dad. Having fun here. Wd like polo pony for birthday. Any chance? Fionnuala xxx."

"It's nice she's keeping in touch," said Jocasta carefully.

"Isn't it? I can't think when she last put kisses after her name."

"I think," she said, "you shouldn't just say yes. You'd just be buying her toys again. Why don't you say you'd like to go and see her, look at some ponies with her?"

"I am not," he said firmly, "going to that filthy place, forced to be courteous to that slimy poof, Carlingford."

"All right. Tell her to come to Ireland, that you'll buy her one here. That you want to be part of the choice."

"She wouldn't come."

"Try her. Go on. Text her back. Here, I'll do it, you're so hopeless at it. I expect it's your age." She smiled at him, reached up to kiss him. "What shall I say?"

"You're the expert. But I'm not sure this is a good idea."

"Yes it is." She began punching out letters, her face very serious. She held it out to him.

"How's this? 'Nice idea, but I'd like to choose it with you. What about you come here? Dad xxx.' "

"OK," he said, after a moment or two. "Send it."

Five minutes later a message came back. "No point. No polo ponies in Ireland. They're all here. F."

"See," he said, "no kisses even. I told you."

"Oh shut up," said Jocasta. "You can't give up that easily." She wrote another message, handed it to him. "OK?"

He looked at it. "No, it is not OK. I told you— Oh, all right. See what she says."

She smiled, reread her message—"I cd come there? xxx."—and sent it.

It was half an hour later, as an increasingly bad-tempered Gideon stalked ahead of Jocasta down to the lake and sat scowling at the brilliant water, that a text message reached his phone.

"Cool. When? Fionnuala xxx."

"See?" said Jocasta. "What did I tell you?"

"Yes, all right," he said, smiling at her reluctantly. "Clever clogs. I hope you realise what this means? I'll have to actually go to the bloody place."

"I promise you," said Jocasta, "it will be worth it."

She was in love with him. Wasn't she? Desperately, terribly in love with him. Of course she was. She felt extraordinarily happy. All the time. She just couldn't believe it. And he was in love with her. He kept saying so. Telling her that he couldn't remember ever being so happy, couldn't believe that anyone so young and beautiful could be bothered with him, "Old and difficult and scratchy as I am."

"You are not old," she said. "You may be difficult, but I haven't seen it yet. And I've seen a lot scratchier. So here I am, youngish—and beautiful, maybe—and amazingly happy to be with you. OK?"

"Very OK," he said.

He was absurdly romantic; she would wake in the morning to find him missing and he would come in, smiling, with a great bunch of wild-flowers he had just picked. He chartered a small plane for the day and flew her over the Mountains of Mourne, simply because she said she had always wanted to see them. They went riding by moonlight, they drank champagne on a boat on the lake, he named one of his thoroughbred foals after her. "Until you arrived, she was the most beautiful female to come to this place all year."

She felt her own past was completely left behind her; she had only the clothes from her rucksack and her phone, nothing else. It was as if she had been set down and told her life was to start over again. It was all too good to be true, exactly what her romantic soul craved. Just the two of them, for a little while, cocooned from the world, feasting on pleasure; looking back, she saw that it was their honeymoon.

And then there was the sex.

The sex was—well, it was good. It was very good. Obviously.

She was enjoying it a lot.

•—•

"Well, I think that's enough." Carla smiled at Kate.

They had a wonderful morning, combing Topshop and then just in case it looked as if they'd paid for the publicity, to Oasis and River Island as well. The last two had been a bit of a rush, as Kate had promised Jilly she'd be home by soon after lunch to get on with her studying; but Carla knew they had enough. Kate had chosen almost everything herself; it always showed, Carla thought, the eye for clothes, not so much in the actual outfits as in the accessories. Belts, scarves, tights, sunglasses: the choices had been unerring, some things which Carla wouldn't even have considered, but which looked wonderful on Kate.

"I think so too," said Kate. "I'm so excited. What time do you want us?"

"As early as possible. I've ordered a cab and I've booked someone from Nicky Clarke to do your hair, and a lovely girl to do the makeup, which I promise won't be much. Now let's get you onto your tube. I don't want your grandmother worried. She's terrific, Kate. You're very lucky."

"I know," said Kate. "She always seems younger than my mum."

"You look a bit like her too. Same colouring."

"Pure coincidence," said Kate.

"Why?"

"I'm adopted," said Kate. "Look, I'd better go. Thanks, Carla. It's been great. Bye!"

Carla looked after her thoughtfully as she disappeared down the escalator, a whirl of blond hair and long, long legs. Adopted? That was interesting. Another dimension to the story, perhaps. She must find out more about that tomorrow.

•─•─•

"The Girl with Tunnel Vision," the article was subheaded. And went on to describe how Martha had been driven all her life—"no serious boyfriends while she was at school, in case they distracted her, working at least a twelve-hour day, and even now, still only one week's holiday at a time . . ."

Jack Kirkland had organised it: the woman's editor was a friend, had said they'd seen the one in the *Sketch* and were looking for a woman in politics to interview. Martha had said why not Janet and he'd said Janet was interviewed out; they wanted someone new, someone younger.

"Well, don't tell Janet that," she'd said.

"Why not? Anyway, I already did."

"Jack! Just think how she'd feel."

"Too late," he'd said. "But she didn't seem to mind. She agreed, more or less, said she was sick of doing them."

Anyway, she hadn't been so scared this time; she'd felt in control of the whole thing. And it read well. She was learning—fast.

She binned the paper, resolving to buy another later. She was out for a run; it was just six, a perfect May morning. Pounding over Tower Bridge, taking in the glorious view downriver, the wonderful tapestry of old and new buildings carved against the sky, glorying in having the city almost to herself, she thought she had never felt quite so happy. She had taken all these risks with her life, stepped outside her own closely defined comfort zone, breathed in the heady air—and found herself still safe. It was hard to believe. She should have trusted herself earlier, she thought; she'd missed a lot. She'd even done something which had astonished her, and been to an audition for *Question Time*, the main political TV show. The publicity department had been over the moon when she was invited; had said people struggled for years to get on the programme. And she'd actually enjoyed it; challenging though it had been, sitting round a table in a dining room in Lime Grove, with the producer and some other potential guests. It wasn't as if she'd had to say a word about herself, she had simply had to talk politics, prove her views were strong enough and that she was sufficiently articulate. She'd felt she'd done quite well, but it had been weeks since then, so probably she hadn't.

Anyway, she was altogether feeling rather bullish. She'd be going on holiday with Ed soon, as he so wanted her to.

"What harm would it do?" he said. "We'd have fun. Heard about fun, Martha? It's what other people have. You ought to investigate it. Just a week, I promise I won't ask for more. Go on: be reckless."

So far she'd said no; but this morning, standing here, astride her life and its success, she could just about imagine—well, maybe more than imagine . . .

◆·◆

"Well, that's about it," said Marc Jones. "You were great, Kate."

"You really were," said Carla. "Fantastic. Those last shots, when you started dancing—well, I'll want to put them on the front page."

"Oh please do!" said Kate. She was flushed, flying, triumphant. For the first time in her life she felt properly confident. Someone in charge of her life, someone who mattered; not someone of no consequence, with no proper footing in the world, no proper roots.

"I doubt we'll get that. But you'll certainly be a double-page spread—hopefully the centre of the paper. Aren't you proud of her, Jilly?"

"I'm terribly proud of her," said Jilly. "I thought she was marvellous. She looked as if she'd been doing it for years."

She did feel very happy about it; entirely justified in her decision. She had seen something happen to Kate that morning, just as Kate had felt it herself; she had shaken off some of her insecurities, her doubts about herself, become someone new. If Helen was upset, Jilly would tell her all that, tell her what it had meant to Kate. A lot more than simply being photographed in the paper. In a funny way, Kate had found herself. It was lovely to see.

Carla was taking them all out for tea: lunch had been a sandwich.

"I thought we'd go to the Ritz," she said. "I've booked a table."

"The Ritz!" said Jilly. "I haven't had tea at the Ritz since I was a girl."

"I'm sure it hasn't changed," said Carla, smiling. "I don't suppose even the waiters have changed."

"Still tea in the Palm Court?"

"Still tea in the Palm Court. We can have a champagne tea, if you like."

"Oh I don't think we should do that," said Jilly.

"Granny! I think we should. We've got a lot to celebrate. Haven't we, Marc? You'll come, won't you?" She was flirting with him. Jilly thought, How sweet.

" 'Fraid I can't," said Marc regretfully. "Got to go back and get this lot processed. But another time, Kate. Another session. I'm sure there'll be one."

"Are you really?"

"Absolutely. The other Kate will be looking to her laurels soon, you mark my words."

"Oh, wow!" said Kate. They did have the champagne tea. Sitting amongst the excesses of the Palm Court, with its crystal chandeliers and huge palms, painted murals and wonderfully old-fashioned pianist. Champagne, and a pile of tiny sandwiches, scones with cream, very fancy iced cakes, meringues and éclairs, and a pot of fragrant Earl Grey.

Jilly was struggling weakly to refuse a second glass when Carla got her notebook out.

"You may as well, Jilly, I've got to ask a lot of boring stuff now. Like Kate's age, where she goes to school, what she's interested in, and what she wants to do. Anything that you might think would give her a bit of colour, as we call it in the trade."

"Well, my full name is Kate Bianca Tarrant," said Kate. "Make sure you put the Bianca in, won't you? Kate's such a dull name."

"Of course. We could reverse them if you like—Bianca Kate sounds better than the other way round." She seemed pleased. "Why Bianca? It's quite unusual. Did it mean something special to your mother?"

"No, not really. I think . . . she just liked it," said Kate. She sounded guarded suddenly. "Anyway, my birthday's August the fifteenth."

"And you'll be sixteen?"

"Yeah. Then I can do what I like!" She grinned happily.

"And what would that be?"

"Oh no doubt about that. Be a model. Now I know how great it is."

"Fine. And what other interests do you have? Hobbies?"

"Don't have many. Clothes. Clubbing," said Kate vaguely. "My sister's the one. She got a music scholarship, and she plays the piano and the violin and belongs to two orchestras."

"Yes, she's very talented," said Jilly fondly. "We're extremely proud of Juliet."

"Is she adopted too?" asked Carla.

Jilly looked at her sharply. "I didn't know you knew that."

"Kate told me about it yesterday, didn't you, Kate?"

"Yes, yes, I did. Juliet's not adopted, no."

"Right. Well, you obviously get on."

"Quite," said Kate. "She makes me look a bit hopeless."

"No she doesn't, darling," said Jilly, patting her knee. "You're just very different."

"Hardly surprising," said Carla, "since you're not real sisters. Kate, do you know who your real mother is? Are you in touch with her?"

"No," said Kate shortly.

"Would you like to be?"

"No, I wouldn't. And it's *birth* mother, not *real* mother," she added, rather severely. "My real mum and my real dad—that's what they are to me—they're the ones who brought me up, they're the ones I care about."

"Of course," said Carla soothingly, "and I'm sure they know that."

"Of course they do," said Jilly. She could see that Kate was getting upset. "They're a very happy family."

"I'm sure. So, any boyfriends, Kate?"

"No. No one serious, anyway."

"And what sort of boys do you like?"

"Oh . . ." A picture of Nat swam into Kate's head. "Cool ones, obviously. Tall. Dark. With really cool clothes."

"And what do cool boys wear?"

"Well, combats. Really good boots. Sleeveless T-shirts. Leather jackets. And they drive cool cars."

"And what's a cool car? A Porsche?"

"No!" Kate's expression was a mixture of pity and disdain. "That's an old bloke's car. No, maybe an Escort, or a Citroën, that's been, like, souped-up, something with a spoiler, that sort of thing."

"Sounds great," said Carla. "And which clubs you go to."

"Oh, all over the place," said Kate airily. "The Ministry of Sound. The Shed in Brixton."

"They have a wonderful time these days," said Jilly, relieved that the conversation had turned away from Kate's adoption. "Of course we did, too. In our own way. I used to come dancing here, you know."

Kate sighed and said she'd like to go to the loo. "It's over there," said Carla, "just down those steps to the right."

"Cool. See you in a bit. I might clean some of this muck off my face."

"Kate seems a little defensive about her adoption," said Carla casually, after several minutes of hearing how Jilly and her husband had been two of the earliest members of Annabel's.

"Yes, well it's not surprising, especially under her particular circumstances."

"What particular circumstances?"

"Oh, she—" Jilly stopped, took a large sip of champagne. "Carla, this is not for publication, is it?"

"Of course not. It's got nothing to do with the article."

"No. Well, she has absolutely no idea who her mother is. None of us do."

"Oh, really? I thought these days it was all very open, that they can go in search of their birth mothers."

"Normally, of course, they can, but because she was just left like that— Oh, Kate darling, there you are. We really should go. I'm worrying about Juliet."

"I've got a car waiting," said Carla. "It'll take you home. Look, I've got all I could possibly need. I'll send some of the pictures over tomorrow, and I could have a couple mounted for your parents, Kate, if you like. As a coming-home present."

"That'd be cool," said Kate. "Thanks."

Jilly said that she didn't know what Kate would do if the word "cool" hadn't been invented, drained her glass of champagne, and followed Carla, slightly unsteadily, out to the front of the Ritz.

What a wonderful day it had been: she felt sure it would prove a huge turning point in Kate's life.

What was she going to write about Kate? Carla wondered, looking at the photograph. Just an extended caption? Or a bit more? She wasn't really particularly interesting. Just one of a million other fifteen-year-olds. Best to concentrate on that. "An extraordinary ordinary girl," she wrote, "who could be working in a branch of Topshop, or—"

No, it wasn't good enough. It just wasn't. She'd read that so many times in other fashion editors' pages. It was a cliché. And she wanted to capture in words as well as pictures the quality of Kate, to make her special, her toughness, her prickliness. All because of the adoption, she supposed. Well, they obviously wouldn't want that written about. And there was nothing special about that really, either. If they'd known who the mother was, it might be different.

Her door burst open; Johnny Hadley, the diary editor, came in, looking flustered.

"Carla. Hi. Look, do me a favour, would you? I'm frantic, got to check a couple of things for the lawyers. I'm running a nice story on Sophie Wessex. A few months ago, Jocasta interviewed some woman in the powder room at the Dorchester Hotel, or wherever it was, when there was all that trouble about the bogus sheik, remember? She said how sweet Sophie was, how she always had a kind word for everyone. It never ran, so could you have a rummage in her desk, see if you can find it. It would make a nice bit of background. God, who's that? Lovely pair of boobs. And talking about Jocasta, she looks a bit like her, wouldn't you say? Or am I imagining it?"

"No," said Carla, glancing down at the pictures of Kate, "I've said it myself. She's my latest discovery. Yes, all right, Johnny, I'll bring the piece in if I can find it."

She went to Jocasta's desk and pulled out the top drawer; nothing in that but a stack of old tapes, some rather dubious-looking lipsticks, and a packet of Tampax. The next one looked more promising: cuttings from the paper, printouts of e-mails, a few drafts of articles. Nothing about Sophie Wessex. The third drawer was total chaos: a mass of papers, notes, typed copy, more printed e-mails. Bloody hell. She'd just have a quick rummage and then say she couldn't find it. It was—

"Oh my God!" said Carla. She sat down suddenly and began to read a set of pages. Feverishly, not once, but two, three times. And then picked them up, took them into her office, shut the door, and read them again.

It was *exactly* what she had been looking for. Only it wasn't an article about the chatelaine of the toilets at the Dorchester. It was something quite different. A printout from the *Sketch* archives, and another from the *Mail* and yet another from the *Sun*, about a baby, abandoned at Heathrow airport. On August 15, almost sixteen years ago. Whom the nurses had named Bianca. And whose mother had apparently never been found.

PART TWO

It was a bit like when President Kennedy was shot, the older people concerned said. And like when Princess Diana had been killed, said the younger ones. You knew exactly what you were doing when you heard about it: or rather read it. And you knew you would never forget the moment as long as you lived.

"Oh, no," whispered Helen, "oh, no, please no," as she read the story, read it again, and again, and then sitting there, white-faced under her new tan, concentrating on the pictures of Kate, the extraordinary pictures of Kate, as if by ignoring the words she could will them away.

Jim, literally speechless with rage, was pacing up and down the kitchen, pausing occasionally to bang his fist on the back door; and Jilly, the one most responsible for the horror, sat in the dining room, too shocked even to think, confronted by the very worst of all the scenarios she had imagined since Carla's phone call, twenty-four hours earlier.

. . . .

Clio, doing a Saturday morning surgery, was shown the article by the receptionist, excited at the rebirth of the story about one of their patients. "It mentions Mrs. Bradford and her shop by name," she said. Clio sat in her room, reading and rereading it, wondering how much Kate had contributed to the story herself, and hoping against hope it had been nothing to do with Jocasta. And wondering how Kate's mother, her real mother, must be feeling when she saw it, as she surely would.

Nat Tucker read it as he sat in his mother's kitchen, ignoring his father's exhortations to shift his bloody arse and get on down to the garage, and wondering not only if he should call Kate or just go round and see her, but how he could never have realised how totally gorgeous she was, and enjoying the very clear description of himself and his car. And, with a sensitivity that would have surprised most of his mates and the whole of his family, thinking that it couldn't be that great, having the fact you'd been abandoned in a cleaning cupboard splashed all over some cruddy newspaper.

Carla, who had seen the pages the night before at proof stage and felt extremely satisfied with herself, was having a little trouble confronting the reality. Of course she had only been doing her job; of course Jilly, clearly shocked and even frightened, had confirmed (Carla having put her phone onto "record" when she spoke to her, as instructed by the lawyers) that yes, it was correct, and abandoned baby Bianca was indeed Kate; and of course nothing had changed and Kate still clearly had a dazzling future as a model. But somehow, seeing her there in the paper, in all her young vulnerability, with her small sad history spelt out for the almost two million readers of the *Sketch* to be entertained by as they ate their breakfasts, Carla didn't feel quite so pleased with herself.

Martha saw the story trailed on the front page of the *Sketch* while she was out on her early run: "The abandoned baby: now tipped as the latest face in fashion. Meet Bianca Kate, modelling for the first time in the *Sketch* today." She read the story, put the paper, folded neatly, into a rubbish bin, ran back to her apartment, showered and dressed in one of her constituency suits, and drove down to Binsmow. She arrived, as promised, at the vicarage at eleven thirty, did a brief legal clinic, and went to a school summer fair. That evening she and her parents attended a charity concert in Binsmow town hall, where she bought five books of raffle tickets and won a rather grubby-looking bottle of bubble bath. She left Binsmow early next morning, after going to communion and then breakfasting with her mother, who was engrossed in the story of Bianca Kate, the abandoned baby, which had found its way into the *Sunday Times* as well as the *Mail on Sunday*. She agreed it was the most dreadful thing to abandon a baby and that she couldn't imagine anyone doing such a thing, then drove back to London and her apartment, where she spent the day working and dealing with personal admin. In the evening she went to the gym, where she did a spinning class and swam thirty lengths of the pool.

Ed, who had left four messages on her landline, several more on her mobile, and a couple of text messages as well asking her to call him to discuss, among other things, a trip to Venice he had organised, was first hurt, then annoyed, and finally seriously anxious when she failed to answer any of them.

And Kate, her golden, dazzling day turned dark and ugly, sat in her bedroom, the door firmly locked, crying endlessly and silently, and feeling more wretched and ashamed than she could have believed possible.

When Gideon found Jocasta, she was sitting on the grass by the lake, still and stunned, holding the paper close to her, wondering how such a thing could possibly have happened, and cursing Carla with a venom which surprised even her.

"Can I persuade you to talk about this?" said Gideon.

"I suppose so," she said, turning a face, swollen with crying, to him. "It's something horrible, Gideon, something I—well, something I was implicated in."

"But you weren't there," he said when she had finished. "It's not your story. It's nothing to do with you."

"Gideon, it is, it is. Oh God, I have to go to London. Go and see Kate. I really have to."

"All right, my darling one. If you have to. Maybe I should come with you. I'm worried about you, you look dreadful."

"No," she said, leaning forward to kiss him, resting her head briefly on his shoulder. "I've got to do this by myself."

"All right. If that's how it is."

"It is. Oh, Gideon, it's such a horrible thing to happen. To a little girl."

"What, being abandoned at an airport? It is indeed. But she has a lovely family now, from the sound of it—and maybe she told Carla herself. Maybe it wasn't your fault at all, nothing to do with you."

"I asked Carla that when I rang her," said Jocasta, starting to cry again, "and she said Kate didn't tell her anything, only that she was adopted. She got it all—she said—from the archives."

"She could well have done."

"Yes, but I had a lot about Kate in my desk; I think she found that. And she certainly didn't warn the poor little thing what she was going to do. She admitted that. Bitch! It's so cruel, so dreadfully cruel."

She blew her nose, managed a wobbly smile. Gideon looked at her, then back at the newspaper.

"I suppose," he said quite quietly, "no one has mentioned any resemblance between you and this girl?"

Jocasta started to laugh: a loud, almost hysterical laugh.

"Yes," she said, "actually they have."

Clio decided she should ring Jilly Bradford. She had liked her so much and she could imagine how dreadful she must be feeling. There were no quotes from her, or indeed from any of the family. Including Kate.

She got a recorded message in Jilly's slightly dated, upper-class accent. She left a message, saying how sorry she was, and then pressed her buzzer for the next patient. What an awful mess. Poor little Kate. God, these newspapers had a lot to answer for. Surely Jocasta couldn't have done this. But it was her paper.

Back in her flat, feeling half ashamed, she decided to call her. Her mobile was on message. Clio left her number, asked her to call, and was still wondering if she could be bothered to make herself anything more than a sandwich, when Jocasta rang.

"Hi, Clio. It's Jocasta. How are you?"

"Fine. I just saw the article about Kate and—"

"It was nothing to do with me, Clio. Honestly. Well, only in the most indirect way and—well, actually I've left the *Sketch*."

"You've left? Why?"

"Oh . . . bit of a long story. Look, I'm in Ireland at the moment, about to fly to London. I'm going to try and see Kate, because I do feel responsible. In a way."

"Jocasta, you're talking in riddles."

"I know. Sorry. Look, if I haven't been beaten up by the Tarrants, could we meet this evening? I could come to you, if you like. It'd be good to talk it through with someone who knows Kate. Would you mind?"

"Of course not. Don't be silly. Just call me."

"Is that Mrs. Tarrant?"

"Yes?"

It was a soft voice with a slightly north-country accent.

"Mrs. Tarrant, you don't know me, but I think I could be Bianca's mother. You see, I left a baby at the airport seventeen years ago—"

"Sixteen years," Helen said sharply. She thought she might be sick.

"What? Oh I'm sorry, I thought it said seventeen."

Helen slammed the phone down and burst into tears; and greatly against her will, feeling every word threatening to choke her, she called Carla Giannini.

Carla had called first thing: bright and confident. Weren't the pictures lovely, didn't Kate look great, they must all be so proud of her. Helen had been so shocked she had mumbled something totally inane.

"Would Kate like to speak to me, I wonder?"

"No," said Helen in the same quiet, numb voice, "no, I'm sure she wouldn't."

"Well, later, perhaps. Tell her I've had several offers for her already."

"What sort of offers?"

"Modelling agencies. Of course, that is entirely up to you."

"I'm so glad something is," Helen said icily. She was beginning to re-gain her confidence.

Carla ignored this. "There is one thing, Mrs. Tarrant—one thing I should warn you about. You could get calls. From women claiming to be Kate's mother. We've had a couple already. I would advise you to let us handle these for you. Put any calls on to us. It's—"

"I don't want you to handle anything for us," said Helen, and she could hear the loathing in her own voice, the rage and the misery. "You've done enough damage—please leave us alone."

And she put the phone down, very carefully. What was she going to do? How were they going to get through this? How?

After two more phone calls from women, she realised, very reluctantly, that they couldn't do it alone.

Carla was brisk and efficient. "Just redirect them all to us."

"And suppose—suppose one of them was genuine?" The words hurt her to speak them. "How would we know?"

"We would ask for proof of some kind."

"What sort of proof?" said Helen, desperately.

"Well, is there anything at all that you know, about the way Kate was abandoned, that wasn't in the story? Like the time it was, or what she was wearing."

"I don't think so," said Helen bitterly. "Every wretched detail is there."

"Try and think of something. And call me back."

So far, Helen couldn't.

She went and opened the dining-room door without knocking, looked at Jilly with cold dislike.

"I think I'd like to take you home. Jim and I both feel we need to be on our own with the girls."

"Of course," said Jilly humbly. "But no need to take me, I'll get a cab. There haven't been any calls for me, have there?"

"I've stopped answering the phone, we've had so many. Jim's going out to buy an answering machine."

"Oh dear, how dreadful. Who from?"

"Other reporters mostly. From other papers. Do we have anything to add, could they interview Kate, that sort of thing."

She didn't tell her about the women, the would-be mothers; she couldn't bear it.

"Helen, I must just say once more how sorry I am. But I really didn't tell this woman anything, she had all the information already—"

"Mummy, for what must be the tenth time, if you hadn't agreed to let

Kate do those wretched photographs, none of it would have happened. How could you, without asking us, when you were supposed to be responsible for her?"

"I—" Jilly stopped. She had no defence, she knew.

"Mummy, it really wasn't just Granny's fault." Juliet had appeared, her face pale. "I told her to go ahead. I said it would be so great for Kate and—"

"Juliet, you are fourteen years old," said Helen wearily. "I hardly think it was very sensible of your grandmother to rely on your opinion."

"But—"

"Juliet, darling, it's nice of you to stand up for me, but your mother's quite right. I should never have agreed. Could I just say goodbye to Kate?"

"If you have to." Helen was disproportionately pleased when Kate refused to let her into her room.

Half an hour later, when Jilly had departed, there was a ring at the door. Helen answered it. It was Nat Tucker. The Sax Bomb stood at the gate, its engine still running, its sound system at full volume.

"Oh," she said. "Nat. Hello."

"Mornin'," he said. "Kate in?"

"Er—she is," said Helen, "but I'm afraid she's not very well."

"Oh, right. Just tell her I came then. And that I saw her photos in the paper."

"Fine. Yes. Of course."

"Nice, aren't they?" he said.

"She looks great. Well, see you later."

And he ambled down the path, pulling a packet of cigarettes out of the pocket of his extremely low-slung trousers. Helen and Juliet, who had heard his voice, stood staring after him.

"How sweet," said Juliet, "how really sweet. Wait till I tell Kate."

Helen caught her arm. "Juliet, you are not to tell Kate."

Juliet stared at her. "Why on earth not?"

"Because I can't face any more upsets this morning."

"Mum! That's horrible. Why should there be an upset? He's the one person in the whole world, probably, who can make Kate feel better just now."

"Don't be so ridiculous," said Helen.

"It's true! She only did it to make him notice her. She'll be pleased he came round. And don't you realise, half of what's making her so upset is thinking everyone'll know what happened to her, that her mother just . . .

well, just threw her away, as she sees it, and she feels it's like a public humiliation. If Nat Tucker doesn't care about it, she'll be much happier—"

"Juliet, Nat Tucker is not the sort of boy I want Kate getting mixed up with," said Helen.

"You sound like Granny," said Juliet, in a tone of complete contempt. "Actually, worse. At least she thinks Nat's good-looking. Anyway, he was nice enough to come round, so I'm going up to tell Kate and you can't stop me."

Kate was wondering how she could ever leave her room again, face a world that knew what had happened to her, that must be either despising her or feeling sorry for her or laughing at her, when Juliet called through her door with the news that Nat had come to the house, had wanted to see her, had said she looked great: it was like—well, she didn't know what it was like. Like being given a present. No, better than that. Like the dentist's drill stopping. She opened the door, let Juliet in, and sat on the bed, staring at her, as if she had never seen her before.

"Did he really? Come here?"

"He really did. He's so sweet, Kate. Honestly. It can't have been easy for him. He obviously does like you a lot. Why don't you call him?"

"Yes, I might. Later. When I feel a bit better. God, I can't believe that. I really, really can't."

"Well, he did." Juliet studied her. "Better not ask him round yet, though. You look awful—your eyes look about half the size. And your face is all swollen and blotchy."

"Yes, all right, all right," said Kate irritably. "God, Jools, think of that. He actually came here. That is so cool. Tell me again exactly what he said. Exactly . . ."

Helen recognised Jocasta; she was looking nervously from behind the curtains in the front room at the slowly growing crowd at the gate. She turned to Jim.

"It's Jocasta. You know, Jocasta Forbes—"

"Well, I'll tell her to bugger off," he said. Helen had never heard him use a stronger profanity than "bloody."

"Jim!"

"Well," he said, his tone infinitely weary, "she was where it all began.

No doubt she told that other woman all about Kate. I don't want her anywhere near us. And if we let her in, those other vultures will follow. Or try to. God, here's another, looks like a photographer. Jesus, Helen, what are we going to do?"

"I think we should let Jocasta in," said Helen bravely. "My mother said it was nothing to do with her."

"Helen, I am not having that woman in my house," said Jim. "I won't allow it. It's as simple as that."

"It's not your house," said Helen, emboldened by the desperate situation. "It's *ours*. And I think she might be able to help."

He said nothing, just sat in his chair, biting his fist.

Helen walked over to the door, shouted through it, "What do you want, Jocasta?"

"I want to talk to you. And to Kate. I want to try and explain. That it wasn't me. I want to tell Kate that. I think it might just help. Please, Mrs. Tarrant. *Please*."

"All right," said Helen. "I'll open the door. I don't know if Kate'll want to see you."

"Thanks. Thank you so much."

"It was totally awful," Jocasta said to Clio later, over a glass of wine. She had arrived on Clio's doorstep, pale and very shaken. "None of them believed me. Kate refused even to see me. She just said she thought she could trust me. That she thought I was her friend. Shouting through her door at me. Oh God, Clio, what an awful mess. What have I done?"

"Nothing—I thought," said Clio.

"Well, I did do one thing," said Jocasta, lighting a cigarette. "Sorry about this, Clio. I really need it."

"That's OK. What did you do?"

"I looked Kate up in the archives. I was—well, I was intrigued. Her grandmother told me she'd been abandoned, and Kate had told me when her birthday was. I printed the story off. It was in all the papers at the time. About Baby Bianca being found. And then Kate told me all about it herself. She obviously finds it really hard to cope with, but she thought if I wrote about it, her mother might come and find her. I certainly wasn't going to do anything without her parents' permission, but I put all the printouts in a file in my drawer. I shouldn't have. If I'd thought for five minutes, I'd have shredded them or something. But—well, I didn't know I was going to leave. I didn't know that cow Carla was going to go through my desk."

"Is that what she did?"

"She must have done. She says she didn't, but I don't believe her. God, I feel so sick. Oh, Clio, what am I going to do?"

"I don't know," said Clio, "but I'm sure Kate will calm down. She's obviously terribly shocked. I just spoke to her grandmother. She was very subdued . . . It turned out she'd agreed to the fashion session while the Tarrants were away. Apparently this Carla woman had called her to confirm the story. Anyway, she said it was all her fault. She said Kate had been shouting at her, telling her she hated her. Clearly," she added, refilling Jocasta's glass, "you aren't entirely to blame."

Jocasta's mobile rang. "Hi," she said. "Oh, hello, Gideon. How absolutely lovely to hear your voice. No, everything's not all right. It's ghastly. It didn't do any good. Look, I'll call you later. I'm with a friend. An old friend." She smiled at Clio. "Yes, you would like her. A lot. We went travelling together. With that bitch Martha I told you about. What? Oh, Gideon! Well, I know I did but— Oh, all right. I might stay in London till you get back. I don't think I can cope with Mrs. Mitchell on my own. Yes, I will. I promise. I love you too."

"Who was that?" Clio asked.

"Gideon Keeble. He's Irish and quite famous—owns dozens of shopping malls all over the world and God knows what else. Several houses. He's had umpteen wives and he's got a nightmare teenage daughter, who he's just off to see in Barbados, that's why he rang, to buy her some polo ponies."

"*Some?*" said Clio, incredulously.

"Yes. One is nothing like enough, apparently. Anyway, he's older than me and a workaholic and it's all completely unsuitable. And I am totally, totally in love with him. I've left Nick, given up my job, given up my whole life here. Just to be with Gideon."

"God," said Clio, "he must be very special."

"He is. I can't imagine how I could have ever thought I was happy until now. I feel—oh I don't know. As if my real life has only just begun. It's so strange."

Chapter 24

. . . .

Helen was laying the breakfast table; she wasn't sure why. No one would come down. Kate was still more or less locked in her room, and since the altercation over Nat, Juliet refused to communicate with her, had eaten supper in Kate's room, and even slept in there. She had become, in Kate's hour of need, her best, her most loyal friend, the only person Kate would talk to. So some good had come out of it, Helen thought wearily.

Jim certainly wouldn't want breakfast; he was still raging, so angry and upset, that he had been up half the night with dreadful indigestion, pacing up and down, snapping at Helen if she tried to say anything. He was asleep now: a fitful, noisy sleep, but at least asleep.

At any rate, the reporters had gone. Jocasta had said they would. "It's not a big enough story to keep them all night. They'll just rehash what's on the files."

Jocasta had asked about cranks, too; clearly it was a standard hazard. She seemed relieved that Carla was doing something to help.

"Have you had many calls?"

"About five now," said Helen. "I've told them all to ring the paper. But I'm so afraid that—well—" She stopped.

"I can imagine," said Jocasta gently. "That one of them might be the real mother."

"Yes. The Giannini woman said to try and think of something that could be a sort of test question. And there is just one thing. She wasn't wearing a nappy. That wasn't ever . . . ever detailed."

"That would do," said Jocasta. In fact it would do wonderfully well. No one would expect a baby to be left without a nappy on. "Tell Carla. Better still, I'll do it for you. Right now. And I do think you should change your telephone number, Mrs. Tarrant, go ex-directory. Otherwise you—well, let's say an answering machine just isn't what you want."

Very shortly after that she left.

Suddenly, Helen heard pounding on the stairs; she looked into the hall. Kate was disappearing through the front door, her hair flying behind her; she was wearing jeans, an extremely skimpy top, and her highest-heeled boots.

"Kate!" she shouted, running to open it again. "Kate, where are you—"

But all that was left of Kate was a roar of exhaust and a screech of tyres; the Sax Bomb was just disappearing round the corner.

"Sorry, Mum." It was Juliet, looking slightly shame-faced. "She won't be long. She says she wants to talk to him. He rang again this morning. We couldn't tell you, because we knew you wouldn't let her go. She'll be back for lunch: promise. Shall I get that?" she said as the phone started to ring.

"No," said Helen sharply. "Let the machine pick it up. And"—as another female voice spoke—"don't listen to it, Juliet. Please."

But it was too late.

When Kate returned, looking flushed and almost cheerful, at one o'clock, Juliet rushed her up to her room.

"Kate! There are people—women ringing, saying they're your mother. Can you believe that?"

"How do you know?"

"I heard one. On the answering machine. Mum's telling them all to ring the *Sketch*. They're dealing with them."

"Dealing with them?" Kate shouted. "What do you mean, dealing with them?"

"Getting rid of them, I s'pose."

Kate stared at her. "But Juliet, one of them might actually be my mother! How can they do that? How can they fucking do that?"

"Shush!" said Juliet.

◆·◆

Clio felt completely bewildered, almost shocked, by Jocasta's behaviour.

She had sent her off for a walk on the Hog's Back. Clio was on call that Sunday morning, but that evening they were going up to London together, to stay in Jocasta's house in Clapham.

The next day was important for Clio; she was having lunch with dear old Beaky, Professor Bryan. She had told Mark—hating to deceive him, when he'd been so kind—that she had to see her solicitor about the divorce. Which was true, she had arranged that too. She didn't have very high hopes of the Bayswater job, but she was determined to try. General practice in a country town was fine, if you had a life outside it; she didn't and she already felt the loneliness beginning to bite.

But as she drove from house to house on her rounds, it was Jocasta, not her patients, claiming her concentration.

For someone of eighteen, like the blithely irresponsible Jocasta she had first met, to turn her back on real life and run away with a rich man, yes, perhaps. But at thirty-five, with a flourishing career and a long-term relationship under her belt—oh, please! It seemed to Clio that Jocasta was standing near a large drain and pouring every treasure she possessed down it.

Gideon Keeble might be very charismatic and charming, in the way of extremely rich men; Jocasta might have been growing weary of waiting for Nick to put a ring on her finger and the life of a tabloid reporter might be losing some of its charm; but did she really think she was going to find happiness in a way of life so totally unfamiliar to her?

Clio did realise, of course, that it was much harder for her to understand, not having met Keeble; he veered in her imagination between being a self-indulgent overgrown child who had to have everything he wanted and a kind of evil enchanter who had bewitched Jocasta and swept her away to his castle.

Well, sooner or later, providing the affair lasted—and Clio found herself devoutly hoping it wouldn't—she would meet Gideon Keeble, and then it might be easier for her to understand. She might even like him. But it did seem rather unlikely.

Jocasta still felt terribly guilty. She didn't seem to have done much for Kate, but then, who could? Kate's refusal to see her had hurt dreadfully; she obviously blamed her. God, it was a relief to be out of all that potential for damage to people's lives. And Clio, so sensible and calm and kind. It had been comforting, talking to her last night, confronting what had happened all those years ago. She'd told Nick about it, but all the time running away from the memories. With Clio she had relived them, and it had been healing, in a way.

Chapter 25

All she had to do was keep completely calm. Nothing could happen, if she did that. No one could possibly think she had the slightest connection with this rather sensational story in the tabloid press. There was no connection. None at all. The only person who might think there was anything disturbing her was Ed, because he had been so close to her. But he couldn't be anymore. He would have to be out of her life. And then she would be safe. As long as she kept calm. Perfectly calm.

And didn't look at the tabloids for the next few days. And certainly not at any pictures of that girl.

Kate had called as Jocasta waited for Clio; she sounded very shaky.

She said she was sorry she'd been so rude to Jocasta and that she totally believed that Jocasta had nothing to do with the story.

"I was just upset. It was all such a—a shock."

"Of course it was. I was so sorry for you. The pictures were lovely," she added carefully.

"Yeah, well. Pity about the rest. But it's not so bad, I s'pose. I don't have to go to school at the moment, because I'm on study leave, so I can avoid the really cowy girls. But I need your help, Jocasta. All these women keep ringing up, saying they're my mother, about a dozen of them now, and I'm so scared one of them really is my mother and I'm going to miss her. I just don't know what to do."

"Well, I'm sure the paper will be keeping names and so on."

"Yes, but I need to . . . to know," said Kate desperately. "I can't lose her now. And what about the model agencies, what should I do about that? Mum is so totally no use, and Dad's gone completely ballistic, and Juliet said we should ask you. Could you help, do you think? Please, Jocasta, please."

Jocasta was so touched by this plea that she was half inclined to rush straight over to Ealing and the Tarrants, but she called Gideon and he had wiser counsel.

"You can't do it, Jocasta, don't be insane. You're too involved and <u>the</u> responsibility is just too much. And very dangerous. Now listen, I have the very man for you."

"Gideon's such an angel. You can't imagine," Jocasta said to Clio. "He's so kind and so concerned for me. Just wait till you meet him, Clio, you really will love him, I promise."

"I'm sure I will," said Clio carefully.

"Meanwhile, you're going to meet a friend of his. Who's going to sort Kate out. Gideon's having him call me. His name's Fergus Trehearn."

Fergus Trehearn was Ireland's answer to Max Clifford, Jocasta explained to a rather bemused Clio, "Only he operates from here now. Not quite so successfully. But, well, anyway . . . You must know about Max Clifford," she added, seeing Clio's puzzled face. Clio said humbly that she didn't and when she had heard what Max Clifford did—"He sort of manipulates everybody including the press"—she said she was surprised that anyone should want to.

"Fergus is a complete sweetheart, apparently," said Jocasta, "and Kate certainly needs him. She—they just can't cope with it all. Fergus will take the whole thing on, sorting all these women out, getting Kate the best contract with a model agency, deal with offers from other papers and magazines for her story—"

"She won't want anything like that, will she?" said Clio.

"Not at the moment, no. But the thing is, you see, as far as the media is concerned, Kate will be Abandoned Baby Bianca for the rest of her life. Any story about her will refer to it and maybe one day, who knows, she might want to tell her story. And if her mother turns up—well, that could be huge. She needs her interests protected. Fergus will draw up contracts, that sort of thing. Stop unscrupulous people taking advantage of her and her parents. Anyway, I said Fergus should come to my house. You don't mind, do you?"

"Of course not," said Clio bravely.

The last thing she wanted was to have to meet some flashy gold-medallion man and sit and listen to him talking about manipulating the press.

But it was not a medallion man who sat in Jocasta's untidy sitting room, listening carefully as she talked; it was someone charming and courteous and well dressed, in a linen suit. He was in his early forties, tall, slim, and extremely good-looking, with close-cropped grey hair and dark brown eyes. He was Irish, garrulous, and funny and she found it hard not to like him. Jocasta introduced her as her brilliant friend who was a consultant physician and he appeared duly impressed, even as she protested and said she was nothing of the sort.

His manner, as he listened, was concerned and sweetly interested. It completely belied the ruthless opportunism that drove him. No one would have thought that this Fergus Trehearn, gently sympathetic over the dreadful wickedness of Carla Giannini, hardly able to believe the depths of her treachery, was the same one who had conducted a telephone auction between two major newspapers for the story of a beautiful refugee girl from Bosnia who had become a call girl (under cover of a chambermaid's job at a West End hotel) and then staged a roasting by a posse of drunken footballers; or who had negotiated a hefty media deal for a young couple arrested for, and duly acquitted of, having sex on the hard shoulder of the M25.

"He will be perfect for Kate," Jocasta said to Clio happily, after he had gone, "keep all the sharks at bay and make her lots of money. And what's more, I know he'll be able to persuade the Tarrants. Isn't he a sweetheart?"

Jocasta called the Tarrants, explained what Fergus did and begged them to see him. Helen, exhausted and still deeply distressed, finally agreed. Jim said he would personally throw him out of the house, but Helen was learning to ignore such threats. They had to get through this somehow and it sounded as if Fergus Trehearn might be able to help. An appointment was fixed for six on Monday evening.

"I know it's a little late," he said apologetically to Helen, "but that's the earliest I can manage. Do you have any of those inky vultures at your gate now?"

Helen, who had thought she would never smile again, recognised this as a description of the press and actually laughed. "They've gone," she said, "but we're still getting so many calls."

"I'll take them all off you," he said, "if you'll let me. I'll see you at six, Mrs. Tarrant, and your husband too, of course. And after we have talked, then, if you're happy with me, I'll meet your beautiful daughter."

"He'd deal with the press," said Helen to Jim, "and the women. And Kate. With all these offers we keep getting."

"And what's that going to cost us?" said Jim. "Don't tell me he's doing it out of the goodness of his heart."

"I'll ask Jocasta," said Helen uncertainly. She hadn't thought of this.

"Oh, that's a really good idea," said Jim, his voice heavily sarcastic. "They're probably hand in glove. You can see him if you like, Helen, but I won't. And don't expect a penny out of me for him, either."

Helen sighed and went to telephone Jocasta. Jocasta was very reassuring about the money.

"He won't want any, unless Kate starts to do well as a model," she said, "then he'll probably act as her agent and take a percentage. They work on a sort of no win, no fee basis, like all the lawyers are doing now."

Had Helen been even slightly worldlier she might have found this a little suspicious; she was not to know that Gideon Keeble had already agreed to pay Fergus's bill until something was resolved with Kate.

◆◆

"Look," said Martha, "I'm sorry. I've said at least three times now I can't go away to Venice. Not at the moment. I don't know why you can't accept that."

It had taken her all day to bring herself to make this call, and every word that she said hurt more than the last. She kept seeing him, sitting there, confused, bewildered by the change in her, and she didn't quite know how to bear it. But it had to be done.

Suppose he'd read about it, asked her about it even, said he couldn't imagine anyone doing such a thing. Or said how dreadful, how awful the mother must be.

No, it was very clear. The need for control was back. And to be in control, you had to be independent, answerable to no one. Ed loved her. And she loved him. And love was powerful, when it came to secrets. Huge, dangerous secrets. It saw them, it found them out.

She took another deep breath. "So I can't go to Venice. Is that all right?"

"Of course it's not all right! Two days ago you said you could." Ed's voice was very quiet. "What's changed?"

"Nothing's changed, Ed. I can't go just now, please understand that. I'm sorry."

"Yeah, so sorry you couldn't even be arsed to call me all weekend, didn't return my calls. Why not, Martha, would you just tell me that?"

"There wasn't an opportunity—"

"Oh, right. All weekend. Not a single five-minute—what do you call it?—oh, yes, window, not a five-minute window to pick up your fucking phone and say hi, Ed, sorry I can't talk now, I'll ring later. Is that right?"

"Yes," she said and her voice was so cool, so steady, it amazed her, "that's right."

"Oh, for fuck's sake," he said suddenly, "I've had enough of this. Don't you care that I was worried out of my skull? Don't you?" His voice was less angry, was cracked with pain.

"Of course I care, Ed, but as I told you, I—"

"You're made of fucking stone," he said, "you know that?"

She was silent for a moment; then she said, "Ed, I really don't like being abused like this. If you can't cope with my life and the way I am, then we would do far better to end this whole thing."

"What whole thing?"

"Our relationship, of course."

"Relationship!" he said. "You call what we have a relationship? Right now, I'd call it a load of bullshit, Martha, total fucking bullshit. You tell me what to do and say and think, where to be and when, and I just tag along behind you, licking your arse. Well, you can find someone else to lick it, because I'm finding it extremely tedious all of a sudden. OK?" And he slammed the phone down.

Martha sat for a long time, completely still, just staring at it. Wanting more than anything to pick it up again, fighting the instinct to say she was sorry, she hadn't meant it, and she loved him, wanted to see him.

But she couldn't. It was too dangerous.

◆

By the end of the weekend, Kate was feeling better. She couldn't help it. Yes, it had been awful, the shock; yes, she felt hideously ashamed still, that everyone knew what had happened to her, that everyone must be pointing her out, saying that's the girl whose mother just threw her away; she still felt as if she was walking down the road with all her clothes off, naked and exposed; and yes, it was horrible to have trusted someone like Carla and then found yourself totally let down. It was appalling to think that one of those women who had phoned up might be her birth mother, and that she was having to wait quietly when the most tumultuous discovery in her life might be within reach. She wanted to rush into the offices of the *Sketch* and demand to see the list, see the women, organise the DNA testing. But it was also quite nice, she had to admit, to have not just the *Sketch* but papers like the *Sunday Times* describing you with words like "beautiful" and "dazzling," and to see your pictures in them, as well.

And to have model agencies ringing up, asking you to go and see them, and even magazines, asking if they could come and interview you—that was pretty cool.

And then there was Nat. It had almost been worth it all, to have Nat calling her twice a day and taking her out in the Sax Bomb and saying what about going to the Fridge this Saturday. She'd said that would be cool, that she'd most definitely come; she'd worry about her parents and what they might say when the time came. The thing they didn't understand—that nobody seemed to understand—was what a nice person Nat was. The first thing he'd said when she'd got in the car was, "You all right?" and, "Yes," she'd said, yes, she was fine, thank you. And he'd said, "I meant about the story in the paper, like, about your mum," and it had completely wiped her out, that he'd understood how she might be feeling, had thought about it. He'd obviously read the article properly, because he'd said, with that grin of his, that he'd liked the way she'd talked about his clothes and his car.

Then he leant forward and started to kiss her; he was a very good kisser. Nice and slow and careful, his tongue moving round, sort of stroking hers. Kate hadn't experienced good kissing before and it was wonderful. They were parked on the edge of a park, under some trees; it was terribly romantic.

"You going to do more of this modelling, then?" he said, when he had finally finished, and lit a cigarette.

"Course," she said.

"Cool. I wouldn't mind coming along, if they ever wanted a bloke," he added.

Kate said she didn't know how it worked, but she could ask, if the occasion arose.

"Yeah, right," he said, and drove her home in silence. Or as close to silence as the Red Hot Chili Peppers, at top volume, would permit.

"So are you looking forward to your lunch with your professor tomorrow?" Jocasta asked.

"Half. And half dreading it. I keep thinking he's asked me to lunch to soften the blow, to say there's no point my applying for the job."

"I really don't think people spend money giving you bad news," said Jocasta. "Polite little notes, more like it. No, he wants to encourage you. Goodness, Clio, a consultant. I shall be proud to know you."

"I'll be pretty proud to know me too. If I am one again."

The only place she felt pleased with herself was at work. It was odd: she felt somehow in charge when she was working; it was like going downhill on a bicycle after struggling up the other side, not easy exactly but exhilarating, everything running smoothly and to order. She sighed; Jocasta looked at her.

"You'll be fine," she said, "I know you will. Let's go for a drink. Just a few quiet ones."

They went to one of the pubs on the common, sat outside in the gathering dusk. A sliver of moon was hanging in the turquoise sky, the sun a vast display of crimson, hugging the horizon.

"It's like a child showing off," said Jocasta. "Look at it, saying let me stay, let me stay. Do you remember those sunsets in Thailand, Clio, so unbelievably dramatic, especially when it had been raining? I must take Gideon to Thailand, he'd love it."

Like everyone in love, she managed to bring every discussion round to the subject of the beloved.

"I can't wait for you to meet him. He's so—so exciting. And interested in absolutely everything. I mean, he'd be talking about your work right now, getting really involved."

"Don't you ever miss Nick?" asked Clio curiously. "He seemed lovely to me."

"He *was* lovely. Just not lovely enough. And the way I love Gideon is quite unlike anything I felt before. For anybody. It's so—so violent, Clio. It's just taken me over. I feel I'm where I ought to be, when I'm with him. It's as simple as that. I didn't feel like that with Nick. I thought I did, but I didn't."

"But you had so much in common with Nick and you cared so much about your work. What are you going to do, Jocasta, stop working altogether, be with Gideon wherever he is?"

"Yes, probably," said Jocasta vaguely. "I haven't thought about it."

•-•-•

"Martha, are you all right?"

Paul Quenell's voice seemed to be coming from far away. It was a long time since Martha had felt like this: swimmy-headed, clammy, as if she was going to be sick. Probably not since she had been at St. Andrews for early communion and having terrible period pains. She sat down abruptly.

"Yes," she said, "yes, I'm fine. Thank you. Just a bit . . . a bit . . . sorry, Paul."

What was it doing here, on his desk, the *Sunday Times*, open at the article about—about— Was he going to show it to her, ask if she knew anything about it?

"Jane," he called through the open door, "bring a glass of water in, would you?" And then, gently stern: "You've been working too hard."

"Well, yes, maybe just a bit."

"It's all this extracurricular stuff," he said, and smiled his swift apology of a smile. "You shouldn't do it, you know."

"Maybe not."

"Thanks, Jane. Just put it down there. You can take this now . . ." He folded the paper, held it out to his long-suffering secretary. "I've seen all I needed." All he needed? Why should he need anything? What did it have to do with him? She felt hot, violently sick again.

"Jane spotted this piece about the new senior partner at Kindersleys." Paul sat down at his desk again. "Hannah Roberts, one of these superwomen, five children at least. Come across her?"

"Once or twice," she said, and relief flooded her, cool, soothing relief.

"Anyway, I'm going to stop the extracurricular stuff for a day or two. I'm sending you on a little trip. Not a long one, a week at the most. But you should be able to grab a couple of days of rest out of it."

"A trip? Where?"

It was actually the last thing she wanted; she only felt safe doing completely familiar things, in completely familiar places. Even going to a new restaurant the day before had been unsettling.

"Sydney."

Sydney! It couldn't have been worse. That was where—when— She hauled herself back to the present. "Why?"

"You don't look as pleased as I hoped. It's such a wonderful place. You've been there, I presume?"

"No! Well . . ." She mustn't start lying. That could become very dangerous. "Well, only for about two days. Long ago. On my way somewhere else."

"Oh I see. Well, you'll love it. It's on Mackenzie business, of course."

"Of course." She was regaining her cool now, back in control, Mackenzie was a worldwide property chain—"intergalactic" as Paul had once said. "They've got some massive new takeover in their sights on the waterfront over there, they need advice."

"Can't the Sydney office manage?"

"Of course. But Donald wants someone from London. He likes to see us earning our fees, as you know."

Martha smiled. "I do indeed." Donald Mackenzie was famous for querying every invoice.

"He asked for me, then when I said it was out of the question, he specified you. I'll get Jane to book your flight and hotel."

On her way back to her own office, she felt dizzy again; she managed to make it to the ladies' and sat on a loo seat for a long time, her head between her knees.

Just keep calm, Martha, just keep calm . . .

•-•-•

"None of those women had left names." Fergus Trehearn smiled at Kate. "And of course, no numbers or addresses."

"Oh," she said. She wasn't sure how she felt: disappointed, she supposed.

"The thing is," he said gently, "it's a criminal offence, abandoning a baby. So they're not going to be terribly upfront about themselves. Although they may not have understood that. But each and every one of them failed the nappy test. Most of them said it had been a disposable nappy, a few had apparently put a towelling one on you."

"Yes, I see." She felt dreadfully bleak. It somehow underlined her poor, destitute, baby self, not just that she'd had no nappy on but that this fact was being used in this horrible mechanical way to catch her would-be mother out. All her would-be mothers.

"I'm sorry," he said, "this must be so difficult for you. But I think I can assure you that you haven't missed your real mother. Whoever she is, she hasn't declared herself."

"What about the first few? Before we thought about the nappy thing? One of them might have been her."

"Kate, if that is true, she will call again. She's not going to give up at the first hurdle."

"She might. It might have taken all her courage to make that one call, and then when—when . . ." She fought back the tears.

"That is a possibility, of course," said Fergus gently. "But I think a remote one. And Kate, it is still possible that you will hear. Very possible. People behave strangely under pressure. Any sort of pressure. I'm no psychiatrist, but I would imagine that if you've kept something like this to yourself for sixteen years, it could be pretty difficult suddenly to acknowledge it. It might seem better to wait until the fuss has begun to die down. And then again, I suppose, she might not have seen the article immediately."

"Not very likely," said Kate. "It's been in most of the papers. And mentioned on the radio as well."

"Indeed. Now that is a relevant observation—*Woman's Hour* are very eager to do something about it, to talk to you, Helen, and to Kate—"

"No," said Helen sharply.

"Why not?" said Kate. "Just why exactly not?"

"Because I don't want this thing prolonged," said Helen wearily. "You've been upset enough, Kate, and—"

"So it's over, is it?" said Kate. "I hadn't realised that. What do you mean, Mum, for God's sake? You don't want it prolonged! How ridiculous is that? What about me? Yeah, I've been upset. But if anything good comes out of it at all, it'll be finding my mother. And I think the radio would be good. I could say what I wanted, not what the paper said I had. Like I really want to see her still."

"It's a very nice programme, Helen," said Fergus. "Jenni Murray is a superb interviewer—she's gentle with her interviewees and very sensitive about her material. If Kate still hopes to find her mother, then it could be a good way forward. There's something honest about radio. As Kate says, they can't distort your words. She could make a direct appeal to her mother. It could be very emotive. But Kate, if your mum doesn't like the idea, then it would be wrong for you, too."

He moved into safer territory: both the *Sun* and the *Mirror* wanted interviews, but he thought not. "You'll just get more of the sensationalism, and I think you've had enough of that," and several model agencies wanted to see her, three of them really good ones.

"And"—Helen hesitated, fearing another outburst from Kate—"are we sure about . . . about the modelling?"

"Mum! What do you mean, are we sure? It's something I can do, make lots of money, be successful, all that sort of thing!"

"But Kate, what about your exams?"

"Oh God! Mum, I'll do my exams. Of course I will."

"And college?"

"Well, maybe. I'll see. Point is—"

"The point is," said Fergus, sweetly reasonable, "she can do her modelling in the holidays. Work round her college terms. A lot of girls do that."

"Do they?" Helen looked slightly less distraught.

"Fergus," said Kate suddenly, "will you be my agent? Do I have to go to one of these other places?"

"I don't know . . ." Fergus's voice was heavily cautious. No one would have suspected that this was what he had been hoping for, ever since Gideon Keeble had contacted him, the long-term reward from this project: this and a good publishing deal for the whole story, when the mother turned up. As he was sure she would. It was a fantastic story; it could be a big money spinner. And the more famous Kate was, the bigger it would be. For the time being, that must be his goal. He smiled modestly. "I'm not familiar with the fashion scene, you know, and—"

"Couldn't you learn? It would be so much nicer. Wouldn't it, Mum? We trust you, I feel like we've known you forever."

"I have to tell you, I think you might do better with a conventional agency, although there are precedents, of course. Twiggy—you've heard of Twiggy, I expect?"

"Yeah, course. She was in a magazine the other day; she's really old now, isn't she? But she still looks OK."

"Well, anyway, she wasn't with a standard agency. Her boyfriend managed her very successfully, and he was a hairdresser."

"There you are. Oh, Fergus, please, I'd like it so much and so would Mum, wouldn't you?"

"But there would be one important condition, Kate," said Fergus, and his voice was quite stern. "You must do your best in your exams. They're important. Very important indeed. You could regret throwing away your chances. Things change, and not every girl who is spotted by a fashion editor makes it big-time. I would be very unhappy if you started doing any modelling at all, until those are over. What would you say to that?"

"I'd say cool," said Kate with a shrug. "As long as they don't all forget about me."

"Don't worry about that," said Fergus. "I won't let them forget about you, Kate, not for a single moment. Now you and your mum have your conversation and let me know what you decide about *Woman's Hour*."

⋯•⋯

Clio felt very tired when she got home: not sure if she was happy or not. The lunch with Beaky had been wonderful; he had told her how much she had been missed and how he hoped that she would apply for the consultant's job.

"I've got a very good team there," he said. "Keen, clever, mostly young. I can hardly bear to think of leaving it. You'd fit in jolly well, Clio. We've got a couple of research projects going, we're doing some trials with a new Alzheimer's drug, and we've got a wonderful new psychiatric chap."

"It does sound wonderful," she said wistfully, "but do you really think I'm up to it?"

"Clio! Is this really the brightest new consultant in the department for years talking? You do put yourself down, dear girl, and you really mustn't do it. I wouldn't have invited you to apply if I didn't think you were absolutely up to it, as you put it. As far as I can see, you're the perfect candidate. You're familiar with the hospital and the workings of the department, you did very well when you were here, everyone liked you—and from what you tell me, you've done a lot of geriatric work while you've been in general practice. I'm sure you can slot back into the rotation system, no one's going to object on procedural grounds."

"Good," said Clio. "I was worrying about that a bit."

"No need." He patted her hand. "Not enough people going into geriatrics. We need you."

She smiled at him, promising to apply, and made her way to the solicitor's office.

She had been warned it would be wretched: it was. It was one thing to agree, however sadly, that your marriage was over; it was quite another to find yourself in an adversarial situation, picking over the balance sheet of that marriage. She had agreed that she wouldn't contest the divorce and had expected a certain generosity in return; but Jeremy was even querying her right to a share of the house, claiming she had walked out on a marriage that she had entered into under false pretences.

"Don't worry, Mrs. Graves, they all start like this." Her solicitor, a very nice sympathetic woman, smiled at her encouragingly. "He'll come down." She passed Clio a tissue from the box on the desk between them. "It's horrid. I know."

"I put so much work into that house," said Clio, blowing her nose. "Sorry about this."

"It's all right. I never remember having a preliminary consultation over divorce when the tissues weren't needed. And of course you worked hard on the house."

"And I paid for a lot of the work on it," said Clio.

"I know. Don't worry. We'll get you everything that's due to you . . ."

•-•-•

"I missed you," said Gideon. "Very much."

They were lying in bed; he had returned from Barbados, leaving an extremely contented Fionnuala behind him, the owner of three superb polo ponies.

"She was so pleased," he said, "and most affectionate. It was all very sweet."

"I expect it was," said Jocasta and hoped her voice didn't sound barbed.

It was early in the morning; they were in his London house, in Kensington Palace Gardens. It had shocked Jocasta, that house: shocked and almost intimidated her. It could only be described as a mansion, a five-year-old Palladian-style mansion, complete with a ballroom, several vast reception rooms, a staff flat, and ten bedrooms. It was a strong statement, about its owner, about the sort of money he had and the sort of taste. Excessive, in all cases. Did a man with almost no family really need ten bedrooms?

"I missed you too," she said. "Terribly."

"I'm pleased to hear it. I would have liked to think you were terribly unhappy. Oh God"—he pushed the sheet back, sat up, and studied her—"you are the most beautiful thing. I can't imagine what you're doing with an old man like me."

"I love you," she said, "old as you are. Believe it or not. I just love you. I can't imagine how I got through even a week of my life without you, never mind thirty-five years. It seems most peculiar."

"I was thinking, while I was away," he said, bending down and kissing first one breast, then the other, "thinking how you told me you loved me, and thinking how much I loved you, and that neither of us really knew the other at all."

"I thought that, too. But I feel I do. I feel I've known you always. I feel I know everything about you. How ridiculous is that?"

"Very ridiculous. And very dangerous. You may have discovered some of my virtues. My vices are mercifully a closed book to you."

"Oh, I don't know. I know you're quite ruthless. I know you have a terrible temper. I know you can be stubborn—"

"That's quite enough. I don't like this game."

"We can talk about my vices, if you like, if that'll make you feel better."

"And what are they? I thought you had none."

"OK. I'm impatient. Self-centred. Cowardly. I dread pain. I'm easily bored. And then I'm vain—"

"With good reason."

"Thank you. And generally rather silly."

"Silliness is not a vice. I encourage it in myself. Let's do virtues now. You're clever. Imaginative. Tenderhearted. Beautiful—"

"That's not a virtue. That's a bit of luck. Let's do yours. You're generous and generous-hearted. Kind. Thoughtful. And I like the way you care about everything so much." It was true: he sought the highest standards in everything; he said that was what life was for, to find the best. From the houses he lived in to the clothes he wore, from the food he ate and the wine he drank to the way he travelled and the people he employed, everything must meet not just his approval but his high approval.

"Anyway, the States next week. Looking forward to it?"

"Of course. I plan to shop for England. And Ireland."

"That's my girl."

•─•─•

Martha got out of the cab, went into her building, pressed the lift button. She felt a little better: her life almost whole again. She'd had a very good meeting with Paul, she was on top of her work, her assistant and her trainee were well briefed for the following week, and the night before she had actually managed to sleep with only one sleeping pill.

No journalist had rung her, and after—what—three days, it didn't seem likely that they would.

The only thing was, of course, how much she was still hurting over Ed. It was awful; it was like the pain of a burn, searing, shocking, beyond the reach of any analgesic. It woke her up, that pain; disturbed her as she worked, dug into her consciousness at the most unexpected times.

But it would pass: of course it would. It had to. There was no alternative. And he seemed to have accepted it; there had been no phone calls, no appearances in reception, no e-mails. Just—nothing.

She was leaving her apartment at five thirty in the morning, so that she could go to the gym; with twenty-one hours on the plane ahead of her, she would need that. She was actually looking forward to the trip now that she had it all properly under control.

And going away now seemed, suddenly and surprisingly, what she needed.

She poured herself a glass of mineral water and carried it into her bedroom, to finish her packing. She had just pulled fourteen pairs of pants (two for each day) out of a drawer when the doorbell rang. That would be the papers Paul had promised to have sent round, extra background information on Mackenzie, so that she could study them in bed.

She went to her door, pushed the buzzer.

"Yes?"

But it wasn't papers; it was Ed.

"You can't stay," she said, staring at him as he stood in her hallway, thinking with complete irrelevance that he looked absolutely wonderful, wearing an open-necked white shirt and jeans, like someone in a film. "I'm packing, I've got a plane to catch."

"I don't care if you've got a fucking rocket to catch," he said. "I want to know what's going on. Something's happened, Martha, hasn't it? I don't care what it is, I don't care if you're in love with someone else, I don't care if you're terminally ill—well that's bollocks, of course I care, but I've just got to know. I can't stand it. You've got to tell me."

"Nothing's happened," she said, fists clenched, meeting his eyes with considerable courage, for what might he read there? "Nothing's happened at all. I'm just—just terribly busy. I'm going to Sydney tomorrow."

"Sydney? How long for?"

"Just a week. We have a client there. A very important client," she added firmly.

"Martha, for fuck's sake, what is it? What's happened to you? You've got to tell me, I'm not going away until you do."

"Nothing's happened," she said, and she was quite frightened now, he looked so desperate.

"Martha," he said very quietly, "I love you. I know you really rather well. I know every inch of you. Literally. I know how you are when you're happy and when you're upset and when you're stressed and when you want sex, and I know when you want to talk and when you want to be quiet and when you're feeling rotten and tired and mean. And I know something's happened to you—I *know* it. This is not about you being busy. It's about you being scared. What are you scared of, Martha? You've got to tell me. What have you done? Nothing you did could shock me, or upset me, unless it was falling in love with someone else. I'd have to get over that, but at least I'd know. Is that it, is there somebody else?"

"No," she said, very quietly, "there's no one else."

"So what is it?"

She was silent.

"Martha, look at me. Tell me what's fucking happened."

And for a moment she wanted to tell him. Just to get it over, to know that someone else knew, it wasn't locked away, struggling to escape, this awful, dreadful shocking thing that she had denied for so long, managed to contain, this fearful obscene monster. Just to be able to say to someone what should I do, where can I go, where shall I start? Instead of crushing it, endlessly, pulping it to—

But she couldn't.

"Nothing's happened," she said finally and then: "You must excuse me, I don't feel very well."

And she rushed into her bathroom, slammed the door, and was violently sick, over and over again, and then sat on the lavatory, shivering and shaking, awful pain driving through her stomach, wondering how she could ever go out of the room again.

She heard him knocking on the door, very gently, calling through it; and she made a supreme effort, washed her face and cleaned her teeth and walked out, facing him, trying to smile into his concern.

"Sorry," she said. "I'm so sorry."

And that was when he had said it: the worst thing he could possibly have said.

"Martha, you're not pregnant, are you?"

She started to laugh; weak hysterical laughter that turned, in time, to tears, shaking her head from side to side, avoiding his eyes. He helped her into the sitting room, sat her down on the sofa, watching her as she wept and wailed and keened, like some wild, primitive woman; and then finally as she quietened, he came to sit next to her and put his arms round her, drew her head onto his shoulder. She sat there, briefly sweetly at peace, where she wanted to be, and she picked up his hand and intertwined it with her own, then raised it to her lips and kissed it.

"Thank you," she said, "thank you so much. I'm sorry."

"Oh, Martha," he said, kissing her hand in return, "I wish you could trust me. Whatever it is you've done, I would understand and I would forgive you. And I shall find out, you know. I'll find out somehow. I won't leave you alone until I do, and I won't leave you alone, even then. I think you need me."

"No," she said, summoning up all her will, releasing his hand, moving slightly from him, "no, I don't. I don't need you, Ed. And you certainly don't need me."

"That's where you're wrong," he said. "I do need you. We need each other. I'm going now. But when you get back—when is that, next weekend?" She nodded feebly. "I'll be here for you. Don't think I won't; don't think I'll give up. I love you too much. Now go to bed and get some sleep, for God's sake. Shall I stay? In here, I mean?" he added, with a faint touch of a smile.

"No," she said, "of course not. You must go. But thank you for the offer. You're very kind, Ed. Very kind indeed."

"No," he said, "not kind at all. I keep telling you. I love you." And then he was gone. She was awake all night. She had set her alarm for five, but she watched the hours, the quarter hours; she felt appalling fear, her heart pounding, her stomach churning. She was sick again: more than once. She had never felt so alone: not even in that dreadful tiled room, in appalling pain, pushing her baby out in abject terror, looking at it.

No, Martha, don't think about that, that of all things, never, ever that. Don't think about that face, that puckered anguished face, so peaceful when you left it, fast asleep. Don't remember, don't, don't.

When the alarm went off, finally, she was sitting on her bed, her head in her arms, trying not to remember. It was the first time her will had failed her. She couldn't stand, couldn't walk, even across the room. She shook in every part of her body, shook violently. She was first hot, then cold. Her head ached, she could hardly see. She lay down on the bed, pulled the sheet over her, closed her eyes. She would stay there, just for an hour. She didn't have to go to the gym, she could get into the office at seven. Or even eight. Eight would be fine, everything was done.

But at seven and at eight, she was still helpless, her body uselessly disobedient; it would not stand or sit, it would not even turn in bed. She managed to put an arm out to put the radio on, heard John Humphrys's wonderful, reassuring voice, like a comforting presence in the room; and then fell suddenly asleep, drifting in and out of dreams, horrible stifling dreams, about obscene creatures behind half-open doors and hiding and falling and darkness and blood. And then woke, finally, to the sound of her daughter's voice.

Chapter 26

·   ·   ·   ·

Well, at least it was over. She had got through it somehow. It was true what everyone had said, Jenni Murray made them feel relaxed and at home, so much so that she had almost forgotten there were millions of people out there listening to them. Kate, of course, had been fine, chatting easily away, wonderfully composed. Where did that come from, Helen wondered wearily, lying back in the car the BBC had kindly provided, that self-confidence, that ability to deal with unfamiliar situations, and then thought, how absurd a question: from one of her parents, obviously.

One of the worst things, she felt, was that she had become relegated to some kind of second division, no longer properly Kate's mother, no longer in charge of her life. Kate no longer seemed her child, seemed not a child at all, indeed, but a newly created being, making her own decisions, constructing her own future.

Tomorrow she was going out with Nat Tucker to a club in Brixton; she had said, perfectly politely but very firmly, that he had asked her and she would like to go. Given everything that was happening to her, it seemed a little absurd to try to stop her. They had compromised on a 2:00 a.m. latest return; Helen had hoped Nat would object to that, and the thing would be cancelled, but he had apparently said it was cool. Cool. Helen often thought she would scream if she heard that word once more.

She had to admit she had been wrong about Nat; his manners were on the primitive side, but he always said hello to her when she answered the door, and asked her how she was doing, and ground out his cigarette butt on the path before coming into the house. And he was very sweet with Kate.

He came round most days, but not until after tea; he seemed to have a great respect for Kate's academic future.

"I know she's got her exams to do," he'd say, as Helen apologised for her nonappearance.

The fact that Kate was more likely to be applying a sixth coat of mascara than rehearsing her French verbs never seemed to occur to him.

A nice researcher had come round and told them more or less how the interview on *Woman's Hour* would go: "Just a few questions on the early days, Helen, how you came to adopt Kate, and then how the story came out. How you're both feeling about it now. And how Kate sees her future, and what she feels about the woman who left her that day."

Which was how Martha came to hear her daughter's voice for the first time. And to learn that she would like to meet her, "Very, very much."

That Friday morning, lying listlessly in bed, trying to summon the strength to get up and go to work—when had she last missed what was already most of a morning? she really couldn't remember—she had woken to hear a light, pretty voice, saying, "I would like to meet my birth mother, yes, of course I would. Very, very much."

"And how do you think you might feel?" Jenni Murray sounded gently intrigued.

"Well, I don't know. Confused, I s'pose. And maybe angry. And really interested in what she was like. What sort of person she was."

"What would you say to her? Have you thought about that?"

"I'd ask her why she did it. That's the main thing I want to know."

"Of course. Well, Kate, Helen, you've been great. Thank you so much for talking to us. And I hope you do hear from your birth mother, if that's what you want."

"It is," said Kate very simply. "It really is."

Martha found that far more moving and disturbing than seeing her photograph in the newspapers.

•◆•

Beatrice also heard *Woman's Hour* that morning for the first time for years: and also from a bed that never saw her after 7:00 a.m. even on Sundays. Thank God, just thank God, she wasn't meant to be in court. But she was supposed to be in Chambers; they had clearly taken a rather dim view of her phone call with the news that she was ill. She wasn't exactly ill: she had an appalling migraine, such as only hit her when life threatened to completely defeat her. It didn't often defeat her, but the night before, her nanny had given in her notice and although she had said that she would work her three months out, Beatrice had found the news almost unbearable.

Nothing can distress the working mother more, however brilliant, successful, and efficient she may be, than the loss of her nanny. On the strength of those hugely expensive, neatly dressed shoulders rests most of the superstructure of her life. Beatrice, deprived of even this comfort and support, felt totally bereft, and the very thought of the process of interviewing made her feel hysterical. She had several important cases coming up, not to mention Charlie and Harry's joint birthday party, and even a holiday of her own, which she badly needed and which would now have to be sacrificed. Christine was paid extremely well, she had her own flat at the top of the house, she had full use of a car, and the girls were well past the most demanding age. But that, actually, had been the reason for Christine's resignation; she liked looking after babies, she said, and much as she loved Charlie and Harry, they became more independent every day.

As Beatrice tossed and turned miserably in her bed, her mobile rang. Checking it, she saw it was her mother. She decided to tell her her problems; her mother was rather brusquely unsympathetic.

"Darling, you've got three months. Surely that's enough. It's not as if they were babies."

"It isn't just that," Beatrice said. "It's having no support of any kind at home, with Josh gone."

"Now you know how I feel about that. You turned him out. It was your decision."

"Mother! He was having an affair."

"Beatrice, none of Josh's little flings have been what I would call an affair. They were more or less one-night stands. They meant nothing. I sympathise with you, of course. But there was no emotion involved; Josh adores you, you know he does."

"He's got a funny way of showing it," said Beatrice bitterly.

"Beatrice, he's a man. It's as simple as that. They can't resist sex if it's offered them. It's beyond them, any of them. And there are far worse things, to my mind, than that. Josh is a very good husband, in a lot of ways. He's wonderful with the children; he pays all the bills, including the nanny, when many men would have seen that as your responsibility. He's good-natured. And he's always nice to me," she added.

"Yes, I know he is. I don't think that's absolutely relevant."

Her mother ignored this. "Does he want to come back?"

"I . . . think so," said Beatrice, recalling Josh's endless pleas to be forgiven, his protestations of remorse, his complaints of loneliness.

"You should consider it," said her mother. "I'm thinking of you, darling, not Josh. You need a husband. It's not as if he knocks you about or anything. And do you really believe it's going to be of benefit to those girls, growing up without their father? Think about it, Beatrice. You're being very stubborn, cutting off your nose to spite your face. Always have been. Now I must go . . ."

Beatrice spent the next hour considering what her mother had said.

And deciding that, to an extent at least, she was right. She did need a husband. Quite badly.

⸻

Somehow Martha managed to get up and shower.

It was one o'clock; her flight was at seven thirty. She called a cab, asked him to come up and get her bags. She wasn't sure she could manage even wheeling them to the lift. Finishing her packing had been hard enough.

She began to feel better as soon as the car pulled away from the building; it was as if she had left at least some of her traumatised self behind in it.

By the time she was in the plane, she felt almost human. She settled into her seat, smiled gratefully at the hostess, took a glass of orange juice.

"And here's the menu, Miss Hartley."

"I won't want dinner," said Martha. "I'm awfully tired. What time do we get to Singapore?"

"Local time, three p.m. Are you disembarking, or going through?"

"Going straight through," said Martha.

She settled back, and almost as if watching a movie, allowed thoughts of sweeter, happier things to drift through her head: of Ed and how much he clearly loved her, and of her daughter with the lovely face and the pretty voice, who had said she wanted to meet her, and for the first time, wondered if it might, after all, be something she would enjoy, rather than endure. She felt changed about Kate: she was no longer something dark and dreadful, to be denied at all costs, rather the reverse, indeed, a source of possible happiness and pride. Even if they could never meet, never know each other; even if she could never explain and Kate never understand. She had been found, that dreadful day, cared for, and had grown up safely, into someone clearly confident and happy, and for that, Martha felt deeply grateful.

There was nothing she could do about either of them, Kate or Ed, and neither of them could be allowed into her life; but for a brief time, they at least moved into an easier place for her.

After a while, she took a sleeping pill and slept for over four hours.

And dreamt: not frightening, dark dreams but oddly sweet ones, of sun-lit beaches and calm blue sea. And after that, instead of working as she always did, she watched one of the appalling movies which are apparently only shown on long plane journeys, and woke up in Singapore feeling refreshed and almost happy.

•••

Helen looked rather nervously at Nat. She had asked him to Sunday lunch; Kate had been rushing off to meet him again, straight after breakfast, and Helen couldn't bear it. Kate was clearly delighted, had thrown her arms round her and kissed her.

"You're ace, Mum!"

"He might not want to come," said Helen hopefully.

"He'll come," said Kate. "Just don't try and make him talk about politics or the news, Mum, yeah? He's a bit shy."

And now here was Jim, stopping mid-carve, saying that these politicians were all the same, totally immoral, and he wouldn't vote for any of them.

"That Mrs. Thatcher, she was all right," said Nat. The entire family stared at him; it was as if he had declared his intention to take up ballet.

"Mrs. Thatcher?" said Kate incredulously. "I thought she was a real old bag."

"No way. She had the right ideas, my dad says, sorted the unions out and that. He says they needed their heads examined, kicking her out. She wouldn't have let all these people in, neither."

"What people?" said Juliet.

"These foreigners. Refugees and that. Taking over all our houses and hospitals and stuff. And Legoland," he added as if this was the final felony, putting a large forkful of Yorkshire pudding into his mouth.

"Legoland?" Helen and Kate spoke in unison.

"Yeah. They sent a whole load of them there free last week. Said in the paper."

"Gracious," said Helen. "I had no idea."

"She was good on the radio, wasn't she?" said Nat after a long, chewy silence, pointing his fork at Kate. "I thought her mum might come on the programme, that she'd be, like, listening."

"It wasn't a phone-in," said Helen gently.

There was a long silence; then: "Yeah? What's the point in that, then?"

Kate stared at him, then she said, "That's a really good idea, Nat. I might ask Fergus about it."

•◆•

Martha stepped out of the English luxury of the Observatory Hotel and into the Sydney sunshine. It was absolutely beautiful: a cool but brilliant day. She smiled up at the blue sky, and asked the doorman to get her a cab.

She was going to the Rocks, to do some shopping, wander round Darling Harbour, go back for an early dinner, and then prepare for tomorrow's meetings. How absurd that she had been worried about being here. About the ghosts. This lovely place was so far removed from the other Sydney, the Sydney where worry had turned to fear and fear to panic. This Sydney was smooth and luxurious and busy and beautiful. She looked down at this Sydney, at the legendary view, the white wings of the opera house carved into the blue sky, the flying sails of the yachts in the harbour, the great bridge arched over it all, and the ranks of dazzling new buildings, gleaming in the sun: and turned her back absolutely and resolutely on the other, the scruffy room, the endless smell of frying food, the relentless heat. It had been another Martha who had lived there, too, an uncertain, frightened, lonely Martha. The one standing here now, in her linen trousers, her silk sweater, with a dozen appointments in her diary, three people waiting to buy her dinner, she had nothing to do with that one, she was no more. Nobody knew about her; she was safe from her, she had escaped.

"Where would you like to go then, on this beautiful day?"

The cabdriver was friendly, good-natured, anxious to help; and of course she wanted to go down to the harbour, to buy T-shirts at Ken Done and to sit in the sun on the quay, drink lattes, maybe take a waterbus across the harbour, then back to the hotel to wait to be picked up for dinner, down on the Rocks. She did not even consider visiting the northern beaches of Collaroy and Mona Vale and Avalon, that was back, not forward, and forward was where she had to go, the only place indeed and—

"Do you have plenty of time?" she said.

"As much as you want," he said with a dazzling smile—Australian teeth were as good as American ones, she thought irrelevantly.

"Could we go up to Avalon, please?" she said.

She got off the bus on the Barrenjoey Road, blinking in the fierce brilliance of the sun. She had seen the beaches, all along the road from Sydney, stuck sweatily to her seat, longing to be in the cool of the water. The two boys she was with were surf-struck, boasting of the waves they would catch, the boards they would ride; Martha listened to them, smiling to herself, wondering just how their English-school swimming would survive the reality of waves and rips.

They had been directed to Avalon by a boy they met at the airport, who was doing the trip the other way round: "It's the only real surfers' hostel near Sydney, really great place."

And so they had heaved their rucksacks onto the bus and sat there for more than two hours as it lurched through the suburbs of the city and out again the other side, riding the high bridges, gazing awestruck at the dazzling harbour below them, out through the smart suburbs of northern Sydney, of Mosman and Clontarf, and then along the endless, charmless highway, studded with car salerooms and cheap restaurants—and surf shops, always surf shops.

She stood on the dizzily high cliffs of Avalon, looking down to the beach; and there it was, not just the sight but the sound of the sea, roaring and rolling in, and the smell of it too, fresh, salty, and altogether beautiful. She stood there for a long time, watching the surfies riding the waves, huge, rolling breakers, deceptively small from her viewpoint; and then she hoisted her rucksack on again, and walked down the steep hill and into Avalon, thinking how inappropriate was its name, so importantly a part of the English myth of Camelot, this infinitely Australian place.

Avalon was built on a crossroads, little more than a village really, and the Avalon Beach Hostel was just along one of the roads forming the cross. It was quite large, sleeping ninety-six, and the first one of its kind in the Sydney area, the warden told her.

Martha looked up at it rather nervously as she walked through the big gates and across the paved courtyard; she was easily intimidated in those days, and the sun-bleached boys sitting on the long veranda overlooking the courtyard, some lolling back with long brown legs propped on the rail, others leaning over it chatting and smoking, looked as settled as if it were home. Which it was to many of them; they stayed here for weeks, months even.

She booked in, was given a room—or rather one-sixth of a room, a hard bunk fixed to the wall by ropes, and a locker. It was very primitive, the floor simply painted concrete, but it was clean and the girls' bathroom, equally spartan and clean, was just opposite her door.

"Stove's here," said the warden, who seemed about the same age as she was, leading her into the large room behind the veranda, half filled with long tables and benches, the walls covered with surfing posters. "And here's the fridges; just bag one of the empty compartments, put your name on it, and it's yours till you leave. Everyone eats in here."

Martha smiled nervously at the boys on the veranda; they grinned back, asked her where she'd come from, where she was going. She felt very happy suddenly; she would like it here.

She did: it was absolutely wonderful. She loved Avalon, the villagey atmosphere, the small shops, and the French restaurant, with its red-and-white-checked cloths, where they very occasionally ate. There was a bookshop called Bookoccino, the Gourmet Deli, where they couldn't afford to shop (but an excellent Woolworth's supermarket where they could), and astonishingly, a cinema, which was apparently owned by someone who had a midday TV show. Whoever he was, he took the cultural life of Avalon seriously and showed foreign films on Sundays. Not that going to the cinema was a priority: it was January and very hot.

She made two good friends there, a boy called Stuart, inevitably named Stewpot, and a girl called Dinah. Dinah came from Yorkshire, and her father was also a vicar. "The worst thing I think," said Dinah, passing Martha the joint she was smoking, "is being so poor and having to be posh. And the whole bloody parish watching you, of course. Can you imagine if you got pregnant or something, what on earth they'd do?"

Martha shuddered, then laughed and passed the joint back.

The three of them became a tight little unit. Stewpot had tried surfing and had a bad fright, caught in a rip, and was content to swim with the girls in the safety of the rock pools, the natural swimming pools filled every day by the sea. Together they roamed the lovely white beaches, went up to Palm Beach, to the exclusive, tree-lined shore of Whale Beach, and to Newport and Mona Vale and Bilgola. At night they sat on the beach at Avalon and smoked and talked with all the others, cooked on the beach barbecues, swam in the black-and-silver sea. Martha preferred this life to the self-indulgence of student Thailand; she liked the colder sea, the comparative order of the hostel, the more familiar food. She loved the Australians too, so easily friendly, upbeat, absolutely lacking in pretension. Looking across from this golden place at the dark, rainy English winter, she even considered, briefly, staying herself.

She told Dinah this as they sat on the beach one night in the warm darkness; she was horrified.

"Martha, you couldn't. It's so unsubtle. And the men are such chauvinists."

"They may be chauvinists, but they're very kind," said Martha. "I'd rather have them any day than some stuffy public-school wally, thank you very much."

"Plenty of those in your prospective profession," said Dinah. "Are you sure you've chosen the right career?"

"Oh yes," said Martha. Without knowing why, she had an absolute certainty that the law would suit her. "But you're right. Especially the barristers."

"Which you're not going to be?"

"No, I'm not. Can't afford it for a start, you need very rich parents for that. You can be years waiting to earn any money. And no thanks, no more beer. I feel a bit queasy. Don't know why. I did last night, as well."

Dinah laughed. "Don't tell me the nightmare's come true, you've got a baby to take home to the vicarage."

"Of course not," said Martha, almost crossly; and then—although she was not remotely worried, she told herself—when she got back to the hostel, she got out her diary. Her periods had been chaotic ever since she had arrived in Thailand. But no, it was all right, she'd had one in Singapore—very light, but nonetheless, a period—and that had been well after Koh Tao. And since then: no sex.

At the beginning of February, Stuart and his harem (as the other boys called them) set off for the north. They got a bus from Sydney, all the way up to Ayers Rock: two and a half days of jolting on the long, endlessly straight roads. It was only moderately uncomfortable; the bus was air-conditioned and it stopped every four hours or so. The worst thing was the boredom: the unchanging scenery for most of the way, the red earth, the flat scrub, the unvarying speed.

The bus was full of backpackers; they made friends, swapped chewing gum, cigarettes, and the sweets Dinah had christened anaesthetics. They stopped at Alice Springs for the night, and then in the morning caught another bus to Ayers Rock. Together they gazed in awe at it, at the great looming cliché, watched it turn purple at sunset, climbed it in the cold desert dawn, stood together, holding hands on the summit, faces raised to the sun, and felt—in spite of all the other tourists—alone in the world, while the desert stretched away from them, absolute emptiness in every direction.

When they got down, Martha felt odd; she sat for a while in the shade, and then was extremely sick; and was repeatedly sick again on the bus, as they travelled endlessly on up north to Cape Tribulation.

"Martha," said Dinah gently, as she wiped her friend's sweaty forehead by the side of the bus—it had stopped for her—"Martha, you don't have anything to tell me, do you?"

Martha said irritably that no, she hadn't; a distant crawling fear had begun to trouble her. But once they arrived at Cape Tribulation, she stopped being sick—and she started her period.

"You see," she said, waving a Tampax triumphantly at Dinah, on her way to the loo, "it's perfectly all right."

Two days later it was over; but that was surely fine?

They stayed at Cape Tribulation, where the rain forest so famously meets the sea, for a month, and made friends with someone who had a boat. He took them out to the reef several times; they snorkelled and explored the underworld, the hills and valleys of coral, the sweetly smiling brilliantly coloured fish, the friendly baby sharks who swam up to investigate them. Martha was entranced by the silence and calm beneath the water, and the gentle slowing of time. She longed to try scuba diving, but couldn't afford it.

She and Dinah got work in one of the beach bars, and made enough money to get back to Sydney by train. It was March by then; the temperature was cooling just a little. The harem broke up: Dinah was going on to California and Stuart was planning to go to New Zealand. Martha planned to fly to New York. But they stayed a few days in Avalon, rediscovering the place, feeling they had come home.

The second evening was quite cool. "I'm going to put on some trousers," said Martha, and delved into her locker to find them, unworn for months. They wouldn't go on. They weren't just a bit tight; they simply wouldn't go on.

She told herself it was all the food she'd been eating up at Cape Tribulation and the beer; it was a well-established fact of travelling that you lost weight in Thailand and piled it on again in Oz, but this was different, her arms were still stick-thin, and, forcing herself, with a supreme effort of will, to look sideways at herself in the small bathroom mirror—she had to stand on the loo to do it—she could see a distinct doming of her flat stomach. She felt sick again, but differently: the sickness of panic. And then told herself that she was being hysterical, that she'd had two periods, after all. Just the same, she went into the Avalon chemist, bought a pregnancy testing kit, locked herself in the bathroom the next morning to use it. An unmistakably distinct blue ring told her that she was pregnant.

Terrified, she gathered all her courage and went to the Avalon doctor.

He was young, with brilliant blue eyes: brisk, cheerful, very Australian.

"Those tests in the chemists aren't always reliable," he said and she could have kissed him. "But let me have a look at you and then we'll know what we're talking about."

He was quite a long time, gently palpating on her stomach, feeling her breasts, doing an internal. A nurse stood watching, her face expressionless.

"All righty, Martha," he said finally, "you get your clothes on. And then we'll have that talk."

He told her she was about five months pregnant. "But I can't be," she said, her mind flying back in hot, black panic to Koh Tao, five months earlier. "I've had periods, one just about a month ago."

"Can still happen. Was it quite light?"

"Well . . . quite."

"How long did it last?"

"About—about two days."

"Martha, I'm sorry, that's quite common. Have you had any nausea?"

"A . . . bit. But not every day, just, well, for a few days. I can't be pregnant, I really can't."

"Are you telling me you haven't done anything to get pregnant?" he said, his blue eyes twinkling at her.

She managed to smile.

"Well, I have. But only . . . only once." Twice actually, she thought, thinking of the next morning, and the immeasurably increased pleasure of it.

"It only takes once. I'm sorry, Martha. There really is no doubt. When was this one time?"

"At the end of October."

"I'm afraid that exactly adds up. Exactly."

He was kindness itself: Did she want to go home to England, was there anyone with her who could help?

"I'll have to have a termination," she said immediately, ignoring his questions. "It's the only thing."

"Martha, I'm very sorry," he said, and his voice was gentle and almost hesitant, "it's much too late for that."

Chapter 27
· · · · ·

The wheeling and dealing that goes on between politicians and the press, their mutual dependence, their ruthless pragmatism towards each other, is one of the most crucial ingredients in political life.

"We don't have any power without the politicians," Nick Marshall had explained to more than one fascinated dinner party, "but we have a hell of a lot of influence over political events. And they're frightened of that influence. Mostly because they don't know where it's going to come from next."

He often said nobody outside the business would believe his life: the mysterious phone calls with anonymous tip-offs, the invitations to meet politicians in the bars of London pubs (most notably the Red Lion halfway down Whitehall, opposite 10 Downing Street, a favourite haunt of the Gordon Brown mob), the offers of leaked documents, the waylaying in the busy corners and corridors of the House of Commons to have a piece of gossip of extraordinary sensitivity whispered in his ear. Or the exclusive stories from high-ranking cabinet ministers and senior civil servants, either in return for his ongoing loyalty to their party's cause or to buy his temporary silence over something that might have caused them embarrassment.

The phone call he got quite early that Monday morning, as he ran across Hampstead Heath, didn't seem particularly intriguing. Theodore Buchanan (Tory MP for South Cirencester) invited him to lunch at the Ritz and told him he might have a nice little story for him. Nick knew Teddy Buchanan quite well, a nice old buffer, traditional Tory, who had a soft spot for Nick because he was a country boy and understood about things like foxhunting, and its importance to the life of the countryside.

Nick was at the Ritz, in the absurdly overdressed restaurant, ten minutes early; he sat there alternately studying the menu and the clientele, who seemed to be getting older and older. The food was as fussily got up as the restaurant itself, everything encased in something else—rich pastry, truffles, double cream—nothing simple at all. He ordered himself a gin and tonic, which seemed in keeping with the place, and reflected rather sadly that nothing seemed much fun at the moment. God, he missed Jocasta. She had left a dark and silent void in his life, and he couldn't imagine how he was ever going to get over her.

The thought of commitment, of marriage even, no longer seemed so terrifying; indeed a life of ongoing bachelorhood seemed a great deal worse. He wondered how long her affair with bloody Keeble would last, and if she'd get over it and come back to him.

He sipped his gin and tonic, and sat back in his chair, trying to distract himself by watching a very pretty girl who had just come in: tall, slim, with long dark hair and wonderful legs; she was wearing what even Nick could recognise as Chanel. Rich then. No, rich daddy, that was more like it; he had come to join her, had kissed her, sat down opposite her. Or rich sugar daddy, more like it still. How could they do it, these lovely things, sleep with these old men? He had heard it referred to by a girl on the paper as antiquing—it was extraordinary—and then realised that Jocasta had done exactly that. Shit! Why had he let her go, why, why? He was thirty-six, more than old enough to settle down; silly bugger that he was, running around like some pathetic adolescent.

A dazzling smile came at him from across the room, a slim, elegant figure crossed towards him, shook him by the hand; it was Fergus Trehearn.

"Hello, Nick. What a wonderful surprise. What are you doing here?"

Nick liked Fergus. He had met him six months ago when he had been handling some sixteen-year-old who had been propositioned by a Tory

MP. Of course he was as ruthless and devious as all the others, but he was a lot more pleasant to be with.

"Hi, Fergus. Waiting for my lunch date."

"A beautiful young girl, no doubt?"

"A rather portly middle-aged politician."

"Well, that's a terrible shame. I'm doing a little better than that. As you will see. She'll be here any minute. With her mother, let me add, before you get any unpleasant ideas. You'll have heard about Baby Bianca, no doubt? The abandoned baby, found at Heathrow."

"I certainly have," said Nick. "Jocasta had some dealings with her. You're not handling her, are you?"

"I am indeed. And I'm doing a very good job for her as well. We're no nearer finding her mother, but we have fashion editors slavering over her and newspapers trying to sign her up."

"And you're buying her lunch at the Ritz?"

"It was her choice. We've just been to see the fashion editor of *Style*, and this is her treat, in return for promising to get on with studying for her GCSEs for the next six weeks or so. Then I hope she'll be back in the public eye with a vengeance. She's a sweetie—ah, here they are now. Do you want to meet her?"

"I certainly wouldn't mind," said Nick, staring transfixed at Kate who had just walked into the restaurant. She was stunning; actually rather more striking than the girl with the sugar daddy. A wonderful mixture of tenderly gawky youth and innocence, and a slightly self-conscious sexiness. She was wearing a black trouser suit with a white vest top, very high-heeled boots, and her hair, her long blond curly hair, was pulled back in a ponytail.

Fergus walked over to them, kissed both Kate and her mother, and led them over to Nick.

"Nicholas Marshall, Kate and Helen Tarrant. My dates for lunch. Nick, aren't I the lucky man?"

Nick stood up briefly, shook both their hands, managed to mumble something at Kate, and then, as Fergus led them off again to a table on the other side of the room, sat down rather heavily. He felt slightly shaken, but not by Kate's beauty or Helen's nervousness: it was the fact that Kate did bear a considerable resemblance to Jocasta . . .

. . .

Teddy Buchanan arrived at almost half past one, full of apologies. He had been held up in a committee meeting.

"So sorry, Nicholas. Have you ordered? No? That a G and T? I'll join you. Splendid idea. Let's order straightaway, shall we, and we can get on with the matter in hand."

"Fine," said Nick, but it was only as Teddy settled to his main course—steak topped with truffles in phyllo pastry—that he suddenly put down his knife and fork, picked up his glass of claret, and said, "Well, you'll be wondering why I've brought you here, Nick."

Nick said yes, he was, but that he was greatly enjoying himself anyway. "Excellent," said Buchanan. "Well, I've got a very good little story for you . . ."

He leant forward, started speaking quietly in Nick's ear. After a few minutes, Nick forgot all about Kate Tarrant, and the girl in Chanel with the sugar daddy, and even Jocasta. It was a very good little story indeed . . .

Chad Lawrence and Jonny Farquarson had been at Eton together; had been good friends, attended on each other's weddings, were godfathers to each other's children. They met occasionally over the years; while Chad fought his way up the political ladder, Jonny ran Farjon, the family engineering business. When the Centre Forward Party was formed, Farquarson asked if he could be involved in any way; he had always had an eye for the political scene. Chad told him yes, he could be a backer, and Farjon donated a million pounds.

In the excitement and panic of the party launch, Chad failed to check on Farjon, as he should have done; the fact that it had gone bankrupt eighteen months earlier had gone unobserved.

It got worse: Farjon, it transpired, had been acquired by a company operating out of Hong Kong. "Which means," Theodore Buchanan had said to Nick, "the Centre Forward Party is being illegally funded by an overseas company, and far worse by one within the People's Republic of China." From every point of view it could not have been worse; there were ugly sleaze associations, the party was open to the dangers of blackmail, and it had been seriously negligent of Chad not to check on the company.

"Would you mind telling me who fed you this fascinating piece of information?" Chad said, when Nick spoke to him about it.

"Now, Chad, you know I can't do that. Not possibly. And it's a very good story."

"Yes, and that's exactly what it is. A story. Load of bollocks."

"Good. Fine. Well, you won't mind my checking it out, then?"

"Of course I bloody well mind! Poking into my affairs—"

"Chad," said Nick almost sorrowfully, "that's my job."

Chad glared at him. "I thought your paper was supposed to support our party."

"Of course. We do. But not against this sort of thing. Look, I've done you the service of warning you. I could have just published and been damned. I'll speak to you soon, Chad. Sorry about all this."

He put his beer down, only half finished, and walked out of the Red Lion; when he looked back Chad was staring into his own glass, his expression murderous.

•◆•

Clio had applied for the job at the Royal Bayswater. It had taken a lot of courage; she knew how devastated she was going to feel if she didn't get it. Her confidence was at an all-time low, and almost every day delivered yet another misery-producing request or phone call or letter from either her solicitor or Jeremy's.

Just the same, she knew herself very well, and she knew that staying in the backwater that was the Guildford practice was going to prove ever more dispiriting. She did love it, but it wasn't what she needed anymore. She needed challenge, new people, and new problems. And she really wanted to get back to London.

She still hadn't said anything to Mark, but she was taking Beaky's advice and visiting the other hospitals in the Bayswater group, had taken a few days of leave to do it. Apart from it being politically astute and impressing the board, it would get her back into hospital procedure and give her some insight into the Bayswater philosophy. The first hospital she was going to visit was in Highbury; they had promised her a day in Outpatients: "And if you can get here by eight, we've a management meeting that might be interesting for you."

The thought of getting to Highbury from Guildford by eight in the morning made her quail.

"Borrow my house," Jocasta had said promptly when she heard. "Honestly, it would enjoy the company and I'd love to think I'd helped you get your job. People next door have the key."

Clio arrived in the early evening, when the pavements outside the cafés and bars of Clapham and Battersea were filling up with pretty, noisy young people; within ten minutes she felt at home. The house was so pretty, every room dizzily crammed with books and pictures and ephemera of every type; Jocasta collected a range of things, advertising memorabilia, silk shawls which were strewn as throws across every imaginable surface, and 1930s books of school stories by people like Angela Brazil. There were also several collages, made up with snapshots from Jocasta's childhood, mostly pictures of her and Josh with their mother, a rather severe-looking woman—and only one with their father, taken at what was presumably Jocasta's eighteenth. That was Jocasta of the year they had met, skinny, very brown, in a strapless black dress with her hair up. Ronald Forbes was what people described as a fine-looking man, tall and blond, very like Jocasta—or Josh—wearing a dinner jacket, standing close to Jocasta, but not touching her and not smiling, either. It was not in a collage, that picture, but mounted in a silver frame. Whatever she said, he clearly mattered to her—very much. Partly the basis for her relationship with Gideon, Clio thought: she had a father complex.

There were other collages, of her schooldays and her travels and even, rather touchingly, of her life with Nick: a dizzy display, taken in bars and restaurants, at parties and out with friends. Poor Nick. Clio, who had liked what little she had seen of him, felt very sad for him. She felt increasingly doubtful about Jocasta's new relationship.

She had brought a few things for her supper with her and had just uncorked a bottle of wine when the phone rang.

"Is that Jocasta?"

"No, it's not, I'm afraid. Who's calling?"

"Is that Clio? What a wonderful surprise to hear your voice." It was Fergus Trehearn.

"Yes. I mean, is it?" God, she must sound ridiculous. "Jocasta lent me her house for a day or so. I've got to be in London and—"

"This is Fergus Trehearn."

"I know. I mean, I recognised your voice."

"Well, it's very nice that it made such an impression on you. My voice, that is. Now it's ridiculous to be calling her there, I know, but she told me she pops in from time to time and I can't raise her anywhere else. Her mobile is switched off. How are you, Clio?"

"Very well, thank you. Fergus, if you want Jocasta, she's in New York. With Gideon. They're staying at the Carlyle."

"Ah, yes. It's one of Gideon's favourites. I'll call her there. It's not urgent, just something about Kate."

"Fine. I hope you get hold of her."

"I will. And I hope your business goes well. Some terribly high-powered medical conference, I expect?"

"No, not exactly," said Clio. "I'm . . . visiting a hospital. I'm applying for a job at my old hospital and this place I'm going to is affiliated to it."

"Applying for a job? As a hospital doctor?"

"Well, yes. A consultant. A consultant geriatrician. Which is what I was before." Why was she telling him all this?

"Geriatrics—that's the care of the elderly, isn't it?"

"It is indeed."

"What a wonderful job, what marvellous work to be doing. It breaks my heart to think of old people being neglected, uncared for. When they've done so much for us. And I wouldn't mind betting they're a little more courteous than your younger patients might be."

"That's exactly right," said Clio, smiling, surprised at his insight. "Anyway, I'm sorry, I'm keeping you—"

"Not at all. I would love to continue the conversation. But, yes, I should call Jocasta. More's the pity. Goodbye, Clio, it's been extremely nice talking to you."

She wished she could dislike him, because she so totally disapproved of what he did. But she couldn't. He had the same effect on her, she reflected, putting the phone down, as drinking a glass of good red wine. Soothed. Pleased. The opposite of irritable.

On an impulse, and prompted by a picture on the wall of the three of them at Heathrow in a backpacking collage, she decided to try and raise Martha Hartley. It was only half past six, and since she had said in her interviews that she frequently worked till midnight, she might just catch her. She called Sayers Wesley and was put through to a girl with a coolly clipped accent, who told her that Miss Hartley was away, but that she would pass on the message.

"But I should warn you, she will be extremely busy for a few days at least. I can't promise anything."

Clio put the phone down feeling ruffled. Snooty bitch. She probably only passed on the messages she thought sufficiently important. For some reason she thought of Martha, all those years ago, talking about her very different life then as a vicar's daughter, the conditions of what she described as "unbelievable respectability," in which she had grown up "in a spotlight of sorts. The whole parish watching."

Well, the parish would be watching her now; it was also her constituency. Binsmow in Suffolk. Now there was a way of tracking her down. She said in the article she went there every weekend, on constituency business. And her parents were bound to be nice people.

Clio suddenly felt rather excited. She would call them, see if they knew when Martha would be back. They would definitely pass the message on. She was intrigued now by Martha, the totally changed Martha. She had become a challenge. She dialled directory enquiries. "Binsmow, Suffolk," she said. "The name is Hartley. It's a vicarage."

—•—

Nick was walking over Westminster Bridge next morning when his phone went; it was Theodore Buchanan.

"Hello, young Nicholas. Nice piece yesterday. Well done."

He had run an item about rural unemployment, quoting several MPs on the devastating effect a hunting ban would have on employment in the area. It was a neat payment for Buchanan's story about Chad Lawrence.

"I just thought you'd like to know," Buchanan was saying, "I'm going to raise the other matter as a point of order this evening. I've given advance warning to the Speaker's Office. It'll be pretty late, probably about nine, because there's a lot of stuff about the Lords Reform. Now, this is what I'm going to say . . ."

Later that day, Nick wrote his story and filed it—after rechecking with Buchanan that he was indeed making his point of order. He had run so many of these exclusive stories and they never failed to worry as well as excite him. The great fear being that with the story set and ready to run, something would prevent that statement (with its consequent parliamentary privilege) from being made.

"So that the newspaper isn't actually reporting what an MP has said at all, but making an actionable statement of its own," he had explained once to Jocasta, "and therefore laying itself open to the laws of libel."

Buchanan reassured him once again that there was absolutely no question but that the point of order would be made, "In roughly two hours from now, I'd say."

Chapter 28

. . . . .

Sometimes they made her feel terribly hunted, her e-mails; they pursued her wherever she went. This morning she was checking them from her suite at the Observatory. Quite a long list, as usual. Mostly administrative matters: could she attend this meeting, agree to that memo, was she available for a session with Paul Quenell the following Wednesday. And there was a list of people who had called. She skimmed through them: mostly from outside the firm concerning committees and charitable boards she had agree to sit on, functions she was invited to attend. Then a name that made her heart lurch: Clio Scott. Would Martha call her about a meeting, as soon as she could?

Martha sat staring at the screen, feeling her mind fracture: Mackenzie, Paul Quenell, Sayers Wesley, Jack Kirkland, Centre Forward were in one part of it, a smoothly controlled, well-conducted place; and Clio was in quite another. What did she want? Why had she suddenly called? What could she possibly want with her, what might she know, what could she do?

Stop it, Martha, stop it; you're panicking. It's panic that's dangerous. The only thing that's dangerous. Calm is everything, calm and control: that's what keeps you safe. Everything was perfectly all right. Maybe Clio wanted to arrange a reunion for the three of them. Jocasta had mentioned something of the sort. Yes, that was actually quite likely. Quite likely.

A sliver of cool was parting the hot panic, sending it away. There was no need to see Clio, talk to her even. She could simply tell her PA to say that she was too busy and she'd call her when her diary was a little less full. That was what she always said to unwelcome invitations and it always worked. Then she never called them, and usually they never called her back. Clio could be banished again, there was no need to admit her any further into her life.

And now she would go to the gym for half an hour before she had to set out for Wesley's offices and another tedious but infinitely controllable meeting with Donald Mackenzie.

At one point she had been afraid she would have to stay on, but they seemed to be nearly there now; and she would fly back on Friday night, and be in London for the one really important event in her political diary, a meeting on Sunday with Janet Frean along with several other party members to discuss a standing committee Janet had been invited to serve on, in connection with benefit fraud. Martha was really excited at the prospect, at politics coming properly alive.

She was amazed how much better she felt out here. The trip to Avalon had, against all odds, done her good. She had looked at the other Martha and wondered at what she had survived and how well, had left her there, sitting on the beach, dressed in tattered Bermuda shorts and baggy T-shirt, staring panicked out to sea, and taken her successful, accomplished self back to Sydney Harbour. Avalon had changed along with her, she thought, had become chic and successful, full of smart pavement cafés, and expensive boutiques. She had even found the time to sit at one of the tables and have a skinny latte and watch the world going by, a world of chic young people and perfectly dressed young families. Only the surfers had not changed: they wandered along on bare feet, carrying their boards, sun-bleached and deep-down brown, and talking, talking endlessly, on their way to ride the waves. Such a lovely lifestyle it had been. Such a lovely lifestyle it clearly still was.

◆

CLEAN SHEET PARTY AND THE CHINESE LAUNDRY

Chad Lawrence, the charismatic MP whose blond good looks and public-school charm made him a favourite with the old Tory Party, has behaved with uncharacteristic carelessness over the funding of his new party's think tank. So claimed Theodore Buchanan, in a point of order in the House this evening.

He asked the House if it was in order "for the Centre Forward Party to be receiving funds from a source within the People's Republic of China? Is it not the case that British political parties—in this House—are forbidden from receiving finance from foreign interests? Mr. Speaker, should not the Committee of Standards and Privileges investigate this disgrace as a matter of urgency?"

At which point Mr. Buchanan sat down amidst a great deal of booing and cheering.

When an old school (Eton, where else?) chum, Jonathan Farquarson, offered the new party a million pounds for party funding last autumn, Lawrence (Ullswater North) failed to check that Mr. Farquarson's engineering company, Farjon, was entirely U.K. based; after a bankruptcy two years ago, it was acquired by a Chinese company operating from the north of Hong Kong. Not only is it against the law for a British political party to receive finance from foreign interests, it is quite possible that Mr. Lawrence could find himself under pressure to secure favourable import tariffs for the company. Once tipped as a future Tory prime minister, he was one of the founding members of the Centre Forward Party, the left-of-centre breakaway group from the Tories.

The party pledged to be squeaky clean, devoid of sleaze and cronyism; unfortunately for Mr. Lawrence, he has found himself in the middle of a row involving both.

Jack Kirkland, sitting with Chad Lawrence on the opposition benches, rose to say that the matter was receiving his full attention and meanwhile he would continue to have every confidence in his Honourable Friend, the member for Ullswater North.

Nobody was remotely deceived.

"What I want to know," said Jack Kirkland, passing a glass of wine to Janet Frean, who had offered him her company that evening, "is who on earth can have tipped Buchanan off. He's not the sharpest knife in the drawer—someone must have helped him. God, what a mess. In just six weeks. Fallen from our shiny pedestal, right down into the murky squalor, along with the rest of them. I suppose it was naïve of me to think our little band was unique. Above this sort of thing."

"Not really. I thought so, too. It's very sad."

"Not sad, Janet, *bloody* stupid. Feckless." He sighed. "I honestly think we may not recover from this, you know."

"Oh don't be ridiculous, Jack," she said, her strong-jawed, rather handsome face full of sympathy. "Of course we can. Tomorrow it'll be someone else, something quite different. How about a new Mandelson scandal? I'd put quite a lot of money on that."

He managed a smile. "You could be right. Well, thank God for you. You're not going to do anything dreadful to me, are you, Janet? You're not going to be found snogging in the press gallery with someone or handing out houses for votes?"

She laughed. "Bob wouldn't like the former too much and I don't have the means for the latter. Sometimes I think I should have stuck to my original profession, the law, and made some money. But no, don't worry, Jack, I won't let you down. Promise."

He looked at her very seriously. "I know you won't. I trust you totally. I've always thought women were a far better bet for politics. Less power-crazed, more genuinely idealistic. I'd forgotten you were a lawyer. Like the blessed Margaret. And young Martha, of course."

"Indeed." There was an edge to her voice that he didn't notice.

"Now there's a clever girl. I think she's absolutely splendid."

"I agree. Although she seriously lacks experience."

"She'll gain it fast. Involve her as much as you can, Janet. I really think it could be worth it. I see her as our future. In an odd way."

"Very odd," said Janet, and this time he did notice her tone, "considering she's had about two months' experience."

"Janet, Janet," he said, patting her hand, "you're not feeling jealous, are you? She may be the future but you're our present. Incidentally, I heard a rumour that Iain Duncan Smith is going to make Theresa May chairman of the Tory Party."

"What? I don't believe it!"

"Oh, I think it's very possibly true. One of his cleverer moves, I'd say. Putting a woman into that job. Just think, Janet, it might have been you."

"Indeed," said Janet briefly.

He stared at her. "You wouldn't have wanted that, surely? With that lot?"

"Of course not," she said.

Shortly after that, she made her excuses and left; when she reached home she poured herself a very large whiskey and went up to her study. Bob found her pacing up and down the room, fists clenched, raging silently; rather wearily, he asked her what the matter was.

"Just go back to bed and leave me alone," she said. "I don't want to discuss it."

He reflected that very few people would have recognised the calm, brilliant superwoman in that near-frenzied creature.

He was never quite sure how much he disliked her. Or even if he disliked her at all anymore, simply felt nothing for her. He had fallen in love with her at university, a brilliant girl, not beautiful but very attractive, reading law, had been flattered by her interest in him and even more so by her desire first to move in with him and then to marry him. It took a time for him to realise this had been largely inspired by his money—he was the beneficiary of a large trust fund—but by then it was much too late. He suited her beautifully, both financially and practically, as support for her ambition to become the second woman prime minister: he paid the bills—including those for her political expenses—babysat endlessly, oversaw the children's upbringing, smiled by her side at functions and interviews.

But as she rose in the political firmament, she became increasingly dismissive of him, ignoring him whenever possible, eating alone, saying she had papers to read, work to do, walking away from him when he tried to talk to her. That was when he began to dislike her.

The only place she appeared to welcome him was in the bedroom—she was sexually voracious, too voracious, indeed, for him. It took a while for him to realise that his role there was as much for the begetting of their children as for satisfying her physically. It suited her career; her large family was a most useful tool in her self-publicity, a kind of shorthand for her image—Janet Frean the mother of five, Janet Frean the superwoman, Janet Frean who showed women they could indeed have it all.

Her career was of prime importance to her, and everything was sacrificed on its altar; primarily Bob, of course, but her children, her friends, her health, her own sanity, it seemed. He had become aware early in their relationship of the fanatical side of her nature, her ruthless destruction of anything in her path, her capacity to drive herself beyond exhaustion.

At first he admired it, then became wary of it, and finally anxious about it, recognising it as something almost manic, a psychological flaw. He looked at her sometimes, white and exhausted after late-night sessions at the House, saw her drained face, her taut neck muscles, her white knuckles as she chatted easily on the phone to constituents, to party workers. Her control was awesome. He often wondered when she would crack; it was only a matter of time. But he knew there was nothing he or anyone could do about it, and she should go to hell in her own way.

•—•

It was Wednesday evening. Clio was packing her things and leaving Jocasta's house, rather regretfully. She had loved the whole of the three days. The morning at the Highbury Hospital had been fascinating, and she had sat in on all the interviews. There were several very sad cases, reminiscent of the Morrises; she had shared her frustrations with the consultant over the problems of getting medication safely organised for the elderly, and the frustrations with the red tape binding up the carers. She had told him how she had taken to visiting her patients personally, with their carefully allotted doses in containers, and he had been impressed.

"You really care about them, your patients, don't you?"

"I do. That's the thing about general practice that I like best, you get really involved, can make a difference."

She had also spent a day in the psychiatric unit of a small hospital in Harrow and was given access to research material on various trials that were being conducted there.

"Dementia and its affiliated horrors are still some of the biggest problems in geriatrics," the consultant told her, "even with all these new drugs. It leads to such dreadful social problems, of course, and isolation from society."

It had been fascinating—and stimulating. She realised she did desperately want this job.

She had done some shopping while she was in London, had bought herself a new suit and shoes for the interview, if she got it; she decided to try them on and was buttoning the jacket when she heard a key in the front door. Jocasta? Couldn't be. Not Nick, please not Nick, she'd be so embarrassed.

"Hello?" she called down rather nervously, and "Who's that then?" came a voice up the stairs.

It was Josh.

"Who called?" said Martha. "Who did you say?"

She had rung her parents to make sure they were all right and that they hadn't been too bothered by constituents the weekend before, and her mother had told her a Clio Scott had rung.

"She was very nice," she said, "apparently you went travelling with her."

How dare she? Worming her way into her most private life, ringing up her parents, for God's sake. What did she want, that she was pursuing her like this, like a stalker almost? It was outrageous, she had no right.

"She only wanted you to ring her, dear," her mother had said half apologetically, clearly surprised by Martha's reaction. "She said it would be wonderful to see you. I don't know why you're so upset. I thought she sounded very nice. We had a little chat about your travelling days."

"You what?" Martha felt hot suddenly, hot and shaky. "What on earth were you doing, discussing that with her? What's it got to do with her? Or you, come to that?"

"Martha, dear, are you all right? You don't sound yourself. I suppose it's the journey. You must be exhausted."

"I'm perfectly all right," said Martha, "I just don't like people pestering me. Give me her number, please Mum, and I'll tell her to stop. It's too bad. What? No, of course I won't be rude to her. Why should I be? Yes, I'll be home next Friday. I'll call you before then."

Clio was making Josh a cup of coffee when her mobile rang.

He had come, he said, clearly deeply embarrassed, to try and find a belt he had lost. "I stayed here recently and I thought it might be here. It was a birthday present from Beatrice—that's my wife—and she keeps asking where it is. I was just passing, sorry if it's an inconvenient moment."

Clio said it wasn't inconvenient at all, that Jocasta had very kindly lent her the house for a couple of days.

"She's been such a good friend to me. I don't know what I'd have done without her."

"Is she with this Keeble fellow?"

"Yes."

"Odd that," he said. "I mean, he's jolly nice, of course, but Nick was so . . . so right for her. And giving up her job. The last thing I'd have expected."

"Well, I'm sure she knows what she's doing," said Clio carefully. "Now, do you take sugar?"

That was when her phone rang.

"Phew," she said, switching it off a few minutes later. "I just got what we used to call a bollocking."

"Oh yes? Who from?"

"From Martha Hartley. Remember Martha?"

"I do," he said, after a moment's pause, "of course." Then he looked at her slightly awkwardly. "Er—Clio . . ."

"Josh, don't say a single word. That was another lifetime. It's really nice we've met again now."

"Happy days, weren't they?" he said, with a grin, taking a sip of coffee.

"So happy. Wonderful kickoff to grown-up life."

"Anyway, what on earth was Martha on about?"

"I've been trying to contact her. Just because—well, just because I thought it might be fun. Anyway, I rang her PA and I rang her parents, and it seems I shouldn't have. She said I had no right to be contacting them, could I please not worry them again, and that she was far too busy to meet me at the moment. And then rang off."

"Blimey. Obviously a complete nutcase. Well, her loss, Clio, not yours."

He was a charmer, she thought—still. Impossible to dislike.

Beatrice reflected, as she got ready for her dinner, that her mother had been absolutely right. Life seemed so much better already. What would she have done this evening, for instance, with the nanny going off for interviews? Got some strange babysitter in, which would have upset the children? They were so happy with Josh: he was absurdly indulgent with them, but he also was a good father, attentive, loving, and really very hands-on. He had been from the beginning, ready to share nappy-changing and mopping up, as well as the fun things.

The atmosphere in the house had definitely lifted since he came home, officially on a trial basis—for both of them, she had added, she didn't want to sound too domineering. And he was so desperate to please her, to show her how happy he was to be back; it was very sweet. Of course he was a bit of a philanderer—but her mother was also right about that, it wasn't everything. Or so she was teaching herself to think. He was also wonderfully generous, while being surprisingly organised financially; he was very good-tempered and extremely kind. And admired her and was actually proud of her success. So the balance sheet could be said to show a large credit in his favour at the moment.

She heard him coming in, in good time as he had promised. He ran up the stairs, came into their room, gave her a kiss.

"Hi. Your resident babysitter reporting. You look gorgeous."

Beatrice knew she didn't, she wasn't the gorgeous type. But it was nice to hear, nonetheless. She returned the kiss.

"Thank you," she said, then stood back and studied him. He was so good-looking. She still fancied him, actually. Which was lucky. They hadn't had sex yet, not since his return. She hadn't been able to face it. Quite.

Suddenly it seemed possible. More than possible. A nice idea even.

"Josh," she said, as he walked towards the door, "try not to go to sleep before I get home. I'd—I'd like to tell you about the evening."

His eyes met hers; he smiled. He knew exactly what she meant.

"I won't be asleep," he said.

"Clio? Clio, it's me, Jocasta. How are you?"

"I'm fine. Back at work. Had a lovely time at your house. How's New York?"

"New York's wonderful. Really wonderful. Clio, I've got some news. Big news. We're married. Me and Gideon."

"Married! But—"

"Don't but. We just did it. Went down to Vegas, actually. Anyway, I'm Mrs. Gideon Keeble now. How cool is that?"

"Very cool."

"Well! Don't you have anything else to say—like congratulations or something?"

Clio felt a pang of remorse. What must Jocasta think, ringing her with such momentous news, clearly expecting her to be delirious with joy for her, and the best she could manage was "very cool."

"Of course I do. I'm absolutely so happy for you. Both of you. It's wonderful, really wonderful. Give my love to Gideon, won't you? Tell him he's a lucky man."

"I will. Anyway, we'll be home in a week, and we're going to give the most ginormous party. In Gideon's London house, probably. Haven't quite got a date yet, but pretty soon. Keep everything clear, won't you?"

"Of course I will," said Clio. "And—and congratulations again."

Mrs. Gideon Keeble. How insane was that? As Jocasta might have said.

Jocasta would actually have said it was reckless, daft even, if she'd read about it in the papers: someone of thirty-five, independent and ambitious, marrying a millionaire—well, a billionaire, actually—of fifty-one, who had three ex-wives and a difficult daughter. She'd have said it must be for his money, that she couldn't possibly fancy him, that the sex must be rubbish.

Well, it certainly wasn't for his money; she knew she would have married him anyway. Although she did rather like the glamour it had brought her, the first-class travel, what she called the ten-star hotels, the limitless amount of clothes she could buy, the beautiful cars, the knowledge that whatever she wanted she could have. And she was, she knew, rather besotted with Gideon's power. It gave him another dimension, made him intriguing and exciting. In every way.

She did fancy him—a lot. He was very fanciable. Amazingly so for someone of his age. The sex was—well, it was fine. Not specially, incredibly interesting, but maybe older men didn't do interesting. Anyway, she'd had plenty of interesting sex with Nick. It just didn't matter. It wasn't important. It was good and she really enjoyed it. They both did.

And she certainly didn't miss her job; she found Gideon much more interesting and rewarding, and being his wife much less demeaning and demoralising than door-stepping unhappy people.

She wasn't sure what she was going to do all day, but there were lots of possibilities. She wanted to buy a house that wasn't his, but theirs. She wanted to see a lot of the world. She wanted to entertain all the immensely interesting and famous (and not famous at all, come to that, but still interesting) people that he seemed to know. She wanted to talk to him forever.

When she met him at Heathrow after he got back from Barbados, he was smiling so much his face seemed fractured in two, and the first thing he said to her was, "You're a magician!"

Hardly right, of course. Her advice had been pretty standard agony aunt stuff—with a bit of personal experience thrown in—but apparently after a sticky start Fionnuala and he had talked more in five days than they had since she was ten.

Obviously the three polo ponies had pleased Fionnuala more than a bit, but she had actually asked him if there was anything he'd like to do on his last day and they'd gone up to Crane Beach, where the surf came in and the water was green, and swum and sunbathed all day and had a fish-and-fries lunch at the Crane Hotel on the top of the cliffs. She'd told him what she really wanted to do was be a doctor, and Gideon had nearly cried with pleasure.

Jocasta hadn't met Fionnuala yet, of course, and it would obviously be sticky when she did, but she'd worry about that when it happened.

So here she was, sated with happiness, with two days of shopping to do, and then home to England. And their wedding party.

She was still slightly reeling from the fact that she was married. It had rather seemed to happen, in retrospect at least, as she told Clio, "by accident. I mean, there we were in Vegas, wandering about after lunch one day, having the most lovely time, and I suddenly thought, This is like a honeymoon, and I said so to Gideon, and—well, I don't know, we just decided to do it. We did the classic Vegas thing, walked into a register office, and asked two people off the street to be our witnesses. And I came out Mrs. Gideon Keeble. Just like that. It was terribly exciting. And Gideon really wanted it. He's a Catholic, you know, and—"

"Jocasta," said Clio, laughing, "I don't think a register office in Vegas would quite satisfy the Catholic Church."

"Wouldn't it? No, probably not. But it was a statement of commitment. A wonderful one. I'm so happy, you can't think."

She had been half shocked, half amused by Gideon's confession of his Catholicism.

"Gideon, you don't really believe all that stuff, do you?"

"I don't exactly know," he said, serious for a moment. "It's pretty deep-seated, you know, when you've imbibed it with your mother's milk. Are you telling me you don't have a God of any kind?"

"No way."

"So your life is your own, is it? Entirely down to you?"

"Not any longer," she said, suddenly serious. "It's yours now instead."

"Oh dear," he said, and the intense blue eyes suddenly filled with tears. "Oh dear, Jocasta, you mustn't say things like that. It's a bit too much for an old man."

"There is just one thing," she said. "You don't want me to have babies, do you? Because I really don't want to."

"Jocasta, the last thing I want is any more babies. To have to share you. That's a promise."

The date of the party was set for June 22; Jocasta had rethought the thing and decided on the Berkshire house as the setting.

"It'll be a midsummer night's dream," she said joyfully. "How lovely! Maybe we should theme it, tell everyone to come as fairies."

Gideon said she could do whatever she liked, but there was no way he was going as Oberon. "I don't have the legs for it."

The guest list currently stood at three hundred and rising; Jocasta kept remembering people she wanted to ask. People she had been at school with, at university with, had worked with. She had invited the entire staff of the *Sketch*, including Nick. She had agonised over that; she knew he wouldn't want to come, but she could hardly exclude him.

She rang him up, said how she'd love him to be there and why; he was short with her, thanked her, said he was going home to the country that weekend, but that he hoped she would be very happy. For the first time since she had married Gideon, Jocasta felt miserable: she thought of all the years with Nick, the fun they'd had, how close they had been, and how much she hated hurting him. She put the phone down and cried for quite a long time.

The formal invitations to the Keeblefest, as Gideon persisted in calling it, went out in the last week of May. It was a little tight, but Jocasta said everyone would want to come so much they'd cancel almost anything except their own wedding.

Cruxbury Manor was ideal for it, a piece of Georgian perfection, standing just slightly above the grounds, said to have been designed by Capability Brown.

"Which I don't believe," Gideon said. "If that man had really designed half the gardens ascribed to him, he would have had to work seven days a week for a hundred years. And he was less than sixty when he died."

She had hired a party planner, Angie Cassell, a silvery stick-thin blonde, and in a few days she had caterers, menus, marquees, bands, and DJs lined up. She also persuaded an extremely camp designer called MM, who refused to reveal his full name, to consider her theme. He dressed in white, did a lot of hand kissing, and had an accent that would have vied with Scarlett O'Hara's. He advised against the midsummer night's dream. "It's just a little too overdone," he said, making Jocasta feel rather small. "I think we should go for Gatsby. The costumes are sooooo flattering. You don't want your guests cringing at their pictures in *Tatler*."

Jazz bands, bootlegger bars, speakeasy-style dining tents, and gun-toting gangsters in spats and trilbies roaming the grounds sounded fun, and it was true: white suits and beaded Charleston dresses were infinitely more flattering than floating chiffon.

"And what about an ongoing ten-minute crash course in the Charleston," said Jocasta, "from a professional, so people aren't afraid of trying?" Angie said she thought that would be the hugest fun, and MM clasped his hands together and cried, "Perfect!"

Clio's first emotion on getting her invitation was panic. All those glittering people, all knowing one another, all those wonderful costumes: and she was a terrible dancer. And who should she take with her? It was hardly something you could go to alone. Could she be ill? Maybe that would be the best thing. She could accept and then phone on the morning with a stomach bug. Yes, that was a really good idea.

She wrote a formal acceptance, feeling quite pleased with herself; Jocasta called the next day, saying she wanted Clio to come the night before.

"I know it'll be difficult for you to get here and someone'll need to hold my hand through the day. What are you going to wear?"

Clio said, trying to sound delighted, that she thought she would hire something.

"Look, I've got a sweet girl making me something. Would you like her to do one for you?"

"Won't that be awfully expensive?" said Clio, while thinking that it would be one huge anxiety out of the way.

"No way," said Jocasta airily. "This is fake stuff, cheap as anything. She's doing one for Beatrice as well, so it can all go on the same bill and we can sort it out later."

Clio tried very hard to believe her.

Chad Lawrence was going, of course. The entire Centre Forward Party— or at least its major players—had been invited.

He wasn't exactly looking forward to it; he seemed to have survived the Farjon scandal by way of an apology to the House for his lack of care, and assurance that the money had already been repaid—thanks to Gideon Keeble. But he was aware that his glossily successful image had been badly dulled. It had been his first serious bit of wrong-footing, and he didn't like it. And his constituency party had not been impressed.

Jack Kirkland, who hated parties, called Martha Hartley to see if she would like to go with him. His irritation when she said she couldn't go, that she was away that weekend, was profound.

"Martha," he said, "you are *not* away that weekend. You are going to the party. Gideon Keeble has just given us another million pounds to bale us out of the Farjon debacle. This is a three-line whip. *You* are going. We are *all* going. Now do you want to come with me, or would you like to bring someone else?"

Martha, sounding rather shaken, said she would very much like to go with him.

Bob Frean was dreading the party. He could cope with Janet's political career, her ferocious ambition, and her absences from home—just. What he objected to was being dragged into it. He did it occasionally— when he had to. But this was different; this was social. The kind of thing he most loathed.

She was in a dangerous mood at the moment: half excited, half withdrawn. It was one he knew well and dreaded. And she had developed one of her obsessions against someone. There was always someone; usually some rival in the party. It was generally another woman; she had hated that extremely nice woman, Amanda Platell, who had masterminded publicity for Hague's last campaign, and Theresa May because of her shoe obsession. Just now it was this new girl, Martha Hartley, who was getting so much attention from everyone. She could hardly bring herself to utter her name.

Fergus Trehearn was euphoric at being invited. It was exactly the sort of occasion he loved best: glamorous, fun, high profile, and crawling with media. He would have a wonderful night. He also adored dancing, loved dressing up, and was never happier than when watching pretty women partying.

Fionnuala Keeble, with wisdom beyond her years, refused the invitation. She did it by way of a text message to her father, which made him smile.

A large Irish contingent was expected, many of them Gideon's relatives.

"It'll be great for them to meet you at last," said Gideon, smiling at Jocasta. She smiled back and thought how sweet it was that his accent always intensified when he was even talking about Ireland.

Josh was longing for the party; he and Beatrice had agreed that, for the time being, they would stay at home, working things out, spending weekends almost entirely with the children, and refusing all but work-based invitations. Of course it was worth it, but the thought of a night of social excitement was extremely welcome. And Beatrice had thrown herself into it, suggested they go as Scott and Zelda Fitzgerald, and had even hired a (fake) Bugatti for them to arrive in. He'd have fun: only of course he'd be very sensible and careful. The two were not incompatible after all.

Ronald Forbes, after carefully considering the invitation to his only daughter's wedding party, sent a note accepting, telling her he hoped she and Gideon would be very happy and enclosing a very large cheque by way of a wedding present. He knew it was a meaningless gesture: as meaningless, indeed, as his acceptance, which he had absolutely no intention of honouring. Nevertheless Jocasta was disproportionately pleased.

"I never thought he'd come, I really never did."

"Well, there you are," said Gideon, giving her a kiss.

Several days after the mass of invitations had been sent out, Jocasta had the idea.

"I'm going to ask Kate Tarrant," she said to Gideon.

"What on earth for?"

"Because she'd love it. It would be the hugest treat for her. And it would sort of make up for all the trouble I've caused her. I'll tell her to bring her boyfriend and maybe a couple of friends. Actually, I'll ask her parents as well, I think; that'll reassure them. Oh, and her grandmother."

"Her grandmother! Jocasta, what on earth are you doing inviting grandmothers to your parties? Unless it's to make me feel young."

"Gideon, I swear you could fancy Kate's grandmother. She's really glamorous. You'll probably spend most of the night dancing with her."

"I doubt it. And what about Carla? Do you think they should come face-to-face?"

"Carla's not coming. She's staying with her mother in Milan. Honestly, Gideon, it'd be fun. And I'd love you to meet Kate. Do you really think it's a bad idea?"

"I think it's a terrible idea," said Gideon.

"But why? What harm could it do?"

"Quite a lot, I'd say," said Gideon. "But I can see you're going to do it anyway. Just don't blame me if the boyfriend's sick all over the speakeasy."

"If that's the worst thing you can think of," said Jocasta, "it isn't very serious."

Chapter 29

Janet had got Martha a ticket to hear Chad speak.

"On Thursday afternoon. About foxhunting. It's an important subject to us, because the rural vote is up for grabs. You really ought to be here, if you can possibly get away. Why don't you come and hear him, then we'll go out after that?"

"Oh—OK." Martha was flattered. "I'd like that. Thank you."

She liked Janet very much: she was so supportive and always friendly, and an evening at her house in the company of a lot of other MPs, not talking about politics at all, had really made her feel much nearer to belonging.

She managed to get away for the debate, slipped into the public gallery, and sat there, enjoying the unfailing sense of excitement that sitting in the Chamber gave her, remembering what had ensnared her in the first place.

Chad spoke witheringly of the "Islington government" and its lack of grasp of what foxhunting meant to the rural communities; said how many jobs would be lost, and how his party and his party alone seemed to understand that. There was a lot of shouting and booing. "Take all your toffs over to China, teach *them* about hunting!" shouted some wit. Chad seemed unmoved. "They'd probably enjoy it, they haven't heard of class envy over there," he shouted back.

There was a lot more; afterwards they met him in the Strangers' Bar for a drink.

"I don't know how you can bear it," said Martha. "All that abuse. I know I never could."

"My darling, you could and you will," said Chad. He was high on adrenaline. "It's rather fun, once you get going. I'm afraid we'll never win this one, though. No hope. The pressure to come in behind Tony will be incredible."

"I don't really understand all that," said Martha. "How does it work?"

"Bargaining. The whips go round the night before a big division, wheeling and dealing. They know everyone personally; they know what they all want. You give us your vote, they say, and we'll see your bill gets a third reading. You give us your vote and you'll get funding for your bypass. You give us your vote, tell your old lady the knighthood's on its way. It's shameless."

"That's terrible," said Martha.

"That's politics. Oh, hi, Jack. Were you in the Chamber just now?"

"No," said Jack Kirkland. He looked grim. "I was at HQ. Hideous results from that focus group research are in. We've lost about ten percent of our potential vote. Just over the last two months. I don't need to tell you why." He glared at Chad. "Mercifully, it was something I commissioned privately. We come in a good fourth. I'd hoped to publish it, if it was good news. As it is, I'm keeping it quiet. It's a rolling disaster, this sort of thing. People see you sinking, wonder what was so wonderful about you in the first place, switch back to something safer."

"Oh God," said Janet, "I'm so sorry, Jack. I suppose saying it's midterm won't help?"

"Of course not. We should be in our heyday still. Shiny new. We look old and sleazy already. Bloody shame. And it's hard on the party workers, this sort of thing. It sends morale right down, makes their job twice as difficult."

"Could I see the research? Maybe it isn't as bad as you think."

"Janet, it's appalling. But, yes, if you like. Keep it confidential, for Christ's sake. You'd better take a look as well, Chad. See what you've done. God, it's depressing."

"I think it'll be all right," said Janet to Martha later. They were eating in Shepherd's in Marsham Street. "We've just had a run of bad luck, that's all. People's memories are very short. A bit more idiocy from Iain Duncan Smith, another gaffe from Mandy and we'll be up there again, flying high, promising the world to the voters. A good conference—not that we can afford one—and we'll be back."

"I was reading about the Social Democratic Party," said Martha, after Jack and Chad had left. "They had their first conference on a train. Took the party to the voters. I thought that was brilliant."

Janet looked at her thoughtfully. Then she said, "Yes, but we can't copy them. People would say that we had no original ideas."

"I see," said Martha humbly.

"Sorry. Didn't mean to crush you. I worry about you, you know. You've got a lot on your plate. Your job, which is terribly demanding, and your constituency duties every weekend. I would imagine those legal clinics you do are a lot of work. And no one to confide in, to talk to. Or have you?"

"Well . . . not in the way you mean," said Martha carefully.

"I know about pressure. And it's very tough, especially for a woman. This place is hard for us. It's such a male club. So any problems you do have, that you need a sympathetic ear for, you know you can always bring them to me. I've been round the block a few times. And you'll find you do need a confidant—someone who knows what the pressures are."

"Thank you," said Martha, slightly awkwardly.

"Don't thank me. It's lovely to have an ally, a female ally. Potentially, anyway. We have to stick together."

First thing the next morning, Janet went to Jack's office to see the research. It was very depressing. She saw what he meant.

"I feel we've squandered everything. Bloody Chad."

"It's not all his fault," she said.

"God. What are we going to do?"

"Just keep trucking," she said. "Now look, I've been thinking: we ought to have a conference."

"I know that. But we can't afford one."

"Not the standard kind, no. But remember what the old SDP did?"

"Of course. The train."

"It was a brilliant idea, a PR coup in itself. I really think we might do something similar."

"It was brilliant," he said, "but Janet, there are enough jibes about copying them already."

"I realise that. But we could make a virtue of it. Come out with our hands up, saying yes, we know it's not our idea, but we're big enough to say so. It would be affordable, it would be brilliant publicity, and it is exactly what we could afford. Think about it, anyway."

"I will," he said slowly. "And this research—it never happened."

"It never did."

He smiled at her rather wearily. "At least I can trust you, Janet."

"You can indeed," she said.

—•—

Jocasta was waiting at Heathrow for Gideon to arrive back from Washington. He had been there for a week, and she had missed him horribly. She had wanted to go with him, but with the party two days off now, with marquees and fountains and flowers and table plans to attend to, even she could see it wasn't possible.

Her father had sent a fax that day, telling her that after all he was unable to come to the party. She had been horribly hurt: it had surprised her how much.

"I should have known better by now," she wailed on the phone to Josh. He tried, helplessly, to comfort her, saying he knew how busy their father was, how he knew he had been looking forward to the party. She was not in the least comforted.

"He went to your wedding," she said bitterly. "I don't think he'd even bother going to my funeral."

"With a bit of luck," said Josh, "he won't be around."

"I bet he will."

She had been at the airport half an hour already and the plane wasn't due for another fifteen minutes. This must be love, she thought smiling to herself, being at arrivals for an hour longer than you needed to be.

•—•—•

Nick Marshall would often walk from Hampstead at least as far as St. John's Wood before getting on the tube. Or get off the tube at Baker Street and walk the rest of the way to the House. It was the best way to see London, and you saw things that you'd never see from a taxi, let alone the tube. Like that Friday, walking down towards Carlos Place from Grosvenor Square, at about three o'clock, when he saw Janet Frean coming out of the Connaught and getting into one taxi, and shortly after her, Michael Fitzroy, Tory MP for West Birmingham, getting into another. Well. Who'd have thought that? She was a dark horse. All that stuff about the importance of the family and her superwoman image, and she was having it away with someone in an expensive hotel at lunchtime. Not quite as straightforward as she seemed then. He might tease her about it, if he got really bored. He felt bored quite a lot these days. Bored and lonely.

Nick was right that Janet was a dark horse, but wrong about the manner of it. As for Michael Fitzroy, as soon as he got back to the House, he called the political editor of the *Daily News* and told him he had an interesting story. When could they meet? It was about the Centre Forward Party and some research.

•—•—•

Nothing had happened, no reporter had arrived on her doorstep, no accusing voice had come on the phone, no angry child had come into her life. It was going to be all right: she allowed herself to think that now. It had died down, as she had told herself it would. Everything was safely and neatly parcelled up again; the past in the past, the present in the present.

But there was one thing straddling the two—and that was Ed.

He simply wouldn't go away. He called her and texted her endlessly. He had been in reception at Wesley her first day back. He was patient, reasonable, not aggressive, not difficult; he said he wasn't into stalking her or pestering her, he just wanted to know she was all right.

A pattern had developed: he would call her every other day or so on her mobile and as many times at home; he sounded surprisingly cheerful, absolutely calm, asking how she was. And she would tell him she was fine, that there was nothing wrong, that he had to forget about her, and he would say it was impossible, until he knew why he should. He would ask her what she was doing, and she would reply that she was working or going to Binsmow, and after a few more pleasantries, he would tell her that he would call her again soon and hang up. It was all very agreeable really: only it hurt more than she would have believed.

She missed him—horribly.

But she was surviving. Everything did seem perfectly all right. And a blank, bland, sexless life seemed a small price to pay for that.

"I'm fine, Ed," she said, picking up the phone now, slightly reluctantly, "really fine. Thank you."

"Good. And are you going to this bash tonight?"

"What bash?" she said carefully.

"The big party that Gideon Keeble and his girlfriend are giving. To celebrate their wedding. I read about it in the *Mail*, about how you have to have a security number to give the guy at the gate so you can get in."

"No," she said firmly. "Why should I be going to that?"

"It said the whole of the Centre Forward Party was going. I assume that includes you."

"No, Ed, it doesn't."

"I don't believe you," he said. "I shall call tomorrow and see how you enjoyed it."

She knew whatever she said, he would. "Bye, Ed," she said firmly.

•◆•

"What do you think then?"

Kate walked into the sitting room, where Nat was waiting for her. She was wearing an extremely short silver-sequinned shift dress, almost backless, with a silver chiffon sash round the dropped waist. Her long legs were encased in white tights, and her shoes were silver also, high-heeled with a bar across the instep. Her hair was in a long, loose plait, draped across her right shoulder; she wore a silver band on her forehead, dangly, glittery earrings, and a slave bangle in the shape of a snake coiled round her upper arm. Her huge dark eyes were heavily made up, with long, overtly fake eyelashes, and her mouth was a slash of red against her white skin. She carried a vast white fur stole draped over one arm. There was a silence. Then he said, "You look pretty—cool."

"Nat! I've been three hours getting like this. You have to do better than that."

"Oh, OK then. You look great."

"That's better. You don't look so bad yourself."

"This OK, is it?" he said anxiously. "I don't look like a tosser?"

"Not a bit. Did you have that suit before?"

"Course not. I bought it, didn't I? What'd I want with a dinner suit?" She considered his life and saw his point.

"Well, it suits you. You look really, really sexy."

"Yeah?" He studied himself closely in the small oval mirror over the fireplace. "So where'd you get that dress, Kate, it's well nice."

"A fancy dress place Fergus took me to."

"Oh yeah?" Nat scowled. He wasn't keen on Fergus; he thought Kate took too much notice of him.

"What about your hair, I suppose Fergus did that an' all?"

"Don't be silly, Nat. He's not a hairdresser. No, Gran did it."

"Yeah? She's all right, your gran. She still coming?"

"Of course. She's coming in the other car with Mum and Dad and some old bloke she calls her date. She's really excited. Mum and Dad aren't exactly looking forward to it," she added. "Dad's really miserable."

"He'll be all right," said Nat confidently. "He can stick with me."

It was a tribute to Fergus's powers of persuasion that Kate was going at all, let alone her parents. They had been completely horrified when the invitations arrived, one for Kate and partner, one for Mr. and Mrs. James Tarrant. Jim had told Helen to put theirs in the bin where it belonged, that Kate would go over his dead body and wild horses wouldn't drag him there.

"Well, you'll have to die then," said Kate calmly, "because I'm going. I'm not missing this, not for anything."

"No harm can possibly come to her," Fergus told them, earnestly. "This will be a grown-up party; in fact she'll probably be bored in no time. But it will be wonderful for her to go, and a lovely reward for working so hard at her exams. And isn't that great, Jocasta inviting you, too? You'll have a wonderful night, I promise you. She told me she was asking Kate's grandmother as well: I think that's a very nice touch."

Finally, because Kate was so determined to go, they all went. She couldn't go alone, with Nat and Sarah and Bernie, Helen thought, and it was asking too much of Fergus to look after her. There was no way Jim would entrust her to Jilly—"She'd be selling her into the white slave trade before the end of the night," he said.

As time went by, Helen was actually beginning to look forward to the party, just a little. It sounded so glamorous. Fergus had helped her with hiring a costume, a very nice silver shift dress, and Jilly had suggested she have her hair pulled back into a loose chignon, wear long glittery earrings, and carry a long cigarette holder. After all, as she said to Jim, no one would expect anything of them, they wouldn't have to talk to anyone frightening, except of course Jocasta's new husband, who was, after all, their own generation. And he must be a very respectable person; Kate had told her that he and Jocasta were going to the concert and fireworks at the Palace for the Queen's Golden Jubilee. That had clinched it, really, for Helen. They could just sit there and eat some food, which she was sure would be very nice, and watch. It would be like going to the cinema.

Jilly was beside herself with excitement, trying on and rejecting dress after dress, discussing her hairstyle endlessly with Laura at Hair and Now in Guildford, over old copies of *Vogue*, practising the Charleston in her sitting room. The invitation had said, "Mrs. Jillian Bradford and partner" and she had agonised over who to take, finally settling on Martin Bruce, who had been best man at her own wedding and was a recent widower.

Sarah and Bernie and two of the more reliable boys they went round with, Cal and Kevin, all invited by Kate, had pretended to be cool about it at first, but as the days went by and the column inches about the party grew, they gave up and became very excited. The rumour that Westlife were going to do a spot really pushed them over the top. OK, they were a bit naff, but still they were—well, they were Westlife, for God's sake. There. In the flesh. To dance to. It wasn't exactly bad.

"Right," said Nat, as the doorbell rang, "that'll be our car then. S'pose we'd better go."

He was interestingly composed; nothing really fazed him. His attitude to life was very attractive, Helen thought: she had become quite fond of him over the past few weeks. He was cheerful, good-natured, and, in a rather idiosyncratic way, nicely mannered. He was also touchingly thoughtful and clearly devoted to Kate. Helen hoped she wasn't being naïve in her confidence that they weren't sleeping together.

Clio was still wrestling with her hair when the first cars started coming up the drive. She had a wild desire to run away. Jocasta would never miss her now—she was standing on the steps of the house in a state of high excitement, greeting, kissing, laughing, hugging. She had done her duty after all, Clio thought, calming her all day and just occasionally wandering round the grounds, marvelling at what imagination, combined with money, could accomplish. Jay Gatsby would have been very satisfied with this.

A massive marquee stood just to the rear of the house, with lanterns strung across the trees above it; there was a jazz band on a platform on one side and a white grand piano, complete with pianist in white tie and tails, on the other. A fountain, made of outsize champagne glasses, played on the terrace; and beside that stood Gideon's pride and joy, a black-and-silver twenties Chevrolet. A photographer was on hand for any guests who might wish to pose in it. Several cocktail bars, complete with barmen, were dotted about the grounds; a flashing sign on a gleaming black-and-silver deco-style structure said CASINO, and next to it, something that declared itself to be a cinema.

Girls in long white crepe dresses wandered languidly about with borzois on leads ("Actually not Gatsby at all, more thirties, but never mind," Jocasta said to Clio), men in Al Capone suits and slouch hats carried trays of drinks, and gangsters' molls, with too much makeup and floozies' curls, offered cigarettes and lighters. After dinner, and before the dancing, there was to be a treasure hunt, a great twenties craze.

It was a perfect evening, warm but not hot, the sky starry, a nearly full moon hanging obligingly in it.

She had met Gideon, and of course she had been totally charmed by him. She could see so easily how Jocasta would have fallen in love with him, how it had all happened. Warm, easy, tactile, and extremely attractive, not only good-looking, in his untidy Irish way, but with that crackling energy and capacity for intent concentration on whomever he was talking to. Clio felt she could have fallen in love with him herself. For a person as romantic and emotionally hungry as Jocasta, he had obviously been irresistible.

Just the same, she thought, observing him over the twenty-four hours, watching as he appeared from time to time, then vanished again, completely uninvolved in the party, in what was going on, while striding about the house, mobile clamped to his ear, jabbing at his Palm Pilot, summoned frequently by the PA he had installed at the house for the day to deal with some crisis or other, to take calls, sign faxes, read e-mails, was this really the husband Jocasta needed?

When the first few months were over would she just become part of his empire, another dazzling acquisition to be displayed and admired, but no longer the absolute object of his attention? Clio feared for Jocasta.

And now the party was about to come to life; all the brilliant, famous, distinguished guests would appear, and Clio felt as close to terrified as she could ever remember. The dressmaker had done her proud, made her a pale blue chiffon dress, ankle-length with a drifting skirt, set off with long ropes of pearls; and her hair lent itself perfectly to the period, curved obediently into Marcel-like waves, held back from her face with a pair of diamanté clips.

But her spirit didn't quite match it. She sprayed herself lavishly with scent, touched up her already brilliant-red mouth—and then sank back on her bed, feeling dreadful. Who ever could she talk to, who on earth would she know? God. What a nightmare. She couldn't do this, she really couldn't.

And then she had the idea. She could leave now. She would just quietly slip away: no one would miss her. Least of all Jocasta. It was perfectly brilliant. Why hadn't she thought of it before? She could call for a cab once she reached the lane that led to the house; it would be easy.

She smiled at herself in the mirror with positive pleasure. Deciding to stay in her costume—she might meet Jocasta on the stairs or something if she changed—she picked up her bag and the fox stole she had hired and cautiously opened her door. The corridor was deserted; she was nearly at the bottom of the stairs, when she heard her name.

"Clio, hello! How lovely to see you."

It was Fergus, smiling up at her, wonderfully handsome in white tie and tails; he came up to her, caught her hand, and kissed it.

"You look marvellous. A real twenties femme fatale! What a lucky man I am, to have caught you on your own."

She smiled at him rather feebly, wondering what she might do next.

"Would you like to take a turn round the grounds with me? Once everyone arrives, we won't be able to see for looking."

"Well, I . . ." This was hugely tempting; Fergus was the opposite of demanding company, so easy and charming and funny. She might begin to feel part of the evening with him, even enjoy it a bit, and then when he found someone better, which he surely would, she could slip away.

"Or," he said, "do you have a beau waiting for you to come down and join him? I expect you do."

"Fergus, I don't have any beau anywhere," she said laughing, "and I'd love to take a turn with you. I've been sitting up there in my room, feeling quite scared."

"You ridiculous woman," he said, "what have you to be scared of? It's going to be fun, just you see if it isn't. And did you know we're on the same table for dinner? With old Johnny Hadley, diary writer on the *Sketch*. He's the best fun in the world and has so many scurrilous stories. We'll all have a wonderful time together. Come along, my darling, and let's take a tour. Now, did you get that hospital job you were after?"

"Good heavens," said Jilly, "isn't this absolutely out of this world? Just look at those lights—oh, thank you so much," she said graciously to the driver. "Martin, dear, take my stole for a moment, would you—and that fountain over there, how absolutely marvellous— Oh, now there is Jocasta. My God, what a dress!"

Jocasta stood on the steps of the house with Gideon, wearing a dress that was a faithful copy of a vintage 1924 Chanel. It was ankle-length chiffon, in palest grey, with a layered petal-like hem, the fabric printed in a spiderweb pattern in a darker grey. When she raised her arms, wings unfolded from the dress in the same floating fabric, falling from her fingers; she looked like a dancer, the star of some exotic revue—a shining, glittering star.

"Jilly, how perfectly wonderful to see you! You look younger than ever. I want you to meet my husband, Gideon Keeble, I've told him so much about you. Helen and Jim, it's nice of you to come, and where is the lovely Kate? Kate, darling, come and give me a kiss. My God, you look wonderful, and who is this desperately handsome man you've got with you?"

"Nat Tucker," said Nat, holding out his hand. "Pleased to meet you. Nice place you've got here," he added, "very nice indeed."

"We like it," said Jocasta, "thank you. I'll catch up with you all later, just a bit busy at the moment—go through there and you'll be looked after."

"She's very nice-looking," said Nat, the first to take a glass of champagne, leading the way through the arch of flowers that led across the side of the house and down to the wonderland below.

"Isn't she? And nice too," said Kate, following his example, sipping at her glass, aware that a great many people were staring at her. "Oh my God, Sarah, look, a cocktail bar and there's another—this is going to be really cool! Let's explore."

"Kate . . ." called Helen feebly, as the six of them disappeared into the lantern-lit twilight. But she was gone.

"I think we should do exactly the same," said Jilly. "Just look over there, it's—my goodness, a casino, and, I don't believe it, there's even a cinema! Do let's see what's on."

"Well, he's certainly pushed the boat out for her, hasn't he?" said Josh. He and Beatrice were settling themselves at their table for dinner: the family table, with Gideon and Jocasta, and Jocasta's godmother and her husband, substituting for Ronald Forbes. Jocasta had changed the table plan through a blur of tears.

The marquee slowly filled, the buzz of conversation rising and falling as people moved to their tables, greeting people on the way; it was almost half an hour before everyone was seated.

"And soul food!" said Fergus to Clio. "What a brilliant idea. Don't look like that, you'll love it. And if you don't, there's an alternative. Of course."

"They really have thought of everything, haven't they?" said Jack Kirkland to Martha. She smiled. "Indeed. It's been quite wonderful." So far it really had been fine; Jack had been a marvellous escort, courteous and attentive, introducing her to anyone who would listen as one of Centre Forward's brightest stars. Janet Frean, rather surprisingly dressed in tie and tails, her auburn hair slicked back—"Well, I don't like dresses"—had been warm and friendly.

A rather subdued Chad told Martha she would greatly improve the standard of looks in the House when she got there. Eliot Griers told her it was nice to see her, and asked her how she was getting on; Caroline Griers was effusively friendly. Sitting next to her was Chris Pollock, the editor of the *Sketch*, whom she had liked enormously when she met him at the Centre Forward launch. Chad was on her other side; she asked him where his daughters were.

"Oh, there's a younger contingent down there," he said gesturing vaguely towards the other side of the marquee. "They're having a wonderful time. Too many cocktails, I'm afraid, but it's that sort of night, isn't it?"

Martha agreed and noticed that, like her, he was hardly drinking. She would have liked a little more champagne, but she knew she couldn't afford to. She still felt the need to be very watchful.

Towards the end of the meal, Gideon stood up. He smiled round the vast space, raised his hands for silence, picked up a microphone.

"He looks marvellous, doesn't he?" whispered Beatrice to Josh. "He really is wonderfully handsome."

Gideon had refused to dress up; he said people his age and size had no business to be embarrassing everyone. His only concession to the theme was a wing collar on his dress shirt.

"No speeches, I've promised Jocasta. Except for two things: thank you all for coming. It's been a wonderful night—so far. I'm told it is yet extremely young. Not being quite that myself, I am hoping I can last a little longer. And I just wanted to tell you all, our friends, our very good friends, how much I love Jocasta and how happy she has made me." He reached down and took her hand; a chiffon wing spread itself across the space between them. "I don't know what I've done to deserve her, but I only hope I can make her as happy in return."

Jocasta promptly started to cry; Gideon leant over and wiped her tears tenderly away with his fingers.

"She's like that," he said, "terribly predictable."

A roar of laughter went up. As it died again, he said, "Next on the programme is the treasure hunt; each table has a list of clues. First back here wins. I shall be waiting patiently. Good luck."

"I'm going to go and visit the Tarrants at their table," whispered Fergus in Clio's ear. "But I will be back, I promise. Don't go off treasure hunting without me."

"I won't," she said laughing and then turned back to Johnny Hadley who was telling her yet another scurrilous story about Charles and Camilla. He could hardly believe his luck in finding a pretty woman who had never heard any of his sort of well-worn gossip before; instead of mocking him, as the media girls did, Clio's eyes got bigger with every story.

She found it hard now to believe she hadn't wanted to come to this party. She'd had a wonderful time. Fergus, she discovered, was not just charming and amusing himself, he made you feel the same. For almost the first time in her life Clio was experiencing the dizzy sensation of making someone else laugh. And although he did disappear from time to time, at the sighting of some new high-profile celebrity, he kept coming back to her.

She just wished he did something else for a living—and then wondered why on earth it mattered to her.

"Martha, isn't it?"

"Yes. Yes, it is. Hello, Josh."

"Hello. Wonderful to see you. Who'd have thought we should all be reunited at a bash like this?"

"Who indeed?"

"What are you doing these days? Law, isn't it?"

"Law, yes. And a foray into politics. And you?"

"Oh, working for the old family firm. Are you—married or anything?"

"No, nothing. You?"

"I'm married. Yes. Very much so. Two children as well. Girls. Dear little things."

"And is your wife here?"

"Yes. Somewhere. Well what a long time ago that seems, doesn't it?"

"It does indeed. Another lifetime altogether . . . Well, I must be getting back to my table. Nice to see you, Josh."

"Nice to see you too. Very nice dress," he added.

Well, that had been all right. She'd got through that. No awkward questions. He still looked pretty good, a bit heavier, maybe, and possibly a bit less hair, but you could still just about see the golden boy there.

Yes, it had been fine. She needn't have worried about that.

"Who was your smooth friend?" It was Bob Frean's voice; Janet had proved a rather enthusiastic treasure hunter and been missing for ages.

"Oh—Jocasta's brother, Josh," she said carefully.

"I didn't know you knew them that well."

"I don't really. Not anymore. I met them when we were young."

She was beginning to feel a bit panicky; she took a deep breath, smiled at him feebly.

"Do you want to go over to the casino? Or have a dance, even?"

"I'd love to go to the casino," she said. She had learnt, when she was feeling like this, that the trick was to keep moving.

He took her hand, pulled her out of her chair. "Want to take a drink with you?"

"No, I'm fine. Are you sure Janet won't be wondering where you are?"

"It'll make a change if she does," he said and smiled just the briefest moment too late. Ah, Martha thought, not quite the perfect partnership then.

They walked slowly away from the table: she felt better already.

"Clio! There you are, my darling. I've been looking for you everywhere. Come along, the nightclub awaits."

She had been walking back from the ladies', had seen him talking to Jocasta rather intently. Probably she'd told him to keep an eye on her that evening, she thought, suddenly less sure of herself.

"Fergus, I'm sure you've got lots of mingling to do," she said, trying to sound cool.

"I haven't. Let's go and dance."

"You really don't have to, you know."

"Now look," he said, sitting on the grass, pulling her down beside him, "Clio, you have to get over this ridiculous inferiority complex of yours. You are an attractive, sexy woman. And a very nice and interesting one. Anyone would be pleased to dance with you, to talk to you. I watched Johnny Hadley drooling over you at dinner. Now come along, I saw you in the Charleston school. You were the star pupil at the time. Which is more than I could say for myself. Maybe you can give me a hint or two."

"Well . . ."

"Oh, stop dithering," he said, "or I really will go and find someone to mingle with. But I don't want to. How do I get that into your extremely beautiful, but it seems rather thick, little head?"

He stood up, held out his hand. Clio took it and followed him meekly to the nightclub.

"Oh, this is so cool."

Kate was overexcited, drunk not only with champagne and cocktails but with the noise, the music, the awareness that a great many people were looking at her, admiring her, pointing her out. "You enjoying it, Nat?"

"Yeah. Pity about the music."

"Well, it's an old-people's party, isn't it? What do you expect? It's still fun, come and dance. Bernie, you coming?"

"No, not for the moment. Cal's not feeling so well."

"Where is he?"

Bernie indicated the bushes.

"I said I'd go with him, hold his head and that, but he said to leave him alone. Oh, here he is now. You all right, Cal?"

"Yeah, fine." He was greenish white; he sat down unsteadily. "Wouldn't mind some water. Well—maybe in a minute." And he disappeared back towards the bushes.

"Well, my ex–star reporter, how is married life treating you? Is it really better than the *Sketch*?" Chris Pollock had invited Jocasta to dance; they were walking towards the disco.

"It's wonderful," said Jocasta. "Truly."

"You don't miss it at all?"

"Not at all. Honestly."

"I suppose I should be happy for you. But we certainly miss you. Conference is not the same without your often daft suggestions. The newsroom is not the same without your legs—"

"Chris! That is so chauvinist."

"Sorry. I was born that way. And the paper is not the same without your byline and the stories beneath it."

"Really?" She stopped suddenly, looked at him, and for a moment she knew she did miss it, and how much: missed the excitement, the pursuit of stories, the absurd panics, missed the easy chat of the morning conference, moving, with the relentless rhythm of a newspaper's day, into the tension of the evening one. Missed the gossip, the absurd rumours, missed the rivalry, missed the fun.

"Well . . . maybe just a bit," she said finally.

"Thought so. Young Nick misses you. That's for sure. He's a man with a broken heart."

"Well," said Jocasta, "if he hadn't been such a commitment-phobe, maybe it needn't have been broken."

"Are you telling me," he said, his eyes dancing with malice, "you married Gideon on the rebound?"

"No, I am not. Of course I'm not. Don't put words into my mouth."

"Sorry, darling. Only teasing. I know love when I see it."

"You? Oh, please!"

"Of course. Nothing more sentimental than a newspaper editor. You should know that."

"Martha! It is you, isn't it? How lovely!" A girl was standing in front of her; a small, slender girl, holding the hand of a rather handsome man with close-cropped grey hair. "I'm Clio. I hoped I'd find you."

She would never have recognised her: tubby, shy Clio, transformed into this pretty, sparkly woman with diamonds in her hair. Martha managed to smile.

"Yes, yes, it's me. Hello, Clio. I thought you might be here. This is Bob Frean. Bob—Clio Scott. We knew each other when we were younger."

"We went travelling together," said Clio, smiling. "In what is now known as a gap year. I've been so impressed with everything I've read about you, Martha. Especially the political bit. Are you in politics, Bob?"

"Thankfully not. But my wife is." He looked rather uncertainly at Fergus.

"Oh, I'm sorry," said Clio, "this is Fergus Trehearn."

"Hi," said Fergus. "Isn't this a fantastic party? And doesn't Jocasta look wonderful?"

"So where are you off to?" asked Clio. "The cinema? The disco?"

"The casino," said Bob Frean. "I'm no dancer, I'm afraid."

"Well, it's worth looking in at the disco," said Clio, "honestly. Just put your head in. We're going that way, we're off to the cinema next, they're showing *The Jazz Singer*."

"How marvellous," said Bob. "I don't think I can resist that. Martha, fancy a movie?"

"No," said Martha hastily. Here was her escape: she could disappear, call a cab, tell Jack she wasn't well, she'd surely done enough for the wretched party for one evening, she could get out safely, before—

"Clio dear! You look marvellous. And Fergus, how nice!" A glamorous woman was hurrying towards them.

"My goodness, Mrs. Bradford," Clio said, "how lovely to see you, that dress is—"

"Would you just excuse me a moment?" said Fergus. "I see Helen on her own over there."

"How sweet of you, Fergus," said Jilly. "What a party, Clio! My dear, I didn't think they did them like this anymore. So generous of Jocasta to invite us all. But I'm sorry, I'm interrupting your conversation—"

"No, it's fine," said Clio. "Mrs. Bradford, this is Martha Hartley, an old friend of mine and Jocasta's. Martha, this is Mrs. Bradford—"

"Oh, Jilly, please. How do you do, Martha. I was just dragging Martin off to look in the disco, the children are all having a ball in there—such fun to watch."

"I said the same," said Clio. "Come on."

"Do you mind, Martha?" said Bob. "It sounds like fun."

"Of course not."

They stood just inside the disco, taking it in, the strobe lighting, the gyrating bodies; the music was loud, very strong. Martha suddenly felt dizzy; she put out her hand to steady herself on one of the tables.

Bob noticed. "Do you want to sit down?"

"No, no, I'm just a bit hot. Maybe I should go back outside—" She did feel very dizzy; she sat down abruptly.

And then it happened.

"Gran! Come and dance. Come on, I'll show you."

"Darling, no. I couldn't possibly—"

"Oh, hi, Dr. Scott. I didn't know you were here. Isn't this cool, isn't it great? Are you enjoying yourself?"

"I certainly am."

She must get outside. She must. She was tall, this girl in a silver dress, tall with long, long legs and wild fair hair. She looked like—she looked just like . . .

It wasn't possible. Of course it wasn't possible. Why, how could it be? Just a girl, they all looked the same, exactly the same. Sit quietly, Martha, sit still, don't stare, they all look the same . . .

"Oh, here's Fergus. You'll come and dance with me, won't you, Fergus? I'm having such a good time. Come on—" She twined her hand in his, pulled him onto the dance floor, walking backwards, laughing. She heard him say, "Kate, Kate!"

Kate. Kate.

"We should go," she said to Bob.

But another girl had come over now; another young one, very young. She seized Bob's hand, and Martin's too, pulled them after her. They were all laughing, the men clearly flattered, old men invited to dance by beautiful young girls.

The room spun, the music seemed to roar; it was hot, poundingly hot, she was going to faint, it was all blurry now, blurry and far away.

She managed somehow to stand up. "Sorry. Must get outside." Away from her. Away from having to look at her.

"You look awful, Martha." Clio's face was concerned. "Here, sit down, put your head between your knees. Jilly, could you find some water?"

She was just beginning to feel a little better, standing again, trying to get outside when: "Gran, come on. *Please.* Your boyfriend's doing awfully well. A real cool dude."

"Just a minute, dear. We're going outside for a moment."

"No need for you to come," said Martha. "I feel better now. Honestly."

"You look better," said Clio, "much better. Let's go outside, into the air."

She took Martha's arm, began to usher her out.

"Darling, get another glass of water, would you?" said Jilly to Kate. "Miss Hartley isn't feeling very well."

"Yeah, sure," said the girl. She grabbed a glass, followed them outside.

"Thank you, darling. Here you are, Martha, dear, drink this. Just little sips. That's right. Deep breaths."

"You do look better, Martha," said Clio. "Less green. Good. It really was awfully hot in there."

"Oh dreadful," said Jilly. "Of course you don't notice it," she added to the girl with the flying hair. The girl called Kate. Sitting so near she could touch her. "Martha, have a little more water. That's right. I don't think you've been introduced to my granddaughter, have you? This is Kate, Kate Bianca Tarrant as she likes to be called these days. Kate, darling, this is— Oh my God. Clio, she's fainted!"

Chapter 30

• • • •

How on earth had this happened? She was in bed in a room in Jocasta's house, with no chance of getting home. Unless she walked. Which she couldn't. What could she do, how could she escape?

It had been all right at first, after she had fainted. Bob had helped her back to the table, and she had persuaded them all that she was fine, that she could just leave in her car, it was here already, waiting for her; she was simply exhausted, had been working too hard, and it had been terribly hot in the disco. It was too early for anyone to leave, it would break up the party, and she was fine. Really fine.

She sat calmly arguing her case, her teeth chattering, despite the heat. She knew what it was: shock. It was hard to conceal. She saw Janet watching her carefully, her dark eyes thoughtful; after a while, she stood up and said, "Martha, we're going to take you home. There's no way you're going off on your own. Come along, I'll bring your things—unless you want to stay a little longer and recover?"

"No," she said, "I don't want to stay." She kept her eyes fixed on Janet's face; she was afraid that if she allowed herself to look around her, she might see—see the girl again. She couldn't allow that. She really couldn't.

Somehow she managed to stand up; her legs obeyed her to that extent. What they wouldn't do, it seemed, was walk; and she suddenly found she couldn't breathe properly either, she was struggling for breath. And then she felt quite desperately ill; she had pains in her chest, and she could feel her heart thudding so hard and beating so violently that she could hardly bear it. She was having a heart attack, she thought, she was going to die, and her last thought was that it was not entirely a bad thing: if she died now, no one would ever know.

She started trembling violently, shuddering in every part of her, and heard someone saying, "Get that other girl, the doctor, for God's sake!"

She came back to herself, very slowly; she was sitting on a chair, and someone, she didn't know who, was holding a paper bag over her face.

"Try to breathe steadily," said a voice, a female voice, vaguely familiar. "You're fine, I'm pretty sure you're just having a panic attack. That's better. Good. Go on, deep breaths."

Martha had heard of people having panic attacks; she rather disapproved of them, dismissed them as hysterical.

She tried to push the paper bag away. "Just leave it a tiny bit longer. It'll help," said the voice again and she realised who it was: Clio, Clio who had been looking after her earlier.

"You're fine, Martha, you really are. Feel a bit better?" Her voice was calm, her smile, as Martha looked at her, very kind. She was nice, Martha thought, she shouldn't have been so rude to her. She'd have to apologise, when she felt better.

"Yes, thank you. I do. A bit."

Clio said, "Fergus, if you could help her into the house, she can lie down, get some rest. That's what she needs."

Into the house, she couldn't go into this house, Jocasta's house. It was much too dangerous.

"Please," she said in a feeble whisper, "I'm fine, I'd just like to go home."

"Not a good idea," said Clio, "not yet, anyway. Now, this very kind gentleman is going to carry you—"

"Well you're certainly not heavy," said an Irish voice, picking her up gently. "What do you live on, air? Or do you allow yourself a little bit of water with it?" He smiled at her, clearly anxious to make her feel better, and he carried her easily through the gardens into the house, then Fergus and Clio were helping her to a couch in some large room and Clio said, "I'll get you some water and a blanket, just stay there and don't worry about anything."

"I should go," said Martha, "some people have very kindly offered to take me home, they'll be waiting."

"They're not waiting, I told them you'd be staying the night," said Clio firmly.

"I can't stay the night," said Martha. "It's out of the question. Please, Clio, do let me go home."

"You're honestly not up to it," said Clio, "and you can't be alone."

"Why not?" asked Martha.

"Because it might happen again. Now look, Martha, calm down, you can go home in the morning—I'll take you myself, if necessary. But right now, you've got to stay put and rest. Jocasta's organising a room for you, she won't be long."

God. Jocasta as well; both of them, in the same house. She felt as if she was held in some terrible trap.

"Hi, Martha." It was Jocasta, smiling down at her, in a way she really didn't deserve. Why did they both have to be so nice? "I've got a bedroom for you. Fergus is going to take you up there and—"

"Please," said Martha for the last desperate time, "let me go home. You've been so kind but I'm all right now and—"

"You can't go home," said Jocasta. "Dr. Scott says so. Now I have some guests to attend to, but I'll see you later. Or in the morning. Just try and rest. The room's on the second floor, sorry."

"It's me you should be saying sorry to," said Fergus.

"Oh nonsense, the exercise'll do you good. Anyway, she can't weigh more than about three stone. Sleep well, Martha."

She gave in, allowed herself to be carried upstairs by Fergus and helped into bed by Clio. And now she felt more alone and more frightened than she had ever been in her life.

Everything had changed suddenly, she realised. That was the most frightening thing of all. She couldn't deny it any longer. The child she had left behind was no longer Baby Bianca, totally anonymous, forever a baby; she had become Kate, a beautiful sixteen-year-old girl. She had been in the same room as her, breathed the same air, seen her, watched her, almost touched her; she had become reality.

She sat bolt upright, feeling the panic coming back, the breathlessness, the sweating.

"God," she said aloud, "what do I do?"

And then the door opened and Janet came in.

Martha was so pleased to see her, a friendly, reassuring person, that she burst into tears. Janet sat down on the bed, held her like a child, and told her to cry as much as she liked. Which Martha did, and for quite a long time: helpless, uncontrollable tears; and Janet just sat there, in complete silence, except for the occasional soothing, hushing noise, until finally Martha stopped crying and lay back on her pillows.

"I'm so sorry," she said, "so terribly sorry."

"Martha," said Janet, smiling at her gently, "Martha, stop apologising. Please. You've done nothing wrong."

Shocked into speech suddenly, she said, "Oh, but I have. That's the whole point, Janet. You don't understand."

"Do you want to talk about it? This wrong thing you say you've done? Which I'm sure you haven't."

This denial, of what Martha knew to be true, made her agitated again; she started to shiver, to feel the breathlessness coming on.

"Janet, I have, I have! I've done something terrible, I—oh God!"

"Well, all right," said Janet calmly, "you've done something terrible. Why don't you tell me about it? Nothing seems as bad once you've shared it with someone, it's a fact. And I would say I'm totally unshockable—having five children and spending a great deal of my life at Westminster has done that for me, at least. Try me. Try talking about it. Please, I can't bear to see you like this. Tell me what it is."

And suddenly, she did. She had to. She couldn't fight it any longer.

She knew she shouldn't, shouldn't admit to it, to this extraordinary, dreadful, shocking thing that she had kept locked away inside her head for all those years, but the deniable had become undeniable, and she lay weak and wretched on her pillows in the dim room, with the noise of the party in the distance, the party where her daughter danced the night away, and told Janet what she had done.

PART THREE

Chapter 31

· · · ·

"She was weird," said Kate, sinking back in the limo, "really weird. Didn't you think she was weird, Nat?"

"Don't know," he said, "didn't really talk to her." I was looking after poor old Cal. He was in a bad way."

"Is he all right now?"

"He looks fine to me," said Sarah, examining Cal's apparently lifeless form. "What a tosser. He must have missed half the party."

"So, who was weird?" asked Kevin.

"That woman," said Kate. "The one who fainted."

"Yeah, she took one look at you and fainted," said Bernie, giggling. "Honest, she was all right up till then, as I said to the doctor woman. What was her name?"

"Clio," said Kate. "She's my gran's doctor."

"What? Who fainted?" Kevin sounded irritable. "You're talking bloody riddles."

"We're not. You're not concentrating. A friend of Jocasta's did," said Kate. "Well, she was her friend when they were young. She was in the paper the week before me, she's in politics and law and she knew Clio as well—that's the doctor, for those of you with learning difficulties."

Bernie giggled.

"Now *she* was nice," said Nat approvingly. "Anyway, it was a good bash. And what about them snappers, Kate, calling your name as we left. You're a celeb now, whether you like it or not."

He sounded rather complacent, as if the credit was largely his rather than Fergus's, who had quietly tipped a couple of papers off about Baby Bianca's attendance at the bash of the year.

"I thought I might be in some of the pictures an' all," he added hopefully.

Jack Kirkland was deep in conversation with Gideon Keeble when Janet rejoined them.

"You've been a while," he said. "Is she all right?"

"She's fine. Asleep. Goodness knows what it was all about, poor little thing."

"I don't think I would describe Martha in quite those terms," said Gideon lightly. "Tough little cookie, if you ask me."

"I think I'd agree with Gideon," said Kirkland. "She is quite tough. Law at the level she practises it is no easy option. And to manage to fit in the politics as well—pretty remarkable."

"That's the whole point about women, Jack, we can do a whole lot of things at the same time," said Janet.

"Like bring up five children and run a political party, you mean?" said Gideon.

"I don't exactly run it, do I? Just turn up at the House now and then."

"Oh Janet, come on, you could run it if I wasn't there. Maybe you should," said Kirkland.

"Oh yes? What about Eliot and Chad?"

"As far as I'm concerned, you're a better contender than either of them," said Jack. "After what's happened."

"Well happily for me, you *are* still there," said Janet. "Nothing I'd hate more. Honestly."

Gideon Keeble, who had not risen from the slums of Dublin without an ability to sniff out a lie at very long distance, looked at them both with interest. Jack clearly believed her, and more important, Janet knew he did.

"Well, that's all right then," he said and went to find Jocasta.

·•·

"Oh, look at this picture of Kate!" Clio passed the *People* across the table. "Naughty girl, leaning out of the stretch window, waving at the cameras. I thought the whole idea was to keep well inside those things. Doesn't she look sweet? And the boy looks rather handsome too."

"He *is* rather handsome," said Jocasta. "And he's a poppet. Who else did they get? God, the nights I've spent with the paps, outside rich people's gates. And now they're my gates and I'm inside."

"Is that right?" said Gideon. "I think they're mine as well, those gates."

"Sorry, Gideon. I'm confused. Still half drunk, I think. God, I loved it. I want to give another. Oh look, here's Jamie Oliver and Jules. I hope he liked the food. And Jonathan Ross, I still can't believe he came, and the gaggle of It Girls, in their gangster car. It was so sweet, everyone going to so much trouble."

It was half past ten. Gideon had already swum and had been making coffee for hours; people were drifting down to the kitchen, including several of Gideon's brothers and sisters. Jocasta embraced them all fondly; she had long since given up trying to work out which of them was which. Beatrice, considerably the worse for wear, huddled behind the newspapers. Josh, most unfairly full of beans, had already been for one walk and was suggesting another.

"There's a whole crowd of people down there still in the tent, Gideon. They appear not to have gone to bed."

"Quite possibly not. It'll be the Dublin lot still exchanging the craic. They're tireless once they get going. I must go down and offer them some coffee."

"I think I should check on Martha," said Clio. "I'm surprised she's not down."

She came back in five minutes. "Down and out," she said. "She's gone. Is that strange behaviour, or what?"

"Very strange," said Jocasta, staring at her. "How did she get away, anyway?"

"She said she got a cab. She's left a note," said Clio holding it out. "It's very polite, sorry to have put us to so much bother, thanking us for all our kindness, but she had to get home."

"She is the strangest girl," said Jocasta. "I think she didn't like it that we'd seen her out of control. I never met anyone quite so tight-arsed in my entire life."

Martha had spent the entire day in a desperate effort to calm down. She felt terrible: her pulse was racing, her heart pounding. She tried to tell herself she was being absurd, that there was nothing wrong—she was in no danger of any kind. But she was. She had committed an act of unbelievable folly: she had done what she had never even considered doing. Obviously it would be perfectly all right: obviously. Janet was the kindest, most dependable woman, and, more important, absolutely discreet. There was no way she was a gossip, no way she would talk to anyone about what Martha had told her. Of course she wouldn't. She just— wouldn't. And anyway, why should she? What would be the point?

It went on all day, round and round Martha's aching head, in desperate convoluted circles, until she felt she might actually go mad. For the first time since, well, since that day, she was no longer in control, was at someone else's mercy.

The phone rang. It was Ed. "Hi, it's me. Just rang to see if you enjoyed the party. I saw the pictures. Why none of you? I'll call again—"

Without thinking clearly what she was doing, desperate just to have someone to talk to, to take herself out of the prison in her head, she picked up the phone.

"Hi, Ed, it's me."

"Hi. You all right?"

"Yes, yes, I'm fine. Thank you."

"Good. Well it's just the usual call. Making sure you're OK. You wouldn't like to come for a drink or anything, I suppose?"

"No," she said quickly, "Ed, I wouldn't. Thank you. Not—not today anyway."

"Tomorrow then?" His voice was hopeful. Something else she shouldn't have said, then.

"No, not tomorrow," she said quickly. "I meant not at all."

"Martha, you sound weird. Are you all right?"

"Yes, I'm fine. Absolutely. Yes."

"OK." She could almost hear the shrug. "I'll call again. Tomorrow probably."

Well, that hadn't helped. Maybe it was Ed she should have told. At least she knew he loved her, wished her well. Why did she tell Janet, whom she didn't know at all? Who might even now—oh God! Of course she wasn't. Of course—

The phone rang again. She snatched it up.

"Ed, please—"

But it wasn't Ed. It was Janet. "Hello, Martha, only me. Wondering how you were."

Her voice was warm, friendly, gentle. Martha felt better at once. How ridiculous she'd been, thinking that this kind, caring woman would do her any harm.

"Hello, Janet," she said, and she could hear the relief in her own voice. "How kind of you. I'm fine, really. Much, much better. And thank you again for last night, you were wonderful."

"My dearest girl, it was nothing, I was just a shoulder to cry on, that's all."

"No! You . . . you saved my sanity, I think."

Damn. Shouldn't have said that. Sounds a bit—desperate.

"You seem pretty sane to me. Listen, I thought—"

"Janet," said Martha, "you . . . you wouldn't tell anyone, would you?"

"Martha! Of course I wouldn't tell anyone. What kind of person do you think me, for heaven's sake?"

God, she'd offended her. Now what might she do?

"No, of course not. I mean—I didn't mean anything like that. It's just that—"

"Martha"—the voice was soothing now, soothing and infinitely kind—"Martha, listen to me. You needed to talk. You couldn't have kept that to yourself forever. Even if she hadn't been there, at the party. It's an intolerable burden—God knows how you've coped all these years. You're clearly making yourself ill. And I'd like to think talking to me helped, just a little."

"It did, Janet, it really did."

Liar, Martha, it didn't help, it's frightened you horribly.

"And of course you're anxious about it. About me talking. I can understand that, I really can. But I won't. Ever. It would be unthinkable. I feel deeply honoured that you confided in me. Showed me that kind of trust. And I won't betray it. I swear to you, Martha. So please stop worrying."

"Thank you, Janet, so much. I won't worry anymore."

She wouldn't. She really, really wouldn't.

·—•·

Clio got home to a letter from the Royal Bayswater. Would she be able to attend an interview board on Wednesday, July 3, for a post of consultant geriatrician?

She felt flooded with happiness and triumph. OK, she hadn't got the job, she'd just got a shot at it. That was a lot. To her at this moment that was a huge lot.

She'd had a very good few days, she thought happily, sitting back on her sofa, what with the party, and this—and Fergus. Did he like her? Really like her? And, more to the point, did she want him to?

Nothing could change what he did, the sort of person he was: and even if she came to understand his work, to see it as less . . . disreputable, could their lives blend in any way?

Oh, for God's sake, Clio, what are you thinking about? Your lives blend? You've met the man precisely twice, talked to him a few times more. He's amusing, he's attractive, he's a man you enjoyed a party with: leave it at that.

She did want to tell someone though, about her interview. That was one of the worst things about being on your own, she had discovered: day to day was all right, even bad days could be coped with, but happiness, however small, needed to be shared.

She decided to call Jocasta; her phone was switched off.

She couldn't tell Mark or anyone at the practice about her interview, and she was just beginning to feel her bright pleasure tarnish slightly, when, as if by magic, perfectly on cue, Fergus called.

"I just wanted to thank you for your company last night. And to make sure you were safely home." Clio told him she was indeed safely home, and that she had been called for an interview for the consultant's job.

"I wonder why I'm not surprised," he said, and she could hear him smiling.

•—•—•

Jocasta had invited Kate to lunch the Monday after the party; Gideon was in his London office and she travelled up with him. She was sitting at a table at the Bluebird when Kate got there.

"Hi! You look nice. Seen anyone today? About your modelling?"

"No, not till Friday now. Then it's this cosmetic company, Smith, and I think I'm getting a spot. I told Fergus and he said they'd be able to see past it."

"He's absolutely right," said Jocasta, "of course they will. He's still looking after you all right, is he?"

"Yeah. Really well. He's cool. Mum likes him. I think she fancies him, actually."

"Goodness! Now what do you want to eat? And then tell me if you enjoyed the party and if your mum and dad did. And your very handsome boyfriend."

Kate said it had been a really cool party and that Nat had enjoyed it a lot.

"He's lovely, your Nat," said Jocasta, "I really like him."

"He's all right," said Kate, and then looked at Jocasta and smiled, quite nervously for her. "I worry a bit he hasn't got any ambition, though. I mean, he's nineteen and he's not getting anywhere, just quite happy to go on working for his dad's garage."

Jocasta said, carefully, that she thought Nat had plenty of time and that Kate shouldn't worry. "Anyway, if his dad's got a garage and Nat took it over one day, that'd be great, wouldn't it? Always money in cars."

"I s'pose so. But he lets his dad think for him—he doesn't have his own ideas. Whatever we're talking about, he tells us what his dad says. It's seriously annoying sometimes."

"I'm sure it is. Men are annoying," she added. "They can't help it. But Kate, how are you feeling about everything now? About your mother and so on? A bit better?"

"I don't know. I mean even after all this, she could still be anyone, she could be Madonna, and she could be the woman who cleans the toilets down at the park. It's horrible. Really horrible, not knowing, always wondering . . ." Her voice shook. She picked up Jocasta's glass and took a large gulp of wine. "Sorry."

"Sweetie, don't be sorry. I'm really sorry. Oh, dear. You're no nearer, are you?"

"No nearer," said Kate. She was obviously extremely upset.

·—·

"Oh, no!" Chad's voice was quiet, shocked. "God almighty, I don't believe it. How, in God's name, did that get out?"

"What?" Abigail got up, walked round the table, and leant over him, reading over his shoulder. "What is it? Oh, yes. I see. Oh dear . . ."

"How the fuck did it happen?" he asked. "I mean, nobody had seen it except just the few of us. *Nobody*. And the research company, obviously. But they wouldn't. They just wouldn't!"

"Wouldn't what?"

"Leak it."

"Does it have to be a deliberate leak?" said Abigail.

"Absolutely deliberate. But who?" The phone rang. "Jesus. Get that, Abi, would you?"

She picked it up. "Abigail Lawrence—oh. Oh, yes, Jack, he's here. What? Yes, I'm afraid he has . . ."

And against a background of Chad, quietly reasonable at first, then his voice rising in indignation—"No, I did not! Of course I didn't. Not to anyone. For fuck's sake, Jack"—she read the story on the front page of the *News*, by Martin Buckley, the political editor.

CENTRE FORWARD'S LOSING STREAK CONTINUES

Left-of-centre breakaway political party Centre Forward, which made its debut only a few months ago, is enduring serious teething troubles. Launched on a platform of sleazeless and crony-free politics, it has been dogged by scandals. A few weeks ago, Chad Lawrence, charismatic MP for Ullswater North (voted the sexiest man in Westminster last year by *Cosmopolitan* magazine), was discovered to have founded the new party's think tank with money from a Chinese-owned company, based in Hong Kong.

Despite its flying start in the polls, the party is beginning to flag, as the scandals bite. A Focus Group Research, commissioned by the putative party leader, Jack Kirkland, showed a ten percent loss of potential followers. Originally Centre Forward captured the public imagination, but it seems now that the electorate's cynicism with the entire political system in this country is extending to the new party.

Unless Centre Forward achieve a big breakthrough in the next few weeks, it could be destined to find its place as the shortest-lived political party in history. Which, given the considerable talent within its ranks, would be a tragedy of some magnitude.

Martha Hartley, reading the report in the *News* with a sinking heart, could not but reflect that a further—and shocking—scandal within those talented ranks could actually prove fatal.

Nick was waiting in the press dining room at the House of Commons for a rather dreary example of a Blair's Babe when he saw Martin Buckley leaving alone.

"Hi, Martin. Nice story today. Intriguing. I'm rather sad about it. I'd have put money on them at least continuing to nip at the others' heels."

"Yes?"

"Yes. A casual observer might imagine someone was out to do them down."

"He wouldn't need to be a genius, your casual observer. The list of suspects would be very long."

"I know. Well, here's my lunch date. See you around."

The Babe looked after Buckley. "That was an interesting story about Centre Forward this morning, wasn't it? Of course I'm not surprised, it was all much too good to be true."

"Indeed. I agree," said Nick.

"I like Martin. He's always very fair to both sides."

"I think that's not quite accurate. He's much more often on your side, if you ask me."

"Not necessarily. I saw him on Monday, lunching with Michael Fitzroy."

"Oh really?" said Nick. "Well, maybe I'm wrong."

Interesting. Fitzroy, having lunch with Buckley.

Michael Fitzroy having lunch with Janet Frean. Didn't necessarily mean anything, of course. But—interesting, very interesting. Maybe a little chat with Teddy Buchanan might be even more so . . .

• • •

"Martha! What do you think?"

"Oh—I'm sorry, Paul."

She met his eyes across the conference table. They were sharp with irritation. This was the second time today she'd lost concentration.

"Maybe you'd like a bit more time." Her. Martha Hartley. Needing more time: not delivering absolutely on the minute. This was serious.

"No, of course not. I'm so sorry. No, I don't think there'd be a tax advantage in holding back. We need to push things forward, surely. It's a time-sensitive merger; they need it settled before the Christmas deadline. There's more money in that, ultimately, than any tax savings."

"And what about changing distribution channels, how much is that going to cost them?"

Shit! Shit! She'd meant to send her trainee into the data room that morning to check on everything—and forgotten. What was the matter with her? What? As if she didn't know.

She took a deep breath. "I'm sorry, Paul. I haven't checked that yet. Maybe I do need a little more time. Perhaps tomorrow morning?" If she had to spend the night in the data room herself, she would.

He sighed. "Yes, all right." He looked at her rather searchingly, and then said, "Martha, I agreed to help you in your political ambitions because I felt sure that, short-term, you'd be able to cope. Please don't let me down. Or I might have to revise my thoughts on the whole thing. See you in the morning, then?"

"In the morning, Paul, yes. Seven thirty."

If only it was her political ambitions that were absorbing her time and concentration. If only.

•—•—•

"Clio, this is Fergus. Again."

"Oh—hello, Fergus."

Damn, she sounded breathless, nervous. Not cool and in control.

"I wondered if you were free on Saturday evening. For dinner."

"Dinner would be lovely. Thank you!"

She put the phone down and tried to compose herself before her next patient came in. She looked in the mirror; she was slightly flushed. Now come on, Clio, this won't do. Fergus is just looking for a pleasant evening. Probably his regular girlfriend is away or something. Calm down. You've got to start taking things in your stride. It's just a dinner date, not a proposal of marriage. Be cool.

She pressed her buzzer. "Send my next dinner date in, would you, Margaret?"

"I'm sorry, Clio?" said Margaret and she could hear her smiling. "What did you say?"

•—•—•

"I must fly." Gideon leant over to Jocasta and kissed the top of her head. She was burrowed into the pillows of the vast bed in their room at Cruxbury and still half asleep. "See you in forty-eight hours."

"Forty-eight!" She stared up at him, blinking her way into consciousness. "I thought you said it was one night."

"It was. It's just become two. I'm relieved in a way—I was thinking of staying over anyway."

"You were?"

"Yes. I was. I was actually contemplating being away from you for two nights and not one. I must be getting bored with you."

"Gideon, that's not funny! You know I'd have come, if it had been more than a night. I said so."

"Did you? I'm sorry, I'd forgotten."

· 397 ·

"Well, I think that's a bit important just to forget. Of course I'd have come. I don't like you going away."

"Well, darling, you can come, if you want to."

"I can't now. There's no point anyway, you obviously don't care if I come or not."

"Jocasta, that's ridiculous," he said, smiling at her. "You're putting words into my mouth. Of course I care."

"Then how can you forget to tell me you're staying away another night?"

He became visibly less patient. "Jocasta, this is absurd. Look, I'm very late, do you want to come or not? Because if you do, you have about five minutes to pack."

"No, I don't want to come. Thank you." She turned away from him, feeling absurdly near to tears. What was happening to her? To the independent Jocasta Forbes. How had she begun to be this dependent, clinging creature, crying because her husband was going away for two days? It was pathetic.

"Gideon, it's fine. Just go. I'll see you in a couple of days."

"I thought I'd come back to London. Can you be there?"

"I'm . . . not sure," she said.

"Do you have business down here?" The dark blue eyes were snapping with irritation now.

"I might have."

"Oh Jocasta, you're being so childish. I'm off—" His mobile rang. "Hello? How are you, darling? No, of course not, never too busy for you." His voice had changed. Totally. It must be Fionnuala. She lay, with her eyes closed, pretending she wasn't listening to every inflection, every syllable.

"Yes, as a matter of fact, I will. I'm going to LA, and then across to Miami. So it couldn't be better. I could easily pop down there for twenty-four hours. Tell Mum to call me. What? I'm leaving Cruxbury now, catching the midday flight. Bye, my love." He looked at Jocasta, smiled at her, his irritation totally gone.

"That was Fionnuala."

"I sort of worked that out."

"She wants me to have a look at another pony for her."

"Another! Gideon, you've just bought her three."

"I know, but this one is special, apparently. Anyway, sorry darling, that means another day, I'm afraid. So I'll be back in London on Friday. Please be there for me. We can spend the weekend in London. You'd like that, wouldn't you?"

"Yes, it'd be really exciting," said Jocasta, struggling to sound ironic.

"Good." Clearly the irony had failed. "Think of some things you'd like to see, places to go, and get Marissa to book them. Love you."

"Bye," said Jocasta and burrowed back into her pillows.

As soon as he'd gone, she felt terrible. How could she behave like that? Like a spoilt child. And she hadn't even said goodbye properly, hadn't told him she loved him. Suppose his plane crashed, suppose— She seized her mobile, tried to dial him. It was on message. Suppose he'd done that on purpose, suppose he was so angry with her he didn't want to speak to her. She tried again, left a message: "Sorry I didn't say goodbye properly. Love you too. Call me when you get this."

She got up, stared out at the garden. It was a beautiful day. So what was she supposed to do? Walk? Do a little light weeding? Swim in the pool? Alone? All day? Shit, this was pathetic. There was so much she wanted to do. What had she been telling Clio so stoutly? Find a new house for a start. A house for them. For her and Gideon. Well, she could do that. She'd call up all the estate agents in—in where? They had houses in the best places in England already. Why buy another? Wales? Not many nice houses. Scotland? So cold. All right then, France. She hated the French. Italy? That might be very nice. Or the States? California? What about somewhere like Virginia? That would be great. She'd never been there, but she'd heard it was fantastic. Horse country. Fionnuala would like that. Did she want to buy a house where Fionnuala was always coming to stay? Probably not.

"Oh shit!" said Jocasta aloud. People never thought of this, people who weren't rich. She certainly never had. When you could have everything, nothing was right, nothing was good enough. Not just houses, but clothes. If you could buy a Chanel jacket and then a Gucci leather coat and then a Valentino evening dress, where was the fun? Shopping was about choices, decisions, what suited you best, not about having whatever your eye lighted on.

Maybe she should do something completely different. Find some new challenge. Like—yes, like learn to fly. That would be really great. She'd always wanted to do that. Always. That'd be something to get excited about, get the adrenaline pumping. That was the main problem: she wasn't making adrenaline. Or rather her life wasn't.

And Gideon's life, of course, was; it was all about work and pressure and deadlines and moving on to the next thing. God, she was going to seem boring to him pretty soon. An empty-headed wife, who had to get all her kicks out of stupid hobbies like learning to fly, or who tagged along after him on business trips, where all there was to do was shop some more and have more stupid hobbies. And the business trips were a big part of his life; Gideon's world was lived largely out of his Vuitton suitcases.

Jocasta felt her heart literally lurch. Had she, after all, been completely sensible giving up her job? Should she have hung on for a bit? Until—well until what? Until she had a family, people would say. That would inevitably be what they would say. But she wasn't going to have a family. She absolutely wasn't.

Oh God. She'd been through all these options and Gideon had only been gone for twenty-five minutes. She had another three whole days to get through. What was she going to do? What?

The old adage about marrying in haste and repenting at leisure drifted into her head; she drove it out again with sheer willpower: but all day, as she swam in the pool and then packed up her things and left Cruxbury, and made her way to London and settled herself into the vast house in Kensington Palace Gardens that was Gideon's, not hers, it kept returning to her. And the thought that she had allowed it into her consciousness so early in her marriage. She had been Mrs. Gideon Keeble for just over a month and she was already not entirely happy about it. What kind of person was she, for God's sake? What kind of stupid, reckless, ungrateful, unloving person?

By five o'clock that afternoon—by now in possession of a Chanel jacket, and with the first of a dozen flying lessons booked for the next day, and a silver BMW Z3 on order—she was still depressed. Depressed and almost frightened.

Chapter 32

. . . .

"Martha, we have to talk." Janet's voice was very brisk, very cool.

Don't panic, Martha, don't.

"What about? Anything important?"

"Depends on your viewpoint, I'd say. I thought you might be able to meet me after work today."

"I'm sorry, Janet, I'm going to be terribly late tonight. Tomorrow might be possible."

"Look." Janet sounded almost impatient now. "I'm busy too, you know. But we've got to do this thing and—"

"Janet, what thing? I'm afraid I don't understand—"

"Oh God. Hasn't Chad called you?"

Chad? Had she told Chad? "No. But I've been in a meeting all morning. He couldn't have."

"Oh, I see. Well, he's arranged for what he calls the female force to be interviewed. By some girl from *The Times* for Saturday's paper. He thinks we can save the party."

"Save what party?" Relief had made her stupid.

"Martha dear, you'll have to do better than that," said Janet, her voice slightly kinder.

The female force consisted of Janet, Martha, and Mary Norton, one of very few defectors from the Labour Party to Centre Forward. Fortyish, sensible, articulate, with a strong northern accent. She was very good with the media and a frequent guest on both *Any Questions?* and *Question Time*. Martha had only met her once and found her even more awe-inspiring than Janet.

"Jack thinks we'll make a good team."

"You and Mary will," said Martha carefully.

"Yes, but Jack sees you as the future," said Janet. She sounded very cool. "And of course," she added, quite brightly, "you are much the best-looking of the three of us."

That was all right then; she was to be cast as the group's bit of fluff. Fine. She would normally have resisted that, but under the circumstances, it was less frightening.

"Your skin is just so, like, totally perfect." The makeup artist smiled at Kate. He was black, with white-blond hair and rather red lips. She smiled back nervously. Crew, as he was inexplicably called, was hard to talk to; he was from New York, for a start, so that cut out any conversations about shops or clubs, and when Kate admired his shirt, he said he bought all his clothes from what he called thrift shops.

He worked exclusively for Smith Cosmetics, so she couldn't ask him what other jobs he did, what famous people he'd made up; and anyway, whenever she tried to talk, he held up his hand and said, "Don't talk for, like, just a tiny moment," and the tiny moment seemed to mean the entire duration of the session.

Every so often the door would open and two women would come in; they were, it had been explained to her, the creative director and the advertising director of Smith and neither of them had talked to her at all, beyond saying, "Hi, Kate, we're just totally thrilled to have you on board," when she was first introduced to them. Since then, they would stand and study her each time, as if she was a shop-window model, not a girl at all, narrowing their eyes at her reflection in the mirror, and then leaving again, talking very quietly and occasionally saying, "Difficult forehead" or "The hair's too full," and telling Crew to try wider eyes. Or fresher skin tone. Or bigger lips. Mostly he just nodded and said he was, like, totally willing to try, but when they said bigger lips, he shook his head and said, without collagen there was, like, no way.

"So I think we should either postpone and go for the collagen, or use what we have, and, like, make the story less is more."

After an hour of this, Kate was convinced they had decided they had made a mistake even to be doing test shots, and was all ready to be told to go home—and thinking she actually would like that.

The photographer hadn't appeared yet, but the way everyone talked about him, he was obviously very big and important in the company. It was, "Oh, Rufus would never consider sleeves" and "Rufus never does curly," as what she might wear or how her hair might be done was discussed. She imagined some huge man with a booming voice and a suit, but when Rufus appeared, he was tiny, about five foot six, dressed in white trousers and a beige T-shirt. His voice was very quiet and in fact everyone had trouble hearing what he said, which irritated him; but he smiled at Kate in the mirror and said hi, he was Rufus Corelli, and then turned her to face him, pushed back her hair, and studied her for what seemed like forever, and then said, "She's sixteen, for fuck's sake. You have to take most of that shit off."

Kate expected the women to argue and Crew to have a tantrum, but they all meekly nodded and Crew said, "But her skin will have to rest, it's, like, so over-absorbing already," and he cleaned her makeup right off and told her to sit very quietly in the reception area of the studio, where it was, like, fresher air.

It was two o'clock before they did the first test shots, and that was fraught as well, because Rufus said he wanted the studio cleared. "I want no one here, except the model," he said, as if she didn't have a name. She was a bit scared of being alone with him, but he actually became much nicer and said she still had too much makeup on, didn't these people understand what young looked like, and offered her a stick of his chewing gum and asked her where she got her jeans.

"The thing is," he whispered, "I'm so tiny, I can wear girls' clothes, it's such a help."

Kate wasn't sure in what way that could be a help, and thought her jeans would be much too long for him anyway, but again she didn't like to say so and told him they were Paper Denim & Cloth from Harvey Nichols. They were actually her only extravagance from her *Sketch* money, but he wasn't to know that.

"Right," he whispered, pulling a Polaroid out of his camera and tucking it under his arm, "what we're going to do is nothing like those obscene roughs. Jed, did you see those roughs, aren't they completely obscene?"

Jed, his assistant, had come in when everyone else had left the studio; he was about twice as tall as Rufus, but no wider, and he also spoke very quietly.

"Completely obscene," he said.

"Now, Kate, this is nice," Rufus said, studying the Polaroid, "but you're trying too hard. I want you to think about nothing at all. Certainly not this—this rubbish. Just empty your head. What I don't want is sexy. Or mannered. Just be. Be you. Before any of this happened to you." She nodded. It was quite difficult, thinking of nothing at all. After three more tries, she was getting upset; and then Rufus suddenly rushed out of the studio and disappeared.

He was complaining she was no good, he wanted another model, she thought; but he was back with a pile of magazines, *Seventeen* and *Glamour* and *Company*.

He gave her one. "Right. Read it. Really read it, find something you're interested in, OK?"

She nodded, opened *Glamour*, which was her favourite, and found an article on how you'd know if you were in love. She was always wondering if she was in love with Nat. She rather thought she wasn't.

"I've got something."

"Good. Now sit there, on that stool, where you were before, that's right, and read it. Really read it."

It was easier than she'd expected. She was just into the second question, wondering if what she felt when Nat kissed her was exciting, very exciting, or totally off the scale, when Rufus said, "Kate!"

She looked up, not sure what he might want. The camera flashed.

"OK," he said. "Carry on."

After three more, he came over to her, with some Polaroids. "There," he said, "how's that?" Kate looked; she could have been her own younger sister; almost no makeup visible, her hair tumbled over one shoulder. She looked slightly surprised, sweetly confused, her dark eyes wide and questioning, her pale lips just parted.

"It's glorious," said Rufus. "Can you do that over and over again, do you think?"

"Oh yes," said Kate, more confident now she knew what he wanted, "I'm sure I can."

Next day, Smith made their offer: a three-year contract for Kate to be the face for their new young range, Smith's Club, for a million dollars a year. The terms of the contract would include a publicity tour in both the States and the United Kingdom, as well as public appearances at Ascot and at Smith's Lawn polo, and at various film premieres, and a free hand for Smith's with press briefings. Fergus told them he would have to discuss it with Kate and her parents and that he would get back to them after the weekend.

He spent the next twenty-four hours wondering how best to present the news to the Tarrants in order to ensure their agreement, while thinking what he could do with twenty percent of three million dollars. And just occasionally considering what the whole thing might do to a vulnerable child of not quite sixteen, with a sad and difficult history: then telling himself that was absolutely no concern of his, that his job was to do his best for her. And securing three million dollars was a pretty good start.

◆

Nick was in the Members' lobby on Thursday morning, only half listening to a story he had already heard too often, about how Gordon Brown was about to demand the leadership before the next election or resign, when he saw Teddy Buchanan moving on his self-important way towards the Chamber.

Nick waylaid him and invited him to dinner the following Monday at the Stafford Hotel, not only a great purveyor of the sort of food and wine Teddy most loved but far more discreet than the Connaught or the Savoy. Teddy accepted with alacrity.

◆

Jack Kirkland was on the phone before seven on Saturday morning. "Know it's a bit early, but wanted to catch you. I know you go off to Suffolk early. Have you seen *The Times*?" Martha had. "I'm extremely pleased," he said, "extremely. It really puts over a new message. Makes us human, sensible, aware of real life. You've all, in your different ways, done a wonderful job. Well done, Martha. I know you don't like this publicity business, but you're going to have to get used to it. You're a natural."

"Oh, not really," she said. "But I'm glad if I've helped. Um—have you spoken to Janet yet?"

"No, Bob said she was sleeping in. Bit unlike her: she's more of a Martha, up with the lark, getting on with all her lives. Have you?"

"No, she wouldn't—didn't want to speak to me, either."

"Well, she deserves a bit of a rest. So do you. You mustn't do too much, Martha, but I know what these legal clinics mean to you—and to your constituents. Very valuable. Very clever idea."

The girl from *The Times* had said that, and put it in her article. It was a very nice article, Martha thought, glancing at it again. Only it did rather flatter her.

THE HEADMISTRESS, THE PREFECT, AND THE NEW GIRL had been the headline: Janet, of course, being the headmistress, was described as one of the leaders of the new party, "passionate about the need to nurture it, educate it, and improve its health both physically and morally." It all sounded a bit, well, nannyish. And Janet looked nannyish in the photograph, wearing her "uniform," her hair rather severely combed back. And then Mary Norton, talking about women's role in politics, the need to expand their power base, for positive discrimination, about women as a force within the trade unions, how she would aim for double the number of crèches in the workplace, paternity leave, increased maternity leave. She sounded very feminist, very left wing. Martha was surprised Jack was so pleased about her contribution. Mary, with her curly, styleless greying hair, her twin set, her obviously makeup-less face, appeared very formidable. And then there was Martha, gazing into the camera, all wide brown eyes and sleek, streaky hair, in a slash-necked T-shirt and a sharply cut jacket, saying she cared most for the little people, male or female, mentioning Lina and the horror of the mixed ward, her own grammar school, wrecked by the "comprehensive ideal," talking about her legal clinics in the town where she had grown up, and about how she viewed politics from "my new-girl point of view."

She came across as charming, thoughtful, and modest; she looked lovely. The writer had singled her out as "perhaps the most human of the three, the one still living in the real world, the one most aware of what she wants from politics and with the charisma to win her seat, and put her ideas into practice. Jack Kirkland, the Centre Forward Party's leader, is certainly right behind her: he says she represents the future of the party."

That was what had worried her most: from the first moment she had read it, late the night before on Waterloo Station, worried her through a restless night. To be so singled out, favoured, was worrying her even more now, after Janet had refused to take her calls.

Because if she were Janet, she wouldn't have liked being cast as the older statesman, wouldn't have liked the nannyish implications—or the unflattering photographs. In spite of protesting that she didn't care what she looked like, Janet did: she cared quite a lot. She had her bob cut at

Nicky Clarke and blow-dried twice a week, and her uniform suits were all from places like Jaeger and MaxMara. Mary really didn't care. She had true political integrity and was absorbed in her ideals. The simple fact was that Janet came over as the least charismatic of the three of them: and charisma was the bottom line in politics. It was what kept Tony Blair so resolutely in place.

Martha tried Janet's number once more, left a second message on her phone—Bob was obviously weary of playing private secretary—checked her e-mails once more in case Janet had written. Nothing from her.

"Martha my dear, forgive me for not getting back to you before. I've had a beast of a morning. Wasn't that a wonderful piece? I thought she got us all to an absolute tee. I was very pleased, especially with the way she got almost all my points across. And I know Jack was. Lovely picture of you. Not so hot of Mary and me—but that's not the point, is it? Thank you so much for making the time."

Martha was driving down the M11 and she felt the car could have taken off and flown, *Chitty Chitty Bang Bang*–style. She should stop worrying about Janet; it was a waste of her precious energy. And there really did seem to be no need.

⁃◆⁃

Clio looked at Fergus across the table, and wondered if she should tell him she didn't have to catch the last train home, that she was once again borrowing Jocasta's house in Clapham.

But it might look a bit . . . forward. Like an invitation. And he was expecting her to go, had twice said, very sweetly, they must keep an eye on the clock—and added that he didn't like the idea of her being on public transport late on a Saturday night, didn't she worry about it? Clio had said she never did, she had spent most of her youth and much of her adult life on late trains and the last one was particularly safe, always packed with people. And her car was at the station. All of which was true.

But she was having such a lovely time; they were in Mon Plaisir, in Covent Garden, and its warm, golden charm, its wonderful food, its pretty young waiters had relaxed her totally. She had been horribly nervous, of course. She had no idea what you wore to a London restaurant these days—studying the fashion magazines all week, it seemed to her shorts, high boots, and a sou'wester would have been just as appropriate as a little black dress. What had happened to clothes? Why didn't she know about them? As Fergus so clearly would.

She had gone down to Caroline B to buy herself something, but Jilly Bradford hadn't been there and she didn't trust the taste of the rather aggressively middle-aged woman who was standing in for her and who had none of Jilly's taste and chic. She bought some tops, all of which she thought would go with a black crepe suit she called her Doubt Suit (when in doubt, wear it), but somehow none of them did. At six o'clock, when she should have been in the bath, she was frantically ironing a cream silk shirt, which was five years old. Fergus told her she looked lovely and she tried to believe him. He was, of course, looking wonderful in a cream linen suit and black silk shirt, which made her feel more dowdy than ever.

But she stopped worrying about her clothes after about three minutes. Fergus had been absolutely sweet all evening, attentive, flattering, and amusing (why did he like her, why?), making her laugh, making her make him laugh (how did he do that?), asking her opinion very seriously on whether he should buy a flat he was considering in Putney.

"Don't ask me," she said, laughing, "I don't know anything about London property. Of course, if I get this job, I'll have to."

"Ah," he said, smiling at her, "but you have huge common sense, and I can't afford this flat, not really, not at the moment, anyway."

"Then don't buy it."

"I knew you'd say that," he said.

"So why ask me?"

"I thought I could talk you round and convince myself at the same time. It is absolutely beautiful, right on the river, and with a little roof garden—well, more of a balcony really. You'd love it, Clio."

She had pondered the relevance of this briefly, and decided, rather sadly, that it was a figure of speech.

He then moved on to all the shows in the West End: What had she seen, what would she like to see?

"*My Fair Lady*," she said promptly, and then realised how hopelessly suburban she must sound and blushed.

"Me too," he said. "So shall we go together? I would also love to see *Les Mis*," he went on. "See how up-to-date I am?"

Clio had been afraid he was just being kind again, humouring her, and said she'd like it too, nonetheless.

"And *Chicago*."

"Then we have a busy time ahead of us," he said, and glanced at his watch. Now he was bored, she thought, checking on how much longer the evening had to be. But, "It's getting late," he said. And that was when he said he didn't like the idea of her being on the train.

So should she say it, or not? That she didn't have to catch the train at all; but how, exactly? What did she say? She sighed, without meaning to; then, as he looked at her, said, "I must go to the loo. Excuse me."

She was a while, tidying up her face, spraying herself with perfume, studying herself in her middle-aged suit; when she came out, there was a girl at the table, sitting in her place, a beautiful girl, with a perfectly carved die-straight bob, wearing a silk wraparound dress. She was sitting sideways on the chair and Clio could see her perfect legs and the high heels of her silver sandals; she glanced down at her own black court shoes and wanted to run away. Probably he had told this girl to come and meet him there. "This woman I'm having dinner with has to leave at eleven," he would have said, "get back to the suburbs, we can go on somewhere then."

She took a deep breath, went over to the table.

"Clio, this is Joy. Joy Mattingly. She and I are old workmates, aren't we, darling?"

"We certainly are," she said, smiling at him, and then up at Clio. "The fun we've had, Fergus, eh?" Her voice was rather deep, with just a touch of an Irish accent; she picked a sugar lump out of the bowl, dipped it in Fergus's coffee, and licked at it slowly. Clio watched her, transfixed.

"Well, I must go," Joy said, standing up slowly; she was incredibly tall. "See you around, Fergus darling. Have fun."

He stood as she left and kissed her, and then sat down again, gesturing at Clio's chair.

"Sorry."

"No, no," she said, "don't be silly. But I must go, Fergus, it's late and—"

"And you'll miss your train," he said, and his voice was very flat. "Of course. I'll see you to a cab. Are you sure you'll be all right?"

"Of course I will," she said.

"Right," said Fergus, and she saw him blow a kiss at Joy across the restaurant and felt more miserable than ever, "let's find you a cab."

And when one pulled up almost instantly, he said quite briskly, "Right, well, safe journey, Clio, I've so enjoyed it. We must do it again sometime."

He hurried back into the restaurant. Clio sat staring at the crowded streets, at all the happy couples in it, holding hands, laughing, their arms round each other, and found it quite hard not to cry.

Inside the restaurant, a depressed Fergus was telling a patently bored Joy Mattingly that he feared Clio, so brilliantly clever, so obviously successful in her career, found him frivolous and rather uninteresting.

"I don't usually admire clever women, but she is something quite, quite different," he said, ordering them both a large brandy. "It's the combination of brains and beauty; it's a very rare thing. Well, it's clearly not to be. I had my hopes, but . . ."

He sighed and drained the glass and then refused Joy's invitation to join her and her party at Annabel's. She stared at him; she had known Fergus for many years and she had never yet known him turn down an opportunity to network.

He must be in love.

Chapter 33

．　　．　　．　　．

"No, young man, I can't tell you that. Honour among thieves and so on."

Teddy Buchanan's face was flushed as he drained his second glass of port. God, this had been a lot of money for nothing, Nick thought.

"Teddy, I only want a name."

"Only a name! You boys never give away your sources, do you? Don't start asking us to do it for you."

Unless it suits you, thought Nick, unless you want to land someone in it, or start a new plot, or fuel an old fire. Then you tell us anything. "No," he said, "no, of course not."

"Still, it's been a jolly good dinner. Thank you."

"We couldn't possibly agree to that," said Helen. She was flushed and on the verge of tears. "Not possibly. Could we, Jim?"

"No, we couldn't. She's too young and too vulnerable. And we don't want any more publicity for her of that sort."

Fergus had expected them to be upset. In a way, he was impressed. Not many people would turn down three million dollars. In a way he even agreed with them. But . . .

"Helen, Jim, this is a lot of money," he said gently.

"We know that," said Helen. "It's part of what we don't like."

"Yes, but think about it. Please. Just for a moment. Any dreams you might have had for Kate, this could buy. Any travelling, university education, all that sort of thing. And what are you going to tell her?"

"Well—can't we say they didn't want her?"

"Not really. Think about it. Look . . ." He hesitated. "What do you think she'd say later in life, if she found out you'd turned this down without consulting her? She'd be very angry. Rightly so, many would say."

"Yes, but we have to think what's best for her now," said Helen. "She's very vulnerable. She's a child, Fergus, not an adult . . ."

After he had gone, Helen and Jim studied the pictures of Kate. "This is very difficult," said Helen.

"Martha? Martha Hartley?"

It was Martin Farrow, head of publicity at Centre Forward House. They needed to talk to her urgently. A request had come through for her to appear on *Question Time* that week; Clare Short had pulled out at the last minute and they'd like Martha.

"They say you acquitted yourself extremely well at the lunch at the studios. They said you were very articulate and opinionated. They want you, Martha."

"Oh, God." Why hadn't she just sat there like a pudding, not saying anything? She felt absolutely terrified. "They should have Janet Frean," she said. "Obviously. Please, tell them to ask her."

Farrow said, slightly awkwardly, "We did suggest her, of course. But they said they'd rather have you. They said you were a new face, and they've already got two political heavies. They'd seen the piece in *The Times* on Saturday, and we sent some tapes of you on local radio and your show reel and—it's you they want."

"Well, I can't do it," said Martha flatly. "I'm frantically busy here, and anyway, I don't want to. And I couldn't, I'd be useless."

"Martha, I keep telling you: they think you'll be marvellous. They know you'll be marvellous, they've heard you talk!"

"That's quite different. I wasn't nervous then. And what would Janet say?"

That was the worst thing—too hideous to contemplate. How Janet must be feeling: turned down for *Question Time*, the most desirable slot on television for a politician, in favour of her. Not Janet Frean, experienced, brilliant professional, but Martha Hartley, inexperienced amateur. She'd want to kill her. She'd want to— Oh, God, what might she want to do? What might she do?

"I can't do it," she said. "Sorry."

Jack phoned, dismissing Martha's decision to turn down *Question Time* as nonsense. Chad called moments later, reminding Martha how most people would give their eyeteeth for the chance she had. Mary Norton refused to accept Martha's insistence that she couldn't go on. Nick wanted a quote about her avoiding the program, then Paul Quenell and even her own mother phoned to scold her.

The only person in the world who didn't seem to want to talk to her was Janet. She had called her at least five times. It was hardly surprising. What was she going to do?

"Martha, dear, this is Janet. I hear they've asked you to do *Question Time*. I think that's marvellous. Of course you must do it. As long as you really think you can cope. It is very frightening. No one knows that better than I—I've done it a few times. Oh, but I'm sure you can. Once you get going, it's absolutely fine. What? No, of course I don't mind. I'm relieved it's not me, as a matter of fact. I'll so enjoy watching you. Now, if you want any tips, we could have a little session, maybe the night before, something like that."

She didn't mind! She didn't mind! It was all right. God, she was so nice. So generous. Well, in that case—just maybe.

•—•

"Is this Kate? Kate Tarrant? This is Jed. Mr. Corelli's assistant."

"Oh, hi."

"He wants to know where you got your jeans. He made a note and then forgot."

"Harvey Nichols," said Kate.

"Harvey Nichols! Well, that is just wonderful. We'll go there tomorrow. Did you like the pictures?"

"I haven't seen them yet."

"Oh, I sent a few over to your agent."

"Yeah? Well, I haven't seen him today. I've been out shopping."

"Oh, OK. I heard they were *very* pleased. The Smith people. You must be *so* excited."

She ended the call and immediately called Fergus.

Kate was in upset mode: flushed, brilliant-eyed, hands clenched. "Thanks for telling me!"

"Telling you what, Kate?"

"You know. About the contract. Fergus said he'd discussed it with you, that I should ask you about it."

"Yes, that's right."

"And you didn't think to talk to me about it?"

"We were waiting for the right moment."

"Well," said Kate, "here it is."

"Your father's not here."

"I don't care."

"Well, I do," said Helen, struggling to sound firm. "This is an important matter and I don't want to discuss it without your father."

Kate walked out of the house, slamming the door so hard the windows drummed in response.

•—•

The waiter eased a salmon steak onto the plate, poured the juices from the pan over it, all with great care, and then leaning over Nick in order to place the vegetables carefully on the table, said very quietly, "Mr. Marshall, there's something in your jacket pocket."

"Thanks. Thanks very much."

Nick was lunching in the press dining room with one of the boys from the Foreign Office; he excused himself as soon as he decently could and walked slowly out of the dining room. His jacket was hanging on a coatrack. He picked it up casually, went into the gents', and sat down in one of the stalls. This was not the first time this had happened: it was a classic way of imparting information discreetly. But it was always exciting—he felt as if he was in a miniseries or something.

There was a note folded neatly in the inside pocket of the jacket, marked Confidential.

"I'd love to have a chat with you sometime," it said, "about Centre Forward and its future. I've got some stuff you'd find really interesting. Maybe you could call me on my mobile."

It was signed Janet Frean.

•◦•

Clio often thought that if she had been a more truthful person, then the whole of her life might have turned out differently.

If she had told Mark what she was really doing the day of her interview board, instead of creating an entirely fictional visit to an orthodontist, which necessitated her leaving the practice at lunchtime, then—well, everything really would have been very different. She would have taken the whole day off to prepare for her interview and gone up to London in the morning, so as to be sure to have plenty of time. But she felt it was tempting fate to tell Mark what she was doing; the interview was late enough to enable her to do her morning surgery and still have time to go home, change into her new suit, and catch a train at around two. All she had to get cover for were her home visits; very few at the moment.

With that in mind, she wore a shirt that was, well, not exactly shabby, but certainly not stylish or even particularly crisp-looking, and a skirt that had also seen better days. And her oldest, most comfortable shoes. Her surgery had overrun, not finished until ten to one, but that was still fine. She could be home by one, and then—

"Clio? It's the Laurels." Margaret sounded diffident. "The matron says it's important. It's about the Morrises."

"Put her through," she said.

Mrs. Morris had died that morning, the matron said. "It was quite peaceful. And Mr. Morris was with her."

"Oh, that's so sad." Clio's eyes filled with tears. Dear, sweet Mrs. Morris, with her sparkly, pale blue eyes and her bright brave smile. Mrs. Morris, baking cakes every day for the husband she loved so much—even if she sometimes didn't put the oven on. Mrs. Morris, so fastidious about her husband's appearance and her own—occasionally popping an apron or a headscarf on him rather than herself, but everything always immaculately clean and ironed. Dear, sweet Mrs. Morris.

"I'm so sorry," she said, "so very sorry. How is Mr. Morris?"

"That's why I'm phoning," said the matron. "He's terribly upset. And asking for you. I wondered if . . ."

"I can't," said Clio. "I have to go to London and—"

Ten minutes later she arrived at the Laurels.

Mr. Morris was sitting with Mrs. Morris, holding her hand. She had been prettily dressed in a clean nightdress and her face wore the neatly peaceful smile of death. Clio pulled up a chair and sat down next to him, took his other hand. He looked at her and said, tears rolling down his face, "She's gone, Dr. Scott. Gone without me."

"I know," she said gently. "I'm so sorry."

"She promised she wouldn't. She promised she'd wait for me. What am I going to do without her?" he said, and a drop fell off the end of his fine old nose. Clio reached out and wiped it gently with a tissue.

"We've been married sixty-two years—I can't manage without her, I really can't. Who's going to talk to me, who's going to listen to me now? 'No one else would listen to you, Trevor,' she used to say, 'you talk too much.' "

"Did she?"

"She did." He managed a feeble smile. "But she talked a lot too. We both did, all our lives. No need, really, in the end—we knew what the other was going to say, but we went on just the same. 'Not that old story again,' I'd say and she'd say, 'If it was interesting the first time, it'll be interesting now.' What am I going to do without her, what?"

"Were you with her?" asked Clio, wiping his tears again.

"Yes. They were very kind; they let me stay all the time. Since six this morning I've been here. Except—just after, you know . . ."

"I know. Well, I'm glad. That you were together then."

"Yes. We were. It was very peaceful. She just drifted away from me. Last thing she said was, 'Sorry, Trevor.' That would have been for not waiting for me. And then a little smile and she was gone." He turned and looked at her. "Do you believe in the next life, Dr. Scott? A lot of people don't anymore."

"I do indeed," said Clio, and in that moment, she was as convinced as she was of anything that Mrs. Morris was up somewhere in a sweet blue heaven, bright and smiling, waiting for her Trevor, with a nicely ironed shirt and a freshly baked cake.

"And you think I'll see her again?"

"Of course you will. Of course."

"I'm so glad you think that." He turned to look at her, and managed a weak, watery smile. "Sometimes I have wondered. Thank you for coming, Dr. Scott. Thank you so much."

It was two o'clock. She screeched down the drive, only just missing the butcher's van coming up it. She hoped it had been worth it. It *had* been worth it. She was glad she'd done it. Whatever the cost.

Now what did she do? If she went straight to the station, she might still catch the two thirty. Which meant she would be able to get there, compose herself and her thoughts, and present herself just about in time, while wearing her oldest shirt and skirt, and her kicked-out driving shoes. On the other hand, she could appear neat, smart—and late.

Clio thought about the people who would probably be sitting on the board and their concerns and decided they would not be focused on her Paul Costelloe jacket and her Jigsaw trousers. She headed for the station.

Clio caught the two thirty—just. She sank into the corner of the compartment, trying to get her breath back, rummaged in her bag for a comb. No comb. Lucky she had a small one in her makeup bag, she could— "Shit," she said aloud. No makeup bag either.

This was grim. Sat-out skirts were one thing; smudged mascara from crying and a seriously shiny nose were another. Well, maybe she could get something from Boots on Waterloo Station. No, she wouldn't have time. Oh God . . .

Now then. The journey from Waterloo to Bayswater was not easy. Cab? Dodgy, and she didn't have that much cash on her. She could go to the cash machine, but there was always a long queue at Waterloo. The tube then: Lancaster Gate was the nearest and only involved one change—one change, yes, and a lot of underground corridors—but then she could get a cab from there. If there was one. The Royal Bayswater was tucked into a difficult little triangle, bordered by Sussex Gardens and the Edgware Road, a truly hideous place to get to. Oh, God. Would it be worth phoning? Saying she might be a few minutes late? Not yet. No point giving herself a black mark before she had to.

She switched on her phone, carefully silenced for poor Mr. Morris; it bleeped. A text message from Fergus, saying, "Good luck with the interview. Hope you're wearing the wedding party dress." What a treasure he was. Maybe he hadn't found her so dull, maybe . . . She texted back.

"Thanks vv much. I wish. Wearing oldest clothes. Look terrible. Clio."

He texted back at once. "Why?"

"V long story. Might not make it."

It was passing the time at least. Was this train going slowly? No, it must be her imagination. It was a fast train. A fast train going slowly. Shit!

"We apologise to customers for any delay. Due to a signal failure at Waterloo, this train will terminate at Vauxhall. Customers are advised . . ."

Customers!

"We are not bloody customers!" she shouted at a hapless ticket inspector who was working through the carriage. "We're passengers. People who want to get somewhere. On your trains. You know?"

He shrugged. "Don't blame me, love," he said and walked on.

Shit shit shit! She just wasn't meant to get this job. She wasn't. She might as well—

Her mobile rang.

"Clio? It's Fergus. Is anything wrong?"

•◆•

Jocasta was rather earnestly preparing for Gideon's return that weekend; she felt like a Stepford wife. She had filled the house with flowers, arranged them herself—and then felt a mixture of foolishness and rage when Mrs. Hutching, the housekeeper, politely said, "I always do the flowers on Fridays, Mrs. Keeble. If you'd rather I didn't—"

"I would rather you didn't, yes," said Jocasta briskly. "I love doing flowers."

She had arranged to have her hair trimmed and the highlights done and she had bought herself a new nightie from Agent Provocateur. She'd probably only have it on for a few minutes, but it was still very pretty. Well, pretty wasn't quite the word. Sexy. All black satin and cream lace, and not much of either. Gideon would like it. He was a bit old-fashioned when it came to underwear. He was a bit old-fashioned altogether.

She had also booked some tickets for a Mozart concert at the Wigmore Hall, which she knew he would enjoy much more than she would, and then a table at Le Caprice for dinner.

She felt delighted with herself. This would please him, would show him she was a mature woman, a suitable wife for him, not an immature selfish brat. Like that bloody daughter of his.

She looked at her watch and sighed: only halfway through Wednesday afternoon. What should she do now? A bit more shopping, perhaps? No, she'd go for a run in the park. It was wonderful to be so near to the park, just be able to walk across the road and into the green of Kensington Gardens, not the scratchy, cigarette-scarred grass of Clapham Common. Nick hated running on Clapham Common.

She suddenly had a vision of Nick taking off on a run from her house on a Sunday morning, his long lean body moving smoothly and steadily down the street, his brown hair flopping, waving to her without turning round. And then her going back into the house and making some coffee, frantically trying to defrost the orange juice she had left too long in the freezer and tidying up the piles of newspapers that covered the bed. They very often had sex on Sunday mornings, lovely slow, lazy sex; how he could run after it she could never understand.

Stop it, Jocasta! That was all very well, and it was terrific fun and the sex was fantastic, but he didn't love you. Well, not enough. Gideon does. Which is wonderful.

She wondered how Clio was getting on; it was her interview today. She was sure she'd get her job. She had been very disappointed in Clio's relationship with Fergus; it seemed to be fizzling out. Their careers were such worlds apart, but there was something about them that was exactly right; they were like two wiggly pieces of jigsaw that suddenly fitted to-gether. Maybe it wasn't too late. Maybe she could organise a dinner party or something, make sure they kept in touch.

•–•

Fergus had said he would meet Clio at Vauxhall. "I can cut across Lon-don, easily. Across Vauxhall Bridge, up Park Lane, you'll be there in a trice. Don't worry."

She had protested, said he must have other things to do, like work, but, "Nonsense," he said. "I'm as free as air this afternoon. Had a hot date with the VAT inspector, but she came this morning instead. Anything else I can do for you?"

"Well . . ." She hesitated; it seemed an awful lot to ask. "Actually, Fer-gus, if you could just—"

He must like her; he must.

They pulled in to Vauxhall Station at 3:35 and he was waiting for her outside, grinning, holding a Boots bag. "And in the back there is a jacket. I think it should fit you. It's not bad, quite nice in fact. A girl I fell out with left it behind, it's Jigsaw, size twelve."

"Oh, Fergus!" said Clio, and careless of whether she might be embar-rassing him or not, she gave him a kiss. "You are an angel."

"Not quite, and that certainly wasn't her view, but—come along now, into the car, you can do your face as we go."

He had even brought some tissues.

At five to four they were at the bottom of the car park that was called Park Lane.

"Clio, hello!" It was Beaky's secretary. "Are you in the building?"

"No," wailed Clio, "I'm at the bottom of Park Lane. Stuck! They're not running late or anything, are they?"

" 'Fraid not. Dr. Smartarse—I didn't say that—your only real rival is in there now. Due to come out any minute. God, Clio, shall I warn them?"

"I think you'd better," said Clio.

At quarter past four they were approaching Sussex Gardens; the traf-fic was still crawling.

"I think you'd be quicker legging it from here," said Fergus. "I'll park and come and find you. Good luck. I'll be waiting."

She wrenched the door open and started running. At least there was one benefit in her old shoes. As she reached the doors of the Royal Bayswater, she realised she had left her notes in the car.

Fergus was trying to reverse his car into a space too small for it, and on double yellow lines, when he caught sight of the notes for the presentation part of her interview on the backseat; the hard stuff about why she wanted the job, about funding, how she saw the geriatrics department fitting in with the rest of the hospital administration and the internal politics. She had been studying them, trying to keep calm as they drove. They obviously mattered. But she was five minutes ahead of him now. At least. And the hospital was still a ways away.

Clio stood in reception, trying to impress upon the woman, who had no knowledge of any interview board, the urgency of her case. "Just call Professor Bryan's secretary," she said. "She'll know where I should be."

God. If only she had her notes. If only. She felt so confused, so brain-dead.

"Clio! Come along. They're giving you till half past, I made them some more tea."

It was Beaky's secretary; she must send her some flowers.

"Clio!"

It was Fergus, waving something at her. Her notes.

"Oh my God," she said, "how did you manage that?"

"I once got a medal for running, the only prize I ever won at school," he said. "I'll wait here. Good luck. That jacket suits you," he added. "Looks much nicer on you than on her."

"Your boyfriend?" asked Beaky's secretary. "What a sweetie."

They all looked at her very coldly when she went into the room. Even Beaky. There were five of them: some familiar, some not. The chief executive of the hospital, an outside assessor, the clinical director, one of the other consultants—and Beaky.

"I'm so sorry," she said, sinking onto the chair they indicated. "I can explain if you like—"

"Not now," said the administrator. "I think we have been delayed enough. If we could just begin . . ."

Astonishingly, once she started, she felt coolly together, all her facts and theories marshalled, her experience summoned, made to seem clearly relevant. She answered all their questions smoothly and easily, expressed her view that as much a part of geriatrics as medicine was the social side, the importance of enabling elderly people to continue in the community by way of careful monitoring, drug therapy, and support from the social services. She had done some research of her own on late-onset diabetes and on stroke management, was absolutely up-to-date on treatment, both in the UK and the States; she could see that impressed them. She discussed her days in the outlying hospitals, said how impressed she had been with the care home in Highbury and its policy of patient independence. And finally, expressed her personal view of the frustration of the carers, prevented from giving out drugs by red tape and meaningless regulations.

"I know this is more politics than medicine," she said, "but it is so important. I firmly believe we would see smaller clinics here, fewer beds needed, less pressure on the homes if we could only overcome it."

And then heard, to her horror, her own voice shake as she said it, felt her eyes stab with tears, thinking with fierce regret that the Morrises might still be safely at home together, had she only been able to ensure that they had got their medication at the right time and in the right doses every day.

"I'm sorry," she said, seeing them look at her oddly, "I've had a bit of an upsetting day with a patient. It's why I was late."

"Perhaps, Dr. Scott," said Beaky gently, clearly seeing his opportunity to push her forward, "you would now like to tell us about it."

She waited outside with the three other candidates. The one who was clearly Dr. Smartarse sat drumming his fingers on his leg, looking at his watch. The other two read their newspapers and weren't very friendly either. She supposed she had held them all up.

Finally she spoke into the tension.

"I'm so sorry I was late," she said, "but you see—"

The door opened; there was an interminable silence; then: "Dr. Scott, could you come back in, please."

She was never sure afterwards when it had gone wrong: when the hugs and kisses outside the hospital, the sense of warm euphoria and sweetly shared triumph ended, and the chill began. He had even bought her some flowers. "I knew you'd earn them," and insisted on driving into Covent Garden—"perfect place to celebrate."

She thought of Saturday's dinner there and hoped he was right.

"Here's to you, Consultant Scott." Fergus raised a glass of champagne to her. "I'm very proud indeed to know you."

"Thank you. A whole bottle! Fergus! Your eyes are bigger than your stomach, as my nanny used to say."

"Your nanny! How very grand," he said. "Where I come from your nanny is your gran."

"Fergus. I only had a nanny because I didn't have a mother," said Clio. She could feel herself blushing. Had that been it? She had certainly felt awkward suddenly, less happy.

"You had no mother?"

"No. She died when I was a baby."

"That's terribly sad."

"Not really. I know that sounds dreadful, but I never knew her, I didn't know any different. Anyway, that's not what I want to talk about. Oh, Fergus! I'd never have done it without you. Never. I just don't know how to thank you."

"You don't have to," he said. "I feel rewarded enough that you got it. You were a long time," he added. "I was beginning to wonder if you'd popped out the back way."

"Fergus! Of course not. There's a lot to discuss at these boards, you know, it's not just like a simple interview—" She stopped, fearing she sounded condescending.

"I daresay. The only interview I ever attended was for the position of filing clerk. It lasted about two and a half minutes. Since then, I've just wheedled my way into places."

"I'm afraid wheedling isn't a recognised interview technique for doctors," she said. Damn. She'd done it again. She smiled at him, still afraid it sounded schoolmistressy.

"Yes, well, our worlds are obviously pretty far apart," he said. And this time he didn't smile back.

She had begun to feel panicky. It couldn't all go wrong today. Not now. Not after all he'd done.

"You were so kind, Fergus," she said again. "So, so kind."

"Now let's not OD on the praise," he said. "It was just what any friend would do."

A friend. Any friend. That was how he saw her. He had just been helping a friend.

"And what are you doing this evening?" he said.

"Oh, just getting back."

"But—you have to?"

"Oh yes," she said quickly. She didn't want him to feel he had to amuse her, go on helping her to celebrate. She'd imposed on him enough.

"Right. Well, I must get back to the office too."

"You certainly must. I've robbed you of hours of useful occupation."

"Debatable I'd say. That it was useful."

"What? Your occupation? Don't be silly."

"It's not exactly a useful occupation, is it? Not like being a doctor." He sounded edgy, almost defensive. "But anyway, it was a pleasure helping you. It really was." A long silence; then: "Can I give you a lift to Waterloo?"

"Oh, no. Honestly. That would be too kind. I'll just make my own way, get a cab probably. I'd much rather actually."

"Right," he said, "fine." His voice had become cool, distant.

It was all going wrong. Horribly wrong. She looked round the bar; it was full of pretty girls, with long brown bare legs and low-cut tops. She felt appallingly out of place, again, in her shabby skirt and kicked-out shoes. And her—oh, God, flesh-coloured tights. And the jacket he had lent her was a bit tight. That girl, whoever she was, had obviously been really skinny. She had to get out of here.

"Well, I'll just go and get a cab. I don't think I could walk another inch." She stood up. "Thank you again for the champagne, Fergus. And for everything."

"There's a lot of champagne left," he said indicating it.

"I'm sure you'll manage." God. Now he'd think she meant he was an alcoholic.

"You couldn't stay for another glass?" he said.

She should have said yes then, she knew she should—he must be thinking she'd just been using him all afternoon and now she wanted to get away—but she could feel everything she said going from bad to worse.

"No, no, I couldn't. I'd love to, but I really must get back. Back to . . . to the Laurels—you know, the nursing home. I said I would."

"OK, fine. I can see that is really important. Well, I'll see you to your cab."

"There's no need."

"I know that," he said and his voice was even slightly impatient. "But I will, just the same. I have been properly brought up, you know. Even if I didn't have a nanny."

"Fergus, that's . . . that's silly."

"I'm a pretty silly fellow. Come on."

Where had it all gone, she thought, all that happiness, all that triumph, all that closeness? She thought of him buying her mascara and lipstick in Boots, pounding up Sussex Gardens, desperate to give her her notes. How had she managed to wreck that, and so quickly? God, she was a disaster. It was hopeless. Completely hopeless.

"Here's a cab," he said.

"Thanks. Thanks for everything, Fergus. I do hope—" What did she hope? Nothing that wouldn't sound boring. Or as if she was forcing herself on him. "I do hope you get everything done."

Now, how crass was that?

"I will," he said.

She got into the cab, leant forward. "Waterloo," she said and turned to say goodbye, only he had wrenched the door open, was climbing in beside her.

"That'll be extra," said the cabbie, pressing his meter.

"That's fine," said Fergus.

"Fergus, what—"

"I want to talk to you," he said. "Get to the bottom of this personality change you go through. It keeps happening. One minute you're you, all warm and chatty, and the next all buttoned-up, holding me at arm's length. What is it, what do I do?"

"It's not you," she said quickly. "Really it isn't, it's me."

"What do you mean, you?"

"I can't explain," she said wretchedly, and she felt, to her horror, the tears well up and she fished in her bag for a tissue and blew her nose. "Hay fever," she said by way of explanation.

"I don't see any hay," he said, taking the tissue away from her and wiping her eyes tenderly. "Come along, Clio, tell me what's wrong, please.

Otherwise"—he looked out of the window, they were on Waterloo Bridge now—"I shall throw myself into the river."

Clio giggled in spite of herself, and then sniffed rather unromantically.

"I can't tell you," she said.

"Rubbish," he said, and started to try to open the door.

"Mind out, guv, it's locked," said the driver.

"Clio! Come on!"

"Well—oh dear!" The tears were flowing fast now. "It's just that—that—"

"That what? Are you in love with someone else?"

"No, no, it's nothing like that—it's just that I'm so—so dull. And middle-aged and—and—"

"What are you talking about?" he said, looking genuinely mystified.

"I'm dull, not exciting. Serious. Not like the people you know. Not like Joy the other night. I don't know why you wanted to have dinner with me, Fergus, I suppose you were just being kind like today, and you were so kind, but—"

"Which entrance?" said the driver.

"Oh, Eurostar will do," said Fergus. "Clio, I wanted to have dinner with you because I love your company—I adore your company. You're so interesting and thoughtful—"

"Oh yes," she said, "very exciting that makes me sound. Interesting and thoughtful—"

"It is to me, you silly bitch," he said.

She stared at him. "What did you say?"

"I said you were exciting, to me. I find you very exciting. And today I was so proud of you and—"

"Yes, but what else?"

"I said you were a silly bitch. OK? I'm sorry."

"Seven quid," said the driver.

Fergus fumbled in his wallet, pulled out a tenner, thrust it at him. "That's all right, keep it."

"Fergus, that's terrible," said Clio, shocked by this piece of wanton extravagance. "You can't just give him three pounds—"

"I can. Of course I can. Come on. OUT!"

She got out, meekly followed him into the Eurostar building, and then up the escalator. At the top he turned and faced her.

"Look," he said, "I don't know how I can convince you that I like being with you. That I find you terribly attractive. You're driving me mad. What do you want, woman? A signed declaration? Here"—he pulled a sheet of paper out of the small Filofax he kept in his pocket—"here you are. I, Fergus Trehearn, find you, Clio Scott—don't know what your married name is, but if I could get hold of your husband I'd punch the living daylights out of him, for doing what he has to you. I find you incredibly exciting and interesting and desirable and I would like to remove all your clothing right here." He tore the paper off, handed it to her. "There. Will that do? Now then, we'd better go and find your bloody train."

Clio stood very still and stared, first at him, then at the piece of paper; then she said, "Fergus, I don't want to get the bloody train. And I don't have to. I want to stay with you. And I want you to remove all my clothing. As soon as possible. Only not just here, maybe."

"Well, where then?" he said, speaking very slowly. He raised his hand, tilted her face up to his.

Clio felt a lurch in what she could only describe as her guts. A strong, probing lurch. It led to part of her anatomy that had been dormant for quite a long time. It wasn't dormant now. It appeared to be on the rampage.

"I believe you've got a flat," she said very quietly. "And could you just say that once again?"

"What?"

"You know, about me being a silly bitch?"

"But why?"

"Well, because it proves you weren't just being polite. It's about the biggest compliment I ever had."

"I can do a lot better than that," he said, "you silly bitch." And he started to kiss her.

Chapter 34

· · · ·

"I don't know what I think. Not really. It's well confusing."

"That's why I asked you," said Kate, her voice exasperated. "I want to be less confused."

"Yeah, I know, but you can't think something to order. I'm not like my dad. You've only got to say something to my dad, like—well, like police, or posh, and he's off."

"What does he think about being posh, then?" said Kate curiously.

"Not being posh, Posh. Like Posh Spice."

"Oh, right. What does he think about her?"

"He says she's addled Beckham's brain, dressing him up in skirts and that. That's why we lost the World Cup, he says, all her fault. I agree with him," he added.

Nat usually did agree with his father.

"Yes, but Nat, that's things he already knows about. What do you think he'd have to say about this contract and me? Just for instance."

"Well, I don't know. I could ask him."

"No, don't," said Kate hastily. She sighed. "So suppose I was *your* daughter. What would you do?"

Nat considered this carefully. "I would worry about it. I mean you're not sixteen yet. You'd only spend it on clothes and that, wouldn't you?"

"No," said Kate, "course not. I'd invest it."

"Yeah, but what in? You wouldn't know. Anyway, it's not the money, is it?"

"Isn't it?"

"Kate, you know that. What it's really about is the publicity and that, isn't it? I mean, you don't want all that stuff in the papers again, do you?"

"Well, no. I don't. But—"

"Kate, you don't. And you heard what Fergus said. It's not going to go away."

"It won't go away, whatever I do," said Kate rather sadly. "And what am I supposed to do, stay in my bedroom for the rest of my life? Not do anything interesting?"

"Course not. But you don't have to do something like modelling, do

· 427 ·

you? I mean you're clever, and you've done your exams. You could be a teacher, or something."

"Nat, I've got a lot more exams to do before I could be a teacher!"

"Yeah? My dad says they're a waste of space, teachers, don't teach kids nothing these days."

"Well," said Kate, "I don't think I want to be something that your dad considers a waste of space." She was getting bored with this conversation. "Let's go for a drive."

"Tell you something else," he said, "there's no rush. Keep 'em waiting, tell Fergus that and all."

"That's a very good point," she said.

She reached across to kiss him; in her high heels, she was almost as tall as he was. "Thanks, Nat. What would I do without you?"

"Walk everywhere," he said, and grinned. "Kate, I wish you could find your mum, then you wouldn't mind all the crap, would you?"

"I s'pose I wouldn't," she said, "not so much anyway. But I don't think I'm going to. Not now."

"You don't know that," he said. "You never know what's round the corner."

"And who says that, your dad?" she asked, teasing him.

"No," he said, very seriously, "my mum. Mind you, she needs to think that, married to my dad. But matter of fact, it's true."

⋅•⋅

Martha woke up on Thursday and thought that whatever else happened, this was the last morning *Question Time* would be hanging over her, like some vast brooding predator. Tomorrow it would be over; she might have made a complete fool of herself, she might have been taken off the air, but at least she wouldn't be dreading it anymore.

God, she was scared. She wondered if anyone had ever actually thrown up on camera. That would be an interesting first.

She got up, put on her running things, clipped her tiny radio to her shorts, and set off for Tower Bridge while listening to John Humphrys on the row over Tony Blair and the Queen Mother's funeral, which was still going on. And the ongoing Hinduja business. And the equally ongoing debate on ID cards. And Cherie and her remarks about the suicide bombers. And who might be Archbishop of Canterbury. And why it still mattered. The trouble was, as Janet had told her, you could think you were right on top of the news, and then the hot topic that night could be something you knew next to nothing about. That hadn't helped to make her feel more confident.

She was going to the hairdresser on her way into the office. She had been told that the studio hairdresser was pretty useless. "They just comb it," Janet had said. "Take a hair styler with you and loads of hair spray."

Janet had been great: coaching her, giving her practice questions, telling her the one cardinal sin was to look at the camera, advising her on her jacket—"not blue, not patterned"—and to try to eat something beforehand, "or your stomach will rumble and your mike will pick it up. It's a nightmare."

Martha felt she was in a nightmare already: How much worse could it get?

For some reason, the other nightmare, the really hideous one, seemed to have receded. She supposed there just wasn't room for it. It would be back, but she was grateful for the respite.

Janet had asked Nick to meet her for an early supper at the Savoy. "Not the Grill. The Savoy Upstairs. It's very quiet there and we can talk as much as we like. Then I can be back in time to watch *Question Time*. You know Martha Hartley's on tonight?"

Nick said he did. And that he was planning to watch it too. "She's very bright. I've met her once or twice. She went travelling with Jocasta, way back in the eighties, did you know that?"

Janet said yes, she did.

It was a very long morning. Martha had a difficult client meeting booked, which she had expected to distract her, but it was cancelled at the last minute; she worked on a presentation document and prepared a report, but it wasn't the all-consuming stuff she needed.

She had to leave at two; the BBC was sending a car for her. She sat watching the clock as it crawled the last half hour; this must be like waiting for the executioner, she thought. She had a fat bundle of briefing material, sent over from Jack Kirkland's office, which she knew more or less by heart, and she had the day's papers to read in the car.

She kept going to the loo, and checking and rechecking the holdall she had brought, containing her precious hair styler and three different tops to go with either of the suits she was taking for final approval (one bright red, which she loved but feared might be a bit much on camera, and one grey-and-white Prince of Wales check, which she also loved but feared might count as the busy pattern Janet had advised her against).

At five to two the phone rang; she let her voice mail pick it up. It was Ed.

"Hi, Martha. I just discovered you're on telly tonight. Mum told me. Cool. Good luck. And—"

Suddenly she wanted to speak to him. Terribly.

She grabbed the phone. "Hi, Ed. I'm here. Just leaving now."

"Yeah? How do you feel?"

"Terrible. Absolutely terrible. So frightened, you can't imagine!"

"Is this the cucumber-cool Miss Martha Hartley, prospective parliamentary candidate for Binsmow? Martha, don't be scared, you'll be fine. Just keep your hands over your nose, dreadful if people spotted that."

"Oh, don't! And I won't be fine, I know I won't."

"Would you like me to come?"

"What? To Birmingham?"

"Is that where it is? Cool, I love Brum, they have some great clubs there, we could go out afterwards."

"Ed, I'll be in no state to go clubbing."

"OK, we'll just sit in the greenroom and watch the reruns. Do you have anything planned for afterwards?"

"Suicide," she said.

"Terrible waste. Look, I mean it—I will come if you want me to. I'd love to."

She was silent for a moment, then: "I'd absolutely love it," she said simply. "It would make all the difference. But God knows if you'll be able to get in."

"I'll think of something. If I can't get in, I'll wait in reception and watch you on the monitor."

"Oh, Ed." Her eyes filled with tears. God, she'd missed him. And God alone knew what she was doing, letting him back into her life. It was hugely dangerous, she was overemotional, frightened, she might say or do anything. It was also exceedingly selfish. But she'd worry about that afterwards.

On the way up, she read the papers again. All of them. She also yet again read the stuff from Centre Forward House. And looked increasingly anxiously at her two suits and wished she'd brought a third.

"Goodness," said Clio, "Martha's on *Question Time* tonight. You remember Martha, don't you, Fergus?"

"Could I ever forget her? I bore her in my arms up to her bedroom, and laid her on the bed, lucky man that I am. She's very pretty."

"Mmm . . ." said Clio.

"Not as pretty as you, though, I don't want any neuroses starting up. And I'm sure her breasts aren't nearly as nice."

He had a bit of a thing about her breasts; he said they were the prettiest he had ever seen.

"They're like you," he said, gazing at them tenderly, as she sat bolt upright in his bed the night before, still slightly shocked by the turn of events. "Sweet and charming."

"Fergus, how can breasts be charming?" she asked, laughing, suddenly relaxed.

"Yours demonstrate it beautifully. Can I kiss them?"

"Of course."

He bent his head and kissed them, slowly and contemplatively, one at a time; her last distinct memory was of his tongue circling her nipples, teasing, caressing, infinitely gentle. And after that it became a blur, a joyful, greedy, melting, astonishing blur. And after that, peace, silence, stillness. And then: "You silly bitch," he said. "You gorgeous, lovely, silly bitch. Think of all the time we've wasted."

"Well, we can make up for it now," said Clio.

"I think the red . . ." The floor manager considered Martha's suits. "It suits you and it looks very zingy. Good. Now if you'd like to get changed, dinner will start in about half an hour. There are some really nice people coming, local dignitaries as well as your fellow panellists, and you can chat away and keep up-to-date with the news at the same time."

"Oh—great," said Martha.

She went into the dining room at about seven; it appeared full. A large table, laid as if for a formal dinner party, was in the centre of the room, with a group of people at one end, at least three with faces she found terrifyingly recognisable. She was introduced to them, given the glass of water she had requested, and left to sink or swim. Two of the faces smiled at her kindly, asked her how she felt, assured her it would all be fine, and then returned to their previous conversations. She longed to run away. She went to the lavatory and guiltily switched on her mobile. There was nothing from Ed. It was almost seven o'clock.

Ed was sitting in one of the biggest traffic jams he had ever seen. His mobile had inexplicably run out of juice, and he was desperate for a pee. Otherwise everything was fine.

Nick smiled encouragingly at Janet. "It's nice up here, I've often wondered about it, but never actually got any further."

"Few people have," said Janet. "It's good for a discreet rendezvous, for that very reason."

"Indeed. Well, Janet, how are things at Centre Forward House? You've had a bit of bad luck lately."

"I know. It's been unfortunate. After all our hard work, people being so courageous and backing us, people in the field that is. Very dispiriting. It does make you wonder, just sometimes, if the game's worth the candle."

Nick often found himself on the receiving end of such reflections—politicians tended to use journalists not just to disperse information stories, or berate them when they didn't write exactly what they were told, but rather surprisingly to share their self-doubt with them, use them as a sort of personal confessional.

"Well I hope you're not giving up," he said.

"Heavens, no!" She suddenly became herself again, brisk, incisive. "Not after all this. I'd be pretty annoyed with whoever spilt the beans over the poll figures if I came across him—or her—but the others were just plain bad luck, stories waiting to be stumbled over."

"Well . . . yes," said Nick carefully. He wondered what she'd say if he told her he'd seen her with Michael Fitzroy that lunchtime.

"Martha, can you come to makeup now, please?"

She followed the makeup girl meekly; this had to be better than discussing the progress of the various planning committees in Birmingham while trying (mindful of Janet's dictum) to swallow some rather tough chicken—where would politics be without chicken, she wondered wildly—and follow Sky News on the television in the corner nearest to her.

She wondered what on earth the point of this dinner was: all any of them wanted to do was to watch the news and see what topics were developing. She felt terribly sick; her stomach was churning, and her mouth was increasingly dry. How on earth was she going to talk coherently for the cameras?

"Lovely colour, your suit," said the girl chattily. "I always think red's so cheerful. Your skin's lovely," she added, "really young-looking."

"Well," said Martha, "it is quite. Young I mean. But thank you anyway."

Maybe the town planners were better than this, after all.

She checked her mobile: there was still nothing from Ed.

"Oh wow!" said Jocasta. "Gideon, guess what—"

"What, darling? You couldn't tie this for me, could you?"

"Course. I always had to do it for Nick."

He was off to a dinner: an all-male dinner, he told her, regretfully; there was no way she could come.

"That's all right. The little woman will be waiting for you when you get home."

She was working very hard on being a good wife.

"In bed, I hope, wearing nothing but your perfume, Marilyn-style?"

"Not that nightie?"

"I prefer nothing."

"Well—depends how late you are . . . There." She considered him, his large powerful body in the perfectly tailored dinner jacket, his tanned face, his brilliant blue eyes, and smiled. "I could really fancy you in that getup, you know. I mean *really* fancy you. Come here . . ."

She reached up to him, kissed him very hard on the mouth. "Why don't you take it all off again, and come to bed with me instead?"

"Darling, I can't. I'm so sorry."

"Oh well. Actually, I just discovered Martha's on *Question Time* tonight. Martha Hartley, you know—I want to watch her."

"Oh, really? I would think she'd be good; she's very articulate and composed . . . Darling, I must go. Sorry. Enjoy your programme."

"Yes, I will, thanks. Love you."

"I love you, too." He disappeared; then she heard his footsteps coming back. He opened the door and looked at her. "Never leave me, will you?" His expression was very serious, very intense. "Never."

"I never will," she said. "I promise."

Nick was beginning to feel frustrated. So far he'd been listening to Janet for an hour and a half and he'd got nothing from her but a lot of rather dull policy statements and a bit of banging on about her personal hobby horses, like NHS reforms.

"We have to get rid of the managers," she was saying now, slightly pink-faced—she had begun to drink during the main course and had actually had rather a lot. Nick was surprised. Usually, in his experience, she was virtually teetotal.

"I tell you, Nick, those managers are a far bigger obstacle to NHS efficiency than lack of funds. And Centre Forward's policy of less interference would extend above all to that sort of thing."

"Yes," said Nick. "Absolutely."

"Bob trained as a paediatrician," she said after a pause, "as you probably know."

"I do. Why did he leave it, go into industry?"

"Because of the system," said Janet, "and there must be hundreds, probably thousands, like him who couldn't stand it any longer. Of course it's not quite industry, Nick, it's pharmaceutical research." She paused for just a beat, not allowing Nick to respond. "Could you excuse me for a moment? I just need to find the loo."

Nick was looking out of the window when she got back. Her demeanour appeared to have totally changed, she looked purposeful, brisk, almost excited.

"Anyway," she said, sitting down again, picking up her glass, "that's enough of the politics. How would you like a bit of gossip?"

"I'd love it. Political gossip?"

"Well you could say that. It concerns a politician. An up-and-coming one. It's quite a story . . ."

· · ·

"Kate, you up there?" It was Juliet's voice.

"Yeah, in my room."

Juliet came in; she was carrying her violin case. "You ought to watch *Question Time* tonight. That woman's on, Martha Hartley, the one who was in the paper the week before you, in the fashion feature. It'd be interesting, wouldn't it, watching someone you knew?"

"Well, I don't exactly know her."

"I thought you said she was at the party."

"She was, but I never spoke to her. She was in the disco and then Gran looked after her when she fainted. I really didn't like her; she was well up herself. But yeah, let's watch it."

"I will if I can. But I've got a lot of practice to do first."

"Juliet," said Kate, "you are just so much too good to be true."

"Oh, come on," said Ed to the girl in reception. "I only want to say good luck."

"I'm sorry, it's more than my job's worth. No one's allowed in without a pass."

"Well, you could give me a pass."

"No, I couldn't. I really can't do that," she said, "but I will get a message to her. If you write her a note, I'll take it to her. OK?"

"It'd be better than nothing," said Ed, and then, seeing her face, "I mean, it'd be great. Really cool. Thank you." He had just started to write when he heard his name.

"Ed! What are you doing here?"

It was someone he'd been at uni with. Judging from his uniform—T-shirt, jeans, clipboard, and headset—he was clearly some kind of technician.

Ed explained his problem and the guy grinned.

"Tell you what I can do," he said. "I'll get a bigger sheet of paper."

They were in position now, sitting at the table. Martha was at the end, two away from David Dimbleby, next to a rotund Tory. He was being very nice to her; so was Dimbleby, they were all trying to put her at her ease, but she felt dreadfully sick. But there was no escape and there was still nothing from Ed. What had happened to him, for God's sake? Probably decided not to come after all: well, she deserved it.

"Right, we're going to put a dummy question to each of you, to get the sound levels," said the floor manager. "Martha, you first. How do you rate your chances tonight?"

"On a scale of one to ten, zero," she said, and everyone laughed; she felt briefly better. And then much worse again.

What happened if she couldn't think of anything to say at all? Some completely wild card might come up. The researchers were moving about amongst the audience now, getting questions, deciding which ones to take; these were written down, but that was only for Dimbleby's benefit—and he kept the paper covered, so that the people on either side of him couldn't get a preview. The first the panel knew was literally when the questions were put, and it was, she had been warned (again by Janet), often hard to hear.

She took deep breaths, trying to calm her heaving stomach.

And then she heard one of the cameramen calling her name, very quietly.

"Martha. Over here."

She looked at him, at camera two or whatever it was: he was grinning at her, and gesturing just below the camera. There was a large hand-lettered sign there.

"Hi, Martha. Go for it! Ed xxx."

She laughed aloud—and suddenly everything seemed much better.

"Nick! Why on earth are you ringing me at this time of night? I'm in bed. What? No, alone. He's out. No, of course you can't, I'd be in the divorce courts— What? WHAT? My God, Nick. Yes, of course. Come at once. I'll let you in. Sure, bye."

Clio was in the kitchen when her mobile rang; Fergus had demanded a cup of cocoa before they went to bed. Who on earth would ring at this time of night?

"Hello? Jocasta! No, I'm making cocoa. Oh, shut up. We don't all live on champagne and— No, I'm listening. What? WHAT? My God, Jocasta. My God!"

An hour later, she and Fergus had arrived at Kensington Palace Gardens; Gideon was still out.

"I'm glad you're here, actually," Jocasta said, hugging them both. "Me being alone in the house with Nick is just a tad compromising. Cocoa? Or something even more exciting? Just look at the two of you, I think it's so wonderful!"

"Cocoa will do fine," said Fergus, smiling at her, "and we think it's wonderful too. And it's all because of you."

"Aw, shucks," said Jocasta. "Now come on, Nick's in the drawing room. I'll go and get the cocoa."

She came in with a tray; she looked absurdly out of place in the vast room, Clio thought, with its heavy brocade curtains, its embossed wallpaper, its chandeliers, its Antique (with a capital A) furniture, dressed in nothing but an oversize T-shirt, padding across the (no doubt priceless) Indian carpet in her bare feet. It somehow seemed to sum up the whole marriage; she didn't belong here, it didn't suit her. But then—Gideon did, she told herself firmly. He suited her perfectly. And she suited him. That was what mattered . . .

"Well, all I can say, Nick," said Jocasta, putting the tray down, "is that Martha was very lucky Janet chose to tell *you*. Not someone from the *Sun*. Or the *Mirror*. It'd be in tomorrow's paper, no messing. I s'pose it's because we—I mean the *Sketch* had the exclusive on the Baby Bianca story. What did you say to her, anyway? I suppose you've got it on tape?"

"Yes. In my pocket, right here." He patted it. "I must make a duplicate before something happens. I just thanked her for giving me the story, said I wasn't sure what would happen next, and legged it as fast as I could. I was terrified she'd change her mind, ask for the tape back. Not that it would have made any difference, but she's obviously a bit deranged."

"Is she?" asked Clio. "Why do you say that?"

"It's a very odd thing to do. If she wanted to discredit that party of hers, she's going the right way about it—it would just about finish it off, all the scandals it's had lately. Incidentally, I'm pretty bloody sure she was behind the leak about the polls. I saw her in what you might call a compromising situation. Yet she talks about the party as if it was another child she adores. I don't understand it. Anyway, what do we do next? What do I, in particular, do next? Chris would have my balls if he knew I was sitting on this. And she could be talking to the *Sun* right now. I could have just been a rehearsal. God, what a mess."

"We have to tell Martha," said Jocasta, "absolutely have to."

"So what do we do?" asked Nick. "Ring her, say oh hi, Martha, nice performance, and we know you're Baby Bianca's mother."

"And there's another thing," said Jocasta. "Who's going to tell Kate?"

"Well, Martha must," said Clio, "of course. My God. No wonder the poor girl fainted."

"What poor girl?" said Jocasta. "Martha? You're not saying you're sorry for her, I hope?"

"Of course I'm sorry for her. Just think what she's been going through for the last sixteen years. It's one of the saddest stories I ever heard."

"Me too," said Fergus. Jocasta looked at him thoughtfully.

"This relationship with Clio is turning you soft, Fergus Trehearn. Now come on, who's going to make this call?"

Martha was half asleep in the car, her head on Ed's shoulder, when her mobile rang.

"Oh, let's just ignore it," she said sleepily. "It won't be anyone I want to speak to. Probably Jack, having yet another orgasm."

Kirkland had already rung twice, the first time to congratulate her in general terms, the second to say how brilliantly he felt she had put the party philosophy over. Chad, Eliot, and her parents had also called.

"Yeah, OK. Speaking of orgasms, I hope you're going to be a bit more alert than this when we get home." Martha turned to him, pulled his face down to hers, and kissed him with great thoroughness.

"That's on account. A sort of down payment. I feel very alert in the relevant department."

They had discussed staying in Birmingham, but Ed said he had to be in London first thing. "So what do you think I'm doing?" Martha had said indignantly. "Sleeping in?"

"Only thing is—my car overheated all the way up. Hate to drive it down now."

"We can both go in the Beeb car. We can drive up and get yours on Saturday. Oh, no, I'll be in Binsmow. Well, Sunday, then. No, I've got a garden party. Sunday night, maybe? No—"

"How about dawn on Wednesday week?"

"You're on."

"You were fantastic, you know," Ed said now. "Really, really good."

"I wouldn't have been," she said, "without your lovely message. Oh, Ed, what on earth was I thinking of, keeping you away from me all this time?"

"If you can't answer that," said Ed, "there's no hope for any of us. When are you going to tell me the reason?"

"I'm not." They reached Canary Wharf just before two. "I'm sorry," she said, as they walked in the door, "I just absolutely have to have a shower. I was sweating like a pig under those lights."

"The cool Ms. Hartley sweating? I don't believe it. All right. Tell you what, I'll join you. How would that be?"

"Heavenly," said Martha. They stood together in the thudding water; Ed began to kiss her, slowly, almost lazily. Martha began to soar; soar into a sweet dark place, pierced with brilliance and promise. Why had she denied herself this for so long, how could she have borne it? Ed's hands were on her buttocks, holding her against him; she could feel him hard and very strong, and her own response to him, liquid and longing. He lifted her slightly, so that she was on him. "I love you," he was saying through the kissing, through the water, and almost before she was ready, it came; she felt herself suddenly, swiftly, gather and tauten and then release in an explosion she could almost see, it was so bright and strong.

"I love you too," she said, smiling, leaning gently against him now. "I love you so much."

"Good," he said, "you've come to your senses. Now let's go to bed."

He wrapped her tenderly in a towel and half carried her to the bed. And unwrapped the towel again, and lay, looking at her, at her face, ravished with weariness and sex, at her body, her neat, tough little body, her mound, perfectly waxed. "There's just one thing wrong with you, Martha Hartley," he said, wiping her face on the sleeve of his bathrobe.

"Only one?"

"Only one. Your pubes. I know you like minimal, but there's a time and place for everything—and right there and as soon as possible, I'd personally like more of a bush. Will you grow it for me? Prove that you love me?"

"I will," she said. "If that's all it takes."

At that moment the landline went, and the answering machine cut in.

· · ·

"At last," said Jocasta, "she said she only just got back. She obviously had someone with her."

Fergus had left. It was agreed that he should, that this was best handled by the three of them. Gideon had come home, and gone straight up to bed. If he was curious at the presence of his wife's ex-lover and her best friend in his house, he didn't show it. "Enjoy your party," was all he said.

"I'm sorry, Gideon, I'll explain everything in the morning."

"Fine. Good night all of you." He left with a wave, and his oddly sweet smile.

"I want to come," said Ed.

"No, Ed, you can't. I'm sorry. It's too . . . complicated. But I will be back, I swear, and I'll tell you everything then."

"All right." He sighed. "But I don't like you driving. You're exhausted, you're upset—"

"I'll be all right. Promise."

"Suppose I drive you over, wait outside?"

"No, Ed. I might be hours."

"I've waited weeks for you already," he said. "What's a few more hours? Please, Martha."

She looked at him. "All right. If you really want to."

"I really want to. And I don't mind how long you are."

Jocasta opened the door; she had put on some jeans under her oversized T-shirt and looked about seventeen. She smiled at Martha.

"Hi. Come in." She peered out at the car. "Is that someone with you?"

"Yes, but he's waiting outside," said Martha. "I don't want him with us while we talk." Jocasta led the way into the drawing room; Clio had made a jug of coffee.

"Hi, Martha. How are you? You were so good tonight."

"Thanks. First and last time, I guess." She managed a cool, slightly sad little smile.

"I'm sorry about this, Martha," said Nick, holding out his hand rather formally.

She took it. "Not your fault." They all sat down again.

"Look," Martha said suddenly, "this is a bit . . . hard for me. I don't really want to talk to all of you at once."

"That's fine," said Jocasta. "We're only all here because—well, because Nick knew I'd be able to get hold of you. And it was obviously urgent. God knows who else she might have told."

"It's not in the other papers," said Clio quickly. "We went to Waterloo and got them, so we've got a few hours at least. Days hopefully."

"But it's got to happen, I suppose? Got to come out?" Martha sounded vulnerable at last.

"I would say so, yes. I'm so sorry."

"No, no, it's very nice of you to try to help, I haven't exactly been very friendly to you."

"Well, we know why now," said Jocasta.

"Anyway," said Clio, "we felt that, perhaps, you might find it easiest to talk to me. I'm a doctor, Hippocratic oath and all that."

"Actually," said Martha, "you were right. I think I would like to start with you, Clio. If you others don't mind."

"Of course not," said Jocasta. "We'll be in the kitchen if you want us."

"I cannot believe I've been so stupid," said Martha suddenly, "telling that bloody woman. I mean—why her?"

"It was at the party, wasn't it?" said Clio. "You were obviously very distressed. Ill, actually, I'd say. And you had just been confronted by it all. Literally."

"I suppose so. But—oh God. Oh God, oh God . . ." She dropped her head into her hands and began to cry. Clio went over and sat next to her, put her arm round her.

"I'm so sorry," Clio said. "Really, I couldn't be sorrier. I can't imagine how you must be feeling. But we do all want to help. We're totally on your side."

"I know," said Martha, pulling a handkerchief out of her pocket. "And I do appreciate it. I'm sorry. Sorry I wasn't more friendly, Clio, so sorry."

"Don't be ridiculous. Look, why don't you try telling me about it? When you're ready. There's no hurry."

And Martha sat there with Clio, in the quiet drawing room, already growing light in the midsummer dawn, and started.

Because she had done it just a few weeks earlier, it was easier than it might have been, but she still had to force every word out of herself, the painful, difficult words. It was a bit like giving birth again, she thought, giving birth to Kate, and she couldn't believe she was releasing them: the words she had kept inside her head, buried deep in her consciousness for sixteen years. Telling of the dreadful days, weeks in Bangkok, in the awful, airless room, the terrible boredom, passing the time by walking, walking miles and miles round the hot, dirty, stinking city, and reading, reading— "I got some of the cheap travellers' used paperbacks."

"So, how long were you there?"

"About two and a half months. It was horrendous at first; I thought I'd go mad. But actually, it got better. I worked myself into a routine, just took one day at a time. I went to the markets a lot, I stayed downtown, on the left bank of the river, there's a kind of ghetto of guesthouses, really cheap. Anyway, I found a room there, without windows—you can imagine how cheap they are—and ate off those street stalls. I tried to eat properly, I realised that mattered, but I must have been spending about a pound a day altogether, and I just waited, waited for the baby to be born. I—well, I sort of hoped I could have it there, by myself."

"By yourself! You thought you could have a baby all by yourself?"

"Well, yes. I mean, people do. I kept thinking about a girl I'd read about in the paper once, who had a baby in her bedroom while her parents watched television downstairs, they had no idea, and then she took it out and left it on a park bench and went back to the house and went to bed. I thought if she could do that, then so could I. I'd bought a medical book in Australia, so I knew exactly what to expect. I knew all about cutting the cord and everything. I bought some really big, sharp scissors and some strong string—"

"Martha, this is a terrible story! God, how brave you must be. And you must have felt so terrible, so alone."

"I did, yes. But I had to manage. There was a lovely old Thai woman I made friends with; she was so kind and she used to give me massages and rub my back and everything. In return I taught her English. I thought she'd help me if—well, things went wrong. And of course, there was no way she could ask awkward questions."

"But what did you plan to do with the baby, Martha? Afterwards? What did you think would happen to it? In a place like Bangkok?"

Martha met her eyes with great difficulty.

"I . . . I decided to take it to a hospital. I investigated them all—you'd have thought I was going to have it there—and finally decided on the Bangkok Christian Hospital. I thought I could leave it there, by the main door, and it would be found by someone, and be really well looked after. And then probably adopted by someone European. I'm sorry, Clio, I can see you think it's appalling of me, but you have to understand how desperate I was. It wasn't really a baby to me. It was something dreadful that I'd done, that I had to . . . to put behind me. Literally. I had to have it, and then leave it behind. So I could go home, and everything would be all right again and I'd be safe."

"Yes. Yes, I see."

"And the baby just wouldn't come. After all those weeks, it wouldn't come. I tried everything, I took castor oil and walked miles and jumped off the bed, and sat in a hot bath, and the old woman gave me an enema, and lots of herbs and stuff, but it wouldn't come and I had to get home. I was completely out of money, completely. I could never have got another ticket, the cheap flights were all booked anyway for weeks ahead. So I thought, Well, I can't stay here forever, I'll just have to go and sort something out when I get back. Maybe go to a hospital somewhere in the north of England—I just wasn't thinking logically at all. And then, it started on the plane. I crawled off it, and headed for a lavatory, and saw this room on the way in marked Staff Only. It had cleaning stuff in it, and a sink, and just room for me to lie down—and I had her there. I just did. It was . . . well, quite awful. But I didn't have any choice. If anyone had known, I'd have been taken off to hospital and I'd have had to give my name, my parents would have been told . . ."

"Martha, couldn't you possibly have told your parents?" Clio's voice was very gentle. "Had the baby adopted after that, fine, but at least told them, got some help?"

"No. I couldn't. Well, I can see now, that just possibly I could have done, but then— Clio, you don't know what Binsmow's like. You can't sneeze without everyone knowing, and discussing where you got the germs from. I was the vicar's daughter and I'd done the most awful thing a girl could do. I'd have brought disgrace on them."

"You're talking like a Victorian novel," said Clio, and smiled for the first time. "Bringing disgrace on them? Martha, for God's sake, this was the 1980s."

"But I would have done. The whole parish respected my father so, he would never, ever have recovered. I honestly believe that he'd have had to move away, he could never have lived it down. I was the star of the family, you see, they were so proud of me, getting into Bristol, getting straight A's in my A levels, doing law, all his parishioners were so impressed, how could I have failed them, said, Sorry, I'm not what you thought, I'm not your darling innocent daughter, I've done something terrible, I've had a baby. And I did think of it like that, as something terrible I'd done—"

"So how did you feel? When you left her?"

"I rested for a bit, and—and cleaned myself up, and then I thought, Well, that's it, it's over, I've done it. And I held her for a little while and then wrapped her up very carefully in a sheet and a blanket I'd bought for her in Bangkok, and laid her in a sort of trolley basket thing with towels in it. And then I went and sat on a bench just opposite, and waited until someone found her. I was very worried because I'd somehow not thought to get her any nappies; I thought she'd pee on the blankets. After all that, and I was worried about a bit of pee. Anyway, someone did find her, some Asian woman cleaner, and she came out calling for help and there was a lot of fuss, of course, and people coming and going and then a police-woman just took her away."

"Didn't you feel—upset?"

"Honestly? No. Not then. Just relief. I thought, She's safe now, and it's over, and that's all I felt. I'm sure you must think I'm dreadful, but I didn't feel sad, or any of the things you might expect. Later on, yes, but not then."

"I don't think you're dreadful," Clio said. "I'm just so sad for you. And full of admiration, that you could be so brave."

"I told you, I had to be. And then I just thought, Now I can go home. Only of course, I couldn't, not straightaway, I didn't dare, my parents might have noticed something. I wasn't feeling very well. I was . . . was bleeding quite a lot. So I went into the ladies', and had a shower—that was so nice—and then I lay down on some seats upstairs and slept for ages. I felt quite happy, actually. I knew the baby was safe, and that was all that mattered. She wasn't my worry anymore. And that was when it be-gan: I just knew I had to put her out of my head. I've read lots of articles since, about women who have given up their babies at birth and even do what I did. And they go into denial, complete denial. They don't allow it into their lives anymore, they block it out, it's just something that hap-pened, that they've put right away from them. That's what I did."

"Yes, I see. I have heard that. So when did you go home?"

"After a couple of days—well, four, actually. When . . . when I seemed to be all right. I went to a YMCA hostel in Hayes; I had just enough money, and I slept a lot and looked after myself as best I could."

"Didn't you get milk?" asked Clio very gently.

"Yes, I did." Tears welled up again. "I wasn't expecting that. It was awful. That did make me cry. I kept looking at it, I didn't know what it was at first, and thinking, This was meant for her. It was horrible. And quite painful. I bought some pad things at Boots and stuffed them in my bra. After a few days it dried up."

"And your parents didn't suspect anything?"

"Why should they? I'd put on some weight, of course, but plenty of people do when they're travelling. I'd bought lots of kaftan things, and those fisherman's trousers, so I wore them. I was all right. I was very tired, but that was to be expected."

"And what about letters, didn't they want some kind of address all that time?"

"Yes, and I gave them the poste restante in Bangkok. Told them I was doing some more travelling in Thailand. I told them I ran out of money, so I couldn't go to America. And I'd done enough to satisfy them. Singapore, Australia, Thailand—it sounds a lot to people who've never left England. Quite enough to fill a year.

"Anyway, I knew I'd done the right thing. And every day I felt safer. I got a sort of high just from doing it, getting away with it. And I knew she was all right, because I read the papers."

"Did you keep the papers?"

She hesitated. "No, I didn't. I know that sounds awful, but it was all part of her not being anything to do with me. I couldn't let myself think about her, because then I'd acknowledge her."

"Yes, I see," said Clio carefully. "And how did you cope? Didn't you feel unhappy at all?"

"Well, in a way, yes. But I just buried it and buried it. And got on with my life. Worked terribly hard, did well. It helped. And developed into the control freak you see before you. But all alone, in private, I'd remember her quite suddenly, remember what she looked like, remember holding her, specially on her birthday—that's always hard—but even that somehow wasn't real. It was like something that had happened to someone else, not me. But over the years, if anything upset me, it would—sometimes, not always—come back to her. I would start crying and go back to that time. I did cry a lot at the beginning. I felt very . . . strange. Very confused. Funnily enough, she never got any older than about one. Not in my head. She stayed tiny, I never grew her up."

"Didn't you long to tell someone?"

"No, I was terrified of telling someone. I was terrified of getting that close to anyone. I had very few friends, always. Men were a bit safer. It wasn't the sort of thing you'd tell a man."

"I suppose. Oh, Martha. What a story."

"It is quite, isn't it? And then all these extraordinary coincidences that have brought us together. That was such a terrible day—I was out running and there she was in the paper: Abandoned Baby Bianca. I did go a bit . . . strange then."

"And now?"

"Now I don't know," she said. "I really don't know what now. I mean, it's the end of my life as I know it."

"Martha, no it isn't!"

"Yes, it is. Look at me, a highly paid lawyer. It's a criminal offence, you know. Abandoning a baby. You can get ten years in jail for it. And worse than that, I'm a prospective parliamentary candidate. For Binsmow, for God's sake. Where my father's the vicar. You have to sign something saying there's nothing in your past that would cause your party any difficulty or embarrassment, you know."

"Yes," Clio said quietly, "I can see you're right. Martha, the father—did he ever have any idea?"

"No," she said quickly, "absolutely none. I couldn't possibly have told him. Not possibly."

"Because?"

"I don't want to go on with this," she said. "Sorry."

"All right. But what about Kate, Martha? She's going to have to be told."

"I know. I know. How on earth is that going to be done? Who's going to tell her?"

"Well, I thought you should," said Clio, very gently. "You're the only person who can make her understand."

Martha stared at her. "I really don't think I can do that."

Chapter 35

· · · · ·

"Poor you. Poor, poor you."

Ed's voice was very gentle. Taking courage from it, Martha forced herself to look at his face. It was tender, concerned, there was no judgement, no shock, even; it was as if she had told him someone dear to her had died. She supposed, in a way, that was right: the cool, efficient, hypersuccessful Martha had died, and in her place was someone flawed and very frightened, someone who had done something so shocking and shameful that she had kept it hidden for sixteen years.

"You're going to have to tell me what to do, Ed," she said. "For the first time I have no idea. No idea at all."

"I'll try," he said. "I'll try very hard. I'd like to meet your friends, talk to them."

"Of course. They're being so good to me. I really don't deserve it, I was vile to them."

"I tell you what's the first thing you should do," he said. "You should stop crucifying yourself. You haven't committed a crime."

"Ed, that's exactly what I've done. I told you. A crime with a ten-year prison sentence."

"Yes, OK, I hear what you say. But it isn't really a crime, not morally. You knew she was all right, you saw her safely taken away, you knew she was being cared for by people who knew what they were doing. After that, you got on with your life. Calling it a crime is just a technicality."

"Ed! I think you're a bit prejudiced. How do you think the press are going to present this?"

"Fuck the press."

"No, you can't say that. They're going to call me a harridan, a monster, a ruthless bitch. That's what people will take in. What kind of woman abandons her child and never goes near it again? Someone kind and caring? I don't think so."

"I think you should go and see her," he said.

"Kate? I can't, Ed. Maybe when she knows, maybe when she's got used to the idea, but—"

"No, not her. The woman. Janet whatever-her-name-is. Find out what she might do next, if your friend doesn't run the story. He must be a great guy," he added. "Most hacks'd have it out on the street by now."

"He is. He's a sweetheart. I always liked him."

"A sweetheart, eh? Not sure I like that."

"Oh, Ed. No one's as much of a sweetheart as you."

She looked at him and smiled tenderly; he was clearly shocked. He was only twenty-three, with very little experience of life. How could he be expected to cope with all this? Then she thought of herself at twenty-three, a first in law under her belt, working as a trainee solicitor in one of London's finest firms, all after coming through almost unbelievable trauma: they were obviously two of a kind, she and Ed.

"I love you," she said simply. "I really, really love you . . ."

"Good God," said Gideon, "the poor child. That is a terrible story, Jocasta."

"I know. Isn't it? Doing what she did, all alone . . ." She shuddered. "I'd rather have died. Well, I probably would have died of terror."

"No you wouldn't," he said. "You'd have done it because you had to. You're a lot braver than you think you are, you know. Now then, let's think what's best to be done for Martha. I have to say, it's a very nasty situation. Very nasty indeed."

"I know. I keep thinking of all the people she ought to tell. Before they hear anyway, in tabloid speak."

"Young Nicholas wouldn't do tabloid speak."

"No, of course not. But the others'll pick it up and run with it. I can see it now. 'The ruthless career woman who abandoned her baby' or 'Baby Bianca's Heartless Mother.' I mean, it doesn't help that Kate's so bloody famous. It's a gift as a story, you must admit."

"Oh, I admit it. Pollock will murder Nick if he finds out. Now, this is only idle curiosity, but has anyone asked Martha if the father knows?"

"No. I don't suppose she has the faintest idea where he is."

"Or even who?"

"Oh, I think she'd know who, Gideon. Martha isn't a sleeper around."

"You didn't think she'd abandon a child until today, did you? You of all people, Jocasta, know how unpredictable people are."

"I know. But I bet she knows. I'd put quite a lot of money on it."

"None of mine, please. Now, I have a fancy she should go and confront Mrs. Frean. If she can find the courage."

Jocasta's mobile went; she looked at it.

"Hi, Martha, how are you doing? What? That's interesting. Gideon said the same. Hold on a minute." She looked at Gideon. "Ed, Martha's boyfriend, says the same thing."

"Then he must be a very bright fellow. A man after my own heart. I wonder if he'd go with her?"

"I'm sure he would. Martha, would Ed go with you?"

"He says he will."

"OK," said Jocasta. "Go for it."

"Martha dear, hello. How lovely to hear from you. I meant to call you last night, you were marvellous. Absolutely marvellous. Congratulations."

Martha was not as surprised by this as she might have been. She was beginning to get Janet's measure.

"Thank you, Janet. I wondered if . . . if I could come and see you."

"When did you have in mind? I'm very busy today and then, of course, it's the weekend. Monday maybe?"

"But it's awfully urgent."

"Really? Well, it'll have to wait, I'm afraid. I'm so sorry."

"But Janet, I—that is—don't you know what it's about?"

"I have no idea. But I really can't see you this weekend. There's no question of it. I won't even be here. I'm sorry."

Martha looked at Ed. "Now what do we do?"

Janet put down the phone and went in search of her husband; he was sitting out in the garden, reading the *Daily Telegraph* and drinking a large mug of coffee.

"Bob, I did tell you, didn't I, that I had to be out of town on Saturday night?"

"I don't know. Anyway, it doesn't matter, we haven't got anything on. Party business, I presume?"

"Of course. Charm offensive has to continue but—you can cope with the children, can you? It's Kirsty's weekend off."

"I usually do," he said dryly.

Martha had broken one of her own unbreakable laws and called in sick. She actually spoke to Paul Quenell, who was so excited by her performance on *Question Time* that she felt he would have given her the whole week off, had she asked.

"Of course, Martha. You must be exhausted. Splendid they mentioned Wesley by name. Well done. You're a clever girl. Enjoy the weekend, see you on Monday."

Martha put the phone down, wondering if she would ever see him again. Once, she supposed, when she resigned.

She felt oddly calm. It was ten in the morning; Ed was asleep, having called in sick himself. She had a shower, then wandered round her flat tidying it, flicking through magazines, organising her laundry, and staring out of the window. Mostly, she stared out of the window. And thought about Kate and what on earth she could say to her and how.

Clio had also called in sick; she had slept for a few hours, but at ten o'clock she was in the kitchen, hoping to find Jocasta. Gideon was there, in a towelling robe; he smiled at her.

"Hello, my darling girl. Excuse my rather informal attire; I've been having my swim. You should try my mechanical pool, it's very clever. Tedious, but clever. How are you? Tired, I expect."

"Not too bad," said Clio. "Is Jocasta about?"

"I'm here." Jocasta came into the kitchen; she looked rather pale.

"Jocasta, I've been thinking," said Clio. "If Martha agrees, I think you should tell Kate. First off, that is. I mean, she doesn't know Martha; it'd be the most awful shock. And she's so fond of you. You won't mind how she reacts, whereas Martha might. Kate's probably going to be very stroppy, very hurt."

"I rather agree with that," said Gideon. "Jocasta, what do you think?"

"I think so too, I'm afraid. The only other thing would be for me to tell her mother and for her to tell Kate."

"It would come better from you," said Clio. "Apart from anything else, you know Martha. But probably her mother should be there. And her father. I don't think they'll help, but they'd be outraged if you told her first."

"God," said Jocasta, "I don't like this!"

Nick was walking through Central Lobby when he saw Janet.

"Look," she said, "our conversation last night—you haven't run the story today, I see."

"No, I needed to do some more research on it."

"Well, don't leave it too long. I'd hate to see it wasted and I'm sure the *Sun* would love it."

"I'm sure they would. Obviously there's a degree of urgency. But I must talk to Martha—and Chris Pollock is the final arbiter."

"Yes. Well, keep in touch."

"Kate darling, this is Jocasta. Look, I wondered—what are you doing today?"

"Nothing, really. Going shopping with Bernie. Seeing Nat later. Why?"

"I . . . thought I might come and see you."

"Cool. But you don't want to come to Ealing. It's not exactly hopping. Why don't I come into town, see you?"

"The thing is, Kate, I'd quite like your mum and dad to be there."

"What? Oh, I get it. It's about my contract, yeah? Is Fergus coming?"

"Oh, I think so," said Jocasta. "Yes. Look, I . . . we'll be over in about an hour. Is that OK?"

"Dad won't be here."

"Is your mum there now?"

"Yeah. Do you want to speak to her?"

"Yes, please."

"Fine. See you later."

Never had that irritating phrase had so much menace in it.

Helen felt physically sick. After all these years, the worst was going to happen: Kate's mother was going to become reality, no longer a distant, shadowy

· 451 ·

figure who could be warded off, talked away, but a person, a dreadfully dangerous person, who could come and claim her daughter. Not literally, of course, but emotionally. The mystery that had hurt Kate so badly for so many years was about to be solved. She would know what her mother looked like, sounded like, she could talk to her, ask her questions, find out why she had done what she had done. This woman would walk in and take her rightful place in Kate's life and she and Jim would be relegated to theirs—second best, understudies, caretakers.

How could she bear it, if Kate wanted to live with her? If Kate fell in love with her, declared her everything she had ever wanted? Helen had often thought that the most dreadful grief possible would be the death of a child; this seemed to her to have echoes of that.

Jocasta had given her no details, only said she knew who Kate's mother was, and that she wanted Helen and Jim to be there when she told her. She was such a nice girl, Jocasta, Helen thought: how badly they had misjudged her.

Jim was on his way home, had said he would be there within the hour; Jocasta said she would wait until he was there before arriving herself.

"Otherwise Kate will start pestering me. I won't be far away, just ring me on my mobile."

"You're not . . . not bringing, you know, *her* with you?" Helen had said, her voice shaky, and no, Jocasta had said, there would be plenty of time for that, when they had got used to the idea and were ready to meet her, "Although I don't think Kate will want to wait for long."

Helen was sure she wouldn't . . .

"Why are they taking so long?" said Martha. She was white-faced, her eyes haunted. "What are they doing?"

"Martha," said Ed, "try not to be so ridiculous. I'd say Jocasta has only been there half an hour and it's not a conversation she can have quickly. Two more hours and I'd say you could start to worry. Right now, I think we should go for a walk."

"A walk!"

"Yes, a walk. You know, one leg after the other, move along the street, that sort of thing. You can take your mobile, you won't miss anything. Come on. Let's go."

Helen went to the corner shop and bought some biscuits. They could have them with the coffee, she thought. As she came out, she saw Kate coming towards her; she was walking very quickly and she waved as she saw Helen. Maybe Jocasta was there already, Helen thought, maybe she had brought Her, maybe Jocasta had already introduced them, and she was coming to tell Helen about her, about this wonderful person who had come at last into her life.

"Hi, Mum. Would you mind if I got Nat round? Thing is, he's quite interested in this contract, he made some really good points about it."

Did she mind? Did she? Probably not. Nat had been part of the family for the past few weeks, and she was very fond of him—he was oddly gentle and thoughtful, might even help ease the emotional tension.

"No, I wouldn't mind," she said.

"Cool. Thanks. You all right, Mum? You look a bit tense."

"No, I'm fine."

Kate put her arm through Helen's. "Mum, I'm sorry I got in such a strop about the contract. Very sorry. Nat said I shouldn't have, he said you were only trying to do your best for me, and of course he's right. He's often right. He's quite clever really, you know, under all that rubbish he talks about his dad and so on . . . Mum, you're crying, whatever is it?"

"Nothing," said Helen, smiling at her through her tears, "nothing at all. And it doesn't matter about you being in a strop, we understood. Oh, look, there's your father now. Go on in and put the kettle on, Kate, there's a good girl."

She watched her striding up the path on her long bare legs, her wild hair falling down her back, pushing the buttons on her mobile to summon Nat: and thought that this was the last time, the very last time Kate would be properly hers . . .

"So why didn't she come herself?" asked Kate. She was white and very shocked, sitting close to her mother, with Nat on her other side, holding her hand.

"I—we—"

"Who's we?"

"Me, and Clio and Martha herself, we all felt it best if I told you," said Jocasta. "You know me, you can yell your head off at me and I won't mind. And your mum and dad know me too. It just seemed more sensible."

Kate nodded. "So does she want to see me?"

"Kate, of course she does," said Jocasta, hoping devoutly this was true. "But she wants you to get used to the idea. I mean, she's a complete stranger to you, isn't she?"

"Yeah . . . Yeah, she is." She sat in silence for a moment, then: "What's she like, Jocasta? I mean, what sort of person is she?"

"I don't really know her either. When we were all your age, well, a bit older, we went travelling together, and I suppose we spent a week altogether in each other's company. Fast-forward sixteen years and I've met her about twice since. Very briefly."

"But do you like her?"

"Well, yes. I think so."

"And she's never told anyone at all?"

"No one at all. Except this madwoman, and that was at the party."

"But . . . had she seen about me in the paper?"

"Well, yes."

"So why the fuck didn't she come and see me then?" She was angry now, two spots of colour high on her cheeks.

"Kate, there's no need to swear," said Jim.

"Yes there is! She's a cow, a stupid fucking cow. I hate her! I hate her already. I didn't like her at the party, I thought she was right up her own arse, and now I like her a whole lot less. Seems to me the only reason she's come clean now is because she's got to. Because she's scared it'll all be in the papers. Not because she gives a toss about me, not because she wants to see me. Cow!" She pulled her hand free of Nat's, folded her arms across her chest. "Well, you can tell her I don't want to see her. Ever. You can tell her she's a stupid bitch, and I hate her."

"Kate," said Nat gently, his face troubled, "you can't hate someone you don't know."

"I don't need to know her. I hate her! I hate what she did to me—God, why did it have to be her?" She started to cry. Nat put his arm round her; she shook it off.

"I'm sorry, Kate," said Jocasta quietly, "so sorry. Look, why don't I go now, give you all a chance to talk about it. You've got my number, if you change your mind, Kate, decide you want to talk to Martha. It might make you feel differently, you know."

"I don't want to talk to her. I never will. Cow. Fucking cow. God!"

She stood up, started pacing up and down the room; they all sat silent, watching her, not knowing what to do. Finally Nat stood up, took her hand.

"Come on, Kate," he said, "let's go for a bit of a drive. OK with you, Mrs. Tarrant? I think it'll calm her down."

Helen nodded, and they watched him lead her out of the room, smiling at her encouragingly, saying, "That's right, come on, it'll be all right," as if she were a small child being led into school for the first time, or to the dentist. Finally Helen said, "That boy is an absolute treasure."

"He is indeed," said Jocasta. "Are you all right, Helen?"

"Yes, I'm fine, thank you. Absolutely fine."

"One thing," said Ed, as they walked along the street, "does the—the—well, does he know?"

"No," said Martha. "No, he has no idea."

"Did he then?"

"No. I never told him—anything."

"But you know who he was?"

"Ed—"

"Look," he said, and for the first time there was irritation, something raw in his attitude, "I've been OK so far. Totally on your side. I think I have a right to ask a few questions, don't you?"

"Of course you do. But I can't answer that one. I'm sorry."

"What, you don't know who it was?"

"I do know who it was. Yes. But I don't intend to talk about . . . about him. Ever."

There was a long silence. "Seems to me it means you don't trust me. Unless you're still in love with him, that is."

"I am not still in love with him. I never was in love with him. It was just—just something that happened. By the time I knew I was pregnant, I had no idea where he was."

"But now you do?"

She was silent.

"You do! For Christ's sake, Martha, don't you think you should tell him? Don't you think she'll want to know?"

"Who?"

"Who? The girl. Kate. Your daughter. God! This is beginning to get to me, Martha. Don't you think the poor little cow has a right to know who her dad is?"

"I don't know," she said. "Does she?"

"For fuck's sake," he said. "Look, I need to be on my own for a bit. Suddenly I can't cope with this. I'll see you later. I'll call you, OK?"

She watched him go, her eyes blurred with tears.

And wishing she could tell him.

She had been half asleep on the boat, coming back from Koh Tao to Koh Samui. She had gone there for a couple of days, having been told it was the most beautiful of all the islands, that she must see it. She had been told that about most of them, but had been half inclined this time to agree; a white-rimmed jewel in the dazzling sea, electricity which only ran in the evenings, and huts so basic they made the ones on Samui seem quite luxurious. The girl she had gone over with had stayed to do some scuba diving; Martha's money didn't extend to that, and ravishing as the island was, it didn't take hold of her heart as Koh Samui had.

The boat seemed unusually rickety, even by Thai standards—very basic, with no toilet on board. She slung her rucksack onto the huge pile with all the others, found a quiet corner, and settled down with her book. She had found it on the secondhand shelf, at the dock at Mae Hat, the first half of *Hitchhiker's Guide to the Galaxy*; it was the custom to rip books in two, to save rucksack space, and leave behind what you'd read. It could sometimes be months before you could find the second half.

The trip was quite long, over three hours, and a wind had come up. Martha, who was a good sailor, had drifted off to sleep, lulled by the rise and fall of the boat; she woke once to see her rucksack tumble onto the mailbags on the lower deck. She reached over and tried to haul it back up, but she couldn't reach it, and went back to her corner. They were about thirty minutes from the jetty at Hat Bophut, when she heard his voice.

"Hi, Martha! I only just realised it was you. Your hair's different."

She struggled to sit up, slightly dazed, and saw him, smiling down at her. "Hi! Oh, the braids? Yes, I had it done on the beach. Were you on Koh Tao?"

She wasn't remotely surprised to see him; that was the whole thing about travelling. People came into your life, you became involved with them, and then you parted, to meet up with them again months later, in an entirely different place.

"Yeah. Been diving. You?"

"No, just snorkelling. Lovely though. Then back to Big Buddha for a few days and then I've got a vague arrangement with some girl to move over to Phuket."

"It's lovely there. And Krabi. And green sea, rather than blue. You been north yet?"

"Yes, it was amazing."

"Isn't it? Can I sit here?"

She nodded; he smiled, slung his rucksack down on top of Martha's and the mail pile, and offered her a cigarette. Martha shook her head.

"So, where are you going now?" she asked.

"Up to Bangkok for a few days. Girl I knew quite well was in a scooter accident on Koh Phangan, pretty badly hurt, she was taken up there. Here, Martha, can you smell burning?"

"Only your cigarette."

"No, it's not that. I'm sure I— Christ! Look, look at that smoke!"

She looked; there was a thick grey cloud pouring out of the engine room. Nobody seemed terribly concerned; the guy who was driving the boat smiled and there was a complete absence of anyone else who might have been considered crew. The smoke grew thicker.

"Shit!" he said. "I don't like this. Jesus, I'm right too, bloody flames now!"

Martha was suddenly very frightened. These boats, old and battered, usually had one lifebelt, at the most.

She looked towards land, at the comforting white curve of the beach, and the stern towering figure of Big Buddha, and felt better. They were surely near enough to swim to shore if necessary. She said so.

"No way, Martha, that's at least a mile and this is shark territory. Shit, shit, shit!"

Everyone was beginning to panic now, pointing at the flames, shouting at the captain, who was continuing to steer his boat doggedly towards the land, grinning determinedly.

"What do we do?" asked someone.

"Jump!" said someone else.

"No, it's much too far," said another.

"Sharks!" said someone else, voice trembling.

The fire was quite obviously out of control now. One girl started to scream, and then another. An old Thai woman started muttering what was obviously a prayer.

"Dunkirk," said Martha pointing. "Look!"

A small armada of longtail boats, their deafening diesel engines at full throttle, was setting out from the shore. One pilot per boat with two small boys perched at the stern of each.

They must have noticed the fire, Martha thought, almost as soon as it began, and simply set off. No official rescue could have been better.

One after another the longtails pulled up alongside the burning boat and people scrambled over the side and down into them. The flames were increasing all the time and there was still a slight swell; some people were clearly terrified, screaming and crying, but the boatmen remained not only calm but cheerful, urging and coaxing them along.

The backpackers left the boat last; being inherently courteous (and English, she said), Martha, hiding her terror, was in the very last one; her last desperate thought as she slithered down the ladder was that she should somehow rescue her rucksack. Only it was at the other end of the boat, near the flames.

As the longtails made in convoy for Hat Bophut, the captain and a boy were struggling to rescue some of the luggage, while the flames began to consume the boat in earnest. Martha gazed at them trustingly; they would surely get her rucksack, they surely, surely would. And then, knowing that even just five minutes later they would have been in very real danger, she found herself crying.

They stood on the shore watching as the ship went up like a fireball. Martha felt sick; she had stopped crying but she was shivering violently, even in the hot sun.

"Hey," he said, coming over to her, putting his arm round her shoulders, "you're cold. Here, have my sweater." He put it round her.

"I think I'm a bit shocked," she said. "I mean, if it had happened even half an hour earlier we'd be dead. We couldn't have swum it, and there were definitely sharks out there."

"I know. But it didn't happen half an hour earlier, and we're not dead. Think of it as an adventure. At last, something worth writing home about. On second thoughts, perhaps not. Hey now, here's baggage reclaim. And Martha—who are the lucky ones? I see both our rucksacks, nobody else's. And you know why? They came in on the mail coach. Look!"

It was true; four mail sacks and two rucksacks had been brought safely in to land. The rest of the luggage was clearly at the bottom of the sea.

Everyone was dreadfully shaken. The tourists left in taxis, the back-packers all went into the café by the jetty that doubled as a ticket office, bought Cokes, swapped cigarettes, fretted over their rucksacks. For many of them it was extremely serious; your rucksack was your life, your home, you never left it without padlocking every pocket separately. Most of them did have their day packs, the small bum bags containing such vital things as tickets, passports, and money, but a few had lost everything. Several girls were hysterical.

Martha looked at them and felt upset herself. "What can we do to help?"

"Nothing," he said, "really nothing. How could we? They'll be all right. They'll go into town, go to the poste restante and cable home, and there are phones there too, and then they'll try the tourist police, who'll probably find them huts to stay in free of charge for a day or two until things begin to get sorted out, and they'll all sit on Big Buddha beach, smoking grass and telling everyone who comes along how exciting it was and what heroes they are."

"You're so cynical," she said laughing. "I feel guilty. It seems so unfair."

"Not unfair. But we were lucky. Right. What shall we do?"

"I don't know," she said, and suddenly started to feel rather bad again, shivery and miserable. "It's all . . . horrid. Isn't it?"

"Mmm. You look a bit green, actually."

"I feel green," she said. "Oh, God—excuse me!" And she bolted into the toilet and was very sick.

"Poor old you," he said when she emerged. "Here, I've got some water for you. Have a sip, that's right. Look, tell you what, I just happen to have rather a lot of money on me—my dad cabled me some extra. Why don't we treat ourselves to a night in a hotel? To be honest, I don't feel exactly great myself."

And indeed he didn't look it; he was suddenly pale under his tan and sweating.

"Sounds lovely. But I don't have any money. You'll have to go on your own."

"I don't want to go on my own. I want you to come with me. I might have nightmares. Don't look at me like that. Two rooms, no hidden agenda, honest. There's a really cool luxury beach resort near Chaweng— Coral Winds. And let's get a cab, none of your bus rubbish."

Martha still felt terrible; she knew he was rich—it was patent from various things he had said—and their shared adventure had indeed made her feel as if he was an old and extremely close friend, or even a relative. She suddenly had a sense of total unreality.

"It sounds wonderful," she said. "Thank you."

There is something about being in a very expensive hotel that is the opposite of character forming. There is a strong sense, born at the reception desk, that the servility and cosseting on offer are an absolute right, to be maintained at all times, and from which the most momentary lapse is an outrage.

Martha, who had been brought up to regard frugality as the ultimate virtue and arrogance as the ultimate vice, found herself settled by the flower- and fern-fringed pool at the Coral Winds Hotel a mere sixty minutes or so after unpacking her rucksack (while picking her way through the bowl filled with peaches and grapes supplied to her room by the management and sending down her crumpled and grubby shorts and T-shirts to the hotel express laundry), waving at the pool boy and asking, just slightly irritably, if her second cocktail was on its way.

Having received a profuse apology, along with the cocktail, she sipped it briefly and then stood up, walked to the edge of the pool and dived neatly in, swam a length or two, and then walked languidly back to her place and lay down again, aware that she was being watched appreciatively by most of the men sitting around the pool. The fact that they were mostly middle-aged and for the most part accompanied by young Thai girls—or boys—increased her pleasure; it felt rather good to be the only Western girl there and to have a novelty value.

"Hi," he said, appearing from inside the hotel. "You OK now?"

"Absolutely OK," she said, "thank you."

"Excellent. Me too. What's that you're drinking?"

"A Bellini." She spoke as if she drank them quite often; she had only ordered it because it was at the top of the menu. It was extremely nice.

"Ah, one of my favourites. I'll join you. I thought we'd have lunch here. They do a very good club sandwich, I'm told. Would that suit you?"

"Perfectly," she said, "but?"—conscience cutting briefly in—"couldn't we just go to the beach or something?"

"No, I really don't want to move. It's awfully hot. We can eat there tonight."

"Fine," said Martha, "my treat."

Lunch was brought and they ate it in a companionable silence, watching one of the men taking endless photographs of his Thai boyfriend.

That evening they wandered along the beach in the soft darkness; every hundred yards or so was a restaurant, candlelit tables set on the sand, a stall of fresh fish laid out on ice, and a barbecue alight to cook it. They sat down, ordered barracuda, and while they waited for it, drank iced beer and watched the water lapping on the shore.

"This is the life," she said. "What a lovely day it's turned out to be. I feel quite different."

"You seem quite different," he said, "different from how I remember you."

"Oh really? Well, I'm the same." Really she wasn't; she had become, just for the duration of the fairy tale, careless and confident, another sort of girl altogether, no longer Cinderella but the princess, and until the clock struck and they left in the morning, so she would remain.

After dinner they walked slowly back to the hotel; there was a jazz singer in the bar, and they sat and listened to her, while drinking more cocktails.

"Honestly," said Martha, "I've drunk more today than I have in the last three months."

"It suits you," he said. "Have another, have a Bellini, that's what you've become, a Bellini girl. I've enjoyed the transformation."

"Thank you."

"No, it's been huge fun altogether. Thank you! It's been a very nice interlude. And tomorrow I fly up to Bangkok—so come on, one more drink and then I think we should go to bed."

That was what had done it, that one more drink. One more Bellini. She had become tipsy, silly, more and more confident.

So that when they were walking to their rooms and he leant forward and kissed her very gently, saying, "It's been really fun," she responded rather more enthusiastically than she had intended. She sensed his slight shock, then his pleasure; and he took her hand and led her along the wooden, palm-fringed walkways towards their bungalows and said, "Tell you what, shall we have yet another last drink? I've got half a bottle of champagne in my mini-bar and I'm sure you have too, so why don't we enjoy them together?"

Which they did; and then, somehow, it seemed really rather a good idea to sit down on the bed and let him kiss her again; and after that, it was just the shortest step to continue being one of those carelessly confident girls who took sex, along with all the other pleasures, not especially seriously.

"You're absolutely gorgeous," he said, "really absolutely. I had no idea, I had no idea at all . . ." And it was so wonderful to be told that, and by someone so beautiful himself. She really wasn't about to become boring, buttoned-up Martha again, until she absolutely had to.

Her last thought, as she lay down and watched him pulling off his clothes, was one of gratitude to a boy who had relieved her of her virginity in the north, in the elephant village near Chiang Mai. That might not have been a beautiful experience, but it meant she could really enjoy this one. Well, concentrate on enjoying it, anyway. As she did. Very much. And even more the following morning, just before dawn, and before he left for the airport in one of the hotel limos, and she became Cinderella again. It had been fun while it lasted, and so very unlike her. But now it was over. Completely and absolutely over. She had no illusions whatsoever about that.

Chapter 36

· · · ·

They'd had another row.

Gideon had a call from a chain of food stores he owned in the southern States; there was a crisis over redundancies, the unions were getting heavy, and he said he really needed to go to Seattle the next day and sort it out.

"Is that OK?" he had said, putting down the phone. "I'm sorry, my darling. You can come too, obviously, and then we'll go down to San Francisco for a couple of days if you like. I'm sure I can fit it in."

She hesitated, then said, "I can't. I really feel I must be around London for the next few days. Kate's rather depending on me at the moment. She keeps calling. And I'm the link with Martha. I feel I can't let her down. Especially if the story comes out."

"I'm really worried about her," Helen had said when she'd called on the Friday evening. "She's very withdrawn, just stays in her room, won't even talk to Nat. I think, really, she ought to meet this . . . this woman, but she says she doesn't want to, ever, that she hates her. She's not going to get over it that way, is she?"

"No," said Jocasta. "Oh, dear. I'll give her a call, Helen, see if I can persuade her. Even if she never sees her again, she's got to confront her. However painful for everyone."

But Kate wouldn't. "She's a stupid cow. Sorry, Jocasta, but I don't see the point."

"OK. But if you change your mind, let me know. I'll come with you. If that would help."

"It wouldn't help, because I'm not going," said Kate. "But I might just call for a chat. I'm so glad you're around, Jocasta. It's difficult to talk to Mum about it."

So how could she go running off to Seattle?

"Quite easily I should say," said Gideon now. "I think you're getting this thing a bit out of proportion, Jocasta. She's not your child, she's not your responsibility—"

"But I feel she is. I'm so involved with her, Gideon, you don't understand."

"No," he said, "it seems I don't. We've only been married a few weeks and I'm beginning to feel marginalised. Already."

"Well, you're a fine one to talk," she said. "Since we got married we've hardly been together. You're always away, I'm always alone."

"Don't be absurd. There is absolutely no reason for you not to come with me, whenever you want. Clearly you don't."

"That's crap!"

"It's not crap. My life is hugely complex, you know that, I have commitments all over the world."

"Yes, and they're the ones that count, aren't they? Yours. Mine are of no importance whatsover, it seems—"

"You're being childish," he said. It was already one of his favourite taunts. Jocasta went out of the room and slammed the door. Later they made up, magnificently, in bed. But it still meant being alone. For at least a week. She decided to call up some of her old friends, see if she could spend some time with them. They were all delighted to hear from her, and she fixed up a Saturday lunch in Clapham, and a couple of her girlfriends asked her to go clubbing that evening. But somehow that didn't feel right anymore, married to Gideon. How could you get drunk and dance the night away in some club, being eyed up by blokes—even if you had not the slightest intention of having anything to do with any of them—if you were a married woman and your husband was thousands of miles away, alone in some hotel room? You couldn't. Better to be alone. Anyway, there was this other wretched business. Maybe she could talk to Clio about that.

But Clio was unavailable; she and Fergus were going to Paris for the weekend.

"Isn't that romantic? He booked it for me as a surprise. Of course I could cancel it but—"

"Clio!" said Jocasta. "Of course you can't cancel it. Don't be ridiculous. Enjoy."

She drove herself back to Kensington Palace Gardens, after her lunch on Saturday, feeling depressed. Even lunch had been not entirely satisfactory; already a gap was opening between herself and her friends. She was not of their world anymore, no longer a career girl about town with a fun boyfriend, but a rich woman with a middle-aged husband.

Jocasta knew whose company she would have preferred herself. She was just parking, when her mobile rang. "Jocasta, hi, it's Nick. Are you busy?"

"I'm going to go and ask her. Will you come with me?" Nat looked at her; her face was very set. "Yeah, if you want. Course I will. Give her a ring. See if she's in. You got her number, haven't you?"

"Yes."

She put out her hand, grabbed his. "Right. Here goes."

Martha had been about to leave for Suffolk when her mobile rang. She knew she had to do it: tell her parents. She couldn't risk it any longer. Just because the story hadn't been in the paper today, or yesterday, it didn't mean it wouldn't be tomorrow. Nick was being wonderful, but there were other papers, and Janet wasn't going to wait forever.

She felt very bad. Ed had not come back. He had called, saying he needed time to think, that he did love her, but he really needed to know more. "It's not fair, otherwise. You're asking me to take too much on trust. This is pretty basic stuff, Martha."

"But Ed—"

"No, it isn't but. I've backed you every inch of the way; I think I've a right to know who this bloke was. I'm the person who loved you, but I can't hack it. Give me a bell if anything changes. I'm not going anywhere. But I do need a bit of help over this one."

So she had phoned her parents, said she was coming, that she needed to talk to them.

"Well, that'll be lovely, dear," Grace had said. "We weren't expecting you this weekend. When will you be here?"

"Oh quite late, around nine or ten."

"Lovely."

No, it won't be lovely, Martha thought, it will be dreadful. But there seemed absolutely no alternative. It had to be done. Too many people knew already, quite apart from the press. There was no knowing what Kate might do, for instance.

And then she rang.

"This is Kate Tarrant. I'd like to come and see you. In about an hour. I presume you'll be there?"

"Yes," said Martha rather weakly, "I'll be here." And rang her parents and told them she'd be much later, to go to bed and she'd see them in the morning. It would be far better anyway: better than telling them late at night.

"I've just had another call from Frean," Nick said. "She says she's going to give the story to the *Sun*, if I haven't run it by Monday. Honestly, Jocasta, this is a nightmare."

"Did you speak to her?"

"No, my phone was on message."

"God, what a filthy mess. But I'm sure there must be something clever we could do. Look—what are you doing now?"

"Nothing. Fretting."

"Well, why don't you come round and we'll have a brainstorming session. I'll order a takeaway—"

"What, give staff a night off? Very democratic of you. Where's Gideon?"

"He's away," she said.

"Then I don't think I should come round."

She knew he was right, and the thud of disappointment she felt proved it. It was completely impossible to have had the kind of relationship she'd had with Nick—absolutely close, very sexy, and for the most part extremely happy—and suddenly just be friends. And the fact that he was being so good about Martha was testimony to his extraordinary niceness.

But she didn't actually love him anymore. Did she? No, of course she didn't. She maybe never had. She'd loved his company and their life together, but was that love? What she felt for Gideon was overwhelming and extraordinarily intense. Yes, he was spoilt, he could be difficult, he could be filthy-tempered, and he liked his own way, but he was, above all things, generous-hearted, thoughtful, and immensely, tenderly loving. And he loved her as she loved him: absolutely.

He was worth being lonely for. And she mustn't let it happen again; he was right. It really was up to her. Once this wretched business with Martha and Kate was settled, she'd never let him go away without her again.

"Hi," said Kate. She was dressed in jeans and a T-shirt that showed a great deal of her flat stomach. Her hair was tied back, and she wore no makeup. She was a lot taller than Martha. Martha tried to feel something, but couldn't: except discomfort.

"This is Nat Tucker," said Kate. "He's a friend of mine."

"Hello, Nat," said Martha. "Do come in, both of you. What can I offer you, a drink or something?"

"Nothing, thanks," said Kate. She walked in, looked round. Nat followed her.

There was a long, frozen silence; Nat broke it.

"Very nice," he said. "Very nice indeed. Good view."

"Thank you," said Martha. "Would you—would you like to sit down?"

Nat dropped onto one of the low black leather sofas; Kate stayed on her feet, turned to face Martha.

"I want to know who my father is," she said. "That's all. Nothing else."

Martha had not really been expecting this; not at this stage.

"I'm . . . sorry?" she said.

"I said I want to know who my father is. Unlike you, he might actually want to meet me."

"I'm afraid I can't tell you that."

"No? Why not? Don't you know?" The dark eyes were very hard. "Was it, like, a one-night stand?"

She's bound to be angry, Martha thought, bound to be hostile. "I just can't tell you," she said.

"Yeah? Are you still in touch with him, then?"

"No. I'm not. But he has no idea. And I don't think it's right to . . . to tell him now. After all these years."

"Oh, you don't think it's right? I see. You think it was right to leave me though, do you? Just left, along with a bit of cleaning fluid."

"Kate—"

"And you thought it was right not to come and see me, when it was in the paper and everything, and you could have done it so easily. That was fine, was it? Funny idea of right and wrong you've got! You left me there, a newborn baby, all alone, I could have died—"

"I waited," said Martha. "I waited until I knew you'd been found, that you were all right—"

"Oh, you did? Well, that was really good of you. I s'pose you thought that was that, did you? You never thought how I might feel, later on. Knowing my mother, my own mother, just wasn't interested in me. What do you think that's like? To be so not wanted. So not important. Don't you think that must be totally horrible? Anyway, luckily for me, I've had a real mother, a proper mother. *She* cared about me. She still does. I reckon I'd have been better off with her, anyway. I don't know what kind of mother you think you'd have been, but I can tell you, you'd have been shit!"

"Kate," said Nat mildly, from the depths of the sofa.

"She'd have been shit," said Kate looking at him briefly, then turning back to Martha. "So I should be thanking you, really. For getting out of my life. Anyway, I don't want to carry on with this, it's totally pointless. But I do want to know who my father was. So if you'll just give me his name, I'll leave you in peace. Which is what you've wanted all along, obviously. Sorry to have had to disturb it."

"Kate, I'm really sorry, but I'm not going to do that. I can't."

She looked at her steadily, trying to equate this girl, this beautiful grown-up creature, with the tiny baby she had left behind, trying to make sense of it, to believe that she had carried her around inside her all those endless months, actually given birth to her, pushed her out of her body. She couldn't.

"I'm sorry," said Kate, "but you've got to. Don't you think you owe me anything?"

"Of course I do. But not that."

"You cow." Kate walked over to her; for a moment, Martha thought she was going to hit her. "You stupid cow."

Nat stood up.

"Kate, there's no need for this. It isn't helping. If she won't tell you, she won't tell you. She's got her reasons, I'm sure."

"Yeah, like she had them for abandoning me. Well, it won't do. I want to meet my father. He might be a bit more satisfactory. Stupid cow," she added.

"Kate!" said Nat again. "I'm sorry," he said, addressing Martha, "she's not usually so rude."

For some reason this amused Martha: so much so that she smiled, almost giggled. She supposed it was a relief from the tension.

Kate walked over to her and slapped her hard across the face. "Don't you laugh at him," she said, "he's worth a million of you."

"Kate, I wasn't laughing at him," said Martha, shocked. She put her hand up and touched her face. "I was laughing at— Well, it doesn't matter."

"Like I don't," said Kate. "Like I don't to you. Not at all. Like I never have. Just something to get rid of, I was, wasn't I? Why didn't you have an abortion? Tell me that. Why didn't you just flush me down the toilet, that would've been much better, wouldn't it?"

And she started to cry, great noisy sobs, that got louder and louder, rose to a scream; Nat tried to calm her, but it was hopeless. She went on and on, beating her clenched fists helplessly against her sides; and then collapsed onto the sofa, her head buried in her arms, her hair showering over them.

Martha looked at her, and suddenly felt something: felt something for

Kate for the very first time. Felt a stir, a stab of sorrow, to see her like this, in such grief, in such pain. It touched her, that pain, and it was like none that she had ever felt before, it was deeper, sharper, more dreadful. She wondered if it was some sort of maternal feeling for Kate, belatedly felt; it was certainly feeling for her, of a kind, and in some strange way, a relief.

She sat down beside her, put an arm rather tentatively round her shoulders; Kate shook it off viciously.

"Don't! Get off me."

But that feeling, that stab of feeling, had given Martha courage. "Could you just listen to me, for a little while?" she said.

"What, and you try to explain? No thanks."

But she had at least looked at her, while sniffing and wiping her eyes on the back of her hand; it was a contact of sorts. Martha went to fetch her some tissues; she took them without a word.

"I think we'd best go," Kate said to Nat, "there's no point staying here."

"Don't you think it might be an idea, Kate, to listen to what she's got to say?"

"No," said Kate briefly, "I don't. Only thing I want to hear from her is my dad's name. Come on, Nat, let's go."

She walked over to the door, had trouble with the lock. Martha followed her, undid it for her.

"I'm . . . so sorry," she said, meeting her eyes. "I know it doesn't mean anything to you, but I am, truly sorry. I wish you'd let me talk to you."

"You could have done that months ago," said Kate. "It's too late now."

And she and Nat were gone.

Janet Frean was getting very impatient. The story was going to lose impetus if it wasn't run soon. The child would be less famous; Martha's temporarily high profile would drop. It was ridiculous. Why weren't they doing it? It was a brilliant story; Nick was a brilliant journalist. The timing—her timing—had been perfect. She had tossed a gift into their laps. She was going to be very angry if it didn't appear. Had Nick gone soft suddenly? Surely not.

She looked at her watch; she had to leave in an hour. She was speaking at a dinner in Bournemouth, a medical conference, and she couldn't be late. She called Nick: no reply. She left a message and went to change. Half an hour later he still hadn't contacted her. She really needed to speak to him, find out what he thought he was doing.

While she was packing her overnight bag, she decided to e-mail him. She could tantalise him with a few more details, make it spicier still. That would at least make him get in touch. There'd be something very wrong if it didn't.

She went into her study, switched on her laptop. There were several e-mails for her, one from Jack Kirkland, telling her to be sure to spell out their policy on health that evening, that their line on it was their trump card at the moment. As if she needed to be told. It was a medical conference, for Christ's sake. God almighty, what did he think she was?

She scrolled through her address book, found Nick's name, and started to write.

"She's sent me an e-mail," said Nick to Jocasta. "She really is not going to wait much longer. Hold on, I'll read it to you. She says she doesn't want the story wasted, now—oh yes, 'Please don't leave it too long. I don't want to have to give it to someone else. Incidentally, I have a bit more to tell you—details of the family tree—let me know if you want it.' "

"What do you think that means? Who the father is? Shit, I'd so love to know."

"God knows. And she says not to delay too long, and then, that if I haven't done it by Monday, she's going to the *Sun*."

"Bloody hell! Bloody, bloody hell, Nick. What are you going to say?"

"God knows. *I* certainly don't . . ."

"Mum! I feel sick."

Janet looked doubtfully at Arthur. He was her second youngest, and his digestion was delicate. He did look very green. She glanced at the clock: she really should have gone.

"Where's Dad?"

"In his study. On the phone. He told me to find you."

"Well, let's get you downstairs, maybe some TV would help— Oh, Arthur!"

Everything Arthur did, he did thoroughly. Including vomiting. Janet's trouser suit was clearly no longer fit for public viewing. By the time she had got Bob off the phone, Arthur cleaned up, and changed her suit, she was extremely late.

She was driving herself; she grabbed her briefcase and her overnight bag, ran to the car, and started it. And realised she had forgotten her handheld. A nifty little device, which could send and receive e-mails—and act as a mobile. Pretty crucial this evening.

She ran back into the house; Bob was in the hall.

"Thought you'd gone."

"I had, but I'd forgotten my BlackBerry."

"What on earth do you want that for?"

"It's got some notes for my speech on it."

He knew that was a lie; he'd already seen the whole speech, neatly printed, lying on her desk. He went back into the house and to Arthur, who was now very cheerfully watching some old *Starsky and Hutch* videos and demanding ice cream.

Martha hadn't realised how tired she was until she was on the A12. Driving out through the endless suburbs of East London at least offered some variety, required the occasional gear change. Confronted by the endless sheet of road ahead of her, she felt her brain begin to glaze over.

Maybe she should stop, stay at a motel, and drive on in the morning. She could call her parents and tell them what she was doing, so they wouldn't worry. She dialled their number. God, what had everyone done before there were car phones? The answerphone cut in. She knew what that meant, that they were watching television. *Casualty*, probably. They never heard the phone from the sitting room. Damn. And they very seldom checked the answer machine until the morning. Well, she could keep trying, but she left a message anyway, saying she might find a B&B and come on in the morning.

She felt her eyes getting sore: another symptom of tiredness. She rubbed them, started playing the number games she always used at these times to keep her awake. Counting backwards in threes, counting upwards in sevens, doubling numbers—it helped for a bit. Maybe she could get there.

She felt terrible. Really terrible. The encounter with Kate had shaken her horribly. For some reason, she hadn't expected quite so much hostility. Naïve really. She probed her feelings for Kate, as if they were an aching tooth. The main thing seemed to be a total lack of them. That was in itself disturbing. Surely she should have felt something, some sort of recognition of their relationship. She was her mother, for God's sake. Not love, of course, that was the stuff of fairy tales, but concern, sympathy, sadness that she had missed so much of her. It wasn't there. Only one thing was there and that was guilt. In spades.

She hadn't even liked her; she had seemed a hard little thing. And distinctly lacking in charm. But then, as situations went, it had hardly been one to bring the best out in her. The boy had been rather sweet, she'd thought; she'd liked him much more.

She was obviously completely lacking in any kind of maternal instinct. Clearly, she was exactly as Kate saw her: tough, uncaring, totally self-centred. It wasn't a very happy thought. She supposed the guilt was something in her favour; she'd never felt it over Kate before. Mostly because she hadn't allowed herself to. Guilt would have meant an acknowledgement of what she'd done, there could be no question of it.

She tried the vicarage again: still no reply. Well, maybe she could make it. She'd have a coffee at a Little Chef and carry on. It would be much nicer to get there, get to her own bed.

Nick had finally replied to Janet's e-mail:

Janet: Doing my best, lot of ends to tie up. Please bear with me. Re family tree, what do you mean exactly? Nick

Janet was not impressed.

Martha was back on the road; she felt quite wide-awake now. She began to try to frame her conversation with her parents, wondering how to lead into it. How could you possibly break such news gently? Maybe she should show them the cuttings about Kate, the story that Carla Giannini had written? And then say, well, what? "I'm actually her mother. It was me that abandoned her in the cleaning cupboard." That would really be easy for them, wouldn't it?

Well, what about the early cuttings? Would that be better?

"This is what I actually did when I got back from travelling. I was too afraid to tell you." How would that make them feel? Or "You've got another granddaughter. She's called Kate and she's sixteen."

"Fuck," said Martha aloud. And this was only the beginning. There was Paul Quenell to inform, and Jack Kirkland. Her friends. What friends? They seemed very few in number suddenly. But they all had to be told and within the next few days, possibly the next few hours, if Janet went to another paper.

Janet e-mailed:

> *There can't be that many loose ends. And what do you think family tree means? Use your common sense. Might speak to Chris myself to push it forward. Terrible waste, if he won't run it. He would have done last Friday I'm sure, with our subject hot off the TV. Maybe you could let me have a draft? Janet*

Shit. Now what did he do? Suppose she did talk to Pollock? Nick began to panic. Better call him himself, warn him. But then he'd want to know what it was about. Shit. He began typing.

> *Janet: What??!! You know we never show drafts. Talk to Chris if you want to, but he's entertaining heavily this weekend, never welcomes interruptions.*

This was true; he was. He always was, he took his Saturday nights very seriously. He and the current Mrs. Pollock, a television executive, gave famously large and starry dinner parties, followed by even larger brunches the following day. Only the kind of headline that took over the whole of the front page was allowed to interrupt them; and however much they all cared about Baby Bianca, she didn't justify seventy-two point. So quite a clever move there.

I'm really doing my best. Obviously family tree interesting.
    Speak maybe tomorrow. Nick

Please God that would keep her quiet.
But:

OK. Let's speak. I'll call tomorrow lunchtime, check on progress. Maybe
you could confirm this is OK.

This was getting very difficult. Maybe he was going to have to run the
story after all. To save Martha and Kate from something much worse.

Martha knew it was crazy, but she rang Ed. She felt so lonely, so besieged
by fate; losing him now when she had found him again, albeit briefly, was
almost unbearable. She was beginning to wonder why she was being protective of—of *him*. She certainly didn't owe him anything. But—she did.
It was ripples in the pond: the wider they went, the worse it got, the more
people were hurt. "Hi, Ed, it's me. Just wondered how you were. Give me
a call if you can, I'm in the car."

It was horribly reminiscent of his endless, caring calls to her, when he
must have known that there was little chance of a response: or the response
he wanted, anyway. It was a measure of how low she was feeling that she
was prepared to put herself at such risk. Martha Hartley didn't do risk.

She was getting sleepy again: very sleepy. She was going to have to
stop. Only there were fewer motels out here, and it was too late to go off
the road, find a B&B. She put a Stones CD on and turned the volume
right up. That often helped.

Then the phone went. Ed's name came up on the screen. Her heart
lurched.

"Hi, Ed."

"Hi. Where are you?"

"About an hour from Binsmow."

"Yeah?" The voice was polite, no more. "Going to see your parents?"

"Yes. And to—well, to tell them."

This was awful. She had only heard his voice this hard once before
and that had been the night of their terrible row, when he had gone for

her, told her how cold and controlling she was. She threw caution not just to the winds but into outer space.

"I'm scared, Ed. So scared."

"Of what?"

"Of hurting them. That's the main thing, you know. That's how it all began."

"Yeah. Well, I'm sure you'll manage."

"Ed . . ."

"Yes, Martha?"

"I'm missing you."

This was unbelievable: that she was talking to him like this, throwing herself on him.

"Well, I miss you too. But like I said, there are limits. I can't cope with all this shit, you know? About the father."

"I know, but—"

"Are you going to tell me or not?"

"No, Ed, I'm not. Not yet anyway. I wish you could understand—"

"Sorry, but I can't, not at the moment. You never change, do you, really? You just call me in when you need me, focussed entirely on yourself, you're still doing it."

"I'm not!"

"Martha, you are. You should listen to yourself. On and on, round and round like a bloody cracked record. Saying how you don't want to hurt your parents, that was how it all began. Assuming I've got time for you, that I'll just drop everything, to listen to you. Well, I can't. I'm busy right now; I'm in the editing suite. Just give it a rest. OK? I'll call you in a day or two."

She managed to say goodbye, and then started to cry, the tears blurring her eyes. She had to stop. Together with her tiredness, it was a fatal combination. She pulled across to the inside lane, meaning to pull over onto the hard shoulder. She missed the fact that a slip road was coming onto the A12 from her left; a large lorry, being driven only a little too fast, was coming down it, its driver momentarily distracted, himself, by a call from his girlfriend. He pulled out to try to avoid her, hit her anyway, and skidded right across the width of the road, taking the Mercedes with him.

Chapter 37

. . . .

🌹 "Martha's very late," said Grace, switching off Michael Parkinson and moving into her bedtime ritual of cushion plumping, cat ejecting, and newspaper collecting. "I hope she's all right."

"I'm sure she is," said Peter. "I'll just go and switch off my computer, read through that sermon again, and see if she's called."

He came back, smiling. "She's probably going to stop on the way. She was very tired, she said, so she might book into a motel and be here for breakfast."

"Well, I'm glad she's so sensible. And we're too tired ourselves to talk to her now. You go up, dear, and I'll make the tea."

Because the accident had taken place on a curve in the road, it was hard to see it coming. Two more cars had piled into the wreckage before a man, driving slowly and carefully enough to spot it in time, stopped to turn on his hazard lights and phone the police. Then he pulled his fire extinguisher out of his own car and ran across to the mass blocking the road. He felt more than a little frightened.

The cars at the rear were not too seriously affected; their bonnets were crushed, and in one case the front wheels were totally buckled, and the horn of the other appeared to be jammed on, but the drivers of both were conscious and had the presence of mind to switch off their engines. The driver of the less damaged car was bleeding from a gash in his head, but otherwise appeared completely unhurt. He climbed rather unsteadily out of his car and said he had no passengers.

"Just getting home. You got a phone, mate?"

"I've called the police. Do you want to phone home?"

"Yeah, please. God, that lorry's in a bad way."

"It does seem to be. What about this car, next to you?" There was the sound of a child crying; they ran over to it, peered in. A baby of about one was yelling lustily in its car seat; a young couple, presumably its parents, were rather dazedly trying to turn round and pacify it. Neither of them appeared hurt either, although the girl was crying.

"Just shock," said the father. He appeared quite shocked himself; he kept rubbing his eyes and blowing on his hands, but making no attempt to get out.

The two men got the little family out, and helped them to the side of the road. By now a couple of other cars had arrived and were parked just short of the crash, all with their hazard lights flashing.

"Best . . . best have a look in the lorry," said the man with the cut head. He mopped it with his handkerchief; it had almost stopped bleeding. "Christ, I've been lucky. Thanks for that." He held out his hand. "Derek Jones."

"Peter Morrison. Didn't do anything." He walked rather nervously round the great hulk of the lorry; the cab was half on its side, the engine still running. Morrison handed his fire extinguisher to Jones and said, "Cover me, there's a good chap. First sign of trouble use this. I'll just get the engine switched off."

It meant climbing up the steps, hauling open the door, leaning in, and switching off the ignition. He was, as he said on his return to his new friend, shitting himself pretty bloody hard. But it had been done.

"Anyone in there?"

"Yeah, driver. On his own. Unconscious. Breathing, though. Don't want to move him. Might do more harm than good."

"Right. Well, we'd better look at the other car, I suppose. Blimey. It's a fucking Mercedes. Bet he was drunk."

They looked almost dispassionately at the car. It seemed impossible that anyone could be in it and live. It was jammed beneath one of the lorry's wheels, its roof entirely crushed, its windscreen smashed in.

"Poor bleeder," said Derek Jones. "Must have copped it."

And then through the darkness, just before the blessed wailing of the police sirens, came the unmistakable sound of a mobile phone ringing from inside the car.

"Fuck," said Ed. She must have reached the vicarage, switched off her phone. There was no way he could call her there, at this time of night. He'd do it first thing in the morning. That was one of the great things about Martha, you couldn't ring her too early; she was always awake by six, even on Sundays. Well, sometimes on Sunday it was half past.

He switched his phone off; he felt bad. He'd been much too hard on her. He hadn't meant to give her such an earful. She hadn't deserved it. She was very upset and he should have been more . . . supportive. Trouble was, he was really rather tired of being supportive, and she absolutely didn't seem to realise that, or be in the least grateful for what he did.

Still—she'd had the sort of forty-eight hours that would have destroyed most people entirely. And in some ways he supposed he should admire her for not telling him who the father was. She obviously wanted to protect him. She must have been very fond of him, to be so bothered, though. That was what had been bugging him. Which was pretty childish really, since it had been sixteen years ago.

Funny sort of bloke, if that had been the case, though, that she hadn't been able to tell him at the time. Well, it was a funny thing, travelling: it did weird things, all those relationships, starting and ending without a backward or a forward glance. She probably didn't know where to contact him; it must have been dead difficult in those days, before there were mobiles. Oh, well. He'd call her in the morning, say he was sorry, try and make it up to her. He went back to his editing.

The police were fucking marvellous, Peter and Derek agreed. Calm, organised, setting up a road block in no time, so there was no danger of anyone else piling in—although they reckoned they'd done a pretty good job of that themselves with their hazard lights. Got the ambulance to the front, using the hard shoulder, and started with the poor bugger in the lorry.

He was going to be OK, actually, the ambulance men said. He was clearly concussed, but he was breathing, and his pulse was steady; which probably precluded any serious internal injury. Every so often he came to and groaned. They were trying to get him out, but it was difficult; they had to cut out the steering wheel before they could free him. Both his arms were broken, they said, and some ribs, but his legs looked OK.

"Bloody lucky," one of them said. "Going to have a bit of a headache tomorrow, but it could be much worse."

Derek asked what the chances were for the other bloke, the one in the Mercedes, and they said God alone knew, they couldn't do anything till the lifting equipment arrived, but it was a miracle it hadn't exploded with the impact.

"Part of this cab's lying on top of him, that's the trouble. He might be all right, might not. Can't say— Ah, here they come. We'll find out pretty soon now."

"You know," said Clio, "I can't stop thinking about Martha."

"Well, that's very fine," said Fergus, "and I admire your Christian spirit, but I can't help feeling it's me you should be thinking about. To the exclusion of anything else. I've brought you here to tell you how much I care about you, and what do you do but tell me you're thinking about your best friend. Or whatever she is."

"Not my best friend," said Clio. "I hardly know her. But I keep thinking what an awful situation she's in, and no one there for her, to hold her hand."

"I thought she had a beautiful young man to hold her hand?"

"She does, and my God he is beautiful, but it's not the same, is it? Not quite."

"Not quite the same as what? A woman? I'm not sure I like that too much, either."

"Oh, Fergus!" She punched him gently on the arm. "Look, it's only eleven thirty in England. She's bound to be awake, she never sleeps, and she'll be worrying and—all alone."

"And suppose she's not all alone, suppose she has the beautiful young man in bed with her, then what?"

"Well then, she won't pick up the phone. Let's just call her, Fergus, tell her we're thinking about her. Come on."

"All right. Here's my phone. You can use it, on condition we go straight back to the hotel and get on with what we were doing at lunchtime."

"It's a deal," said Clio, leaning over the table to kiss him. She called the landline: Martha's cool tones told her that she was busy right now, but that she would call her back.

"Don't worry, Martha. Hopefully that means there's someone with you. Or you're asleep. This is Clio. Fergus and I were just thinking about you, hoping you're OK. We both send our love. Over and out. Now, Fergus, I'll just try her mobile— Oh dear, horrible noise. Listen."

Fergus listened. "It's out of range, or out of order, or something. I think we've done all we can. Now, how about the rest of the arrangement?"

"Can't wait. We can ring her again in the morning, can't we?"

"For God's sake stop talking about Martha Hartley," said Fergus, "and get your delicious little arse out of here. She's fine. I'm absolutely certain of it."

"Well, she's alive," said the paramedic, "losing quite a lot of blood, and her chest is crushed, but she's breathing. Blood pressure's very low. Can't say more till we get her to hospital. 'Scuse me, mate."

Derek looked at Peter. "Fucking hell. What a waste. A girl. Owning a car like that."

"Is that the Reverend Peter Hartley? I'm sorry to ring you in the middle of the night, sir. This is the police. I'm afraid there's been an accident . . ."

He put the phone down and looked at his wife. Her eyes were wide with fear. He didn't need to tell her.

"Is she alive?" she said. "And where is she?"

"She's alive. But in intensive care. In Bury St. Edmunds Hospital."

"Well, let's go," she said, climbing out of bed, very calm, reaching for the clothes she had laid out for the morning, as she always did. "Quickly, Peter. She needs us."

As he pulled on his own clothes (adding his clerical collar; it could be very useful, he had discovered), Peter Hartley started to pray silently. He could pray while he did anything: drove the car, did the supermarket shop, weeded the garden, tidied his study. He didn't stop until they reached the hospital. And then prayed briefly that they were not too late.

Janet Frean couldn't sleep. She never could, after she had made a successful speech. She felt wired up, reliving the evening, the applause, the sense that she had the whole room with her—a lot of people, more than three hundred, you couldn't beat a medical conference—and she really had felt she had convinced them of the rightness of the Centre Forward policy. They had clapped for what had seemed a long time, and then come to her table, an endless flow of medics, all telling her they hadn't heard so much sense talked for a long time. A lot of them had promised to vote for Centre Forward, to switch from their present parties.

"At last," said one rather arrogant surgeon—well, were any surgeons not arrogant?—"a politician who seems to understand our profession, doesn't seem hell-bent on undermining it. Jolly good. Well done."

She saved that up to tell Jack next day; it was all grist for her mill.

There had been a disco after that, for the younger contingent, and the older ones were settling down to some hard drinking. A lot of wives had slipped upstairs; Janet decided to follow their example.

In her room, she kicked off her shoes, and looked at her handheld. Now, what from Nick Marshall? There had better be something. Something very tangible. Otherwise she wasn't going to wait even till Monday.

The worst thing, they had been told, was her abdominal injuries: her spleen was ruptured.

"Which has resulted in considerable blood loss," the hollow-eyed houseman told them. "We're giving her transfusions, obviously, but we're going to have to remove the spleen. She also has several fractured ribs, and her left arm is broken. But those are not serious."

"And the spleen is?"

"I'm afraid so. That and the subsequent blood loss. But she has no head injuries, for which we can all be grateful. She was lucky to escape them. She was lucky to escape with her life."

"Can we . . . see her?"

He hesitated. "You can. But it might be distressing for you."

"Why?" said Grace, her voice tremulous. "Is she . . . disfigured?"

"No, no. Well, not permanently. She's cut and bruised about the face and head, but she's got drips up and God knows what else, and these bleeping machines we use." He smiled at them rather wearily. "But you'll have watched *Casualty*, I expect; no surprises for you there."

"No," said Grace, "we were watching it tonight, as a matter of fact, it was about a car crash—" And then realised not only how absurd she must sound, but that it had been *Casualty* which had prevented them from hearing the phone that evening, and speaking to Martha. The words "for the last time" tried to surface in her shocked brain; she managed to suppress them.

"And she's absolutely unconscious. Probably will be for many hours."

"Yes, well, we'd still like to see her, if we may."

"Fine. Nurse, take Mr. and Mrs. Hartley up to ITU, would you?"

Helen couldn't sleep either. This was not an unusual state of affairs; indeed, since the first story about Kate had hit the front pages, it had become more or less the norm. It was particularly bad at the moment.

At five she eased herself from beside the snoring Jim, and went downstairs to make a cup of tea. It was already light, and very warm. She opened the kitchen door and stepped out onto the patio, and sat there amidst the birdsong, trying to think what she should do. She felt she had to do something. Make some gesture. Kate's rage and hostility towards Martha Hartley were increasing almost by the hour, and they were bad for her.

She had waited, in a state of great agitation, for Kate and Nat to return from their visit to Martha; Kate was white and tear-stained and went straight up to her room. Nat sat and told them what had happened.

"She was very upset," he said, "very upset indeed. Not too nice to the woman."

"Oh dear," said Helen. She had the inconsequential thought that Martha would think she'd made a bad job of bringing Kate up, never taught her any manners.

"But I think she understood. Miss Hartley, that is. She was quite patient with her."

I expect she was, Helen thought, she's never had to deal with her before this.

"She seems a very nice sort of person," said Nat, accepting the beer Jim had handed him. "Cheers. Very nicely spoken and that. Course she would be, doing that job. And lovely place she's got," he added. "Lot of money, I'd say."

"Yes, I'm sure she has," said Jim. "She hasn't had to spend any of it raising a family, has she?"

He was nearly as angry with Martha as Kate was; Helen felt she was alone in a desire to be at least a little conciliatory.

"That's true," said Nat, "and anyway, lawyers, they're all well rich, aren't they? My dad says they're just parasites, what with the—what you call it—the compensation culture and all. He says we'll soon be suing our own parents for not doing well enough for us."

"I'd say your dad was right there," said Jim.

"Yeah, well, I don't think Kate'll be suing you," said Nat. "I'm always telling her how lucky she is."

"Oh Nat," said Helen, "thank you."

So how were they to help Kate? she wondered now. She obviously wasn't going to fall into Martha's arms with cries of "Mother"—and, even in her anxiety, Helen was forced to admit that the hostility was easier to bear than that particular alternative—but it would be much better for Kate if she could accept her, think in more positive terms about her, try to understand why she had done what she had done. Otherwise she was going to be angry and bitter for the rest of her life. Maybe, just maybe—and even the thought was quite difficult to cope with—she should go to see her herself, see if they couldn't find some way together of explaining to Kate, making everything less difficult for her.

The more she thought about it, the better an idea it seemed. It would be horribly difficult and she would need to summon all her courage, but she could. For Kate. She could do anything for Kate. Anything in the world.

She would ring Martha in the morning and try to fix an appointment. She just hoped Martha would agree.

It was eight o'clock. Martha had survived the hours of surgery, but she was very ill. Her blood pressure had dropped alarmingly with the blood loss, and the surgeon had told the Hartleys that at one stage he had been quite worried. He was still in his thirties, the caricature of a surgeon, confident, arrogantly tactless. But he was kind, as well; he came striding down the corridor from theatre to where they sat in silence, holding hands, Grace frozen with fear, Peter continuing to pray, and said immediately, reluctant to give them one minute more terror than was necessary, "Well, so far, so good. I tell you, if she wasn't so fit she wouldn't have made it. She's an example to us all. Not an ounce of spare fat on her, heart like an ox. Jolly good."

Grace thought of all the times she had tried to make Martha eat more and felt ashamed.

"So is she all right now?"

"Well, can't quite say that for sure. Sorry, but I don't want to mislead you. She really has lost so much blood, and her pulse is very erratic. There's always a fear of secondary infections in these cases. But we're pumping her with blood and antibiotics and all sorts of other stuff, and of course she's had no head injuries. Lucky escape. It could have been so much worse."

"She hadn't been drinking, or anything," said Grace. She was anxious that he should know. "She'd been working all day, and she was just driving down to—to see us, have a bit of peace and quiet. Oh, dear—" She started to cry. The surgeon patted her shoulder.

"No, no, there was no alcohol in her blood. Don't worry about that. But you know, tiredness is as big a cause of road accidents as alcohol. Anyway, she's been lucky—so far. I should go home, get some rest if I were you."

Grace wondered if he had any children and decided not; if he had, he'd never have suggested anything so absurd. And Peter thought of the hours of prayer he had sent up for Martha, and knew that it had not just been luck that had seen her through.

"We'll stay," they said, simultaneously.

"Fine, it's up to you. Coffee machine down the corridor. Try not to worry."

And with another dazzling smile, he was gone.

Peter called his curate at seven, told him he'd have to take the communion service—"And the rest actually, I'll be here all day."

The curate said that would be the least he could do and that of course he would include prayers for Martha at every service.

Which was how Ed's mother, Mrs. Forrest, who had gone to early communion rather than evensong as she usually did, learnt about the accident. She was very upset.

Grace was dozing, her head against Peter's shoulder, when a nurse came running past her. She stared rather sleepily after her. And then felt a clutch of fear at her heart. She had read a great many of the Sue Barton books when she was a girl; Sue Barton who rose from being a student nurse to Sister with rather dizzy speed. Sue Barton was told on her first day on the wards that a nurse only ran for three reasons: flood, fire, and haemorrhage. There was clearly no flood or fire. Therefore . . .

Nick was rather halfheartedly beginning to put together the draft of a piece about Martha and Kate, when Janet called him.

"Hi, Nick, I wondered how you were doing?"

"Fine. Yes. Just working on it now."

"And have you talked to Chris?"

"For God's sake, it's eleven on Sunday morning! The Pollock brunch party will be just warming up. It would be more than my job was worth. And you wouldn't want that right now, would you?"

"Oh, I don't know. The *Sun* might be a bit quicker off the mark than you. Anyway, we'll speak later. I'm still in Bournemouth. At a medical conference. I'm doing a bit of work before I leave for the bedlam I call home." She was clearly trying to be funny. "So if you'd like to e-mail me any thoughts you've got . . ."

She was like a fucking ferret, Nick thought.

Martha was back in surgery; there was some unexplained internal bleeding, they told the Hartleys, and her blood pressure had dropped again. For the time being, they couldn't tell them any more.

Ed was eating his usual Sunday morning breakfast—a doughnut and a coffee in Starbucks—when his mother rang.

"Edward? Are you busy, dear?"

"No. Not at all. You OK, Mum?" She sounded a bit funny. He thought hard: he'd been down two weekends ago; she couldn't be trying to hint that he should be there, surely? It would be totally out of character, anyway.

"I'm fine. I've just been to church."

"Oh yeah? How was the Rev?"

"He wasn't there, dear. That's why I'm ringing. Andrew took the service."

"Yeah? Cool." He took a large bite of doughnut. Hardly worth a phone call—she'd obviously not got enough to do.

"Yes. Poor Mr. Hartley was at the hospital."

"The hospital? What's wrong with him?"

"Nothing, dear. But I thought you'd want to know. It's their daughter, the lawyer. Martha, you know." The doughnut was turning to something very unpleasant in Ed's mouth; he spat what was left of it out into his napkin, took a swig of coffee.

"What's happened to her?"

"She's been in a terrible accident. A car crash. She's still alive at the moment. But it's very serious, apparently. Anyway, I wanted to tell you, because I knew you'd met her. She drove you up to town once, didn't she, one Sunday night? Very kind, that was. They're such a lovely family."

"Yeah, I know that. Can you—can you tell me a bit more, Mum?"

"Well, not a lot, dear. She had a collision with a big lorry. Last night. Her car was under it, apparently. There were several cars involved. She's had surgery and she's in a critical condition, Andrew was saying. Poor girl. After all she's trying to do for Binsmow as well, with her legal sessions—"

"What hospital is she in, Mum, do you know?"

"Bury. She's in intensive care. You sound quite upset, dear. Did you ever see more of her?"

"A bit," said Ed, and put the phone down.

Quite a bit. All of her, in fact. All of her lovely, skinny, sexy body, all of her tough, awkward, fierce mind; he knew every mood of her, knew her loving, knew her laughing, knew her angry, knew her—very occasionally—calm. Usually when they'd had sex.

And now she was lying in intensive care, her body crushed and broken, dangerously, critically ill. Her car under a lorry: last night. After he had spoken to her, after he had been so cruel to her. She had rung him for help and he had refused it. It could all have been his fault.

Ed suddenly felt terribly sick.

"I'm sorry, you can't see her now." The Sister in ITU sounded rather dismissive. "There would be no point. She's very ill, she's completely unconscious."

"I realise that. But I'm her father."

"I'm afraid that doesn't make any difference."

"I'm also a priest," he said, very gently, "and I would like to be with her while I pray for her."

She looked at him, looked at his face, looked at his clerical collar and hesitated, and he could see that he had won. There was only one authority higher even than the consultant in hospital life, and that was God. God was permitted to be with the most desperate cases, the most dreadful situations, borne by His earthly representatives; and God, she had seen for herself, from time to time, had wrought what appeared to be miracles. The doctors would have none of it, of course, said it was coincidence, but Sister knew otherwise. There were too many such coincidences for that to be true.

She hesitated, and then said, looking rather nervously up and down the corridor, "All right. Just for a few minutes." And Peter Hartley took God in with him to see his daughter.

"Is that Jocasta Forbes?"

Now, who was that? The voice was vaguely familiar. Jocasta, surfacing from a very deep sleep, said, "Yes. Well, Jocasta Keeble, if you're being pedantic."

"Jocasta, this is Ed. Ed Forrest. Martha's friend."

Of course. The gorgeous boy. Nothing had surprised them all more than Martha's choice of boyfriend. They'd expected some smooth, buttoned-up lawyer, and had met instead this easy, beautiful creature who seemed far too young for her. Who clearly adored her.

"Oh, hi, Ed. What can I do for you?"

"I thought you ought to know, Martha's had a terrible accident. A car crash, she—she's in intensive care. I don't know much more than that . . ."

"Oh Ed, no! I'm so sorry."

"I'm going up there right away," he said, "to see her. But I thought you should tell Nick— Sorry, I can't remember his name, but the journalist—"

"Yes, yes, of course."

"So he can tell that woman. Get her off our backs, I mean. She won't do anything now, will she?"

"I shouldn't think so," said Jocasta quickly. "God, how awful. Where is Martha? Which hospital?"

"Bury St. Edmunds. So—quite a way. I must go."

"Of course. Ed, give her our love. I'm sure she'll be fine. And don't worry about Janet Frean. We'll deal with her. I'll call Nick right away."

"Thanks."

·   ·   ·

The *Sun*'s stringer in Colchester had got the story about Martha. He called the news desk. Chad Lawrence had one of the best-known mobile numbers in Westminster: he was also one of the best-known faces. At midday a reporter from the *Sun* called.

"I expect you've heard about Martha Hartley, Mr. Lawrence."

"No," said Chad shortly, "I haven't."

"No? Well, she's in hospital. Critical condition. Terrible car crash. We're doing a paragraph for tomorrow's paper, wondered if you had a quote you could give me about her."

"That's appalling," said Chad, and he was indeed very shocked. "I had no idea, no. Is she all right?"

"Like I said, she's critical. Not well at all, from the sound of it."

"God!"

"So could you give me a quote? I know she's one of the new stars of your party."

"No, I couldn't," said Chad and put the phone down. He called Jack Kirkland and told him.

"Good God, how dreadful. How did you find out?"

"I had a call from a bloke on the *Sun*. He wanted a quote about her. I said I wouldn't give him one."

"Why on earth not? I'll call them myself."

Funny bugger, Chad thought, putting down the phone. He felt genuinely upset. He was very fond of Martha.

Kirkland spoke fulsomely and at some length about Martha; about her brilliance, her promise, how she was the future of the new party; the reporter, who was only planning a paragraph, grew impatient.

"Thanks very much, Mr. Kirkland," he said, cutting into a pause.

"That's my pleasure. Oh, and perhaps you should talk to Janet Frean. She's the female face of our leadership. She's been very good to Martha, helped her along, and taken a motherly interest in her. You should speak to her. I'll get her to call you."

"That's terrible," said Clio. "I'm so, so sorry. We tried to call her last night, couldn't get an answer. We know why now. Oh, God. Can we send flowers or something?"

"I don't think she's quite up to flowers," said Jocasta soberly.

She would have liked to talk to Gideon; he was very fond of Martha. She looked at her watch: no. He'd be fast asleep; it was about four in the morning in Seattle. She felt very lonely, and very upset. She decided to call Nick back.

"Bob, hello. This is Jack Kirkland. Sorry to intrude on your Sunday morning."

"That's fine, Jack," said Bob Frean. "I'm on nanny duty. Nice to talk to a human being. What? Oh, good God. How appalling. Poor Martha. Is she on the danger list? God, how dreadful. Yes, of course I'll tell her as soon as she gets here. She shouldn't be long."

Nick picked up the phone. "Janet, Martha's had an accident. A car crash. She's very seriously hurt. I imagine this changes everything, for the time being."

"Of course. How dreadful. Yes, we'll speak later." Janet drove on, feeling thoughtful. Actually, it would make the whole story more brilliant still. Give it an added edge. A poignancy even. She could see it now. Yes. It would work very well. As long as Martha lived, of course.

At this rate, Ed thought, his tyres screaming between lanes on the A12, he'd be joining Martha in intensive care. Which wasn't going to help either of them. He tried to calm down, but all he could think of, all that was in his head, running and rerunning, was his conversation with Martha, his last words to her: "Just give it a rest. OK?" What sort of man said that to the woman he was supposed to love? A pretty bloody rotten one.

"Bastard," he kept saying aloud to himself, "you bastard."

Helen called Jocasta's number; she was very apologetic, this being Sunday morning, probably Jocasta and her new husband were busy, giving a grand lunch party or something. But there was no time like the present.

"Helen, it's fine. Honestly. But—"

"I won't keep you a minute. I just wanted Martha Hartley's phone number. I thought it might help Kate if I went to see her, tried to—"

"Helen, I'm afraid you can't go and see her. Well, not at the moment, anyway, although I think it's a lovely idea. She's in hospital. She's had an accident, she's been very badly hurt."

"Oh," said Helen. "Oh dear— Is it very bad?"

"Very bad, I'm afraid," said Jocasta.

Helen put the phone down, wondering how Kate would react to this, and decided that until they knew a little more, she wouldn't tell her.

"I thought we might ask Jocasta over for lunch," said Beatrice. "She's all on her own, and it'd be nice to see her."

"Good idea," said Josh. He was heavily involved with Jeremy Clarkson, as he always was on Sunday morning.

Beatrice came back into the room a few minutes later, looking shaken.

"She can't come. She's with Nick."

"Nick? What on earth's she doing with him?"

"I'm not sure," said Beatrice, "helping him with a story, I expect."

"What, with Gideon away? Bit odd, I'd have thought."

Beatrice gave him a look that meant he was no arbiter of any kind of behaviour and said, "Anyway, apparently that girl Martha Hartley's in hospital. You know, the one who was ill at the party, who rushed off in the morning—"

"Yes, yes. Why is she in hospital?"

"She's had an accident. A car accident. She's in intensive care. Unconscious. Poor thing. I mean, I didn't actually meet her, but you knew her, didn't you?"

"Well . . . hardly. Haven't seen her for seventeen years. But we had a little chat at the party. How ghastly. Is Jocasta going to keep us informed?"

"I expect so. Anyway, she was very upset. I was quite surprised how much; she said after the party she really hardly knew her."

"Yes, well, it's always a shock when something like this happens to someone you know," said Josh. "I feel a bit shaken myself, to tell you the truth."

"You do look a bit pale," said Beatrice briskly. "Why don't you take the children to the park for an hour or so, while I do lunch? Bit of fresh air will do you good."

Jocasta was also surprised to find how upset she was.

"It's not as if we were friends," she said to Nick. "I hadn't seen her for nearly seventeen years, and she was pretty vile when I went to interview her. But she has had a basinful, poor girl. It was probably worrying so much that caused it, she wasn't concentrating. Ed was so upset. Distraught. He obviously really loves her. It's a weird relationship, though, isn't it?"

"I don't see why."

"Well, he's so much younger than her, for a start. And what can they possibly have in common?"

"You're a fair bit younger than Gideon," said Nick, "and what do you two have in common, after all?" His tone was quite hostile; Jocasta stared at him.

They had met for coffee at Starbucks in Hampstead; Nick was writing a quick piece about Peter Hain and Europe. "Well, I'm not doing anything," Jocasta said, "so I'll come up to you."

She wasn't sure why she wanted to be with him; she told herself it was because of their joint involvement in this extraordinary drama. Talking to anyone out of its loop would have felt irrelevant that morning. They sat in the sunshine, drinking lattes. It was like the old days, Jocasta thought, the old Sundays—and then crushed the thought firmly.

"I'm still worried about Janet," said Nick, "I just don't trust her."

"Nick! No one's going to rat on someone when they're lying in intensive care. They just aren't."

"I'm not sure. Anyway, I don't know that I spelt out how bad Martha was to the bloody woman. I might just ring her again."

But the usual enraging voice told them that the number they were calling had been switched off and suggested they leave a message, adding brightly, "or why not send a text?"

Nick threw his own mobile across the table. "Bloody woman. Bloody, bloody woman. What is she up to now?"

·   ·   ·

Ed knew he couldn't risk it, the petrol gauge had been running on empty for miles; he would have to stop at the next garage. He pulled in and could smell the burning rubber of his own tyres as he got out of the car. He put twenty litres in, decided that would get him there, and ran into the pay station.

"Fifteen quid, mate."

Ed fumbled for his credit cards. "Shit," he said, and then again, "shit."

"Left your cards at home?" The expression on the man's face was not attractive.

"Yes, I have, Look—I'll leave you my watch. I won't be long."

"Yeah? If you could see the pile of watches I've got here, mate, you'd wonder why I didn't open a shop. Funny thing, their owners never come back. Never pay for the fuel either. I'll have to call the police, I'm afraid."

"But my girlfriend's in intensive care, I've got to get there!"

The man shook his head. "We get a lot of them and all. Now if you just wait over there, while I make the call . . ."

Ed stood staring at him, frozen to the spot. Then he said, "Can I go and look in the car again. I might find some cash."

"Only if you leave your keys."

"Yes, OK."

He threw them at the guy, walked out to the car, feverishly started searching it again. Nothing. Not in the glove compartment, not on the backseat, not in the boot, not in the door pockets . . .

And then—"Shit," he said. "Fuck me."

Falling out of his *A to Z* was a twenty-pound note. What was that doing there, how did it get there? Then he remembered. It was Martha; she'd tried to pay for some petrol, months ago, but he wouldn't let her and she'd stuffed the money into the *A to Z*. She'd even written "Love from Martha" in her neat writing in the corner. It was—well, it was—

"It's a bloody miracle," he said, staring at it, and rushed up to the man who was tidying a row of cigarettes behind him.

"Give me my keys, please," he said. "Quickly."

"Oh. Right. Don't you want any change?"

But Ed was gone.

When Janet got back to the house, it was unnaturally quiet. The only child present was Lucy.

"Hi, Mum. Go well last night?"

"Yes, fine. Everything OK here?"

"Yes, I think so. We weren't expecting you yet. Jack Kirkland rang. Wants you to ring him."

"OK, I will. Any other messages?"

"Don't think so. Anyway, I'm watching *EastEnders*, see you later."

A major earthquake in the next street would not keep Lucy from *EastEnders*.

Janet went up to her study, rang Jack.

"Hello, Janet. You heard about Martha?"

"Yes. Very sad. Is there any more news?"

"No. I just wanted to make sure Bob had told you about the *Sun*."

"The *Sun*? No." Surely they couldn't have got a hint of the story already?

"Yes, they want you to ring them with a quote. About Martha. I've already given them one, but I thought it would be nice if you did, too. As a fellow woman politician. Do ring this chap, he's waiting to hear from you. His name's . . ."

Janet scribbled down the name, her head whirling. If ever there was a piece of serendipity, it was here.

Martha was not very well, Sister told Peter and Grace. Her blood pressure was falling again; she had bleeped the doctor. Yes, if they wanted to see her for a moment . . .

"Dear God," whispered Grace.

Ed had arrived at the hospital. He screeched to a halt in the only space he could see, which stated clearly that it was reserved for medical staff only, and rushed into the building.

"I've come to see one of the patients," he said to the woman on reception, "Martha Hartley."

"Hartley, Hartley—let me see . . ."

An officious-looking man came up behind him. "That your car, sir? The old Golf?" He put the emphasis on the word "old."

"Yes," said Ed, without looking at him. The woman was clicking keys endlessly on her computer.

"Going to have to ask you to move it, sir, I'm afraid. That's a consultant's space."

"Yes, well, he's not here, is he?"

"She's on the second floor, Ward F. But you won't be able to see her."

"Can I go up there?"

"There's no point."

The door to reception opened sharply. "Who's parked in my space, Evans?"

"I'm sorry, Mr. Thompson, sir. This gentleman—"

"Look, I've got a seriously ill patient in surgery and I can't waste time with bloody cars. Get it moved, will you? Here are my keys."

"Yes, Mr. Thompson. Right away." He turned to Ed, put his hand on his shoulder.

"Now, sir, would you please move your car? At once. As you can see, you're disrupting serious medical procedures—"

"Oh fuck the cars!" said Ed. He threw the keys at him. "Move it yourself. Sorry," he added, seeing the man's face, "but my girlfriend's desperately ill, I have to get to her."

"You won't be able to," said the woman again. But Ed was gone.

"Is that the news desk? Yes? This is Janet Frean, I think you're expecting my call. It's about Martha Hartley, the girl in the car crash. Yes, I'll wait."

Ward F was very quiet; even hospitals seemed to respond to the mood of Sunday mornings. Ed ran along the corridor, desperately trying to find anyone, anyone at all.

He saw a door marked ITU. He tried to open it, but it was locked; there was a bank of numbers on the door. Bloody combination lock. Shit. He hammered on the door. An irritable face appeared.

"I think my girlfriend's in there. Martha Hartley?"

"If she is, you certainly can't see her. This is ITU. No visitors."

"Oh, God. Please, PLEASE!"

"I'm sorry, no. Please wait outside, and someone will help you in a minute."

"But— Oh, Mr. Hartley. How are you? I mean, how is she? I mean—"

Peter Hartley's face was ravaged with grief.

"She's not very well, Ed," he said simply. He showed no sign of surprise at seeing him there. "Couldn't you let this young man in, Sister? Just for a moment? It can't make any difference now . . ."

Bob stood in the doorway of Janet's study. His face was very cold, very blank.

"Janet—"

She raised her finger to her lips, put her hand over the receiver. "Sorry, talking to the *Sun*. Won't be long—"

Bob walked forward and put his hand on the receiver.

"Bob! What are you doing, you've cut me off!"

"Good," he said, "that was what I intended. And before you ring them back, I have just one thing to say to you, Janet. If you tell the *Sun* anything at all unpleasant about Martha Hartley, I shall tell them a great many unpleasant things about you. Starting with your rather odd relationship with Michael Fitzroy." He smiled at her, quite politely, and then turned and walked out again. Janet sat staring at the telephone, listening to his footsteps going along the corridor.

Martha's eyes were closed; she looked perfectly peaceful, her face slightly swollen and bruised, but no worse. Tubes seemed to be coming out of every part of her; drips hung above her on both sides of the bed, one delivering blood, the others, he supposed, drugs of some sort. A bank of monitors to her right blinked various incomprehensible messages: the one comfort he could find was that there was no dreadful straight line on any of them, the line so familiar to viewers of hospital soap operas, signalling, as it did, the end of a story.

But this was not a soap opera and this was not a story line. And the person on the bed was not an actor, but Martha, his Martha, whom he loved more than he had ever even realised. And who it seemed he was about to lose.

He looked, panic-stricken, at the Hartleys: Grace was very calm, sitting by the bed, her eyes fixed on Martha's face; Peter was holding one of her hands.

Ed moved round the bed, and carefully picked up the other hand. She had very small hands, she was quite small altogether, he thought; it was rather as if he was realising this properly for the first time. The hand felt warm. Well, that had to mean something good.

"Can I—am I allowed to speak to her?" he said, very quietly, remembering, from his own father's death, that hearing was the last sense to go.

"Yes, of course," said Grace.

She sat there watching him now, as he bent down, totally unself-conscious, and said very gently, very quietly, "Martha, it's me. Ed. I'm here now. I'm here with you."

If this was *Casualty*, Grace thought, Martha's eyelids would flicker, she'd move her head, she'd squeeze his hand. But it isn't, it's real life and none of those things will happen. Real life isn't like *Casualty*; real life is much harsher, much crueller than that.

And Peter thought, if she recovers now, it would be a miracle. And struggle as he might, in that moment he didn't believe in miracles.

Ed was still talking in the same gentle voice: "Martha, I'm so sorry. What I said last night. So sorry."

Still real life. Still no miracles.

"I don't care about Kate. I don't care about any of it. I love you, Martha. Very, very much. I really, really love you."

And then it happened, against every possible expectation, and Grace and Peter watched, awed, as Martha's eyelids did indeed flicker and she turned her head, just very slightly. No more than a hair's breadth but enough to be seen, in Ed's direction, and a glancing shadow of a smile touched her face; and two great tears, Ed's tears, fell on the hand that had—almost imperceptibly—squeezed his.

It was only a small miracle: but in some ways it was enough.

Afterwards, real life came swiftly in again: the line on the monitor grew straight and Martha's story was written gently out of the script. But Ed, who had both worked and experienced the miracle, felt, as he bade her farewell, just a little comforted.

And thought later, as he sat outside the room, numb with shock, while Martha's parents said their own goodbyes to her, that it had actually been the second miracle that day.

Chapter 38

"I don't know why I feel so upset," Jocasta said. She was sitting in Nick's flat in Hampstead, weeping; his arms were round her, and he was tenderly stroking her hair. "It's not as if I'd been close to her, or anything. I suppose it was Kate; she came with Kate, in a way. Oh dear. Nick, it's so sad."

"It is sad," he said, "dreadfully sad. I can't believe it, not any of it."

"But at least Ed got there. That's something. He was so distraught, Nick, I can't tell you. He said he was going to stay with his mum tonight, in Binsmow, and he'd see us tomorrow. He said"—she swallowed hard, sniffed loudly—"he said he thought they'd like us to be at the funeral. He said we'd done so much for her. I wish."

"Well, we tried," said Nick. "We did our best. I think Janet must be feeling pretty bad."

"I bloody well hope so," said Jocasta.

"That's dreadful," said Helen, "I'm shocked. I mean, I never even met her, but obviously—well, she's part of us now, after all. It's an odd feeling. Kate's in a very strange state."

"I expect she is," said Jocasta, "poor little thing."

"I feel awful," said Kate. "Really bad. Just think, my mother, all my life I've been looking for her, and then I find her and all I ever said to her was horrible things. God, Nat, I really am a right cow!"

"No, you're not," he said. "You weren't to know. And you don't owe her nothing, don't forget. It's not like she was your real mum."

"Nat!" said Kate. "She *was* my real mum. That's the whole point, don't be stupid."

"No, she wasn't. She didn't, like, look after you, did she, didn't bring you up? I'd say your mum, downstairs, she's your real mum. Think how you'd feel if it was her."

"Oh, don't!" said Kate. "I'd rather die myself."

"Well, there you are."

"I know, but she, Martha, must have died thinking I hated her. That's not very good, is it? And then, just think, finally I found her, finally I could've got to know her, and now I've lost her again forever. It's not fair, Nat, it really, really isn't fair!"

Nat left shortly after that. Kate was crying again and he was beginning to feel he'd had enough. But before he went, he looked in on Helen, who was in the kitchen, rather feebly peeling potatoes, and told her that Kate had just said that, if it had been Helen who'd been killed, she'd prefer to be dead herself. He thought she'd like to hear that, but it seemed he was wrong. Helen burst into tears.

Nat's dad had often told him women were a complete mystery and it was a waste of time and energy to even try to understand them. Nat decided he agreed with him.

"Oh, it's so, so sad," said Clio. Her eyes were red with weeping; like Jocasta she couldn't quite work out why she was so upset. Fergus told her it was because she was tenderhearted, but she knew it was more than that. In a few short weeks Martha had wound her way into their lives, just as insistently as if they'd had the annual meetings they had promised one another all those years ago. She kept thinking of Martha as she had last seen her on the beach in Thailand, brown, smiling, her hair sun-streaked, no longer touchy and inhibited, but happily easy, and thought of the dreadful ending to that happiness, the long days in the hot, filthy city, waiting in dread for her baby to be born, and then of what must have been the nightmare of that birth, all alone, with nothing and no one to help her through the pain. And then she thought of her making her new life, her perfectly accomplished and successful new life, and all the time with her dreadful secret, and she thought that Martha was, without doubt, not only the bravest person she had ever met but the bravest that she was ever likely to meet.

Beatrice had called Jocasta for news of Martha; she expected to be told she was better, or at least holding her own. She went to tell Josh, and he had been clearly upset as well; it was just that it was a shock, they agreed, as they sat drinking larger-than-usual gin and tonics before dinner that night. Of course neither of them had known her at all well, they said, in fact Beatrice had scarcely met her, it was just the thought of that lovely, brilliant girl, with so much promise and life before her, being no more, her light put out forever.

They agreed that there was no reason for them to go to the funeral, but that they would send some flowers.

Jack Kirkland called Janet Frean. "It's about Martha. Dreadful thing. She's died."

There was an endless silence, then: "Died! But I thought—Jack, are you sure?"

"I'm very sure. Nick Marshall just rang me."

"Nick Marshall! What's it got to do with him?" Her tone was very harsh.

"She and Jocasta were friendly, as you know. They went travelling together when they were girls. Anyway, she died. Around lunchtime today. Janet, are you all right?"

The line went suddenly dead; puzzled, he rang off, waited for her to ring him back, and then called Eliot Griers and Chad Lawrence.

Half an hour later, he rang again. Bob answered the phone.

"Hello, Bob. I was talking to Janet about half an hour ago, and we were cut off. Could I speak to her?"

"I'm afraid not." Bob sounded awkward. "She's—lying down. Not very well."

"Oh, I'm sorry. She does too much. I thought she sounded rather odd when I told her about Martha. She was very fond of her, of course."

"Indeed."

"It was about the funeral. Obviously we should all go. It's at her father's church in Suffolk; he's taking the service, poor man. Next Monday. Chad and Eliot and a great many others will be there. I know Janet will want to come."

"Yes, of course. I'll tell her. I'd like to come myself, if that would be all right. I was very fond of Martha."

Bob went into the bedroom that he and Janet occasionally shared. Most of the time he slept in another room, on the next floor. She was lying on the bed, staring up at the ceiling, ashen-faced, very still. She looked almost lifeless herself.

"That was Kirkland."

She said nothing.

"It was about the funeral. Martha's funeral."

Silence still.

"It's next Monday. Jack said they were all going and naturally would expect you. I said we'd both go."

"I can't go," she said, her voice as expressionless as her face.

"Janet," he said, "you're going."

Martha had not been unlike her in some ways, Bob thought. She had that same capacity for self-control. The same near-fanaticism in pursuit of her own success. But she was a much nicer person. Janet was not a nice person.

He'd had no clear idea what she was going to tell Nicholas Marshall or the *Sun* about Martha; but he knew something was going on by simply reading her e-mails, latterly on her BlackBerry. He had been doing that on and off for a while. Thus Bob learnt about a great many tedious things—select committees she was asked to serve on, local planning laws she had pledged to fight, NHS reforms, the Lords Reform, European regulations, important divisions, and a few more interesting ones. Such as this latest, concerning Martha. It astonished him that Janet had never realised he might do so: perhaps she did, and her contempt for him was such that she never thought he would do anything with the knowledge.

"How did you know?" she said that morning, lying on her bed, white-faced and hollow-eyed.

"Oh, Janet," he said in his courteous voice, "you really think I'm very stupid, don't you? I've been reading your e-mails, of course."

"But you couldn't have. The most recent ones hadn't even been opened."

"I'm afraid they had. That latest little gadget of yours, the BlackBerry, I've had a lot of fun and games with it. You'd be surprised what you can do with a password and a bit of know-how. Not nice, what you had planned for Martha. Well, I'll leave you to rest, shall I?"

As he went back to the garden, he thought sadly that although he might have saved Martha from Janet, it was of little use to her now.

·   ·   ·

Gideon Keeble found himself very moist-eyed when Jocasta told him the news. "Silly old fool that I am," he said to her, "but she was a lovely thing, and so charming and clever. What a waste, what a dreadful waste."

"The funeral's next Monday, Gideon, will you be able to come? Will you be back? I'd so love it if you would."

"Of course I'll come. If that's what her parents want."

"I think the more people who come, the better. Nothing worse than a small funeral. And they've invited me, through Ed, who seems to be doing a lot of the organising, and if I'm there, I want you to be."

"I'll be there."

"Thank you. I love you, Gideon."

"I love you too, Jocasta. Where are you, incidentally? I've been calling the house."

"I'm at Nick's," she said, without thinking.

Before Ed went home to Binsmow, he drove back up the A12 to the petrol station where he had filled his car earlier in the day. The same man was on duty.

"Hi," said Ed heavily, "remember me?"

The attendant looked uneasy. "Yeah."

"I wondered if you could very kindly give me that twenty-pound note back. Here's another."

He had found his wallet on the floor of the car, under his seat. Had he been calmer, he'd have noticed it.

"You want the same note back? You'll be lucky."

"Yes, I realise that, but I'd like you to try. It . . . was signed. By my girlfriend."

"Oh yeah? The one that was in intensive care? S'pose she's OK now, is she?"

"No," said Ed, very quietly, "she isn't. She died."

He hadn't often seen a jaw drop; he saw it now. And a red flush rising from the man's neck, up to his forehead.

"Sorry, mate," he said, "very sorry."

"Yes, well, perhaps you'd be kind enough to look through your till. You'll know it, if you see it—I'm sure not many of them are signed."

The man pulled out the drawer, sorted through the row of notes.

After a minute he pulled one out, handed it to Ed in silence. Ed walked back to his car, looking at the note, at the writing, the neatly inscribed "Love from Martha."

It wasn't much to have of someone, but it was something. He had very little else: a few shirts, a couple of books—they, too, were signed the same way, nothing effusive, but then she wasn't, hadn't been, effusive—a few CDs. A couple of photographs of the two of them on her balcony and the one in her bed, that he'd framed, all taken with the auto on his camera. And a lot of memories.

The loss of her suddenly hit him, almost physically; he felt breathless, weak, and absolutely alone. He put his head on his arms on the steering wheel and sobbed like a small child.

"I think I'd like to go to the funeral," said Kate.

Helen stared at her; she was pale, but otherwise composed, not hysterical. "Kate, love, are you sure?"

"Yes, of course I'm sure. Perfectly sure. Why shouldn't I be?"

"But you didn't know her," said Helen, realising the absurdity of this statement, even as she made it.

"Mum! I know that. But I'd like to say goodbye to her. Properly. I . . . well, I wasn't very nice to her when I met her. I feel bad about it."

"Oh dear." Helen sighed. She wasn't at all sure about this. For all sorts of reasons. Not least—"Kate, what do you think Martha's family will think about it? This is no time for you to be upsetting them."

"I'm not going to upset them. What do you think I am, some kind of moron?"

"But won't they wonder who you are?"

"I'll tell them I'm a friend of Jocasta's, that I met Martha through her. I've thought of that."

"I'll see what your father thinks," said Helen.

"I don't care what he thinks. It's nothing to do with him. I'm going, OK?"

"Oh dear," said Helen again. "Kate, I don't think I can go. Even if you do. It would be very difficult. I don't expect you to understand, but—"

"Oh Mum!" Kate's expression suddenly softened; she put her arms round her mother. "Of course I understand. You do think I'm a moron, don't you? Of course you don't have to come, it'd be hideous for you. I'll go with Jocasta. She'll take me. And Fergus will be there. I'll be fine. Honestly."

Jocasta thought it was a good idea for Kate to go to the funeral.

"I can see it sounds a bit strange, but I think it will help her. And of course she can come with me. It's kind of final, draws a line for her, as much as anyone."

"She's really not herself," said Helen. "She's very quiet, not going out anywhere. Nat's been banished."

"The lovely Nat? Poor little Kate. It's very difficult for her, isn't it? She's lost her all over again. Without learning anything."

"I'm afraid so," said Helen with a sigh.

"Beatrice . . . I know this might sound a bit odd, but—I think I'd like to go to Martha Hartley's funeral."

"Really? Why?"

"Oh, hard to explain. I'd just like to. I feel I should. No need for you to come, of course."

"No, it would be out of the question anyway. Well, I suppose if you want to, Josh. It seems totally out of proportion to me."

Janet was in a very odd state, even by her own standards, Bob thought. She had hardly emerged from the bedroom in twenty-four hours; she hadn't left the house on Monday, and had even missed PM's *Question Time* on Wednesday. She appeared for family meals, but sat rather silently, listening to the racket but taking no part in it and certainly not instigating the political discussions she managed to dredge up, as Lucy had once rather forcibly put it, from almost any topic.

She clearly wasn't sleeping, Bob heard her moving around the house in the middle of the night, when it was quiet, and assumed she was working, but when he went to her study to check, she was never there, and he would find her sitting in the drawing room in total darkness. She refused to talk to him. But as the week wore on, she became increasingly distracted, shouting at the children, snapping at anyone else who crossed her path; the only time she became alive and herself again was when she went off on Friday night to make a speech at a charity dinner in the constituency. Then she appeared, wearing her favourite evening trouser suit, her hair done, her makeup immaculate, sparkling at the driver waiting in the hall for her, and came back, flushed with triumph, saying it had been superb and everyone had congratulated her on what she and the rest of Centre Forward were achieving.

Bob had thought that Saturday might see the more familiar Janet back. It didn't. What price superwoman now?

It was Sunday night; with enormous determination, Peter Hartley had taken two of the three Sunday services, but was now lying down, exhausted. Grace, who had hardly slept at all, was pretending to read the papers, and wondering when, if ever, the wild pain she was experiencing might even begin to ease.

Martha had been brought home; her coffin lay in the church and an enormous number of people had been to pay their respects, some of them spending quite a long time with her, kneeling in prayer. If only she knew, Grace thought, how many there were, how fond people were of her; and then felt guilty, because Peter would have said, of course, that she would know. His faith appeared unshaken; Grace's was becoming very frail indeed.

She felt daunted at the thought of what was clearly going to be a large funeral the next day, but comforted too; she had always worried that Martha didn't have many friends, but clearly an enormous number had loved and admired her. Her boss, Paul Quenell, had phoned Grace and said he would, of course, be there, and that he was bringing several of Martha's colleagues—including her friend Richard Ashcombe, who was flying over from New York. The thought of someone flying from America to attend Martha's funeral impressed Grace almost more than anything.

"I always wondered about Martha and him," she said to Quenell, "whether something might, well, come of it. She was always talking about him, they seemed so fond of each other."

Quenell said, without more than a second's hesitation, that he too had been struck by their close friendship.

"But of course we were wrong, she chose a local boy in the end, Ed Forrest, I don't know if you ever met him?"

"I didn't, but I heard he was absolutely charming." Paul had not even been aware of Ed's existence until that moment; but he was sure this, too, was what Martha's mother would want to hear.

"And of course she thought so much of you. She was always talking about you. It'll be a pleasure to meet you at last."

If only, Paul thought, as he said goodbye to her, if only the meeting could be a pleasure, rather than a dreadful tragic duty.

There was a ring at the bell: it was Ed. He was pale and didn't look as if he'd been sleeping much, but he seemed fairly cheerful.

"I just popped round to see you. And Martha," he added. "And Mum says is there anything more at all that she can do for tomorrow?"

Mrs. Forrest had already made ninety-six vol-au-vents; Grace said she had done enough.

"Are you all right, Ed dear?"

"Well, you know. I'll be glad when it's over. In a way."

"I know what you mean," said Grace. "We've still got her at the moment. We haven't said goodbye yet."

She smiled at Ed; if only she'd known that he and Martha had been—well, been in love, she would have been so happy. It had always been her dearest wish that Martha would come home to Binsmow, perhaps work as a solicitor there; her political ambitions had seemed a promising step along that road. And with Ed—so handsome, so charming, such a wonderful son—it would have been too good to be true. As it exactly had been: too good to be true. She looked at him now and her eyes filled with tears; he put his arms round her and they stood there, the two of them, remembering Martha and thinking how much they had both loved her.

Later that evening, Gideon phoned. "Jocasta, my darling, I'm going to fail you. I can't get there in time for tomorrow."

She felt disproportionately angry and upset. "Why? What's happened?"

"Some kind of breakdown in air traffic control. So I can't even charter anything. Darling, I am so, so sorry. I've been trying to get something sorted for hours. I didn't want to ring you until I knew it was hopeless."

"Yes, well, now you have," said Jocasta.

"Darling one, don't sound so angry."

"I *am* angry. If you'd left a day earlier, as you should have done, anyway, to be sure of getting back in time, you'd be here by now."

"Jocasta, I haven't exactly been on holiday, you know."

"I do know, and I shouldn't think you ever will be. Oh never mind, doesn't matter. I'll get by without you."

Fergus wondered if he could talk to Kate about her contract with Smith before the funeral and decided he couldn't. She was, Helen told him, very worked up about everything. Fergus said of course he understood, but it really couldn't be left much longer.

"They think we're playing games and they're getting impatient," he had said to Kate earlier in the week.

"Well, let them. I don't really care. Honestly. I've got the magazine work, haven't I?"

Two e-mails from Smith later and he was getting worried. And it wasn't just that Smith would be disenchanted with Kate soon; word would get round that she was awkward, difficult, played games. She wasn't so successful that she could afford to mess people around. These were very early days.

And he had his own agenda, although he tried not to think about it: his commission on the magazine work would be small change compared to the Smith contract. On the other hand . . . Fergus knew very well what the other hand held: more unwelcome publicity, increasing media pressure on Kate—"How do you feel about not knowing who your mother is, Kate?" "Do you think you'll ever know who your father is?" He knew in his heart of hearts she would be better without it. But what would three million dollars do for her as a start in life? A very great deal. And he continued to try to crush the thought of what twenty percent of it could do for him.

He had tried to discuss his dilemma with Clio, but they had already had a fierce argument about it.

"I don't know how you can even think of putting pressure on her at a time like this. Beastly people can wait."

Fergus said he was trying not to put pressure on her, but that it wasn't a decision he could take for her, and that Smith, with the best will in the world, could hardly have known Kate was having a difficult time and they simply needed to have the whole thing settled.

"It's a commercial matter, Clio, they have deadlines to meet."

"Then tell them she's having a difficult time, for heaven's sake. I'm sure they'll understand. And if they don't, they don't deserve her anyway."

It was at such times that Fergus worried about their relationship, so far apart were their attitudes to his career. To Clio it was something distinctly shameful; to him it earned him more than a few crusts in the only way he knew, and for the most part enjoyed.

The whole thing didn't quite add up.

"You two go down together," said Jocasta to Clio, "and Nick can take Josh. Beatrice isn't coming and it won't be much fun for him driving down alone. I really can't imagine why he's going at all, but it's very sweet of him. And I'll bring Kate. I think it's best she's alone with me, she might be very upset. Just as well Gideon isn't coming, really."

"Does Josh know about Kate?" Clio asked. "I mean, who does he think she is?"

"He knows she's Baby Bianca, but he has no idea she's anything to do with Martha. I just told him that she met her at the party and wanted to come. He's awfully thick, you know, he never thinks anything much at all."

"Jocasta," said Clio, "that's rubbish! He's terribly clever, he got a first, didn't he, and God knows how many A levels when he was about twelve?"

"Yes, but he's incredibly stupid when it comes to real life," said Jocasta, "just misses the point of everything."

"Oh I see," said Clio. "Are you all right, Jocasta?"

"Yes. Course. I'm fine. Why shouldn't I be?"

"I'm not sure. You just don't seem quite yourself."

"I'm absolutely myself." Clio decided to let it rest.

The funeral was to start at two. By just after one, cars began to fill St. Andrew's Road. By one thirty people were standing awkwardly about outside, greeting those they knew, smiling uncertainly at those they didn't. At twenty to two, they moved into the church.

Martha's coffin was standing now in the vicarage porch. The flowers inside the church had been done, as always, by the ladies of the Women's Institute: great fountains of lilies and lisianthus and white roses on the altar and in the huge urns on either side of the nave, vases of roses on each window, and on the side of every pew a simple posy of sweet peas, Martha's favourite flowers, tied with white ribbons.

It was a tremulously perfect English summer day: a blue, blue sky, a few white scudding clouds, the lightest breeze. Grace, who had woken to it before dawn, listened to the birds in their heartlessly joyful chorus and hoped that crying so much then would save her later on. It did not.

St. Andrews was not a large church, but it was not a small one, either; by ten to two it was full. The older members of the parish had come in force, all wanting to say goodbye to the little girl they had watched grow up; and Martha's constituents too, wishing to show their gratitude for the help she had given them so freely, albeit for so brief a time.

There were several middle-aged ladies, Martha's teachers at the grammar school—"Such a brilliant girl," they kept saying to anyone who would listen, "the cleverest of a clever year. It was a privilege to teach her."

And then there were the Other People, as Grace called them to herself, the people from London, carloads of them: a large contingent from Sayers Wesley, many of the younger partners, Martha's contemporaries, and the older ones too, all marshalled in by a stony-faced Paul Quenell. The Centre Forward Party had come in force: Jack Kirkland and Chad Lawrence and Eliot Griers and their wives, Janet Frean, horribly pale and almost haggard-looking, with her husband. Martin Farrow, the publicity director and his team, and then another whole row of party members, other candidates, and the secretaries from Centre Forward House. Colin Black, Martha's political agent, was there, his face sombre. And a small Asian family, a beautiful teenage girl and an embarrassed-looking boy, and their father, smiling awkwardly: Lina's family, come to show their respects to Martha for what she had tried to do for Lina.

And finally, her friends: Jocasta, with a stricken-looking Kate, and Clio, Josh, Fergus, Nick, all filing in together. Ed saw them first, as he walked in behind the coffin, together with Martha's brother and father; they gave him courage as he heard the awful words, in Peter Hartley's beautiful voice, "I am the resurrection and the life," and wondered in genuine bewilderment how they could possibly apply to the person he had loved so much, the person who was such an important and lovely part of his life, who was lying in this flower-drenched coffin, with his own small wreath set beside her parents' larger one, a ring of white roses with the words "Martha, my love always, Ed" on the card, written in his own untidy, near-illegible hand.

She had been right, Jocasta thought, a full church did make a funeral more bearable. So many people, so determinedly there for Martha. She stood, holding Kate's hand, singing "Lord of All Hopefulness," and thought how it had to bring some comfort to the Hartleys. Lovely people, both of them. She had hugged Grace and told her what a good friend Martha had always been to her—such things could not be said too often—and watched Peter Hartley now, looking at his flock over his daughter's coffin, and wondered how anyone could be so brave. She smiled encouragingly at Kate, who did not smile back.

The elderly organist, who had played at Martha's christening and confirmation, was pouring his heart into Elgar's "Nimrod" for her, tears blurring his eyes. Nick, sitting with Clio and Fergus, looked at the two political rows, the only people he properly knew here, apart from Jocasta, and wondered what Martha could have found in these self-seeking, power-obsessed people that could have lured her under their spell. What was it about politics that people found so irresistible, and worth sacrificing so much for? To observe, to be entertained by, to pronounce upon it, that was one thing: to be a part of it quite another. And if she had resisted them, then she would, very probably, have been alive today. He tried not to dwell on that; it was too awful.

Richard Ashcombe was standing up now, moving to the lectern; deeply touched to have been asked by Grace and Peter to read St. Paul's letter to the Corinthians. He only hoped he would not fail them. He felt desperately upset; the last time he had seen Martha had been at his leaving party, in fact she had made a brief speech; he could see her now, her small face laughing at him, pushing back her hair, holding out his present (a gold champagne bottle stopper, engraved with his name), telling him that the London office would be more sober, and more effective, with him removed, "although a great deal less fun," and then giving him a kiss. How could she be gone, how was it possible? He reached the end—just.

It was with the words "the greatest of these is charity" that Ed's heart felt as if it might explode with pain; he gripped the pew in front of him and bowed his head, fighting his tears back; Jocasta, who was sitting behind him, reached forward and placed her hand on one of his shoulders to let him know she was there and wept too. They all loved her, Grace thought, noticing this. How can she have gone and left us alone?

Paula Ballantine, who sang at every funeral in the district and had done for forty years, was giving Martha an *Ave Maria* all the richer for her voice occasionally losing its certainty. Fergus, who had an Irish love of music, found himself deeply moved. It was the waste, he thought, looking at the coffin, the waste of a bright and lovely life: albeit filled with hidden darkness, and thought then that she had taken her secrets with her and that no one need know them now. No one who was not deemed fit to know them; he thought how hard her parents would have found it, and wondered if, in fact, they would ever wish to know. It was a very difficult question.

And then, praying for enough strength to do it, Peter Hartley spoke the briefest of eulogies.

"You must forgive me," he said, "if I am unable to finish this. But with God's help I will. I want only to say a very few words of farewell to Martha. She was not an effusive person, and as most of you know, anything flowery irritated her. Although I think she would have liked this church today. She was a remarkable person and, allowing for some natural prejudice, strong as well as gentle, kind as well as ambitious, brave as well as tenderhearted. She was a perfectionist, as many of you will also know, and hard at times to live up to. We were always immensely proud of her, and although it was sad to lose her to the big city and her high-flying career, we could see that was where she belonged. But this year she had come back to Binsmow, and was working for the community in a new way in her guise as a fledgling politician. Who knows what might have happened to her? Maybe a future second woman prime minister grew up in this parish and in the house next door. We shall never now know. But what we do know is that while she was"—his voice shook—"while she was with us, for that too-short a time, she failed no one. Not her family, not her colleagues, not her friends. And we all loved her.

"There could be no better epitaph than that. Thank you all for coming to say goodbye to her. My wife and I thank you from the bottom of our hearts."

Kate was aware of something strange happening to her, which had begun as they first went into the church, a little melting of the cold around her heart. This mother of hers, this woman who had abandoned her as a baby and pursued her own interests ever since, had begun to change—just a little. That person, had she been as cold and as selfish as she had imagined, could not have earned all these flowers, all these people, all this love. It wasn't possible. There must have been a different Martha, a kind and generous one, who meant a great deal to a great many people—who were those Asian people, for instance? And who was that gorgeous bloke, sitting and crying right in front of them? He was quite young, maybe a brother or something. She must have been not at all as Kate had thought. Better. Not all bad. And Martha's poor mum, she looked really nice, and her dad too—that had been brave, standing up and saying all that. How could they have had a daughter who had done what she did to her? And what would they say, if she said, "Hi, I'm Kate. I'm your granddaughter, thought I'd just say hello." The inappropriateness of this, the tension of the occasion, suddenly had a dreadful effect on Kate; she felt an overwhelming desire to giggle. She bit her lip, looked at Jocasta, and at Clio, Martha's friends, her real mother's friends; they were both crying and it sobered her. They were both so nice, so cool. How could they have cared so much about the monster she had created in her head?

God, if only she'd known her, if only she'd been a bit nicer that day.

Bach's Toccata and Fugue in D minor filled the church now from the organ loft. Clio, who had been sitting clutching Fergus's hand, listening and watching and remembering as if in a dream, saw the whole thing almost detachedly, as if she was watching a film, a strange, disconnected series of images. The pallbearers picked up the coffin, turned very slowly; she looked at Jocasta, wiping her eyes, and at Kate, her small face frozen with confusion, and thought, for the thousandth time, how absurdly alike they were.

And then the coffin began to move slowly, so slowly down the nave, the flowers spilling over it, the sunlight streaming so determinedly in—she would always think of Martha in sunshine, Clio thought, only not here, not in this church, but on a sun-drenched white beach. And then she looked at Ed, ashen-pale, his eyes red-rimmed and still full of tears, moving off behind the coffin, and thought she had never seen such pain on so young a face, it was too soon, far too soon. And then Martha's mother she supposed it was, leaning on a young woman's arm, her other daughter obviously, sobbing in a dreadful silence.

She looked at Nick, at dear, sweet, good Nick, who had struggled so hard to save Martha from pain, and thought how special he was, and then at Josh, standing next to Jocasta—how strange that he had wanted to come. They had all been so surprised, and he looked really upset, white and heavy-eyed. Why, when he had hardly known Martha? God, they were alike, he and Jocasta, like twins, as she had thought when she first saw them, and then it was her turn to leave and she began to move slowly down the aisle, holding Fergus's hand. Outside, it was all confusion; the hearse bearing the family was already gone to the cemetery, and another car behind it, clearly with more relatives; she had become separated from the others now, had become caught up somehow in the political lot. She saw Eliot Griers, and Chad Lawrence, totally subdued, and Jack Kirkland, blowing his nose repeatedly on his handkerchief; and the hideous Janet Frean. God, she had a nerve coming. Clio supposed she should admire her in a way, so much easier to have feigned illness and she did actually look ill, dreadfully ill, her eyes huge and staring in her gaunt, almost grey face, her mouth set rigid—well, good, she deserved to be ill.

This wouldn't do, she must get back to the others, Jocasta might need her, Kate might be very distressed. There they were now, the three of them standing together, Kate between them, they could almost be a family, they all looked alike. Josh and Jocasta could have been the parents, young, young parents, and Kate the child—and then everything really did move into slow motion, and the sound around her was echoey and the sunlight dazzled her and she began to hear things, over and over again, echoing through her head . . . they could be twins . . . Kate looks just like Jocasta . . . why should Josh be coming, I wonder . . . Josh seemed really upset . . . And Fergus said "Clio, are you all right, you look a bit faint" and she said "Shush" quite fiercely and the thoughts and the words kept on coming at her, relentlessly, words and memories. Martha saying she couldn't tell her who the father was, studying the old photographs of them as children, so amazingly alike, she had thought, and someone at the party saying how alike they still were . . . Kate looks so like Jocasta . . . Josh seemed really upset . . . I can't tell you who the father is . . . And then it was there, right there, as it had been all the time, in front of their eyes, and she looked again across at Jocasta and Josh, standing there together, so alike, so fatally, extraordinarily alike, and Kate so like both of them, like both of them, like a family, just like a family: and Clio knew in that moment, in a roar of shock and with an absolute certainty, who Kate's father was.

Chapter 39

· ·   ·   ·

He was really nice, Kate thought, Jocasta's brother. Very kind and jolly; she liked him a lot. Jocasta didn't have time to introduce them until after the service—he'd been almost late, arriving with Nick with about five minutes to spare. Jocasta had been furious, spitting tacks at him as he slipped into the pew about three along from them.

It didn't seem that bad to Kate—they got there, and that was all that mattered—but Jocasta kept muttering things to Clio like "typical" and "this is just so Josh."

Since it turned out it had been Nick's fault, and not even his, really—he'd had a puncture—this seemed pretty unfair; but Kate was beginning to learn that the Jocasta she had for a long time considered perfect did actually have some faults, and one of them was jumping to conclusions, often wrong, and overreacting accordingly.

As they walked out into the sunshine (she'd been feeling pretty odd, upset and a bit happier at the same time), he'd held out his hand to her and said, "Hi. I'm Josh, Jocasta's little brother. You must be Kate."

He didn't look that old, he was a bit fatter than Jocasta and very tall, with the same blond hair and the same blue eyes; he was wearing old people's clothes, of course, a suit and so on, but quite a nice one, dark grey. Clothes for funerals were obviously a sort of uniform; her mother had been very worried about what she should wear today and sent her down to Guildford to her grandmother, who had bought her a black shift dress and long jacket in Jigsaw, and some black pumps as well; she'd felt like some old woman, but once she got there she could see Jilly had been right, and she'd have felt a total idiot in the light blue trouser suit she'd wanted.

She'd smiled at Josh and said yes, she was Kate, and he'd said something like it was jolly nice of her to come when she'd hardly met Martha. "It's a lovely day for it, anyway," he said, moving into grown-up rubbish, and then asked her how her exams had gone, he'd heard she was doing her GCSEs.

"Oh, fine, thanks," said Kate, and then Jocasta told her to come over to the house, and that the Hartleys would probably be quite grateful if she wouldn't mind passing plates of food round. It seemed quite odd to Kate that something so emotional and sad should have turned into a sort of party, with people shouting "Nice to see you" and "How are the children" at each other, but she was glad to have something to do. She'd been a bit worried that people might be wondering what on earth she was doing there and who she was, but mostly they didn't, just smiled vaguely at her and took their vol-au-vents or whatever, and if they did ask, she simply said she had met Martha through her best friend, which was what Jocasta had told her to say. She still felt totally dazed, and hoped they wouldn't have to stay too long; she was dreading she might have to meet Mr. and Mrs. Hartley.

The Asian family were standing alone, looking lost; she went over to them with her vol-au-vents, but they shook their heads.

"And how do you fit into this gathering?" the man said and she made her small speech and asked, because she was genuinely curious, how they had known Miss Hartley, as she called her. Martha felt a bit overfamiliar, somehow.

"Oh, she was extremely good to my wife," said the man. "She has died now, but she worked for Miss Hartley, cleaning her office, and she was always so kind, took such an interest in Jasmin here, my daughter, and her studies, found books from her own collection that would help her. And also she visited my wife when she was in hospital, and fought a battle with the authorities for her, tried to get her moved into another ward. She really was the most kind person."

Kate smiled and moved on with her plates, feeling more confused and upset than ever.

Jocasta appeared at her side and said, "I think we'll leave in about ten minutes, Kate. I'm sure you won't mind and we're not really needed here. I'd just like to say hello to the Hartleys and then we'll slip off."

At this point she heard someone saying, "You must be Kate. I'm Ed, hi!" and she turned round and felt she must be looking at a picture in a magazine or something. It was the gorgeous bloke in the church, he was blond and quite tall, with the most amazing smile, and although he was wearing a suit, it wasn't an old person's suit, it was really cool: very dark navy, lined in dark green, with a lighter blue shirt, the colour of his eyes. Kate's knees felt quite weak.

"Hi," she said, smiling at him, taking the hand he offered, wondering wildly who he was and how he fitted into the day's proceedings; and then he said, "It's very nice to meet you, Kate. I'm Martha's . . . friend. Well, I was. It's lovely of you to come."

She remembered now: Jocasta had told her about him, as she had about lots of people on the way down, and of course she knew Martha's boyfriend would be there, but she hadn't expected he'd be like this, more like the one from New York, probably, who'd read the lesson. Not young and looking like something out of a Calvin Klein Eternity ad. How had Martha done that? Got a bloke as fit as this one? He must be at least ten years younger than her. Weird.

It felt a bit weird altogether, talking to him; presumably he must know who she was. Kate felt more and more as if she had walked into some strange film.

"Oh, hi, Ed. Lovely to see you." It was Jocasta; she kissed him and gave him a hug. "I see you've met Kate."

"I have indeed. Thank you for coming, Jocasta, it's really good to have you all here."

"It's the least we can do," said Jocasta, "and I'm just sorry Gideon hasn't made it. He's been held up in Canada. I won't ask you how you're feeling, because it must be perfectly dreadful, but I'm going to call you later in the week, and get you round for supper with Clio and me. Only if you can't face it, just say so, we'll totally understand."

"I think I'd like that," he said, "and thank you, but I'm not sure how next week will be, how I'll be feeling . . ."

"You can decide an hour before," said Jocasta, giving him another kiss, "half an hour if you like, five minutes. Now, if you don't mind, we're going to go. Nick had a puncture on the way down and he's got to get back to work, and we've promised to follow him up to London, make sure another one doesn't go. I've spoken to Mrs. Hartley—she was completely dazed, obviously didn't have the slightest idea who I was."

"No, she's in a bit of a state, poor lady. Anyway, thank you again. You two could be sisters," he said suddenly, adding, "Sorry, Kate. Don't suppose that's exactly a compliment to you."

"Well, it is to me," said Jocasta, "so that's fine. And we're always being told that. Aren't we, Kate? It's only our hair."

.   .   .

They set off in convoy; Clio said she wasn't feeling too good and was happy to leave. She did look a bit rough, Jocasta thought, exhausted and very pale. Well, it had been a hell of a day. She didn't feel great herself; she wondered when Gideon would be home. She really didn't feel up to the Big Welcome.

As they reached London, Nick drove off with a wave of his hand, and Josh got into their car. Kate moved into the back; she had been asleep and said she had a headache.

"Poor old you. Are you all right?"

"Yes, I'm fine. Just a bit . . . confused. But I don't want to talk about it. I'm glad I went, though."

"Have you decided what you're going to do about your contract?" said Jocasta.

"No, I can't. I know everyone thinks I'm stupid when it's so much money, but I sort of agree with Mum. It's too much; in a way, it's scary."

"What's this?" said Josh.

"She's been offered a fortune to model some makeup range," said Jocasta.

"What sort of a fortune?"

"Lots of noughts," said Jocasta briefly, giving him a look.

"So why don't you want to do it, Kate?"

"I'm not even sure I don't want to, but I feel like I'm signing my life away."

"Take it from me, young Kate," said Josh, swivelling round to look at her, "if you're not sure, don't do it. No point doing some job you don't like, just for the money. I should know. I've spent my life doing exactly that. Ask yourself if you'd do it for nothing. Or very little. That's the test."

Kate was silent for a while, then she said, "I don't think I would. I mean, it's so boring. Everyone thinks it's glamorous and it's not. I can't stand all this where-did-you-get-your-Botox-done rubbish. And acting like your jeans were a religion." Josh laughed, and Kate told him about Rufus and Jed, and their whispering, and Crew as well. "They're completely insane. Not like lovely Marc, who did the shoot for the *Sketch*," she added to Jocasta. "He's really quite normal. Although in that business, abnormal is normal."

"You ought to be a writer," said Josh, "like my sister. You have a great turn of phrase."

"I did think of it for a while," said Kate, sounding at least forty-five, "but I don't think it's for me. I tell you what I would like—I'd like to be a photographer. That seems much more fun to me. You're really doing something then, aren't you? Making something, I mean, not just sitting there."

"How extraordinary," said Josh. "I've often said that's what I'd like to do, given my time over again. Remember all those pictures I brought back from Thailand, Jocasta? Some of them were really quite good. I was looking at them the other day."

"I don't, actually," said Jocasta.

"Well, anyway, Kate, I think you've really hit on a good career there. Much better than modelling. Tell you what, I've got a whole drawerful of pretty good cameras I never use. Bit antique, some of them, but they're what the real boys use, none of your automatic nonsense."

Bought by our father, thought Jocasta tartly, when it was that month's fad. "I could give you one if you like, get you going," Josh was saying. "Give you a couple of lessons, even."

"Josh," said Jocasta warningly. She gave him an icy look. She could see he was very taken with Kate. Silly bugger. How Beatrice stood it, she couldn't imagine.

On the way back to London, Janet Frean was repeatedly and violently sick; when she got home, she locked herself in her bedroom and refused to come out. Bob found it hard to care; she'd done what she needed to do, attended the funeral of the woman she must realise she had—possibly—helped to kill, and she now had to face her demons. He made her a cup of tea, called to her that it was outside her door, and went to see his children.

Clio didn't know what to do. She could be wrong. Josh might never have slept with Martha and it was hardly something you could ask. She had no proof at all. Jocasta always said that the only real similarity between her and Kate was their hair. And how awful if she was wrong: if she accused him of something he was totally innocent of. And even if he weren't, what good would it do now if it came out? It would create dreadful problems in his marriage and he had enough of those. Maybe she should just remain silent. But she knew, as surely as she knew anything, that she wasn't wrong. There was more to that likeness than hair: it was a smile, a way of standing, and an overall impression. And it all added up. If it had been some bloke Martha had just met travelling, she would have told them. She had said—what had been her exact words? "I couldn't possibly have told him. Not possibly."

That fitted too: she couldn't possibly, not then. It would have been too late, he could have been anywhere, and what could he have done? And later—well, Clio could see why not later. The humiliation, the admission of incompetence, running after the glamorous Josh—who wouldn't want her, who would be horrified—saying, "Do something, I'm about to have your baby." Or even, "I've had your baby." Some girls would do that, wouldn't see it as a humiliation, but as a bringing to book, a demand for justice. Not Martha.

She fell into a feverish sleep, woke to find the car stopped and Fergus smiling down at her. "Whatever's going on in your pretty little head? You've been muttering all kinds of nonsense."

"I . . . had a bad dream," she said, managing to smile at him. "Sorry. Can we stop and have a cup of tea? I've got an awful headache."

·◆·

Gideon Keeble arrived home at Kensington Palace Gardens at seven that evening, exhausted and on the edge of extreme bad temper. He had hoped to find Jocasta waiting for him with dinner organised; he found instead an empty house and a note to Mrs. Hutching.

> *Mrs. Hutching, don't worry about dinner, going out. See you in the morning. JFK.*

She was very tickled with her new initials, he thought, momentarily less irritated. He went into his study, expecting to find a note from Jocasta: there was none. Nor in their bedroom, nor in his dressing room. He called her mobile; it was on message. He checked his own: there were none.

It is virtually impossible for extremely—or even moderately—rich people not to expect to get what they want, whenever they want it. They may imagine themselves reasonable, patient, easy; the fact is that the various people who are dependent upon them work to make their lives so agreeable that they do not have to become unreasonable, or impatient, or difficult. This process is in direct proportion to how rich they are; and Gideon Keeble was extremely rich. As nobody that night was making the slightest effort to make his life agreeable, he lost his temper very thoroughly.

He didn't lose it immediately. He called Mrs. Hutching down from her flat and asked, very nicely, for a light supper; he didn't ask her if she knew where Jocasta was, that would have been humiliating. And then he went into his study to do some work and wait for her. She surely wouldn't be long; she surely would call him.

She was a very long time; and she didn't call. And her phone remained on message. He didn't leave one for her; that too, he felt, was undignified.

At ten o'clock he went, exhausted, to bed; at eleven thirty he heard a taxi throbbing outside. He heard her come in, heard her pause—presumably while Mrs. Hutching told her he was back—heard her running upstairs. She came in; she was flushed, had obviously had more than a glass of wine. She smiled at him uncertainly.

"Hi."

She bent down, gave him a kiss; he could smell the wine on her breath. It wasn't very attractive. "Hello, Jocasta. And where have you been?" He managed to sound playful, good-natured, even; he saw her relax.

"Just having dinner."

"With . . . ?"

"With friends."

"Oh, yes. Which friends? Nicholas Marshall, for one?"

"For one, yes."

"Any others?"

"Of course others. Gideon, I've had a shitty day, you weren't here, I didn't want to be at home on my own—"

"Which other friends?"

"People from the old days, on the paper. You wouldn't know them. What is this, some kind of inquisition?"

"I think I have a right to know who you've been with."

"Oh, really? A right? That sounds very old-fashioned to me."

"It does? I happen tō think that as your husband I do have rights. Old-fashioned, yes. Reasonable—again yes. You seem to take a different view of these things."

"Oh, Gideon, stop it." She sounded exhausted; she sat down on the bed. The flush had faded now and she looked very tired. "I've had such an awful day. You can't think how sad it all was, the funeral and everything."

"I'm sure. I, too, have had an awful day. Trying to get on flights, changing at absurd places like Munich, all to get home sooner to you. And what do I find? An empty house, no note, nothing arranged for me, and you out with your previous lover—"

"It's so dangerous."

"What is?"

"Implying that I'm back with Nick."

"And that's not dangerous, I suppose? Your being with him? As you were the other day."

"I— What?"

"You were with him on Sunday morning. I asked you where you were and you said you were at his flat."

"Gideon, for fuck's sake, I wasn't at his flat. I was dreadfully upset; I needed to be with someone. We met at a coffee place."

"Oh yes. And you were with him this evening, by your own admission."

"Yes, I was with him. And about ten other people. At a bar in Soho. Perhaps you'd like me to call them, get witnesses—"

"Oh, get out of here," he said, suddenly switching off the light, turning away from her. "Just get out. I'm extremely tired, I need some rest."

Jocasta got out.

"I just can't cope with this," she said tearfully to Clio next morning on the phone. "I'm beginning to think I've made a terrible mistake."

Clio had a full surgery; she couldn't really give this the attention it deserved. Just the same it seemed too absurd to ignore.

"Jocasta, don't be ridiculous, you've told me often that you love him, that you never knew what love meant before, that—"

"Yes, and it's true. I do love him. So much. But I don't see how I can live with him, be his wife. It's a horrible, awful, pointless life and I hate it."

"But Jocasta, don't you think that's a bit . . . childish?"

"Oh, don't you start on that one. It's Gideon's line." Clio felt a wave of sympathy for Gideon.

"Look, Jocasta, I can't talk now. I've got patients waiting. I'll call you later. Try to calm down. I'm sure you'll feel differently later."

"I'm perfectly calm!" Jocasta's voice was rising now. "And I won't feel differently. I wish I'd never told you if you're going to start talking crap like that."

She slammed the phone down. Almost gratefully, Clio pressed the buzzer for her next patient.

Five minutes later, Jocasta tried to ring her back. The receptionist said Dr. Scott was with a patient and that she'd get her to call back later. Jocasta burst into tears.

Gideon had left for work at seven, without even saying goodbye. She felt dreadfully alone, and shocked with herself at being so unpleasant to Clio of all people. What was happening to her? What was she turning into? Some kind of spoilt bitch, who had too little to do. Like the three other Mrs. Keebles, perhaps. God, it was difficult being married. If she'd realised . . .

The phone rang; she snatched it up. Clio. Thank goodness. "Clio, I'm so—"

But it wasn't Clio, it was Gideon. "I'm sorry, my darling," he said, "I'm so sorry. I behaved like a brat."

"I was just thinking the same," said Jocasta, a laugh rising through her tears, "about me, I mean."

"No, no, you didn't. You'd had a dreadful day and I should have been more understanding. Is there anything I can do to make you love me again? How about lunch?"

"Lunch?" Was that the best he could do?

"Yes. I thought we might go to the Crillon."

"The Crillon? Gideon, that's in Paris!"

"I do know that."

"But it's almost ten o'clock."

"I know that too. If you can get over to City Airport, I'll meet you there in an hour. Table's booked for one o'clock. Please say you'll come."

"I . . . might," said Jocasta.

It was a very good lunch; at the end of it, she leant across the table and kissed him.

"Thank you. That was gorgeous."

"Good. So, am I forgiven?"

"Totally. Am I?"

"Nothing to forgive. Now—little walk across the Place de la Concorde? Or a little lie-down? You choose."

"Lying down sounds nicer. But where?"

"I have a suite booked," he said. "If you wouldn't think that too corny."

"I love corn." Suddenly she wanted him terribly. She stood up, took his hand. "Come on, let's go."

Later, she lay smiling at him, thinking how much she loved him, wondering at the raging anger she had felt only a few hours earlier. How could that happen, how could this simple biological event, this fusion of bodies, heal hurt, soothe anger, restore tenderness?

"Clever old thing, isn't she?" he said. "Mother Nature."

"That's just what I was thinking. Sort of."

"Well, there you are. Like-minded or what? As you would say." He bent and kissed her breasts, then said, "So—a new beginning, Mrs. Keeble?"

"A new beginning. And I will try to be better."

"I don't think," he said, "that you could be better, in one regard, at least."

And kissed her again.

◄•►

At half past eleven that night, an ambulance arrived outside the Frean house. Janet had taken an overdose: whether or not it was too late to save her, nobody could say.

But Bob, pacing up and down the hospital corridor an hour later, as they administered various drugs and antidotes, thought that he really should have foreseen the possibility of it, and felt an appalling remorse. In spite of everything.

Chapter 40

. . . .

A dreadful rage was building up in Grace. She was angry with everyone: with her husband, who appeared to be coping with the loss of Martha far better than she was, by burying himself in his work; with Anne, who was still alive, while Martha was dead, and who kept telling her she must try to concentrate on the positive things in her life; with her son, who was not only still alive but also had a new girlfriend, who was a therapist of all things, and kept offering her skills to Grace, who most assuredly didn't want them.

She was also very angry with everyone in the parish who kept on asking with infinite kindness how she was, when they could perfectly well see how she was, which was in a dreadful state of misery; with the GP who had called round and suggested she perhaps consider some medication for her insomnia, when the only good which could come of that, as far as Grace could see, was that if she took them all at once, then her misery would be well and truly over. She managed to say that, so the doctor would understand; he patted her hand and told her she was too good and too sensible to even consider such a thing. That made her angry too.

She was terribly angry with God, for allowing such a thing to happen, and also because He appeared to be withholding from her any of the comfort He was clearly showering down upon her husband.

She was angry, too, with Ed, for not telling them he was in love with Martha, and denying them the happiness it would have brought, however briefly.

And worst of all, she was angry with Martha: that she could have been so reckless, so stupid, driving when she was tired, driving that ridiculous car which went much too fast, trying to do so much with her life, spreading herself too thin. And for leaving nothing of herself behind, nothing except this awful, bleeding blank.

Every day she got angrier.

"My darling, could we have a little talk?"

Jocasta was lying in bed, watching Gideon while he dressed. This was increasingly a pattern; she had nothing to get up for, so she would wait until he had gone, and then lie in the bath for up to an hour, making non-plans, as she thought of them, to fill her day. It was actually quite nice, the watching; she would comment on his clothes, he would consult her on which tie he should wear, and tell her what he was doing for the rest of the day. On a good morning he would suggest what they might do in the evening, or even (occasionally) for lunch; he had been in London now for over a week and said he had at least another two before a big trip to the States she was to accompany him on. Life was rather more as she had imagined it.

"Goodness, Gideon," she said, "when my father said things like that, it meant I was in serious trouble."

He smiled at her, came over to kiss her. "Not serious."

"Unserious trouble?"

"Not trouble at all. But are you all right, darling? You look very tired."

"I'm not tired at all, thank you. I'm fine."

"You said you had a headache last night."

"I did. But it's gone now."

"Actually, I had a bit of a headache too, maybe it was that wine, I thought it tasted a bit off."

He took his health rather seriously; Jocasta tried to tell herself that anyone who'd nearly died of a major heart attack would do. She still found it irritating.

"It might have been," she said, "I didn't notice." She sighed. "Gideon, what did you want to talk about?"

"I know," he said, a note of triumph in his voice, "you're premenstrual."

"Oh Gideon, for God's sake! What is this, the ladies' changing room? I don't get premenstrual, I don't have my period, I don't have a headache, and I just want to get on with this conversation. OK?"

"All right. Sorry. Right. It goes like this. I want to give a couple of big dinner parties within the next month. In London. Mostly business, but a few friends. Could you liaise with Marissa, and then get planning with Mrs. Hutching on menus and so on. I'll do the guest lists, obviously—"

"I'm sorry?"

"I said I'll do the guest lists. These are mostly business affairs. I have to do them."

"You said a few friends."

"Yes, I know, but I meant—" He stopped.

"You meant *your* friends?"

"Well, yes. But I very much hope they will become our friends."

"What's wrong with mine?"

"Jocasta, please. There's nothing wrong with them, but most of your friends wouldn't fit in with a large, rather serious dinner party with a lot of middle-aged people."

"And would I?"

He looked at her awkwardly. "Well, you're different, aren't you? I mean you're my wife."

"So you're stuck with me at this rather serious dinner party, which I won't fit in with? Thanks!"

"You're being difficult."

"I am not being difficult. And I would venture to suggest that if you want to have a dinner party which I won't enjoy, you should have it at a restaurant. Or in your boardroom. Or I'll go out."

"Oh, for God's sake," he said, irritable himself now. "I think we'd better stop this. If you're not prepared even to organise a dinner party for me—"

"Even? What do you mean even?"

"Well, let's say that so far, you haven't exactly troubled yourself with domesticity, have you? Mrs. Hutching says when she tries to discuss menus, or the flowers, or even general arrangements, where we might be when and so on, you just tell her to go ahead and do what she thinks best."

"That's not true. I said I liked to do the flowers."

"Yes, she did say that. But that you appeared to have forgotten lately."

"For God's sake! What's wrong with her doing it all? She's much better at it than I am."

"That's hardly the point. I would like *you* to be good at it, to run our lives. In the way you want. Obviously."

"Gideon, there's no question of running our lives in the way I want.

· 525 ·

We live your lives. In your houses, with your staff, in your way. I don't come into it at all, except trying to fit in."

"Well, as far as I can see, very little trying is going on. Oh, forget it. I'll speak to Mrs. Hutching myself."

"Yes, and give me the dates and I'll make sure to be out." He looked at her with intense dislike and slammed the bedroom door without saying another word.

She lay in her long bath, wondering what non-plans she could make for the day, feeling miserable. What was she supposed to be, some kind of secondary housekeeper? She didn't know anything about that sort of thing, menus, guest lists, table linen, not even flowers. It wasn't what she was about.

So what was she about? She really didn't know anymore. She got out of the bath, wrapped herself in her bathrobe, and, greatly to her surprise, she started to cry. What was the matter with her? Maybe she was premenstrual. She probably was. Yes, that was it. She didn't often get premenstrual, but when she did, it was awful. Only she'd been feeling like this for weeks. So it wasn't that. It wasn't at all. It was because she felt so useless. So lost.

She got dressed, went down to the kitchen, made herself some coffee, and drank it quickly before Mrs. Hutching could appear and offer her breakfast, ask her if she'd be in for lunch—God, it was awful, not living in your own house—and almost ran out of the front door.

As she stood waiting for a cab, Nick called her. She was so pleased to hear from him, she burst into tears again.

"What on earth's the matter?"

"Oh, nothing. Just me. Sorry. Rewind, yes, Nick, nice to hear from you, how are you?"

"I'm fine," he said, "thanks. I rang you because I had a clear-out at the weekend and I found a few of your things. Wasn't sure what to do about them."

"What sort of things?" She felt rather bleak suddenly, seeing his bright white flat, with its tall ceilings, looking over Hampstead Heath, where she had spent so much time during the past few years.

"You know. Jewellery mostly. One of your innumerable watches, a baby G. A gold bracelet, the one your dad gave you—"

"Oh yes." She remembered that episode: her birthday, her father had cancelled a dinner with her and sent it instead, clearly horribly expensive; she had sat looking at it and crying and Nick had tried to comfort her, and they had ended up in bed.

"And a few bits of rather expensive-looking lingerie."

She thought he might have wanted to keep that, as a memento. The tears started again.

"Just throw it in the bin, why don't you?" she said and switched off her phone abruptly. It rang again.

"Jocasta, is something wrong? Want to talk? I'm free for lunch."

"Well . . ." It was so tempting. So terribly tempting. And if Gideon saw her as little better than a glorified housekeeper, then why not? Why the fuck not?

"Yes, all right," she said finally, "that'd be lovely."

·•·

Bob Frean called Jack Kirkland.

"Sorry, Jack, you'll have to manage without your female lead for a while."

"Oh really? Is she not well?"

"I'm afraid she's very unwell indeed," said Bob. "She's had a complete breakdown. She's in the Priory."

"What? I don't believe it. She's so strong, tougher than any of us. What a dreadful thing, Bob, I'm sorry. What on earth brought that on?"

"Life, I think," said Bob and put the phone down.

·•·

Helen got more worried about Kate every day. She simply wasn't herself. She was quiet, withdrawn, touchy—well, that, at least, was like herself. She didn't want to go out, she said, she didn't want to do anything.

"I just feel horrible," she said to her mother. "I can't explain why. I suppose it's like I said, I had her for a few days and now I've lost her forever. And I don't know any more about her than I did. Or why she did it, or anything. It's worse than before. At least then I had a chance of finding her."

Helen said it wasn't really worse than before, surely, and that at least

Kate knew who her mother had been, and a bit about her. Kate clearly found this immensely irritating.

"You don't understand," she said, "nobody could."

She had told Fergus she still couldn't decide about Smith and that she might not want to model at all, but do a photography course instead. Jim was investigating this; he felt at least it was something he could do for her. He felt even more helpless than Helen; Kate wouldn't talk to him at all; she was polite and little more.

Nat had also been banished. "There doesn't seem to be much point seeing him," she said to Sarah. "I don't seem to actually love him, and he loves me, so it's just not fair on him."

Sarah said if that was really the case, could she tell Bernie; Kate said what for and Sarah said Bernie still fancied Nat.

"Well, he doesn't fancy her," said Kate, "and no, you can't."

"You're just a bitch in the manger," said Sarah. "You don't want him, but you don't want anyone else having him. Classic!"

"Oh, piss off!" said Kate.

•••

"I just feel . . . lost," said Jocasta, stirring her fork round and round her rocket salad. They were in Rumours, in Covent Garden, not usually a stamping ground for retailing billionaires. "Anyway, I don't care," she had said, when Nick proposed the venue, "I don't care if he sees me with you or not."

Nick was unable to decide whether this meant that she saw him as someone of very little importance, or Gideon as someone worthy of very little consideration; he hoped the latter.

"In what way lost?"

"Oh, I don't know. I feel sort of incompetent. As if I've got some terrific part in a film and the cameras are turning and I don't know my lines. Or what to do, even."

"You could try to learn them," he said carefully.

"Nick, I can't. Anyway, I don't want to."

"Well, those are rather different things."

"But I don't know how to be a good wife. I don't know about running houses and giving grand dinner parties and telling staff what to do. It's not me."

"Well, sweetie"—the endearment slipped out—"it's got to be you, don't you think? You've married someone who wants you to do those things. He's a high-maintenance husband, he needs a highly maintaining wife."

"Then he's got the wrong one."

"Jocasta, you've married him, for God's sake!" He sounded angry. She looked at him: he was angry.

"Look," he said, "I don't think this is a very healthy conversation. Do you?"

"Why not?"

"Jocasta, if you don't know why not, you are truly stupid. It isn't healthy and it isn't very kind."

"Who isn't it kind to?"

"To me, for crying out loud," he said and there was a note in his voice she had hardly ever heard before. "Can't you see how hideous it is for me to sit here, listening to you wailing about your marriage and what a mistake it seems to be, when I still"—he stopped—"care about you? Just grow up, Jocasta. For God's sake. Try thinking about someone other than yourself for a few minutes, why don't you?"

He left the table, settled the bill at the front desk, and left without another word.

When Gideon got home that evening, an immense bunch of flowers in his arms, Jocasta was sitting in the kitchen with Mrs. Hutching, a sheaf of menus fanned out between them. She got up and went into his arms, kissed him fondly.

"I'm so sorry about this morning," she said.

"Me too. So very, very sorry."

Mrs. Hutching gathered her menus and hurried upstairs.

•◆•

Kate kept thinking about the Hartleys. Her grandparents. Of course they didn't know they were her grandparents, but they were. And they had seemed incredibly nice. She felt so sorry for them. It must be awful, knowing your own child had died. She wondered if there was anything she could do to make them feel better. Certainly not telling them who she was. But she could write a note to them, say she hoped they were feeling a little better, saying how lovely the service had been, and—goodness knows what else.

She consulted her mother; Helen said she thought that was a lovely idea. "The shortest note would do. I'm sure they'll be very touched."

"I'll do it then. Would you read it, make sure it's all right?"

When she'd done that, she thought, she must ring Fergus.

Fergus managed to sound a great deal more cheerful than he felt—he'd had a very bad morning. A client he'd thought pretty much in the bag, a footballer accused of rape, had gone to Max Clifford instead. True, he had that cute little singer who was in dispute with his dad over his earnings, but that wasn't going to pay many bills. Wouldn't even pay the rent for this place, never mind a mortgage for the riverside apartment in Putney. And he was badly out of pocket with Kate; her earnings so far were non-existent and although Gideon had offered to pay the preliminary expenses, Fergus's professional pride wouldn't allow him to take him up on it until he had managed to show something for her.

"Fergus, I've made up my mind. I don't want that contract."

"Right." Fergus tried to suppress the slug of disappointment. "Right, I see. Are you sure?"

"Absolutely sure. I know it's a lot of money and everything, but—I just can't cope with the rest of it."

"Like what, Kate?"

"Oh, you know, the publicity. It'll all start again, just as it's beginning to die down. Asking me about my mother and everything. And now I know, well, I can face it even less. Sorry."

"That's all right, I understand."

"Anyway, I don't really like it. In fact I hate it. The cosmetic stuff anyway. It's so, like, totally boring. And I hate the people, they're just crap. Fashion's better, I could still do that."

"Yes?" Well, that was something, he supposed. A few hundreds commission, instead of a few hundred thousands, but—

"Yes, I think so. Although not yet."

"Kate, I'm sorry, you've got your first cover session with *Style* in a couple of weeks. You'll have to do that."

"I don't think I can. I'm sorry, Fergus, I just feel so down."

Fergus counted to ten silently. This was a nightmare. Silly, arrogant little thing, imagining she could play games with these people, tossing a three-million-dollar contract down the drain as if it was a used Kleenex, saying she didn't think she could do a cover session for one of the country's leading magazines because she was feeling down. Who did she think she was? Naomi Campbell?

"Kate, my love, you really will have to do that. Everything's booked, they confirmed it this morning, makeup artist, hair, photographer, you can't—"

"Fergus, I told you. I can't. They'll have to find someone else. Sorry," she added rather reluctantly.

He was staring out of the window, trying to pluck up the courage to ring *Style* and tell them, when Clio rang. He felt better at once.

"Just calling about tonight. Is dinner still on?"

"I hope so. God, I hope so. I've got nothing left to look forward to."

"What's happened?"

"Oh, Kate's being impossible. Totally impossible. She's refusing to sign the contract with the cosmetic people and now she won't even do the cover session with *Style*. It's all booked. It's too bad of her, it really is. Totally unprofessional."

"Fergus, she's only sixteen. She can't be expected to—"

"At sixteen I'd been hard at work for over a year, learning not to let people down."

Clio thought about this, as she often did. About Fergus's difficult childhood and the success he had made of his life against considerable odds. It had been a remarkable achievement, however much she might dislike the way in which he had done it.

"I'm sorry," she said carefully, "really sorry. Maybe Jocasta could talk to her about it; Kate seems to think the sun shines out of her every orifice. At least make her think really hard about what she's doing."

"That's a good idea," he said, his voice brightening. "Oh, Clio, you're a star. I wish it were dinnertime now. I'm missing you dreadfully."

"Fergus, it's only two days since we were together."

"You have a heart of stone. That's forty-eight hours. How early could you meet me?"

"If you came down here, at about six o'clock."

"I'm on my way."

She was really totally happy with him, apart from what he did. He was sweet, kind, thoughtful. He was sitting outside the surgery when she came out that evening, with a ready-to-cook meal that he had bought on the way down; she sat watching him as he bustled about her kitchen, thinking how lucky she was to have found him.

She was a bit low herself. Mark had been very upset that she was leaving, and although he had been extremely nice about it, she could see he was annoyed. She could understand it; he had taken her back once after she had given in her notice, and now she was doing it again. She'd have been pretty annoyed herself—but it had taken the edge off the intense pleasure of getting the job. And then she had visited Mr. Morris at the Laurels that morning and become very upset in the face of his helpless grief.

Fergus listened to her patiently while she ranted against the matron of the Laurels and her authoritarian approach to her patients, as she insisted on calling them—"They're not patients, Fergus, they're just old people who need a little help"—and against the daughter, who had been too busy and too callous to find someone who could help them to remain at home. He told her the Morrises had been lucky to have her as a doctor—"I don't think so, Fergus, I don't think so at all, and anyway, what could I do? Against that bloody system. It's a cumbersome load of crap, and—"

"Hey now," he said, "this is no language for a lady." She smiled at him through her tears.

"Sorry. But it makes me so angry. And what can I do?"

"I'm not sure. Launch an appeal. Try to get a campaign going. Interest some politicians. See if one of those people in the Centre Forward Party could help. It's the sort of thing politicians like, a cause that will make them appear noble and altruistic, rather than the self-seeking creatures they really are. I'll help you, if you like, draft something, maybe put out a press release."

"Oh Fergus . . ." She looked at him very seriously. "You are a complete mystery to me. I mean, you spend your days helping greedy, badly behaved people manipulate the media—"

"Hey," he said, "that's not entirely fair. Would you call Kate greedy and badly behaved?"

"No. Of course not. But she's a little bit unusual, as your clients go, you must admit. Anyway, in spite of all that, you have this heart of pure gold, beating away."

"Maybe it needs polishing up, my heart of gold," he said. "Would it seem too terribly insensitive of me to ask for another glass of that very delicious wine? And to let me put my arms round you for a moment or two?"

"Terribly," said Clio, "but it wasn't very sensitive of you to call me a silly bitch, was it? And look where that got us."

She longed to tell him about Josh; somehow she couldn't. Maybe, in a day or two. There really was no hurry. And there were enough dramas to be going on with.

• ◆ •

Jocasta was trying very hard now to be a good wife. She was too frightened not to be. She had to make this work, she just had to. It had been a moment of terrible truth, her lunch with Nick. She had seen with horrible clarity how he saw her: spoilt, self-centred, and totally immature. Yes, he had asked her to lunch, but he had been worried about her, thought she was properly unhappy. All she had done was bemoan her fate—her rather luxurious fate.

And so she had planned the dinner parties, twenty people at each, twenty people she didn't know, and as well as arranging the menus, had discussed flowers with Mrs. Hutching, and even the music with Gideon. He was rather charmed by that idea; he said he didn't usually like background music but that it could be the emblem of the new era—the Jocasta era.

She had also made tentative suggestions about the decor of the house, starting in the kitchen. "It's so old-fashioned, Gideon, and over the top. Doesn't do for a kitchen these days, I thought something totally minimal—"

"Any other room my darling, but not the kitchen. That's Mrs. Hutching's, she hates change."

She opened her mouth to argue, and then shut it again. "OK. What about the garden room? I'd love to tack on a conservatory, and have a lovely tiled floor—"

"Sounds wonderful. Just go ahead and do it." She was a bit disappointed by his lack of interest and indeed in the fact that she was doing it at all, but she was determined to be mature and spent the next three days poring over *Interiors* and *Elle Decoration*. After that she rather lost interest.

She had also broached with him the subject of a house. "Ours, not just yours. It would be lovely. I wondered about France, sort of Biarritz way. Or maybe America, the East Coast, Maine, somewhere like that."

"Darling, I rather think we've got enough houses. But yes, if you think it'll make you happy, see what you can find."

She called all the estate agents and began to put together a portfolio to show Gideon. It felt a bit of a solitary task, but some of the houses were lovely, and it would be fun going to see them. The only problem was finding a space in his diary to do it. "How about a year next January?" she said, exasperated, and he smiled at her.

"Sorry, darling. I did warn you, you've married a workaholic."

She thought that he hadn't actually, but she didn't say so. She was learning to hold her tongue; it was against her nature and lowered her spirits.

She sat through a couple of dinner parties, too, trying to make conversation with people with whom she had nothing in common; the men had been all right, although clearly regarded her as a complete airhead, a bit of arm candy Gideon had been clever enough to acquire, but the women were horrendous, bored and boring, obsessed with their looks, their houses, their children, their sports coaches and personal trainers, and treated her as if she was some interesting but distinctly inferior species. They had even all gone upstairs without the men for an hour, "To discuss detox and Botox," Jocasta said to Clio next day. She thought of the old dinner parties she and Nick had given, easy sprawling affairs, the atmosphere funny and flirty, with everyone getting steadily and happily drunk and sometimes stoned as well. But she managed to tell Gideon that she had enjoyed it; she was amazed when he seemed to believe her.

She had rung Nick to apologise for whining at him over lunch that day; he was friendly but brisk with her, said it was fine, and had all her things sent back to her with a perfectly nice but cool note. She felt rejected and miserable for days.

Anyway, she felt she was getting somewhere with learning to be Mrs.

Keeble. It was bound to take time, to settle into all this. She'd get used to it. Of course she would.

And then it happened.

It had started quite gently: he asked her to go on a business trip with him in a few weeks' time. It wouldn't be the most exciting event in the world, he said, it was a three-day weekend for captains of industry in Munich, but he thought she would manage to enjoy it and he would really benefit from her being there.

Jocasta tried to feel enthusiastic; she smiled and said it sounded nice and she had never been to Munich and she was sure it would be fun, but she could hear her own voice being rather sure it wouldn't be fun, or even nice. She wasn't feeling very well, nauseous and headachy, she said to Gideon, anxious he might think she simply didn't want to go on the trip.

"Darling, I'm sorry. I hope you're not pregnant."

"Of course I'm not pregnant, Gideon," she said.

"You sure?"

"I'm absolutely sure. I couldn't be surer actually, as of about six hours ago. All right?"

"All right. Sorry, darling, I didn't mean to annoy you. But anyway, I think you'll enjoy this trip, there's quite a nice spousal programme, lots of shopping and sightseeing—"

"A what?"

"A spousal programme. Surely you know what that is."

"Actually, Gideon, I don't. Sorry to appear so simple."

"What a very sheltered life you've led. It's what wives do while the husbands do business."

"What, all together? Me and the other wives? A load of old trouts?" Gideon said they wouldn't all be old trouts, there were bound to be some younger wives for her to make friends with and—

"For young read forty-five," said Jocasta, "like at that dinner the other night, with perma tans and discussing their face-lifts. Oh, Gideon, don't make me, please!"

"I'm not making you," he said, his face developing the rigid look that she knew prefaced a loss of temper. "I'm saying it would be very nice for me, and helpful too."

She was silent. He sighed, then said, "This marriage seems to be turning into a bit of a one-way street, Jocasta."

"And what's that supposed to mean?"

"I mean, it only goes the way you want. For God's sake, you don't have to do much—"

"Oh really? Not sort out your meals and your housekeepers and wait quietly until you deign to come home, and—"

"I don't consider that very onerous. Actually. In return for—"

"In return for what, Gideon? Do tell me." Her stomach hurt and she was tired; his words touched a raw nerve.

"In return for quite a lot. Like that." He indicated a pile of unopened bags in the corner, from Harvey Nichols, Chanel, Gucci—she was getting into her stride now, with the shopping. "And flying lessons and cars—"

"Oh, so it's a credit-and-debit arrangement is it, our marriage? I hadn't realised that. Well, let me see, perhaps we should set a price on a few things. How much for two hours, just waiting for you to come home for dinner, a whole morning sorting out your wardrobe—"

"Jocasta, don't be childish!"

"Don't say that to me! It's a disgusting thing to say. Insulting, horrible."

"This is a disgusting argument."

"I'm sorry, but you started it. Talking about what I did in return for your fucking money. And talking about fucking, what about sex, Gideon, is there a price on that? How should we set that, how much does a high-class tart earn these days? I'm sure you know."

"Can we just stop this horrible conversation?" he said, the white line appearing now round his mouth.

"No, I don't think we can. I want to get it sorted out. And little things like trips to Paris for lunch, is that set against my account as well?"

He came over to her, his face heavy with rage; she really thought he was going to hit her. She stood up quickly and knocked over her bag; a bundle of credit card slips fell out. He picked them up, started going through them.

"Don't do that, Gideon, please. They're mine, nothing to do with you."

"Unfortunately, they almost certainly are. Look at this, thousands of pounds all on a lot of rubbish."

"Well, I'm so sorry. I'll take it all back tomorrow."

"And lunch for two at Le Caprice. Pretty pricey, even by their standards. Champagne, eighty pounds. Who did you share that with, Jocasta? Nicholas Marshall?"

"No," she shouted, "no, no, no. It was my mother, actually."

"You took your mother to Le Caprice and bought her vintage champagne? I find that very hard to believe."

"Ask them," she said, handing him her mobile. "Go on, check up on me. Do you really think I'd take Nick to Le Caprice if I were having an affair with him? What is this, Gideon? You're getting obsessed with this idea, why on earth should I be having an affair with anybody?"

"Let's just say your behaviour doesn't inspire confidence," he said.

Jocasta went upstairs and packed a rather minimal bag, containing none of the new clothes she had bought, and then went down again, and into his study.

"I'm leaving," she said, "and I'm not coming back. I can't. Not until you apologise."

Gideon said that as far as he could see, he had absolutely nothing to apologise for, and told her to pull herself together and grow up. For the very first time, Jocasta felt a pang of sympathy for Aisling Carlingford. She went out and called a cab—for how could she take her new car?—and directed it to Clapham.

Chapter 41

· · ·

She sat in her house for three days, waiting for him to call. He didn't. She couldn't ever remember feeling so lonely. Normally she would have rung friends, but she felt she couldn't face them. She kept thinking of the party, only a few weeks ago, of that excessively lavish display of the new Jocasta and her new life and how everyone would laugh at her, or at best feel sorry for her, and say how stupid and immature she had been, how anyone could see it wouldn't work, and how she had only left Nick in some fit of pique. She simply couldn't bear it.

More than anything, she dreaded Nick hearing about it, Nick who had berated her, told her to grow up, Nick who clearly despised her now. Whatever would he think of this latest demonstration of her childishness, as he would see it, walking out on a three-month-old marriage with cries of how horrid Gideon was to her and how it wasn't fair? For some reason, she minded the thought of that more than anything.

Finally she called Gideon and said she was sorry for her part in their quarrel and asked if they could meet and discuss things. It was agony; she had to have several drinks before she could get up the courage, but she did it. If anything meant she had grown up, she thought, that did.

He was in a meeting, said he'd call her back.

"A meeting? Gideon, it's eight o'clock in the evening."

"I do know that. I said I'll call you back."

That was all; not the slightest gesture in her direction, not even thank you. She had another two glasses of wine, telling herself his pride was hurt, she must make allowances; it was another hour before he rang her back.

He was going to be very late; he'd like to talk tomorrow. Would the evening be all right? He hoped she was all right.

Jocasta took a hugely deep breath and said yes, it would.

"Fine," he said, "let's have dinner. I'll call you." And then added, "Thank you for phoning."

He rang off, and Jocasta, not sure whether to laugh or cry, had her revelation. Seeing things very clearly, as she always did when she was drunk, she suddenly knew what had happened to their marriage. She'd got it wrong. She was trying too hard. She was becoming someone different, not the person Gideon had fallen in love with. It was so obvious she laughed aloud.

The person she was turning into wouldn't have scaled the wall of Dungarven House in order to get into his sanctuary; nor would she have fallen over her own feet dancing at the conference, nor told him how to treat his own daughter. All she had to do was become that Jocasta again and all would be well. Gideon would fall in love with her again. It was easy. And life would be fun again. She would fill the house with her friends, who Gideon did adore, he had told her so, and infiltrate them into his boring dinner parties, where everyone would laugh a lot, and get drunk; she might even tell him she wanted to go back to work.

She had a shower, pulled on her skimpiest top, some jeans, and her highest heels, and called a taxi to take her to Kensington Palace Gardens.

"It was horrible," she said to Clio, her voice broken with tears next morning on the phone. "He was so cold and distant and he wouldn't talk to me, told me I was drunk, and he wouldn't even have sex with me. And I'd gone there, ready to try so hard, meet him three-quarters of the way, and I've been so good, Clio, you've no idea, organising his horrible dinner parties, even agreeing to be part of a spousal programme—did you ever hear of anything so absurd in this day and age? I can't believe that lovely, gentle, kind person was actually such a monster. He's a time warp, Clio, he wants a Stepford wife."

Clio didn't say that she had been part of several spousal programmes on Jeremy's behalf, nor did she say that if you married someone nearly twenty years older than you were, he was almost certainly in a time warp anyway. She knew it was completely fruitless.

She tried to soothe and comfort Jocasta, told her she'd come and see her if she liked; Jocasta leapt on this and begged her to come to stay the night.

"I will come," said Clio, "but only if you promise to discuss it all sensibly."

Clio spent the evening struggling to appear nonpartisan, agreeing that yes, Gideon was very unreasonable, but that surely Jocasta could see he was having to make huge adjustments too.

"He isn't, Clio, that's the whole point. He isn't making any adjustments at all."

"I think he probably is," said Clio, "but maybe you can't see them. Any more than he can see yours. You were so in love with him, Jocasta, it can't have all just . . . gone."

"Of course it hasn't! I still adore him, really. That's why I went round there last night, and he was just so—horrible."

Clio could imagine the scene rather clearly: a tired and exasperated Gideon, confronted by an overexcited and emotional Jocasta, slightly the worse for drink, expecting him to be deeply touched and grateful for her visit. It wouldn't have been an ideal marriage-mending scenario.

"Well, look. I'll call again in the morning. No, I'll call now—it's only ten o'clock—and see what happens. Then you'll at least know I've tried. And see what I'm up against." She started to cry.

"Jocasta, don't call now. You've had a lot of wine and it'll be the same thing all over again."

"You think I'm a lush, don't you?" said Jocasta with a watery smile.

"Of course not. But right now, the state you're in, you're not going to get anywhere at all. Let's go to bed."

Later, when Jocasta was asleep, exhausted by emotion, Clio went outside and called Fergus. "I'm sorry; I hoped I might be able to get away. It's awful, Fergus, I really think the whole thing is going to come crashing down. They are just so—unsuited, that's the real problem, their lives are completely incompatible. They might love each other, but it isn't enough."

Fergus said he hoped that it was enough in their case and Clio said she thought they were sublimely suited, compared with Jocasta and Gideon, and that she'd see him the next evening.

In the morning Jocasta called Gideon on all three numbers—the house, his mobile, and the office—saying she wanted to talk; an hour later there had been no response. After another hour, during which she raged and ranted, she left another message, saying that if he didn't call, he wouldn't hear from her again—ever. He called then and said how dared she threaten him; she put the phone down. After several hours, he rang again: Didn't she think she owed him an apology? She said she'd made several and if he couldn't even acknowledge that, then there could be no future for them of any kind. Gideon said as far as he was concerned, that would be a happy release and that she should go back to Nick, which was clearly what she wanted.

"I've just been a device, as far as I can see, to make him come to heel. Well, I don't like it, Jocasta. I'm not prepared to put up with it. Please don't call again."

Jocasta phoned Clio, told her everything that had happened, and said that was it—it was over.

"I couldn't have tried harder, Clio, I really couldn't. So that's it. End of chapter. Thanks for everything and please don't tell anyone but you can stop trying to help. Sorry."

Clio still didn't take it terribly seriously, in fact she could hardly believe the absurdity of it: two adults, behaving like extremely spoilt children. Giving up on a marriage after three months! It was ridiculous. It would blow over; they'd be all right.

Fergus, when she told him, was more doubtful. "I've seen Gideon through two of his divorces, you know. And once he thinks he's been wronged and he's dug those well-shod heels in, that's it. Trying to budge him is like taking an elbow to the Rock of Gibraltar."

"Fergus, he hasn't been wronged, as you put it, she's done nothing except—well, except be Jocasta."

"She's left home. He would see that as being wronged. Not in the traditional sense. I'm sure all this stuff about Nick is just a smokescreen. What he minds is her not accommodating him, one hundred percent. That's what he expects. It comes with the territory, Clio. Just be thankful that I'm not rich and powerful."

Clio said she didn't mind in the least and said goodbye, feeling very sad. She thought of her struggles to preserve her own marriage, and then thought that it had done her little good and maybe it was better that Jocasta's was ended, anyway. Perhaps it had all been a fantasy, a display of self-indulgent, self-deluding emotion. How could it possibly survive more than a few weeks of real life?

•—•

Several days had passed with Grace hardly eating at all, and Peter observed a pattern forming. She would lie in bed until about eleven, then get up and do minimal housework, have a cup of tea while he ate a lunch that he had prepared, take a rest, serve a perfunctory supper, which she would pick at, and then retire to bed again. She hardly spoke to him; she had withdrawn into a solitary, silent world.

And pray for guidance as he might, Peter found himself beginning to resent it.

•—•

"I wish you'd tell me what the matter is," said Nat. "I can't help you if you don't."

He had phoned to ask Kate if she wanted to go out; she had said she thought it better not.

"And I can't tell you what the matter is, because I don't really know myself. Except that it's worse than ever."

"What is?"

"Not knowing about my mum. At least before I'd found her, I could keep hoping."

"Hoping for what?"

"Well, that she'd be the sort of person I'd like. Which she wasn't."

"You don't know that, though, do you? You only met her once."

"Yes, and that was a real success, wasn't it? And now she's gone, and I'll never know anything about her, why she did it—anything. No answers, Nat, just more questions. I'm sick of it!"

"So you don't even want to go to the cinema. There's that *Matrix* film, you'd like that."

"No," said Kate with a sigh, "I don't think so, Nat. You go. And I've turned that contract down, and all. That's made me feel bad."

"But you didn't want to do it."

"I know that. But you think about turning down three million dollars. It's well scary."

"I'd rather not," said Nat with a shudder.

Kate went out into the garden; her mother was watering the roses. "Hi, Mum."

"Hello, love. You feeling any better?"

"Not really. I don't know what's the matter with me."

"I do," said Helen, "you've had too much to cope with, that's what's the matter. What with finding out who your mother was, and then what happened to her, and all this worry about the contract. It's too much for anyone, let alone someone of your age."

"Yeah, I suppose so. I feel bad about Nat, too. He's been so good and I just can't be, well, very nice to him. I don't feel sort of—positive about anything."

"I think that'll get better," said Helen, "I really do. I hope so." She smiled at Kate. "I miss him. Him and his dad."

Kate smiled and put her arm round her mother's shoulders. "Thanks, Mum. You've been great. Don't know what— Shit, if that's Nat again, tell him I'm asleep or something! Why's he ringing the landline anyway? He's such a tosser sometimes."

"Don't swear, dear," said Helen rather feebly.

•◆•

Nick was packing; the parliamentary summer recess had begun and he was going home for a couple of weeks to stay with his parents. He did it every year and could never see anything remotely odd about this: his friends went off scuba diving in the Maldives or sailing off the coast of Ireland or trekking in the Himalayas. But Nick was perfectly content to help on the farm, lounge in the garden, hike across the Somerset hills, go on riding picnics with any small nieces and nephews who might be around, chat with his brothers and sisters, and trounce everyone at Monopoly or backgammon after dinner. If that was what he enjoyed, why pretend he wanted to do anything else? In his holidaymaking, as in everything else, it was generally agreed, Nicholas Marshall was an absolute one-off.

He pulled down the battered old leather Gladstone bag from the shelf in his bedroom and tipped its contents out on the bed. This was always an interesting moment; he could never be bothered to finish unpacking when he got back from the trips the paper sent him on—usually to follow sundry politicians around the globe—and this evening's yield, following a trip to Washington in the early spring, was no exception. A couple of half-read paperbacks, three American newspapers, several packs of chewing gum—intended for Jocasta, to help her in her biannual struggle to give up smoking. A pair of socks—clean, thank God—and some gold cuff links his father had given him. Thank God for that too—he'd thought he'd lost them.

And a tape recorder, still in its box; a present from Jocasta for the trip. "It's a nice modern one, that old clockwork one of yours is going to die on you one of these days, probably interviewing Bill Clinton," she'd said. Although he'd thanked her, he'd never even used it, preferred his old one, tried and true as it was.

It was a very nice one about a quarter of the size of his old one, with tiny tapes; one was labelled "Play me." Curious, he slipped it into the machine and pressed play. Jocasta's voice came out.

"Hello, darling Nick. This is your devoted—well, fairly devoted—girlfriend, wishing you *bon voyage* and *bonne chance* and all that sort of thing. Have fun, but not too much and don't forget the Hershey bars." (Of course he had.) "Love you loads and loads and thank you for the best time last night. Lovely dinner, lovely everything. Kiss kiss."

Nick played it again, and then again. Thinking about her, about how that tape was just like her, sweet and funny and loving. And thinking how much he had loved her. Still loved her. And that he really hadn't been very nice to her last time they had met. Still less so when he'd sent her stuff back. It was terrible to think of all that love, evaporated into coldness and distance. Forever.

He picked up the phone and rang her.

Jocasta was lying in bed, feeling extremely sorry for herself. She'd had a long and lonely weekend, and had sent out for a curry on Saturday evening; it had been the first meal she had eaten for days, and she gorged herself on it, washed it down with an entire bottle of rather rough red wine, and finished off with some ice cream, over which she had poured a melted Mars bar, one of her favourite puddings. Whether it was the curry, the gorging, or the wine, she had been extremely ill much of Saturday night and most of Sunday. She was only just beginning to feel better. And still terribly lonely.

Nick's voice was, therefore, even more irresistible than she might have expected.

"Hi," she said carefully, "it's lovely to hear from you."

"Hello, Jocasta. I just thought I'd phone. Make sure you were all right."

"I'm fine, yes. Thank you. That's very sweet of you."

"You sound a bit . . . tired."

"I had some bad curry on Saturday night."

"I'm sorry. I wouldn't have thought curry of any kind would be on the menu for Mrs. Gideon Keeble."

"No, well, obviously it wouldn't normally. But he was—he was out, and I just fancied it. You know."

"Oh I do. In the old days you'd have had ice cream and melted Mars bar to follow."

"I did," she said without thinking.

"Jocasta! The staff must have had the night off."

"What? Oh, yes. Yes, they did. Um—where are you, Nick?"

"Just packing. To go down to Somerset for a couple of weeks. And I found the tape recorder you gave me. In my bag."

"Oh yes. I hoped it'd be useful. Obviously it hasn't, if it's still in your bag."

"Oh, it has. Of course it has. And I played the tape you put in for me. Again, I mean. It was very sweet, and I just wanted to thank you."

She could remember the tape. She had wanted him to have it, to have something of her. She could remember the whole thing, making the tape and sending it to him, because it had been his last trip abroad, just before the whole drama had begun: Centre Forward, Gideon, Kate, Martha. God, it had been a year. Less than a year. It felt like five. Anyway, she'd intended to give the recorder to him, and they'd gone out to dinner but she'd had too much wine, as usual, and got very emotional about him going away. Then they'd gone home and had the most mind-blowing sex, and she'd completely forgotten until next day, when she'd found it in her bag and sent it over to his office. First making her little recording.

"That's OK," she said, smiling at the memory.

"So where are you?"

"Oh, at home," she said without thinking.

"What, at the Big House?"

"Of—of course."

"And you're really all right?"

"Of course I'm all right, Nick. Why shouldn't I be? I took your words to heart—it was the best thing anyone ever said to me, and I'm a reformed character, learning to be a good wife and—"

"I'm pleased to have had such an excellent effect on you," he said. "And you're happy?"

"Terribly happy," she said. "Yes, thank you. Oh—hang on, Nick, there's someone at the door. Won't be a minute."

Nick sat there waiting; he could hear the roar of traffic in the background, a police siren, hear her saying, "Yes, that's for me, thank you, do I need to sign, fine, there you are," heard the door slamming, heard her walking back across the wooden floor—the wooden floor? Roar of traffic? Answering the door herself?

"Jocasta, where are you?"

"I told you—"

"I know what you told me," he said, "but I don't recall traffic roaring up and down Kensington Palace Gardens. I would have thought staff would take in parcels. And I seem to remember a lot of carpeting everywhere, and quite a distance from the front door to anywhere."

There was a silence; then she said, "I'm in Clapham, Nick. I've just—come to collect a few things."

"So why lie to me about it?"

"Oh, I don't know. It seemed simpler."

"Jocasta, what's happened? Please tell me."

She wouldn't let him come to Clapham; it was too dangerous. She said she'd meet him in Queen Mary's Rose Garden in Regent's Park. It had been a favourite place of theirs, in the early days, halfway between both their houses. She looked at him sitting there on a bench, his long rangy body stretched out in the sunshine, his untidy brown hair flopping into his eyes, and thought how she missed him more every single day, and that even this was not exactly sensible. She sat down beside him; he gave her a kiss.

"That allowed?"

"Of course." She smiled at him, and told him some of what had happened: very unemotionally.

"I'm really not complaining, Nick," she said carefully. "I can see a lot of it was—*is* my fault. Most of it. But it just isn't working at the moment. It might still. I hope so."

It was a lie: of course. She didn't think so at all. She just couldn't let him think it was over, that she was throwing herself at him, expecting to be taken back.

He was very sweet, unreproachful. He said if that was the case then he certainly wouldn't want to be the cause of it not working out; he said he would like always to be her friend, her best friend; he said he missed her terribly.

"I miss you too," she said, brightly, "so yes, let's be friends. Best friends."

She stood up, smiled down at him, and had just managed to say, "Well, I must be getting back then," when she felt suddenly terribly dizzy and faint. She supposed it was the emotion, the tearing, mixed-up emotion, and also because she hadn't really eaten since she had left Gideon, apart from the thrown-up curry. She swayed visibly and was unable to walk calmly and steadily towards the entrance of the garden, as she had planned, but had to sit down again, her head between her knees.

And after that, it was only a very short—and logical—progress to his car and thence to his flat. He bought some food on the way, good, bland, binding food, he said firmly, eggs and bread and Vichy water—"full of minerals." And then he cooked her an omelet, made her some toast, and—well, somehow after that, there they were, alone, in his flat, and try as she might, she couldn't remain unemotional and said she thought she should go. To which he suddenly said, quite sweetly, that she should never have left him, and that reminded her exactly why she had, and she got angry and told him.

"I loved you," he said. "So much."

"And how was I to know that?"

"I kept telling you."

"But you didn't show me," she said. "You never showed me."

"Oh, this is ridiculous!" he said. "I couldn't show you then, not how you wanted. I didn't know—" He stopped.

"Didn't know what?" she asked, but he wouldn't answer her, just turned away and looked out of the window, and then suddenly it was the old situation starting again, and she couldn't bear it and she said, wearily, "I must go."

"Yes, I think you should. I'll call you a cab. I'm very sorry, Jocasta. For all of it. I hope it works out for you, I really do."

"Thank you," she said.

"Can I kiss you goodbye? Old times' sake?"

"Old times' sake . . ."

He bent to kiss her on the cheek; only somehow she moved and his mouth met hers instead. And—that was that, really.

How she did it, she afterwards never knew; one moment she was feeling frail, dizzy again, wretchedly confused, the next full of a powerful, surging energy and certainty. Nick was there in front of her, and she wanted him, and she had to have him; and he felt it—she saw him feel it, saw him smile, saw him acknowledge it, saw him certain too.

They were naked before they reached the bedroom; she flung herself back onto the bed, holding out her arms to him, saying his name over and over again, hearing him saying hers, both of them talking fast, feverishly, "Want you, missed you, love you," and then his mouth was everywhere on her: her throat, her breasts, her stomach, her thighs, and hers on him, moving over him, frantic for him, a great tangle of desire growing and growing in her, pushing at her. She lowered herself onto him, feeling him, moving on him, round him, melting, softening, sweetening for him, crying out as the sensations grew, sitting on him now, riding him, twisting, turning, journeying through some dark, wonderfully difficult place, reaching for the light at the end of it, feeling herself growing, clenching, climbing, struggling, and then yes, yes, that was it, the height, the peak and she was there, shouting, yelling with triumph and then she felt him come too and she came again, in great warm, easy, spreading circles, until finally she fell into a deep, sweet peace.

"Now what?" he said, and his brown eyes, smiling into hers, were very sweet, very tender.

"God knows," she said, and went suddenly and happily to sleep.

Clio had finally told Fergus about Josh. About Josh and Kate, that was. When she had finished he said, "Of course. How clever of you. It was all so obvious, wasn't it? Staring in our faces all the time."

"So obvious. But Fergus, I don't know what to do. I just don't. Whatever I do, I shall upset Josh—"

"I shouldn't worry too much about him, spoilt brat of a man that he is."

"Fergus, that's not true! He may be spoilt, but he's very sweet really. But think what it would do to poor Beatrice. And their rather strained marriage."

"Think indeed."

"But then Kate *needs* to know. I really think it would help her now. She's so—bewildered, still. Martha dying has just made her worse. You said yourself she was very down. So what do I do? I feel as if I'm holding a time bomb. And Jocasta about to—well, I don't know what she's about to do. She's in the most extraordinary state. Not miserable anymore. Excited, almost, but incredibly emotional. Saying one minute she wants a divorce, the next she doesn't, not yet anyway."

"There's nothing any of us can do about that," he said, "and you must just wait with this Josh business. It's been a secret for many years and it will keep a few more weeks. Although I agree, it would probably help Kate. But the moment will arrive. It always does."

"I hope so," said Clio miserably. "I can't stand much more of this."

⊷

Jocasta had said goodbye to Nick and gone home. He had not argued, had not tried to detain her. It was all rather unnerving.

The afternoon in his flat had acquired a dreamlike quality—there were even times when she thought she must have imagined it. Nick was being as evasive, as enraging as ever: if she had been looking for some great expression of commitment, she would have been sadly disappointed.

He simply told her he would always love her, that he would always be there for her, her very best friend as he had said—and then agreed that the best thing for both of them was for him to go home as planned and for her to go back to Gideon.

"Back to the Big House?"

"Of course. I'll send you a postcard," he said. "I know how much you like getting postcards."

"Thank you," she said.

"And I certainly don't see any need for foolhardy confessions, or anything like that."

"Of course not," she said, bravely bright. "It was just a bit of lovely, naughty fun."

But when she got home to Clapham, digested what had happened, thought over what he had said, she felt a disappointment so crushing she could hardly bear it.

She would have been comforted and totally astonished over the next few days, had she heard him talking endlessly to his favourite brother, telling him how much he still adored Jocasta, loved her more than ever, indeed, but that she had made it very plain she was still hoping to salvage her marriage and it would be dreadfully wrong of him to do anything to scupper that.

⋅•⋅

"Grace, dear, you must eat." Peter Hartley looked at yet another untouched breakfast tray. He had to leave her that morning, to do some parish visits, but he had prepared a tempting breakfast: muesli, yogurt, fruit—all the things she liked—in very small portions.

"I can't eat. It was very nice, but I just don't want it. Please, take it away." She pushed it aside fretfully, and lay down again, pulled the covers over her head.

Peter took it away.

⋅•⋅

Janet Frean wasn't eating very much either, but it was enough, as her doctor reported to Bob that morning. "She doesn't need a lot of food, and don't worry, we're keeping a careful eye on it." She was doing very well really, he said; she'd had several sessions now with the resident psychiatrist, who had prescribed drug therapy, one-to-one sessions with him or one of the other psychiatrists, and possibly, as she began to feel better, group therapy.

"It often helps, to hear other people describing their own torments," the psychiatrist said to Bob.

Bob told him he didn't think anyone could have had torments more dreadful and complex than Janet's; the psychiatrist patted him on the arm.

"There you would be very wrong," he said.

"Has she told you anything yet?"

"A little. I don't have time to discuss it with you now, I'm afraid. But don't worry, she's a far from hopeless case. Believe me. Try not to worry too much."

They didn't understand, Janet thought, lying back on her pillows after a particularly exhausting attack of rage on her therapist—she probably shouldn't have attacked her physically like that, but she had made Janet so angry, with her soothing rubbish—they absolutely didn't understand.

Nobody could. They all thought it was because of Martha Hartley, her breakdown. It wasn't at all. Of course she was sorry about Martha, and she did feel some degree of guilt—but not to the extent they all thought. Martha's secret would have come out, it was too big, too dangerous; she could not have hoped that the concentric circles she had built so carefully about her life to protect her would remain so; sooner or later another event would have exploded into them, pushing them together, forcing a revelation. And really, what happy ending could there possibly have been for her, once the revelation was out? Her career, her personal life, certainly her political life would have been fatally damaged. It could be argued Janet had done her a favour.

No, the reason she had wanted to end her own life was because everything she had ever worked for, hoped for—and taken such risks for—was now gone from her forever. Irretrievably gone. She could never have it back. And if the Centre Forward Party survived, Jack would be its leader, probably with Chad as his chief henchman.

And if it did not, how could she go back to the Tories now? The best she could have hoped for with the new party was the post of deputy leader. Which would have almost satisfied her. She would have even considered that winning: a uniquely high-profile position. Given that she was a woman. She had got rid of Martha. There was just Mary Norton to deal with now. And that should be quite easy; a few hints about her lesbian friends, and the electorate would start wavering. Then she'd find something else. Well, maybe all was not lost. Maybe. She could still come back. She could. She would . . .

"Mrs. Frean is asleep," her nurse reported to the psychiatrist ten minutes later. "The sedative has worked very well. I'll let you know if there's any change."

•—•—•

Smith Cosmetics had thanked Fergus for his e-mail and said that they were now looking at other young girls. They said in the unlikely event of their not finding anyone else, they might contact him again, should Kate change her mind. They said there might be some leeway on the financial front, but they couldn't possibly give any undertakings on the publicity side of the contract, which he'd told them was what worried Kate most.

"As you must know, the press make their own decisions about what and what not to print."

It was a very friendly and gracious response, Fergus thought, given all the time and money they had wasted on Kate, a testimony to how much they had wanted her. Still wanted her. It comforted him, just a bit. Things might change.

Fergus was the eternal optimist.

•—•—•

Clio spent Sunday with Jocasta; she found her still in an odd mood, on an emotional seesaw, overexcited one minute, tearful the next. She said she was just trying to work out what to do, that she might go back to work, might do something quite different—when pressed on what, she said vaguely that she'd thought of property, or maybe interior design. Clio had said what a good idea; there was no point arguing with her. She was beyond reason.

She had arrived still hoping she might help to effect a reconciliation, because she did still think that was what Jocasta wanted. She tried reason, humour, appeals to common sense. But it appeared to be a complete impasse.

There had been another very ugly row the day before; Gideon had demanded that she meet him to try to have a reasonable discussion about what they were going to do next, and Jocasta had said it wasn't possible to have a reasonable discussion with a person so unreasonable that he was actually unstable. Each confrontation was infinitely worse than the last, making that one seem comparatively pleasant, almost an exchange of views.

Right in the middle of telling Clio this, Jocasta burst into tears, and when Clio asked her if there was anything particularly the matter, said there was, but she couldn't talk about it. She was still drinking and smoking far too much, seemed unable to rest or settle to anything for more than five minutes. All she wanted to do was talk interminably about Gideon and his shortcomings. In the end, Clio gave up and said she must go home.

"Oh, please don't go," said Jocasta. She had been talking to someone on the phone, sounding increasingly hostile. "That was Josh. He's threatening to come round; he thinks he can make me see sense, as he puts it. Such a wonderful arbiter of relationships, such an example to us all."

Clio sighed. "Well I've failed. Maybe he will be able to help."

"Clio, he won't. And it's not a question of you failing. It's the marriage that's failed."

"Jocasta, I must go. It's Monday tomorrow and I've got an early surgery. And I do want to see Fergus this evening before I go home."

"You're so lucky to have such a normal, stable relationship," said Jocasta wistfully. "Oh, Clio, don't go! You can't leave me with Josh; he's going to upset me. Stay and go down in the morning, you always say how easy it is. Please, Clio, please."

Clio hesitated.

"Please! You can't fail me, and you're such an angel, such a good friend."

Clio wondered what on earth Jocasta would say or do if she knew the real reason for her reluctance to see Josh.

She stayed for his visit, of course. She could never quite work out how Jocasta managed to persuade people to do what she wanted, how she used that intense will of hers, a mixture of charm and absolute determination: she had a hunch that Gideon might have been subjected to the full force of it. Would he really have wanted to get married, after being with Jocasta—what—three weeks, if he hadn't? The fact was, she was absolutely irresistible.

And here Clio was, in Jocasta's sitting room, trying not to look too often at the photographs on the table of Jocasta and Josh as children, while Jocasta sat ordering a takeaway from the local Thai restaurant.

"I haven't eaten all weekend and suddenly I'm hungry. Hope it doesn't make me ill, like the curry did."

Josh arrived, finally, almost an hour late, so that the Thai was half cold; it wasn't even very nice. Clio sat picking at it miserably, wishing Josh would stop telling Jocasta that she was being immature and unrealistic, wondering what the point of her being there could possibly be.

"The thing is, Jocasta," he was saying now, "marriage is almost impossible, even when you're trying really hard. If you're not—well, forget it."

"That's *exactly* what I'm doing," said Jocasta. "Or was trying to do, I mean."

"But I thought you loved Gideon."

"I do. Anyway, thought I did. But I can't live with him; he's a monster, leading a monstrous life. I should have seen that long ago."

"But he's such a nice man," said Josh. "He's kind and generous and he obviously adores you—that's what you have to concentrate on, Jocasta, Beatrice always says that."

"What does Beatrice always say?" said Jocasta, her tone deceptively mild.

"Well, that in a marriage you tend to just take the good things for granted, and only notice the bad. That's what finishes most of them off."

"What nearly finished yours off," said Jocasta, "was your inability to be faithful to Beatrice. And what saved it was her incredible facility for forgiveness. Don't ever try and get a job as a therapist, will you?"

"Oh, piss off!" said Josh. He had gone rather red. "I'm only trying to help, I can't bear to see you two making each other so unhappy."

"I know and I'm very grateful," said Jocasta, suddenly remorseful, "but honestly, you're not doing any good at all. Let's talk about something else. What's in that bag?"

"Oh—I found my pictures of Thailand. They were in the bottom of a cupboard, with my cameras. I thought they might amuse you."

"Now you're talking," said Jocasta. "Let's have a look. Come on, Clio, let's clear the table."

He pulled them out: batch after batch, in no kind of order, shots of the steaming jungle up in the north, shots of elephants, of monkeys, of the hill villages, the sweet, smiling children; of the temples and palaces and floating markets and canals in Bangkok—"God, I can smell it just looking at them," said Clio—of the chaos of the Khao San Road, the lady-boys in Pat Pong—"They obviously fancied you, just look at them vamping it up," said Jocasta. The tuk tuks, the longtail boats on the great river: and then the islands, endless shots of sweeping white beaches backed by green hills, of waterfalls, of lakes, of palms tipping gracefully into water, of sheer cliffs, of brilliant flowers, of shrines, of Big Buddha—"Dear old Big Buddha," said Clio, "I still think about him sometimes, sitting there, those eyes of his following you everywhere. Golly, this is a trip down memory lane, I feel eighteen again."

There were shots with people in them, some occasions they remembered—"Look, there we are at the airport," said Josh, "all of us, that nice old chap took it, remember?"—frozen in time, smiling, tidy-looking, everything ahead of them.

And then there was island life, hundreds of people, most of whom they couldn't remember, smiling, always smiling, smoking, drinking, waving, hugging each other; lying on the beaches, sitting in the boats, swinging on ropes over lakes, swimming under waterfalls, elephant riding, snorkelling. There were some frenetically blurred shots of the full-moon parties, people dancing, the beach covered in candles, and, "Here, look at this, remember the reggae boat?" said Josh.

"Yes thanks," said Jocasta, "that was how I got dengue fever, from a mosquito on one of those lakes, too stoned to feel it."

"What on earth are you doing there?" asked Clio, intrigued, looking at a shot of Josh lying on a rug, inhaling from a large pipe.

"Taking opium."

"Josh! You never told me. What on earth was that like?"

"Absolutely nothing," he said, laughing. "I think it was talcum powder."

"God, it was all fun," said Jocasta, "such, such fun. Hey, Josh, what's this, posh hotel, or what? And who's this? Martha? By that amazing pool? And on that terrace? Josh, you never told me about this, whatever happened?"

"God—didn't know that was there," said Josh, flushing a dark red, and went on rather hurriedly to explain that he'd bumped into Martha leaving Koh Tao, there'd been a fire on the boat and they'd all nearly drowned. "No, it's true, I'm not making it up."

They'd both felt pretty rough, and he'd had plenty of money on him, so they'd gone to a hotel near Chaweng, stayed there one night.

"Mmm," said Jocasta, her eyes dancing, "you dark horse. You pair of dark horses. You never said. When was that? You obviously had lots of fun. Is that why you wanted to come to the funeral?"

"No. Well, sort of. I mean—yes, it was, actually."

"I think that's very sweet."

Clio had been literally praying for some bell, however faint, to ring in Jocasta's head. It clearly wasn't going to. She had to do it. And it was now or never. She took a deep breath, and said, "Josh, when exactly was that? Can you remember?"

"I don't know," he said. "Does it matter?"

"Yes. It—could."

"Clio," said Jocasta, "what are you on about?"

"I, well, I just thought of something. I was just thinking about—about Martha. That's all."

"What about her? Except that she was obviously a darker horse than we thought. I mean—with Josh! And never telling us. And— Oh my God! You don't think—I mean—Josh—oh my God!"

"What?" he said irritably. "What's the matter with you both?"

"Just tell us when you and Martha had your little . . . fling." Jocasta was speaking very slowly. "It's terribly important."

"I'll try. But I don't see—"

"Josh! Think!"

"Well, it was before Christmas, definitely, because I was in Malaysia then. Sometime around October, November, I suppose. You know how meaningless time is out there, weeks feel like months and vice versa."

"Josh, you've got to do better than that."

"I'm trying, for God's sake. Right—well, actually, it must have been October, yes, it definitely was, because I was on my way up to Bangkok, to see my girlfriend, well, not exactly my girlfriend, but we had been pretty involved, and she was in hospital, she'd had a scooter crash on Koh Phangan, and I had my birthday up there, my eighteenth, I do remember that."

"And on the way you took Martha to a hotel. Josh, Josh, you are—oh God, you're so awful!" said Jocasta.

"Yes, I get the message. I thought you wanted to know when I was there with Martha."

Jocasta looked at Clio. "So that's October the twenty-sixth, his birthday. And Kate was born in the middle of August, so it would have had to have been November, wouldn't it?" she said.

"Sorry," Clio said. "Kate was nearly three weeks late. Martha told me. That was the whole point, why she was here when she had her. So the end of October would be just right."

"What are you two going on about?" asked Josh. "You really have lost me."

"Josh," said Jocasta, filling his glass to the brim, "drink that. You're going to need it. You really are . . ."

Chapter 42

. . . .

Josh had hardly slept. He felt he would never sleep again. He had spent the night tossing fretfully on the spare room bed—he told Beatrice he had indigestion, that he'd keep her awake.

It seemed to him it was impossible to do the right thing. He either had to tell Beatrice, who would be horrified, not to mention terribly hurt, probably finally throw him out—and what on earth would the little girls make of it, suddenly having a big sister? Or he could just not say a word and live with this awful, oppressing piece of knowledge for the rest of his life.

It wasn't as if she was just any old girl either: she was famous. Well, quite famous. What was it Jocasta was always saying? Once something was in the cuttings, it was there forever. It would be like a time bomb, waiting to go off. He supposed this must have been exactly what Martha had felt, and wondered how on earth she had stood it. God, she must have been brave. Brave and tough.

And then there was Kate. Kate his daughter. The vision of her kept rising before him, all night. The girl at the funeral, so lovely, so funny, so clearly clever, discussing her future with him, was his daughter. He had a grown-up daughter. It just didn't seem remotely possible. He thought of

Charlie and Harry, still babies really, clambering all over him, pulling his hair, tweaking his nose, giggling, making faces at him, splashing him with their bathwater, lying on his lap, sucking their thumbs while he read them stories. They were the sort of daughters he wanted. That he could cope with. Not a dangerously attractive girl of sixteen. He had fancied her himself, he thought, and his blood curdled.

And how could you start being a father to someone you'd met for the first time at that age? She was grown up, processed, done. He'd had no part of her, she was nothing to do with him; another man had done all that, read to her, bathed her, played with her, chosen her schools, laid down the rules. There was nothing of him in her.

But there was, of course, he thought, sitting up suddenly, there was half of him in her. One night with someone, one pretty good night actually, as far as he could recall, at the age of seventeen, well, nearly eighteen, that's all he'd been, one and a bit years older than Kate herself, carefree, happy, just enjoying life, having fun and—there you were, a father. It was a bad system, that, very dangerous. He had no idea how it could have happened; he'd always been jolly careful, always used french letters, but everyone knew they could fail, spring a leak. That was obviously what had happened.

Why hadn't the bloody girl had a termination? They weren't hard to come by, so why on earth had she hung on to it? Why had she never tried to find him, for that matter? He'd have helped her out, helped her decide what to do, given her money. At this moment, Josh suddenly had a clear vision of himself at seventeen, utterly selfish, totally immature, and thought rather sadly that he could actually see very clearly why she hadn't sought him out. He wouldn't have seemed to her a very good bet.

And anyway, she might not have been sure it was him. She might have been promiscuous, sleeping with every guy she came across. She'd certainly been pretty keen, hadn't taken much persuasion. But clearly it had been him. Kate was his. She looked exactly like him. Or to be precise, like Jocasta.

And what would she want? This new, problematic daughter? Jocasta and Clio had both told him she was very hurt by what had happened to her, that she had been searching for her mother all her life, ever more confused and upset.

"She just wants to know where she belongs," Clio had said, "where she came from, if you like. You can see how dreadfully confusing for her it all is. She loves her parents dearly but they can't supply the answers. And Martha's death has been yet another blow; she didn't provide any, either."

Whatever he decided, they all agreed, Beatrice must be told. "She's so bloody marvellous, she'll probably be magnificent," said Josh gloomily, "offer Kate a home and—"

"Kate doesn't need a home," Jocasta said sharply. "She's very happy where she is. She doesn't lack for love or attention and her adoptive parents are great. She just wants to know how and why it all happened. She's got the dearest boyfriend," she added.

Josh groaned. "I can't cope with her," he said, "let alone her boyfriend."

When the clock struck four, he went downstairs to make himself a hot toddy.

‧◆‧

Peter Hartley had been in church since very early. He had spent a little time on his knees alone, remembering Martha, and quite a lot of time in the vestry tidying up, hanging up the choirboys' cassocks and sweeping the floor; it was only when he found himself sorting out the prayer and hymn books, a job that the verger and his wife always did, and indeed enjoyed doing, that he realised what he was really doing: postponing his return to the vicarage and to Grace.

He felt very bad; it was only a few weeks since Martha had died and he missed her terribly and the brilliant light she had shone into his rather drab life. Nobody knew it was drab, of course, or, rather, that he found it so. His unshakable faith helped a great deal, and the knowledge that he was doing it all for God; and there were wonderful moments, at weddings and confirmations particularly, but also when he was taking the communion service, or delivered what he felt was a good, rather than an all right, sermon. But the fact remained that day to day, his life was filled with thankless and tedious tasks.

His other prop and mainstay was his beloved Grace, and being apparently robbed of her, as well as of Martha, was proving almost unbearable. What had begun as bewilderment and moved to reproach was now turning to hostility: based, as far as he could see, on a deep resentment that he was finding comfort from God and she was not.

"It's all right for you," she had actually said. "You've got comfort—I haven't got any."

Meanwhile, she continued not to eat: or rather, as he was beginning to see it, to starve herself.

When he got back to the vicarage, the post had arrived; the usual junk mail and two proper letters, as he thought of them. One from a parishioner, asking if he would sponsor her son on a trans-Siberian cycle ride, and another, written in a very childish hand, from someone called Kate Tarrant.

I just wanted to say that I've been thinking of you both a lot, and I do hope you are beginning to feel a little bit better now. I only met your daughter twice, but she seemed a very nice and interesting person. It was a very good experience to be at the funeral and to learn more about her and all the things she had achieved in her life.

With very good wishes, yours sincerely,
Kate Tarrant

Kate Tarrant: now who on earth was she? She'd been at the funeral, she said, but he had no idea who she might have been. Until he saw her helpful PS on the other side of the paper: "I came with Jocasta Forbes," she had written, "one of the girls your daughter went travelling with before she went to university."

Now Jocasta he did remember; she had come up to them and talked for quite a while. A beautiful girl, charming. There had been two other girls with her: one who had also gone travelling with Martha, very nice, a doctor he seemed to recall, one much younger, with long blond hair: perhaps that had been Kate. Grace might remember. Or young Ed—he had seemed to know that particular crowd. It would give him something to talk to Grace about later, perhaps even lift her from her dreadful lethargy. His busy, bustling Grace: lethargic. It was terribly hard to bear.

He took it up to her.

"Now look, we've had such a nice letter. From one of the young people who came to the funeral. You remember Jocasta, with the blond hair who went travelling with Martha all those years ago?"

"Peter, it's all a blur."

"Anyway, there was another girl with her, much younger. Nearer Ed's age, I'd say. It's from her. Kate's her name. Such a sweet little note."

"Well"—she shrugged—"that's nice. What does she say?"

"I'll leave it here, you can read it for yourself."

"I've got a terrible headache. I really don't feel up to reading."

"It's very short. I'll go and get your tea. If you haven't read it when I get back, I'll read it to you."

He laid the letter on her bed and walked out; when he looked back, she had picked it up and was reaching for her glasses. It was odd, the way these young friends of Martha's seemed able to cheer her up. Or at least interest her.

Grace did remember Kate now. Pretty girl. She'd noticed her because she had that lovely fair hair and then those huge, dark eyes, a bit like Martha's. Her mother was lucky. She still had her daughter. She hadn't seen her wiped out, her brilliantly promising life ended, all through a bit of stupidity. She hadn't got to go on living on a planet that didn't contain her daughter, full of people who didn't matter because they weren't her.

She wished she and Martha had been closer; she'd always had the feeling that Martha was keeping her just slightly at arm's length. Never discussing her boyfriends, her private life, only her career, always her career. She'd probably be alive today without that career. She wouldn't have been driving up from London, far too late and much too fast, in that car. She'd be working safely in Binsmow, where they could keep an eye on her. .

Ed had obviously known her very well. She wondered if they'd got engaged or anything like that. Of all the people who kept coming to see her, she only enjoyed seeing Ed. She could talk to him about Martha, learn a bit more. She would like to see more of Jocasta, too. And Clio, the pretty dark-haired one, she'd liked her too. Between them, they probably knew more about Martha than she did. Well, it was no use thinking they'd have time to come all this way to see her. They were young, they had their own lives, and they were busy, happy . . .

Grace turned on her side again and started to cry. She felt so alone in her grief. Peter had his God. She had no one.

Jocasta would not have said she was pleased about the drama of Josh and Kate, but it gave her something else to think about, apart from her own worries and misery.

In spite of everything they had said, she had expected to hear something from Nick. If only a note. Or a call on her mobile. Or the promised postcard. Just to check that she was . . . well, she wasn't sure what he would be checking, but they had shared a fairly amazing experience that afternoon—God, already over a week ago—and a complete silence was a bit unnerving. Maybe now he just saw her as another girl; but that wasn't right, he had said he would always love her. And that he would always be her best friend. Did being your best friend really include having that sort of amazing, stunning sex? Maybe it did. And oh, God, it *had* been amazing. Every so often she just sat very still and concentrated on remembering it, and became hideously excited.

Whatever else it had done for her, that afternoon, it had made her realise she couldn't go back to Gideon. Sex with Gideon was, well, dull. It was fine, it could be very good in fact, at worst it was extremely pleasant and, obviously, bonding—but it was always the same. She felt terrible comparing him with Nick in bed, it made her feel dreadfully disloyal, and even a bit of a trollop, but she couldn't help it.

She had expected thunder and lightning, given his intensity and his experience and his dangerously seductive tongue, and she had got only a sunlit afternoon. A very nice sunlit afternoon, to be sure, but one that just went on and on. In fact—and she would never have believed this possible of herself—she had come to be quite grateful for the nights he fell asleep, while she sat beside him reading. Or even—on some truly awful occasions—carrying on and on reading until he went to sleep. She had heard girls, usually ones in long-established relationships, saying things like that and been quite shocked. And very sorry for them. Now she understood.

Sex with Nick had always been good; always, always. Not necessarily extraordinary, but good. Sometimes fun, sometimes more serious, occasionally really quick, now and again very, very long—Sunday sex, as she thought of it—when she came and came and wanted it never to end. But never dull. And they were absolutely honest: that had to be important. If she didn't want it, she said so and he never minded; if he was too tired, he said so and she understood. They told each other if they didn't like something, or if there was something they thought they might try, which often led to giggling failures and an agreement that the missionary position had a lot to be said for it. She couldn't imagine that sort of honesty with Gideon.

And then they had it in all sorts of places, some more unlikely than others, sitting in the bath, standing in the hall, on the beach, in the woods, even occasionally, and rather riskily, in Nick's car. The point was it was an integral part of them being together, as much a part of their lives as eating or drinking or working; she could no more imagine a sexless life with Nick than one without conversation. She could very easily imagine a sexless life with Gideon.

Well, life with him just wasn't going to happen: sexless or otherwise. She had written to him now, telling him that she thought they should get a divorce as soon as possible, that she could see no hope of their ever being able to live together happily, and that prolonging matters was just making them worse. She gave him the name and address of her solicitor, and said she would hope to hear from him shortly. She supposed she should feel sad, but she didn't; apart from being lonely, her only emotion was still anger.

Maybe she should write to Nick, but saying—what? That she missed him, that she still loved him, that she wanted to see him? No. That was out of the question. He would think she had come back to him on the rebound, or that she was whining again. She had to get his respect back; she had to be strong. If, in the fullness of time, he heard that she had left Gideon, that would be quite different, but he mustn't think it was anything to do with him. That would be emotional blackmail; it wouldn't be fair.

Gideon read her letter and then tore it up and threw it in the wastepaper basket. If she thought he was going to make things easy for her, so that she could marry Nick sooner, she was very wrong. He had managed to convince himself that she had left him because she had gone back to Nick. His vanity would not allow him to consider any alternative. A young rival was better than an intrinsic fault in himself.

•→•

Beatrice had been absolutely wonderful. Josh had called her from his office at midday, unable to stand it any longer, and asked if they could meet after work for a drink.

"What on earth for, Josh? Why not at home?"

"Because I've got something I want to talk about and I don't want the girls around. Or anyone, come to that."

They met in the American bar at the Connaught. Beatrice arrived, looking rather pale. She clearly thought Josh was going to tell her he had some new girlfriend.

"Which I suppose, in a way, he had," she said to Jocasta, brightly.

The news had been so extraordinary and shocking that she had found it difficult to find an appropriate reaction at all. What exactly did you say, when your husband told you he had just discovered he had a sixteen-year-old daughter? "How nice," or "I can't wait to meet her"? Or "How could you?" Or "How dare you?" Or "Never darken my doors again"?

None of them seemed right. Beatrice sat and looked at him, at this person she really did love, who had hurt her and humiliated her a great deal, who had vowed never to do so again, this charming, good-looking, troublesome person, and found that her overwhelming emotion was sympathy. She waited for this to be replaced by something less noble, like rage, or outrage, or jealousy—and it wasn't. Sympathy remained: and she said so.

"For heaven's sake, Josh," she said quite sternly, "a lot of seventeen-year-old boys sleep around. That was just incredibly unfortunate."

"Yes," he said, "I suppose it was."

"And certainly Martha was. Poor Martha."

"Yes," he said, "poor Martha."

"I can't imagine why she didn't tell you. Or her parents. I suppose she just felt she couldn't."

"I suppose."

"What a sad, sad story."

"Absolutely. I feel bad," he said suddenly, "that she had to cope with it all, and I just got away scot-free. It seems so terrible."

"Yes, well," said Beatrice, slightly brisker, "you have a certain talent for getting away scot-free, Josh."

The sympathy was waning now—just a little. She looked ahead and saw enormous problems. Did they tell Kate? What did they tell Kate? Did they tell the girls? *What* would they tell the girls? How would they understand? Josh and Beatrice had only just begun to broach the subject of babies in mummies' tummies growing from little seeds.

What about the media, did they need to know? And most problematic of all, how did she fit into this new relationship? Not very comfortably. People would talk, laugh even: she would appear foolish, naïve, cuckolded all over again. Josh might have been only seventeen at the time of Kate's conception, but the fact remained that he had been caught with his trousers down. Very far down. People would remember the last time. And the time before that. And would they believe that he had known nothing about it? Probably not.

"I think I need some time on my own," Beatrice said, "just for a while. I'll see you at home."

She went for a walk. It was a perfect evening, golden and warm, the buildings all touched by the late sunlight, the streets, if you caught them at the right angle, did indeed seem paved with gold. She walked through Berkeley Square and into Bond Street, wandered up and down it, looking in the shop windows, in Aspreys, and Chanel and Tiffany and Ralph Lauren, finding them strangely distracting from Josh's clumsy, painful story, and even managed to admire a coat here, a bracelet there.

And then through into Regent Street, where she contemplated, as she always did, the perfection of its architecture, and marvelled that she could do so, crossed it and went beyond, into the seediness of Soho. As she walked among the strip joints and the blaring music and the pimps and the throbbing motorbikes and the shop windows filled with underwear and studded leather and impossibly high-heeled feather-trimmed shoes, all serving as half distraction, half background, she saw a girl, no older than Kate, her face horribly childlike, despite its heavy lipstick and fake eyelashes, hanging around a doorway with a man dressed in a flashy suit and a lot of gold jewellery, clearly old enough to be her father, clearly her pimp. And she thought what an obscenity that was, and that it should be stopped, somehow, that children should be children, should be safe from adult life and its ugliness. And that brought her rather tortuously to Kate, where her emotions somehow settled, shook down into some sort of order, and she discovered, above all, a concern for Kate. Her childhood might have been happy, but it had its ugly, dark side—a mother who had abandoned her, and a father vanished, no one wanting her, coming to claim her. That was ugly.

Of them all, Kate had had the worst of it and she deserved the best now. She was a child and they were adults; if Josh found the situation distressing and she found it painful and Kate's adoptive parents found it difficult, that was their problem. Kate must come first, and they should all do what was best for her. It was perfectly simple.

She called Josh and said she was coming home.

It was Jocasta's suggestion that she and Josh go together to see Kate.

"I know it seems I keep muscling in on these occasions, but she does know me best. I don't even know that we should tell her, not straightaway. I think we should take her out for a drink or something, and just chat and she can get used to Josh—not that anyone ever could, but she obviously liked him a lot the other day, after the funeral—and relax her a bit and then we can decide whether we should even tell her then, or wait till another time altogether. Not another great solemn sit-down, like when we told her about Martha. What do you think, Beatrice?"

Beatrice said she thought that was probably rather a good idea, and hopefully less shocking for Kate. "God," said Jocasta, "you are being stunningly wonderful, Beatrice. I'm totally filled with admiration." Beatrice felt she didn't have much option, but she smiled politely and said she'd go for a little walk while Jocasta called Helen.

Helen had taken the news with remarkable calm; so much had happened to her over the past few weeks that she would hardly have been surprised if Jocasta had told her Prince Charles was Kate's father. Or Brad Pitt. Or David Beckham.

It actually seemed a fairly happy option. At least it was someone they had all met and who Kate liked.

"I suppose that explains the similarity between you and Kate," she said to Jocasta.

She agreed that Jocasta and Josh should tell Kate together. "It will come much better from you. And he can answer lots of her questions. Including hopefully about—about Martha." She still found it difficult to refer to Martha as Kate's mother.

She told Jim, who was less pleased.

"Public school, I suppose," he said irritably. "Like his sister."

"Well, yes."

"Any idea which one?"

"Eton, I think."

"Well, that's all I need."

Helen opened her mouth to tell him not to be so silly and shut it again. She knew what this was about: what she had been through a few weeks earlier. When Jim had done his best to comfort her, but not really understood at all. He did now. Fearing rejection, criticism, comparison. Most of all comparison.

She also knew that despite his passionate socialism, his total commitment to the comprehensive ideal, and his hostility to the public-school culture, Jim felt threatened by the innate confidence which an expensive education provided. The thought of his beloved Kate being the offspring of an old Etonian made him feel physically ill.

"Did we meet him? At the party?"

"No, I don't think so. But I did see him. Jocasta pointed him out to me."

"Oh yes. What did he look like?"

"Well, he looked—you know. Tall. Blond. Slightly overweight. He was dancing the Charleston, rather well actually, with some girl."

"His wife?"

"Oh no, I don't think so. She's a barrister. This girl looked about eighteen."

"Dear God," said Jim, "a lecher. That's all I need."

"Don't be silly, dear," said Helen.

"I'm not being silly. What sort of man makes a fool of himself with young girls?"

"Jim, he wasn't making a fool of himself. He was just dancing."

"I would call that one and the same thing. Well, I don't think that's going to impress Kate at all. She's far too sensible. I don't want him coming here," he added abruptly.

"Jim! He's bound to come here, if Kate likes him. Be sensible," she said gently, "whatever he's like, and however much or little Kate likes him, you really don't have to worry. She's much too sensible and she knows where she belongs. She knows who her father is and it's not him. Not really."

"Yes, it is," he said and walked out of the room.

They took Kate out for a meal: to the Bluebird. "She loves it there," Jocasta said. "It's become our place, hers and mine."

She had walked in looking stunning, not, for once, in jeans, but a long, bias-cut floral skirt and a white T under a denim jacket, her hair hanging loose over her shoulders. Heads had turned.

"Oh, God," said Josh.

Jocasta patted his arm encouragingly. "It'll be fine."

They both stood up as Kate reached the table, kissed her. "This is so nice of you," she said. "I've been looking forward to it all day."

"So have we."

"I thought I'd bring you those cameras I was talking about," said Josh, "show you how they worked, maybe later."

"Cool."

She smiled at him. Jocasta had told her that he knew about Martha being her mother. "But if you don't want to talk about her, that's fine. It's up to you."

"It's really very kind of you," she said now, "to lend them to me."

"Not at all. Pleasure."

"They look expensive, I'll take great care of them."

There was a slightly awkward silence. "Let's choose," Jocasta said, "then we can relax."

"Glass of wine, young Kate?" said Josh.

"Yes please." She grinned at him. "It's really weird, you calling me young Kate. It makes you sound like some elderly uncle. Which you're not."

"Sorry."

"No, it's cool."

Another awkward silence. Jocasta hadn't expected this, had expected Kate would chatter away as she usually did.

"I finally decided about the contract," she said, into the silence. "Did Mum tell you? Or Fergus?"

"No, what did you decide?"

"Not to do it. Now I'm really worried it was the wrong decision. I mean, it's just so much money to say no to. Think what it could have done for us all, me and Mum and Dad. And Juliet, of course. She's going to be very expensive with her music."

"Well, it wouldn't have done anything for you," said Josh, "not if you hate it as much as you say. And I'm sure your mum and dad would rather take care of everything, anyway. They wouldn't like being indebted to you. Uncomfortable for them, I'd say."

"I hadn't thought of that. Yes, of course. If there'd been no question of that money, they'd be finding a way to pay for her somehow, wouldn't they?"

"Of course."

She smiled at him. "Thanks for that. I feel better now."

"And *Style*?" said Jocasta. "When's that shoot?"

"I told Fergus I couldn't do it."

"Why? Kate, they'll have everything booked."

"Yeah, I know. Don't you start. I just don't feel I can do it, I feel so down still."

"Sweetheart, I'm sorry. What sort of down?"

"Well—you know." She looked at Josh, clearly uncomfortable at discussing it in front of him. "The usual. Like I said to you, no further forward really."

"No?" said Josh. "But you know who—who your mother was now."

"Well, yeah. But she's, well, she's gone, hasn't she?"

Jocasta decided this was getting too heavy too soon. She changed the subject.

"I'm thinking of going back to work."

"Really? Why?"

"I miss it."

"I thought you would," said Kate, rather complacently. "You're much too clever to be sitting around all day, waiting for your husband to come home."

Josh laughed. "Beatrice would agree with you. She doesn't wait for me, either."

"No? What does she do?"

"She's a barrister."

"So she must be pretty clever."

"She is. Cleverer than me, I can tell you that."

"I'm sure she's not," said Kate politely. "But anyway, Jocasta, that's really cool. I mean, I'm sure Gideon wouldn't have expected you to give it up for long—and it's not as if you've got a baby, or anything."

"No," said Jocasta quickly, "absolutely not!"

"Would you like to have one?"

"Oh, I don't think so, no."

"What, never?" Kate was looking at Jocasta interestedly. "Because you'd be a very good mother, I think."

"Now why do you say that?" asked Josh.

"Well, she's so cool. She wouldn't fuss. And she's so sympathetic, always knows how you feel. And she's fun. My mum's great, but she's a bit . . . old. She doesn't know what's going on."

"But if Jocasta did have a baby, she'd be old too, when it was your age," said Josh. He was so genuinely interested in the conversation, he had almost forgotten why they were there.

"Yeah, I suppose. But I think Jocasta'd stay young."

"Well, I'm not going to have a baby and that's that," said Jocasta.

There was another silence, then: "Gideon's got a daughter about my age, hasn't he? She must be pretty spoilt."

"Well, in some ways. In others, far from it. He never sees her, she lives with her mother, when she's not at her boarding school."

"Were you two spoilt?" Kate asked, looking at them. "I mean, your dad's pretty rich, isn't he?"

"Not like Gideon is," said Jocasta, "and we weren't spoilt, no. I suppose we had everything we wanted. But our parents were divorced and we—I—never saw my dad. My dear little brother did, though."

"Yeah?" said Kate, turning to Josh. "And do you get on with your dad?"

"Oh, you know. OK."

"I think that's awful," said Kate. "I can't imagine being sent away like that, not seeing your parents every day. I mean, mine are gruesome in some ways, but we're all together and we know what we're all on about at least. My mum has this thing about us eating together and I'm just beginning to see the point of it. I didn't when I was younger. What sort of a dad are you?" she asked Josh. "I mean, you've got kids, would you send them away to school? Probably you would, I s'pose."

Josh took a very deep breath; if ever the Almighty had delivered a cue, this was it.

"What sort of a dad am I?" he said. "Well, that's a very interesting question. I try to be a good one. I like to be with my children a lot and I don't want them to be sent away to school. Um—Jocasta, what sort of a dad would you say I was?"

Jocasta had heard the cue, heard the deep breath also. "Pretty good,

I'd say," she said. "Really pretty good. Now—Kate, when you've finished that, let's go, shall we? Go for a walk or something?"

She looked at them, clearly puzzled by this swift ending to the meal; she had been looking forward to the pudding.

They called for the bill; Josh paid it in silence. He couldn't remember ever feeling so frightened, not even when he had been left at his prep school for the first time, at the age of seven. He led the way outside.

"I've got my car," he said, "let's go down to the river, shall we?"

"Cool car," said Kate. It was a Saab convertible and he put the hood down. At the river, he parked it, rather recklessly, on a yellow line, on a corner.

"It'll be OK," he said. "Come on, let's walk."

He pulled Kate's arm through his; Jocasta did the same. Kate looked at them both and smiled.

"We look like a family," she said.

"Funny you should say that," said Jocasta.

"Why?"

"Well—Kate, this is going to be a shock." They were on the river walk now. "Let's sit down," said Jocasta, indicating a seat. "Come on. Kate, darling, hold my hand. Josh, this is your story. Off you go."

Kate sat in silence listening, looking up at him intently and occasionally at Jocasta. He stumbled along: it was difficult. He told her that he and Martha had been quite close, had done some travelling together—he and Jocasta had agreed that a one-night stand was not an attractive notion—but that afterwards he had moved on to Australia, and she hadn't been able to get in touch with him.

"No mobiles, you see. All we had were poste restante addresses, and nobody knew where anybody was going to be, or when."

"And I think, then, she decided to manage on her own," said Jocasta, "she was a very independent lady. That much you must have learnt. And as I told you the other day, she felt she couldn't tell her parents."

"That's so weird," Kate said, "I've thought about that so much. About feeling it was worse than just—just leaving your baby, I don't understand it."

"I know," said Josh, "it does seem jolly odd. I think you just have to accept it. They might be lovely people, they are lovely people, but Martha obviously felt they wouldn't have been able to stand it, the shame and so on, because he's a vicar."

"This is so much the sort of thing I wanted to talk to her about," said Kate sadly. "Only she would have been able to help me understand, only she could have made sense of it. And why didn't she come forward when the story was in the paper? None of it makes sense to me still. And what did I do, the one time I met her? I just shouted at her and said all I wanted to know was who my father was."

"And—what did she say?" said Josh.

"She said she couldn't tell me. She said he—*you*—didn't know and she didn't think it was right to tell you after all these years."

There was a silence; then Kate said, "I was shouting at her. A lot. I wish I hadn't now. And she said she wished I'd let her try and explain. She said, 'Could you just listen to me, for a little while?' I said no and left in a strop. I wish I had," she said and started to cry, "let her try. It might have helped."

They all sat there for a while, staring at the river, then she said, "The thing is, though, that whatever she said, it comes down to the same thing: she was ashamed of me. Ashamed of having me. That isn't very nice to know."

"Well, I'm not," said Josh and put his arm round her, kissed the top of her head. "I'm very proud."

⋅

When she got home, Helen and Jim were reading. Helen smiled at her; Jim didn't look up from his paper.

"How was it, dear?"

"It was—fine. Yes. I s'pose Jocasta told you, he's my dad. Her brother Josh."

"Yes, yes, she did. But we thought they should tell you. How do you feel about that? Oh, dear, what a silly question."

"No, it's not. When I've got used to the idea, I think I'll be quite pleased. He's nice. I mean really nice. And he came to tell me straight-away, the minute he knew. I think that's lovely. Not like her. Still," she added, "I even feel a bit better about her now."

"What's he do, then?" said Jim. "This paragon?"

"Jim," said Helen warningly.

"He works for his dad. He doesn't like it much. He wishes he'd been a photographer."

"His dad seems to pay him plenty of money," said Jim. "Nice car, that."

"Yes, it's cool."

"Well, I expect you'll be seeing a lot of him now," said Jim, "now you've found him."

"Quite a lot, I expect, yes. I hope so, anyway."

She looked at Jim and then went over to him and wriggled onto his knee, put her arms round his neck.

"He is very nice," she said, "and he's quite good-looking and I can see he's fun. But you're my dad. You so are still my dad."

Chapter 43

· · · · ·

"And what happened exactly?" The doctor looked anxious: for a doctor, very anxious.

"She fainted. I heard a thud and rushed upstairs and—there she was. Out cold on the floor. She must have hit her head as she fell."

"Well, her pulse is rather low, and of course, where she hit her head there's going to be a nasty bruise. But I don't think she's concussed. She's got very . . . thin," he added. "Worryingly so."

"I know. She's just not eating. It's a nightmare, Douglas. I've tried everything. It's as if she—"

"Doesn't want to go on? Poor Grace. I don't know how you're standing it, yourself." Douglas Cummings was of their generation, had looked after all their children.

"Well," Peter Hartley sighed, "I'm not too sure, either. I suppose one just does. But Grace really isn't coping. And she has this obsession that I have my faith to sustain me, which she doesn't. She says she's lost hers. That it's easier for me. And maybe she's right. I wouldn't say easier is the word, though. A little less dreadful, perhaps. Anyway, that makes her angry. And she's feeling totally bereft. She did adore Martha. Mothers don't have favourites, but—"

"If she did, then for Grace, poor soul, it would have been Martha," said Dr. Cummings. "Well, she was an exceptional young woman."

"Indeed she was. I find it so hard to bear, you know, all that brilliance, just lost, nothing to show for her life. The only time Grace cheers up at all is when young Ed comes round. She sees him as a link with Martha. But he's gone back to London, of course, so— Oh God—I just don't know what to do for her, how to help her . . ."

"I'm afraid," said Dr. Cummings, "that time is the only cure. Although we must try to get some nourishment into her. Self-starvation is one of the hardest things to deal with. Whatever the age of the patient," he added. "Try to get her to take one of the food supplements. I'll put my thinking cap on, I certainly don't want to hospitalise her. But—"

"Oh, dear God, no. Please don't even think about it!"

"I'm afraid we might have to," said Dr. Cummings.

After he had gone, Peter went upstairs and looked at Grace. She was asleep now; her face oddly pinched-looking, an ugly bruise forming on her forehead where she had hit her head. She looked very small, almost shrivelled; she was also cold. He fetched another duvet from the spare room and laid that gently over her, then decided to sit with her for a while. She had seemed confused while the doctor was there; he didn't want her to wake alone.

She had always been so full of life. Even when her back had hurt her so much, she had struggled on, insisting she was fine, refusing to let it win, as she put it. She had taken too many painkillers, he kept telling her she shouldn't, but she had said it was the lesser of two evils. Nothing had ever got the better of her, until now. She sighed, opened her eyes. He smiled at her.

"Hello, Grace."

She didn't smile back; she just stared at him, rather blankly, and then turned on her side, away from him.

"Would you like some tea, dear?"

"No thank you," she said, very politely. "I don't want anything. Just leave me alone, Peter, please."

•─•─•

Clio felt irritable. Fergus and she had arranged a little holiday in Italy, towards the end of August, just a long weekend, really, but she had been looking forward to it so much, a proper stretch of time together, to enjoy each other, away from all the hysteria of Jocasta and Gideon and Josh and

Kate. Sometimes she wondered if she shouldn't stay peacefully in Guildford, working as a GP. It might not be exactly the sharp end, but it wasn't one long exhausting drama, either.

She was due to start at the Royal Bayswater on October 1; plenty of time to work out her notice, put her flat on the market, find somewhere in London to live. And go on a little holiday.

Only Fergus had called and said he might not be able to make it.

"Oh Fergus! Why on earth not?"

"I might just have got a very hot new client. Which could run for several weeks."

"And that takes precedence over our holiday? Great!"

"Clio, I'm sorry, but I have to be practical. I don't have any money in reserve. If I don't work, I don't get paid. I haven't done at all well lately, you know. Kate's let me down—"

"Fergus! I think that's stretching things a bit. She's a little girl. She's been through no end of an upheaval. She needs support, not pressure."

"Of course. But it is difficult, you know: you arrange things, and we're not talking chicken feed here, this is big money, important assignments, and everything goes hang on the whim of a sixteen-year-old."

"Exactly. A sixteen-year-old. Anyway, who or what is the client?"

"Oh it's another rent-boy story. Been totally screwed in both senses by his manager, he's a singer, and now the bastard's—"

"Fergus, please don't go on. *That's* what's coming between us and Italy?"

"Yes. It's work, Clio. I know you despise it, but it earns me my crust and, as I've said before, I don't know any other way. I can't, unfortunately, get a highly paid job as a hospital consultant, and be a pillar of the community, as you can."

"Oh, for God's sake," said Clio, "don't start that!" And she put the phone down.

Half an hour later, she rang to apologise, but got the answering machine. She decided not to leave a message.

Fergus was in a financial mess. He was seriously out of pocket over Kate. Gideon's promise to pick up the tab until she began to make money for him had not been honoured, and though he knew Gideon had simply forgotten, Fergus didn't feel able to ask him for it. He had, the last time he'd checked, about seven hundred pounds in the company bank account, and a large overdraft on his personal one. He'd have to get an extension to the overdraft, simply to pay the rent. He felt angry with Clio, and bitter at her judgmental attitude towards him and his work; and he was buggered if he was going to run back to her just because she'd snapped her fingers.

She rang him again the next morning. "I'm sorry," she said, "about yesterday."

"That's all right."

"Look, if I pay for the holiday would that help?"

Fergus felt a flood of rage towards her. "No, Clio, it wouldn't. In the first place, I still need to be around, I've got this client now, and in the second, I've no wish to be beholden to you."

"That's ridiculous! I'd like to pay for you."

"Well, I wouldn't like it. However kindly it's meant. I'm trying to run a business, Clio. I know you have trouble recognising it as such, and you see it as little better than running a brothel—"

"Of course I don't!"

"Well, that's the message that comes over very loud and clear. You obviously don't realise it. So let's cool it for a bit, OK?"

"Absolutely OK. I just wanted to relieve you of feeling you had to put any pressure on Kate."

"That's a filthy thing to say!" he said and rang off.

•◦•

Jocasta was wandering aimlessly round the supermarket when it hit her. Hit her with the force of a rather large truck. And left her almost physically reeling.

She was feeling very miserable. It was the middle of August and everyone was away; she couldn't have seen any of her old friends if she'd wanted to. She really must make contact with them all in September; she couldn't avoid them forever. Even if it did mean admitting to everyone that her marriage was over.

Even Clio seemed to be avoiding her; she had been rather odd, almost distant, said she wasn't coming to London this weekend, when Jocasta had asked her, and hadn't invited her down to Guildford, either.

She had heard nothing from Nick: not even the promised postcard.

Every day she told herself she'd ring him in the morning and every morning she didn't. She mustn't. She wasn't going to appear to be chasing him.

She had heard nothing from Gideon, either, not even from his solicitors; but there had been a picture of him, in the *Evening Standard*, the day before, smiling and looking rather pleased with himself. He looked a lot happier than she was. The caption said he was going on a business trip to the East Coast of America. She had thought of the houses she had lined up for him to look at there and just for a moment she felt sad instead of angry. She could have gone with him and they could have seen them at the same time, maybe even chosen one; that would have given her something to do.

And then the really dreadful thought came, that perhaps even now it wasn't too late. She had crushed it hastily, but it had still disturbed her. She must be feeling very bad.

Come on, Jocasta, concentrate. Coffee, tea, better get some milk; the last lot had been off. Bread, got that. Toiletries—shampoo, soap, Tampax—and that was when it hit her.

Now, this was absurd. One day, one day late: well, two. Actually, she could remember that last time so clearly, it was the night she had walked out on Gideon, that terrible Thursday. Two days was nothing. Nothing.

Actually, though, it was, when you were so regular you could literally set the clock by it. Well, that was the pill of course. No need to worry, she was on the pill. You didn't get pregnant on the pill. You just didn't. Unless you forgot to take it. Which she never, ever did, it was too important.

Or—and this was the second ramming by the truck—you had a stomach upset. Which she'd had. A truly terrible one. Throwing up, diarrhoea, the lot, for two days. And hadn't even taken the bloody thing for one day. Actually, two. She decided there was no point, especially as she wasn't having sex.

Only—she had, hadn't she? Sex with Nick, amazing sex with Nick, a few days after the stomach upset, right bang in the middle of her cycle.

Oh God. Oh—my—God!

Calm down, Jocasta. You're one day late. All right, two days late. It's nothing. It happens sometimes. Maybe not to her, but to other people. So it could perfectly well happen to her too. That was all it was: she'd missed a period.

Anyway, no need to worry about it. She could do a test. You could do them on the very day your period was due, and it was something like ninety-eight percent accurate. She'd go to Boots, buy a test, take it home and it would be negative and then everything would be all right and her period would probably start straightaway.

She looked at her watch: five twenty. If she legged it over to Boots now, or to the chemist in the North End Road, she should be just in time.

When she got to Boots it was shut. So that meant either one of the late-night chemists, or waiting till tomorrow. It was no contest. There was one in Wandsworth, open until seven, she was sure. But when she got there, that was closed too: from one o'clock every Saturday, a sign informed her, with an infuriating smugness. She drove home and started frantically leafing through the Yellow Pages.

◆

Kate was getting ready to go out with Nat.

It was extraordinary how much happier she felt all of a sudden, knowing Josh was her father, knowing he had wanted to tell her, wanted to be her friend. He'd actually said that: "I don't feel quite like your father, not yet anyway, it seems so—odd. Maybe we could start by being friends."

Kate had liked that so much; she had never entertained any ideas about falling into her birth parents' arms, she had simply wanted to know who they were and to find out how it had all happened. Of course it wasn't exactly nice to discover you were the result of what amounted to a holiday romance, but they'd been awfully young: only a bit older than she was now.

She could tell from some of the answers Josh had given her about Martha that he really hadn't known her at all well. She'd have preferred it to have been some passionate, forbidden affair. But Josh was so nice, even if he was a bit silly, so she was sure he must have liked Martha quite a lot, it hadn't been just sex. And if he'd known about—about her, he would have helped Martha. She could tell. She'd never know why Martha hadn't told him, she'd never know an awful lot of things, but she was discovering that a great many people had liked Martha, thought a lot of her. Which was nice. You didn't want your mother to be a one hundred percent bitch. You wanted her to be nice. And Ed, that gorgeous Ed, he was so nice too, and he'd really loved Martha. She'd never seen a man cry like he did at the funeral; it had been very upsetting.

Anyway, feeling happier had made her want to see Nat again. There seemed some point in it. There seemed a point to quite a lot of things. She thought she might even go and see Fergus, and really talk through the contract with Smith. Maybe it wasn't too late. He'd said something about the door still being open. Three million dollars really was a lot of money to turn down. She'd already told him she'd do the *Style* cover, which had seemed to cheer him up a bit. She was quite looking forward to that, mostly so she could talk to the photographer.

She was just trying to untangle her hair, when Jilly rang. "Hello, my darling, how are you?"

"I'm fine. Mum told you about Josh? Jocasta's brother?"

"She did indeed. What an extraordinary coincidence. Although not really, when you think about it. Just imagine, Kate, if I hadn't fallen on the step that night, none of this would have happened."

"Yeah, I know. I was thinking that."

"And I hear you like him?"

"I do. I really like him. He doesn't feel like my dad, exactly, but he's good fun and it's lovely talking to him and everything. He can't answer all my questions, but he tries. He's well posh, Granny, you'll love him."

What had her mother said? Oh, yes: "Just wait till Granny knows where he went to school, she'll have a heart attack with excitement."

"There's more to liking someone than their social class," said Jilly slightly stiffly.

"Course there is," said Kate.

—•—

Jocasta stood in her bathroom, her heart thudding so hard she felt her body could hardly contain it. She had gone to Boots in Piccadilly in the end, because it was always open round the clock. The pregnancy test had cost her £90 so far, because she couldn't find anywhere to park, and so she'd left her car on a yellow line in Jermyn Street with a note on it thinking she'd only be five minutes, and of course she had been about fifteen, by the time she'd found the wretched things and read all the instructions and decided which one would be best and then queued to pay for it. It had been a long queue. A long, hot queue, composed largely of tourists. There was also a very long queue at the pharmacy end, presumably all the druggies getting their stuff. Anyway, by the time she got back to her car, it had a ticket. A self-satisfied-looking female warden was just placing it on the windscreen.

Anyway, she had the test. She would go home and use it and get the matter settled. Maybe she was getting her period anyway, she felt a bit . . . achy.

She did the test.

The instructions were very clear; you had to hold the end of the stick thing—it looked a bit like a thermometer—into your pee for five seconds only (this bit was in bold type) and then keep it pointing downwards for one minute. There were two little windows at the other end of the stick. At the end of the one minute, a blue line should appear in the end window and then you could read the result window. A plus meant pregnant, a minus not.

She timed the five-second dip into the pee she'd collected (in a clean dry container as they had said, a large breakfast cup actually) and dipped what they called the absorbent sampler into it. And then waited. For one minute. In one minute she'd be fine, in one minute a nice neat minus sign would tell her she was not pregnant, and— God! It was there! Unmistakably a minus. She wasn't pregnant. She was fine. For heaven's sake. How ridiculous to think she could have been! How could she? Of course she wasn't. She felt quite dizzy, light-headed with relief. She— The doorbell rang. She stuffed the box into the cupboard under the bathroom sink and went to answer it. It was a young man, asking her to sponsor him on a trek over the Himalayas. Jocasta gave him £25 and then opened a bottle of champagne to celebrate.

·-•-·

"You look rotten."

"Thanks. I expect it's the heat. You know how much I hate it."

Gideon was not on a business trip in the States, as he had told the reporter at Heathrow, he was in Barbados.

"Possibly." Aisling Carlingford shrugged her slender, pale brown shoulders, took a sip of her crushed fruit cocktail. "You didn't have to come."

"I know that. I wanted to see Fionnuala."

"Well, you've seen her now. There she is, swimming up and down. So you can go again, back to the rainy mists of Ireland. She does look lovely, doesn't she?"

"Very lovely."

Fionnuala saw them admiring her, got out of the pool, dived neatly back in again, and swam the length of it underwater. She surfaced near them and smiled, inviting him to join her. He refused irritably.

Aisling looked at him rather intently. "So where's the lovely young wife?"

"I told you. In London. Possibly in Berkshire. Not sure."

"And why did you leave her behind?"

"Aisling, I was hardly going to bring her here."

"It's gone wrong, hasn't it?"

Gideon hesitated, then said with great reluctance, "Yes. It has."

"You shouldn't have married her. It was a terrible mistake."

"I think it probably was. She hasn't turned out as I hoped."

"I meant it was a terrible mistake for her, Gideon. Mistake on your part. Wrong of you, you know?"

"I think that's a little unfair."

"Is it? Anyone could see, just looking at her, she was completely overwhelmed by you."

"Aisling, she wasn't some naïve child. She was a very sophisticated girl, a successful journalist. Her father is a rich and successful man."

"Oh come on, Gideon. What did she know of your life? Of what it meant? She's nearly twenty years younger than you for a start. Marriage has come to mean something very different in the last twenty years, for girls like her. There's no way she could be expected to understand her role as your consort. I feel very sorry for her."

Gideon raised his eyebrows. "This is a ridiculous conversation."

"Don't start losing your temper. Just think about it for a bit. I suppose you thought you were in love with her."

"I was very much in love with her. I still am."

"Rubbish. You're in love with love, you always have been. You're a romantic old thing, that's why I fell in love with you. And I'm sure it tickled your fancy, having a lovely trophy like that on your arm. 'Look what I can still catch,' that's what that said. Honestly, Gideon, you ought to be ashamed of yourself. I suppose she was more impressive as a wife than a girlfriend, but still—"

"She was very anxious to marry me," said Gideon. "It was all her idea, she practically dragged me into the registry in Vegas."

"Oh, yes, and you're such a pushover, aren't you? It's so extremely easy to make you do something you don't want! Gideon, honestly, you can't expect me to believe that. It's all horribly plain to me. And then the honeymoon was over and that wonderful party, that sounded fun, I'd have liked to be there, and you got back to work, and she was left alone twiddling her pretty little thumbs. Feeling all the worse for the fact that she'd actually had a career before. So what are you going to do?"

"Oh, I don't know. She wants a divorce."

"Well, give it to her. I know you find that hard, but what's the point otherwise? You're probably not even properly married, anyway. Think of it as a wedding present for her," she said, and started laughing at her own joke.

Gideon stood up and dived into the pool, swam a few lengths, and then settled at the other end, looking at his ex-wife. His second ex-wife. She was a lovely thing—still. Blond, reed-slim, but full-breasted, her sleek body and almost unlined face a testimony to the wonders of cosmetic science. He had loved her so much. As much as he had loved Jocasta. Probably more. Aisling was right; he *was* a romantic old fool. And he shouldn't have married Jocasta. Who he still loved—in a way. Enough, just maybe, to set her free again.

•—•—•

Jocasta sat staring at the little blue plus sign. Plus. Not minus, this time, but plus. Plus meant pregnant. It was very simple. She was plus something. Plus a pregnancy. Plus a baby. Plus Nick's baby.

She felt odd, very odd indeed. Not entirely as she would have expected. She felt shocked and horrified and terrified; but she felt something else, as well. Almost—awed. That it could have happened. That she and Nick could have made a baby. They had made love and made a baby. Something that was partly her and partly Nick. It was an extraordinary thought.

Only, of course it wasn't a baby: it was a cluster of cells. She was—what was she? Three weeks pregnant. Three and a half weeks. Whatever it was, it was pinprick size. A tiny, pinprick-size cluster of cells. It was not a baby. And she could get rid of it. Quickly and easily.

She must get rid of it. Obviously.

What on earth would Nick do or say, if he knew? Nick, who still couldn't contemplate any sort of commitment, not even living together, certainly not getting married, how would he react to the news that he was a father? Well, not a father, but going to be a father. It was absolutely unthinkable.

She decided to go and see Clio.

Clio—of course—gave her all the wrong advice.

Like she shouldn't do anything too hasty. Like she should wait a few more days, these tests weren't entirely reliable, whatever they said, it was very early days. Like was she really sure it was Nick's. Like she ought to tell Nick.

"Tell Nick! Clio, are you mad? Of course I can't tell Nick. He'd be horrified, he'd run away, he'd hate it, he'd hate me. No, I must just have a termination as soon as possible and—"

"Jocasta, I think you should tell him. If you're really pregnant and it's really his, you should tell him."

"But why?"

"Because it's his baby too. It's wrong not to. It's a terrible thing to do, deciding to get rid of a baby, without telling its father."

"Clio, you don't know Nick and I do. He would not want a baby. He doesn't even want *me*. And if you're even contemplating telling him yourself, you'd better just stop right away, at once, you've got to promise me not to, promise, Clio, all right, now, at once, on your life—" She was crying now; Clio went over to her, put her arms round her.

"Of course I won't tell him. I promise, on my life, I won't."

"Never, ever?"

"Never ever. Come on, sit down, have a cup of tea."

"Coffee, please. Nice and strong."

"Fine." She went into the kitchen; Jocasta followed her, sat down at the table.

"You might not be, you know. When was your period due?"

"Last Thursday."

"That's a very short time. It could all be a mistake. You don't feel . . . funny or anything? Sick, or tired or—"

"Absolutely not," said Jocasta.

"I should wait a few more days, then do another test. Go and see your doctor, or your gynaecologist, see what she says. Various things can affect these tests—I presume you're still taking the pill. Here's your coffee."

Jocasta took one sip of it, put it down, made a face.

"God, that tastes disgusting. What have you put in it, Clio? It makes me want to heave."

Clio looked at her very soberly, in silence. Then she said, "Jocasta, I'm sorry, but I would say that rather clinches it. You definitely are pregnant."

Sarah Kershaw confirmed Clio's diagnosis.

She had been Jocasta's gynaecologist for years; she was in her early forties, high-powered, sympathetic.

"I'll do a lab test, of course. We can do it now, this afternoon. Think you can pee?"

"God, yes," said Jocasta. "I never stop."

"That's another symptom, I'm afraid. Sorry, Jocasta. We'll do the test, anyway. Now, what do you want to do about it?"

"I want to have a termination. And I want to be sterilised at the same time."

"That's a very drastic decision. You're upset, your hormones are in a state of total upheaval—"

"I'm not upset, Mrs. Kershaw. Or in a state of upheaval, actually. I feel very calm. That's what I want to do."

"Well, it's your decision of course. Have you—talked it over carefully with your husband?"

"No. We're getting divorced. So no point."

"He might feel differently."

"What about? The divorce?"

"Obviously I can't tell you that. I meant about the baby."

Jocasta was silent; there was no way she was going to tell Sarah Kershaw that the baby was not her husband's, that it had been conceived in adultery, one dizzy afternoon.

"Look," Sarah Kershaw said, "this is your decision, obviously. You're clearly distressed about your marriage, but has the marriage actually broken down? Irretrievably?"

"Sorry," said Jocasta, "I haven't come to discuss my marriage."

"I know that. But even if you don't realise it, you're not thinking entirely clearly. Perhaps not the best way to be taking extremely important decisions."

"I'm thinking very clearly. I'm feeling perfectly well. I don't understand all this fuss about pregnancy making you ill. I haven't felt sick once and I've got loads of energy."

"Well, you're very lucky. I'm happy for you. Even so, believe me, you're not quite yourself. And this is a bigger decision than perhaps you actually realise. Especially the sterilisation."

"Mrs. Kershaw, please. I don't want bloody counselling. I don't need it. I want a termination and I want to be sterilised. What do I have to do?"

"If I was just having the termination," she told Clio, "I could have what they called a con-op, first a consultation, then the termination, all on the same day. But as I want to be sterilised, they'll counsel me, as they call it, and then book me in for another day. But there's no problem. I can do it."

It sounded terrible to Clio. "What did she say about telling the father? Does he have a right to know?"

She knew he didn't, but she was hoping Jocasta's mind might have been at least alerted to the possibility.

"She said I didn't have to, and he couldn't stop me having the termination. It's totally up to me. The doctors and me. All I need is a legal justification and of course I've got one. 'Change of life circumstances,' it's called. So in about ten days, with luck. Will you come with me?"

"I don't think I can," said Clio and slammed the phone down. She found it hard to believe that, even in her manically self-absorbed state, Jocasta could be asking her to go with her to get rid of her baby. Could be so grossly insensitive not to have remembered Clio's grief on the subject of her own infertility. It hurt almost more than she would have believed.

The phone rang again almost at once: she picked it up, feeling remorseful. She had misjudged her, Jocasta had phoned to apologise . . .

"Clio, don't know what happened then. Look, I've heard from

Gideon, he wants to see me, discuss things. I'm absolutely petrified, he wants me to go round to the house tomorrow afternoon, can you come up afterwards?"

"No," said Clio, "I can't. I do have a life of my own, you know, Jocasta. I can't actually drop everything, just whenever it suits you. Sorry."

There was a silence: then Jocasta said, her voice absolutely astonished, "OK, OK. Easy. I thought you'd want to help."

Clio said she was getting a bit tired of helping, and put the phone down for the second time.

She was a fine friend, Jocasta thought. When she really needed her, where was she? Having a hissy fit in Guildford. Well, too bad. She could manage without her. She could manage without anyone. She was just fine. She was getting her life back. As soon as she'd had this . . . thing done next week, she would go to see Chris Pollock. She couldn't imagine how she could ever have thought she could give up her job. And her freedom and her independence. She must have been completely mad. Gideon had driven her mad.

She wondered what on earth he was going to say to her tomorrow. She hadn't been making it up when she told Clio she was terrified. But it had been a nice and very friendly e-mail; she really felt she should agree to see him.

•◆•

Nick was still in Somerset. He had been showing off to the children when they were all out riding one afternoon, and fell off, breaking his radius. An extremely painful four hours later, he was back at the house with his arm in a sling and ordered not to drive, or indeed do anything much, for two or three weeks.

"You are an idiot," his mother said, "galloping off like that over the moor. I bet it was a rabbit hole, wasn't it?"

"Yes, I think so," said Nick humbly. "Sorry, Mummy."

"I'll get you some tea. And they gave you painkillers, I presume."

"Yes. But it's wearing off already. I couldn't have a whiskey, could I?"

"I think that's a terrible idea, on top of painkillers. Go on up to bed."

"Thanks. You couldn't bring my mobile, could you? I must let them know at the office."

"Of course. Although I really can't think it could matter much if you're not there for a bit. Those dreadful people you write about, they're all away. There was a picture of the Blairs this morning, in Tuscany I think, or was it the Bahamas? I don't know why they can't holiday in this country."

She brought Nick his mobile with the tea; he checked it to see if there was a message from Jocasta. That was the real reason he wanted it. There wasn't—again. God, he missed her. God, it hurt. Much more than his arm.

·—·

Jocasta drove up to Kensington Palace Gardens. She had dressed very carefully, in a short black linen shift that was just slightly too large for her. She knew her boobs were slightly bigger than they had been and she was terrified Gideon would notice. Notice and guess.

She knocked on the door tentatively. Mrs. Hutching opened it, smiled at her rather awkwardly.

"Hello, Mrs. Keeble."

"Hi," said Jocasta. She had tried to get Mrs. Hutching to call her Jocasta; it had never worked, and now the poor woman was embarrassed, whatever name she used.

"Mr. Keeble isn't here yet. He asked me to give you tea in the garden room. He said he wouldn't be long."

"Lovely. Thank you."

As she walked through the hall, she glanced at the letter rack; there were two postcards in it. Two sepia-tinted postcards. She pulled one of them out. It was a picture of Exmoor and it was Nick's writing.

"This is for me," she said. "Why didn't you send it on?"

"I don't think it is for you, Mrs. Keeble. It's addressed to a Mrs. Cook. It's certainly this address. I thought perhaps one of the agency cleaners we have in August might claim it."

"It's OK. It's from a friend of mine. A sort of—joke."

"Oh, I see. I'm so sorry."

"It's OK."

OK! When she had been waiting for this for two and a half very long weeks. Why hadn't she thought of this: of course Nick would have sent it here, he thought she was living here.

Dear Mrs. Cook,

Thank you so much for a very pleasant afternoon. I enjoyed it enormously. I hope your health has improved and that you are able to get out and about in this lovely summer weather. It is wonderfully beautiful down here; I know you don't admire the countryside, but the moors are amazingly lovely. The air is so very clean and clear; I wish I had been able to persuade you to join me here occasionally in the past.

Yrs, with every good wish,
James Butler

The other card was slightly less enigmatic.

Dear Mrs. Cook,
I am worried that you might not have got my last card and hope you continue in good health. Do let me know.

James Butler

She slipped them into her bag, feeling much happier, and went into the garden room to wait for Gideon—who was actually very nice, friendly, and courteous. He said he was sorry things had got so bad between them, that he had never intended it and he saw himself as at least partly to blame. He had been doing a lot of thinking, and if she wanted a divorce, then he would not contest it, however sad he might feel. He was sure they could come to an amicable arrangement over a settlement; she must let him know . . .

At this point, Jocasta could bear it no longer. The old Gideon had come back: kind, gentle, charming. How did it happen, where did the demons come from? Clearly she released them in him; it wasn't a very nice thought.

"I don't want a settlement, Gideon," she said. "I don't want anything. Nothing at all. Really. I couldn't possibly take any money from you."

"Of course you could."

"I couldn't. Honestly. I really don't want anything."

"Jocasta—"

"No, Gideon, I don't. I feel bad enough already."

There was a silence, then he said, "Well, you may change your mind. You look tired—are you all right?"

"I'm absolutely fine," she said quickly.

How on earth would he react if he knew she was pregnant? With another man's baby, the ink on their marriage licence hardly dry? Or thought it might be his? It was terrifying. God, she was a disaster!

"Good. I would really like you to have something. So if you change your mind—"

"I won't," she said. "I know I won't."

"Well, at the very least take the clothes," he said. "They are clogging up cupboard space and they don't suit me at all."

She smiled. "Oh, Gideon. This is so sad. We should just have had an affair."

"But you didn't want an affair," he said, "you wanted a marriage. Come along, Jocasta, admit it."

"I . . . admit it," she said.

"But I encouraged you."

"Yes, you did. And most of the time, it was great fun."

"I'm glad you thought so," he said. "I enjoyed it too. Most of it. Now drink up your tea, and then you must excuse me. I have to go back to the office. And before that I have to pick up some luggage. I'm—"

"Going away tomorrow," she said and laughed. "Oh, Gideon. I'm so sorry. I behaved so badly."

"I behaved badly also. And I am sorry for it. Well, it was a short marriage but mostly a merry one. Thank you for coming today. I just wanted us to part friends."

"Friends it is," she said and went over to his chair, bent to kiss him. "Goodbye, Gideon."

"Goodbye, Jocasta. And I would be hugely grateful if the press didn't hear of this just for a little while."

"They won't. I promise."

They wouldn't. The press getting hold of it was the last thing she wanted. Especially one member of the press.

Just the same, Nick had sent a postcard. Two postcards. And had clearly been thinking about her. That was nice.

The minute she got into her car, she called his mobile; it was not Nick who answered.

"Hello. Pattie Marshall. Can I help?"

"Oh, sorry, Mrs. Marshall. It's Jocasta here, Jocasta Forbes."

"Hello, Jocasta." The voice was very cool; they had never liked each other. "I expect you're wondering why I'm answering Nicholas's phone. He's broken his right radius—"

"What's that?" Pattie always used medical terms; it had been one of the many things that got up Jocasta's nose.

"It's one of the bones in the forearm. He fell off a horse—bit of a shame. It isn't serious, but he's asleep at the moment, and he asked me to switch off his phone and I forgot."

"I'm so sorry. So, he's staying with you?"

"Yes, of course. I'm certainly not up in London with him."

"Of course not. Please give him my best wishes. Tell him I'm sorry. And thank him for the postcards. When will he be back in London?"

"Oh, not for a couple of weeks, I should think. I'll get him to call you."

"Well, only if he—if he feels like it. Thank you."

"And are you at home?"

"Yes," she said, and then quickly, "tell him I'm at the Big House. He'll know what I mean."

"Very well."

When Nick woke up, Pattie Marshall told him that Jocasta had called and sent her best wishes. And that she was staying at the Big House.

"She says you'll know what that means."

Nick did; it meant she was staying at the Big House—not leaving it. He'd lost her, again.

Chapter 44

· · · ·

This time tomorrow it would be over. Just—over. She wouldn't be pregnant anymore. Fantastic. She hadn't really felt pregnant anyway; it had never been real. It had been a nonhappening. One missed period and now nearly another. That was all. She'd never felt sick, she'd never felt anything; people made an awful fuss about nothing, as far as she could see. And she certainly hadn't felt emotional. Not in the least. She just wasn't maternal; she didn't have any maternal feelings. She'd have been a terrible mother.

Jocasta looked down at her stomach; it was totally flat. It was impossible to believe there was anything alive in there, certainly not a baby. A child. Hers and Nick's child. Maybe it was all just a fantasy, something she'd imagined. But she'd done three tests altogether and Sarah Kershaw had done hers; there was no doubt. Nick's baby was in there.

She wondered what on earth Nick would say if he knew she was pregnant. He'd be absolutely terrified. He'd want to just run away. And what if he knew she'd had a termination without telling him? Well, that was a bit—tricky. He might be cross. He might say he'd had a right to know. But he still wouldn't want it. So it was certainly infinitely better he didn't. Much better. He'd never know; the only person who did know was Clio, and she'd never tell. Nick was still down in Somerset: that was lucky. She was sorry he'd broken his arm, or whatever it was, but it was lucky.

Clio was still being weird, very cold and distant when she'd called her, not even interested in how Josh was getting on with Kate. She didn't know what the matter with her was. She'd asked Fergus and he'd said he had no idea; he hadn't spoken to her for a bit. He'd sounded quite down, but when she asked him if there was a problem, he said of course not. Obviously there was; they'd had a row or something. It would blow over.

Anyway, she'd be fine tomorrow. They had warned her she might feel very sore, but that it was a relatively minor procedure.

The counselling had been crap. Had she really thought about it? Was she absolutely sure about sterilisation? It was a very big step. Jocasta said she knew that and she had thought about it. It was what she wanted. Definitely.

"I see that you and your husband are separating," the woman said.

"Yes, that's right."

"Which is a perfectly acceptable reason for a termination, as far as we're concerned. Now how is your general health, Miss Forbes? Any problems, anything we should know about?"

They had told her she would be in for the whole day; that she would have a general anaesthetic, because of the sterilisation; that someone should come and collect her, she wouldn't be able to drive herself home. Well, if Clio wouldn't come with her—and she wouldn't—she would go on her own, get a cab home. She'd be fine.

She wondered if Martha had felt like this: that it was just a matter of time and then it would be over. Probably. Only Martha'd had to have a baby first. Whenever she thought about that, Jocasta felt physically faint, clammily nauseous. All alone in that dreadful screaming pain: How had she stood it, how had she coped with the mechanics of it, the reality? It was just—unthinkable. She could never have done it. Never. Well, she didn't have to. After tomorrow. Fine. Just fine. Much better.

The phone rang sharply; she picked it up. It was Clio.

"Hi, Jocasta. It's me."

"Oh—hello," she said, just a little cool.

"I wanted to talk to you."

"Oh yes? What about?"

"This baby. I know it's nothing to do with me, but Jocasta, I still think you should tell Nick, it's his baby too. It's wrong not to. I—"

"Clio, I'm not very interested in your opinion on this, and you're right, it isn't anything to do with you. It's me that's pregnant, and it's my body and my decision. Nick's a commitment-phobe. He wouldn't even live with me. He will not want a baby."

"But—"

"Look, what would be the point? Just tell me that? All I'd be doing is upsetting him. And you're upsetting me, come to that. For nothing."

"Not for nothing, Jocasta, for a baby. And you might—you just might change your mind. At least don't be sterilised yet."

"Oh for God's sake, Clio. I'm not having it. You know I can't, and anyway, I don't want it, can't have it, and tomorrow I'm just going to—to have the termination, and that'll be it. Over, finished, done and dusted."

"I wish you wouldn't talk about it like that," said Clio quietly. "It's a baby you've got in there, Jocasta, not some sort of parasite."

"Babies are parasites, as far as I'm concerned. Right from conception."

"Oh shut up," said Clio. She suddenly sounded quite hysterical. "Just shut up, will you?"

"You started this," said Jocasta, "so don't tell me to shut up. Perhaps you'd like me to have it, and then you could adopt it. What about that for an idea?"

"It's about the only way I'm going to get a baby," said Clio, and her voice cracked with hurt, "adopting one."

There was a dreadful silence; in the middle of it, Jocasta remembered. Remembered what she should never have forgotten for a moment, remembered what would have made the whole thing of telling Clio, saying she was going to have an abortion, savagely cruel. Asking her to go with her when it was done, for God's sake. How had she done that? How had she been so totally, utterly callous to Clio, poor sweet Clio who wanted babies more than anything, but could never have them?

What was the matter with her, how had she turned into this monster? It was Gideon's fault, he'd done it . . .

"Clio," she said, "Clio, I'm so, so sorry. I forgot. I'm so totally wrapped up in myself at the moment. God I'm a cow, a foul, hideous cow, Clio, I'm so sorry—"

"It's all right," said Clio and rang off. When Jocasta tried to ring her back, the answering machine was on and her mobile was on message.

She felt so guilty, she felt sick. She actually thought she was going to be sick. How could she have done that, been so brutal, how could she have forgotten? Clio was supposed to be her best friend, and she'd hurt her in that awful, vicious way.

She kept ringing the number, kept saying, "Please Clio, pick up the phone," but she wouldn't.

Jocasta rang Fergus; it seemed the next best thing to speaking to Clio. He was short with her.

"I'm afraid Clio and I aren't really in touch at the moment."

"Oh Fergus, why on earth not? What's happened? You were made in heaven!"

"Call it a clash of ideologies," he said, rather stiffly, "so, not made in heaven at all."

"I'm sorry. Are you going to tell me any more?"

"I don't think so."

"But the thing is, Fergus, I need to contact her. I've done something really dreadful and I need to speak to her and she won't speak to me. Won't even pick up the phone. Could you help?"

"I don't think I could," he said, and his voice was very sad. "She won't pick up the phone to me, either. I'm sorry, Jocasta. I'd love to help, but I can't."

He sounded dreadful; she felt quite anxious about him. "How are things generally, Fergus, darling? You're wonderfully busy, surely?"

"Oh, you know. Difficult. Not a lot of work coming in, to be honest with you."

"I'm sorry. And Kate isn't coming to anything, is she? In the financial sense. Not doing the Smith work?"

" 'Fraid not. No."

"I hope my soon-to-be-ex-husband paid you for her," said Jocasta suddenly. "I do remember him promising to, but he might need chasing on it. Just at the moment."

"Well, he hasn't, Jocasta, as a matter of fact. Obviously it's slipped his mind, rather more important things on it." She could hear his voice, determinedly light, almost amused.

"Oh, Fergus, I'm so sorry. That's unforgivable. I'll ring his PA—"

"I have rung her, of course. I'm sure it'll be through soon."

"Look," said Jocasta, "I'll ring Gideon myself. It's all right; we're back on speaking terms. And I've still got a joint account chequebook. I'll write you a cheque on that, if all else fails."

"My darling, I don't think you'd better do that. He might be very cross."

"He can be as cross as he likes. I don't care. You need your money. You've got bills to pay. And we landed you with Kate. Anyway, I'm sure he's just forgotten. I've probably driven everything out of his head. He does have his faults, but he's certainly not mean. I'll call him right away."

Gideon said he was very sorry; he'd have a cheque sent round to Fergus within the hour.

It might help both him and Clio a bit, Jocasta thought. At least she'd been able to do something for them.

•—•

Peter Hartley was sitting in the kitchen, as close to despair as he had ever been, when Maureen Forrest arrived with a large bunch of dahlias.

"I brought these for Mrs. Hartley. I'm sorry I'm so early, but I'm on my way to work. Ed said she didn't seem too good when he came on Saturday."

"She isn't, I'm afraid. She's—well, she's so frail. And this morning early, she just fainted dead away."

"Oh, I'm sorry. Is she all right?"

"I'm afraid she is very down. I can't get her to eat—Dr. Cummings says he'll have to hospitalise her soon, if it goes on."

"I'm so sorry, Mr. Hartley. You've got enough to cope with yourself, without this."

"Oh, I'm all right. It was nice of Ed to come and see her at the weekend. Somehow he seems to get through to her when no one else can. I suppose because he was so close to Martha. She feels he's a link."

"Well, I'm glad it helped. Ed's very down himself, of course. Although—it's a dreadful thing to say, but he's young. You and I both know he'll get over it one day. Not completely, of course, and he'll never forget her, but—he'll find someone else. Of course I wouldn't say that to him, he wouldn't believe me, and it sounds rather—" She stopped.

"Heartless?" he said and smiled.

"Yes. But it's not. He's only twenty-three; what you and Mrs. Hartley have lost is so much worse. When John was dying, I kept thinking, At least it's not Ed. Does that sound very bad?"

"Of course not," said Peter and patted her shoulder. "Yes, it's the worst loss of all. I—well, I'm afraid I'm finding it almost unbearable. It's the wrong order of things. I can't make sense of it."

"I'm so sorry for you both. Anyway, I'll pop in again in a day or two. And I'll tell Ed what you said. He'll be pleased."

•━•

Jocasta had decided to go and see Clio; it was too important not to. She hadn't got anything else to do, for God's sake. She was just leaving, when Beatrice rang.

"Jocasta, how are you?"

"I'm fine. You? You amazingly wonderful and selfless woman."

"Don't know about that. Not too thrilled with Josh."

"I'm sure you're not. But it is a long time ago. Sixteen years, or whatever."

"Yes, I know. But it still hurts, I don't know why. I suppose because—oh I don't know. It just doesn't help me to trust him. Silly, I know. But clearly, this sort of thing is in his genes."

"Not silly at all. I'd feel exactly the same. But he has been behaving himself lately, hasn't he?"

"Oh, yes," said Beatrice quickly, "he really has." She managed a laugh. "I sound like his mother, don't I? Or his big sister."

"You take a much better view of him than his big sister," said Jocasta. "You must love him a lot, Beatrice."

"I suppose I must. Anyway, it's obviously best for Kate. Josh tells me she's really happy about it."

"Yes, I think she is. You haven't met her yet?"

"No, she's coming to tea next Sunday. I do want to meet her properly and we thought it would be easier if she came here."

"I think you'll like her," said Jocasta, "she's sweet. Very bright. Presumably you're not going to tell the girls?"

"Not yet. Now, Jocasta, I've actually rung up to ask you something. Are you going back to Gideon?"

Jocasta was caught off her guard. "Of course not. Absolutely not."

"I see. We've been worrying about you. We'd hoped that things might be better."

"Well, they are better. We seem to be friends again. Probably because we haven't seen each other for weeks and weeks. But we are getting divorced. And I'm altogether fine, I feel extremely happy, as a matter of fact, happy as a lark, just don't worry about me, please."

"Good. I'm delighted."

"Anyway, sweet of you to call. I've got to go now, sorry. Speak soon, you're a total heroine."

"I wish," said Beatrice.

·◆·

Ed was drinking his third coffee of the day and wishing he could feel the slightest interest in what he was doing, when his mother called. She did most mornings; he wasn't sure whether it helped or not.

"How are you today, dear?"

"Oh—you know. Bit bad, I think."

"I know," she said gently. "It comes and goes, doesn't it? Mostly it comes, especially at the beginning."

"Yes. Well, you should know, Mum."

His parents' marriage had been particularly happy; it was, he had told Martha, how he knew about love. "Proper love. The on and on sort. The you and me sort."

"I do," said Maureen softly. "And I tell you what, Edward, after a while, the memories become happier. They really do."

"Good," he said, "something needs to. Thanks, Mum."

"I popped in at the vicarage this morning. Poor Mr. Hartley's so worried about his wife. She had a fall this morning, and apparently she won't eat, she's just turned her face to the wall. The doctor says he's going to have to put her in hospital, in a day or two."

"Oh dear. I'm sorry."

"Anyway, the real reason I rang you was that Mr. Hartley says the one thing that's cheered Mrs. Hartley up lately was your visit. He said he thinks it was you being so close to Martha, it brings her back, in a funny way."

"That's nice," said Ed. He wished someone could bring Martha back for him in any way at all. Funny or not.

"Yes, well, take care of yourself, love. I'll ring in a day or two."

⚫⚫⚫

Nick had decided he must get back to London. It was all very well being at home with his parents when he was haring round doing things and enjoying himself, but being marooned there, confined to the house, was rather different. Most of the family had left; he had nothing to do but read and go for solitary walks.

And think: to a large degree about Jocasta. And what a fool he'd been. An absolute bloody fool. Why hadn't he moved in with her, married her for God's sake, if that's what she wanted? From his lonely perspective now, that looked a pretty attractive proposition. All his three brothers, one of them younger than him, were married, and they seemed perfectly contented. And they had all these children, jolly little things. He often thought he'd like some children. He got on with them terribly well.

He kept conjuring Jocasta up, warm, laughing, happy, talking nonsense—and as she had been that last afternoon, lying in bed, her lovely body naked, her astonishing hair splayed across the pillow, her huge eyes brilliant as she looked at him, holding out her arms to him, telling him she loved him. Yes, she had said that, there had been no doubt about it—wanted him, talking her way through lovemaking as she so engagingly did: "That's lovely, so lovely. God it's gorgeous, fantastic . . . here I go now, Nick, I can't bear it . . . go on, go on . . ."

He snapped his mind shut. This was ridiculous. She'd gone back to Keeble, and who could blame her. He had to get on with his life. And he'd start by going back to London. The very next day.

Jocasta reached Clio's flat at six o'clock; it had taken her much longer than usual. She had developed a headache, driving into the sun, and was feeling rather nauseous. She wondered if this was the beginning of the pregnancy sickness. If she was going to start feeling ill, then the—well, what she was going to do tomorrow was even better timing.

She pressed the bell. "It's me, Jocasta. Can I come in?"

There was a silence, then: "Sure."

She was looking rotten: white and drawn. She had obviously been crying.

"Oh, Clio," said Jocasta, "I'm so sorry to have been so beastly, and insensitive, and sorry about you. Please forgive me. I don't deserve it, but please do."

Clio managed a smile. "Of course. I understand."

"I expect you do," said Jocasta, "understand what a brat I am, what an unfeeling, pathetic brat. I need my bottom smacked very hard. Would you like to do it?" she added, with a smile. "I'm sure it would do me good."

"I wouldn't dream of it," said Clio. She managed a weak smile. "What would the neighbours say?" And then two tears trickled down her face.

"Oh Clio," said Jocasta. "Here, let me give you a hug." She opened her arms and Clio went into them, and sobbed for a long time.

"It's so unfair," she said, "so, so unfair!"

"I know. I know it is. It's dreadful for you. There really is nothing you can do?"

"Apparently not. My tubes are buggered and that's it."

"Well you should know. What—what about IVF?"

"It's a possibility of course. Quite a good one—in theory."

"And in practice?"

"It's a pretty miserable business. Someone's got to love you an awful lot to submit themselves to it. Dodgy, too. I mean it doesn't work all nice and neatly the first time. There are very long waiting lists. And going privately, it's thousands of pounds a time."

"Couldn't you jump the queue? Being in the business and everything?"

"Of course not!" Clio sounded quite shocked. "I wouldn't dream of it. Anyway, I don't know why I'm being so pathetic; who's going to give me a baby anyway? In some new relationship? I'm already thirty-five."

"Fergus?"

"I'm afraid not. That's dead in the water."

"Clio, are you sure? That's not the impression I got."

"What do you mean?"

"I rang him to see if he could help me get through to you. He said you weren't getting on very well, said something about a clash of ideologies? Anyway, he'd been trying to ring you. He said you wouldn't speak to him. Doesn't sound quite a corpse to me."

"Maybe not now. But it would never work, Jocasta. In the first place, I can't approve of what he does."

"Why?"

"It seems to me the very worst sort of cashing in on other people's misfortunes. I know you see it differently but—"

"Clio, it *is* different. It's helping people through them."

"What? People like footballers who've been shagging six girls at a time, presenting their cases in the best possible light?"

"But it's not all that. Look at what a lot he's done for Kate, and he hasn't even been paid yet, not a penny, I've just discovered. By my beloved nearly-ex-husband. Well, he has now. I hope."

"Gideon! What's he got to do with Kate?"

"He said he'd pay Fergus until Kate could. That was the whole basis for the deal. And the poor guy hasn't had a penny out of him. Anyway, don't you think that was amazingly nice of Fergus? When he'd never met Kate, didn't know the first thing about her?"

"No," said Clio, "it was only money."

"Oh, shut up! Now, come on, what else does the poor bloke do wrong? Apart from earn a crust the only way he knows?"

"Nothing, really," said Clio feebly. Jocasta left quite soon after that: her headache was worse, and she was very tired. They had, by common assent, not discussed her situation; she had made up her mind, she told Clio, and nothing was going to change it.

"I know you think it's wrong of me, but we'll have to agree to differ. At least we're friends again."

"You—wouldn't like me to come back with you? Be with you tonight?"

"Oh, God, no. I am so not worried about it. Honestly. And it would be awful for you. I'll be fine. I really will. Just totally, totally fine. Bye, Clio darling, and please go on forgiving me. Lots of love. I'll call you in a day or two. And give Fergus a ring. Go on."

·—·

Nick was on his way to London. He was driving; his mother had been absolutely horrified, but he said his arm was fine out of its sling, he could do most of the driving with his left arm. "I'm sorry, Mummy, but I've got to get back. So much to do. And I swear I'll go and see my own quack first thing tomorrow. OK?"

Pattie Marshall sighed. "I can't stop you, I know, but I think it's very foolish. And you'd better not have an accident. The police would throw the book at you."

Nick promised not to.

·—·

Jocasta walked into her house and sank onto her bed. She felt absolutely dreadful. Less sick now, but lonely, frightened, bereft. The thought of what she had to go through in the morning suddenly seemed rather—unpleasant. It wasn't the pain; Sarah Kershaw had assured her it would be minimal. "You'll just be sore. And bleeding rather a lot, at first. You have arranged for someone to drive you home?"

"Of course," said Jocasta. "No problem. Absolutely no problem at all." She had booked a cab: both ways. So what was troubling her about the morning? She wanted to be rid of the—pregnancy. She would never have to worry about another. She wasn't afraid of the procedure. Nick would never know. She'd have her life back after it. She'd be fine. It was just a bit . . . sad. Yes, she did feel a bit sad. That was natural. You'd be pretty odd if you didn't feel anything about getting rid of—ending a pregnancy. Actually, she was almost relieved that she did. That she wasn't totally hardhearted after all. Of course it wasn't a baby: she kept telling herself that. It was a pregnancy, that was the thing to hang on to, a medical condition, which she was dealing with, in a very adult way. The fact that if she didn't deal with it, in something like eight months there'd be a small creature in the world that had been put there by her and Nick didn't merit even thinking about. She wouldn't think about it. There was nothing to think about.

She poured herself a glass of red wine, had a long bath, and grazed through the papers: she was still horribly awake. Maybe she should take a sleeping pill. Maybe not: on top of the red wine, which had made her feel sick. Maybe she should watch TV; that always sent her to sleep, it was like flicking a switch. There was a good movie on, *When Harry Met Sally*. She'd watch that. She always loved it.

Halfway through the orgasm scene, she switched it off. It was annoying her. Really annoying her. As if anyone would sit in a café and pretend to have an orgasm that loudly. Stupid. She poured herself another glass of wine and reflected she'd only faked one herself a couple of times: when she'd been just so tired and all she wanted was to go to sleep. It was amazing how they didn't know. Couldn't tell. She'd certainly never, ever faked with Nick. Their sex had always been amazing. Had made a baby even.

Stop it, Jocasta. It is not a baby. It really is not a baby.

She was still awake, and horribly frightened again. She looked at the clock. Only half past twelve. How was she going to get through the rest of the night? Shit. This was awful.

But it was the last one. The very last one.

•◆•

Nick woke early. It had been a hell of a drive but he'd done it, and fallen exhausted into bed in Hampstead at midnight. But the pain in his arm had woken him up; he struggled into the kitchen, took a couple of the painkillers—they were bloody strong, made him feel quite woozy—and made himself a cup of tea. Maybe he should go for a walk, clear his head. God, he'd be glad when he could run again; at the moment it jarred his arm too much, destroyed the pleasure. Yes, he'd go for a stroll, buy the papers, come back and have breakfast, and then head down to Westminster. There was bound to be something going on, and it would be good to get back there. He'd really missed it: funny old place.

He walked down to Heath Street, bought *The Times* and the *Guardian* and the *Daily Mail*—between them they would put him back in touch with the country, his parents only took the *Telegraph*—then dropped in at the deli for a couple of croissants and went home.

He was halfway through the second croissant when a feature in the *Mail* caught his eye: Holiday Getaway Gear, it said, and was a piece about what to wear when travelling and how to look as good—or as bad—as the rich and famous. Lots of shots of people leaving airports, over the past few days: Madonna, Nicole Appleton, Kate Moss, Jude Law, Jonathan Ross, Jasper Conran—and Gideon Keeble. Terrifically well-dressed as always—probably better than most of the others—in a linen suit and panama hat. Bastard. All that money, and looks and style as well.

The captions said where they were all going: mostly to the sun. Workaholic Keeble, as they called him, was off to Melbourne on a business trip. God, he really was a workaholic. No Jocasta in sight; not famous enough, he supposed. Not that Keeble was, really; they must have been scraping the barrel, needed a last person to fill the page. Maybe she hadn't gone: maybe she was still in London, in that absurd mansion. Or down in—Wiltshire, was it? Or Berkshire?

He could try. He could ring her; she had phoned and left that message he'd never responded to—well, it had been a bit cool, and unmistakable in its meaning, and he'd been a bit cross, actually, that she'd been so long in acknowledging his postcards. But he could ring, tell her that he was fine, back in London if she needed him. No, that would be wrong, why should she need him—well just back, thank her for calling—

It took him a few minutes to decide actually to do it; then telling himself they had agreed to be friends, and it was what any friend would do, he called her mobile.

It was switched off.

Well, best leave it then. Only maybe he could try the house. Just see if she was there. Why not? No reason, it was much less clandestine, really, than using her mobile. It proved how innocent his call was. Simply—friendly.

He dialled the Big House; a foreign voice answered. A Filipina-sounding voice.

"Mr. Keeble's residence."

Slightly odd phraseology. Surely it was the Keeble residence now?

"Good morning. Is Mrs. Keeble there?"

"Mrs. Keeble? No, Mrs. Keeble not here."

"Oh, fine. She's away with Mr. Keeble, then? Or in the country."

"Mrs. Keeble not living here now. She—"

There was a sort of scuffle at the end of the line; then Mrs. Hutching, he recognised her voice, said, "Good morning! Can I help you?"

Nick's heart was doing slightly peculiar things.

"Mrs. Hutching, isn't it? Good morning. You won't remember me, but I'm a friend of Mrs. Keeble's, Nicholas Marshall, I came to the house once or twice. I wanted to speak to her, if she's around."

"I'm sorry, Mr. Marshall, she isn't here. She's away."

"With Mr. Keeble? Or in the country?"

"I'm not absolutely sure. I'm sorry. If you'd like to leave a message—"

Nick left a message and then put the phone down. He felt slightly dizzy. Must be the pills, of course. But the first woman, she'd said Jocasta didn't live there anymore. Of course she was foreign, and might have meant something different, like she wasn't living there at the moment. But then Mrs. Hutching had sounded pretty bloody odd, as well.

Shit. Had Jocasta actually left Gideon? She couldn't have. She couldn't. She'd have told him. Surely. And if she hadn't told him, the outlook wasn't too good for him anyway.

Nick stood, walked up and down his small kitchen a couple of times, and then rang Clio. She'd know. She'd tell him.

Jocasta had been awake for three hours; the longest three hours she could ever remember. She had just lain there and watched the clock tick the seconds past, longing for it to be later. It took its time. It was still only half past six. She felt altogether dreadful; her headache was worse and she felt terribly sick. If this were indeed pregnancy sickness, thank God this would be the last day of it.

She felt really frightened and alone. If only she had someone to talk to. To tell her not to worry, that she was doing the right thing, that she'd be fine. Even Clio, telling her she was doing the wrong one would have been preferable to this. But there was no one. And three more endless hours stretched ahead of her.

She couldn't stand any of it any longer; she decided to go for a walk.

All Clio could think about when she woke up was Jocasta. How she must be feeling; for all her brave tough words, Clio knew she was frightened and upset. The more Jocasta talked and protested, the more upset she was. She was talking a lot at the moment.

She would call her, and arrange to go to see her that evening. She'd be feeling awful—even if she weren't upset—sore, and tired. And no matter what anyone said, from Clio's experience at any rate, it wasn't true that what most women felt after a termination was relief. They did feel relief, of course: they also felt guilt and misery and regret.

She rang the house: the answering machine was on.

"Only me," she said. "I'm just calling to see if you're OK, wish you luck. I thought I'd come and see you this evening. No need to call back, I'll be there about seven. Unless you don't want me. Lots of love."

She looked at the clock: nearly seven. She might as well stay up now. Get a good start on the day. She had a shower, was just starting to get dressed, when the phone rang. Hopefully Jocasta, having got her message.

But it wasn't Jocasta; it was Nick.

Jocasta was in the middle of Clapham Common when she felt faint. She sank rather dramatically onto her haunches, dropped her head in her arms, taking deep breaths, and tried not to panic. Now what should she do?

"You OK?" A girl, a jogger, had stopped, was bending over her. Jocasta looked up at her, tried to smile, and then threw up onto the grass.

"Sorry," she said, "so sorry. Yes, I—well, no, I don't feel too good. Have you got a mobile?"

"Sure." She rummaged in her bum bag, handed her phone to Jocasta. Even making the call was almost beyond her.

Clio felt dreadful. She was the worst liar in the world. She had done her best, had stumbled through her story that she hadn't seen Jocasta for a while, that she didn't know if she was still with Gideon, and that she didn't know where she was. It had been totally pathetic. Nick had actually said that. He'd said, quite nicely, "Clio, that is just so pathetic. Of course you know where she is. Come on. At her house? In Clapham. Look, I can see you're protecting her for some reason. She probably made you swear not to say. So if you don't say anything I'll assume it's Clapham, OK?"

Clio was dutifully silent. Nick got into his car and set out for Clapham.

"You are just so stupid," said Beatrice severely, helping Jocasta up the steps of their house and into the sitting room. It had taken her five minutes to get to the common and twenty-five to get back in the building traffic. During which she'd had to stop twice for Jocasta to be sick. "You should have told us before."

"I couldn't," said Jocasta wearily, dropping down onto the sofa. "I just couldn't bear to talk about it. Or think about it. Bit like Martha, I suppose."

"I think you're a little better off than she was, poor girl. I presume Gideon knows about this?"

"Well—"

"Jocasta! I can't believe this. Of course you must tell him."

"It isn't Gideon's baby," said Jocasta.

Nick stood outside Jocasta's house alternately ringing the bell and banging on the door. He was convinced she was in there, hiding, that she knew it was him.

After five minutes he decided to let himself in. Even if she wasn't there, he might get some clue as to where he could find her. Or what had happened. Thank God he had never given the key back.

She wasn't there: but she had clearly only just left. Her duvet was flung back, there was the usual incredible mess in her bedroom, several used cups piled up by the dishwasher. She always did that, never put them in it. It had driven him mad. Even the radio was on: Chris Tarrant burbling cheerfully away. She would obviously be back any minute.

God, his arm hurt. So much. They'd obviously known what they were talking about, telling him to rest it. Bloody agony. And he'd left his pills behind, of course. Jocasta always had plenty of painkillers; she was a bit of an addict. He'd take some of hers, have a cup of tea, and wait for her. He put the kettle on, went to the cupboard under the bathroom basin.

It was a shrine to her messiness; two or three Tampax packets, one of them empty, a very exhausted-looking toothbrush, a mass of hair bands, a spilt box of cotton buds, two packs of dental floss, both in use; a half-empty bottle of mouthwash, two rather evil-looking flannels, and—yes—rummaging a little, bravely on, two bottles of painkillers, not particularly strong ones, she usually had more than that, two large tubes of fake tan, several AA batteries, a packet of something that called itself a natural sleep remedy, an enormous bottle of vitamin C tablets and—what was this? God in heaven, what was this? It couldn't be—no, it wasn't—yes it was, it really indubitably, really horribly was, a pregnancy testing kit, and sweet Jesus, another, both used, the instructions for one crumpled up and pushed back into the box, the other still neatly folded, clearly unread.

What was this, what had been going on here, what had she been doing, why hadn't she told him? Absurd, ridiculous, pointless, cretinous questions. And how long ago had this happened, when had she bought these tests, was the baby Gideon's? Must be, that would explain her extraordinary behaviour, avoiding him. It surely couldn't be his—could it? If there was one? And how did he know that, even? What had she done since? He would have put nothing past her, nothing at all. Why hadn't she told him? It must be Gideon's, must be, must be, otherwise she'd have told him surely, surely.

Nick walked out of the bathroom and sat down, his legs having become suddenly weak, totally devoid of substance; and then rang Clio again. She didn't answer.

"Look, Beatrice, I'm not having it. Nick won't want it. I know he won't. You know what he's like; the last thing in the world he'd want is a child."

"That's not quite the same thing as not knowing he's got one. In the making, at least."

"Beatrice, I can't tell him. Believe me, I can't."

"Well, I do beg to differ. Look—I'd love to stay with you, but I can't, I have to be in court in under an hour. We can discuss it all tonight. Are you going to stay down here, or do you want to go up to bed? Christine'll look after you. She's taking the children to school now, but I'll leave her a note. Josh is away, somewhere up in the Midlands."

"Fine. Thank you so much, Beatrice."

"That's OK. Now promise me, rest."

"I promise."

Good thing Beatrice was going out, thought Jocasta. She felt much better. She had an hour still; she'd have a shower, borrow one of Beatrice's rather severe tracksuits, and set off. God, and change the cab arrangement. Better do that first.

Josh was still asleep when Beatrice rang. He'd had a bit of a night with the sales force, his head was agony.

"Josh, this is Beatrice. Look, I've got something to tell you. You are coming back tonight, aren't you?"

"Of course."

"Right, well, Jocasta will be there."

"Jocasta! Why?"

"She's pregnant."

"Pregnant!"

"Yes. And—wait for it—it's not Gideon's. It's Nick's. And she's clearly planning a termination."

"Nick's! How terrible. Can't we stop her?"

"I'm not sure. But the point is, he doesn't know. And he really should. She swears he wouldn't want it, but he ought to have a chance to say so himself. He can't stop her legally, of course, but—anyway, do you have his number?"

"I think so. You really think he ought to be told?"

"I really think so."

"Lord. Poor Jocasta."

Clio was frantically worried; Jocasta appeared to have gone missing. She had tried her several more times and each time there had been more bleeps on the answering machine and no reply on her mobile.

She actually picked up the phone to call Nick once or twice and then put it down again hastily. He had called her, but she hadn't picked up the phone. God, she was a coward. Or was she just being a good friend, keeping Jocasta's counsel?

She wished she could talk to Fergus about it all. He would know what to do. That was one of the wonderful things about Fergus, he was so sensible. And sympathetic. He was such a Jekyll and Hyde, he had been so sweet about the Morrises, for instance. Stop thinking about Fergus, Clio, concentrate on Jocasta and what's going on.

Her phone rang: she jumped, but it wasn't Nick, it was Josh. Did she have Nick's mobile number? Or even his flat? It was urgent . . .

"Well . . ."

"Oh, Clio, come on."

"Do you know where she is?"

"Yes, she's at our house."

"Thank God. I've been so worried about her. Yes, of course, I'll give you his number. But don't say I gave it you. And you can tell him what you like. Only, I swore I wouldn't—"

"Thanks. You don't happen to know when—if—she might be having a termination, do you?"

"Well, yes. She is. This morning, I'm afraid. And she's going to be sterilised—"

"Jesus! Where?"

"I don't know. She wouldn't tell me. I think she thought I might tell Nick; we'd had a row—"

"Look, call her at our house, Clio, would you? Try to find out where she's going, try to delay her. And I'll ring Nick."

Jocasta was feeling much better. She could go to the clinic. She'd be fine. She had three-quarters of an hour before the cab came. She might just have a bath rather than a shower, it would be more relaxing.

Sitting in the bath with the door shut and Capital Radio on loudly, to distract her, she didn't hear the phone ringing.

"Nick? This is Josh."

"Josh! Thank God. Maybe you can help. I'm terribly worried about Jocasta, I don't know where she is and—"

"She's at our house."

"At yours?"

"Yes. Now the thing is—that is— Oh God, this might be a bit of a shock, Nick, but she's—well, she's pregnant. Sorry to spring it on you, but . . ."

"I did—think she might be," said Nick. He was speaking rather slowly. "I just found some tests. I'm at her place now. But why are you ringing me?"

"Because it's yours." Nick felt as if he was falling through a large silent space, with Josh's voice echoing in the heart of it.

"My baby? Are you absolutely sure?"

"Well, Jocasta is. She told Beatrice."

"Good God," said Nick. "Dear, sweet Jesus."

"Yes. And she's about to have a termination." There was a silence. "Nick? You still there?"

"Yes. Yes, I'm still here."

"Nick, I'm so sorry. Bloody awful thing to hear out of the blue. But Jocasta's at our house, if you want to stop her."

"Of course I want to stop her, for God's sake!"

"Well, call her. Got the number? I think you really have to put your skates on, Nick, and—" But Nick had already cut him off.

• ◄ •

"Mr. Hartley, hello. This is Ed Forrest. I just heard from Mum, she said Mrs. Hartley might have to go into hospital. I'm so sorry. How is she now?"

"Nice of you to call, Ed. Yes, she isn't very well. Dreadfully low, I'm afraid. Just as you must be. How are you feeling?"

"Not too bad," said Ed quickly. He didn't like talking about how much he hurt; that was his property, part of Martha and of how much he had loved her, not to be shared.

"Your visit was the one thing which seemed to cheer my wife up. I was so grateful to you, Ed. Oh, and could you thank Kate? Her letter seemed to help, as well. It was kind of her to write. I've been meaning to write to her, but I've been so busy. I think Grace feels Martha's friends bring her closer, somehow."

"Yes, well, that's nice. And I will tell Kate, yeah. I'm not sure if I'll be up again this weekend, Mr. Hartley, but if I am, I'll certainly come and see her again. Cheers. Take care."

"It's Grace who needs to take care. But thank you, Ed, so much."

Poor old chap. Poor, poor old chap. He'd tell Kate. She was a nice kid. Pretty too. Bit spiky. Like her mother.

"Miss Forbes, isn't it? Yes. And you're booked in for—yes, a termination this morning. And a sterilisation." The nurse smiled at her encouragingly.

"Yes," said Jocasta, "that's right."

"If you'd like to come with me, I'll take you up to your room. We can do your admission; check everything's in order, ask you to sign the consent form, all that sort of thing. You've had nothing, since six o'clock, to eat or drink?"

"No, I haven't."

"Good. Now I think we'll start with taking your blood pressure."

"I'm sorry, Mr. Marshall, but Jocasta's gone." The nanny was clearly anxious. "Yes. She left about—oh, I don't know, about half an hour ago. I'm sorry, I didn't—what? In a cab. Yes. No, it was a minicab. I have no idea, I'm afraid—oh hang on, he's left a card. I can't stand the way they always do that, can you? Oh, sorry, yes, Clapham Cars, does that ring a bell? Yes? Well, the number's—"

•◆•

Kate was on her way to see Fergus; she had definitely decided to sign the contract, if Smith hadn't found anyone else. It was only three years, it was such a lot of money, it would set her up for life, as a photographer maybe, or whatever else she decided to do.

It was all very well for Josh to tell her not to, if it bored her: he had plenty of money already. She could see how it would help her parents, and Juliet for that matter. And now she was feeling so much better about everything, she thought she could handle the publicity.

She knew Fergus would be pleased. And rather better off as a result. So it would benefit everyone, really. After all, it was only three years. . . .

•◆•

Peter was in the middle of dealing with some correspondence when Grace called him. "Could I have some painkillers, Peter, please? My head is dreadful."

"Of course. I'll bring them up." He walked in; she looked terrible. "Poor old love. Here they are. I'll get a couple out for you—" The phone started to ring as she took the bottle from him. She tipped out a couple of the tablets, and swallowed them and had just started to replace the cap when something stopped her. She sat looking at the bottle. There were plenty more. She could just take a handful. That should do it: quite quickly. The other way was taking too long and making her feel too bad. Lucky whoever it was had called then. Really lucky . . .

◆

"Would that have been a Miss Forbes?"

"I—would imagine so. Yes."

"Let me see. She changed the booking, from Haines Road, to Old Town pickup—yes, here we are. She's booked to Gower Street. That sound right?"

"Yes, definitely."

"OK. The GG & O Clinic, Gower Street, it was. Just down from UCH. Pickup this afternoon, time to be confirmed."

"Thank you," said Nick, "thank you so much." If she was having this awful thing done this morning it could be anytime. It could be now. He'd better get his skates on, as Josh had said.

◆

"Kate, my darling, come along in. You're looking perfectly gorgeous, as usual. How are you?"

"I'm good, thanks, Fergus. Now who's that— Excuse me, sorry—"

It was extraordinary, the way the young responded to their mobiles, Fergus thought, as if every call was far more crucial than anything else they might be involved in. You saw them, sitting in a group, a large group, and half of them, at any given time, were on their mobiles. Very odd. And they didn't seem to think breaking off whatever conversation they were having was remotely antisocial.

"Sorry. I'll switch it off now. That was Ed. You know Ed? Martha's boyfriend."

"I do. Rather handsome, as I recall."

"Handsome or what! Yeah. Anyway, apparently Mrs. Hartley, that's Martha's mum, she's really low. And I wrote to them both. I was thinking, you know, that she was my gran really, another gran, and she seemed really lovely, and I felt so sorry for her, and Mr. Hartley said my letter had really cheered her up, can't think why, and could Ed let me know. It's a pity we can't tell them, in a way—"

"I do hope you won't," said Fergus anxiously. "I don't think that would be a good idea, at all."

"Fergus! I'm not that stupid. Anyway, I've come to talk about the contract with Smith. I really do think I should sign it. I feel so different now and . . ."

•◆•

Nick roared along Knightsbridge and cut up into the park; please God don't let the Horse Guards be going along it. They were. He sat there in agony for a moment or two, then did a U-turn and screeched back, cutting up into the Bayswater Road. The traffic there was fairly solid too: he shot across it, and took a back route, weaving round the narrow streets and squares, cutting up other motorists (surprised at their outrage, he was driving as he always did, only faster), nearly killing two dogs, one cat, and frightening the life out of a rather grand-looking old lady, stepping out into the road without looking, as grand old ladies tended to. She shook her fist at him, and when last seen in his rearview mirror, she was pointing out his car to a passerby. He shot across Baker Street, wove his way along Welbeck Street, and then struck north, his mind wiped clear of everything except the need to get to Gower Street in time. At one point he found himself confronted by a No Entry sign and a one-way street; it seemed entirely logical to take it on. He was lucky.

In Gower Street, he had to find the clinic, right at the top it had been, the man had said. Where was the bloody place—ah, there. No meters of course, only double yellow lines everywhere.

He abandoned the car and faced a traffic warden who asked him what he thought he was doing. "Saving a life," he said.

The man had clearly heard this before. "I'll have to give you a ticket," he said.

"Great. Fine. I'd really like that. Just go ahead." The warden stared at him and then started to write the ticket, shaking his head.

And there it was, a discreet, freshly painted door, with GG & O Clinic on a brass plate. GG & O—what sort of bloody nonsense was that? He pushed on the bell; the door opened with a self-important burr.

There was a reception desk in the hall, with a vast urn of flowers on it; to the left of the urn was a smiling young woman in a navy suit and a flowered shirt, with a bow at the neck. "Good morning," she said. "How can I help you?"

"By telling me where—where my wife is," said Nick. He somehow felt they'd be more helpful if he assumed husband status. He sat down breathing heavily. He felt rather odd.

"Would you like to give me her name?"

"Keeble. Jocasta Keeble."

"And who is she seeing today?"

"I'm afraid I can't tell you. I don't know."

The woman started to press the keys on her computer. Enough keys, it seemed to Nick, to be writing a book. Or certainly a very long article. What a bloody waste of time and energy those things were. All she needed was an appointment book and a pencil.

"Keeble, you say, Keeble. No, I don't have anyone of that name this morning."

Her phone had just rung. "Gower Gynaecology and Obstetrics. Mr. Cartwright? Yes, if you could just wait a moment." More key-tapping.

"Look," said Nick, "this is so urgent, I can't begin to tell you. Please, please tell me where she is."

"Just a moment, please. So sorry, Mr. Cartwright, just putting you through now." She smiled at him; a less friendly smile.

"Now: no Keeble today. Definitely."

"Well how about Forbes?"

"Forbes, Forbes . . . oh, yes. Yes, here she is. Good. If you'd like to sit down over there, I'll let Mrs. Miles know you're here. Do help yourself to tea or coffee."

"I don't want any coffee and I certainly don't want Mrs. Miles. I want my—wife."

"Mrs. Miles is looking after your wife today. Please try to be patient. Hello? Susan, it's about a Mrs. Forbes. One of Mrs. Miles's patients. Her husband is here. Is she in theatre? Ah, yes, I see. Thank you." She sat back in her chair, gave Nick an even more gracious smile.

"I'm so sorry, Mr. Keeble. Your wife has already left."

·•·

He could see at once what she had done. She was looking . . . odd. A mixture of defiant and excited. The paracetamol bottle was placed neatly on the bedside table, with its cap on. She glanced at it. He picked it up. It was empty.

"Oh, Grace, Grace, my darling, you shouldn't have done that, I know why, but—God, let's ring Douglas—dear God—"

Grace started to cry.

Douglas Cummings's advice was succinct. "Get her into hospital. At once. It's a lethal drug. However she seems, just bring her in. Do you want an ambulance?"

"No," said Peter wearily, "it's only five minutes away. I'll drive her." He hoped very much it wouldn't be the last thing he did for her.

·•·

Nick walked slowly back to the car. It had been clamped. He decided he couldn't sort it out yet; he would just leave it.

The one good thing about being clamped was that the car was safe.

He felt rather sick, and terribly tired. Apart from that, nothing: not sad, not angry, just—nothing. His arm hurt. He hailed a cab, directed it to Hampstead. He sat in it, staring out of the window, at the rather depressing upper reaches of Gower Street, looking at people, lucky people, who had normal relationships and happy families.

He tried very hard not to think about Jocasta and even harder not to think about the baby she had just thrown away. He failed. His mind felt as if it would never think of anything else again. Of her, and how much he had loved her—still loved her, so, so much—and how he would have behaved, what he would have wanted, if he had known. And he knew he would have wanted it. Very much. Even now, thinking about the baby, a baby that no longer existed, he felt new and totally unfamiliar things. He wasn't quite sure what they were, but there seemed to be pride there, and a fierce protectiveness and a degree of awe at what they had accomplished, Jocasta and he. Yes. No doubt. He would have wanted it: his baby.

It would have been absolutely terrifying: it would have meant not only commitment, absolute commitment, abruptly and forcibly entered into, but a new and entirely different life. There would have been no period of adjustment for the two of them, no time to learn to live together, no time for him to come to terms with his new condition. He would have had to make the leap from single man to husband and father, with scarcely time in between to take breath. It would have been very difficult. But it was what he would have wanted.

And as he sat there, astonished at the sadness of it, of what he had lost, they had both lost, he thought it was as well he wasn't going to see her, for he would not be able to answer for what he might do to her; and then he leant forward and tapped on the window and said to the cabbie, "Could you change that, take me to Clapham, North End Road, instead. Please."

•―•

She would probably be all right, they said, because he'd acted so quickly.

"The trouble with paracetamol is that it doesn't seem to have had any effect and all the time there's appalling liver damage going on," said the young doctor. He had come out of the room where Grace lay, to find Peter, head in hands, weeping quietly. He was very young, the doctor; he normally found patients' grief extremely difficult to deal with, but his father was a clergyman and this sweet man seemed somehow familiar.

"I really think she'll be all right. We've given her a very powerful antidote, washed her stomach out, of course, and she's sleeping now. Try not to worry. She seemed quite peaceful."

Peter nodded; he was unable to speak.

"Look," said the doctor, "I know she's frail and not so young, but she has a huge spirit. I could tell that, just from being with her, and she kept saying she was sorry. Try not to worry," he said again.

"Yes," said Peter, wiping his eyes. "Yes, thank you."

"Get yourself a cup of tea, I would."

Peter watched him as he hurried off in response to another patient,

· 614 ·

another crisis; he hardly looked old enough to be in charge of a medicine chest, let alone a busy Casualty clinic.

Suddenly the young man turned and came back to him.

"There was something I forgot to tell you," he said to Peter. "Your wife said it had been an accident. She said that about three times. She's obviously regretting it terribly. I think that's good news. The really serious cases are when they don't want to be brought round."

Peter thanked him. But he knew Grace would actually have loved to go. Go to join Martha.

•-•-•

"Call for you, Clio. I think it's your journalist friend," said Margaret. "Shall I put her through?"

"Oh yes. Please do. Jocasta, hello, are you all right?"

"Oh, Clio, Clio—" Jocasta got no further; huge sobs came down the line.

"Oh, Jocasta, darling, what happened, what is it?"

"It was all so terrible, so awful. I was so frightened and I— Oh God. Clio, please come. As soon as you can. Sorry, Clio, so sorry, I'm all right really, I just—"

"Jocasta, you shouldn't be alone. You should have someone with you. Where are you?"

"At home. I'm fine, honestly. I'll be all right."

"I can be there by about five," said Clio. "Is that all right?"

"Yes. Thank you." She sounded terribly weepy; Clio rang off and buzzed for her last patient.

Maybe she could get the new young locum to take her afternoon surgery.

•-•-•

"You can see her now, Mr. Hartley." The young nurse smiled at him encouragingly. "She's had a little sleep. She says she wants to go home, but because of her age and everything, we feel she should stay in for a couple of days. Just so we can keep a check on her liver and so on. We've got a room in Florence, we'll move her up there as soon as we can."

"Thank you," said Peter. He wondered rather distractedly how many millions of hospital wards were called Florence, and went in to see Grace.

She was lying on her back, staring up at the ceiling; she was rather yellow-looking. "Hello, Grace darling."

She turned her head and looked at him—and dissolved into tears. "Oh, Peter, I'm so sorry. It was wrong of me. Please forgive me."

"Of course I forgive you. I'd forgive you anything. You know that. I love you so much, Grace."

"I know. And I love you. But everything seems so hopeless. So dreadfully hopeless. I looked into that bottle and saw the answer."

"I know, darling, I know."

"It just hurts so much. I don't know how to bear it. I don't seem to have God anymore, as you do. Not helping me, as He is you. Please forgive me, Peter, please."

"Grace, He isn't helping me very much, either, at the moment. I can't imagine ever feeling any better."

"Really?" she said.

"Really. There have even been times when I felt I had lost my faith entirely."

"Oh, Peter. I didn't realise, I thought—"

"You thought wrongly. But I know He will help. Sooner or later. I just have to hang on. As you must. I can't afford to lose you, as well," he added with a weary smile.

Grace looked at him. It seemed dreadful to feel better because she knew Peter felt worse. But somehow, it helped. Knowing they were in it together, knowing she wasn't enduring the worst of it all alone. She managed a smile back.

"I'm so sorry," she said again, and then, "I must look so awful!"

"You always look beautiful to me."

"Oh don't," she said, turning her head away. The endless tears started again.

Peter sighed. She still had a long way to go. But he felt an important marker in the road had been passed. They were at least together again. He could feel it.

"Edward?"

"Yes, Mum." He could hear his own voice, slightly irritable; he must be careful. But this was getting a bit much: second time today.

"Edward, I've got some rather sad news. Poor Mrs. Hartley—"

"What's happened now?"

"She took an overdose, Ed. So sad."

"Oh no! Is she—"

"No, no, she's going to be all right. But think how dreadful she must be feeling. Poor soul. She's still in hospital, Dorothy told me, you know, she's my friend from Weight Watchers—"

"Yes, Mum."

"She's a nurse. Of course she shouldn't have told me, but I thought you'd like to know."

"Yes, I'm glad you told me." He felt sharply depressed. How long and how far were the effects of Martha's death going to spread? "Yes, I'll send her a card."

"Could you? And perhaps you could ask that girl—Kate, was it?—to do the same? I found cards, the briefest note, so helpful. Just to know people are thinking of you."

"Sure. I will."

He'd ring her later; he couldn't face it now.

⋅◆⋅

"Clio, this is Fergus. I just wanted to tell you something—"

"Look, Fergus, I'm sorry, but I'm terribly busy. I've got to—well, do something, leave Guildford in a couple of hours and see a waiting room full of patients first. Another time—"

Fergus rang off without even saying goodbye.

Nick stood looking at Jocasta's little house for a moment, listening to the taxi drive away. He felt almost frightened to go in, afraid of how he might feel about it and her, of how dangerously it all might have changed. Of how dangerously she had changed, from someone easy and irresponsible and transparent into someone capable of huge deception and terrible arrogance—and great courage. To do what she had done, entirely alone. He almost wanted to go away, to keep her as she had always been; but he knew he had to see her, face her, find out what she had become and why. He raised his finger and pressed the bell; there was quite a long silence. And then he heard her voice.

"Who is it?"

"Nick."

A moment's pause, he could hear her shock. Then he heard the chain being undone, watched the door open, saw her.

She looked dreadful; she was very white and her eyes were red and swollen with crying. Her hair hung lankly round her face, and she was twisting a handkerchief in both hands. She was wearing one of the most hideous tracksuits he had ever seen. She managed a half smile.

"Hi!"

"Hello?"

"Do you want to come in?"

"If I may."

"Of course . . ." She led him into her sitting room; surprisingly tidy, by her standards. "Would you like a cup of tea?"

"No thanks. How are you feeling?"

"Terrible."

"Ah."

There was a long silence; then she said, "Excuse me," and rushed out of the room. He heard various unpleasant noises coming from the lavatory; she emerged finally, whiter than ever, stood twisting a tissue in her hands.

"Sorry."

"The anaesthetic, I suppose," he said.

She looked at him sharply. "You know?"

"Yes, I know. I've just come from the clinic."

"From the— Nick, who told you?"

"I'm quite a good detective," he said. "It's part of being a journalist. As you know."

"Yes, but—"

"Oh, I had a little help."

"From Clio, I suppose?"

"No. Not from Clio. She wouldn't tell me anything." He looked at her and shook his head. "This is a fine thing that you've done, Jocasta. A very fine thing. Why on God's earth didn't you tell me? Don't you think I had a right to know? About—about a baby that wasn't just yours but mine as well. Ours. Don't you think I would have wanted to know, to talk about it, to tell you what I felt? How could you decide all on your own what was best, for—for all of us? It was arrogant and it's made me terribly unhappy."

"Unhappy?"

"Of course. Jocasta, I love you. I love you so much. How could you think I should have no part in all this?"

"Nick—Nick, you don't mean—you don't mean you'd have wanted me to have a baby?"

"Of course I'd have wanted you to have our baby. I might not have chosen it, just now. But that doesn't mean I'd have wanted you to—to throw it away. Given the choice. Of course I wouldn't."

"Oh," she said, "oh I see. Yes."

"And I can't begin to think how you could have done that. Without talking to me."

"No. No, indeed. Well—well, you see, the thing is—"

"The thing is, what? I don't think I can cope with any justifications."

"You're not going to get any. The thing is, Nick," she said, slowly and very gently, "actually, it is rather a fine thing I've done. I think."

He stared at her. "What do you mean?"

"I mean I couldn't do it," she said, "not in the end. I just couldn't. I got into that room, and I lay there, thinking, really thinking, about what I was doing, what was going to happen, and then after a bit, I just got up and left. So actually, Nick, I'm still pregnant. What are we going to do about that?"

Chapter 45

·   ·   ·   ·

Clio looked, with great foreboding, up at Jocasta's windows. She was terrified of what she might find. It wasn't going to be easy. She was actually finding it very hard. Even now. That someone, especially someone she was fond of, could so carelessly—literally—discard a baby, hurt her a lot. But Jocasta's reasons, however tortuous, had seemed insurmountable to her; and it was Jocasta they had to look after now.

Very tentatively she pressed the bell; after a few minutes, she heard Jocasta's voice. She sounded remarkably cheerful; she looked remarkably cheerful, as she opened the door. She was very pale, but—yes, unmistakably cheerful. She was recovering very fast, Clio thought, and tried to suppress her irritation.

"Hello, darling Clio. Let me give you a hug. Come in, it's so lovely to see you."

"I came as soon as I could—"

"I know. You're an angel. Thank you."

She led the way into the sitting room. Clio followed her. Jocasta seemed perfectly all right. She could have given her patients a bit more attention this afternoon after all.

"Well, how do you feel?" she asked.

"Dreadful. I keep being sick."

"Oh, Jocasta, I'm sorry. You've been very unlucky. The anaesthetics don't usually do that, these days."

"Don't they? I wouldn't know."

"You what? You mean, they didn't give you anything?"

"Nothing. Nothing at all."

"Jocasta—" Clio looked at her; her eyes were sparkling in her white face, she was smiling.

"I didn't have it. I didn't have the termination," she said. "I'm still pregnant. I can't think how I'm going to cope with it, but—I am. I walked out. Told them not to do it, just as they were coming in to get me. They were awfully cross," she added.

Clio felt as if someone had given her irrefutable evidence that the earth was flat. She sat there, staring at Jocasta, trying to work out what she felt. Finally she realised: irritation. Major irritation.

"You cow," she said, "you absolute cow. Letting me break the speed limit all the way here—I've probably got all my points at once, this afternoon—worrying me, crying like that. Oh, Jocasta!" She started to cry herself.

"Clio, darling, don't, don't, I know it's hard, but—"

"No," she said, going over to her, giving her a hug, "it's not hard. Not at all. You getting rid of it was hard. I'm actually really happy for you."

"Oh, good. Because I'm happy for me too. Very happy. I'd be ecstatic, if I could stop being sick. Serves me right for being so snooty about it."

"Yes, maybe it does. Have you told Nick?"

"Yes. He came round."

"What did he say?"

"Clio, he was terribly happy about it. He was actually excited. And until he knew it was all right, he was terribly upset. I can't quite believe it—"

"Jocasta," said Clio, "I hate to say this, no, I don't hate to say it, I'm enjoying saying it, but I did tell you so!"

"Where is Nick?" she said, half an hour later, after she had made Jocasta some chamomile tea.

"God knows. Yes, I do. He's had to go and sort out his car—it got clamped. He belongs to some weird thing that stays with the car for you, while they come and unclamp it, but it was too late, they'd taken it away, so he had to go and find it. Silly bugger," she added fondly.

Her mobile rang. "Hi, Kate. How are you—oh God," she handed it to Clio, "I've got to go back to the loo. Sorry."

Clio made sympathetic faces and said, "Kate, it's me, Clio."

"What's the matter with Jocasta?"

"She's . . . got a tummy bug."

"Oh no. Poor thing. I'll come round and see her, shall I, bring her some flowers? I've got Nat with me, we're in Clapham, just down the road from her, we've looked it up on the *A to Z*."

"Kate, I really don't think—" But she had rung off.

Jocasta was surprisingly pleased by the prospect.

"I'd love to see her. Honestly."

"And Nat? Are you sure?"

"Well maybe just for a minute or two. I know why she's coming, she called me yesterday: it's about the Smith contract. She's changed her mind, she's going to do it."

"Oh yes?" said Clio. She didn't think she wanted to hear about Kate and her contract. Her contract and Fergus.

Thinking about Fergus made her feel suddenly terrible. She was happy for Jocasta, of course, and for Nick, but—here she was, alone again. Very alone. With no prospect of being less so. No doubt that was why Fergus had called her; to tell her what a wonderful contract he had fixed for Kate. He was so bloody insensitive. And self-centred.

Kate came in, looking radiant, holding a large but rather inelegant bunch of flowers.

"Darling, they're lovely," said Jocasta.

"I hope so. We got them from the garage. Nat chose them, while I was in the toilet."

"They're lovely. Thank you, Nat."

"That's OK. Sorry you're not feeling so good."

"You know something?" said Jocasta. "I'm feeling perfectly wonderful!"

"Really?" said Kate. "Clio said you had a tummy bug."

"Oh, did she? No, I haven't got a tummy bug. I'm going to have a baby, Kate. What do you think about that?"

"I think that's really cool. Like I said, you'll be a great mother. Don't you think so, Nat?"

"Yes," he said, his face very solemn, obviously thinking about it. "Let's hope so, anyway."

Jocasta smiled at him. "I'm hoping so, too."

"Gideon must be pleased."

"It—isn't Gideon's," said Jocasta carefully. "Gideon and I are getting divorced."

Kate looked very confused. As well she might, Jocasta thought. "So whose is it then?"

"It's Nick's."

"Nick, who used to be your boyfriend? Who came to the funeral?"

"The very one."

"Oh." She digested this for a bit. "So—are you going to marry him now?"

"Probably. He's a bit anti actual marriage. But he seems very keen on the baby."

"Well, that's a good thing, I s'pose . . . I'm sorry about Gideon, though. I really like him."

"Oh, Kate, so do I. But it's all right. We should never have got married in the first place. It was a stupid mistake. Mostly on my part. And we're still good friends."

"Cool." She was clearly baffled, out of her depth.

Jocasta decided she should change the subject. "Now, tell me all about your contract," she said. "Have you actually signed it, and when are you going to start with them?"

"I'm not," she said. "I didn't sign it. Fergus told me not to."

"Fergus told you not to?"

"Yeah. I was all set to, went in to see him for a meeting, and he told me not to. He said I just didn't realise what I was letting myself in for, he said it would all start all over again, with the press and that, and—well, he just wouldn't let me. I'm really relieved now," she added. "Even in spite of the money, deep down I didn't want to."

"Yes, well money isn't everything, it is?" said Nat.

"It absolutely isn't. Clio, where are you going? Clio—"

Clio drove as fast as she could to Fergus's office. More speeding tickets, probably. She prayed he'd still be there. This wasn't something that could be settled on the phone. As she reached the North End Road, and his building, she saw him standing at the first-floor window, staring down at the street. He looked terribly unhappy. She parked the car, careless that it was on the zigzag lines next to the crossing, and ran across the road, pressed her finger on the bell.

He was a long time answering it. Supposing he'd seen her, supposing he didn't want to let her in? She wouldn't blame him; she'd been so vile to him.

Finally he spoke on the intercom. "Who is it?"

"It's Clio. Please let me in."

"OK." He didn't sound exactly pleased to hear her voice. She took a deep breath, pushed on the door, and ran up the stairs. He was sitting in the minute room that he called his reception area, and looked at her rather coolly.

"Hello."

"Hello, Fergus. I've come to—to apologise to you."

"What?"

"Yes. I'm so sorry I said all those things about you being cynical and trading on people's misery and all that. Very sorry."

"I see."

"Yes. It was terribly wrong of me, I had no right to say any of them."

"No."

This wasn't going very well. Maybe she'd hurt him too much for him to forgive her. Oh, God.

"Fergus, I . . . Fergus, I really want you to know that I—I—well, that I care about you so much. I've missed you terribly. I was thinking only today how much I missed you, that I shouldn't have been so stupid and—"

"That's all right," he said. He was still staring at her, his face expressionless.

This was terrible. She really had obviously upset him, beyond redemption. Well, it served her right. She was a pompous, self-righteous woman; she didn't deserve someone as lovely as Fergus. She should have trusted him, she should have known better. She looked at him again. Still the frozen face.

"Well," she said finally, her voice trembling, "that's all I came to say. It needed to be said. I thought."

She turned towards the door. If she could only get out without crying, that'd be something.

"Where are you going now?" he said.

"I don't know. Home, I suppose, to Guildford."

"You are not," he said, "you are most definitely not."

"What?"

"You're staying here with me."

"Staying here?"

"Yes," he said, "staying here. I love you."

"You love me?" she said.

"Yes. I love you. Love you an awful lot. You silly bitch," he added.

◆

"Grace, dear, you've got some visitors." Peter's voice was slightly tentative. "Can I bring them up?"

"Oh—oh dear. I'm not sure. I'm very tired."

"We won't stay long, Mrs. Hartley."

"Oh," she said, and they could all hear the pleasure in her voice. "Oh, Ed. How nice. Yes, do bring them up, Peter."

"There's two of us," said Ed. "I've brought Kate with me."

It had been arranged on the spur of the moment; he had called Kate to tell her that Grace was in hospital and she'd said she'd send a card; and then he said he was going up this weekend, after all: one of his mates was having a party, and he'd take it.

"Fine," she said and then a bit later, she called him back.

"I was thinking," she said, "should I come with you? Like, to see her. Just for a little while?"

"It's a long way, Kate, for a little while." Ed sounded doubtful.

"Doesn't matter. Nat could bring me. He's got some new wheels for his car and he wants to show them off."

"Yeah. What's he got then?"

"Saxo."

"What, the bomb?" He sounded very impressed; they cared more about their cars than anything, Kate thought.

"Yeah."

"Wow. I couldn't—hitch a ride, could I?"

"Course you could. He loves showing it off."

"Well, OK then. You'd better ask him."

"Oh no," she said, her voice absolutely confident. "He'll be pleased. Honest. I'll tell him to be."

"Good. Well, thanks." She was a one-off, Ed thought, switching off his phone.

Absolutely totally gorgeous and funny and really quite bright. He liked her a lot. Of course, he could never fancy her. Not really. She was Martha's daughter and that made it unthinkable. But he did like her. Somehow, she comforted him. Made him feel just a little less desperate. She wasn't Martha, but in a funny way she was. Part of her. There was something about her voice, for instance, a note in it that was Martha. And when she giggled, that was Martha too. And her eyes, those huge dark eyes, they were Martha's eyes. It ought to hurt, and in a way it did. But in another, it absolutely didn't.

"Well, here she is. Only been home for a couple of days and she gets very tired, but—just a few minutes."

"Hello, Mrs. Hartley," said Ed. "How are you?"

"Oh, you know. A little bit better."

"You remember Kate?"

"Yes, of course I do. It's very good of you to come, dear."

"It's cool. Here, we brought you these." Helen had chosen the flowers and they were beautiful. "How sweet of you. Peter, go and put them in water, love. It's a long journey you've done," she said to Kate.

"Oh, not really. My boyfriend brought me. In his car. He's gone to buy something for it," she said hastily, clearly anxious that Grace might feel she should ask the boyfriend in, as well. "It needs a new trim, or something."

"I see." She looked at her. "How old are you, Kate?"

"Sixteen."

"You're still at school?"

"Yes."

"And what do you want to do?"

"I think I want to be a photographer. But then again, I might be a lawyer."

"A lawyer! My goodness. Like Martha."

"Well, yeah. And Ally McBeal."

"Who, dear?"

"Ally McBeal. She's a lawyer on TV. You ought to watch it, it's really good."

"I'll look out for it. And how is Jocasta? That's right, isn't it?"

"Yes, that's right," said Kate. "She's fine. She's going to have a baby."

"A baby! How lovely. I'm so pleased."

"Yes." She paused, looked at Ed for a moment, then said, "She sent you her good wishes and she said—"

"Yes? What did she say?"

"She said if it was a girl," said Kate, and she smiled, with great sweetness, at Grace, "she said to tell you that, if it's a girl, she's going to call her Martha."

Excerpt from

An Absolute Scandal

By Penny Vincenzi

*Available in hardcover from Doubleday
in May 2008*

Chapter 1

22 APRIL 1988, MORNING

She wasn't even going to think about having an affair.

It was something she totally disapproved of; it wasn't just immoral and selfish, it was deeply dangerous. She was married, very happily, to someone she not only loved but admired, and there was no way she was going to break her vows (and risk breaking Nigel's heart) and put her marriage and her very happy life at risk. So that was absolutely that. And if he phoned—which he almost certainly wouldn't; he'd been drunk and probably hadn't meant a word of what he said—she would simply say just that: "No, I'm sorry, it was lovely meeting you, but I'm happily married and—well, I'm happily married." That would be enough. Surely. He'd know what she meant and he'd probably come out with some jokey reply and that would be that. And if she had to spell it out—well, she would. A fun encounter: that's all it had been. She might have been a bit silly; she *had* been a bit silly. But that was all. Blame the champagne. And luckily Nigel hadn't noticed anything . . .

He came into the bedroom now, from their bathroom, offering his wrists to her so she could put in his cufflinks; as she did so, her fingers unusually fumbly—blame the champagne for that as well; she seemed to have a bit of a hangover—she suddenly found herself looking at him as if she had never seen him before. Was he really, as *he* had said so rudely, a bit of a caricature? She supposed, honestly, that he was: tall, blond—well, blondish, going just slightly grey now—very slim, pretty good-looking really, perfectly dressed in his Turnbull & Asser shirt, his pinstriped suit, his Lobbs shoes. (*He* had been wearing Lobbs shoes; he'd told her: "Only posh thing about me. I get a real thrill going in there, them getting the old last out.")

"Lucinda! Do concentrate, darling, I can't stand here all day."

"Sorry. There you are."

"Thanks. You having breakfast this morning?"

"Oh—no." The thought made her feel sick.

"Hope you're not overdoing the dieting?"

"Nigel, of course I'm not. I'd have thought you only had to look at me to see that."

"Well, you look pretty good to me. Anyway, I'm hungry. Not enough to eat at that thing, was there?"

"No, not really. Gosh, it's late, I didn't realise."

She mustn't be late for work today, of all days. She worked for Peter Harrison, the publishers, as secretary to Graham Parker, one of the editors, and he had an important meeting with some Americans. Being Americans, they had suggested an eight o'clock meeting; Graham had managed to persuade them to move it forward an hour, to nine, but she'd have to be there well before then, with coffee brewed, biscuits and herself ready to greet them. It would be fun.

One of the things Lucinda loved most about her job was the social aspect; there was always something going on—book launches, marketing meetings, sales conferences, press jaunts . . . She'd been working for Graham for a year now; she was hoping to be an editor herself one day, but her ambition was slightly half-hearted; she didn't intend to go on working after she had a baby. That was something else she disapproved of: working mothers. She intended to be like her own mother, always there, putting her children first. But—come on, Lucinda, don't start thinking about that now. You've got to get to work.

She caught sight of herself in the hall mirror and tried to see herself through *his* eyes: longish fullish skirt (Laura Ashley); blue shirt with a turned-up collar (Thomas Pink); and her twenty-first-birthday pearls, of course; navy sleeveless Puffa jacket; flat shoes (Charlie Jourdan); blond hair scooped back in a velvet band.

There really was no way she could possibly appeal to *him*, not really. He'd like one of those sharp eighties girls in short-skirted suits with padded shoulders, girls with big hair and big ambitions. He wouldn't even be able to remember her this morning, never mind ringing her . . . and as she stood there, checking that she had her wallet and her keys, the post came through the letter box. A couple of quite nice-looking things, clearly invitations, a bill or two, a postcard from Verbier, from the skiing party she'd wanted to join and Nigel hadn't, and a letter from Lloyd's. Lloyd's of London. One of the whiter-than-white envelopes that arrived once a year, containing a statement of their account and followed in due course by a large cheque. Nigel was a Member of Lloyd's; it was one of the things that had pleased her father most when he and Nigel had had their Little Chat, just before she and Nigel got engaged.

"Not only all that land, down in Norfolk, but he's a Name as well; that'll stand you in good stead in the years to come."

One of her uncles had been a Name in quite a big way, apparently. When she was young, she'd heard her mother talking about it, and asked her what it meant: "Well, darling, it means you become a sort of sleeping partner," Margaret Worthington had said rather vaguely. "They insure big things, like ships and buildings, and they make a big profit on it. If you're a Name, you get a share in those profits."

"What happens if the ships sink?" she'd asked, and her mother had said, "Well, there's more than enough money to deal with that. They still make a profit. Ask Daddy about it, he'll tell you more, I don't really understand it. Except that it pays all your cousins' school fees," she added.

It hadn't sounded interesting enough for Lucinda to ask her father, but she did know now that there was enough money coming in from Lloyd's every year to boost their income quite a bit. Which they didn't need at the moment, of course; Nigel's salary as chairman of the family business was perfectly adequate, and he had quite a big portfolio of stocks and shares, but it would be wonderfully helpful when they wanted to move to the country and buy a house.

That was the plan—to move as soon as they had children. Not to Norfolk; that was too far, and the last thing Nigel wanted was to run the farm, but he also didn't want to spend the rest of his life in London. Nor did she; she'd grown up in the country herself and loved it.

"Where did you live when you were a child then?" *he* had asked last night. "Some pile in the country, I s'pose?"

"Well," she'd said, "not exactly a pile, but quite a nice house, yes, in Gloucestershire, near Cirencester."

"Oh, yeah? Ponies?"

"Yes. Yes, I did have a pony, actually."

"Very nice," he'd said, "very nice indeed. I'd like my kids to have all that, ponies and boarding school; you go to boarding school?"

"Yes, when I was thirteen."

"Like it?"

"Quite. I got awfully homesick and missed my pony. And Mummy, of course, and my brothers."

"And where were they at school? Eton or Harrow or some such?"

"Um—Eton, yes, actually."

"And Hubby, he go to Eton?"

"Yes, he did."

That was when he'd said Nigel was a caricature. And— Stop it, Lucinda, stop thinking about it.

She started ripping open the envelopes to distract herself. Invitations: oh, fantastic, Caroline's wedding. And that looked like Philippa's writing (it was)—brilliant, party in the country—and Sarah's baby's christening, and— damn! She'd opened a letter addressed to Nigel by mistake, pulled it half out. Not that Nigel would mind—at least, she didn't think so. He always said he had no secrets from her. She'd just say she was sorry and— Now the letter wouldn't go back into the envelope. Lucinda pulled it out to refold it and couldn't resist reading it. The letterhead read JACKSON & BOND, MEMBERS' AGENT, LLOYD'S OF LONDON, and the letter itself was quite brief:

Dear Nigel,
I thought I should warn you ahead of the final account that, as I feared, you did make a loss for the year just closed. Not a big one, just a few thousand pounds . . .

A loss. How extraordinary. That had never happened before. She didn't know how many thousands of pounds Lloyd's would regard as "just a few." Maybe ten thousand, or even more? Surely not. But she did know they dealt in very big numbers. Nigel would know. They'd have to talk about it tonight.

God, she was late; she must go. She left the letters on the hall table and slammed the door behind her.

Despite her resolve, she began to think about *him* again: him and the night before. She'd never met anyone quite like him. It had been at a party to celebrate the publication of a book edited by Graham Parker about the financial markets just before and just after Big Bang—that extraordinary day in October 1986, when the stock market became totally computerised and a free-for-all, rather than the gentlemanly domain of the traditional stockbroker. Lucinda organised and attended all the editorial department's parties; it was part of her job and she enjoyed it. The guest list had looked like a Who's Who of the Square Mile. Nigel had been invited, but not because he worked in the city; he worked for a large manufacturing company that had been founded by his grandfather, but he had a large share portfolio and Graham had kindly suggested to Lucinda that it might be interesting for him. *He,* on the other hand, *did* work in the city.

He was one of that entirely new breed of traders, the market makers, sprung not from the great public schools but from the East End of London. "I'm one of your electronic barrow boys, so called," he'd said, grinning at her, as he allowed her to refill his glass. "Not the sort the city used to give the time of day to, unless we was in our proper place in the back office." He held out his hand. "Gary Horton. Known these days as Blue. Pleased to meet you"—he peered at her name badge—"Lucinda Cowper." He pronounced it wrongly, as people so often did; it always annoyed her.

"It's pronounced Cooper," she said briskly. "The *W*'s silent."

"Yeah, I see," he said, looking mildly amused, and then, his dark eyes moving over her, "are you really called Lucinda?"

"Yes, of course. Is that so unusual?"

"Well, where I come from it is. I mean, that is a posh name, isn't it? Seriously posh."

"I—I don't know," she said.

"I don't s'pose you would. Don't s'pose you know anyone who isn't posh, do you?"

"Well, of course I do," she said, rather helplessly.

"Oh, okay. What, like Daddy's chauffeur and Mummy's cleaner?"

"I think you're being rather rude," said Lucinda, "if you don't mind my saying so. Now if you'll excuse me, I—"

"Sorry," he said, putting out an arm, stopping her. "I was out of order. Sorry. It interests me, all that Eton and ponies stuff, not sure why. Probably because I can't understand how they—you—have done it."

"What do you mean?" she said, reluctantly interested.

"How you've survived so long. I mean, most dinosaurs die out, don't they? Oh, shit. Now I've been rude again, haven't I?"

"Yes. Very," she said coolly, unable to laugh it off; she looked for Nigel, went over and refilled his glass.

"You all right?" she said. "Got enough people to talk to?"

"Oh, yes, of course. Jolly good party, Lucinda. Well done." He smiled at her. It was one of his more endearing characteristics, that he enjoyed life enormously; his work, his social life—although he got a bit irritated with her more giggly friends—his tennis, his shooting. He was seldom out of sorts, always cheerful, almost always good-tempered. He was quite a bit older than she was, forty-two to her twenty-four, but it had never been a problem. She rather liked it; it made her feel safe.

She was in earnest conversation with one of the other editors when Blue Horton appeared at her side again.

"Look," he said, waiting patiently until the editor moved away, "I just wanted to apologise. I've got a real gift for saying the wrong thing. Can't help it, really."

"It's all right," she said. "Now if you'll excuse me, I really have to go and talk to some more—what did you call them?—oh, yes, dinosaurs . . ."

"No, don't go," he said, putting his hand on her arm. "Please. One of the reasons I got carried away was because I felt—I don't know—thrown by you."

"Thrown? Why?"

"Well, because you're so bloody gorgeous," he said. "I just totally forgot myself. Looking at you."

Lucinda felt a blush rising up her throat. "Don't be ridiculous," she said.

"I'm not being ridiculous. I'm a shy, retiring sort of fellow."

"Now you are really being ridiculous." She smiled in spite of herself.

"You're about as shy as—as—" she struggled to think of someone suitably self-confident. "Mrs. Thatcher."

"Ah, now there's a lady I admire," he said, surprising her. "She's responsible for all this"—he waved his arm round the room—"all this enterprise; she's freed up the market, she's made it possible to do whatever you want, given enough ambition and energy and that. It's getting more like the States every day here, and I like it. I think that's what I was really trying to say," he added with a grin, "when I said your lot were dinosaurs. I meant, everything's changed and you've managed not to. And still done well. Very admirable."

"Well, all right. I'll try to accept that."

"Good. So how long you been married then?"

"Three and a half years."

"And kids? Got any kids?"

"No. Not yet."

"Okay. And where d'you live? Don't tell me, somewhere not too far away from Sloane Square."

"Well, yes, actually. In dinosaur country."

"You're not going to let me forget that, are you?"

"No, I'm not. Now I really do have to circulate a bit more."

"I'll come with you."

"Blue—" She stopped suddenly. "Why Blue, when you were christened Gary?"

"It's a nickname," he said. "We all have them, and they all have some sort of reason. I mean, there's Luft, short for Luftwaffe; he's got blond hair and blue eyes and very, very right-wing views. And Croydon, because his surname is Sutton; and Harry, he's one of your coloured gentlemen, so Harry, as in Belafonte; and Kermit, who looks like a frog. Blue Buttons were the runaround boys on the old Stock Exchange floor. Looked after the brokers, kept them supplied with tea and coffee—and info, of course. You'd hear people shouting for them: 'Where's the Blue? Hey, Blue, over here!' I was one of them, before Big Bang. In fact, I got to be the head Blue Button. So the name stuck. I quite like it. Don't you?"

"I—well, yes, I think so," she said doubtfully.

"Good. Come on, let's do some of this circulating then. You introduce me to some of these people. And to your husband, if you like."

She hadn't introduced him to Nigel. It didn't seem a very good idea;

she wasn't sure why. For the next half-hour he followed her round the room, carrying a bottle of champagne himself to assist with the glass re-filling. And then, somehow, she found herself alone with him in the little kitchen; a lot of people had gone, the catering people were packing up glasses, and he said suddenly, "Would you have lunch with me one day?"

"No," she said, staring at him, quite shocked. "Of course not."

"Why 'of course'?"

"Well, isn't it obvious?"

"Not really, no."

"Mr. Horton," she said firmly, sorting empty bottles from full. "I'm—well, I'm married, you know that."

"And married ladies never have lunch with gentlemen? Is that right?"

"Not—well, not like that."

"Like what?"

"You know—" She stopped. "You know perfectly well what I mean. Perfectly."

"No, I don't."

"Yes, you do. Oh, this is silly."

"Yes, it is," he said, "just a bit."

And then he leaned forward and kissed her. On the mouth. Only very briefly, but it was enough to create the most extraordinary sensations, somewhere deep inside her. She pulled away, stared at him; he smiled at her. He had, she noticed, even in her confusion, extraordinarily nice teeth. He wasn't very tall, only a little taller than she was in her heels; his dark hair was close cropped, his eyes a deep brown. He had long, almost girly eyelashes, a very straight nose, and quite a wide mouth (showing the very nice teeth). He wasn't fat, but he was very solidly built, broad-shoul-dered, with rather large hands and feet, and he seemed to emit a lot of en-ergy; he was restless, permanently fidgeting. It was oddly attractive.

He leaned forward and kissed her again, for just a fraction longer. She could feel herself responding to him, feel her lips parting, moving just a little; it was terrible, scary—

"Please stop it," she said, "I really must go."

"Okay," he said, "that's fine. I'll call you in a day or so, see if you've changed your mind. I don't give up easy. Bye, Lucinda." And he was gone.

READERS' GUIDE

1. We join Martha, Jocasta, and Clio at Heathrow Airport a year before a baby is born to, and abandoned by, one of them. We then get to know each of them a little better in the early chapters. Purely on the basis of their personalities, which of them seemed the most likely to have done something so shocking and wretched, and why?

2. Did you guess correctly? Did you spot the qualities in this character that made such a course of action possible? And if you were wrong, what specific things misled you?

3. Did you sympathize with the woman who abandoned her baby? What would drive someone to such desperate action? Can you imagine a situation or a time in your life when you might have done something equally devastating? Can anyone (mother or child) ever recover from such an event?

4. In England in the 1980s it was fairly common for children from well-to-do families to spend a year traveling the world between high school and college. Discuss your own experiences of travel during that or any period in your life. How did travel change you? Would

you allow your teenage daughter to travel alone to Bangkok and the Far East in this day and age?

5. Female friendships can be very complex. What do you suppose drove Martha, Clio, and Jocasta apart? Have you ever lost touch with a friend and then reconnected with that person later in life?

6. English politics, an essential ingredient of the book, are very idiosyncratic; the personal politics of several of the characters could be described as equally so. Yet the less ambitious characters—Helen, Kate's adoptive mother, and Nat, Kate's boyfriend—have been declared some of the more multi-dimensional characters in the book. Would you agree with this, and if so, why?

7. It could be argued either that Jocasta acted completely against her own character in marrying Gideon Keeble, or that it was in absolute accord with her desire for love and security. Which do you think?

8. Kate is deeply distressed by the loss of Martha, when she had spent her whole life railing against her. Why do you think this is?

9. Vincenzi describes several married couples in *Sheer Abandon*: Helen and Jim Tarrant, Jocasta and Gideon Keeble, Clio and Jeremy Graves, Grace and Peter Hartley, Beatrice and Josh Forbes. How does each couple deal with strains on their relationship? What factors help dictate whether these marriages endure or fall apart?

10. Martha, Clio, and Jocasta all struggle to balance a successful career with their relationships with family, friends, and significant others. How does each character prioritize her life? Do you know women facing similar difficulties?

11. How does the book address the struggle for an adopted child, like Kate, to come to terms with her parentage? Who does she ultimately consider to be her "real" mother? How does her relationship with Jim differ from her relationship with her biological father?

12. Did you enjoy the experience of reading *Sheer Abandon*? How fast did you read it? What kept you hooked?